DEMIHUMAN DEI[TIES]

Eric L. Boyd

Contents

Credits

Design: Eric L. Boyd
Original and Source Material Design: Ed Greenwood, Robert J. Kuntz, Colin McComb, Roger Moore, Carl Sargent, and James M. Ward, the primary authors of the demihuman pantheons in *Deities & Demigods*, *Best of the Dragon Volume III*, *Dwarves Deep*, *Drow of the Underdark*, *Monstrous Mythology*, and *On Hallowed Ground*. Also inspiration or original source material from: Lynn Abbey, L. Richard Baker III, Jim Bambra, Wolfgang Baur, Tim Beach, Grant Boucher, Jim Butler, Loren Coleman, William W. Connors, David "Zeb" Cook, Monte Cook, Bruce R. Cordell, Elaine Cunningham, Michael Dobson, Dale Donovan, Nigel Findley, Karen Wynn Fonstad, Ed Greenwood, Jeff Grubb, Gary Gygax, Scott Haring, Paul Jaquays, Steve Kurtz, James Lowder, David E. Martin, Julia Martin, Colin McComb, Frank Mentzer, Blake Mobley, Roger Moore, Rags Morales, Robert S. Mullin, John Nephew, Bruce Nesmith, Douglas Niles, Kate Novak, Chris Perry, Jonathon M. Richards, Chris Perry, Anthony Pryor Tom Prusa, David S. Reimer, Carl Sargent, R. A. Salvatore, Steven Schend, Dave Simons, slade, Bill Slavicsek, Keith Francis Strohm, Rick Swan, John Terra, James Ward with Robert Kuntz, Steve Winter, Peter Dosik. We apologize for anyone we missed.
Editing: Julia Martin
Proofreading: Linda Archer
Brand Manager: David Wise
Cover Art: Todd Lockwood
Priest Color Plates, Interior Illustration, and New Deity Symbols: Ned Dameron
Interior Page Layout Design: Dee Barnett
Interior Page Layout Art: Red Hughes
Typesetting: Eric Haddock
Production: Matt Adelsperger
Research Assistance: Brian "Volo" D. Gute (for compiling all the demihuman deity lore in all of the Volo's Guides), Thomas "Marduk" M. Costa and Bryon "Dracolich" Wischstadt (for help with proofreading), Thomas "Marduk" M. Costa (for his help in cross-balancing avatars and specialty priests), and Alistair "Realms Moderator Emeritus" G. Lowe-Norris, Andrew "Realms Moderator" Hackard, Ariane "Cnith of Fenrisulven" Fournier, Austin "AFrisbie" Frisbie, Bobby "Cat Dragon" Nichols, Boedyn, Brian "Volo" D. Gute, Bryon "Dracolich" Wischstadt, Christopher "Demihuman Deity" Dwinell, Christopher "Seldarine" D. Perry, Damir "Maki" Makovica, Daniel "Highmoon" M. Perez, David "Mulhorand" Wellbaum, Elric, Ezra "Sneezy" S. Freelove, George "Phalorm" Krashos, Grant "Scribe" Christie, John "Bishop" R. East, Jay "Pukje," Jeff "Sacred12" T., Jenn "Kethry" Millington, Kain "CullA" T. Whitehouse, Lestat d'Lioncourt, Malcolm "Agrivar Nekros" the Undead Paladin of Tyr, Mark "Northern Journey" Oliva, Martin "Prescient" Brabander, Matthew "Arawn" McSorley, Mike "Warlock666" Hill, Nigel "Eilistraee" Bennington, Phillip "Sleyvas" Wallace, Rich "Bushcat93," Rick "Maul1," Russell "Wastri" Timm, Ryan "the Silent Sword" McCoy, Thomas "Marduk" M. Costa, and Toby "Runedarspace" Mekelburg. Eric apologizes for anyone he missed.

To Letitia for her unconditional love and support, to my family for their understanding, to the members of the Realms list for their inspiration and thought-provoking posts, to David Wise for his patience, to Ed Greenwood and Steven Schend for their invaluable assistance and ready answers, and to Julia Martin, the visionary, original designer, and editor of this trilogy of supplements who took a chance on a dedicated Realms fan and novice author.

9585XXX1501

ISBN 0-7869-1239-1

U.S., CANADA, ASIA, PACIFIC, & LATIN AMERICA
Wizards of the Coast, Inc.
P.O. Box 707
Renton, WA 98057-0707
800-324-6496

EUROPEAN HEADQUARTERS
Wizards of the Coast, Belgium
P.B. 34
2300 Turnhout
Belgium
+32-14-44-30-44

Visit our website at www.tsr.com

PANTHEONS OF THE REALMS

Demihuman Deities is a companion product to *Faiths & Avatars* and *Powers & Pantheons*. In the Forgotten Realms, the gods and goddesses of the Realms are referred to as *powers*, and they are grouped into collections of gods referred to as *pantheons*. *Demihuman Deities* details the pantheons of the demihuman races, including the dwarves, elves (and drow), gnomes, and halflings.

Ownership of the *Player's Handbook*, the DUNGEON MASTER® Guide, and the *Tome of Magic* are required to use this product. Ownership of *Faiths & Avatars*, *Powers & Pantheons*, *Pages from the Mages*, *Prayers from the Faithful*, the MONSTROUS MANUAL™ tome, the assorted MONSTROUS COMPENDIUM® Annual volumes, the PLANESCAPE® MONSTROUS COMPENDIUM appendices, and the four volumes of the ENCYCLOPEDIA MAGICA™ tome is strongly encouraged and would supplement the information presented here. Without them, DMs will be forced to substitute their own information from some heavily referenced material. Other products mentioned in this book are of tertiary importance; information referenced from them is summarized in this volume or may be omitted completely without significantly influencing the flavor of the entries presented here.

To avoid excessive duplication between the three supplements, only an overview of the format of each deity entry is repeated in *Demihuman Deities*. For a general overview of divine powers in the Realms, the reader is referred to *Faiths & Avatars*. For details on the new priest classes referred to in this supplement, such as the crusader, mystic, and shaman, the reader is referred to either *Faiths & Avatars* or PLAYER's OPTION™: *Spells & Magic*.

Format of Deity Entries

The entries for the powers detailed in all three supplements follow a standard format. Notes on that format are given here in a format mimicking that used in the text:

Name of Deity

(Common Title and Epithets)

Power Ranking of Plane Name, Alignment

Alignment abbreviations used throughout each deity's entry are: LG=lawful good, NG=neutral good, CG=chaotic good, LN=lawful neutral, CN=chaotic neutral, N=true neutral, LE=lawful evil, NE=neutral evil, CE=chaotic evil.

PORTFOLIO:	These are the topics, things, ideas, or emotions over which the deity has dominion, power, and control and about which the deity is concerned.
ALIASES:	Other names the power is known by are given here. These may be "puppet gods" the deity has wholly subsumed, regional names, older names, or simply alternate names.
DOMAIN NAME:	The layer of the plane the deity's domain is found on is listed here, followed by the domain's name. If the plane the domain is on is undivided, the plane name is repeated. (Note that some planes also have layers with the same name as the plane they are part of.)
SUPERIOR:	If the deity takes orders from another power, that power is listed here.
ALLIES:	Traditional allies are given here.
FOES:	Traditional foes are given here. Powers the god rivals or competes with are not foes. These are discussed in the text, not here.
SYMBOL:	A brief description of the deity's symbol is given here.
WOR. ALIGN.:	The alignments required of dedicated worshipers of the deity are given here. Powers generally try to be as liberal as possible to attract as much worship as they can.

This introductory paragraph describes the way a power is generally depicted (or actually looks) if it is different from the deity's avatar form. It gives the accepted pronunciation of the power's name. It details additional titles and epithets the power is known by, common worshipers of the power, and the qualities attributed to the deity, such as its general demeanor, bearing, and personality. It also discusses any relations between the power and other powers not covered by the "Allies" and "Foes" entries above.

Deity's Avatar (Character classes and levels)

This paragraph describes the avatar's appearance and the schools or spheres of magic from which it may draw spells. When discussed in this avatar section, a deity's avatar is spoken of as the deity, not as "the avatar of so-and-so," to economize on space. The avatar's statistics use this format and these abbreviations:

AC Armor Class; MV movement rate, Fl flying (maneuverability class is assumed to always be A), Sw swimming, Br burrowing; HP hit points; THAC0 To hit Armor Class 0; #AT number of attacks per round
Dmg typical damage done per attack (weapon, if one is used, Strength bonus notation, weapon specialization notation)
MR magic resistance; SZ Size notation (size in feet)
Str Strength score, Dex Dexterity score, Con Constitution score, Int Intelligence score, Wis Wisdom score, Cha Charisma score
Spells P: number of priest spells per spell level including Wisdom spell bonuses, W: number of wizard spells per spell level
Saves (saving throws) PPDM poison, paralyzation, or death magic saving throw; RSW rod, staff, or wand saving throw; PP petrification or polymorph saving throw; BW breath weapon saving throw; Sp spell saving throw

Special Att/Def: This entry discusses any special attacks or defenses the avatar has, its magical items of note, and any particularly distinctive tactics it tends to use.

Other Manifestations

This section discusses other manifestations of a power aside from its avatar. These manifestations are much more commonly encountered than the actual avatar of a deity. They often convey benefits to the faithful or indicate favor, direction, danger, agreement, or disagreement by the deity. Sometimes they are merely used to comfort and assure their worshipers that they are aware of a situation or appreciate their followers' devotion.

The Church

In the headings in this section, the following abbreviations are used for character classes: C=cleric, Cru=crusader, D=druid, SP=specialty priest, Mon=monk, Mys=mystic, Sha=shaman, F=fighter, Pal=paladin, R=ranger, W=all wizard classes, M=mage, Abj=abjurer, Con=conjurer, Chr=chronomancer, Div=diviner, Enc=enchanter, Ill=illusionist, Inv=invoker, Nec=necromancer, Spell=spellsinger, Tra=transmuter, T=thief, B=bard. Note that the chronomancer wizard character class is described in *Chronomancer*, the spellsinger wizard class is described in *Wizards and Rogues of the Realms,* and the crusader, monk, mystic, and shaman priest classes are found in *Faiths & Avatars.*

CLERGY:	The different character classes open to members of the clergy are listed here. Always remember that a religion can have lay members of the clergy who have no character class. They are treated as 1st-level fighters unless otherwise specified.
CLERGY'S ALIGN.:	Members of any class who belong to the clergy must be one of these alignments (within the constraints of the alignments to which the class is restricted). The allowed alignments of specialty priests are specifically noted in that section.
TURN UNDEAD:	Abbreviations for all character classes of clergy and whether they can turn undead
CMND. UNDEAD:	Abbreviations for all character classes of clergy and whether they can command undead

Bonus proficiencies or other game-relevant material applicable to all priestly members of the religion's clergy are presented in this introductory paragraph.

Following paragraphs in this overview of the church discuss the regard of the public for the religion, typical details of temple or shrine construction, names different forms of the clergy call themselves by, distribution breakdowns of kinds of character classes within the clergy, church hierarchy, and titles of different ranks of clergy. Further information on the church is broken down into subheadings:

Dogma: Here are detailed the beliefs, tenets, doctrines and sayings of the religion.

Day-to-Day Activities: Typical activities of the church are described here. This entry covers what the church does, as opposed to what the religion believes. This entry also discusses what believers and priests of the religion are expected to tithe or donate to the church or sacrifice to the deity.

Important Ceremonies/Holy Days: Important ceremonies and major holy days in the religion are discussed in this entry.

Major Centers of Worship: This entry describes major centers of the deity's worship. These may be the largest temples of the god, those with the most far-reaching influence in the religion, or those of historical importance in the religion.

Affiliated Orders: Knightly and military orders affiliated with the church are briefly discussed in this entry. They are named and the character classes their members belong to are mentioned. The functions and duties of these orders and other information pertaining to their relationship to the church are also touched on briefly.

Priestly Vestments: This entry describes the ceremonial vestments of priests of the deity and any differences between the vestments of different kinds of priests who serve the deity. Differences in garb according to rank or in different regions are also discussed here. Typical coloration or construction materials of symbols and holy symbols of the god are mentioned here if they are important.

Adventuring Garb: This entry describes the typical priest's adventuring garb. It also discusses any differences between the adventuring garb of different kinds of priests who serve the deity.

Specialty Priests (Class name, if applicable)

The experience progression table for all priest types is found in *Faiths & Avatars.* An optional specialty priest experience point progression table is found in Appendix 1: Demihuman Priests.

REQUIREMENTS:	Minimum ability requirements for this type of specialty priest
PRIME REQ.:	Abilities that must have a score of 16 or above for the character to receive a 10% experience point bonus
ALIGNMENT:	Specialty priests must be the same alignment as their god, unless specifically noted differently here.
WEAPONS:	Types of weapons specialty priests are allowed to use
ARMOR:	Types of armor specialty priests are allowed to use
MAJOR SPHERES:	Spheres of priest spells to which specialty priests have major access
MINOR SPHERES:	Spheres of priest spells to which specialty priests have minor access
MAGICAL ITEMS:	The kinds of magical items specialty priests are allowed to use
REQ. PROFS:	Nonweapon or weapon proficiencies specialty priests must purchase with proficiency slots at 1st level
BONUS PROFS:	Nonweapon or weapon proficiencies specialty priests receive without spending a proficiency slot. Specialty priests may spend additional slots as normal to improve their skills.

- The first bullet point in this section notes the races and/or subraces and genders allowed as specialty priests by the power.
- The second bullet point notes multiclass combinations that a specialty priest of this power is allowed to be part of and which kits, if any, she or he may apply to his or her class or classes.
- This section contains a list of special powers granted to specialty priests of this deity. Clerics do not receive these abilities unless that fact is specially noted. (Usually changes to other priest classes of a deity are noted earlier in the first text paragraph of the description of the church.)
- Spell-like abilities are often expressed in terms of the spells they are similar to. When specialty priests receive such an ability, it is usable *in addition* to their normal spell complements. It should not be read as a restriction on the number of times that the priest can cast the comparable spell per day or per tenday. Such spell-like abilities require no verbal, somatic, or material components to use, and function as innate abilities in combat (discussed in the Innate Abilities subsection of the Special Attacks section of the Combat chapter of the DUNGEON MASTER *Guide*). They have an initiative modifier of +3 no matter what the casting time of the spell they resemble is.

Spells

Here are listed the religion-specific spells of a faith. Unless the Dungeon Master makes an exception or an exception is noted, only priests of the religion where the spell is listed are allowed to cast these spells. Priests, rangers, and paladins of a particular religion can always cast these religion-specific spells, even if the spells do not fall within their normally allowed spheres of access. When used as a material component, holy symbols are *never* consumed in the casting of a spell. An asterisk (*) indicates a cooperative magic spell.

Extended Calculated THAC0s

Group	1	2	3	4	5	6	7	8	9	10	11	12	13	14	15	16	17	18	19	20
Priest	20	20	20	18	18	18	16	16	16	14	14	14	12	12	12	10	10	10	8	8
Rogue	20	20	19	19	18	18	17	17	16	16	15	15	14	14	13	13	12	12	11	11
Warrior	20	19	18	17	16	15	14	13	12	11	10	9	8	7	6	5	4	3	2	1
Wizard	20	20	20	19	19	19	18	18	18	17	17	17	16	16	16	15	15	15	14	14

Group	21	22	23	24	25	26	27	28	29	30	31	32	33	34	35	36	37	38	39	40
Priest	8	6	6	6	4	4	4	2	2	2	0	0	0	–2	–2	–2	–4	–4	–4	–6
Rogue	10	10	9	9	8	8	7	7	6	6	5	5	4	4	3	3	2	2	1	1
Warrior	0	–1	–2	–3	–4	–5	–6	–7	–8	–9	–10	–10	–10	–10	–10	–10	–10	–10	–10	–10
Wizard	14	13	13	13	12	12	12	11	11	11	10	10	10	9	9	9	8	8	8	7

Extended Priest Spell Progression

Level	1	2	3	4	5	6*	7**
1	1	—	—	—	—	—	—
2	2	—	—	—	—	—	—
3	2	1	—	—	—	—	—
4	3	2	—	—	—	—	—
5	3	3	1	—	—	—	—
6	3	3	2	—	—	—	—
7	3	3	2	1	—	—	—
8	3	3	3	2	—	—	—
9	4	4	3	2	1	—	—
10	4	4	3	3	2	—	—
11	5	4	4	3	2	1	—
12	6	5	5	3	2	2	—
13	6	6	6	4	2	2	—
14	6	6	6	5	3	2	1
15	6	6	6	6	4	2	1
16	7	7	7	6	4	3	1
17	7	7	7	7	5	3	2
18	8	8	8	8	6	4	2
19	9	9	8	8	6	4	2
20	9	9	9	8	7	5	2
21	9	9	9	9	8	6	2
22	9	9	9	9	9	6	3
23	9	9	9	9	9	7	3
24	9	9	9	9	9	8	3
25	9	9	9	9	9	8	4
26	9	9	9	9	9	9	4
27	9	9	9	9	9	9	5
28	9	9	9	9	9	9	6
29	9	9	9	9	9	9	7
30	9	9	9	9	9	9	8
31	10	10	9	9	9	9	8
32	10	10	10	9	9	9	8
33	10	10	10	10	9	9	9
34	11	11	10	10	9	9	9
35	11	11	10	10	10	10	9
36	11	11	11	11	10	10	10
37	12	12	11	11	10	10	10
38	12	12	11	11	11	11	10
39	12	12	12	12	11	11	11
40	13	13	13	12	12	11	11

Extended Wizard Spell Progression

Level	1	2	3	4	5	6	7	8	9
1	1	—	—	—	—	—	—	—	—
2	2	—	—	—	—	—	—	—	—
3	2	1	—	—	—	—	—	—	—
4	3	2	—	—	—	—	—	—	—
5	4	2	1	—	—	—	—	—	—
6	4	2	2	—	—	—	—	—	—
7	4	3	2	1	—	—	—	—	—
8	4	3	3	2	—	—	—	—	—
9	4	3	3	2	1	—	—	—	—
10	4	4	3	2	2	—	—	—	—
11	4	4	4	3	3	—	—	—	—
12	4	4	4	4	4	1	—	—	—
13	5	5	5	4	4	2	—	—	—
14	5	5	5	4	4	2	1	—	—
15	5	5	5	5	5	2	1	—	—
16	5	5	5	5	5	3	2	1	—
17	5	5	5	5	5	3	3	2	—
18	5	5	5	5	5	3	3	2	1
19	5	5	5	5	5	3	3	3	1
20	5	5	5	5	5	4	3	3	2
21	5	5	5	5	5	4	4	4	2
22	5	5	5	5	5	4	4	4	3
23	5	5	5	5	5	5	5	5	3
24	5	5	5	5	5	5	5	5	4
25	5	5	5	5	5	5	5	5	4
26	6	6	6	6	6	5	5	5	5
27	6	6	6	6	6	6	5	5	5
28	6	6	6	6	6	6	6	6	5
29	7	7	7	7	7	6	6	6	6
30	7	7	7	7	7	7	6	6	6
31	7	7	7	7	7	7	7	7	7
32	7	7	7	7	7	7	7	7	7
33	7	7	7	7	7	7	7	7	7
34	8	8	8	8	8	7	7	7	7
35	8	8	8	8	8	8	7	7	7
36	8	8	8	8	8	8	8	8	8
37	8	8	8	8	8	8	8	8	8
38	8	8	8	8	8	8	8	8	8
39	9	9	9	9	9	8	8	8	8
40	9	9	9	9	9	9	9	8	8

Expanded Bard Spell Progression

Level	1	2	3	4	5	6	7
1	—	—	—	—	—	—	—
2	1	—	—	—	—	—	—
3	2	—	—	—	—	—	—
4	2	1	—	—	—	—	—
5	3	1	—	—	—	—	—
6	3	2	—	—	—	—	—
7	3	2	1	—	—	—	—
8	3	3	1	—	—	—	—
9	3	3	2	—	—	—	—
10	3	3	2	1	—	—	—
11	3	3	3	1	—	—	—
12	3	3	3	2	—	—	—
13	3	3	3	2	1	—	—
14	3	3	3	3	1	—	—
15	3	3	3	3	2	—	—
16	4	3	3	3	2	1	—
17	4	4	3	3	3	1	—
18	4	4	4	3	3	2	—
19	4	4	4	4	3	2	—
20	4	4	4	4	4	3	—
21	5	4	4	4	4	3	—
22	5	4	4	4	4	3	—
23	5	5	5	4	4	4	—
24	5	5	5	5	4	4	—
25	5	5	5	5	4	4	1
26	5	5	5	5	5	4	1
27	5	5	5	5	5	5	1
28	6	5	5	5	5	5	1
29	6	6	5	5	5	5	1
30	6	6	6	5	5	5	1
31	6	6	6	5	5	5	2
32	6	6	6	6	5	5	2
33	6	6	6	6	6	5	2
34	6	6	6	6	6	6	2
35	6	6	6	6	6	6	2
36	7	6	6	6	6	6	2
37	7	7	6	6	6	6	2
38	7	7	6	6	6	6	3
39	7	7	7	6	6	6	3
40	7	7	7	7	6	6	3

* Usable only by priests with 17 or greater Wisdom.
** Usable only by priests with 18 or greater Wisdom.

Priest of Arvoreen

Priest of Cyrollalee

Priest of
Sheela Peryroyl

Priest of
Urogalan

Priest of
Yondalla

Priest of Brandobaris

Priest of
Deep Duerra

Priest of
Berronar
Truesilver

Priest of
Abbathor

Priest of
Gorm
Gulthyn

Priest of
Haela Brightaxe

Priest of
Dumathoin

Priest of
Thard Harr

Priest of
Laduguer

Priest of
Vergadain

Priest of
Marthammor
Duin

Priest of
Sharindlar

Priest of
Moradin

Priest of
Garl Glittergold

Priest of
Gaerdal Ironhand

Priest of
Segojan Earthcaller

Priest of
Urdlen

Priest of
Callarduran
Smoothhands

Priest of
Flandal Steelskin

Priest of
Shevarash

Priest of
Baravar Cloakshadow

Priest of
Sehanine
Moonbow

Priest of
Solonor
Thelandira

Priest of
Baervan
Wildwanderer

Priest of
Rillifane
Rallithil

Priest of
Erevan Ilesere

Priest of
Labelas Enoreth

Priest of
Aerdrie
Faenya

Priest of
Fenmarel Mestarine

Priest of
Hanali Celanil

Priest of
Deep Sashelas

Priest of
Eilistraee

Priest of
Selvetarm

Priest of
Lolth

Priest of
Ghaunadaur

Priest of
Vhaeraun

Priest of
Kiaransalee

DROW PANTHEON

The Ssri-Tel'Quessir of Abeir-Toril, the dark elven subrace of the Fair Folk, have long been divorced from the Seldarine, the traditional elven pantheon of Arvandor. The drow, as they are now known, venerate a wide range of dark powers, the most prominent of which are presented hereafter. The deities of the drow are a pantheon in name only, united only by the common heritage of their worshipers, long-ignored familial ties among four of them, and occasional, short-lived alliances forged only as a matter of convenience.

By Corellon Larethian's decree, the destiny of the dark elves was placed long ago in the hands of his consort, Araushnee the Weaver. At that time she was a minor, but secretly ambitious, elven power and member of the Seldarine. After a series of betrayals of her fellow gods, Araushnee was banished to the Abyss by Corellon for plotting against her lover and for secretly assembling a host of evil deities—the anti-Seldarine—to assault Arvandor, home of the Seldarine, in a bid to replace Corellon as Coronal of Arvandor. After her banishment, Araushnee assumed the name Lolth, Demon Queen of Spiders. She set about establishing her new realm in the Abyss and driving off or subjugating rivals like Ghaunadaur, Kiaransalee, and Zanassu. Araushnee was not the only elven power to be cast out of Arvandor and the Seldarine, however, for her webs ensnared her two children as well. When his mother's perfidy was exposed, Vhaeraun, son of Araushnee and Corellon, was banished to Abeir-Toril for his complicity in the Weaver's plots to replace Corellon as head of the Seldarine. Vhaeraun's sister, Eilistraee the Dark Maiden, agreed to exile as well, although she was only an unwitting participant in her mother's plots.

Lolth dominates all the other powers and brooks (or at least admits) no challenge to her ultimate authority. Only Kiaransalee and Selvetarm acknowledge the Spider Queen as head of the pantheon, an unavoidable acknowledgment of Lolth's great power. Eilistraee, Vhaeraun, and Ghaunadaur remain independent of the Spider Queen's control, but none of them is strong enough to challenge her directly, and their mutual enmity precludes any possibility of alliance against her. Kiaransalee only recently fought free of Lolth's shadow, but she has little influence (and few worshipers) in the Realms. Selvetarm is still firmly enmeshed in his grandmother's webs, despite the efforts of his followers to break away from the Spider Queen's cult. Eilistraee and Vhaeraun are brother and sister, children of Araushnee (Lolth) and Corellon Larethian. Selvetarm is the offspring of an ill-fated tryst between Vhaeraun and Zandilar the Dancer (Sharess), a goddess of the Yuir elves. Ghaunadaur is a primordial evil who joined the other members of the anti-Seldarine in the assault on Arvandor. Kiaransalee is a once-mortal dark elf of another world who achieved divinity and was named drow before the fall of Araushnee.

With the notable exception of Eilistraee, the dark powers of the drow pantheon are intimately involved in the lives of their followers, demanding absolute obedience and exclusive veneration in exchange for great power. Aside from the Dark Maiden, the gods of the drow pantheon care nothing for the fate of their followers except as it advances their own personal power. All but one dwell in the Abyss or other dark realms, embodying the banishment of the drow from the Lands of Light. Eilistraee seeks to redeem the fallen dark elves and lead them back to the great forests of the surface world that their ancestors forsook many millennia ago. However, the Dark Maiden is quite constrained in her actions by the power of Lolth and the other gods of the pantheon, and she acknowledges the need for individual drow to find their own path to redemption that heavy-handed interference on her part would preclude.

The origin of the drow is firmly enshrined in the minds of all the elven subraces whose ancestors fought in the great Crown Wars that split the Fair Folk. While the other elven subraces recall with horror the depraved actions of the Ilythiiri, as the dominant tribe of dark elves was known, that led to the Descent, the drow weave their own lies regarding the perfidy of the Seldarine and the other elven races whom they hold turned on the Ssri-Tel'Quessir and unjustly banished them to the Underdark. Only those drow who have answered the redemptive call of the Dark Maiden recall and preserve the elven myths regarding the ancestry of the Fair Folk, for such tales are of little interest to those who seethe in anger at the Creator they now scorn, Corellon.

Drow culture is distinguished by a curious mixture of monotheism and polytheism uncharacteristic of most human and demihuman cultures of the Realms. Most drow cities—such as Guallidurth, Menzoberranzan, and Ched Nasad—are ruled in the name of Lolth by priests of the Spider Queen and even the mention, let alone the worship, of other gods is forbidden. A few drow cities—such as Llurth Dreier (Ghaunadaur) and V'elddrinnsshar (Kiaransalee)—are ruled by the clergy of the other drow powers in similar fashion, but they too forbid the worship or mention of all other gods. The few drow cities that exhibit the open worship of two or more deities—such as beleaguered Eryndlyn, located beneath the High Moor, or Golothaer, from whence the founders of Menzoberranzan and Ched Nasad fled—are riven by strife and are usually destroyed by civil war within a generation of such a split appearing. Nevertheless, most of the drow gods have a few secretive worshipers in every drow enclave, as such devotions afford dissidents the opportunity for additional weapons in their endless quest for increasing personal station. Aside from the faithful of Eilistraee, who venerate the Dark Maiden in a fashion resembling the veneration of the Seldarine by elves of other races, most drow venerate one (or in some cases two) deities out of fear, respect, and a desire for additional power of their own, not out of any sense of true piety.

Over 10,000 years ago, the Crown Wars exposed the depths to which most dark elves had fallen in the service of fell powers such as Vhaeraun, Ghaunadaur, and Lolth, despite the mitigating efforts of the good-hearted Eilistraee. As a result, by means never discussed by the Fair Folk, the dark elves were forever banished to the deep tunnels beneath Faerûn by the Seldarine and the allied elven nations and thereafter named drow (originally *dhaeraow*, an elvish term meaning *face of shadow, heart of night, traitor*), circa –10,000 DR.

The first drow civilizations arose in the Underdark of southern Faerûn circa –9,600 DR. The first great kingdom of the drow was Telantiwar, with its capitol in the great cavern of Bhaerynden, the conquered heart of the first great kingdom of the Stout Folk seized by the drow in –9,000 DR. The drow fought among themselves, noble against noble, priest against priest, for rule of their new realm. This all-out war ended amid great magical explosions that brought down the roof of Bhaerynden. The ceiling collapsed entirely, burying many drow and the shattered dwarven cities that they had seized. The cavern, now open to the sky, became known as the Great Rift, and the chasm and the surrounding caverns were later resettled by the ancestors of the gold dwarves to form the Deep Realm. In a great diaspora known as the Scattering, the surviving drow nobles and priests gathered what people, slaves, and equipment they could seize and fled into the Underdark in search of places to dwell. Since that time, countless cities and smaller settlements have risen and fallen, and the drow are now found throughout the deep tunnels beneath all of Faerûn and even farther afield.

The web of chaos and cruelty that enmeshes the drow is embodied in the constant strife between the gods they venerate. Likewise, the hatred they hold for all other races, particularly the Fair Folk of the surface world, is played out as well in the never-ending conflict between the Seldarine and those they banished long ago. Only a small fraction have returned to the surface lands of their forefathers, typically by way of the welcoming hand of Eilistraee.

General Drow Priest Abilities: The general abilities and restrictions of drow priests, aside from the specific changes noted later in this section for each drow faith, are summarized in the discussion of drow priests in "Appendix 1: Demihuman Priests."

Eilistraee

(The Dark Maiden, Lady of the Dance, Lady Silverhair)

Lesser Power of Ysgard, CG

Portfolio:	Song, beauty, dance, swordwork, hunting, moonlight
Aliases:	None
Domain Name:	Nidavellir/Svartalfheim
Superior:	None
Allies:	Callarduaran Smoothhands, Haela Brightaxe, Lurue, Mystra, the Seldarine, Selûne
Foes:	Deep Duerra, Kiaransalee, Laduguer, Ghaunadaur, Lolth, Malar, Selvetarm, Vhaeraun, Blibdoolpoolp, the Blood Queen, Diinkarazan, Diirinka, Great Mother, Gzemnid, Ilsensine, Ilxendren, Laogzed, Maanzecorian (dead)
Symbol:	A silver long sword outlined against a silver moon, with silvery filaments (Eilistraee's hair) around all, in a nimbus
Wor. Align.:	LG, NG, CG

Eilistraee (Eel-iss-TRAY-yee) is the goddess of the good drow—those rare dark elves who yearn for a return to life on the surface Realms, existence akin to that enjoyed by elves of the woodlands, left behind by the drow long ago. She is a goddess of song and beauty, goodness and light, worshiped through song and dance—preferably in the surface world, under the stars of a moonlit night. Eilistraee aids her faithful in hunting and swordcraft, and worship of her is usually accompanied by a feast. Eilistraee also has worshipers of human, elven, and in particular, half-elven stock (particularly around Silverymoon), and she looks kindly upon the Harpers. She is usually seen only from afar, but her song (of unearthly beauty, driving many to tears) is heard whenever she appears.

The Dark Maiden is the sister of Vhaeraun and the daughter of Araushnee, who was cast out and became Lolth, and Corellon Larethian. After Eilistraee nearly slew her father with an arrow during a great battle between the Seldarine and a host of evil deities bent on conquering Arvandor, the Dark Maiden forswore the use of ranged weapons (although she permits them to her followers). Although her arrow went astray because of Araushnee's treachery, Eilistraee chose banishment from Arvandor (and the Seldarine) along with her mother and brother, foreseeing a time when she would be needed to balance their evil. On Abeir-Toril, the Dark Maiden strove for centuries against the hatred of Vhaeraun and his corrupting influence on the Ilythiiri (southern, dark-skinned elves). Eilistraee's power ebbed with the death of many of her faithful in the Dark Disaster, and the rise of Lolth and Ghaunadaur among the dark elves marginalized the influence of the Lady of the Dance for millennia. Only in recent centuries has Eilistraee's faith regained a small amount of prominence in Faerûn, as the Dark Maiden seeks to lead the fallen drow back to the long-forsaken light.

Eilistraee is a melancholy, moody drow female, a lover of beauty and peace. The evil of most drow banks a burning anger within her, and when her faithful are harmed, that anger is apt to spill out into wild action. It is not her way to act openly, but she often aids creatures she favors (whether they worship her or not) in small, immediately practical ways. Eilistraee is happiest when she looks on bards singing or composing, craftsmen at work, lovers, or acts of kindness.

While the Dark Maiden and the Seldarine remain allies, it is a strained relationship that reflects the divisions that persist among the elves. Among the elven powers, Eilistraee is only close with Erevan Ilesere, and she has only recently worked out an uneasy truce with Shevarash. Eilistraee is unusually close with the human goddess of magic, Mystra; Qilué Veladorn, seventh of the Seven Sisters, serves both goddesses as Chosen of Mystra and as Chosen of Eilistraee. The Dark Maiden hates the corruption and unredeemable evil that both Lolth and Ghaunadaur represent, and she mourns her brother's enduring cruelty and selfishness.

Eilistraee's Avatar (Bard 29, Cleric 24, Ranger 21, Fighter 21)

Eilistraee appears as an unclad, glossy-skinned female drow. She is 9 feet in height with ankle-length, sweeping hair of glowing silver. Her hair and wandering silvery radiances cloak her body in a smoothly, continuously moving array of beauty. Eilistraee can call on all spheres and schools of magic, but favors spells from the spheres of animal, creation, healing, and plant and the enchantment/charm school.

AC –2; MV 15, Fl 18; HP 165; THAC0 0; #AT 7/2
Dmg 1d8+12/1d8+12 (*singing sword of dancing +3* ×2, +7 Str, +2 spec. bonus in all swords)
MR 50%; SZ L (9 feet high)
Str 19, Dex 20, Con 16, Int 21, Wis 22, Cha 23
Spells P: 12/12/12/12/11/8/3, W: 6/6/5/5/5/5/1
Saves PPDM 2 RSW 4, PP 4, BW 4, Sp 5

Special Att/Def: Eilistraee wields twin *singing swords of dancing +3*, each with all of the powers of a bastard *sword of dancing* (but with a fixed attack and damage bonus) and of a *singing sword* (see below). When she wishes to appear clothed, the Dark Maiden is garbed in a set of deep brown leather boots with all the powers of *boots of elvenkind*, *boots of varied tracks*, and *boots of the north* that allow her to *pass without trace* and move in total silence at will. She also wears a dappled green cloak that shifts its colors to match the

foliage around it, providing concealment similar to that of a *cloak of elvenkind* and a *ring of chameleon power*, but providing 100% invisibility in natural surroundings.

Eilistraee has *true seeing* (continuous, but otherwise functions as the priest spell) and can unleash nine silvery *magic missiles* per round in addition to her normal avatar melee combat and spellcasting attacks for a round. These missiles unerringly inflict 2d4 points of damage each to all creatures except evil beings and undead creatures, who suffer 4d4 damage per *missile*.

Once per turn, Eilistraee's avatar can employ *spell turning* as the ring, but the effect works against all magic directed against her in that round. This replaces her *magic missile* attack for the round. Once per turn, the avatar can also *regenerate* damage to herself, restoring even lost limbs with-

Drow Powers: Eilistraee

out a system shock roll and healing 1d4+1 points of damage per round. (This process can continue for 4 continuous rounds and precludes spellcasting, but not other activities or combat.)

At will, the Dark Maiden's avatar can create moonfire (see the *Eilistraee's moonfire* spell below), silvery *light*, or *dancing lights*; cause harp, horn (a far-off horn is her sign), or flute music to sound; and sing. At will, her song can affect undead and evil creatures of 3 Hit Dice or less as a *repulsion* spell; can stun any one being (saving throw vs. spell at –2 to avoid) for 1 round; or can act as a *knock* spell (as if cast by an 11th-level wizard). She can also *levitate* at will (self only, horizontal move of up to 160 feet per round). She can only be struck by +1 or better magical weapons.

Other Manifestations

The Dark Maiden seldom takes a direct hand in the affairs of mortals, but she sometimes appears in the midst of a dance in her honor, leaping amid the flames of the feast unharmed. She also appears, radiance dimmed and clad in a plain, cowled cloak, at the campfires of wayfarers in the woodlands by night to test their kindness.

Most worshipers see Eilistraee only from afar, perched on a hillock or battlement, silver hair streaming out behind her. She appears to show her favor or blessing and often rallies or heartens creatures by causing a high, far-off hunting horn call to be heard. (On several occasions, this has frightened off brigands or orc raiders, who thought aid for their quarry was on the way.) When Eilistraee's hunting horn is heard but no foes are present, her followers interpret it as a sign that someone nearby needs their aid.

Eilistraee's most used manifestations are a silvery radiance, sometimes accompanied by a wordless snatch of song or a few echoing harp notes. If the radiance surrounds an item (almost always a sword or other bladed weapon), that item typically gains the following two powers for 6 rounds: full possible damage (maximum roll, plus all bonuses) and immunity to breakage or other damage (automatic success of all item saving throws). If the radiance envelops a being, Eilistraee's favor typically gives any or all of the following three aids for 4 rounds: the ability to strike first in any round, an increase in Armor Class of 2 points, and a bonus of +4 to all attack rolls, including the ability to strike creatures normally affected only by magical weapons of a +2 or greater bonus.

Eilistraee sometimes manifests to a worshiper or nonworshiper who honors her with a solitary dance as a silver radiance that transforms the recipient's hair into a mane of silver fire for a month or even permanently. Eilistraee has also been known to aid her worshipers by providing a faint silvery radiance when they need to find something dropped in darkness, or follow an unknown trail by night through dark woods, or when childbirth occurs in darkness. She sometimes sends a flutter of silvery swallowtailed moths to show her favor, join in a dance, or lead her faithful that have become lost or need some indication of the best direction to take.

In rare circumstances, males who worship Eilistraee—or beings without any priest powers who work to further Eilistraee's aims and need her visible blessing and support (or just some light)—will temporarily manifest moonfire (see *Eilistraee's moonfire* below). Such manifestations are at the will of the goddess; the lucky recipient has no control over the duration, intensity, and location of the radiance.

Eilistraee is served by aasimar, aasimon (particularly lights), asuras, cath shee, einheriar, eladrins, mercury dragons, elven cats, feystags, frosts, hollyphants, incarnates of faith and hope, lythari, mist dragons, moon dogs, moon-horses, mortai, pixies, radiance quasielementals, reverend ones, silver dogs, silver dragons, sprites, sunflies, a tiefling or two, and silver-striped tabby cats or normal-looking animals with solid silver-colored eyes. She demonstrates her favor through the discovery of mithral, moonbars, moonstones, and silver, and the sudden inspiration to write a beautiful song or poem or the skilled to craft a gorgeous sword. Eilistraee indicates her displeasure with the sudden rising of a cold breeze, the disfavored one's hands or feet growing chilled, a sudden lack of inspiration for or capability in any artistic endeavor, or the inability to catch anything while hunting.

The Church

CLERGY:	Clerics, crusaders, mystics, specialty priests
CLERGY'S ALIGN.:	LG, NG, CG
TURN UNDEAD:	C: Yes, Cru: No, Mys: No, SP: Yes
CMND. UNDEAD:	C: No, Cru: No, Mys: No, SP: No

All clerics (including multiclassed clerics), crusaders, mystics, and specialty priests (including multiclassed specialty priests) of Eilistraee receive religion (drow), religion (elven), and reading/writing (drowic) as bonus nonweapon proficiencies. All clergy of Eilistraee must be female, but they may be of any intelligent race. Multiclassed priests are permitted if normally allowed by race. (In other words, if they are not dark elves.) Note that the base and mature spell-like powers as well as the magic resistance and saving throw bonus vs. magical attacks of nearly all priests of the Dark Maiden have either faded due to extended sojourns on the surface or were never even acquired. A player character dark elven priest of the Dark Maiden *never* receives any such powers.

The followers of Eilistraee are figures of legend in both the Underdark and the Lands of Light. They are the subject of superstitions and wildly inaccurate mistruths, held by surface dwellers to be the evil vanguard of the Spider Goddess's plot to plunge all of Faerûn into darkness under her rule and held by those drow who follow the Way of Lolth (or other evil gods) to be faerie (surface elf) invaders masquerading as dark elves in preparation for the coming war of annihilation. Rare is the individual—dark elf or not—who appreciates that Eilistraee is forging her own path, one that welcomes beings of all races who revel in life and the free form expression of all that entails.

The clergy of Eilistraee are collectively known as Dark Ladies, although individual temples often have a unique collective name for the Dark Maiden's priests. Acolytes and aspirants to the clergy who wish to join a temple or who have not yet attained full priesthood are known as Maids.

The titles of individual priests vary widely—and at some temples are personally selected during a private Flame Song—but some common examples include Moon Dancer, Moon Singer, Dark Huntress, Argent Maid, Living Sword, Unsheathed Blade, Sword Smith, Bright Edge of Darkness, and Ghost of the Moonstruck Night. Specialty priests of the Dark Maiden are known as sword dancers and, including multiclassed specialty priests, make up the vast majority (90%) of her clergy. The fraction of clerics (including multiclassed clerics) in Eilistraee's service (6%) has always been small and is continuing to shrink. A small fraction (2%) of Lady Silverhair's clergy, found predominantly in the South, although that has started to change in the aftermath of the Time of Troubles, are crusaders, and all are members of the Darksong Knights. An even smaller fraction (less than 1%) of those who venerate the Lady of the Dance are mystics. Such priests invariably discover Eilistraee on their own and come to worship the Dark Maiden outside of any established church environment.

Temples of the Dark Maiden are typically established in the mouths of dark caverns and in dim forests on the surface world from which her priests can venture forth at night to brave the moonlight. It is rare for clergy of Eilistraee to found a temple below the surface, even one so close to the world above as the Promenade (see below). Eilistraee's places of worship are chosen and developed in a manner similar to those of the surface elves dedicated to the Seldarine. The Dark Maiden's clergy seek out pristine, natural sites that need little modification. Temple complexes typically include a glade in which to dance and from which the view of the moon is unobstructed, a dark place removed from the light of day, a thick tree canopy, a lively fresh water stream that playfully dances and sings, a forge and smithy for crafting swords, an access tunnel to the Underdark, and a vein of iron or some other metal suitable for the crafting of swords. However, the simplest shrine of the Dark Maiden requires naught but a moonlit glade and a song (audible or imagined) that draws one into a dance.

Dogma: Aid the weak, strong, grateful, and churlish alike; be always kind, save in battle with evil. Encourage happiness everywhere; lift hearts with kind words, jests, songs, and merriment. Learn how to cook game and how best to hunt it. Learn new songs, dances, and ways with weapons, and spices, and recipes, and pass this learning on whenever possible. Learn how to play, make, and repair musical instruments. Practice music and swordwork. Defend and aid all folk, promoting harmony between the races.

Strangers are your friends. The homeless must be given shelter from storms, under your own roof if need be. Repay rudeness with kindness. Repay violence with swift violence, that the fewest may be hurt and danger fast removed from the land.

The faithful must aid drow who are in distress. If the distressed are fighting with other drow, the combat is to be stopped with as little bloodshed as possible. So long as the drow met with are not working evil on others, they are to be aided and given the message of Eilistraee: "A rightful place awaits you in the Realms Above, in the Land of the Great Light. Come in peace, and live beneath the sun again, where trees and flowers grow."

Priests of the goddess are allowed to keep and accumulate money given them as offerings—with the understanding that this wealth is to be used to buy food, musical instruments, and other tools (such as good swords) to serve the will of the goddess. Priests of Eilistraee are allowed to go adventuring, so long as they feed, aid, and defend the needy along the way. They are encouraged to aid adventuring parties, with the price of their aid to be provision of some sort of beneficial magical armor they can use (or failing that, an enchanted sword of some sort).

Faithful of Eilistraee are encouraged to give food to others in need with a prayer to the goddess, to act with kindness, and to give food and money they can spare to their priests. Priests are to feed themselves by their own gardening and hunting skills as much as possible and to try to convert at least one stranger per moon to the worship of Eilistraee. Leading a convert in a prayer to the Dark Maiden is itself an offering to the goddess, who often (68%) manifests as a sign to the convert. When priests of the goddess must fight evil, they are to burn the bodies of the evil creatures they slay as an offering to the goddess—unless such creatures are edible and nonsentient, and there are hungry folk near.

Any hungry travelers met with, who offer no threats, are to be fed by the faithful of Eilistraee. While traveling, priests are to carry food with them for this purpose at all times. Where food cannot be purchased or received, it must be gathered or hunted for. Faithful of Eilistraee are to set aside food and give it as often as possible to strangers in need, particularly outcasts and those of other races. If food yet remains, it is to be given to the priests of Eilistraee, that they may do the same, and none shall go hungry. In times of plenty, store food for lean times ahead. In harsh winters, patrol the lands about to find and take in the lost, the hurt, and those caught in the teeth of the cold. Whenever possible, food should be eaten with the accompaniment of song. Except for properly sad occasions, a feast should be accompanied by merriment; the faithful of the Dark Maiden are commanded to promote happiness and gaiety whenever possible.

When faithful and allies of a priest fall in battle, any priest present must, if possible, provide burial, a funeral song, and comfort to the bereaved.

Day-to-Day Activities: Whenever and wherever possible, faithful of Eilistraee encourage drow to return to the surface world and work to promote harmony between drow and surface-dwelling races in order to establish the drow as rightful, nonevil inhabitants of Faerûn. They nurture beauty, music, the craft of making musical instruments, and song wherever they find it, assist hunters and hunting, and help others in acts of kindness whenever they see ways to do so. Priests must be skilled in the playing of at least one of the Dark Maiden's favored instruments—horn, flute, or harp; be adequate singers; and be fit, graceful dancers. They gather songs and musical knowledge constantly and acquire training in the use of the sword when they can.

Holy Days/Important Ceremonies: The customary worship to the Dark Maiden is a hunt, followed by a feast and dancing, and a Circle of Song, in which the worshipers sit and dance by turns in a circle, each one in succession leading a song. If possible, this is done out of doors, in a wooded area, on a moonlit night. Daily prayers are sung whenever possible, and priests try to lead others in a song or two every evening, even if no formal ritual is held.

Worshipers of Eilistraee try to let out all of the gathered emotions of the day with an *evensong*. An evensong is a personal thing, often wordless and done in private. Priests of the Dark Maiden who have the coins to do so are expected to hire any strange minstrel or bard they meet for a song or two; lay worshipers are encouraged to do so.

Whenever a sword is finished or first taken into use by a worshiper of the Dark Maiden, a priest tries to call down the blessing of the goddess upon it. This is done by planting the blade point-down in the ground, out of doors and by night, and dancing. The Sword Dance circles the blade and involves the priest drawing blood from each of her limbs by dancing momentarily against the blade. If successful (45% chance, per night attempted), the blade glows with a silvery radiance. For three months, it does not break or rust (if a drow weapon, it is also made immune to sun and removal-from-radiation damage for the same period), and though lacking a bonus or dweomer, can strike creatures normally hit only by magical weapons.

The High Hunt is celebrated at least once in each of the four seasons: a night-time hunt of a dangerous beast or monster, led by priests of Eilistraee. By tradition, the hunters may use any bladed weapons, and wear anything—except the priests, who go naked, carrying only a single sword. If the quarry is slain, a chanted prayer and circle dance to the goddess is held.

At least once a year, priests of Eilistraee undertake a Run. Those who are not drow blacken their bodies with natural dyes and oils. All priests, drow or not, boil certain leaves and berries to make their hair silvery, and go wandering (on the surface world). (Hostile drow say their silver hair indicates that the brains within the head are addled, though many drow who do not worship Eilistraee have silver hair.) Trusting to their music, kind ways, and sword skills to keep them from being slain as drow, priests of the Dark Maiden go where they are strangers, making an effort to seek out elven communities and bring them game, kindness, and helping hands. They try to learn new songs, music, and sword ways, and do not come to preach their faith or make a mark for themselves.

In the end, all priests who do not die in battle hold their greatest ritual: the Last Dance. In old age, Eilistraee's priests hear the goddess singing to them by night, calling them to her. When the song feels right, they go out unclad under the moonlit sky and dance—never to be seen again. Those who have observed such dances say that the goddess comes and sings overhead, and the aged priest begins to dance more effortlessly, looking younger and younger. Her hair begins to glow with the same radiance as the Dark Maiden's, and then she becomes slowly translucent, fading away as the dance goes on. In the end, only a silvery radiance is heard, with two voices—the goddess and her priest—raised together in melancholy, tender song.

Major Centers of Worship: Before the elven Crown Wars, Eilistraee's faith was strong in Miyeritar, and she had small numbers of faithful in Ilythiir and the other elven realms of the time. The Dark Disaster, unleashed during the Third Crown War, transformed Miyeritar into the blasted wasteland now known as the High Moor and dealt a devastating blow to the ranks of the Dark Maiden's followers. When the Ilythiiri were transformed into the drow and banished from the sunlit lands at the end of the Fourth Crown War some five hundred years later, Eilistraee's church effectively collapsed and was not reformed for millennia. A few ancient, sacred sites of power built before the Crown Wars survive in the Misty Forest, along the borders of the High Moor, and in the Shar, scattered across the once-verdant savannah.

In the Year of Shadows Fleeting (−331 DR), the drow of the Twisted Tower fell to the armies of Cormanthyr and Rystal Wood was left in the hands of good-aligned dark elf allies. Within a century, the Tower of the Dark Moon was Eilistraee's greatest temple in the Realms. The Dark Maiden's temple fell once again to the drow beneath Cormanthyr in the Year of the Apparition (190 DR) and survives today as Shadowdale's primary redoubt where it is known by its original name, the Twisted Tower. All that remains of the Dark Maiden's legacy is the swirl of *Eilistraee's moonfire* that envelops any follower of Eilistraee who mentions her name within the once-sacred halls.

The Promenade of the Dark Maiden, also known as Eilistraee's Promenade or simply the Promenade, occupies a large ruined city located to the east and north of the lawless, subterranean city of Skullport on the third level of Undermountain deep beneath Waterdeep, the City of Splendors. Of the four major caverns that comprise the temple, one cavern contains many two- and three-story buildings that serve as living quarters for the faithful; another cavern—the Cavern of Song—serves as open space and as an amphitheater for the hymns of the Dark Maiden's worshipers; the third cavern serves the priests as living quarters; and the fourth cavern houses guards' barracks, storehouses, armories, and living quarters. A large side cavern leads off from the Cavern of Song to Eilistraee's Mound, site of a great statue of the Dark Maiden hewn from a jagged mound of rock. Adjoining the main temple is the Hall of Healing—once a temple of Moander that was destroyed by an unknown band of adventurers in the service of Tyr long ago—which serves as a sick nursery for the care and tending of the temple's wounded as well as those unfortunates who suffered from the dangers of the Under Halls and were rescued by the Dark Ladies. A fixed one-way *teleport* spot from the sixth level of Halastar's Halls delivers adventurers and an infrequent monster to the northwestern corner passage north of the Hall of Healing itself. Priests of the Promenade heal any who come to the Hall, offering the hand of friendship oft denied to those of the Shunned Races.

Many races live among the community of faithful, and their numbers are drawn from escaped slaves, former adventurers, and the Chosen of Eilistraee, as the dark elven priests are known. Prominent individuals resident in the Promenade include: Qilué Veladorn, High Priest of the Promenade, Chosen of the Chosen, and Chosen of Mystra (see *Seven Sisters* and *Heroes' Lorebook* for additional details on the least-known of the Seven Sisters); Elkantar Iluim, Right Hand of the Lady; Arrikett Uruth, Hand of the Protectors; Iljrene Ahbruyn, Hand of the Protectors. The Protectors of the Song, who wield the temple's sacred *singing swords*, serve as the temple's guards. Their ranks include 24 drow (nine females), 9 dwarves, 27 humans (12 females), and 4 halflings.

Daily activities in the temple include food-growing, temple-building chores, patrolling the temple caverns and passages, and practicing diplomacy beyond the immediate temple area. The Chosen of Eilistraee work tirelessly to further the Lady's aims toward the peaceful coexistence of drow with other races of the Realms and to fulfill her commandments about preventing the return of Ghaunadaur.

Centuries ago, Eilistraee appeared to Qilué Veladorn and commanded the young dark elf and her playmates from part of the now-vanished drow settlement of Buiyrandyn—a small, poor gathering of drow families too small to be considered a city—to take up the *singing swords* provided by the Dark Maiden and destroy the Pit of Ghaunadaur. The Pit was a mile-deep shaft whose upper terminus opened into the third level of Halaster's Halls. After a great battle that resulted in the destruction of an avatar of the Elder Eye as well as the most of its slithering, oozing, and creeping worshipers, the Pit was filled with rubble and the caverns around its opening collapsed. (The rubble-filled Pit of Ghaunadaur is located in the area north of Skullport and west of Eilistraee's Promenade. The only remaining access to the

rubble-filled Pit is via a long, twisting staircase capped by Eilistraee's Mound.) Qilué and the rest of the Chosen of Eilistraee then took up responsibility for patrolling the region in armed, vigilant tours mockingly referred to as *promenades* by other inhabitants of the area.

In the years since their great victory, the number of battles the Dark Ladies have been forced to fight—particularly with the minions of Ghaunadaur—has continued to increase. After centuries of conflict, the Chosen began construction on a temple complex where they could receive the guidance and aid of their goddess late in the Year of the Harp (1355 DR). Although construction continues, the temple was largely completed and habitable by the end of the Year of the Prince (1357 DR). Since that time, the Chosen of Eilistraee have continued to patrol the surrounding tunnels of Halaster's Halls, but with the added security of a fortified redoubt to which they can retreat when prudent. In the spring of the Year of Maidends (1361 DR), the Dark Maidens participated in a daring raid of a slave ship berthed in Skullport that resulted in the death of the deep dragon Pharx and the destruction of the Dragon's Horde consortium, a merchant band led by a priest of Vhaeraun. Several years later in the Year of the Banner (1368), the Promenade came under attack by Ghaunadaur's cultists who led a full-scale assault on the temple that lasted for several months before the Elder Eye's followers were driven off.

Aboveground temples of Eilistraee are known to exist in the Moonwood north of the village of Quaervarr and at the northern end of the Velarwood in Harrowdale. The Mouth of Song, as the former temple is known, is located in a cavemouth beneath a treeless hill—atop which the dark elven priests and a few half-elven and elven faithful from Silverymoon dance in a great ring on moonlit nights—a day's travel north of Quaervarr. The Shadowtop Glade, as the latter temple is known, is located in a series of caves that line both sides of a steep-sided overgrown gully dominated by a grove of towering shadowtop trees. Dark elven priests of the temple armed with enchanted silver swords and moon-worshiping lycanthropes from the nearby Howling Hill join together to conduct sacred hunts to Eilistraee and Selûne when the moon is full.

Smaller shrines of the Dark Maiden have been spotted in the Misty Forest, the High Forest (where the Dark Ladies are led by Ysolde Veladorn, daughter of Qilué), the Forest of Shadows, the Lake Sember region, the Grey Forest, the Forest of Lethyr, the Yuirwood, and the Chondalwood. Hidden temples of Eilistraee may exist in the hearts of such forests as well. Temples of the Dark Maiden are conspicuously absent on Evermeet, the Green Isle, despite the recent rapprochement engendered by the dark elven ambassador, Lady Karsel'lyn Lylyl-Lytherraias.

Affiliated Orders: The Darksong Knights are an elite order of Eilistraeen crusaders active of late in South beneath the lands of ancient Ilythiir. Composed entirely of crusaders and warrior/priests, each members of this order is expected to devote her life to the furthering of the Dark Maiden's ethos, and in particular, the destruction of the Abyss-spawned yochlol, also known as the handmaidens of Lolth.

Priestly Vestments: Priests of Eilistraee wear their hair long, and dress practically for whatever they are currently doing. For rituals, they wear as little as possible. Otherwise, they tend to wear soft leathers for hunting, aprons while cooking, and—when battle is expected—armor. When relaxing, they favor silvery, diaphanous gowns. The holy symbol of the faith is a silver sword pendant the length of a Dark Lady's hand. Such symbols are typically worn as pins or hung around the neck on a slender silver or mithral chain.

Adventuring Garb: Eilistraee's clergy must garb themselves in either magical armor or armor of drow make. Whenever possible, priests of the Dark Maiden must use swords in battle. If no swords are at hand but other bladed weapons are available, they must be used in preference to other weapons. Long bows and silver-tipped arrows are also commonly employed as secondary weapons.

Singing Swords

XP Value: 1,600 *GP Value:* 10,000

The favored weapons of priests of Eilistraee are *singing swords*. Some are sentient and aligned to chaotic good, but most can be wielded by any being capable of lifting them. A *singing sword* is a silver *bastard sword +3* that sings constantly and loudly when unsheathed. When and if silenced, the weapon loses its attack and damage bonuses. Its song makes its wielder more confident, so she need never make any morale checks while using the *singing sword*. The *sword* also renders its wielder immune to *charm*, *command*, *confusion*, *fear*, *friends*, *repulsion*, *scare*, and *suggestion*. If *emotion* is cast on the wielder, the only result is rage directed at the caster of the *emotion* spell. The *sword*'s song also negates the songs of harpies, stills shriekers, and can entrance creatures of 2 Hit Dice or less (except undead beings or creatures from other planes). Such creatures must succeed at a saving throw vs. spell whenever they are within 60 feet of the song or be subject to an automatically successful *suggestion* from the *sword* wielder. This *suggestion* ability functions as the spell of the same name. Note that the *sword* wielder can enact a different *suggestion* on each creature affected. Also note that a bard can easily negate this latter power of the blade by singing a countersong.

Specialty Priests (Sword Dancers)

REQUIREMENTS:	Dexterity 16, Wisdom 9
PRIME REQ.:	Dexterity, Wisdom
ALIGNMENT:	LG, NG, CG
WEAPONS:	Any (swords preferred)
ARMOR:	Only magical or drow armor (of any kind)
MAJOR SPHERES:	All, combat, creation, elemental, guardian, healing, necromantic, protection, sun, wards
MINOR SPHERES:	Animal, charm, divination, summoning, travelers, weather
MAGICAL ITEMS:	Same as clerics
REQ. PROFS:	Ancient or local history, artistic ability, hunting
BONUS PROFS:	Dancing, musical instrument (horn, flute, or harp), singing

- Sword dancers can be of any intelligent race, but they must be female.
- Sword dancers can multiclass as a sword dancer/fighter or as a sword dancer/ranger provided that their race is allowed to multiclass as a cleric/fighter or cleric/ranger, respectively. Half-elven sword dancers are allowed to multiclass as sword dancer/bards.
- Sword dancers can use a *sword of dancing* to great effect. On any round in which the blade's plus is not a 1 (for example, round 2, 3, 4, 6, 7, 8, etc.), a sword dancer can release the *sword of dancing*. At 5th level, sword dancers can release the weapon on any round after the first round; the *sword of dancing* fights on its own for a number of rounds equal to the priest's level before returning for 1 round. (The cycle of pluses continues unaffected by when the priest actually grasps the blade.)
- Sword dancers can cast *Eilistraee's moonfire* at will, once per day for every level of experience they possess.
- At 5th level, sword dancers can cast *magic missile* (as the 1st-level wizard spell, four missiles per spell), or they can temporarily enchant an edged slashing weapon to ignite with a fiery blue-white glow visible to all and strike with a +3 attack bonus (but not a damage bonus) in the next round (in addition to any other bonuses it has). They can either cast *magic missile* twice in one day, enchant a weapon twice in one day, or use each ability once in one day.
- At 7th level, sword dancers can cast *enchanted weapon* (as the 4th-level wizard spell) three times per day by touch on any bladed weapons. Blades so enchanted glow with a silvery radiance and exhibit a +2 attack and damage bonus for 7 rounds, regardless of how many attacks they land or how many *dispel magic* spells are launched against them.
- At 10th level, sword dancers can cast *spell turning* (as the 7th-level wizard spell) once per day.
- At 13th level, sword dancers can cast *commune* or *true seeing* (as the 5th-level priest spells) once per day.
- At 15th level, sword dancers can cast *stone tell* (as the 6th-level priest spell) or *plane shift* (as the 5th-level priest spell) once per day.

Eilistraean Spells

Two unique spells widely employed by the Dark Maiden's followers are *lesser spellsong* and *spellsong*. The use of these spells has given the clergy of Eilistraee the name *spellsingers* in the North. Sword dancers should not be confused with spellsinger wizards who cast spells in the same way, but who worship Mystra and other gods, with other aims. (Spellsinger wizards are detailed in *Wizards and Rogues of the Realms*.)

In addition to the spells listed below, priests of the Dark Maiden can cast the 2nd-level priest spell *stalk*, detailed in *Faiths & Avatars* in the section on Mielikki.

2nd Level

Eilistraee's Moonfire (Pr 2; Alteration)

Sphere:	Sun
Range:	Variable
Components:	V, S
Duration:	1 round/level
Casting Time:	1 round
Area of Effect:	Up to 1 cubic foot/level
Saving Throw:	None

By means of this spell, the caster can conjure controlled moonfire. Moonfire can range from a faint glow to a clear, bright (but not blinding) light, varying in hue as desired: blue-white, soft green, white, and silver. It serves as a source of light for reading, finding one's way, and attracting others to a desired location. Moonfire is the same as the strongest moonlight for all purposes.

Eilistraee's moonfire lasts for one round per level of the caster. Concentration is not required to maintain it, but it can be ended at will by the summoner, by a successful *dispel magic* spell, or by any *darkness* spell cast against it for this purpose (which the *Eilistraee's moonfire* negates during its own destruction).

Moonfire always appears to emanate from some part of the body of the priest casting the spell, but it can move about as the user wills. Priests of 4th level or higher can cause moonfire to move away from their bodies altogether, drifting about in the manner akin to *dancing lights*. Moonfire moves about the caster's body as rapidly as desired, but when no longer in contact with the caster it can drift in any direction (and through the tiniest openings) at a rate of up to 40 feet per round. Moonfire can fill as large or small an area as the priest desires, up to the volume limits of one cubic foot per level.

3rd Level

Bladedance (Pr 3; Conjuration/Summoning)

Sphere:	Combat
Range:	Touch
Components:	V, S, M
Duration:	1 round/level
Casting Time:	6
Area of Effect:	1 bladed weapon
Saving Throw:	None

This spell enables a single bladed melee weapon touched by the caster to animate and attack a chosen creature. The spell confers only the ability to move and fight; it does not confer any other magical abilities or properties. If at any time the caster and the weapon are separated by more than 60 feet, the spell ends and the weapon falls to the ground.

Any time after the spell is cast, the bladed weapon can be cast into the air by the priest and commanded to attack. The weapon flies toward the target creature by the most direct route. It attacks any creature that tries to block its way. If left to itself, it will fight its way to the intended target through all opposition; however, the caster can, at will, take direct control of its flight, its positioning, and its attack. Doing so requires full concentration on the weapon for the entire round; otherwise, the blade attacks on its own.

The weapon attacks once per round, as if wielded by the caster. If *bladedance* is cast on a magical weapon that has powers activated by a wielder (such as the *radiance* effect of a *sun blade*), the caster must concentrate on the blade in order to use them. The dancing weapon does not take normal melee damage, but any attack that might destroy the weapon under normal circumstances can affect it, and of course the *bladedance* is subject to dispelling. If the weapon is engaged in non-lethal combat, it defends as if it was the caster. While the blade is acting on its own, the caster can take any other actions: resting, discharging missiles, spellcasting, melee, and so on.

At 5th level, a priest can cast *bladedance* on any size S bladed melee weapon. At 7th level, she or he can cast the spell on any size S or M bladed melee weapon, and at 9th, a size S, M, or L bladed melee weapon can be affected.

The material component is the priest's holy symbol, which is touched to the weapon.

Lesser Spellsong (Pr 3; Evocation)

Sphere:	Creation
Range:	As spell created
Components:	V, S
Duration:	As spell created
Casting Time:	1 round, or variable depending on the value of the material components used in the spell created
Area of Effect:	As spell created
Saving Throw:	None

This spell enables the caster, by song and supplication to Eilistraee, to cause an effect equivalent to almost any desired priest spell of 3rd level or less, in effect casting the spell with normal effects, range, duration, saving throws, and so on, but without the usual gestures or (most often) material components. However, spells that require material components in excess of 100 gp in value require an additional round of singing to be added to the casting time for each 100 gp of value or fraction thereof of the material component. Spells that specify that the material component cannot be eliminated or substituted for cannot be created with *lesser spellsong*.

The caster must be able to move (hands and shoulders at least) and sing free of magical silencing. Priests of Eilistraee are trained to sing when in pain and can sing while dodging about in combat.

6th Level

Spellsong (Pr 6; Evocation)

Sphere:	Creation
Range:	Special
Components:	V, S
Duration:	Special
Casting Time:	1 round, or variable depending on the value of the material components used in the spell created
Area of Effect:	Special
Saving Throw:	None

This spell enables the caster, by song and supplication to Eilistraee, to cause one of several effects. If other priests of Eilistraee are present, the options for the possible effects this spell can produce increase. The caster and any additional choral participants must be able to move about freely to dance and sing free of magical silencing. Priests of Eilistraee are trained to sing when in pain and may sing while dodging about in combat. Choral work by multiple priests involves a circular dance around the person to be aided, a fire, or other focal point. Failing anything else, a long sword driven point-down into the ground or a tripod of sticks surmounted by the holy symbol of the caster can be used.

This spell can perform one of the following functions:

(1) *Spellsong* can cause an effect equivalent to almost any desired priest spell of 4th level or less, in effect casting the spell with normal effects, range, duration, saving throws, and so on, but without the usual gestures or (most often) material components. However, spells that require material components in excess of 100 gp in value require an additional round of singing to be added to the casting time for each 100 gp of value or fraction thereof of the material component. Spells that specify that the material component cannot be eliminated or substituted for cannot be created with *spellsong*.

(2) Alternatively, a *spellsong* may be used to recall to memory and the immediate ability to cast any one spell of 4th level or less cast by the *spellsong* caster earlier in the last 48 hours, not including any spells cast from scrolls.

(3) It can also, with different wording, bestow *spell immunity*. If a *spellsong* is cast when more than one priest of Eilistraee is present, the other priest or priests can join in the song without using a spell themselves. In this case the spell immunity is not only applicable for a spell known to the caster by casting or by the experience of having it cast on or against her, but also can be applied from any spell known to others in the choral group by casting or having it cast upon or against one of them.

(4) A differently worded *spellsong* can heal 1d4+1 points of damage to the caster or to any creature touched. Each additional singing priest who touches the injured creature while the *spellsong* continues heals

1d4 more points of damage. (This choral addition can be used only for healing points of damage, not in other healing uses of the spell.)

(5) If seven or more priests of Eilistraee are present, they can work a *cure blindness*, *slow poison*, or *cure disease* instead of curing points of damage if they will it so and sing together.

(6) If nine or more priests are present, a *dispel magic*, *remove curse*, or *neutralize poison* can be worked. *Dispel magic* or *remove curse* takes effect at the level of the highest choral participant.

(7) If 12 or more priests are present, a *regeneration* can be worked instead or an experience level lost within the last day restored.

Ghaunadaur

(That Which Lurks, the Elder Eye, the Ancient One)

Lesser Power of the Paraelemental Plane of Ooze, CE

Portfolio:	Oozes, slimes, jellies, outcasts, ropers, rebels, all things subterranean
Aliases:	Ghaunadar, Gormauth Souldrinker, Juiblex, the Elder Elemental God
Domain Name:	Paraelemental Plane of Ooze/The Cauldron of Slime
Superior:	None
Allies:	Bwimb (dead), Moander (dead)
Foes:	Deep Duerra, Eilistraee, Gargauth, Laduguer, Lolth, the Seldarine, Selvetarm, Vhaeraun, Lolth, Malar, Selvetarm, Vhaeraun, Blibdoolpoolp, the Blood Queen, Diinkarazan, Diirinka, Great Mother, Gzemnid, Ilsensine, Ilxendren, Laogzed, Maanzecorian (dead), Psilofyr
Symbol:	Purple circle, outlined with an inner ring of violet and an outer ring of black with a single black-rimmed, violet-on-mauve eye in the center of the circle or (older symbol) an inverted triangle of amber on a purple background, with amber lines inside of it forming an upside-down "Y" shape whose arms end by bisecting the sides of the triangle.
Wor. Align.:	LN, N, CN, LE, NE, CE

Ghaunadaur (GONE-ah-door) is a fell deity that has plagued the darkest reaches of the Realms since the dawn of time. That Which Lurks appears as an amorphous, dark purple blob with many tentacles. It is venerated by the largest slimes, oozes, slugs, and other crawling things—some of which are said to possess intelligence, albeit alien. Once all such beings worshiped Ghaunadaur, but it struck most of them mad in a fit of fury for some transgression—said by some to involve its failure to defeat Lolth shortly after her banishment from the Seldarine—and stole their intellects. As a result, many of its worshipers, and most of its power, ceased to exist. That Which Lurks and its giant roper servants have been venerated for eons by various creatures of the Underdark, particularly lone or subintelligent monsters and other outcasts (whom it occasionally aids, in return for adulation), as well as the few intelligent amorphs that remain. Evil beings seeking an alternative to established deities—including drow dissatisfied with the rule of Lolth—have also begun to worship That Which Lurks. Most humans find the worship of Ghaunadaur disgusting, but there are secret, subterranean altars and cults to the Elder Eye all over Toril, particularly in the older and more degenerate lands of the southern Sword Coast, Thay, and Kara-Tur.

Although Ghaunadaur is a distinct entity unrelated to the tanar'ri lord Juiblex, the Faceless Lord, or the otherwise unnamed Elder Elemental God, neither of the latter two powers is active in the Realms, and Ghaunadaur has assumed both of their aspects within the crystal sphere of Realmspace. Gormauth Souldrinker may have once been the name of a separate power, but if so, it has long been totally subsumed by That Which Lurks. Some rumors hold that Ghaunadaur occasionally lurks on the Elemental Plane of Earth and the Paraelemental Plane of Smoke, while others place him in the Abyss.

Ghaunadaur is unpredictable by human standards. It may aid worshipers who merely pay lip service to its rituals—even expending great power to grant permanent magical boons—but may also devour or maim them, without warning. Ghaunadaur enjoys watching the hunting and devouring activities of large horrible monsters and the suffering they cause. Ghaunadaur is silent and terrible when outside the Inner Planes, but old records tell of gibbering, bestial language spoken in the deity's great court of mingled mud and gelatin pools. Ghaunadaur only communicates telepathically with blunt and simple communications (for example, "Approve," "No," "Not," "Slay," "Come to Me," "Go to [mental picture of desired place]," and so on).

Ghaunadaur's Avatar (Fighter 27, Cleric 25, Mage 21)

Ghaunadaur appears as a reddish-purple giant slug, but at will it can alter its form into an amorphous free-flowing shape like a jelly, rear up into a giant roper with up to 10 long purple tentacles, or appear as a sticky green substance that emerges from the ground. It favors spells from the chaos, combat, elemental, sun (reversed), thought, and war spheres and from the alteration and conjuration/summoning schools, as well as all elemental wizard spells. However, it can cast spells from any sphere or school. Elemental magic wielded by it always has the maximum possible effect.

AC –1 (–3); MV 12; HP 205; THAC0 –6; #AT 10
Dmg 2d6 (corrosive touch)
MR 50%; SZ G (26 feet long or in diameter)
Str 24, Dex 19, Con 22, Int 18, Wis 18, Cha 7
Spells P: 11/11/10/10/9/8/4, W: 5/5/5/5/4/4/4/2
Saves PPDM 2, RSW 3, PP 4, BW 4, Sp 4

Special Att/Def: Ghaunadaur creeps along silently and can cloak itself at will in mauve or violet mists that eddy and flow, foiling attacks that require their target to be seen, including spells such as *magic missile*, and improve its Armor Class to the value given in parentheses above. The mists foil heat-related detections of all sorts but can be pierced by *true seeing* magic. Any being within Ghaunadaur's mists must succeed at a saving throw vs. breath weapon every round or be slowed (as by the spell) on the round that follows. The Elder Eye can emit its violet and mauve mists once every third round to maintain a continuous cloud surrounding it in a 5-foot radius. (However, the mists do not move with Ghaunadaur, who must keep emitting them to maintain them when it moves or there is significant air movement in its vicinity.) Once per turn it can jet thick purple mist, with the same effects, that extends the cloud outward to a 20-foot radius for 2 rounds. Immediately thereafter, however, the mists dissipate entirely and cannot be renewed until another round has passed. Ghaunadaur always has *true seeing*, even through its own mists.

Once per day, Ghaunadaur can *cause blindness* in creatures that it desires to affect within a 20-foot radius. Targets must succeed at a saving throw vs. spell with a –3 penalty or be blinded. Their condition lasts until a *dispel magic* or *remove curse* is applied. (Rest and *cure blindness or deafness* spells do not suffice.)

Ghaunadaur's normal attack is to lash out with four to six tentacles. Each tentacle can extend 30 feet and is studded with barbed hollow teeth. When a tentacle hits a target, it grips with Ghaunadaur's full strength. The target suffers 2d6 points of damage as corrosive fluids well out from its teeth, and the target's movement is halted. Victims are dragged 6 feet closer to Ghaunadaur each round but suffer no further damage until they reach Ghaunadaur's mouth. Ghaunadaur's saw-toothed maw does 3d4 points of damage to creatures dragged to it. Ghaunadaur never employs more than two tentacles against the same creature; the rest are held in reserve for other foes. The tentacles are AC 6 and have 14 hp each.

Victims (and those who aid them) must make a successful Strength ability check to avoid being dragged toward Ghaunadaur. On any round in which the target's Strength roll equals or exceeds Ghaunadaur's, the target can try to tear free from the tentacle by making a successful Dexterity check. Tearing free does the target 1d4+1 points of further damage. Lost tentacles are reabsorbed by Ghaunadaur.

Ghaunadaur is immune to all acids, drugs, and poisons. It can only be struck by +1 or better magical weapons.

Other Manifestations

Ghaunadaur frequently (compared to most powers) manifests to aid priests or worshipers who call on it and always in the same fashion. He can also be summoned by great and audacious evil. One to three rounds after a supplication (one to two if the worshiper has just drawn blood from another creature), a roiling purple mist appears that grows in size to a cloud 4 feet to 6 feet across. From the center of this cloud comes a 12-inch-diameter gold eye that opens its lids to bathe the favored creature in a fiery orange light. The light gradually fades to deep red, then a dark purple. The entire cloud darkens to black and shrinks away to nothingness. The process typically takes 8 rounds, and this manifestation grants the following aid to favored beings: a +6 bonus to the being's Strength ability score (with attendant attack and damage bonuses), double damage with every strike for 1d8 rounds, and a one-time healing (which occurs in the first round of its gaze) of 3d4 points of damage. It also regenerates severed limbs, lost faculties, and permanently negates any diseases and/or poisons present in the creature.

In the presence of an altar dedicated to its worship, Ghaunadaur can manifest its eye within the unholy object and create up to three tentacles emanating from the altar. Such tentacles have all the powers of Ghaunadaur's avatar's tentacles, and the eye has all the abilities described above as well as one of the following effects. (Roll 1d12 to determine the fate of each creature seeing the eye.)

Roll	Effect
1	Death (or catatonia*, at the DM's option)
2	Insanity* (gibbering, drooling feeblemindedness (as the *feeblemind* spell) broken by periods of incoherent frantic activity)
3	Rage* (attack companions until all are disabled or have fallen—physical attacks only)
4	Fright and weakness* (50% instant Strength loss, with the probable attendant need to discard armor, large weapons, and heavy treasure)
5	Unconsciousness for 1d4+12 turns. During this time the vistim visibly ages 2d12 years.
6–12	No effect (looked away in time)

  * = Curable by application of a *remove curse* by a 12th-level caster spell.

Ghaunadaur occasionally acts through the appearance or presence of alkiliths, darktentacles, deadly puddings, gelatinous cubes, giant ropers (also known as ghauropers, they have 15 Hit Dice and many unique magical abilities), gibbering mouthers, ghaunadan, jellies, oozes, metalmasters, mephits (ooze), ropers, slimes, slithering trackers, slithermorphs, slugs, and storopers. He also shows his attention—for widely varying reasons—through the discovery of solitary mauve roses that drip blood from their thorns or amethysts, jasmals, purple luriyls, rosalines, Shou Lung amethysts, violines, or yanolite (ophealine) from the depths of which stares a single, baleful, golden eye.

The Church

CLERGY:	Clerics, crusaders, specialty priests
CLERGY'S ALIGN.:	CN, LE, NE, CE
TURN UNDEAD:	C: No, Cru: No, SP: No
CMND. UNDEAD:	C: Yes, Cru: No, SP: Yes

All clerics (including fighter/clerics), crusaders, and specialty priests of Ghaunadaur receive religion (drow), religion (elven), and reading/writing (drowic) as bonus nonweapon proficiencies.

Ghaunadaur is little known on the surface of Toril except for a few small cults in large, decadent cities. Those who are aware of his existence recoil in horror from the foulness of the Elder Eye's evil. In the Underdark, Ghaunadaur is more widely known, particularly among the dark elves. While speaking the Elder Eye's name is a crime punishable by death in most cities dominated by priests of Lolth, most drow are at least tangentially aware of the existence of this rival of the Spider Queen.

Any living creature—even oozes and jellies—may join the clergy of the Elder Eye, as Ghaunadaur values devotion over ability. All ghaunadan are considered as members of the clergy, as are many slithermorphs. Titles vary widely among Ghaunadaur's solid (nonamorphous) clergy, but examples include Loathsome Ooze, Spawn of the Pit, Eater of Wastes, Noxious Slime,

Creeping Doom, and Amorphous Annihilator. Specialty priests of Ghaunadaur are known as amorphites and make up over 60% of the clergy. Clerics, fighter/clerics, and crusaders make up 12%, 8%, and 5% of the clergy, respectively, and the remainder includes a wide range of miscellaneous creatures who are not priests. Almost all (95%) of the solid clergy are male.

Temples of Ghaunadaur are found throughout the Realms in surface cities such as Bezantur (where it is known as Juiblex), Calimport, Holldaybim (a drow city in the Forest of Mir), Waterdeep, and Westgate. In the Underdark in the cities of the drow, the Elder Eye's temples are found in strife-torn cities where the clergy of rival powers are weak—Eryndlyn, located in hidden caves beneath the High Moor, is riven by civil war between the faithful of Lolth, Ghaunadaur, Selvetarm, and Vhaeraun—or absent altogether—Llurth Dreir, a city of 400,000 dark elves and countless slimes, jellies, and oozes located under the Shaar, northwest of the Deep Realm of the dwarves, is ruled by the clergy of the Elder Eye. Ghaunadaur's temples are sometimes located in the wilds of the Underdark, far from the influence of cities led by the Spider Queen's priests. One such example, beyond the reach of the priests of Guallidurth but better known for having housed the *Living Gem* for many centuries, is located beneath Forest of Mir.

Temples of the Elder Eye are typically lit by purple, mauve, and lavender rays of light, radiances, and drifting, eddying luminous mists. These temples are usually located underground, but sometimes can be found concealed in remote ruins. The walls are decorated with mosaics depicting beings of all races crawling in self-sacrifice to be eaten by vaguely squidlike creatures, each with 10 hairy tentacles. The devouring creatures (Ghaunadaur's long-unseen bodyguard ropers) are purple, violet, and mottled mauve in hue. Temples to the Eye always have well-polished floors, usually of porphyry, obsidian, red and black hornblende, or black marble. Where black and purple materials are not available, carpets and tapestries of those hues are used.

The altar chamber sports ceiling support pillars of polished obsidian, malachite, or serpentine, graven with runes and symbols of Ghaunadaur. When possible, these pillars are imbued with magical effects created by priests of the Eye. (Ghaunadaur itself, if summoned with the proper prayers, endows these magical effects with *permanency*.) Pillar enchantments radiate magical fields of effect. These typically include magical unease and insecurity affecting all beings who do not worship Ghaunadaur. At least one pillar in each temple has a *teleport* rune, known only to its priests. If the rune is touched, the priest is transported to a prearranged sanctuary or a city location. Some of these runes are traps: If a command word is whispered, they go to a safe destination; if no word is uttered, they transport the activator instead into a monster lair or other dangerous area or discharge electricity or other baneful effects. Temples to Ghaunadaur typically have a pillar-flanked aisle leading to the altar in three ascending tiers. On the second tier is the altar, a dull, porous-looking, rusty black rectangular stone. On the first tier, surrounding it on the second, and hanging above the third are usually an assortment of gongs, chimes, drums, candelabra, and braziers.

Dogma: All creatures have their place, and all are fit to wield power. Those who hunt weed out the weak and strengthen the stock of all. Those who rebel or who walk apart find new ways and try new things and do most to advance their races. Creatures of power best house the energy of life, which Ghaunadaur reveres and represents.

The faithful of Ghaunadaur are to make sacrifices to the Eye, persuade others to sacrifice themselves to Ghaunadaur or in service of the Eye, further the knowledge and fear of Ghaunadaur, and in the end give themselves to Ghaunadaur in unresisting self-sacrifice. Priests of Ghaunadaur are to convert all beings that they can to worship Ghaunadaur. They must slay all clergy of other faiths, plundering their temples and holdings for wealth to better their own lot and to further the worship of Ghaunadaur.

Day-to-Day Activities: Priests of Ghaunadaur must do whatever pleases Ghaunadaur best and serve the Eye absolutely. Priests of Ghaunadaur have simple duties: They are to ensure, by force or threat, that a ready supply of sacrifices reaches Ghaunadaur's altars. The god supplies them with spells and *tentacle rods* to ensure success in this. Most of all, Ghaunadaur delights in creatures that offer themselves to him without resistance (regardless of whether these sacrifices have been magically charmed or otherwise coerced by its clergy). Priests who can bring such offerings to the Eye's altars often are highly valued and favored by the god.

Priests of Ghaunadaur are encouraged to become familiar with the use and manufacture of acids, poisons (including gases and incenses), and flaming oils of all sorts. (Temples and priestly abodes are typically well supplied with such weapons in a ready state.)

Holy Days/Important Ceremonies: Ghaunadaur expects a prayer of adulation and praise, accompanied by a sacrifice, at least once per day. If live sacrifices cannot be procured that often, the Elder Eye accepts offerings of bones and food burned in oil. Braziers of perfumed incense are also burned.

If a priest is unable to procure such offerings, the priest must pray while holding one hand in an open flame. The priest's hand must be covered with any magical oil or potion. (*Oils* or *potions of fire resistance* are instantly converted to lamp oil, with the appropriate results.) If the prayer is accepted (55% chance), the hand is healed of any damage it sustains immediately after sustaining it.

In any place of worship to Ghaunadaur, all cloth furnishings and garments worn by priests are to be of hues pleasing to Ghaunadaur's eye. Acceptable colors are copper, amber, flame-orange, russet, gold, dark red, plum, purple, amethyst, violet, heliotrope, mauve, lilac, lavender, black, and silver.

Smoke and flame are to be a part of all sacrifices to Ghaunadaur. No creature should speak out against the will of Ghaunadaur in the presence of the Eye, its avatar, or its manifestation. If such defiance occurs, a sacrifice of appeasement must be performed (preferably involving the creature who defied the Elder Eye).

Major Centers of Worship: In the South, deep beneath the heart of Sarenestar (also known as the Forest of Mir) is a place of great power sacred to Ghaunadaur. This ancient subterranean site was discovered by Clan Hune of Ilythiir prior to the Fourth Crown War. Following their discovery, the dark elves built a great temple around a massive pit in which dwelt a monstrous creature of evil placed there by the Elder Eye. When the temple, known as the Elder Orb of Ooze, was completed, the leaders of Clan Hune sought to draw on Ghaunadaur's power in preparation for the coming conflict with Keltormir. The inscrutable Elder Elemental God was displeased, however, and it lashed out at the fools who dared call on its name by causing countless oozes, slimes, jellies, and other horrid monsters to erupt from the pit and attack everything they encountered. Many of Clan Hune's leaders were destroyed, and the temple was abandoned shortly thereafter. Although its location has been long-since forgotten, the ruined temple still exists today, its defenses still active. Ghaunadaur assuredly inflicts his wrath on any solid foolish enough to profane his place of power, and some believe that fate of the wizard **Shond Tharovin** was sealed when the would-be tyrant removed the *Living Gem* from the temple.

In the North, the Elder Eye's place of greatest power was the Pit of Ghaunadaur, located deep beneath Mount Waterdeep. Several years after her birth in the Year of the Awakening Wyrm (767 DR), Qilué Veladorn, Chosen of Mystra and Eilistraee, led a handful of her dark elven playmates from their tiny, now-vanished settlement of Buiyrandyn in an assault on the Pit of Ghaunadaur. After destroying an avatar of Ghaunadaur resident therein and causing its minions to flee or be destroyed, the Chosen of Eilistraee (as the dark elven children were collectively known) sealed the downward fissures and tunnels in the temple by which Ghaunadaur's surviving minions had fled and caused a rockfall that filled what was left of the Pit of Ghaunadaur. After centuries of patrolling the passages around the Pit, the Chosen built a temple of Eilistraee, which they named the Promenade, atop the long-sealed Pit. That Which Lurks has never accepted the loss of its place of power in what is now the third level of Undermountain north and east of the subterranean city of Skullport, and its minions have remained active in the region. For several years, a circle of ghaunadan based in a small temple to the Elder Eye in a hidden cellar beneath a warehouse in Dock Ward and Halastar's Halls have been active in Waterdeep. In the Year of the Banner (1368 DR), Ghaunadaur's cultists—12 ghaunadan commanders and approximately 50 semi-intelligent slimes and oozes—began a full-scale assault on the Promenade from the northern and eastern caverns that lasted several months. While the Chosen of Eilistraee ultimately prevailed—thanks in part to the assistance of Qilué's sister, Laeral Silverhand—and drove off their foes, the followers of Ghaunadaur were not destroyed, and the cult continues to rebuild its strength in preparation for another assault.

Affiliated Orders: The Fanatics of the Overflowing Pit were an elite order of dark elven crusaders of Ghaunadaur in ancient Ilythiir—the moon and dark elf domains in the woods south of the Lake of Steam in the forests that once covered the Shaar—who waged endless war on the clergies of rival faiths. While Ilythiir fell over ten thousand years ago with the Seldarine-mandated Descent of the Drow, it is believed that the order survives in some form in the city of Llurth Dreier underneath the Shaar.

Priestly Vestments: As listed above, the vestments of all priests of Ghaunadaur must be of hues pleasing to the Elder Eye. Typical raiment includes a full-length robe with voluminous sleeves, a dark tabard emblazoned with the symbol of the Elder Eye, and a gleaming, silver skull cap. All priests wear their hair long and unbound, but beards and mustaches are not permitted. The holy symbol of the faith is a sphere of black obsidian at least 3 inches in diameter, which is sometimes worn on a chain around the neck. Such spheres are often eveloped in a nimbus of mauve-hued *continual faerie fire*.

Adventuring Garb: When adventuring, Ghaunadaur's clergy employ whatever weapons, armor, or equipment is most appropriate to the task at hand. Most priests are careful to always wear hues pleasing to the Elder Eye, however, just in case it is observing their performance, even going so far as to tint their armor and weapons.

Tentacle Rods

Any Lesser Rod:	XP Value: 3,000	GP Value: 15,000
Any Greater Rod:	XP Value: 5,000	GP Value: 20,000
Master Rod:	XP Value: 7,500	GP Value: 25,000

The favored weapons of drow priests of Ghaunadaur are *tentacle rods*. The construction of these fell items is a secret held by drow who worship the Elder Eye, but it apparently involves *animate object*, *enchant an item*, *permanency*, and some sort of *monster summoning*. *Tentacle rods* come in an assortment of types, but all are 2-foot-long, dark rods with a thickened handgrip at one end and three, six, or seven 8-foot-long tentacles at the other. These lifelike arms reach and writhe of their own accord when the *rod* is used as a flail. The color of the tentacles denotes the type of *tentacle rod*. These *rods* function in the hands of priests of any evil alignment, and then only if a specially enchanted *ring of tentacle rod control* is worn as well. Such a *ring* can control any *tentacle rod* of the type to which it is linked. If a *ring of tentacle rod control* is not worn, a *tentacle rod* exhibits none of its special powers and functions only as a magical horseman's flail doing 1d4+1 points of damage; it has no attack or damage bonuses but still radiates a dweomer. No saving throws are allowed against the special effects of these weapons. All *tentacle rod* sale values assume that a *ring of tentacle rod control* for the same type of *tentacle rod* is included; otherwise, deduct 75% of the given price.

Lesser Tentacle Rod
Lesser tentacle rods are 2-foot-long dark rods with a thickened handgrip at one end. They have three 8-foot-long tentacles, all of a single color.

Purple: When wielded in an attack, each arm attacks the same target individually at THAC0 13, inflicting 3 points of damage on a successful attack. If all three arms strike the target in a round, the victim suffers double damage (18 points) and is slowed for 9 rounds (as by a *slow* spell). If struck by all three arms again during the slowed period, the victim is slowed for 9 rounds after the latest strike. In other words, the duration the victim is slowed is not cumulatively extended by each triple strike. This *rod's ring of tentacle rod control* is made of rune-carved hematite (material value 500 gp).

Red or Russet: This *tentacle rod* inflicts the same damage on a successful attack as a *purple lesser tentacle rod*, but its successful triple strike inflicts total weakness in the victim's right or left arm, whichever takes the brunt of the attack. (Determine by situation or randomly.) The limb cannot be lifted or used to strike, grasp, or carry things for 9 rounds. This *rod's ring of tentacle rod control* is made of rune-carved rhodochrosite (material value 500 gp).

Yellow: This *tentacle rod* inflicts the same damage on a successful attack as a *purple lesser tentacle rod*, but its successful triple strike dazes a victim for 9 rounds. Being dazed costs the victim a –1 penalty on attack rolls and prevents the concentration necessary for spellcasting, though magical items can be wielded and command words spoken. This *rod's ring of tentacle rod control* is made of rune-carved lapis lazuli (material value 500 gp).

Greater Tentacle Rod
Greater tentacle rods are 2-foot-long dark rods with a thickened handgrip at one end. They have six 8-foot-long tentacles, all of a single color.

Amber: When wielded in an attack, each arm attacks individually at THAC0 7, inflicting 6 points of damage on a successful attack. The six arms can attack up to three different targets so long as sufficient targets are within 10 feet. If three arms strike the same target in a round, the victim is numbed and strikes at a –4 attack penalty for the next 3 rounds. If all six arms hit a single target, the victim is soul-burned, bursting into flame for 1 round and suffering 4d4 points of damage, 1d6 of which is a permanent loss of hit points. All worn or carried items of a soul-burned victim must succeed at an item saving throw vs.

magical fire or be destroyed. This *rod's ring of tentacle rod control* is made of carved ruby set with a cabochon-cut piece of amber (material value 12,200 gp).

Black: This *tentacle rod* inflicts the same damage on a successful attack as an *amber greater tentacle rod*, but if all six arms strike a single target, that victim is soul-chilled, suffering 6d6 points of internal cold damage, 1d8 of which is permanent. The victim is also slowed (as if by a *slow* spell) for 6 rounds. This *rod's ring of tentacle rod control* is made of obsidian set with a black opal (material value 2,500 gp).

Jade: This *tentacle rod* inflicts the same damage on a successful attack as an *amber greater tentacle rod*, but if all six arms strike a single target, that victim is feebleminded (as the spell). Its *ring of tentacle rod control* is made of jade set with a diamond (material value 5,500 gp).

Violet: When wielded in an attack, each arm attacks individually at THAC0 7, inflicting 6 points of damage on a successful attack. The six arms can attack up to three different targets so long as sufficient targets are within 10 feet. If three arms strike the same target in a round, the victim is blinded and attacks at a –4 penalty for the next 3 rounds. If all six arms hit a single target, that victim is blinded for 6 rounds and loses 1 point of Dexterity for 1d4+1 years. A properly worded *limited wish* or a *restoration* restores this loss (though this is not the normal function of a *restoration* spell), but a *heal*, *regeneration*, *dispel magic*, or *remove curse* does not. This *rod's ring of tentacle rod control* is made of amber set with an amethyst (material value 2,500 gp).

Master Tentacle Rod
These extremely rare items have seven multicolored tentacles, one of each hue of the other types of *tentacle rods*. The arms attack at THAC0 4, inflicting 10 points of damage each on a successful strike. They may be directed at multiple targets within 15 feet of the caster, extending with lightning speed to 16 feet in length and retracting an instant after striking. If three arms strike a target in a round, the victim is robbed of 1d4 senses for the next 6 rounds. If all seven arms hit a single target, that victim is simultaneously affected by any two six-arm effects of a *greater tentacle rod* chosen by the *rod* wielder. This *rod's ring of tentacle rod control* is made of carved malachite set with a star sapphire (material value 6,500 gp).

Specialty Priests (Amorphites)

REQUIREMENTS:	Wisdom 9
PRIME REQ.:	Wisdom
ALIGNMENT:	LE, NE, CE
WEAPONS:	Any
ARMOR:	Any
MAJOR SPHERES:	All, animal, chaos (nonlawful amorphites only), combat, elemental, guardian, healing, necromantic, sun (reversed only)
MINOR SPHERES:	Charm, creation, divination, numbers, protection, summoning, weather
MAGICAL ITEMS:	Same as clerics
REQ. PROFS:	Survival (Underdark)
BONUS PROFS:	Blind-fighting

- Amorphites may be of any race capable of becoming a priest. Most amorphites are male dark elves. Except for a minuscule minority of other races, humans comprise the remainder.
- Amorphites are not allowed to multiclass.
- Amorphites are immune to diseases, even magically induced ones.
- At 3rd level, amorphites are immune to all poisons.
- At 3rd level, amorphites can resist the effects of acids, corrosives, and caustic substances once per day, for 1 round per level. Mild corrosives cannot harm the priest at all, although they can still damage his gear. More intense acids and corrosives (black dragon breath, *Melf's acid arrow*, and the natural attacks of various puddings, oozes, slimes, and jellies) inflict only half the normal damage. If the attack requires a saving throw, the priest gains a +3 bonus, sustaining half damage with a failed saving throw or one-quarter damage with a successful saving throw.
- At 5th level, amorphites are immune to all acids and corrosive fluids and substances.
- At 5th level, amorphites can cast *mists of Ghaunadaur* (as the 3rd-level priest spell) or *Evard's black tentacles* (as the 4th-level wizard spell) once per day.

- At 7th level, amorphites can protect themselves from the attacks of any of the various amorphous monsters, including slimes, jellies, oozes, puddings, cubes, and slithering trackers, once per day. An amorphous creature is any monster that has an amorphous or fluid body, attacks through acids or secretions of some kind, and is a native of the Prime Material Plane. The priest is guarded by a protective barrier that amorphous creatures will not touch, and the natural attacks (including ranged attacks) of such monsters automatically fail. If the priest makes an attack against an amorphous creature or if he forces the barrier surrounding him against the monster, the protection immediately ceases.
- At 10th level, amorphites are immune to breath weapons.
- At 13th level, amorphites can cast *amorphous form* or *elder eye* (as the 5th-level priest spells) once per day.
- At 13th level, amorphites are immune to all spells from the school or sphere of elemental magic, as well as all related magical effects.
- At 15th level, amorphites can cast *wall of tentacles* (as the 7th-level priest spell) or *acid storm* (as the 7th-level wizard spell) once per day.

Ghaunadauran Spells

3rd Level

Mists of Ghaunadaur (Pr 3; Conjuration/Summoning)

Sphere:	Elemental Air
Range:	0
Components:	V, S
Duration:	1 round/level to a 1 turn maximum
Casting Time:	5
Area of Effect:	The spellcaster
Saving Throw:	None

By means of this spell, the caster can cloak himself or herself in mauve or violet mists that eddy and flow giving him or her effective invisibility, foiling attacks for which one must see the target (including spells such as *magic missile*), and thwarting infravision and heat-related detecting abilities. The spellcaster also receives a +2 Armor Class bonus. The *mists* can be pierced by *true seeing*. The caster's vision is unhindered by the enveloping *mists of Ghaunadaur*.

5th Level

Amorphous Form (Pr 5; Alteration)

Sphere:	Animal
Range:	0
Components:	V, S, M
Duration:	1 turn/level
Casting Time:	1 round
Area of Effect:	The caster
Saving Throw:	None

By means of this spell, the spellcaster can assume the form of an deadly pudding, ooze, slime, jelly, or roper. Like a *polymorph self* (the 4th-level wizard spell), this spell grants the spellcaster the form, physical mode of locomotion, and mode of breathing of the selected creature. No system shock roll is required. Unlike a *polymorph self* spell, this spell also gives the new form's other abilities (attack, magic, special movement, etc.), with the exception of the ability of those creatures who can split into multiple forms (voluntarily or involuntarily) and attack. Situations that would normally cause the caster to split up do so, but the multiple shapes only rejoin the next round into one form. Also, the caster cannot assume a different form than the form selected when the spell is cast at any time except to resume his original form, which immediately ends the spell.

The type of form that can be assumed depends on the level of the caster; of course a caster can choose a lesser form if desired. Available forms include:

Caster Level	Form
9–10	gray ooze, crystal ooze, gelatinous cube
11–12	mustard jelly, ochre jelly, slithering tracker
13–14	deadly pudding (black, white, dun, or brown)
15+	roper

When *amorphous form* is cast, the caster's equipment, if any, melds into the new form. (In particularly challenging campaigns, the DM may allow protective devices, such as *rings of protection*, to continue operating effectively.) The caster retains all mental abilities, but she or he cannot cast spells or use psionic abilities derived from the psionicist class. A caster not used to a new form might be penalized at the DM's option (for example, a –2 penalty to attack rolls) until she or he practices sufficiently to master it.

Employing this spell does not run the risk of the priest changing personality and/or mentality. However, there is a 1% noncumulative chance per use of this spell that the spellcaster is permanently transformed into a ghaunadan (with attendant loss of priest abilities) when this spell expires.

The material component of this spell is a vial of ichor/fluid from the kind of amorph into which the priest wishes to transform.

Elder Eye (Pr 5; Abjuration)

Sphere:	Necromantic
Range:	0
Components:	V, S
Duration:	7 rounds
Casting Time:	1 round
Area of Effect:	The caster
Saving Throw:	Neg.

When this spell is cast, one of the caster's eyes is transformed into a glowing golden orb of evil for 7 rounds. Each round, the caster may balefully glare at a single living creature within 20 feet with the *elder eye*. If the creature fails its saving throw vs. spell with a –3 penalty, a magical blindness results that persists until a *remove curse* or *cure blindness or deafness* spell cast by a 9th-level caster is applied. The caster can cast spells or engage in combat in addition to the effect. The caster's gaze can be reflected back on himself or herself by spells or magical effects that do so.

There is a 1% noncumulative chance per use of the this spell that the caster's eyeball is permanently blinded when the *elder eye of Ghaunadaur* expires. In such circumstances, nothing short of a *heal* or *regenerate* restores the caster's sight in the affected eye.

7th Level

Wall of Tentacles (Pr 7; Conjuration/Summoning)

Sphere:	Elemental Earth
Range:	0
Components:	V, S, M
Duration:	1 day/level
Casting Time:	1 round
Area of Effect:	Wall-shaped area (freestanding, if desired), 6 inches thick, and with a surface area on one side of up to 10 square feet/level
Saving Throw:	Special

This spell enables the caster to create a special sort of quasiliving elemental barrier. On the safe side (the inner side), it appears as a shadowed section of wall. On the outside, it initially appears as rough, purple-brown stone. The caster and priests of the same faith can move freely through the *wall* as though it does not exist. If any other creature (except when in physical contact with a living, mobile priest of Ghaunadaur) touches this plain wall, four tentacles emerge to grasp the being and begin a loud hissing and champing noise to alert the clergy to the presence of an intruder.

The *wall* can extrude 20 16-foot-long tentacles and two beaks. These shift about its surface but can make only four attacks per round on any single opponent. Only the tentacles attack initially; the beaks are saved for a second stage of continued attack or resistance (see below). Each tentacle strike inflicts physical damage and forces the victim to succeed at a saving throw vs. spell or be magically held (similar to a *hold person* spell). Affected beings get a saving throw to break free of the *hold* effect (only one saving throw, regardless of how many tentacle strikes are suffered). While held, victims are attacked by other tentacles at a +2 attack bonus and dragged 4 feet closer to the wall per round. Severing a tentacle automatically breaks its *hold*. A tentacle can be severed by causing it more than 12 points of damage in a single round, which causes it to vanish.

The *wall of tentacles* has the following statistics:

Wall of Tentacles: AC –2; MV 0; HD 10; hp 200 (special to the spell); THAC0 11; #AT 22 (maximum of 4 16´ tentacles and two beaks per target); Dmg 1d20 (×20 tentacles) and 1d10 (×2 bites); SA poison bite, *hold* ability of tentacles; SD *darkness 15´ radius*, immunity to nonmagical weapon attack and to all spells *dispel magic* (inflicts 50 points of damage), *disintegrate* (inflicts 100 points of damage), or *symbol of persuasion* (allows all beings of the same alignment as the caster—and others whom they escort, while touching—to pass through the wall unharmed); SZ H–G (140 square feet minimum); ML fearless (20); Int non (0); AL N.

The poison of the beaks is debilitative; it takes effect in 2d4 rounds and reduces all of a character's ability scores by half during its duration. All appropriate adjustments to attack rolls, damage, Armor Class, and so on, from the lowered ability scores are applied during the course of the illness. Furthermore, the character moves at one-half his or her normal movement rate and cannot heal by normal or magical means until the poison is neutralized or the duration of the debilitation elapses. The poison's effects last until *neutralize poison* ends them or until 3d4 days have passed.

If the *wall* is attacked by any spell or spell-like effect or is reduced to 99 or fewer hit points, it creates *darkness, 15´ radius* outward from its outside surface and bites any victims it can reach.

The material component of this spell is any sort of snake, living or dead, and the beak from an octopus or any avian.

Kiaransalee

(Lady of the Dead, the Revenancer, the Vengeful Banshee)

Demipower of the Abyss, CE

Portfolio:	Undead, vengeance
Aliases:	Kiaranselee
Domain Name:	113th Level/Thanatos
Superior:	Lolth
Allies:	Hoar, Myrkul (dead), Velsharoon, Lolth, Malar, Selvetarm, Vhaeraun, Blibdoolpoolp, the Blood Queen, Diinkarazan, Diirinka, Great Mother, Gzemnid, Ilsensine, Ilxendren, Laogzed, Maanzecorian (dead), Psilofyr
Foes:	Deep Duerra, Dumathoin, Eilistraee, Kelemvor, Laduguer, Jergal, Lolth, Orcus (dead)/Tenebrous (undead), the Seldarine
Symbol:	Female drow hand wearing silver rings
Wor. Align.:	LE, NE, CE

Kiaransalee (KEE-uh-ran-sa-lee) is the drow deity of both vengeance and the undead. She is called upon by those seeking retribution, the dark arts, or to prolong life. Although the Lady of the Dead has historically demonstrated relatively little interest in the lands of Faerûn or the Underdark beneath them, the recent rise to prominence of the Cult of the Goat's Head in Vaasa under the leadership of Zhengyi the Witch-King renewed her interest in the Realms and fueled the emergence of the Vengeful Banshee's cult as a power in the north central Underdark.

Kiaransalee's ascension as a dark goddess of evil predates even the banishment of Araushnee from the Seldarine, but the Lady of the Dead has long been an unwilling vassal of the Queen of Spiders, capable of only small acts of rebellion (such as assisting the elven heroine Kethryllia in rescuing her beloved from Lolth's demesne). Kiaransalee was once mortal, a powerful dark elven necromancer-queen on a world known as Threnody. The Revenancer was named drow an d banished by her husband, the king of Threnody, for her unholy experiments on the once-living. Kiaransalee fled with a small group of followers who she then transformed into undead servitors to ensure their loyalty. The Lady of the Dead continued her unholy experiments in secret for centuries before raising an army of undead to exact her vengeance. In the wake of the Revenancer's army, Threnody was a dead world, and the architect of its destruction fled with her unthinking servants into the Abyss—where she eventually assumed a measure of divine power herself—to escape the wrath of the Seldarine.

Only in recent memory has Kiaransalee achieved a measure of independence from the Spider Queen, a result of a successful attack on a rival power long resident in the Abyss. Not too many years ago, Kiaransalee wrested Thanatos, a cold plane of ice, thin air, and a black, moonlit sky known as the Belly of Death, from Orcus, the former Abyssal lord of the undead, in revenge for some long-forgotten slight. Although she lacked the power to eliminate the very memory of Orcus from the minds of the multiverse after killing the Prince of the Undead, Kiaransalee magically erased the name of the late Abyssal lord wherever and however it had been recorded. With her foe slain and his corpse adrift in the Astral Plane, the Lady of the Dead slew all the servants and proxies of Orcus (save one, whom she accepted into her own service) and hid the legendary *Wand of Orcus* where none could ever find it—or so she thought. Recent events suggest that Orcus returned, at least for a time, as an undead god who called himself Tenebrous. It is unknown, even to Kiaransalee, whether the Prince of the Undead has successfully transformed himself into an undead god, has been destroyed forever, or simply waits for another opportunity to return to (un)life. Regardless of the truth, Kiaransalee is convinced that her former foe will eventually return, and thus the Lady of the Dead is consumed with renewed efforts to find and eliminate every last trace of both Orcus/Tenebrous.

The Lady of the Dead has long chafed under Lolth's suzerainty, and only the Spider Queen's overwhelming strength has kept Kiaransalee's long-planned vengeance in check. Consumed as she is with the unknown fate of Tenebrous, Kiaransalee has little interest in interacting with other powers. Nevertheless, her activities on Faerûn have earned the Lady of the Dead the enmity of Dumathoin, Kelemvor, and Jergal and the possibility of an alliance with both Hoar and Velsharoon.

The Lady of the Dead is cruel, twisted, and consumed by thoughts of vengeance. Kiaransalee descended into madness long ago, but she retains her twisted cunning and clear recollection of every slight or insult done to her—real or imagined. The Revenancer is powerfully chaotic and swift to anger, and she schemes dark revenges against all who have wronged her. Kiaransalee prefers the mindless company of the undead, whom she can manipulate at will, to sentient beings capable of independent thought. She prefers to solve problems herself rather than trust someone else to do justice to her vision.

Kiaransalee's Avatar (Necromancer 25, Cleric 23)

Kiaransalee appears as a sinuous drow female wearing only silver jewelry and black silk veils. She favors spells from the spheres of all, chaos, healing (reversed only), necromantic, and sun (darkness-creating reversed spells), and the school of necromancy, but she can cast spells from any sphere or school (including illusion/phantasm and enchantment/charm).

AC –2; MV 15, Fl 24; HP 144; THAC0 6; #AT 1
Dmg 1d4+4 plus special (*dagger +4*)
MR 65%; SZ M (5´6´´ tall)
Str 13, Dex 21, Con 18, Int 23, Wis 18, Cha 22
Spells P: 11/11/10/10/9/7/3, W: 6/6/6/6/6/6/6/6/5*
Saves PPDM 2, RSW 3, PP 5, BW 7, Sp 4
   *Numbers assume one extra necromancy spell per spell level.

Special Att/Def: Kiaransalee wields *Cold Heart*, a curved *dagger +4* that continuously drips acid, inflicting 1d4 points of acid damage for 1d4 rounds after a successful attack. Curative spells end this additional damage. When she wishes, Kiaransalee wears the *Mantle of Nightmares*, a cloak of rattling bones that causes *fear* in all living creatures that hear it, requiring a successful magic resistance check or a successful saving throw vs. paralyzation with a –4 penalty to avoid its effects. The Lady of the Dead sometimes loans the mantle to favored worshipers for short periods of time.

In any given round Kiaransalee can command absolute loyalty from any undead creature within 100 yards that is not of semidivine or divine status, and she can animate any corpse she touches. (Typically she can animate 10 corpses per round if they are placed close together.) If she forgos her melee attack in a round, she can make two spellcasting attacks in a round.

Kiaransalee is immune to poisons, death magic, special attack forms from undead, and has permanent *free action*. She can *charm person* at will and can keep up to 66 Hit Dice or levels of creatures charmed at any one time. Opponents have a penalty of –4 to their saving throws when saving against her spells from the necromantic sphere or the school of necromancy. She is immune to spells from the school of illusion/phantasm. She can only be struck by +1 or better magical weapons.

Other Manifestations

Kiaransalee rarely manifests in the Realms, preferring to husband her personal power and work indirectly through the actions of her servants. When she does manifest, however, the Lady of the Dead uses one of three forms.

Kiaransalee's favorite form is to cause a skull to rise up several feet above the ground and rapidly whirl about for several seconds. When the skull stops rotating, it bears the visage of a comely female dark elf. The goddess then addresses those present (typically communicating a cryptic bit of information), threatens vengeance for some insult or slight, or simply utters a maniacal laugh. The skull then vanishes, or if Kiaransalee wishes, utters a *wail of the banshee* (as the 9th-level wizard spell) and then disappears.

Kiaransalee sometimes manifests as a dry, chuckling laughter tinged with madness coupled with the distinct sensation that someone has stepped on the grave of every creature hearing her mad chortle. This effect reduces the Wisdom and Constitution ability scores of everyone present by 1d4 points for the next 24 hours and duplicates the effects of a *fear* spell. Since there is no obvious threat present, however, those who hear the goddess's laughter flee in a random direction, as adjudicated by the DM.

The Revenancer's most terrifying manifestation always comes without warning. This manifestation only occurs while the target is standing on soil at least 6 feet deep (in other words, ground that could conceivably be dug up to serve as a grave). A pair of giant skeletal hands burst forth from the ground and drag the unfortunate victim into the earth in the blink of an eye. The victim is dragged 6 feet under the ground and held as if by a *sink* incantation (identical to the 8th-level wizard spell). If Kiaransalee is feeling generous, the effect ends after 4 turns, and the subject is forcibly expelled from the ground. If the victim has slighted or insulted the Vengeful Banshee, however, the victim remains imprisoned until rescued by his or her comrades (assuming they have the means and opportunity to do so). In either case, after being freed the victim has a –4 penalty to all saving throws vs. death magic for the next year.

Kiaransalee commonly acts through the appearance or presence of apparitions, banshees, coffer corpses, crawling claws, crimson deaths, ghasts, ghosts, ghouls, haunts, heucuva, kiaranshee, larvae, lhiannan shee, liches of all sorts (including fallen baelnorns), maurezhi, nightmares, penanggolans, phantoms, quasits, revenants, shadow fiends, shadows, shee, sheet ghouls, sheet phantoms, simpathetics, skeletons, skuz, slow shadows, spectres, wights, wraiths, vampires of all sorts, vargouilles, yeth hounds, and zombies, as well as even rarer forms of undead. The Lady of the Dead shows her favor through the discovery of chalcedony, chrysoberyl, chrysocolla, epidote, irtios, ivory, king's tears, meerschaum, moonbars, samarskite, silkstone, tomb jade and her displeasure through the discovery of skulls that split cleanly into two pieces and bones that collapse into dust when touched.

The Church

CLERGY:	Crusaders, necromancers, specialty priests
CLERGY'S ALIGN.:	CE
TURN UNDEAD:	Cru: No, Nec: No, SP: No
CMND. UNDEAD:	Cru: No, Nec: No, SP: Yes, at priest level +2

All crusaders and specialty priests of Kiaransalee receive religion (drow), religion (elven), and reading/writing (drowic) as bonus nonweapon proficiencies. The DM is encouraged to allow Kiaransalee's clergy members access to the necromantic spells detailed in the *Complete Book of Necromancers.*

Kiaransalee and her followers are little known in the Realms, even among the drow themselves. Even those dark elves who learn of her existence usually assume she is simply some sort of lich with delusions of godhood. On the surface of the Realms, Kiaransalee is almost wholly unknown, aside from a few reclusive sages. In Vaasa, rumors of Zhengyi's harem of undead drow mistresses haunting the Black Holes of Sunderland are beginning to spread in Darmshall and have drawn the attention of one or more members of the Spysong network.

Kiaransalee is worshiped in solitary secrecy in cities dedicated to Lolth in simple shrines hidden away from prying eyes. Such shrines are simply

black marble sarcophagi adorned with carved depictions of the dead rising up to take their revenge on the living. To venerate the Lady of the Dead, a priest of Kiaransalee simply lies within her personal sarcophagus while holding her holy symbol clasped in two hands across her breast. According to legend, if a living priest of the Revenancer is disturbed while so engaged, Kiaransalee grants her the powers of a vampire for the next 24 hours. While the only true temple of the Lady of the Dead found in the Realms is the Acropolis of Thanatos (described below), smaller chapels exist in the wilds of the Underdark across the length and breadth of Faerûn. Such chapels are typically small caves in which the skulls and bones of countless long-dead creatures have been partially absorbed by the walls, roof, or floor of the cavern. Kiaransalee is said to guide small bands of worshipers to such sites far from the prying eyes of the Spider Queen's priests where they can worship in secret and plot their vengeance on their spider-loving kin.

Kiaransalee's clergy are known collectively as the Crones of Thanatos. Novices of the Revenancer are known as the Commanded. All other members of the clergy are known as Nighthags. Titles used by Kiaransaleen priests vary widely across temple hierarchies, but those used at the Acropolis of Thanatos include Bones of the Dead, Flesh of the Zombie, Terror Touch of the Ghoul, Chill Touch of the Shadow, Raking Claws of the Wight, Life Leech of the Wraith, Rot of the Mummy, and Spirit Harvest of the Spectre. High-ranking priests of the Lady of the Dead have unique individual titles. Specialty priests are known as yathrinshee. As one might expect, many of Kiaransalee's faithful are transformed into undead servitors either by their own hands, by the hands of other priests, or—in very rare cases—by the hand of the goddess herself. High-ranking priests may become banshees, liches, vampires, or—if truly favored—kiaranshee. (Kiaranshee are banshees who retain their spellcasting powers, whether they were necromancers or priests.) The clergy of Kiaransalee includes only living and undead female dark elves. Kiaransalee's clergy includes specialty priests (80%), necromancers (12%), and crusaders (8%).

Dogma: Death comes to all, and cruel vengeance will be exacted on those who waste their lives on the petty concerns of this existence. True power comes only from the unquestioning servitude of the once-dead, mastery over death, and the eventual earned stature of one of the ever-living in death. Hunt, slay, and animate those who scorn the Revenancer's power, and answer any slight a thousandfold so that all may know the coming power of Kiaransalee.

Day-to-Day Activities: Kiaransalee's priests are rare, secretive, and usually found in small drow communities or special enclaves. They are agents of vengeance, plotting revenge on those who have slain, harmed, or insulted the priesthood in any way. They also regularly go out on missions to kill others to acquire corpses for animation or to steal the corpses of the recently buried. They take a prominent role in persecuting slaves of the drow.

Holy Days/Important Ceremonies: While each priest performs a handful of minor devotions to Kiaransalee every month, the Crones of Thanatos venerate the Lady of the Dead on a single annual holy day—the Graverending—celebrated each Midwinter Eve. The Graverending is celebrated individually, with each priest animating as many undead creatures as she can. All such undead—known as the Vengeance Hunters—are consumed with thoughts of revenge against their killers and unerringly seek them out over the next 24 hours. If destroyed, a Vengeance Hunter does not rise again. Vengeance Hunters return to their graves, if possible, once 24 hours have passed since their animation or once they have exacted their revenge.

Major Centers of Worship: Deep beneath the Galena Mountains and the cold plains of Vaasa is a great subterranean lake fed by the icy waters of the Great Glacier and inhabited by hundreds of giant water spiders. The Vault of Gnashing Teeth is so-named for the thousands of skulls embedded in the roof whose collective cacophonous chomping echoes throughout the great cavern. At the center of the freshwater sea is a large island, nearly a mile in diameter, dominated by a steep-sided plateau at its center. All that remains of V'elddrinnsshar—once a drow city dedicated to the Spider Queen that encircled the central mesa—are crumbling ruins, stalked by a legion of banshees awakened by Kiaransalee's faithful, and the bones of the city's former inhabitants (drow and slaves of various races). V'elddrinnsshar fell in the Year of Many Bones (1278 DR) to the ravages of the Ascomoid Plague and was plundered by duergar scavengers a decade later. The city sat unoccupied until the Year of the Wandering Maiden (1337 DR), when it was explored by Reaper of Souls Larynda Telenna and a small band of acolytes. At their goddess's direction, the priests began construction of a brooding temple of black marble atop the central plateau, a massive stalagmite whose tip had been sheered off centuries before by the followers of Lolth for a similar purpose. When the Acropolis of Thanatos was completed a decade later, Larynda had expanded the ranks of Kiaransalee's faithful a thousandfold, and the skulls of V'elddrinnsshar's dead had been enchanted and mounted in the cavern's roof to form an unholy choir. Since the temple's completion, the priests of Kiaransalee have relentlessly combated the Cult of the Goat's Head, active in the lands of Vaasa above. In the decade since the defeat of the Witch-King and the destruction of Castle Perilous, Kiaransalee's priests have nearly exterminated the remaining clergy of Orcus in the Bloodstone Lands—many of whom took refuge in the Black Holes of Sunderland and thus were readily accessible to attacks from below—and destroyed most of the goblinkin tribes who venerated the Prince of the Undead while the Witch-King reigned in the Lands of Light. Although they do not realize it, King Gareth Dragonsbane and the people of Damara owe a great deal of their success against the forces of the Witch-King to their subterranean neighbors.

Affiliated Orders: The Legion of Vengeful Banshees is an order of Kiaransaleen crusaders dedicated to the destruction of Tenebrous's undead tanar'ri servants, known as visages. While Banshee Knights are found on many worlds, in the Realms all are based in the Acropolis of Thanatos deep beneath the Galenas. From their chapter house within the temple grounds, the members of the order mount long-ranging hunts on the surface and in the Underdark for Tenebrous's minions. The Banshee Knights have apparently developed some sort or spell or magical item that allows them to detect and defend against the use of a visage's *lucidity control* power. Crusaders of the order are fanatically dedicated to their goddess and the destruction of all visages; they stop at nothing to see one destroyed, regardless of the collateral damage.

Priestly Vestments: The church of Kiaransalee favors loose black robes with hooded cowls stitched with bone and ivory. The clergy wear gray skullcaps on their shaven heads and thin silver rings on every finger save the thumb. They spread a grayish paste made of the ashes of incinerated corpses over all uncovered skin, such as the face, hands, and feet. The holy symbol of the faith is the silver rings worn on as noted above.

Adventuring Garb: Priests of Kiaransalee are forbidden to wear any sort of armor, preferring to trust their own magical defenses and the combat skills of their undead bodyguards. Many priests substitute a silver *ring of protection* for one of their ceremonial rings to supplement their defenses. Members of the Revenancer's clergy are trained in a wide variety of weapons, but most favor slim poisoned blades, garrotes, and maces so as to minimize the damage to bodies that could later be animated.

Specialty Priests (Yathrinshee)

REQUIREMENTS:	Intelligence 9, Wisdom 9
PRIME REQ.:	Intelligence , Wisdom
ALIGNMENT:	CE
WEAPONS:	Any
ARMOR:	None
MAJOR SPHERES:	All, charm, combat, divination, elemental (earth), guardian, healing (reversed only), necromantic, sun (reversed only)
MINOR SPHERES:	Astral, chaos, elemental (fire), protection, summoning
MAGICAL ITEMS:	As clerics
REQ. PROFS:	Dagger, spellcraft, singing
BONUS PROFS:	Necrology

- Yathrinshee must be drow females.
- Yathrinshee are not allowed to multiclass.
- Yathrinshee are immune to the special attack forms from undead beings including level-draining, energy-draining, statistic-draining, *magic jar*, aging, and so on, provided they are initiated by an undead creature. They are always protected by the equivalent of the 3rd-level priest spell *negative plane protection*. This does not make them immune to physical damage inflicted by an undead creature.
- Yathrinshee can cast wizard spells from the necromancy school as defined in the Limited Wizard Spellcasting section of "Appendix 1: Demihuman Priests."

- Yathrinshee can cast *animate dead* (as the 3rd-level priest spell) once per day. They can animate one corpse for every two experience levels they possess.
- At 3rd level, yathrinshee can cast *chill touch* (as the 1st-level wizard spell) or *invisibility to undead* (as the 1st-level priest spell) once per day.
- At 5th level, yathrinshee can cast *vampiric touch* (as the 3rd-level wizard spell) or *speak with dead* (as the 3rd-level priest spell) once per day.
- At 7th level, yathrinshee can cast *contagion* or *enervation* (as the 4th-level wizard spells) once per day.
- At 7th level, yathrinshee can cast *cure critical wounds* (as the 5th-level priest spell) once per day on themselves only.
- At 10th level, yathrinshee can heal 2d4 points of damage+1 point per level to an undead creature by touch.
- At 13th level, yathrinshee can cast *heal* (as the 6th-level priest spell) once per day on themselves only.
- At 15th level, yathrinshee can cast *energy drain* (as the 9th-level wizard spell) or *wail of the banshee* (as the 9th-level wizard spell) once per day.
- At 20th level, yathrinshee can cast *slay living* (as the reverse of the 5th-level priest spell *raise dead*) or *destruction* (as the reverse of the 7th-level priest spell *resurrection*) twice per tenday.

Kiaransaleen Spells

2nd Level

Threnody (Pr 2; Necromancy, Enchantment/Charm)

Sphere:	Necromantic, Charm
Range:	0
Components:	V
Duration:	Special
Casting Time:	1 round
Area of Effect:	30-foot radius
Saving Throw:	Special

Also known as *Kiaransalee's song of lament*, this spell enables the priest to evoke images of lost friends and family in the minds of those who are facing the undead, hindering their ability to attack those who bear the guise of their loved ones.

After 1 round of singing *threnody* (the casting time), anyone within or who enters the spell's area of effect while the singing continues must succeed at a saving throw vs. spell or fall under the sway of *threnody* for as long as she oe he remains within the area of effect. Anyone unaffected who remains within the area of effect in subsequent rounds must continue to roll a saving throw vs. spell with a +2 bonus or fall under the sway of *threnody*. The only way to escape the lament's effects is to stay more than 30 feet from the singer of *threnody*.

To a being under the sway of *threnody*, undead creatures in the area of effect appear to be deceased persons for whom the subject being cared deeply. As a result of *threnody*'s magic, affected beings attack undead opponents with a –2 penalty to attack and damage rolls.

A fortunate few persons—typically the very young or the very sheltered—have never lost a loved one or family member or witnessed a death. Such individuals (as adjudicated by the DM) are immune to *threnody*. At the other extreme of experience, if a being who falls under the sway of *Kiaransalee's song of lament* who actually encounters the animated remains of a love one or comrade while subject to the spell's effects is incapable of attacking that foe and suffers a –4 AC penalty to avoid the undead creature's attacks.

This spell requires no material components, but the priest casting *threnody* must be a proficient singer.

5th Level

Haunted Reverie (Pr 5; Necromancy)

Sphere:	Necromantic
Range:	Touch
Components:	V, S
Duration:	Special
Casting Time:	8
Area of Effect:	One elf
Saving Throw:	Special

This insidious incantation affects only elves, drawing them into a world of nightmares when they attempt to enter the reverie. After casting *haunted reverie*, the priest must make a successful attack roll against an elf, ignoring any nonmagical Armor Class adjustments (including shields and the base AC rating of armor, but excluding Dexterity and magical adjustments), within the next turn or the spell dissipates without effect. Only one elf is affected by this spell.

A latent *haunted reverie* effect can be removed by a *remove curse*, *limited wish*, or *wish*, but not a *dispel magic*. Once an elf enters the *haunted reverie*, only a *wish* or a *remove curse* cast by a 12th-level caster can extract him or her from its effects.

The subject of a *haunted reverie* attack suffers no effects from the magical attack until the next time she or he enters the reverie. Upon entering the reverie, the targeted elf must succeed at a saving throw vs. spell with a –3 penalty to avoid its effects. If the saving throw is successful, *haunted reverie* is held in abeyance until the next attempt to enter the reverie. Each subsequent attempt by the elf to enter into the reverie requires another saving throw vs. spell, but the penalty decreases by one with each success. If the elf suceeds at four successive saving throws against the spell, the magic of *haunted reverie* dissipates without effect. However, upon failing any of the saving throws, she or he enters into the *haunted reverie*, a nightmarish parody of the true reverie sought.

An elf who enters the *haunted reverie* thrashes about in agony but cannot be awakened except by means of a *wish* spell or a *remove curse* cast by a 12th-level caster. The elf is consumed by horrific visions of Thanatos, Kiaransalee's realm in the Abyss. Memories of friends, family, and favorite places are intermixed with visions of death, the undead, and decay. Each turn an elf remains in the *haunted reverie*, she or he must succeed at a saving throw vs. spell—with a cumulative –1 penalty for every turn entrapped in the *haunted reverie* (round down)—to escape its nightmarish dreamscape. For every turn an elf remains in the *haunted reverie*, she or he loses 1 point of Intelligence in the first round, then 1 point of Wisdom in the second round, and then 1 point of Constitution in the third round. If any attribute drops to 0 (zero) in this manner, the elf's psyche is drawn into Kiaransalee's grasp, and the elf is permanently dead, beyond the reach of all magic save a *wish* spell.

Once an elf escapes the *haunted reverie*, the spell ends, even if the elf has not yet succeeded at a saving throw vs. the effect on four separate occasions. Lost Intelligence, Wisdom, and Constitution attributes return at a rate of 1 point each every hour.

Although elves are normally resistant to *sleep* and *charm* spells, *haunted reverie* is designed to undermine the defenses of elves to such effects, and, as a result, the normal elven magic resistance to such enchantments is ineffective in defending against *haunted reverie*.

6th Level

Curse of the Revenancer (Pr 6; Necromancy)

Sphere:	Necromantic
Range:	Touch
Components:	V, S, M
Duration:	Special
Casting Time:	8
Area of Effect:	One living creature
Saving Throw:	Special

This spell *curses* a single creature to be haunted by the vengeful spirits of the dead. *Curse of the Revenancer* requires the priest to make a successful touch attack within 3 rounds of casting this spell or the spell dissipates harmlessly. A victim touched within that time can avoid the *curse*'s effects by making a successful saving throw vs. spell, but otherwise nothing short of a *wish* or a *remove curse* cast by a 14th-level caster can end the *curse of the Revenancer*.

Once the *curse of the Revenancer* is successfully laid on a victim, any foe killed by the victim has a 5% chance of rising from the grave as a revenant, regardless of the foe's ability scores. If the foe's Constitution is at least 18 and either Intelligence or Wisdom is 17 or greater, that chance increases to 30%. If the foe is a follower of Kiaransalee, the chance of the foe rising as a revenant increases to 50%. If the foe is the priest who laid the *curse of the Revenancer*, the chance of the foe rising as a revenant is 100%.

The effects of the *curse of the Revenancer* become more pronounced the more deaths the victim of the *curse* is responsible for. If the victim of the *curse* kills a large number of creatures shortly after the *curse* is laid, she or he may awaken an army of revenants seeking vengeance before even noting the presence of the curse. For the purposes of this spell, the victim is deemed to have killed a foe if she or he delivers the killing blow via magical, psionic, or physical assault or by poison.

The material components of this spell are a pinch of dirt from a freshly dug grave and the priest's holy symbol.

Lolth

(The Spider Queen, Queen of Spiders,
Demon Queen of Spiders, Demon Queen of the Abyss,
Queen of the Demonweb Pits, Weaver of Chaos, the Hunted,
the Mother of Lusts, Dark Mother of All Drow,
Lady of Spiders)

Intermediate Power of the Abyss, CE

PORTFOLIO:	Spiders, evil, darkness, chaos, assassins, the drow race
ALIASES:	Araushnee, Lloth (Menzoberranzan and Uluitur), Megwandir, Moander, Zinzerena
DOMAIN NAME:	66th level/Lolth's Web (the Demonweb Pits)
SUPERIOR:	None
ALLIES:	Loviatar, Malar, Selvetarm
FOES:	Deep Duerra, Eilistraee, Ghaunadaur, Gruumsh, Ibrandul (dead), Kiaransalee, Laduguer, Moander (dead), the Seldarine, Vhaeraun, Blibdoolpoolp, the Blood Queen, Diinkarazan, Diirinka, Great Mother, Gzemnid, Ilsensine, Ilxendren, Laogzed, Maanzecorian (dead), Psilofyr
SYMBOL:	Black spider with female drow head (at bottom of figure) or black cloak and short sword (Zinzerena aspect)
WOR. ALIGN.:	LN, N, CN, LE, NE, CE

Lolth (LOLTH) is the goddess of the drow race and drow society. She is responsible for the nature, customs, laws, and survival of most drow communities. The Spider Queen maintains her absolute rule over drow cities by means of her clergy, who tirelessly seek out and destroy all traces of dissent, disobedience, rival faiths, or sacrilege and who ruthlessly enforce the Way of Lolth. The Spider Queen foments unending chaos in drow society and sets the drow eternally at war with each other both for her own amusement and to prevent complacency, runaway pride from asserting itself, or the rise of other faiths. Lolth is also venerated by chitines, a small spiderlike race that are castoffs of the drow.

As Araushnee, Lolth was once a lesser power of the Seldarine and the consort of Corellon Larethian. She was the patron of artisans, the goddess of elven destiny, and—later, by Corellon's decree—the keeper of those elves who shared her darkly beautiful features. The Weaver of Destiny bore Corellon twin godlings—Vhaeraun and Eilistraee—before she turned against her lover and betrayed him. First she aided Gruumsh One-Eye, chief among the orcish gods, in one of his perennial battles with the Creator of the Elves, and then she set Malar on the trail of the weakened Corellon after observing the Beastlord defeat Herne on Faerûn. When these plots failed as a result of Corellon's skill at arms and Sehanine's interference, Araushnee raised a host of hostile powers—the anti-Seldarine—to assault Arvandor. Despite the treachery of Araushnee, and to a lesser extent, Vhaeraun, the assault failed and the perfidy of Corellon's consort and son were revealed. By order of the Council of the Seldarine, Araushnee was transformed into a spider-shaped tanar'ri and banished to the Abyss.

As an Abyssal Lord, Araushnee assumed the name Lolth and conquered a considerable portion of that foul plane, driving off Ghaunadaur and subjugating Kiaransalee in the process. The Spider Queen then turned her attentions toward corrupting the mortal children of the Seldarine and reclaiming her divinity. Lolth's attentions were drawn once again to Abeir-

Toril by the intrusion of the moon elven heroine Kethryllia Amarillis into her domain, and the Spider Queen immediately began to cultivate followers among the most cruel and corrupt of Corellon's children in Faerûn. In the centuries that followed, Lolth made great inroads among the warlike Ilythiiri, who had long since spread across the South conquering their kinfolk under the careful guidance of Vhaeraun, and to a lesser extent, Ghaunadaur. Lolth's machinations among the drow culminated in the Crown Wars, and eventually, the descent of the drow into the Underdark, but by that time she had enmeshed most of the dark-skinned Ilythiiri, now drow, in her webs and engendered the death of countless elves and the destruction of much of elven civilization in Faerûn.

In the centuries since the Crown Wars, Lolth's followers have continued to spread throughout the Underdark, from Dusklyngh to T'lindhet and from Guallidurth to now-fallen V'elddrinnsshar. While other powers contest her rule, the Spider Queen's dominion over the dark elves continues to expand, albeit more slowly than before. Lolth's followers have been occupied with the conquest of the Underdark and the destruction of the faerie elves of the surface, and the Spider Queen has never ceased in her efforts to destroy the elven sanctuary of Evermeet.

Since the Time of Troubles, Lolth has assumed additional aspects as two of her many stratagems to increase the ranks of her faithful and thus her own personal power. In the drow city of Menzoberranzan, in the Underdark beneath the North where Lolth—or Lloth, as she is known there—appeared during the Time of Troubles, the Spider Queen has allowed rumors to spread of a new demipower of chaos and assassins, Zinzerena the Hunted. While Zinzerena was once a legendary drow assassin and later an emerging demipower of a world other than Abeir-Toril, the Spider Queen recently slew Zinzerena—or at least banished her influence from the Realms—and assumed her aspect as a test to see if additional divine aspects increased or decreased the total (albeit fragmented) divine power available. In the Lands of Light, Lolth has long found that the deeply imbued racial antipathy of the surface elves toward the Spider Queen interferes with her attempts to seduce otherwise eminently corruptible individuals. With the death of Moander, always a more comprehensible (and tempting) force of evil to the nature-loving surface elves than the Spider Queen, Lolth has assumed the Darkbringer's aspect and portfolio of rotting death, decay, and corruption and revived its cult in a bid to add elven, half-elven, and human worshipers to the ranks of her faithful.

Although the Spider Queen detests all the members of the Seldarine, Lolth reserves her deepest hatred for her former lover, Corellon Larethian, who banished her to the Abyss and named her tanar'ri. The Spider Queen particularly loathes Sehanine Moonbow, long her rival, for her part in foiling Lolth's bid to replace Corellon as head of the Seldarine. The Spider Queen has also vowed vengeance against Fenmarel Mestarine, who spurned her after initially falling to her seductions.

Lolth is a cruel, capricious goddess, thought by many to be insane. She delights in setting her worshipers at each other's throats, so that the strongest, most devious and most cruel survive to serve her. Lolth roams the Realms often, appearing in answer to the rituals of drow priests, and working whatever harm she can to the enemies of drow. (During the Time of Troubles, Lolth appeared in the northern city of Menzoberranzan for a short period of time.) The Spider Queen secretly wants to be worshiped by humans and elves of other races on the surface Realms, and sometimes journeys among their communities, whispering of the power Lolth can bring. Lolth is malicious in her dealings and coldly vicious in a fight. She enjoys both personally dealing and causing death, destruction, and painful torture. Even more, Lolth enjoys corrupting elves and humans to her service. Lolth can be kind and render aid to those she fancies—but she really cares only for herself; her favor and aid can never be relied on. The Spider Queen enjoys the company of and can converse with spiders of all sorts.

Lolth's Avatar (Cleric 33, Mage 31, Fighter 20)

Lolth can appear as a giant black widow spider with crimson eyes, or she can change into the form of a human-sized, exquisitely beautiful female drow. In this form she often clothes herself entirely in clinging spiders, but sometimes wearing drow chain mail styled into artful dresses or tunics. She can also combine the two forms, appearing as a giant spider with a coldly beautiful female drow head. This is the form in which she is usually found in the Abyss, and it is thought to be her true form. Lolth can call on any sphere or school of magic for her spells.

AC −2 (drow) or −4 (spider); MV 15 (drow) or 9, Wb 24 (spider); HP 210; THAC0 1; #AT 1 or 3/1 (drow) or 3 (spider/drow) or 3 (spider) Dmg 1d10+9 (fist, +9 Str) or by drow weapon type (+3 drow weapon bonus, +9 Str) (drow); 1d4+special (webs) and 4d4+poison (bite) (spider/drow); or 1d4+special (webs) and 4d4+poison (spider) MR 70%; SZ M (6 feet tall—drow) or L (12 feet diameter—spider) Str 21, Dex 21, Con 21, Int 21, Wis 17, Cha 23 (3 in spider form) Spells P: 12/12/11/10/9/9/9, W: 7/7/7/7/7/7/7/7 Saves PPDM 2, RSW 3, PP 4, BW 4, Sp 4

Special Att/Def: Statistics for Lolth's spider and combined spider/drow form are nearly identical. Changing from drow form to either spider or spider/drow form (or the reverse) takes an entire round, during which Lolth can take no other action, is AC 0, and cannot use any spell-like powers. Changing from spider form to spider/drow form (or the reverse) is instantaneous.

When summoned to the Realms, Lolth likes to roam the Underdark, basking in the terrified worship of drow. She customarily takes any magical items they offer to her (or that strike her fancy). When encountered, she typically has 1d4 such items, of the DM's choice. She can employ these in any form, regardless of class limitations. When she employs a weapon or weapons in combat (she can fight two-handed when she desires at no penalty), they are drow weapons of +3 enchantment of variable type.

Lolth can cast her priest and wizard spells only in drow form and can then cast two spells in any round in which she forgos her physical attack, rather than the normal one spell/one physical attack sequence combat capabilities of avatars. In addition, Lolth can (in any form) use any one of the following spell-like powers in a round at will: charm arachnid (a spiders-only charm monster with no saving throw; intelligent beings who have magically assumed spider form receive saving throws vs. spell at a −5 penalty), comprehend languages, confusion (creature looked at only—the victim need not meet Lolth's gaze to be affected but gets a saving throw vs. paralyzation to avoid the effects), darkness 15′ radius, dispel magic, dimension door, ESP (drow only, one target per round), summon spiders (01–20%: 1d8+8 large spiders; 21–50%: 1d6+6 huge spiders; 51–90%: 2d4 giant spiders; 91–00%: 1d4 phase spiders), tongues, and true seeing. Lolth can use the following spell-like powers once per day: change self, clairvoyance, domination, mind blank, and Evard's black tentacles. The Spider Queen can also cast phase door and read magic twice per day and heal three times per day as spell-like abilities.

When in drow form, Lolth's direct physical embrace, if she wishes, can act as a charm person (with a −4 penalty to saving throws vs. spell) on a human or demihuman of either sex. She customarily leaves a poisonous spider to aid, guard, and keep watch on someone who serves her, and gives them any one magical item that she possesses or can seize.

In spider or spider/drow form, Lolth can cast up to 30-foot-long web strands from her abdominal spinnerets. These webs are equal in effect to a web spell and are covered with a flesh-corrosive secretion that inflicts 1d4 points of damage per round of contact unless a successful saving throw vs. poison is rolled. Lolth can swivel her spinnerets to fire in all directions (except through her own body) and can cast 2 strands per round as well as biting or using a spell-like power. Lolth's bite does 4d4 points of damage; the victim must succeed at a saving throw vs. poison at −4 or die in 1d2 rounds of in twitching agony.

Lolth can only be struck by +2 or better magical weapons. She is immune to all poisons. Cold and electrical attacks do only half damage, but Lolth suffers extra damage from holy water. (Each vial does 3d6+3 points of damage from a direct hit and 6 points of damage from a splash.) She has 120-foot infravision and 90-foot-range telepathy. She is not harmed or discomfited by light.

Other Manifestations

Lolth rarely aids her worshipers directly, preferring to watch and enjoy their sufferings and struggles. If she wants someone to know that she is watching, Lolth causes a smirking pair of sensuous lips to appear on any spider present. The spider is always outlined in a flickering purple faerie fire. If no spider is present, Lolth creates a smiling, spider-shaped shadow of giant size.

More rarely, Lolth acts directly. In such cases, her power may be seen as a flickering black, mauve-edged radiance around a person or object temporarily imbued with her power. The Spider Queen's power typically gives one or both of the following aids to affected things: double damage (triple to giant-type creatures) or immunity to breakage or other damage (automatic success on all item saving throws). It also gives any or all of the following aids to affected beings for 1 turn: the ability to strike first in any combat round, a +4 bonus to Armor Class, and a three-level improvement in fighting ability. (For this lasts, phantom hit points are gained and all damage inflicted is subtracted from these points first; when the phantom points disappear at the end of the turn, only any excess damage is actually suffered by the character.)

Lolth's laughter—soft, cruel feminine chuckling—is often heard by drow who have lost her favor or who have gone mad. It is also heard by foes of the drow, especially when beings of these sorts are alone and/or fleeing in the endless caverns and passages of the Underdark. Beings of less than 2 Hit Dice flee uncontrollably, as if affected by a *fear* spell, until they die, are knocked unconscious, or can hear her laughter no more.

Lolth typically acts through the appearance of yochlol, the handmaidens of Lolth, or myrlochar, the soul spiders. She also acts through the appearance or presence of abyss ants, aranea, bebiliths, brambles (petty faeries), cildabrin, darkweavers, deep dragons, driders, fallen and corrupted eladrin, ettercaps, greelox, kalin, living webs, pedipalpi (large, huge, and giant varieties), quasits, retrievers, shadowdrakes, solifugids (large, huge, and giant varieties), spiders (brain, hairy, large, hook, huge, gargantuan, giant, phase, sword, vortex, watch and wraith varieties), spiderstone golems, tanar'ri, red widows, wall walkers, webbirds, and werespiders. Lolth has never been known to employ steeders as minions, and their use as steeds by the duergar hints at an ancient pact between Lolth and Laduguer. The Spider Queen shows her favor through the discovery of arachnids encased in amber, black sapphires, datchas, and webstone, and her displeasure by causing items of value (usually gems) to shatter into eight pieces of roughly equal size.

The Church

CLERGY:	Clerics, crusaders, specialty priests
CLERGY'S ALIGN.:	CN, LE, NE, CE
TURN UNDEAD:	C: No, Cru: No, SP: No
CMND. UNDEAD:	C: No, Cru: No, SP: Yes

All clerics (including fighter/clerics), crusaders, and specialty priests of Lolth receive religion (drow), religion (elven), reading/writing (drowic), and ancient languages (high drow) as bonus nonweapon proficiencies. Members of Lolth's clergy always gain access to the spells *faerie fire* and *continual faerie fire* (detailed in *Prayers from the Faithful*). Members of Lolth's clergy must be drow or chitines, although little is known about the latter, even among the dark elves themselves.

The Spider Queen is the subject of terrifying legend among most surface dwellers and seen as virtually synonymous with the greatly feared drow. In the Underdark, she is a well-known evil, hated for the cruel power of her priests by dwarves, svirfneblin, and other races. Few elves are even willing to discuss their deep-dwelling kin, let alone the dark goddess who is blamed in large part for their depravity and for leading them into evil. Only the dark elven priests of Eilistraee are even willing to discuss the Spider Queen, and their fury at her enslavement of their kin exceeds even that of the other elven subraces. Lolth is hated and feared even by her most devout priests; they venerate her for the power she provides, not out of any sense of affection or loyalty or principles. Dark elves who venerate other evil gods as well all male drow who pay her homage revile both the Spider Queen and her priests for the power they possess, not that they would not seize such power for themselves if they could.

Noble Houses have their own private temples, and every drow city has at least one large, open public gathering-area for large rituals, calls to war, and the like. Most cities also have a grand temple to the Spider Queen, used for training priests. In every temple, despite large differences in size, opulence, and importance, certain constants apply. Inner chambers are reserved for the worship and business of Lolth, including most spellcasting. These chambers are always shrouded in darkness, except for the radiances involved in spellcasting and rituals. Antechambers are set aside for war-councils, and most business wherein priests meet with drow males and outsiders. Most temples have guardian creatures, often hidden, and occasionally magical in nature (such as *jade spiders*). These usually include spiders of all sorts. In the event of an attack, even the harmless sorts of spiders can be equipped with armor-sheaths, strapped to their backs, that bear House defense runes—or even, in the case of intelligent, *charmed* spiders, *house insignia* with active magic powers may be wielded. Statuettes of the Spider Queen, usually worked of black stone, are present in all temple chambers. Marble and obsidian are favored materials for statuary and temple furniture. There are always large, ornately carved (with spider shapes) braziers, and at least one altar of black stone.

Titles used by Lolthite priests vary widely from city to city but are strictly enforced within their respective domains. As an example, in Guallidurth, deep beneath Calimshan, Lolth's clergy are known collectively as Yorn'yathrins. In ascending order, the hierarchy of titles for the Temple City of Lolth include Noamutha, Khalessa, Kyorla, Alura, Quartha, Talintha, Elamshina, and Xundusa. High-ranking priests of the Spider Queen are collectively known as yathtallars. If they rule a noble house they are known as Ilharess (Matron Mother), but otherwise they are titled Streea'Valsharess (Black Widow). Specialty priests are known as arachnes. The clergy of Lolth includes dark elves (94%) and chitines (6%). Of the dark elves, 96% are female; there are male priests of Lolth (4%), but the Spider Queen very rarely allows them to rise above 7th level of experience. Lolth's clergy includes specialty priests (40%), clerics (30%), fighter/clerics (20%), and crusaders (10%), although the relative fractions of each vary from city to city.

Dogma: Fear is as strong as steel, while love and respect are soft, useless feelings that none can lean on. All drow who do not worship Lolth must be converted or destroyed. All weak and rebellious drow must be weeded out. All who impugn the faith must perish. Males or slaves of other races who act independently of Lolth's dictates (and those of her priests) must be sacrificed to Lolth. Those of the faithful whose loyalty is weak must be eliminated. Children are to be raised as loyal worshipers of Lolth, and each family should produce at least one priest to serve the Spider Queen better than his or her parents. Arachnids of all sorts are to be revered, and anyone who mistreats or kills a spider must die.

Such are the commands of Lolth—but the priest who follows them blindly is on a slippery path leading to swift death. Success in the service of Lolth lies with those who are attentive to the ever-changing, often contradictory will of Lolth. Lolth's capricious nature makes hard-and-fast rules few and uncertainty great. Of course, questioning Lolth's motives or wisdom is a sin. Aiding nondrow against drow is a great sin, as is ignoring the Spider Queen's commands in favor of love. (Lolth often tests her priests by ordering the sacrifice of a favored consort.) Drow who lose the favor of Lolth are always given a single chance to redeem themselves. This is usually a dangerous or difficult mission, though Lolth may test certain individuals by setting no task at all and observing what they do. Those who willfully fail are destroyed. Lolth commands other worshipers to do this (in turn, testing *them*). Those who fail through mischance or poor planning or execution are usually transformed into driders. Lolth often plays favorites among her drow worshipers, but those who ride high one season are warned that Lolth can turn her dark face upon them without warning and undoubtedly will sometime soon.

Day-to-Day Activities: Lolth's priests are the rulers, police forces, judges, juries, and executioners of drow society. They wield power daily, and most do so in a manner in keeping with the cruel and capricious nature of Lolth herself. Priests of Lolth strive to act as Lolth wishes and to manipulate (often by brutal force) their fellow drow to do so too. The ultimate aim of every priest is to achieve and keep the Favor of Lolth. The spirits of priests who die in her favor are believed to go to the Abyss, where they become yochlol and other servant minions. Those who die in Lolth's disfavor are thought to pass into torment on another plane somewhere, perhaps to someday return to the Realms as a snake or spider. (Drow beliefs are confused on such matters, and often change with time and location.) The duties of a good priest, then, are to do whatever is necessary to gain and to keep the Spider Queen's favor. Although treachery and cruelty are often rewarded, Lolth does not look kindly on those who let personal grudges and revenge-taking bring defeat or shame to their House, clan, city, or band.

Holy Days/Important Ceremonies: Lolth requires homage—submission in prayer, plus offerings—regularly from her priests. Ceremonies involving the sacrifice of surface elves are performed monthly during nights of the full moon as deliberate affronts to Sehanine, Lolth's hated rival. Rituals to Lolth are customarily practiced in female-only company in a sacred room or area. Rituals requiring extraordinary power or a public display may be celebrated in the open and in all sorts of mixed company. When Lolth's aid is required, sacrifices must be made. These are traditionally the blood of drow faithful and/or captured foes, spilled with a spider-shaped knife whose eight descending legs are blades (2d6 points of damage). In other cases, gems or other precious objects may be burned in braziers, as prayers of offering are chanted. In large, important rituals, priests of Lolth customarily use eight braziers to provide additional flame material and in homage to Lolth (the flames represent her eight legs). The most powerful rituals to Lolth defy detailed description and are seldom seen by nondrow.

Rituals to Lolth involve the burning of precious oils and incense, live offerings, and riches of all sorts, particularly gems. These are customarily placed in a bowl-shaped depression in a black altar (or burning brazier). These offerings are always consumed in the flames of Lolth at some point in the ritual. If Lolth is particularly displeased, or impostors are present, the black-and-red flames that leap from the braziers to consume the offerings may also arc to consume other valuables present, such as magical items, jewelry, and clothing. Typically, Lolth's flames do little more than humiliate a burned priest, destroying his or her garments and dealing him or her 1d4 points of damage, but an impostor or intruder receives a searing flame attack that does 6d6 points of damage (half if a saving throw vs. spell at a –2 penalty succeeds). If this occurs, every priest of Lolth present in the chamber instantly receives a free *darkfire* spell to wield, even if she or he is carrying a full load of spells or has other *darkfire* spells memorized. The spell comes with the strong command to use it, forthwith, to blast those who would so insult Lolth.

Lolth enters the Prime Material Plane in avatar form or allows herself to be contacted only when it pleases her to do so. Otherwise, Lolth's servant yochlol are reached. Such contact rituals require the use of a brazier of burning oils, coals, or incense—burned in a vessel fashioned of a valuable black material (such as onyx, obsidian, or a golden bowl whose interior is studded with black pearls). The flames provide material that the magic transforms into an interplanar gate temporarily linking the 66th layer of the Abyss with the Prime Material Plane. Through this link, the yochlol appear, using flame material to fashion semblances of themselves. If called with sufficient force, a yochlol can emerge fully from its *gate*. Lolth usually orders her handmaidens to remain in the Prime Material Plane only so long as the flames that brought them remain—the dying of the summoning flame then allows a yochlol the safety of being sucked instantly back to the Abyss. Yochlol who are summoned can keep the *gate* that brought them open while they communicate with Lolth and others in the Abyss. (Such communication demands their full attention, causing their Prime Material forms to go momentarily blank faced and unhearing.) They can also send one creature of the Abyss into the Prime Material Plane, loose of all control and against the wishes of the summoner. This act causes the destruction of the *gate* and the disappearance of the yochlol. Such sends are usually myrlochar.

Major Centers of Worship: Deep beneath the deserts of Calimshan and the southern tunnels of Deep Shanatar is Guallidurth, the Temple City of Lolth. The Matron Mothers of twenty-one noble Houses sit on the ruling Council of this ancient city, each representing one (or more, in some cases) sect, cult, or faction of the Spider Queen's faithful. One measure of a sect's relative influence is the magnificence of the house of worship it can afford to construct. As a result, Guallidurth contains hundreds, if not thousands, of temples dedicated to Lolth ranging in size from simple shrines to modest chapels to grand cathedrals. Many of the city's temples are ruined—their congregations long since murdered in the endless religious strife that rages across the city—or abandoned—their congregations able to afford more ostentatious (and defensible) houses of worship. Only the unforgivable heresy of dark elves worshiping other gods—such as the cities of Vhaeraun worshipers in Sarenestar (the Forest of Mir)—unites the Lolthite clergies of Guallidurth in common cause and even such endeavors are usually doomed to failure by the infighting among members of the various sects.

Affiliated Orders: The Militant Myrlochar, also known as the Order of Soul Spiders, is an elite military order composed solely of male crusaders and found in the few dark elven cities where Lolth is revered and males are permitted to enter her priesthood. The Militant Myrlochar directly serve the ruling Matron Mothers of the city in which they are based as agents of uncontrolled destruction, tirelessly hunting any creature designated as their quarry or who interferes with their pursuit and wreaking havoc until recalled (which rarely happens) or destroyed (their most common fate).

The Handmaidens of the Spider Queen is an order of female crusaders with no permanent ties to any individual city. Also known as the Daughters of the Yochlol, the Handmaidens serve as instruments of Lolth's will in times when the Spider Queen needs to bring an entire city into line. At least three times in recorded history the Handmaidens of the Spider Queen have assaulted and destroyed an entire dark elven city that threatened to drift from Lolth's web of chaos. When not assembled into an army of chaos and vengeance, the Handmaidens work in small companies scattered throughout the Underdark, harassing merchant trains that look to Vhaeraun for protection and conducting hit-and-run raids on cities ruled by clergy of the Masked Lord or That Which Lurks.

Drow in the Realms have embraced offshoots of the major faiths, usually following a charismatic mortal leader who claims to be something more. The only such cult known to be still active, albeit in a debased form, is the She-Spider Cult, a Thayan-based sect that tried to link worship of Shar with devotion to Lolth. Opposed in the end by both goddesses, the Cult enjoyed initial success as a secret society operating slaving and drug-running operations in Mulhorand, Unther, and southern Thay. They eventually degenerated into a criminal gang without divine support. The Cult still stages fake rituals to thrill worshipers and to slay foes under the guise of sacrifices.

Priestly Vestments: When participating in rituals, priests of Lolth work unclad or wear robes (black, trimmed with dark red and purple—or, for lesser or novitiate priests, dark purple or red trimmed with black). In some cities ornate helms carved to resemble writhing spiders are worn by Lolth's clergy, while in others heads are always left uncovered. Jewelry worn by the Spider Queen's priests consists of spider medallions and other spider designs, all made of platinum. The holy symbol of the faith is a platinum disk at least 3 inches in diameter with an embossed depiction on both its obverse and reverse in jet black enamel of a black widow spider or a platinum spider figurine on a platinum or mithral chain necklace.

Adventuring Garb: Lolth's clergy favor drow chain mail with magical bonuses ranging from +1 to +5. Typically such armor is enchanted to have a +1 defensive bonus for every four levels of the priest. Some priests also carry adamantite bucklers with similar properties to that of drow chain mail and with magical bonuses ranging from +1 to +3. Clerics of the Spider Queen typically wield adamantite maces—again with similar properties to that of drow chain mail—with magical bonuses ranging from +1 to +5. In addition to maces, crusaders and arachnes sometimes wield adamantite short swords and long daggers, with magical bonuses ranging from +1 to +3 (+4 if they are of noble blood). Priests who are not clerics may also employ hand-held crossbows that shoot darts up to 60 yards and inflict 1d3 points of damage, in addition to being coated with drow sleep poison that renders a victim unconscious for 2d4 hours if she or he fails a saving throw vs. poison with a –4 penalty. Likewise, crusaders and arachnes sometimes employ small javelins coated with the same poison as the darts, with a range of 90 yards and attack bonuses of +3 (short range), +2 (medium range), or +1 (long range). Most senior priests of Lolth carry snake-headed *whips of fangs*, and delight in using them often.

Drow Chain Mail

XP Value: Varies   *GP Value:* 2,000 gp; 1,000 more for +4 and +5
Drow chain mail is a finely crafted, satiny black metal mesh that does not encumber its wearer in the least. It is similar but not identical to magical elven chain mail. It is typically fashioned into tunics, as dark elves share their forest-bound cousins' preference for armor that adequately protects without being overly weighty or restrictive.

Like elven chain mail, drow chain mail has a base Armor Class rating of 5. However, drow chain mail is crafted from an adamantite alloy that absorbs the radiation of the drow homelands, giving it properties similar to a magical bonus ranging from +1 to +5 but undetectable to *detect magic* or similar spells. If drow chain mail is ever exposed to direct sunlight for more than 2 rounds (or any exposure totaling 5 rounds in a five-day period, even if composed of brief instants), decay sets in. Within 2d6 days, the chain mail loses its pseudomagical properties and crumbles into worthless powder. If carefully protected from full sunlight, it still loses its pseudomagical properties 1d20+30 days after it is removed from areas of radiation (in other words, the Underdark) if it is not reexposed to the radiation for two days per day spent above ground (in other words, twice as long as it was removed from the drow lands). Drow chain mail is still useful as chain mail if no longer pseudomagical, so long as it is never exposed to sunlight; however, it cannot be reforged into another item to reuse its adamantite alloy. The drow radiations that permeate it transform its structures in such a way that sufficient exposure to heat to reforge chain mail causes it to instantly break down as if it had been exposed to sunlight.

The resale value for drow chain mail is doubled if it is known to have never been removed from the reach of Underdark radiation.

Whip of Fangs

XP Value: 1,000   *GP Value:* 1,000+500 per living head

These whips (often carried at the belt) have adamantite handles, but their mulitple tendrils are living snake heads, 1d4+1 in number. Evil priests are the only beings able to employ these horrific weapons. In drow communities, only priestesses are allowed to possess and use them. The whips, once enchanted, are attuned to a specific individual and may only be used by another being after another attunement ritual has been performed, since they attack anyone who touches them except their attuned wielder. The ritual of attunement requires the consent of Lolth, and priestesses consider such whips personal gifts from her, believing that they cease to function or even turn on their wielder if they are used in an act against the will of the Spider Queen. Forbidden acts usually include using a whip against a matron mother or other ruling priestess.

Living serpents are required in the making of these weapons. The weapons they become part of are enchanted extensions of the will of their wielders, hissing, coiling, writhing, and reaching in response to her thoughts. The whip of an angry priestess can knot about her belt and menace the beings she is angry with without her ever touching it.

The whip's tendrils are from 1 to 3 feet in length. Each is AC 8, has 2 HD, and attacks (THAC0 14) for 2d4 points of damage. The serpent heads have no poison effects, but their long fangs bite deep, leaving scars and injecting waves of magic that both numb and shoot waves of muscle-knotting pain through the victim.

Angry drow priestesses typically use these whips indiscriminately on slaves, servants, pupils, male relatives, and casual acquaintances. Injured heads regenerate 2 hit points per day. Slain heads cannot be healed, nor do they regenerate.

Specialty Priests (Arachne)

REQUIREMENTS:	Wisdom 13
PRIME REQ.:	Wisdom
ALIGNMENT:	CE
WEAPONS:	Any
ARMOR:	Any
MAJOR SPHERES:	All, astral, animal, chaos, combat, elemental, guardian, healing, necromantic, protection, summoning, sun (reversed only)
MINOR SPHERES:	Charm, creation, divination, time, wards
MAGICAL ITEMS:	As clerics
REQ. PROFS:	Etiquette, weaving
BONUS PROFS:	Animal training (spiders), spellcraft

- Arachnes must be drow or chitines. In some dark elven cities of the Underdark, the clergy of Lolth is exclusively female, but in other cities a few drow males are tolerated in the lower ranks of the priesthood. (None rise above 7th level.) No males are admitted into the ranks of Lolth's clergy among the chitines.
- Arachnes are not allowed to multiclass.
- Arachnes are immune to all spider venoms.
- Arachnes can communicate with spiders of all kinds, and spiders never harm them in any way (except if desired by Lolth).
- At 2nd level, arachnes can cast *spider climb* (as the 1st-level wizard spell) or *spidereyes* (as the 1st-level wizard spell found in *Wizard's Spell Compendium*, Volume 3 or the 1st-level priest spell in *The Drow of the Underdark*) once per day. If *spider climb* is cast, it does not prevent spellcasting so long as two limbs grip the surface being climbed, and light objects do not stick to the priest's hands and feet. *Spidereyes* allows the caster to see through the eyes of a single normal or giant arachnid within 60 yards, but it does not grant any control over the arachnid's movements or direction of gaze.
- At 5th level, arachnes can cast *dispel magic* (as the 3rd-level priest spell) or *web* (as the 2nd-level wizard spell) twice per day.
- At 7th level, arachnes can cast *summon shadow* (as the 5th-level wizard spell) or spider summoning (as the 5th-level priest spell) twice per day.

- At 10th level, arachnes can cast *true seeing* (as the 5th-level priest spell, but with twice the normal duration) or *spiderform* (as the 5th-level priest spell) twice per day.
- At 13th level, female arachnes can cast *domination* (as the 5th-level wizard spell) once per day. Male drow must roll saving throws to avoid the effects with a –4 penalty. Elves and half-elves of all races do not get their normal racial magic resistance to avoid the effects.

Lolthite Spells

Many spells developed by the clergy of Lolth long ago have been requested in parallel form from other drow powers or other nondrow powers and have passed out of exclusive Lolthite usage. Of them, only *darkfire* is detailed here. Note that any spell once specified as either a drow priest spell or Lolth priest spell that has passed into general usage is still available as a religion-specific Lolth priest spell; priests of Lolth can still receive the spell no matter what its sphere.

1st Level

Cloak of Dark Power (Pr 1; Evocation, Alteration)

Sphere:	Necromantic
Range:	0
Components:	V, S
Duration:	3 rounds+1 round/level
Casting Time:	4
Area of Effect:	The caster
Saving Throw:	None

This spell creates a dark aura of coursing, swirling power around the caster. The caster's body and anything she or he wears or carries is protected by this aura from the effects of full sunlight, even under the open, daytime sky of the surface world. Arms and armor imbued with the radiations of the Underdark that are worn or carried by the caster do not begin to lose their power, and the drow caster suffers no bright light combat penalties while under the effects of a cloak of dark power. A *continual light* spell cast directly agianst a *cloak of dark* power negates both spells.

A priest shrouded in a *cloak of dark power* functions as if she or he possessed one additional level of experience in all dealings with undead. Arachnids (and others using arachnid forms) attack a *cloak*-wearer at a –3 penalty.

2nd Level

Darkfire (Pr 2; Alteration)

Sphere:	Elemental Fire
Range:	Touch
Components:	V, S, M
Duration:	2 rounds/level
Casting Time:	5
Area of Effect:	One fire source
Saving Throw:	Special

This magic was developed for use in rituals of worship to Lolth, but has since been adapted into an offensive battle spell. The spell transforms a normal fire or ignites unlit fuel into *darkfire*.

Darkfire gives off no light at all, although creatures with infravision see darkfire as brighter signature than regular flame. All of its combustion is bent to producing heat and magical energy, which it does very well: Contact with a brazier, lantern, or lamp of *darkfire* typically inflicts 2d4 points of damage, plus flammable items or garments worn or carried by the target must succeed at item saving throws vs. magical fire.

In battle, *darkfire* is usually caused to emanate from one of the caster's hands. It does not harm the caster at all, except to burn away clothing it touches. A blow from a flaming hand inflicts 1d8 points of fire damage.

Darkfire from a flaming arm can be willed into handfuls and thrown. One ball per round can be so thrown, and such a ball attacks as if the caster were striking directly and has a 10-foot range. Thrown *darkfire* does 1d3 points of damage plus 1 point per level of the caster upon striking, to a maximum of 10th level. In the event of a miss, its flame affects wherever it lands. When it misses, it rages where it lands for 1d2 rounds before burning itself out.

3rd Level

Conceal Item (Pr 3; Illusion/Phantasm)

Sphere:	Protection
Range:	Touch
Components:	V, S, M
Duration:	1 turn+1 round/level
Casting Time:	1
Area of Effect:	One item
Saving Throw:	None

This magic enables the caster to render utterly undetectable, except to himself or herself, any single nonliving item smaller than his or her total body mass as long as she or he is carrying or touching it. The spell conceals even magical or alignment auras and shows *true seeing* a blank, wavering area of white fog where the item is.

This spell is usually used to conceal a carried magical item or weapon; priests of Vhaeraun typically use it to hide holy symbols. (When cast on any holy symbol, spell duration is tripled.) Developed by a priest of Lolth, this spell has been requested of Vhaeraun by most of his priests and granted to them also.

Its material component is a small handful (about 2 ounces) of the dust of any powdered gemstone. (Cheap stones, such as quartz, are fine.)

5th Level

Undead Focus (Pr 5; Necromancy)

Sphere:	Necromantic
Range:	Touch
Components:	V, S, M
Duration:	Special
Casting Time:	5
Area of Effect:	One undead creature
Saving Throw:	None

Undead focus allows one undead creature to become a spell focus for the caster. The undead creature can be controlled by the command undead priest ability or by spells without hampering this spell, but the spell does not grant automatic control of the undead creature. The caster can funnel any chosen currently carried spell through the undead being. Such spells are emitted from the undead creature, but the priest performs all casting activity, including component use. The amount of space between the caster and the undead creature does not matter, but priest and undead creature must remain on the same plane. Unless the caster keeps the undead being and its surroundings in sight, other spells are used to see it and its surroundings, or it is in an extremely well-known location, spells must be hurled blindly from the creature.

Spells to be cast through the undead can be chosen as needed. A priest can cast multiple spells, one per round, through the undead creature until it is destroyed or a maximum of one spell per level of the priest has been cast, exhausting the undead *focus spell*. The spell also expires after 10 turns per level of the caster have expired.

With this spell, a hidden priest can avoid direct combat, employing an undead being as a spellcasting fighting focus. It can be cast on undead creatures affected by *revenance* and/or *undead battlemight*, and the spells function simultaneously. A *dispel magic* cast on such an augmented undead creature ends only one of these spells (choose which randomly).

The material component is a drop of the caster's blood.

Spiderform (Pr 5; Alteration, Necromancy)

Sphere:	Animal, Necromantic
Range:	Touch
Components:	V, S, M
Duration:	4rounds+1 round/level
Casting Time:	2 per target to a maximum of 1 round
Area of Effect:	One small living animal or arachnid/level one drow
Saving Throw:	None

This spell enables a priest to turn one or more small living animals or arachnids into giant spiders. (See the Spider entry in the MONSTROUS MANUAL tome; these spiders are the giant spiders that are similar in shape and abilities to large spiders.) Unlike normal giant spiders, the bite of the spiders created by this spell is not a fatal poison; instead, failure of the poison saving throw results in the victim being stunned (no attacks or deliberate activities) for 1 round and slowed (as the *slow* wizard spell) for the rest of the spell duration.

Even if a transformed creature is an arachnid that is normally poisonous, the spell transforms it into a giant spider as described above. The giant spiders created are unable to spin webs but can readily navigate in existing webs, even the sticky strands of *web* or *spellweb* spells.

If spellcasting is interrupted for any reason or the arachnids to be transformed already bear a magical dweomer (for example, they are other creatures polymorphed into spiders), the spell is ruined, and the would-be caster is stunned (unable to think or act coherently) for 1 round.

If this spell is used on any drow and overcomes his or her magic resistance, the drow is temporarily transformed into a drider under the caster's control. (See the Elf, Drow entry in the MONSTROUS MANUAL tome for a description of driders. Note that transformed drow retain their own spells, hit points, intellect, and many class abilities.)

This control is like a *charm* spell and lasts for 1 round per level of the caster. It is broken instantly if the drider is commanded to do anything contrary to its nature, the known wishes of Lolth, or its superiors, or that would be anything clearly fatal to itself. Transformation to and from drider form takes 1 round, during which time the drider can take no action, and occurs at the spell's expiration or upon the verbal command of the caster. The affected drow usually (unless Lolth desires otherwise) remembers nothing of its time and actions as a drider.

The material component of this spell is a spider of any type small enough to be held in the caster's hand.

Spider Summoning (Pr 5; Conjuration/Summoning)

Sphere:	Animal
Range:	0
Components:	V, S, M
Duration:	1 round+1 round/level
Casting Time:	8
Area of Effect:	1d4 spiders
Saving Throw:	None

This spell calls 1d4 large spiders (detailed in the MONSTROUS MANUAL tome) per level of the caster to serve the priest. Only true arachnids are summoned by this spell, not similar insect creatures or beings using magic to take arachnid form (such as Lolth or a wizard using *spider shape*). They appear within 100 feet of the caster on the round of the spell's casting and obey the caster's command on the round thereafter. They have their natural maximum hit points and poison reserves and fight to the death for the caster with utter loyalty, following the caster's silent mental urgings as to targets, direction to move, and tasks to do. The caster can cast other spells without ending this spell's control. When the spell expires, any surviving spiders disappear, returning whence they came.

The spell's material component is a dried arachnid corpse.

6th Level

Meld of Lolth (Pr 6; Enchantment/Charm)

Sphere:	Charm
Range:	Touch
Components:	V, S
Duration:	1 hour/level
Casting Time:	1 turn
Area of Effect:	One being
Saving Throw:	Special

Often used by a priest to link herself to a powerful drow male before a battle (to control him when necessary), this spell enables the caster to join minds with another creature. The *meld* allows the caster to see through the other being's eyes, read its thoughts, and communicate telepathically with the linked being.

The caster can act, speak, and cast spells normally without ending the link and is able (whenever not casting another spell or using any psionic abilities) to *dominate* the linked being completely, controlling its body regardless of distance. The spell is broken if caster and linked being end up on different planes. The caster can use the linked being as the focus (source of emission) of a currently memorized spell, casting it *through* the linked being, but this ends the *meld* instantly.

If the linked being's Intelligence is less than the caster's, it is allowed a saving throw vs. spell once per turn to break the *meld*. If the linked being is as intelligent as the caster or more so and is or becomes unwilling to be in the *meld* (for instance, when ordered into danger), it gets a saving throw vs. spell once every other round to escape the *meld*.

Whenever the linked being suffers damage, the caster must succeed at a saving throw vs. death. If the saving throw fails, the pain-wracked caster suffers 1d6 points of damage. If the linked being dies, the caster must succeed at a system shock roll or die instantly. The caster can willingly end a *meld* 1 round after deciding to do so.

Spider Bite (Pr 6; Evocation)

Sphere:	Combat
Range:	0
Components:	V, S
Duration:	Special
Casting Time:	9
Area of Effect:	The caster
Saving Throw:	None

Also known as *venom bite*, this spell confers the poisonous biting ability of a spider to the caster. A successful attack roll is required to administer the poison, and the caster can only bite exposed or clothed flesh; armor cannot be bitten through. The number of times the bite has venom effects, and the power of those effects, depends on the caster's level:

Level	Uses	Rounds to Onset	Poison Effects if Save Failed/Succeeded
11–13	1 bite only	2d6	20 points/1d3 points
14–16	1 bite only	1d4+1	25 points/2d4 points
17–18	1 bite only	1d2	30 points/2d6 points
19–20	2 bites	1d2	30 points/2d6 points
Over 20	2 bites	Immediate	Death/20 points

Spider bite can be saved for hours or days after casting. However, a bite delivered, whether it successful in poisoning a victim or not, is considered to expend one use of the magic. Victims receive a saving throw vs. poison at −3 to avoid the bite effects.

For the entire time this spell is in effect, the caster is immune to poison. No more than two *spider bite* spells can be active on the caster at one time.

7th Level

Cloak of Gaer (Pr 7; Necromancy)

Sphere:	Healing
Range:	Touch
Components:	V, S, M
Duration:	Special
Casting Time:	1 round
Area of Effect:	Creature touched
Saving Throw:	None

This powerful spell surrounds the protected creature with a faint magical aura. It takes effect (days or perhaps years later) when the being it is cast on is forced to make a system shock survival roll or when the being reaches 6 hit points or less. It can also be cast on a just-injured being.

In the round that the protected creature must make a system shock survival roll or is reduced to 6 hit points or less, the *cloak of Gaer* is triggered and the following occur:

- The system shock roll succeeds automatically, regardless of the creature's Constitution.
- The protected creature regenerates severed or missing limbs or body extremities.
- The *cloak* purges the protected creatures of all poisons, diseases, insanity, *charm* effects and outside mental influences, *curses* and *geas* effects, possession or symbiotic/parasitic life (even if friendly and desired), and *feeblemindedness*. It also cancels the effects of any *forget* spells previously cast on the protected being.

- The *cloak* restores the being to full wakefulness, alertness, sobriety, and and a pain-free state.
- The *cloak* heals the protected being of 4d8 points of damage.

If this spell is cast on a hurt being within 2 rounds after the major injury that reduced it to 6 hit points or required a system shock survival roll, it has the above effects and allows a victim who has failed a system shock survival roll and died a second chance. This roll is made at a+22% bonus. If it fails, death occurs, but the *purge* and *regenerate* effects still occur to the corpse.

If this spell is applied 3 to 9 rounds after a being has been stricken, it allows a second system shock survival roll, but without any bonus; other spell effects occur as noted here. If the spell is applied later, it only *purges* and *regenerates* (even on bodies).

The spell's material components are four drops each of holy water, the caster's blood, and dew. A *dispel magic* cannot end this spell while it waits to be activated. This magic has enabled many dead drow to return and hunt down foes. Certain drow wizards are rumored to use a similar spell.

Repulsion (Pr 7; Abjuration)

Sphere:	Guardian
Range:	0
Components:	V, S, M
Duration:	1 round/2 levels
Casting Time:	7
Area of Effect:	Creatures in a 10-foot-wide path that is 10-feet long/level of caster
Saving Throw:	None

When this spell is cast, the priest is able to cause all creatures in the path of the area of effect to move directly away from his or her person. Repulsion occurs at the speed of the creature attempting to move toward the caster. The repelled creature continues to move away for a complete round even if this takes it beyond the area of effect. The caster can designate a new direction each round, bur use of this power counts as the caster's principal action in the round. The caster can, of course, choose to do something else instead of using the repulsion attack.

This spell is not effective against any drow or creatures of chaotic evil alignment, but other evil creatures are affected. The priest must be able to confront the creatures to be affected: She or he must see them and be seen. As the casting ends, flickering black flames seem to emanate from the caster, streaming outward to define the pathway of effect of the spell.

The material components are the priest's holy symbol; a miniature sword blade, normal dagger, or knife; and a flame, spark, hot coal, or ember.

Selvetarm

(Champion of Lolth, Thane of Lolth, the Spider That Waits, the Spider Demon, Prince of the Aranea, Lord of the Venomire)

Demipower of the Abyss, CE

PORTFOLIO:	Drow warriors
ALIASES:	Zanassu
DOMAIN NAME:	66th level/Lolth's Web (the Demonweb Pits)
SUPERIOR:	Lolth
ALLIES:	Garagos, Lolth
FOES:	Deep Duerra, Eilistraee, Ghaunadaur, Laduguer, the Seldarine, Sharess, Vhaeraun, Blibdoolpoolp, the Blood Queen, Diinkarazan, Diirinka, Great Mother, Gzemnid, Ilsensine, Ilxendren, Laogzed, Maanzecorian (dead), Psilofyr
SYMBOL:	Crossed sword and mace overlaid with spider image
WOR. ALIGN.:	LN, N, CN, LE, NE, CE

Selvetarm (SELL-veh-TARM) is the Champion of Lolth and the patron of drow warriors. Seen as the embodiment of unequaled fighting prowess, Selvetarm is worshiped by a few drow in the northern and western reaches of the Underdark beneath Faerûn, particularly in the city of Eryndlyn beneath the High Moor and in the dungeons of Undermountain beneath Waterdeep. The Spider Demon is also venerated by many of the aranea of the Spider Swamp in southern Calimshan where he is known as Zanassu, the Spider That Waits. A few drow in the Forest of Mir as well as a handful of Volothanni seeking any advantage to advance themselves politically in the Gem City of Calimshan round out the ranks of Selvetarm's faithful.

Selvetarm is the offspring of an ill-fated tryst between Vhaeraun and Zandilar the Dancer, a demipower once venerated by the elves of the Yuirwood. When the Dancer's elven followers began to falter in the face of relentless assaults by Lolth's minions, Zandilar sought out the Masked Lord and seduced him in an attempt to either gain information or elicit his direct assistance in battling the Spider Queen. The Masked Lord betrayed Zandilar and imprisoned her, and only the timely assistance of Bast, an errant Mulhorandi demipower, allowed the Dancer to escape. Selvetarm was birthed shortly thereafter when the weakened Zandilar voluntarily merged her essence with that of Bast, creating the goddess now known as Sharess.

Selvetarm walked a solitary way for many centuries, spurning both of his parents, for he was not wholly given over to evil but neither was he aligned with the forces of light. Eventually his path crossed that of his aunt, Eilistraee, and he began to appreciate the goodness of the Dark Maiden, as exhibited in her teachings and deeds. By way of Selvetarm's redemption, Eilistraee hoped to begin to heal the breach between the majority of dark elves and the Seldarine. The Dark Maiden's hopes were dashed, however, by the insidious plotting of Lolth.

The Queen of Spiders had long resented the existence of Zanassu, a minor Abyssal Lord with pretensions of suzerainty over spiders, nearly as much as she disliked the possibility of Eilistraee winning an ally—Selvetarm—among the pantheon of the drow. When the Spider Demon lost much of his power after a conflict on the Prime (against Qysara Shoon V of the Shoon Empire), Lolth convinced Selvetarm to destroy Zanassu and seize the Spider Demon's burgeoning divine power. She did so by suggesting to Selvetarm that a victory would increase his personal power and win him favor in the eyes of Eilistraee, whom he greatly admired. While Selvetarm prevailed in battle over the Spider Demon, the absorption of Zanassu's wholly evil and chaotic nature overwhelmed Selvetarm's nascent beneficial aspects and weakened him sufficiently that he could not escape the traps by which the Spider Queen bound his will tightly to her own.

Cruel and malicious by nature, Selvetarm cares only for battle and destruction. The Champion of Lolth harbors a deep hatred for all living things, including his dominating mistress, and the only beauty he can appreciate is a well-honed and deadly fighting style. Selvetarm can exhibit a great deal of patience while waiting for prey to fall into an ambush he has set, but he prefers the wild abandon of battle frenzy to a careful and deliberate attack.

Selvetarm's Avatar (Fighter 24, Cleric 16)

Selvetarm appears as a large black spider, sometimes with the head of a drow male. He wields a long sword and mace in his front appendages. He prefers spells from the spheres of all, animal, chaos, charm, combat, elemental, guardian, healing, protection, sun (reversed only), travelers, and war, though he can cast spells from any sphere.

AC –2; MV 15, Wb 21; HP 180; THAC0 –3; #AT 7/2 and 1 bite
Dmg 2d8+poison (bite) and 1d8+15 (long sword +5, +8 Str, +2 spec. bonus in long sword) and 1d6+12+special (footman's mace +3, +8 Str)
MR 70%; SZ L (15 feet across, 6 feet high)
Str 22, Dex 20, Con 20, Int 15, Wis 18, Cha 16
Spells P: 9/9/8/7/4/3/1
Saves PPDM 3, RSW 5, PP 4, BW 4, Sp 6

Special Att/Def: In his right hand Selvetarm wields *Venomace*, a *footman's mace +3* that continuously oozes a noxious sludge of acid and venom that inflicts an additional 1d4 points of poison damage (if a saving throw vs. poison is not made) and 1d4 points of acid damage every round for 3 rounds after a successful hit. In his left hand, the Spider Demon wields *Thalack'velve*, a *long sword +5, defender*. Victims bitten by Selvetarm must succeed at a saving throw vs. poison at a –4 penalty. A failed saving throw results in death in 1 round, but even if the saving throw succeeds, the poison inflicts 3d6 points of damage.

Selvetarm is immune to poison and sustains only half damage from cold, electricity, and lightning attacks. He is only affected by +1 or better magical weapons. Magical cold iron weapons get a+2 damage bonus when striking him.

Selvetarm can at will, one at a time, use any of the following spell-like powers once per day instead of casting a spell: *charm monster, charm person, command, darkness 15´ radius, detect good, detect invisible, dimension door, dispel magic, fly, infravision, invisibility, know alignment, protection from good 10´ radius, speak with monsters, telekinesis* (up to 5,000 gp), *teleport without error, unholy word,* and *web*. The Spider Demon can *summon spiders* (01–20%: 1d6+6 large spiders, 21–50%: 1d4+4 huge spiders, 51–90%: 1d6 giant spiders, 91–00%: 1d2 phase spiders) at will, once per round, instead of casting a spell.

Other Manifestations

Selvetarm rarely bothers to simply manifest in the Realms when entreated by his followers, as he prefers to either dispatch his avatar directly or ignore the supplication. He occasionally manifests when his avatar is otherwise occupied and the outcome of the fray is of great interest to him. In such situations, Selvetarm manifests as a tiny sphere of absolute blackness that slowly grows in size over the course of 3 rounds from about 1 inch in diameter to about 1 foot in diameter and then explodes in a shower of blades equivalent in effect to the 6th-level priest spell *blade barrier*, though it grants its victims no saving throw vs. spell against its effects.

Selvetarm commonly acts through the appearance or presence of myrlochar (soul spiders), retrievers, and spiders of all sorts. The Spider Demon shows his favor through the discovery of rogue stones, pieces of dried silverbark, and webstone, and his displeasure by causing steel weapons and armor to shatter in combat even after a glancing blow.

The Church

CLERGY:	Clerics, crusaders, fighters, specialty priests
CLERGY'S ALIGN.:	NE, CE
TURN UNDEAD:	C: No, Cru: No, F: No, SP: No
CMND. UNDEAD:	C: Yes, Cru: No, F: No, SP: No

All clerics (including cleric/fighters, a multiclassed combination allowed to drow priests of Selvetarm), crusaders, and specialty priests of Selvetarm receive religion (drow), religion (elven), and reading/writing (drowic) as bonus nonweapon proficiencies.

Outside of the Spider Swamp, the city of Volothamp, and the dungeons beneath Waterdeep, Selvetarm is little known on the surface world. He does appear in a few Calishite tales as the Demon of the Swamp in which he is depicted as a lurking evil capable of insidious charms and unchecked battle fury. Aside from the drow city of Eryndlyn, where Selvetarm's name is synonymous with the nigh-unstoppable battle prowess of drow male warriors in the service of Lolth, the Spider Demon is known in the Underdark in only a few drow cities that follow the Way of Lolth. Few drow are aware that he is divine being, as most tales depict him simply as a powerful tanar'ri and a minion of Lolth.

The few temples of Selvetarm that exist are typically large subterranean chambers dominated a huge black stone spider idol. The Chapel of the Sericeous Sargh, a small shrine on the first level of Undermountain (Room #12) beneath the streets of Waterdeep, is fairly representative of the style. The idol appears to merge with the center of the room's eastern wall. A darkly stained altar sits before the idol, and two of the spider's legs are outstretched in front of the altar. Another two legs are raised up high, above the altar, suspending an unlit brazier from each leg. The spider's other legs bend up and set down close to its sides, forming large arches along the sides of the idol. An eerie, purplish-blue radiance emanates from the statue's eyes, providing the chapel's only illumination when the braziers are not lit.

Selvetarm's clergy are known collectively as the *Selvetargtlin*, which is drow for *warriors of Selvetarm*. Titles used by Selvetarm's clergy vary widely across temple hierarchies, but those used in the city of Eryndlyn include Edge of the Axe, Crush of the Mace, Steel of the Blade, Tusk of the Boar,

Hunger of the Swarm, Claw of the Cave Bear, Talon of the Wyrm, and Bloodlust of the Berserker. High-ranking priests of the Spider Demon have unique individual titles. Specialty priests are known as spiderswords. The clergy of Selvetarm includes both male (70%) and female dark elves (8%) as well as male (15%) and female aranea (7%). Selvetarm's clergy includes specialty priests (35%), crusaders (25%), cleric/fighters (20%), fighters (15%, including nonpriest multiclassed fighters), and clerics (5%).

Dogma: War is the ultimate expression of individual power, and only through battle and death can one realize the respect of one's comrades. Hone fighting skills constantly and teach those who will follow into the fray. Never give or receive quarter, and die amidst the bloodlust of battle against overwhelming odds. Cultivate as many different weapon tricks and combat maneuvers as a spider has arms, and never fear that hidden venom, like a secret vengeance waiting to strike, will serve you ill.

Day-to-Day Activities: Selvetarm's faithful spend most of their days guarding fortifications, honing their fighting skills, participating in patrols, guarding slave caravans, and getting into fights over status and petty slights. Many spend much of their time training other warriors in the art of war. While the Selvetargtlin are rightly known for their skill in battle, the teachings of the faith place little emphasis on tactics or strategy and thus few members of Selvetarm's clergy achieve a high military rank.

Holy Days/Important Ceremonies: Selvetarm's faithful are expected to observe the rituals of Lolth, as directed by her priests. (Those who have recently emigrated from Eryndlyn have abandoned this practice, so far without divine retribution, and are said to be praying for guidance in new ways of honoring the Spider Demon.) Selvetarm does expect all who take up arms in his name to cry out his name in the bloodlust of battle as they deliver the killing blow to a foe. Since there is always the chance that any attack will be a fatal one, the Selvetargtlin tend to constantly scream out their god's name during a battle.

The aranea of the Spider Swamp venerate Zanassu with a totally different set of rituals, notable in comparison for their emphasis on patience, craftiness, and subtlety. Such ceremonies involve animal sacrifices to the Spider That Waits—typically a boar or lizard—and repeating litanies beseeching him to return. The holiest day of the year is the 6th of Kythorn, the day on which Zanassu returned after his millennial exile. On this day all of the aranea celebrate their deliverance through fasting and ritual combat.

Major Centers of Worship: In the northern reaches of the Spider Swamp of Calimshan lies a ruined city known as Lost Ajhuutal, rumored to have been the capitol of the Maridlands millennia ago. The ruins have been inhabited by a race of werespiders for centuries. The aranea are large, intelligent spiders capable of assuming a single humanoid form. Originally all could assume drow form, but increasing numbers assume a human or half-elven form identical in all ways to Calishites of the same racial mix. In the center of oft-rebuilt Lost Ajhuutal stands the Apostolaeum of the Spider That Waits, one of the city's few buildings that is still relatively intact. The temple has a massive stone spider as its central dome, with stone webs spreading out to the four minarets flanking it at the corners. Less than one hundred priests and followers of Zanassu dwell within the temple, impatiently awaiting opportunities for hunting or wars, but content to serve The Spider Who Waits and the community by defending the temple. Recent expansions of the aranea's territory into the southern reaches of the Forest of Mir have given Zanassu's clergy the opportunity to war with the community of wereboars who are resisting the incursions, but the primary worry of the Spider Demon's priests is the concern that they may lose their fullblood status as fewer and fewer of the aranea keep only drow changeforms.

According to legend, the aranea were created by Calishite wizards during the Night Wars to infiltrate the ranks of the drow and destroy them from within. With the defeat of the dark elves and the end of 260 years of warfare in –530 DR, the aranea were cast off by the Calishites and either killed or driven into the Spider Swamp. Among the dank fens of the Venomire, as the Spider Swamp is also known, the aranea developed a relatively pacifistic, neutral culture, trading in silk, herbs, and poisons with the coastal city of Volothamp. During this time some aranea began to manifest humanoid forms other than that of dark elves, facilitating their ability to move unhindered through Calishite cities and towns. When Qysara Shoon V cast the spider-people as scapegoats for a plague that ravished Almraiven in the Year of Full Cribs (290 DR), the aranea were nearly destroyed by the resultant backlash from Volothamp's military and populace. In response, some of the aranea turned to Zanassu, then a minor Abyssal Lord, to defend

them against the Shoon Empire. Zanassu was banished back to the Abyss by the qysara in the Year of Frostfires (292 DR), but by that time the Spider Demon's cult had taken root among the once-peaceful aranea. Since early in the 4th century Dalereckoning, the aranea have dwelt relatively peacefully in the City of Maridsorrows, their safety secured by the militant followers of Zanassu.

For ten centuries, Zanassu's aranea priests foretold the triumphant return of their deity after his ignominious defeat by Qysara Shoon V. While the Spider Demon was rumored to have stalked the Spider Swamp on multiple occasions during his millennial absence, his avatar did not actually return to the Apostolaeum until the Year of the Wandering Waves (1292 DR), 1,000 years to the day after his banishment. For 66 years (a baleful portent given the Spider Demon's lair in the 66th level of the Abyss), Zanassu—or a powerful tanar'ri claiming to be him—dwelt within the heart of the Apostolaeum. Zanassu did not emerge from his temple until the Fall of the Gods in the Year of Shadows (1358 DR), at which time the Lord of the Venomire stalked northward toward the Forest of Mir and did not return. During the nearly seven decades of his rule, Zanassu's minions infiltrated the corridors of power in Volothamp and the surrounding region so thoroughly that the then-reigning vizier, Ramslett N'door and a number of his senior advisers fell victim to Zanassu's *charms*. During the Time of Troubles, however, Zanassu's hold over the government of Volothamp swiftly dissipated in the magical chaos of the time. With the strife of the Darkstalker Wars of the Year of the Serpent (1359 DR) following on the heels of the Avatar Crisis, 66 years of unseen tyranny vanished with barely a trace.

Affiliated Orders: The city of Eryndlyn, located in hidden caves beneath the High Moor, is characterized by barely contained hostilities between the worshipers of Lolth, Ghaunadaur, and Vhaeraun. During the Time of Troubles, the avatar of Selvetarm rampaged through the drow city, attacking strongholds of the followers of Ghaunadaur and Vhaeraun. Priests of Lolth hailed the monster as the swordarm of Lolth, sent to demonstrate her absolute rule. The avatar of Selvetarm was finally driven into the wild Underdark by an alliance between the victimized cults, but not without great losses. It is unknown whether Selvetarm's avatar still remains in the Underdark or if he has returned to the Abyss.

As a result of Selvetarm's rampage through Eryndlyn, droves of drow worshipers in that strife-torn city have allied themselves with the priests of Lolth. A new military order called the Selvetargtlin—a name also associated with the clergy at large—has shifted the balance of power in the cult of Lolth's favor and consequently driven the worshipers of Ghaunadaur and Vhaeraun into an uneasy alliance. It is uncertain how this will affect the long term balance of power in the city.

A few drow in Eryndlyn began to worship Selvetarm in his own right. This displeased Lolth's clergy immensely, and the blasphemers were quickly driven from the city and into exile. These drow are believed to have recently settled in the Underdark beneath Waterdeep in the hopes of building their own city. Patrols of Selvetarm's faithful have been encountered exploring the dungeons of Undermountain—where they recently constructed the Chapel of the Sericeous Sargh, detailed above—and searching for new magic with which to defend the exiled cult.

Priestly Vestments: Priests of Selvetarm wear long, rich, scarlet robes lined in chain mail. They wear their long hair in thick braids, the tips of which are soaked in blood and allowed to harden into rock-hard clumps. (In desperation, a priest can employ his braids in close quarters as a flail by whipping his head to and fro. Such attacks are made at at a –2 attack penalty and inflict 1d4 total points of damage.) Steel gauntlets are worn on the hands, each of which sports a sharp blade—equivalent to a dagger—on the back of the hand emerging from the knuckles at the base of the fingers. The holy symbol of the faith is a platinum disk at least 3 inches in diameter with an embossed depiction on both its obverse and reverse in jet black enamel of a crossed sword and mace overlaid with the image of a spider.

Adventuring Garb: Selvetarm's faithful employ the best armor and weapons available, although they eschew the use of shields—with the notable exception of spiked bucklers—and missile weapons such as bows and crossbows. Most dark elves who venerate the Spider Demon employ drow boots, a drow cloak, and drow chain mail inscribed with Selvetarm's symbol on the breast. Most Selvetargtlin are trained in the use of two melee weapons. Favorite combinations include sword and dagger, sword and mace, and sword and axe.

Specialty Priests (Spiderswords)

REQUIREMENTS:	Strength 13, Wisdom 9
PRIME REQ.:	Strength, Wisdom
ALIGNMENT:	NE, CE
WEAPONS:	Any; no missile weapons
ARMOR:	Any; no shields except spiked bucklers
MAJOR SPHERES:	All, animal, chaos, charm, combat, healing, sun (reversed only), war
MINOR SPHERES:	Divination, elemental, guardian, protection, travelers
MAGICAL ITEMS:	Same as clerics and warriors
REQ. PROFS:	Blind-fighting
BONUS PROFS:	Tracking

- Spiderswords must be drow or aranea.
- Spiderswords are not allowed to multiclass.
- Spiderswords are immune to all spider venoms.
- Spiderswords are immune to magical fear and need never check morale.
- Spiderswords receive Constitution hit point adjustments to their Hit Dice as if they were warriors.
- Spiderwords can select nonweapon proficiencies from the warrior group without penalty.
- Spiderswords can incite a berserker rage in themselves. The rage lasts for 10 rounds. During this time, a spidersword has a +2 bonus to attack, damage, and all saving throws. A spidersword may use this ability once a day. If the spidersword runs out of enemies to fight, he must either attack the closest living target in the area (even a friend) or suffer 5 points of damage for each of the remaining rounds. This is a conscious choice of the berserk spidersword.
- At 3rd level, spiderswords can cast *remove fear* or *protection from good* (as the 1st-level priest spells) once per day.
- At 5th level, spiderswords can cast *aid* (as the 2nd-level priest spell) or enchant an edged, slashing weapon to ignite with a fiery blue-white glow visible to all once per day. It strikes with a +3 attack bonus (but not damage bonus) in the next round in addition to any other bonuses it would normally accrue.
- At 7th level, spiderswords can cast *prayer* (as the 3rd-level priest spell) once per day.
- At 7th level, spiderswords can make three melee attacks every two rounds.
- At 10th level, spiderswords can cast *charm monster* (as the 4th-level wizard spell) once per day.
- At 13th level, spiderswords can make two melee attacks per round.
- At 15th level, spiderswords can cast *haste* (as the 3rd-level wizard spell) once per day. They do not age from using this ability.

Selvetarmite Spells

2nd Level

Fortitude (Necromancy)

Sphere:	Necromantic
Range:	Touch
Components:	V, S, M
Duration:	2 rounds/level
Casting Time:	5
Area of Effect:	Creature touched
Saving Throw:	None

This spell gives the recipient the ability to ignore mortal wounds and continue fighting for 1d4+1 rounds after being brought to 0 to –9 hit points. Beyond that the creature dies instantly. The effects of the spell end once the subject dies or collapses into unconsciousness.

The material components of this spell are the priest's holy symbol and several drops of cave bear blood.

4th Level

Venomous Blade (Necromancy)

Sphere:	Necromantic
Range:	Touch
Components:	V, S, M
Duration:	Special
Casting Time:	1 round
Area of Effect:	One bladed weapon
Saving Throw:	None

By means of this spell, a priest can enspell a single bladed weapon so as to envenom the wounds inflicted by the three first attacks with the blade. Any creature so wounded automatically suffers 1 additional point of damage per round in subsequent rounds until the wound is bandaged or 10 rounds (1 turn) expire. Note that successive wounds continue to cause damage in the same manner as the first. The spell fades after three attacks or 24 hours expire, whichever comes first.

Similar to wounds inflicted by a *sword of wounding*, injuries caused by a *venomous blade* cannot be healed by regeneration nor by potion or spell short of a *wish*. Damage usually can be healed only by natural means—rest and time. However, the underlying magic that prevents the wounds from healing is can be removed by an entire *elixir of health* or a *cure disease* cast by a 9th-level caster. After such a measure is employed, the impediment to magical healing is removed.

The material component for this spell is a poisonous sludge of venoms other noxious ingredients that must be smeared on the blade to be envenomed.

Vhaeraun

(The Masked Lord, the Masked God of Night, the Shadow)

Lesser Power of the Carceri, CE

PORTFOLIO:	Thievery, drow males, territory, evil activity on the surface world
ALIASES:	Vhaerun
DOMAIN NAME:	Colothys/Ellaniath
SUPERIOR:	None
ALLIES:	Mask, Shar, Talona
FOES:	Cyrrollalee, Deep Duerra, Eilistraee, Ghaunadaur, Laduguer, Lolth, the Seldarine, Sharess, Blibdoolpoolp, the Blood Queen, Diinkarazan, Diirinka, Great Mother, Gzemnid, Ilsensine, Ilxendren, Laogzed, Maanzecorian (dead), Psilofyr
SYMBOL:	Black half-mask
WOR. ALIGN.:	LN, N, CN, LE, NE, CE

Vhaeraun (Vay-RAWN) is the god of thievery and the furthering of drow aims, interests, and power in the Night Above, as the surface world is known to the faithful. He is also the god of drow males opposed to the matriarchy of Lolth, teaching that males are as skilled and valuable as females, and thus passively opposing the teachings of Lolth's priesthood on this point. He believes that drow should work with the other elven races for common advancement and never associate or trade with duergar, svirfneblin, or other dwarven and gnome races. (Humans and halflings can be tolerated.)

Vhaeraun is vain, proud, sometimes haughty, bears grudges of legendary length, and never forgets slights or deceptions. Any underhanded means and treachery is acceptable to him if it furthers his aims or is done in his service—but if others so treat him or his people, it is a deep sin that cannot go unpunished. He actively involves himself in drow affairs and moderately often sends an avatar to assist the work of his priests if the proper rituals are performed and the need is genuine.

Vhaeraun is the brother of Eilistraee and the son of Araushnee, who was cast out and became Lolth, and Corellon Larethian. The Masked Lord was cast out of the Seldarine and banished from Arvandor, along with his mother and sister, when his complicity was revealed in Araushnee's plot to destroy Corellon. While he hates all of the Seldarine, Vhaeraun harbors a particular enmity for Sehanine Moonbow, who escaped the Masked Lord's prison at great cost to herself and unmasked the culpability of both Vhaeraun and Araushnee. Likewise, the Masked Lord nurtures an abiding hatred of Eilistraee. The Dark Maiden always held Corellon's favor more than her hateful brother, and she thwarted Vhaeraun's early efforts to bring all the Ilythiiri (southern, dark-skinned elves) under his sway, enabling Lolth and Ghaunadaur to make great inroads among those who would become the drow. Vhaeraun reserves his greatest hatred for the Spider Queen who gave birth to him long ago. The Masked Lord lacks the strength to challenge Lolth directly, so he works against her in shadow, undermines her in silence, and looks to unite the other drow powers against her.

Vhaeraun's Avatar (Thief 30, Fighter 25)

Vhaeraun frequently dispatches his avatar to answer a summoning ritual performed by his priests. He appears as a well-muscled, slim, graceful, handsome drow male with eyes and hair that change in hue from red (for anger) to gold (triumph) to blue (amusement) and green (puzzlement or curious interest) to reflect his mood. He never wears armor of any sort, but he always wears a long, flowing black cloak.

AC –2; MV 15; HP 191; THAC0 –4; #AT 7/2
Dmg 1d8+10 (long sword +4, +4 Str, +2 spec. bonus in long sword) and 1d6+5 (short sword +1, +4 Str)
MR 65%; SZ H (16 feet high)
Str 18/76, Dex 24, Con 18, Int 20, Wis 14, Cha 21
Spells P: See below, W: See below
Saves PPDM 3, RSW 4, PP 4, BW 4, Sp 5

Special Att/Def: Vhaeraun wields *Nightshadow*, a jet-black *long sword +4 of quickness* that is invisible in darkness and *Shadowflash*, a silver *short sword +1* that can flash with an eerie light equal to a *continual light* at will. (Those who witness such a flash, apart from Vhaeraun, must succeed at a saving throw vs. spell to avoid being blinded for 1d4+1 rounds.) While holding *Nightshadow*, he can create a magical *bladebend* effect once every 6 rounds. The *bladebend* causes the blade of any one edged weaon currently held within 70 feet of Vhaeraun to twist about to strike its holder for maximum damage. (The blade then instantly returns to normal.)

Those looking at *Vhaeraun's cloak* in darkness can see through it the stars, the moon, or whatever else is behind it even if Vhaeraun is obviously within the portion they are observing. *Vhaeraun's cloak* melts into nothingness if removed from him or if he is slain. Its folds can harmlessly absorb seven spells of any level per day and also attract both *magic missiles* and area-of-effect spells such as *fireball,* completely protecting the wearer (and nearby beings who would otherwise be harmed) as if the cloak were some sort of infinitely charged special *brooch of shielding.*

Vhaeraun can use magical items given to him by worshipers regardless of class restrictions, so long as they function for beings of his alignment. The Masked God has no spellcasting ability of his own, but in addition to his physical attacks during a round, he can duplicate any priest or wizard spell in the mind of a priest or follower of his faith who is within 180 feet, regardless of school or sphere. Vhaeraun always *passes without trace* and can turn *invisible* at will. Vhaeraun can cast *bladebend* once every 6 rounds, and such attacks always hit for full damage.

He is immune to the effects of illusions (apart from those created by a divine being) and cannot be charmed. He can only be struck by +1 or better magical weapons.

Other Manifestations

Vhaeraun prefers to appear as an avatar but only comes when summoned by a magical ritual. (In fact, he forbids his priests to use spells from the summoning sphere or sphere as they are only to summon him.) When he cannot send his avatar (in other words, when the ritual of summoning has not been performed), he sends a flitting black shadow. It cloaks a favored being about the face like a half-mask and remains for 9 rounds. During that time, the favored being is empowered with *true seeing;* empowered to strike creatures normally hit only with the most powerful magical weapons, such as those struck only by +3 or better magical weapons, even if the weapon employed is not magical; unable to fall, fumble, or miss its footing or a leap or

catch; able to move silently and *pass without trace*; and healed of 2d4 points of current damage. This manifestation never favors the same being more than once per day.

Vhaeraun may also send a manifestation to signify his displeasure or his defiance of rivals or enemies of his people. This takes the form of a floating, insubstantial half-mask of shadows that drifts silently to confront the beings he wishes to (passing any magical barriers, and entering any place, regardless of guards, holiness to another deity, etc.). The mask can only move and (twice per appearance) utter a chilling, mocking laugh. Those hearing it must succeed at a saving throw vs. spell or be affected as if by a *fear* spell.

Vhaeraun also acts through the appearance or presence of gehreleths (farastu, kelubar, and shator), mephits (air, smoke, and earth), shadow dragons, shadow fiends, yeth hounds, and undead shadows. More commonly he sends a region of absolute, impenetrable darkness, black cats, ravens, dead spiders, agni manis, black opals, black sapphires, black-hued chalcedony, crown of silver, hematite, horn coral, black-hued jasper, jet, black-hued marble, obsidian, black-hued onyx, black-hued pearls, ravenar, or samarskite to show his favor or displeasure and as a sign to inspire his faithful.

The Church

CLERGY:	Clerics, crusaders, specialty priests, thieves
CLERGY'S ALIGN.:	NE, CE
TURN UNDEAD:	C: No, Cru: No, SP: No, T: No
CMND. UNDEAD:	C: Yes, Cru: No, SP: Yes, at priest level –2, T: No

All clerics (including cleric/thieves, a multiclassed combination allowed to drow priests of Vhaeraun), crusaders, and specialty priests of Vhaeraun receive religion (drow), religion (elven), and reading/writing (drowic) as bonus nonweapon proficiencies. All priests of the Masked Lord must be male, with the rare exception of suborned priests of Lolth. Priests of Vhaeraun may not cast any spell from the sphere of summoning or the school of summoning that does not directly summon the avatar of the Masked God of Night or request his favor (such as *blessing of Vhaeraun*). Spells that are strictly of the conjuration school are permitted

Vhaeraun is little known on the surface world among nondrow or in the Lolth-dominated cities of the dark elves in the Underdark. Among those nondrow aware of the activities of his followers in the surface world, the Masked Lord is often confused with the human god of thieves, Mask. Very few surface dwellers appreciate the threat Vhaeraun and his followers represent to the established order. In the wilds of the Underdark, the faith of Vhaeraun is seen to be slowly expanding in power and influence, and the followers of the Masked Lord are viewed with fearful respect. To priests of Lolth, priests of Vhaeraun are the enemy, to be hunted down by any means possible—torture of suspected drow is a favorite tactic—and eradicated on the altars of Lolth to earn the maximum glory of the goddess and derive the most personal enjoyment out of one's efforts. To dissatisfied, city-dwelling drow, particularly males, who somehow learn of the Masked Lord, Vhaeraun's faith is seen to offer a means of escape from the enslavement the Spider Queen.

In the Underdark, Vhaeraun is worshiped in deep caverns cloaked in multiple, overlapping *darkness* spells. Such temples are typically natural amphitheaters, with soaring ceilings studded with sparkling beljurils spaced to resemble stars. In the Night Above, the Masked Lord is venerated in shallow woodland caves cloaked by layers of leaves of deep forest canopies that allow little light to reach the forest floor. Such shrines are typically located near or in small communities of surface-dwelling drow who seek the return of the drow to the Night Above as the Masked Lord has called for. One such temple and community may be found in the western fringes of the High Forest, just two days south of the River Dessarin's headwaters near the Lost Peaks.

Vhaeraun's clergy are known collectively as the Masked. Novices of Vhaeraun are known as the Uncloaked. All other members of the clergy are known as Nightshadows. Titles used by Vhaeraunan priests vary widely across temple hierarchies, but typical titles (in no particular order) include Ascendant Darkness, Black Moon, Dark Mantle, Deep Rogue, Enveloping Night, Raven's Caw, Shadow Hunter, Silent Sable, and Twilight's Herald. High-ranking priests of the Masked Lord have unique individual titles. Specialty priests are known as darkmasks, and traitorous priests of Lolth are known as masked traitors. The clergy of Vhaeraun includes only dark elves, over 99% of whom are male. Vhaeraun's clergy includes specialty priests (55%), thieves (25%, including nonpriest multiclassed thieves), clerics (10%), cleric/thieves (7%), crusaders (2%), and masked traitors (1%).

Dogma: The shadows of the Masked Lord must cast off the tyranny of the Spider Queen and forcibly reclaim their birthright and rightful place in the Night Above. The existing drow matriarchies must be smashed, and the warring practices of twisted Lolth done away with so that the drow are welded into a united people, not a squabbling gaggle of rival Houses, clans, and aims. Vhaeraun will lead his followers into a society where the Ilythiiri once again reign supreme over the other, lesser races, and there is equality between males and females.

Priests of Vhaeraun must encourage, lead, or aid bands of drow and allied chaotic evil creatures in thievery and instigate plots, intrigues, and events to continually increase drow influence and real power in the surface Realms. They must manipulate trade, creatures, and intrigues designed to lessen the power of and frustrate the plans of drow priests (particularly those who serve Lolth), and continually foment rebellion or disobedience among drow males. Drow thieves in need must be aided (even if female): healed, bailed out of jail, or forcibly rescued. Drow men oppressed or under attack by drow women must be physically aided in any circumstances. Cruelties against drow men must be avenged.

Day-to-Day Activities: Vhaeraun's priesthood is nearly exclusively male and practices passive opposition to Lolth's priests. They are also active in the surface world, and some preach a heresy of the unity of elven races and their need to work together for dominion. They specialize in intrigue, trickery, and treachery and foment disobedience and rebellion among males. In drow communities, Vhaeraun's priests often disguise their allegiance, for obvious reasons.

Contact and marriage with other elven races is encouraged. Half-drow usually breed true back into the drow race; Vhaeraun sees this practice inexorably raising drow numbers in surface lands. Every priest works to establish some sort of permanent drow settlement on the surface world, and either support that settlement's needs personally, or (preferably) make it self-supporting. (The settlement of Vhaeraun worshipers in the High Forest, as discussed above, was established by the drow wizard Nisstyre, captain of the merchant band Dragon's Hoard, before his death in a clash with the Dark Maidens of the Promenade in chambers beneath Skullport.)

Poison use, manufacture, and experimentation is also common. Especially effective spells, poisons, and tactics devised by a priest are to be shared with the Masked Lord—and thence, all clergy.

Holy Days/Important Ceremonies: The most important attacks, negotiations, and other activities of the clergy must occur at night. Priests of Vhaeraun utter prayers to the Masked God of Night whenever they accomplish something to further his aims. Offerings of the wealth and weapons of those they vanquish (enemies of the drow, or regalia of female drow priests) are to be melted in black, bowl-shaped altars. Offerings of magic and wealth are made regularly. The more and the more value, the more Vhaeraun is pleased, though he favors daily diligence more than rare, huge hauls.

Midwinter Night, known to Vhaeraun's followers as the Masked Lord's Embrace, is the most sacred time of the year to the followers of the Masked Lord. This annual holy day is celebrated by the Masked Lord's followers with daylong introspective rituals of total sensory deprivation. Each worshiper is expected to cloak himself in a region of magical *darkness* and *levitate* at the middle of the effect for a full 24 hours while contemplating Vhaeraun's teachings and dreaming up schemes to advance the Masked Lord's goals in the coming year. All followers of Vhaeraun who wish to perform this ritual are granted the ability to employ both spell-like effects on this day, with the necessary extended duration, by a special boon of the Masked Lord.

In the Night Above, nights of the new moon are considered sacred to the followers of the Masked Lord. Such occasions are observed with midnight stag hunts that range over miles of shadowy woodlands, such as the Forest of Lethyr, the Forest of Mir, the Frozen Forest, the Lurkwood, Rawlinswood, the Trollbark Forest, and the Winterwood. Packs of Vhaeraun worshipers, mounted on riding lizards brought up from the Underdark, run down a noble hart and then sacrifice its rack of antlers and still-beating heart to the Masked Lord in dark rites that pervert the ancient ways of the surface elves.

Major Centers of Worship: One of the largest, if not the largest, concentration of dark elves on the surface of Faerûn is found in the northern reaches of Sarenestar, also known as the Forest of Mir, on the border of Tethyr and Calimshan. The drow who reside within this great timberland are concentrated in three separate settlements, all connected by tunnels and caverns created during the Night Wars. Each city consists of a few buildings dotting the surface and extensive caverns below. Unlike the egalitarian Holldaybim where both males and females rule, most of the drow who inhabit Dallnothax and Iskasshyoll are ardent Vhaeraun worshipers. Both patriarchal societies have been engaged in a centuries-long conflict with the Spider Queen's followers in Guallidurth, a drow city deep beneath Calimshan from which their ancestors escaped long ago. As part of this unending, intermittent conflict, the small temples to the Masked Lord found within Dallnothax and Iskasshyoll—the Hall of Midnight Bloodshed and the Onyx Labyrinth, respectively—have been sacked on several occasions by Lolth's worshipers. Both shrines serve their true purpose, however, by diverting attacks from the true center of the Masked Lord's worship in the region, a vast underground temple hidden beneath the flanks of Mount Sarenegard known as the Vault of Cloaked Midnight. Under the able leadership of Envenomed Edge Masoj Naerth, the southern Nightshadows have recovered much of their strength since the near disintegration of the Calishite-based cells of the Dark Dagger (see below) in the Darkstalker Wars of the Year of the Serpent (1359 DR).

Affiliated Orders: The Dark Dagger, composed of drow who venerate Vhaeraun, is a whispered name of growing weight in the dark alleys around the Inner Sea lands. Individually powerful but few in number, Dagger agents habitually use poison (which they are largely immune to, thanks to lifelong incremental dosage procedures). Active in Skullport (in Undermountain, beneath Waterdeep), in Turmish and the Vilhon Reach, and to a lesser extent in Amn and Calimshan, the various Points of the Dagger are now beginning to infiltrate coast cities all around the Sea of Fallen Stars. They like to take control of local thieving guilds and fellowships behind the scenes, hire skilled human and humanoid agents, and establish hidden temples to Vhaeraun. They recruit disaffected half-elves and humans to worship the Masked Lord, whose symbol is identical to that of Mask, the Lord of Shadows.

Very rare, but greatly feared in Lolth-fostered drow folklore and among living priests of Lolth, is the traitor priest who serves Lolth and another deity (usually Vhaeraun). It is for this reason that male drow who aspire to be priests in Lolth's service seldom rise very far in levels: even if they overcome the hatred and resentment of any female drow clergy they must work with, the Spider Queen simply does not trust them—they tend to end their days quickly, being used as temple enforcers or guards. In this role they face many spell battles with intruders (such as drow trying to settle grudges with enemies in the clergy) or priests who are rebellious, or feuding, or who have succumbed to insanity under the pressures of their station or contact with lower-planar creatures. There are priests who serve Lolth on the surface, and Vhaeraun underneath. The reverse is almost unknown, though the destructive potential of such an individual keeps the idea a dark and secret dream that fires a glint in the eyes of many a high priest. The glory for training and placing such a one would be very great, but finding suitable candidates and steering them alive through the perils of preparation without losing their loyalty to Lolth and to their handler is unlikely in the extreme—and so far, as far as it is can be told from the news of the Underdark, so unlikely as to be unknown.

How can such treachery be tolerated by the Spider Queen? Surely she knows the heart of every worshiper, and could prevail over any influences of a god of lesser power, such as Vhaeraun? The truth is that Vhaeraun is not so much less powerful than the Spider Queen—he simply uses his power in subtle, hidden, behind-the-scenes ways, not in the tyrannical, exultant, and brutal-naked-force manner so beloved by Lolth. He also watches over the drow in any place ruled by Lolth where he does have worshipers (such as the drow cities of Menzoberranzan, Tlethtyrr, and Waerglarn) often and attentively, looking into their minds for doubts and misgivings. If he finds great hatred or open rebellion against the dictates of the Spider Queen (or against her local high priests) and can find an opportunity for a private audience with the wavering Lolth worshiper, Vhaeraun manifests as a shadowy black face mask, and telepathically speaks to the individual. If the individual is discovered or attacked by others, Vhaeraun typically leaves—after using spells to destroy the beings who discovered or attacked his intended faithful. In doing this he manifests a sign of his power over Lolth and preserves the intended worshiper for another attempt at conversion later.

A double agent priest or priest continues to advance in Lolth's service and to gain spells normally. If the individual's loyalty to Vhaeraun is ever discovered, Lolth typically alerts nearby drow, and refuses to grant any further spells to the traitor—but does not strip the drow of any presently memorized spells. If the drow survives long enough to flee Lolth worshipers and any community they control, she or he continues at the same priest level and spell power, losing only access to spells specifically and only granted by Lolth (note that the *conceal item* spell is granted by other deities than the Spider Queen, and there may well be other Lolth-granted spells that have been granted in parallel for, by rival deities). The double agent becomes a cleric or specialty priest of Vhaeraun (although the dress and manners of a Lolth worshiper may be retained for use as a disguise), and typically travels to near-surface drow holdings or trading communities used by several races (such as Skullport). Drow tend not to speak the names or want to remember such traitors—their Houses disown them for safety's sake, and other drow are urged by the yochlol not to remind people of treachery to Lolth by keeping alive names of those who have so sinned.

Priestly Vestments: Vhaeraun's clergy garb themselves in half-masks, loose silk shirts, form-fitting pants, and leather boots, all of which are jet black. They are never without at least one black-edged bladed weapon on their persons, and most are bedecked with half a dozen or more such weapons. The god's holy symbol is a black half-mask that can, of course, be worn and used like any mask. Priests of Vhaeraun need only be within a mile of their holy symbol to use it in working spells given to them by the Masked Lord. It need not ever be on their persons (except when they first wear it to become attuned or linked to it) or brandished in spellcasting or dealing with undead.

Adventuring Garb: No priest of Vhaeraun can wear any type of armor except leather armor, and dark garb is always preferred. Vhaeraun's clergy favor daggers, short swords, and long swords, but they always select the most appropriate weapon for the task at hand. The Masked Lord's priests are well versed in the use of poisons, and typically prepare several varieties of widely varying onset times, methods of application, and strengths before embarking on a dangerous undertaking.

Specialty Priests (Darkmasks)

REQUIREMENTS:	Dexterity 12, Wisdom 9
PRIME REQ.:	Dexterity, Wisdom
ALIGNMENT:	NE, CE
WEAPONS:	Any
ARMOR:	Padded, leather, studded leather, drow chain mail, or elven chain mail; no shield
MAJOR SPHERES:	All, chaos, charm, combat, divination, elemental (air, earth), guardian, healing, necromantic, sun (reversed)
MINOR SPHERES:	Creation, elemental (water, fire), protection, time, travelers
MAGICAL ITEMS:	As clerics
REQ. PROFS:	A black-edged bladed weapon, disguise, herbalism
BONUS PROFS:	Alertness, blindfighting

- Darkmasks must be male drow.
- Darkmasks are not allowed to multiclass.
- Darkmasks have limited thieving skills as defined in the Limited Thieving Skills section of "Appendix 1: Demihuman Priests."
- Darkmasks may select nonweapon proficiencies from the rogue group without penalty.
- Darkmasks can cast *darkfire* (as the 2nd-level priest spell detailed in the Lolth entry earlier in this chapter) once per day. Use of this ability increases one time per day each time an experience level divisible by five is reached (at 5th, 10th, 15th, etc.) to a maximum of four uses at 20th level.
- At 3rd level, darkmasks can cast *pass without trace* (as the 1st-level priest spell) once per day for every level of experience above 2nd.
- At 5th level, darkmasks are immune to penalties from *light, continual light,* or spells with similar effects. (This granted power does not confer any protection against true sunlight or extend to any magical items possessed by a darkmask.)

- At 5th level, darkmasks can cast *alter self* (as the 2nd-level wizard spell) once per day.
- At 7th level, darkmasks can cast *dark embrace* (as the 3rd-level priest spell) once per day.
- At 10th level, darkmasks can cast *locate object* (as the 2nd-level wizard spell) once per day.
- At 13th level, darkmasks can magically create a *cloak of protection +4* once per day for 1 turn. The *cloak* fades away to nothingness if removed or when the duration expires.
- At 13th level, darkmasks can cast *Lorloveim's shadowy transformation* (as the 6th-level wizard spell) once per day.
- At 15th level, darkmasks can create a *dagger of venom +2* that injects poison on a natural roll of 18, 19, or 20. This costs them three months of time (during the final month of which they can pursue no other activities other than personal grooming, eating, and sleeping), 15,000 gp, two black star sapphires of at least 1,000 gp value each, and a suitable chunk of either mithral or adamantite to have the weapon forged from. If the black star sapphires are worth over 3,000 gp each, there is a 50% chance the dagger created can hold a +3 enchantment (but the poison injection chance does not change).

Specialty Priests (Masked Traitors)

REQUIREMENTS:	Wisdom 9
PRIME REQ.:	Wisdom
ALIGNMENT:	CE
WEAPONS:	As priest of Lolth
ARMOR:	As priest of Lolth
MAJOR SPHERES:	As priest of Lolth
MINOR SPHERES:	As priest of Lolth
MAGICAL ITEMS:	As clerics
REQ. PROFS:	None
BONUS PROFS:	None

Masked traitors are priestesses (including clerics, crusaders, and specialty priests) who serve Lolth on the surface and Vhaeraun underneath. The abilities and restrictions of masked traitors, aside from the changes noted above and later in this section, are identical to those of the type of priest of Lolth (cleric, crusader, or specialty priest) they pretend to be on the surface. All suborned priests of Lolth retain their nonweapon proficiency in ancient languages (high drow).

- Masked traitors must be drow and are almost always female, but need not be the latter.
- Masked traitors are given access to all spells known to Vhaeraun's faith, notably *chaotic combat* (which works only when cast by the priest on herself, or another faithful of Vhaeraun, regardless of class), *create holy symbol, divine inspiration, mindnet, reversion,* and *seclusion.*
- Masked traitors can cast *blessing of Vhaeraun* once per day.
- Masked traitors can cast *deceive prying* once at will at any time after entering the service of the Masked Lord. Thereafter the spell must be prayed for normally, occupying a regular spell slot, assuming the priest is of sufficient level to cast it.
- Masked traitors receive the personal attention of Vhaeraun in the form of useful information imparted to them from time to time in their dreams. The Masked Lord richly rewards those who do well in his service, and he often (falsely) hints he is willing grant immortality to worthy traitors or even elevate them to the role of his consort.
- Masked traitors can function without any penalties in full or bright light, in part because the eyes of the faithful are shaded with the shadow of Vhaeraun's power. Note that this does not negate the effects of sunlight on drow armor and weapons.

Vhaeraunan Spells

Priests of the Masked Lord have devised many spells, some of which have passed into general use. If not combat-oriented, such spells can be sold to wizards of other races—serving as templates on which to base similar wizard spells—to enrich the priesthood of the Masked Lord.

In addition to the spells listed below and those spells common to all drow priests, the Masked Lord's clergy can also cast the 3rd-level priest spell *conceal item*, detailed in the Lolth entry in this chapter and the 5th-level spell *air walk* found in the *Player's Handbook*.

2nd Level

Blessing of Vhaeraun (Pr 2; Conjuration/Summoning)

Sphere:	Combat
Range:	Touch
Components:	V, S
Duration:	1 turn or until used
Casting Time:	5
Area of Effect:	Creature touched
Saving Throw:	None

This spell enables any one single use of a thief skill or single weapon attack of the caster or a touched spell recipient to be performed with a +3 attack roll bonus or +15% ability bonus. Any damage caused by this action (harmful or beneficial to the recipient) is the maximum possible on a 1d8 roll of 1–6; otherwise, determine damage normally. The spell lasts for up to 1 turn or until the single use or attack is made. When the aid granted by the spell is to be used, the spell recipient must state so aloud before making the skill check or attack roll. The latent bonus granted by the spell also dissipates unused if a successful *dispel magic* is cast on the recipient before the round in which the *blessing* is used.

4th Level

Dark Embrace (Pr 4; Conjuration/Summoning)

Sphere:	Combat
Range:	10 yards+10 yards/level
Components:	V
Duration:	1 turn+1 round/level or until used
Casting Time:	7
Area of Effect:	Special
Saving Throw:	Special

This spell manifests as a dark shadow that flits about the spellcaster for a few moments before coalescing into a half-mask of black velvet on the spellcaster's face. Vhaeraun's *dark embrace* lasts for at most 1 turn plus 1 round per level of the spellcaster before dissipating into nothingness.

Once clad in the black half-mask created by Vhaeraun's *dark embrace*—although not in the same round in which the *dark embrace* is cast—a priest can unleash another memorized spell of 3rd level or less with a single word of power: in other words, a casting time of 1. Such spells must be touch spells or must be area effect spells that have no physical manifestation. For example, *cause light wounds* or *hold person* could be delivered by a *dark embrace*, but a *flame strike* could not.

Upon the utterance of the command word, the black half-mask dissolves once again into a dark shadow that then moves to envelop the intended target. The *dark embrace* acts as a carrier of the second spell: No magic resistance check or saving throw is allowed against it. Instead, the target creatures receives magic resistance checks and saving throws only against the spell delivered. Such magic resistance checks are made with a –10% penalty, and all saving throws are made with –3 penalty. Only the target creature is affected by the transferred spell, even if it is normally an area effect spell.

If the spell transferred by means of a *dark embrace* requires a holy symbol as a material component, the black half-mask created by the *dark embrace* serves as such.

6th Level

Deceive Prying (Pr 6; Divination)

Sphere:	All
Range:	Touch
Components:	V, S, M
Duration:	1 hour /level to a maximum of 1 day
Casting Time:	9
Area of Effect:	Creature touched
Saving Throw:	None

Priests of Vhaeraun use this spell to hide from those trying to discover their identities. This spell protects the priest or another touched being from magical and psionic examination (not attack). The alignment aura, faith, and thoughts of the recipient are overlaid by a false alignment and set of beliefs chosen during casting, and random surface thoughts are supplied by the spell in response to what the being sees happening and the false alignment and faith chosen. The being can cast spells without breaking this protection, and conduct any mental activity desired (including the use of psionics or *telepathy*) behind the mental screen. A *deceive prying* spell provides no protection against enchantment/charm spells or psionic attacks except to give a +1 bonus to the initial saving throw against a *charm person* or *charm person or mammal* magic (not the more powerful *charm monster*) by making the attacker's mind assault less precise.

The material components are a drop of cranial fluid and a small cube of iron.

7th Level

Soultheft (Pr 7; Alteration, Necromancy)

Sphere:	Necromantic
Range:	Touch
Components:	V, S, M
Duration:	Special
Casting Time:	1 turn
Area of Effect:	Special
Saving Throw:	Neg.

This spell enables the caster to steal the soul or spirit of a recently slain being to empower magic. The caster's holy symbol must be touched to the corpse within 1 turn per level of the caster of its death. If the target succeeds at a saving throw vs. death magic, the spell fails. The spell calls the life force of the dead being back into the holy symbol. It escapes again, by itself, if the holy symbol is not touched to another specially prepared magical object within 4 turns. (Note that the corpse is not harmed by the *soultheft*.)

The object to receive the life force must be touched by the holy symbol as a secret word is spoken. The transfer takes 6 rounds to occur. If the transfer is interrupted, the life force snaps back into the holy symbol, but the transfer can be attempted again.

Once transferred, the life force empowers an item to function magically for 1 month or 10 charges per level or Hit Dice (in life) of the dead being. The spell uses a trapped soul or spirit as an engine to power a previously enchanted magical item. It cannot be used to turn a plain item into a magical one; in other words, one cannot use *soultheft* to turn a sword into a *holy avenger +5*. The magical item must either be specially crafted to harness a stolen life force (in which case the time duration is used) or must be a charged item that is already enchanted (in which case the recharging function applies). Once this duration is at end or these charges are used (such charges are always used first), the spirit is released unless the spell is renewed.

Renewing *soultheft* involves simply recasting the spell on the enchanted item and does not require the original corpse. When such a spell is renewed, the imprisoned life force must make a system shock survival check or it is annihilated.

The being whose life force has been stolen cannot be contacted, raised, wished back, or otherwise called back to living existence unless the object empowered by the stolen life force is identified, seized, and held by the being doing the raising. The enchanted object betrays the fact that it holds the essence of the particular being to any magical scrutiny—in other words, a *detect magic* not only shows a magical aura, but also reveals the ghostly image of the stolen soul trapped within the item.

The material component of this spell is the priest's holy symbol. A suitable enchanted item must also be prepared, but need not be present at the initial casting of the *soultheft*. (It must, of course, be present at any renewal.)

DWARVEN PANTHEON

The Stout Folk of the Realms worship a pantheon of deities collectively known as the Morndinsamman, a term that can be loosely translated shield brothers on high or the high dwarves. The composition of the pantheon varies slightly from clan to clan (and even more so from world to world), but the powers presented hereafter are venerated or at least acknowledged in most dwarven settlements of Faerûn. (Diinkarazan and Diirinka are no longer considered a part of the dwarven pantheon, nor are they detailed in this book. They and their followers, the derro, have largely been forgotten among the Stout Folk, though a handful of sages know of them.)

Although the term *Morndinsamman* is commonly used to refer to all acknowledged dwarven gods, formal membership in the pantheon is determined by Moradin. The good and neutral dwarven gods, including Moradin, Berronar, Clangeddin, Dugmaren, Dumathoin, Gorm, Haela, Marthammor, Sharindlar, Thard, and Vergadain, have always been members in good standing. Abbathor is still a member, as his treachery has never been proven, although most of his fellows detest him. Laduguer was banished by the All-Father long ago, and Deep Duerra was exiled immediately following her apotheosis and ascension, but both are considered members-in-exile. Diirinka and his mad brother, Diinkarazan, are the only dwarven powers who are truly no longer members of the Morndinsamman.

The dwarven gods are said to have sprung from stone and earth, beginning with Moradin. Berronar is universally held to be Moradin's wife, and many dwarven theologians hold that all the other dwarven powers are their descendants, although the exact ordering and ancestry vary from myth to myth. After Moradin and Berronar, the oldest dwarven powers are thought to be Dumathoin, Abbathor, Laduguer, Clangeddin, Sharindlar, and the twins Diinkarazan and Diirinka. The next group of dwarven gods commonly worshiped in the Realms includes Thard Harr, Gorm Gulthyn, Marthammor Duin, and Dugmaren Brightmantle. Recent additions to the dwarven pantheon, said to be the grandchildren of Moradin and Berronar, have included Haela Brightaxe and Deep Duerra.

The Morndinsamman are intimately involved with the lives of their worshipers, and the Stout Folk as a whole are an unusually devout race. Faced with the slow decline of dwarves across Faerûn, the dwarven powers have become increasingly active as they seek to reverse that trend. Correspondingly, dwarven religion has assumed an increasingly important role in dwarven culture and society. The dwarven pantheon is predominantly male, reflecting the population imbalance between the two genders. Unlike the elven pantheon, the members of the Morndinsamman are scattered across the Outer Planes. This may be symbolic and reflective of the dwarven desire for territory and living space; just as mortal dwarves are ever exploring new territory below the surface world, the deities themselves live apart as well. An oddity of the dwarven deities is that most can, if they wish, have their avatars appear huge in stature—up to 20 feet tall in the case of Moradin. Dwarven theologians believe this reflects their activist natures and inspirational roles as leaders among the dwarves.

While some nondwarven scholars claim that the Stout Folk migrated to the Realms from another crystal sphere early in the history of Abeir-Toril—perhaps through a *gate* located in the heart of the planet—the collective dwarven racial memory holds that their ancestors sprang fully formed from the heart of the world itself. The All-Father is said to have secretly fashioned dwarves of iron and mithral in his Soul Forge, using his huge magical hammer to beat the bodies into shape and then breathing on his creations to cool them and to give them souls.

One is struck, in a study of dwarven theology, by the relationship between procreation and metalcraft; perhaps more than one dwarven smith has looked upon a finished piece of work and felt as if she or he had breathed life into the metal and given it a soul of sorts, as Moradin did long ago. Moradin taught the first dwarves the skills of smithing and metalworking, enabling them to exploit the riches of their homes in the mountains and craft items to allow further exploration. These early dwarves also learned toolmaking and weaponcrafting from Moradin, who watches over these activities still. No dwarven deity has a sacred or totem animal, and the holy symbols used to represent them are invariably not living objects. This derives in large part from some of the teachings of Moradin, who ruled that the dwarves must hold no other race above them; having an animal as a symbol would imply that that animal was better than the dwarves. Likewise, Moradin said that the dwarves should not ever worship each other, so no dwarf or part of one is ever used as a holy symbol.

In many versions of the myths concerning the founding of the race, the earliest dwarves must fight their way up from the world's core to the mountains above, overcoming many dangers on the way. These are usually great monsters and physical hazards that the dwarves overcome by strength, combat, and physical skill, rather than by wit or trickery. These early myths are fully consistent with the way in which dwarven theology stresses the pragmatic and practical. There is absolutely no place for the arcane or mystical in dwarven myths, legends, and beliefs.

It is unknown when or where dwarves appeared in the Realms, but most dwarven legends trace the earliest settlements of the Stout Folk back tens of thousands of years to the great mountain range known as the Yehimal. It is believed that in a great exodus from the Yehimal, the Stout Folk split into two (or possibly three) major branches as they spread across Faerûn, Kara-Tur, and Zakhara. Those who came to Faerûn are believed to have first settled beneath modern-day Semphar before spreading westward, eventually fragmenting into four dwarven subraces.

The first great kingdom of dwarves in Faerûn was centered in the great cavern of Bhaerynden deep beneath the Shaar. The first great schism among the Stout Folk came with the founding of Shanatar beneath the lands of Amn, Erlkazar, Tethyr, Calimshan, the Land of Lions, and the Lake of Steam. Emigrants from the Deep Realm merged with the scattered enclaves of dwarves already resident in the region to form a distinct subrace of the Stout Folk known today as the shield dwarves (mountain dwarves). Shield dwarves eventually founded most of the great dwarven nations of the North, from Oghrann to Gharraghaur. (The D'tarig of Anauroch are descendants of shield dwarves and humans, though their dwarven blood is now so thin that they are essentially a short human race and have totally forgotten the dwarven cultural ties.)

From the earliest shield dwarves, Dumathoin then created the urdunnirin. After the Crown Wars and the descent of the dark elves, Bhaerynden and the surrounding territories fell to the drow, and the dwarves of southern Faerûn were driven into exile and scattered. Those dwarves who fled as far as the jungles of Chult abandoned their subterranean homes and interbred with the small enclaves of dwarves already dwelling in the jungles. Their offspring were the ancestors of the wild dwarves (jungle dwarves) who dwell on the Chultan peninsula today. After the first drow kingdom of Telantiwar tore itself apart in civil war, the great cavern of Bhaerynden collapsed to form the Great Rift. Those dwarves who resettled the caverns of the Deep Realm surrounding the Great Rift were the ancestors of the gold dwarves (hill dwarves).

The last great schism among the Stout Folk occurred when an entire clan of shield dwarves, Clan Duergar, was enslaved by illithids some time before the founding of Deep Shanatar. The gray dwarves, as the duergar came to be known, were long absent from Shanatar before their rediscovery, and they spread through much of the Underdark during the intervening period. It is speculated that the legendary derro may be the result of breeding experiments by the illithids between gray dwarves and humans, but this has never been proven. Other minor branches of the dwarven race, including the desert dwarves of Maztica, the arctic dwarves of the Great Glacier, and the albino dwarves of Chult, are simply isolated clans of shield dwarves. Legends of a race of aquatic dwarves in the Sea of Fallen Stars have been conclusively discredited by every scholar who has looked into the question.

Various schisms in the dwarven pantheon have mirrored the fragmentation of the dwarven race in Faerûn. The shield dwarves and gold dwarves still worship and perceive the Morndinsamman similarly, and both generally revere, or at least acknowledge, all of the High Dwarves. But the gray dwarves venerate Laduguer and Deep Duerra to the near exclusion of the other dwarven gods. Likewise, the legendary derro speak only of Diirinka, and in a handful of cases, Diinkarazan, much as the wild dwarves revere only Thard Harr.

There are those among the dwarves who blame the gods for the present decline of the race or who feel that the old gods are simply too weak or too out-of-touch with the wider world in which the dwarves must live to aid their folk successfully in the ages to come. Many dwarves have dabbled in new beliefs, including one that advocates mastery of wizardry as the key to the race's survival, one that promotes interbreeding with humans and gnomes coupled with secretive diplomacy (so as to dominate and eventually absorb these more fecund races), and so on. Most of these new beliefs have tended to come and go as passing fads, embraced for a time by each successive generation of young dwarves. Details of the cults that have arisen throughout the long history of the dwarves could fill a work many times the size of this one. DMs are urged to devise their own cults, particularly for use as the sources of relics found in old, abandoned dwarven holds and as active religions in isolated dwarven communities.

Only two long-established or recurring cults are discussed briefly below in the Abbathor and Clangeddin entries. These have been successful enough that some divine power—whether it be a dwarven deity operating in secret to further his or her ends (such as Abbathor, Clangeddin, or Diinkarazan), a deity of another race seeking to influence the dwarves, or even a heretofore unknown dwarven deity—has come to support the pleas and deeds of each by granting spells to the priests.

General Dwarven Priest Abilities: The general abilities and restrictions of dwarven priests (including duergar), aside from the specific changes noted later in this section for each dwarven faith, are summarized in the discussion of dwarven priests in "Appendix 1: Demihuman Priests." Due to long-standing tradition, most dwarven priests of dwarven deities before the Time of Troubles had to be of the same gender as their deity. Since the Time of Troubles, this stricture is not longer the absolute that is was, and all dwarven faiths now accept priests of either gender—reluctantly. Priests of the gender opposite their deity are likely to be treated gingerly or with slight resentment by their same-gender fellows and to be called upon to prove their commitment to their vocation often. Dwarven culture is very slow to adopt new customs.

Abbathor

(Great Master of Greed, Trove Lord, the Avaricious, Wyrm of Avarice)

Intermediate Power of the Gray Waste, NE

PORTFOLIO:	Greed
ALIASES:	None
DOMAIN NAME:	Oinos/the Glitterhell
SUPERIOR:	Moradin
ALLIES:	Task, Vergadain
FOES:	Berronar, Brandobaris, Clangeddin Silverbeard, Cyrrollalee, Dumathoin, Moradin, the gnome pantheon, the goblinkin and giant pantheons
SYMBOL:	Jeweled dagger
WOR. ALIGN.:	LE, NE, CE

Abbathor (AB-bah-thor) the Avaricious is the dwarven god of greed, venerated by most evil dwarves and nearly all evil dwarven thieves. He represents the worst aspect and major weakness of dwarven character. Many dwarves and even nondwarves consumed with treasure lust and greed, or those who seek to steal valuables, make offerings to him.

The Great Master of Greed was once interested purely in the natural beauty of gems and metals, but became embittered when Moradin appointed Dumathoin the protector of mountain dwarves—a position Abbathor felt should be his. From that day onward, Abbathor has become ever more devious and self-serving, continually trying to wreak revenge on the other dwarven gods by establishing greed, especially evil greed, as the driving force in the lives of all dwarves.

The Trove Lord maintains an uneasy truce with the god Vergadain, but he is otherwise estranged from the dwarven pantheon. Abbathor particularly hates Dumathoin and Moradin for denying him his rightful place in the pantheon, and he secretly works against both. He hates Clangeddin for Clangeddin's self-righteous noble stance and certain past insult, and Clangeddin returns the favor. Berronar loathes Abbathor's deceitfulness, and Dumathoin shields treasures from the Great Master of Greed, to Abbathor's unending frustration and fury. Unlike Laduguer, however, Abbathor is tolerated by the other dwarven gods, although none trust him. Despite the fact that he embodies everything they teach their followers to avoid, he has sided with them in epic battles of the past and is still a valued member of the group. Abbathor never helps any nondwarven deity or being, however, with the notable exception of Task, draconic god of greed.

Abbathor is squat and hunched, despite his height. He seems to slither and sidle along as he walks, never making much noise but often rubbing his hands together. If carrying gems or gold, he often caresses these in a continuous, unconscious, overwhelmingly sensuous manner. At times, this has made ignorant folk attack him, overcome by lust to gain the treasure he holds. The Great Master is said to have burning yellow-green eyes (blazing yellow when eager for treasure or when pouncing upon it, hooded and green while scheming or when thwarted). He has a sharp hooked nose like a giant eagle's beak and always dresses in leather armor and furs, both fashioned from the skins of creatures who have opposed him and died to regret it. He is said to have a harsh, husky, wheedling voice and a quick temper, hissing and spitting when angry. Abbathor is governed by his insatiable lust for treasure, especially gold, and is treacherous in his dealings with dwarves. He roams many worlds, including the Realms, in avatar form in search of treasure. Abbathor uses any means, no matter how evil, to further his ends, which typically involve the acquisition of wealth. Should the Great Master of Greed see treasure worth more than 1,000 gp or any magical item, he attempts to steal it outright or slay the owner and then take it anyway. If frustrated in an attempt to steal an item, Abbathor tries to destroy it so as not to be tortured by the memory of his failure.

Abbathor's Avatar (Thief 35, Wizard 28, Cleric 18, Fighter 15)

Abbathor appears as a very large dwarf clad in leather and furs. He is fat and piggy-eyed with sallow skin. He favors spells from the spheres of divination, guardian, sun (reversed), and protection, plus the schools of divination and illusion/phantasm, although he can cast spells from any sphere or school.

AC –5; MV 12 or 15; HP 211; THAC0 3; #AT 5/2
Dmg 2d12+15 (*dagger +5*, +8 Str, +2 spec. bonus in dagger)
MR 65%; SZ M (6 feet tall) or L (8 feet tall)
Str 20, Dex 22, Con 21, Int 20, Wis 18, Cha 10
Spells P: 10/10/9/9/6/4/2, W: 6/6/6/6/6/6/6/6/6
Saves PPDM 4, RSW 1*, PP 5, BW 4, Sp 4
    *Includes dwarf +6 Con save bonus to a minimum of 1. The Con save bonus also applies to saves vs. poison to a minimum of 1.

Special Att/Def: Abbathor wields a diamond-bladed *dagger +5* with jewels set into the hilt. It does 2d12 (base) points of damage and can detect the presence (type and amount) of precious metals in a 20 foot radius. It repowers itself by draining life energy from all mortals who grab it: one experience level is lost at the first touch, and one per round or partial round thereafter that the blade is held. (It does not drain life energy on an attack, just when grabbed—like when someone tries to steal it.) In addition to his physical and spell attacks, the Great Master of Greed can cast *detect illusions*, *detect metals and minerals*, or create *treasure lust* (see the first manifestation power, below) at will, one per round.

Abbathor often carries a pair of golden lions (*figurines of wondrous power*) concealed in a pocket. If hard-pressed, he hurls these, commanding them to fight for him. If they are overpowered and the god must flee, he simply returns to steal them back and slay their new owner as soon as it is convenient.

When expecting trouble, Abbathor also bears a shield that can cast a 30-foot range *blindness* spell at any one creature, once per round. Targets must succeed at a saving throw with a –6 penalty, or a –3 penalty if they continually face away from the shield. (This latter option forces them to fight with a penalty of –4 to their attack rolls and Armor Classes.) He can be struck only by +2 or better magical weapons.

Other Manifestations

Abbathor manifests purely to work his own ends, typically in one of four ways:

- He can create a sudden *treasure lust* in dwarves, gnomes, humans, or halflings (to avoid, succeed at a saving throw vs. spell at a –2 penalty; –4 if dwarven). Affected beings do anything Abbathor (in other words, the DM) wants for 6 rounds, in an attempt to seize known treasure and keep it, slaying all witnesses if that seems necessary. Combat with friends or loved ones allows repeated saving throws, one per round, to break free of Abbathor's power.
- Abbathor can cause any dwarf to be suddenly made aware of the precise location, nature, and value of hidden gems within 10 feet.
- Abbathor can cause magical *silence* and *darkness, 15´ radius*, both lasting 1 turn, to aid the escape of a dwarf who has stolen something.
- Finally, whenever a treasure chest is opened or a hoard pile is disturbed, Abbathor tries to cause gems and/or coins to leap of their own accord. He makes them fall and bounce or roll away into crevices or other

hiding places from which he may recover them later. Allow a 2 in 6 chance of this happening; if it occurs, roll 1d12 to determine how many valuables are affected, and allow PCs to make Dexterity checks to trap, catch, or retrieve them, according to how they act.

Sometimes, when Abbathor's avatar is present in the Realms, two other manifestations occur. First, when Abbathor hears his name spoken (in the way all avatars can), a handlike invisible force snatches and clutches at the purse, pockets, worn jewelry, or sacks of the speaker, by way of warning. If anything comes loose (apply item saving throws and/or Strength and Dexterity checks as the circumstances suggest), treat the objects as leaping into hiding (as above) for Abbathor to claim later.

Second, when Abbathor's avatar or a being (almost always a dwarf) upon whom he is concentrating walks close to gems (either cut and finished or natural and still embedded in stone), the jewels sing with a high-pitched, multitoned chiming, rather like the sounds made by the glass and metal wind chimes popular in the South. This singing is audible to all and serves to guide Abbathor or his chosen being to the gems.

Abbathor is served by aurumvorae, crysmals, dragons consumed with avarice, earth elemental vermin, earth weirds, ghost dragons, hetfish, incarnates of covetousness, khaasta, rappers, rust monsters, tso, werebadgers, and xavers. He manifests his pleasure through the discovery of gold and jewels of all sorts and his displeasure through the despoiling of treasure—causing gems to split apart, sacks of gold to tear, and so on.

The Church

CLERGY:	Clerics, specialty priests, thieves
CLERGY'S ALIGN.:	LE, NE, CE; CN (noroghor only)
TURN UNDEAD:	C: No, SP: No, T: No
CMND. UNDEAD:	C: Yes, SP: Yes, at priest level –4, T: No

All clerics (including cleric/thieves, a multiclass combination allowed to dwarven priests of Abbathor) and specialty priests of Abbathor receive religion (dwarven) and reading/writing (Dethek runes) as bonus nonweapon proficiencies. Clerics of Abbathor can use any weapons, not just bludgeoning (wholly Type B) weapons. Clerics of Abbathor (as well as cleric/thieves) cannot command undead before 7th level, but they always strike at +2 on all attack and damage rolls against undead creatures. At 7th level and above, clerics (including multiclassed clerics) can command undead as other clerics do, but as a cleric of four levels less than their current level. All clergy members of Abbathor were male until the Times of Troubles, but since then some females have joined the church.

While Abbathor is publicly reviled in dwarven society ("gone to Abbathor" is a dwarven expression for lost treasure), most dwarves have been consumed on more than one occasion with the lust for treasure that he embodies. Rare is the dwarf who does not recognize the streak of avarice infecting the Stout Folk, and thus the Trove Lord's rightful place in the dwarven pantheon. Like an unliked and self-serving member of the clan who nonetheless is not known to have ever betrayed his kinfolk, the Great Master of Greed is venerated as a member of the Morndinsamman by most dwarves, even as they decry his beliefs.

Temples of the Great Master of Greed are always in underground caverns or secret, windowless rooms. Sacrificial altars are massive, plain blocks of stone, blackened by the many fires laid and burnt upon them. (Note that nondwarves tend to panic when sacrificial fires are lit, and the smoke begins to billow!) Abbathor's places of worship can easily be mistaken for treasure vaults, as they are typically painted in gold leaf and filled with a cache of purloined treasures. In fact, the most sacred places of the Trove Lord are caverns that once housed the hoards of ancient wyrms.

Novices of Abbathor are known as Goldseekers; full priests are known as the Hands of Greed. In ascending order of rank, the titles used by Abbathoran priests are Coveter of Copper, Seeker of Silver, Luster of Electrum, Hoarder of Gold, Plunderer of Platinum, and Miser of Mithral. High Old Ones have unique individual titles but are collectively known as the Masters of Greed. Specialty priests are known as aetharnor, a dwarvish word that can be loosely translated as *those consumed with greed*. The priesthood consists of gold dwarves (50%), shield dwarves (40%), gray dwarves (9%), and jungle dwarves (1%). Abbathor's clergy is nearly evenly divided between specialty priests (35%), cleric/thieves (33%), and thieves (32%), with the remainder being clerics (10%). Male priests still constitute most of the priesthood (97%). Abbathor secretly supports some leaders of the Wyrm Cult (described below); such specialty priests are known as noroghor, a dwarvish word that can be loosely translated as *beast followers*.

Dogma: Seek to acquire all that shines or sparkles, and revel in the possession of such. The wealth of the earth was created for those dwarves strong and crafty enough to acquire it by any means necessary. Greed is good, as it motivates the acquisition and the holding of all that is truly precious. Do not seize wealth from the children of the Morndinsamman, however, nor conspire against the favored of Abbathor, for such strife in the name of avarice weakens the clan.

Day-to-Day Activities: Like their deity, priests of Abbathor strive to enrich themselves, taking advantage of their positions and influence to steal or deal themselves some personal wealth. Such funds are typically cached in remote, fiendishly well-trapped hideaways, as amassing enough loot to retire in luxury is a game and a driving motivation among priests of this god.

As noted above, however, there is one strict rule: No priest of Abbathor can steal from any other dwarf, or influence events to cause harm to the person or wealth of any rival priest of Abbathor. This is the infamous Abbathor's Commandment, of which dwarven thieves are often reminded. Priests of Abbathor do not like to remember so readily that it was uttered purely in order to preserve some followers of the god after angry fellow dwarves had slaughtered thief after thief in the robes of Abbathor's clergy.

The wider aims of the priesthood are to enrich all dwarves, working with the clergy of Vergadain and Dumathoin where possible toward that end. Across the Realms, priests of Abbathor are always looking for a chance for common dwarven profit (and their own personal gain) through underhanded and shady arrangements. The underground ways known to dwarves make them ideal smugglers, and many borders are undercut by tunnels enabling dwarven merchants to avoid duties and restrictions in transporting goods from one land to another. Dwarves are prevented from dominating the smuggling trade purely by their aversion to water, which effectively excludes them from shipborne activity.

Priests of Abbathor trade (on the sly) with *anyone*, including duergar, drow, illithids, Zhentarim, orcs, giants, and other undesirable creatures or traditional enemies of the dwarves. Dwarves have been slain by axes sold to orcs by priests of Abbathor on more than one occasion. This contrariness, however, is an essential part of the dwarven nature, as is the goldlust that drives many dwarves on occasion—at such times they are said to be under the spell of Abbathor or in Abbathor's thrall. Priests of Abbathor can be considered to be permanently in this condition, but to have learnt subtlety and devious cunning in its pursuit, rather than simple, crude acquisitiveness.

Beings who need something underhanded done can always contact priests of Abbathor if they know where to find them. (Usually only dwarves know how to do so.) For a fee, a known worshiper of Abbathor will often arrange a meeting between an outsider (such as a human) and one of the god's priests. The priest and the worshiper will both work to arrange the meeting so that the priest is in little danger of attack, kidnapping, or arrest.

Priests of Abbathor secretly work to undermine the faith of Dumathoin and Berronar—the former in revenge for the Silent Keeper's assumption of a position meant for the Trove Lord, and the latter in response to the Revered Mother's concerted efforts to prevent thefts. Since such actions must always be kept secret from all but their fellow clergy members and may never endanger the immediate safety of the clan, the Hands of Greed must proceed very slowly in this task.

Holy Days/Important Ceremonies: Solar eclipses and days when volcanic eruptions or other causes bring darkness during daytime are always considered holy days.

Once a year, priests of Abbathor sacrifice a creature on an altar. It must be an enemy of dwarves but can be anything from an elf to a boar. Orcs, trolls, and giants are the most favored sacrifices. The faithful of Abbathor then bring gems in offering to the god, and these are placed upon the body; they must touch the blood of the sacrifice. The value of the sacrifice is said to determine the amount of Abbathor's favor that will benefit the offerer in the year to come. Even priests refer to this practice as "buying grace." The sacrifice is then burnt to ashes, gems and all. If magic or especially valuable gems are sacrificed, these sometimes disappear before the body is consumed, taken by Abbathor for his own (or pocketed by the priests for their own use, some say).

Abbathor's favor is said to include minor things like causing guards to sleep or become distracted, shaping shadows and moon-cloaking clouds to hide the features or exact position of a fleeing dwarven thief, or allowing a trapped thief an occasional battle-aid (in the form of an initiative roll bonus). Dwarves in need of Abbathor's immediate favor may make offerings at other times throughout the year. It is also customary to make an offering when one first worships at a particular temple.

Major Centers of Worship: Aefarn, the House of Gold, is a fortified temple complex housing much of the collected wealth of Abbathor's clergy. The temple is located deep beneath Turnback Mountain, the southernmost peak of a mountain range of similar name running north-south along the eastern border of Anauroch and north of the frozen steppes known as the Tortured Land. The treasure vaults of the Hands of Greed are located in a cavern complex hewn millennia ago from the surrounding granite by the great red wyrm Ragflaconshen, Spawn of Mahatnartorian, before he died defending his hoard from the avaricious Abbathor. In the Year of the Wailing Winds (1000 DR), a trio of Abbathoran priests stumbled across the wyrm's long-hidden lair after following a trail of gold coins placed—or so they suspected—by the Great Master of Greed. After an arduous adventure bypassing the long-dead wyrm's many traps, the three priests finally penetrated Ragflaconshen's inner sanctum early in the Year of the Awakening (1001 DR). There they discovered that the great wyrm had survived, after a fashion, as a ghost dragon, his spirit unable to rest until his fabulous horde was replaced in kind. The Trove Lord then appeared to the three priests in a vision and directed them to muster the faithful (along with their personal hoards) scattered throughout the Cold Lands—the territory loosely incorporating the lands between the Moonsea, Anauroch, and the Great Glacier—in the ghost dragon's lair. This mass assemblage of treasure would allow the spirit of the Trove Lord's ancient antagonist and kindred spirit in greed to rest at last. When this was done, Abbathor appeared to his assembled worshipers in avatar form and directed them, under the leadership of the Three Coinlords (as the trio was thereafter known), to build a temple honoring him. This structure would house the assembled trove of treasure (possibly the most valuable to ever exist in the Realms), as well as all new wealth that its clergy acquired in the wider world. In the nearly four centuries since the founding of Aefarn, the caverns that make up the House of Gold have been entirely covered with gold leaf and studded with precious gems. The three seniormost priests of the temple compose the ruling triumvirate (still named for its founders), although Abbathor's assembled priests work collectively to defend the House of Gold from interlopers. Each priest has his own heavily trapped set of chambers in which his personal share of the temple's wealth is hoarded. Thus those seeking to plunder the House of Gold find themselves faced with innumerable smaller fortresses in addition to the formidable collective defenses.

Affiliated Orders: While Abbathor has no knightly orders associated with his faith, the Great Master of Greed has secretly embraced one of the most prominent cults in dwarven society as his own and begun granting spells to its priests, who are known as noroghor. The Wyrm Cult can be found in isolated dwarven communities throughout Faerûn, but it seems more common in the North than in areas south of the Inner Sea lands. Its priests are few and secretive, employing dwarven sympathizers as spies and rewarding them for their aid by allowing them opportunities for recreation or revenge in beast form. The Wyrm Cult worships various beasts (especially dragons and other powerful creatures that dwarves treat with respect) and seeks to increase the power and wealth of its adherents by slaying and confounding enemies with the powers of beasts. Consumed by a burning anger against all types of creatures who have oppressed or slain dwarves in the past, Wyrm Cult priests have taken to attacking all nondwarven adventurers who wander within their reach throughout the wilderlands of the North. Currently in need of wealth and power, they seek both through increased influence and greater numbers of worshipers as well as through the acquisition of magical items and controlled territories.

Priestly Vestments: Priests of Abbathor always dress in red—a brilliant scarlet, worn as underclothing for everyday use and as over-robes for ceremonial occasions. Over this they wear leather armor with leather caps (never helms). If this armor must be discarded, dark crimson robes are worn to echo—and yet conceal the brightness of—the scarlet underclothing. Clergy of Abbathor never wear wealth openly because of the god's saying: "The best is always hidden." The holy symbol of the faith is a gold coin at least two inches in diameter, which is stamped with the symbol of Abbathor on both faces.

Adventuring Garb: When expecting open combat, the Trove Lord's priests gird themselves in the best available armor and weapons with which they are proficient, in the fashion of most dwarven warriors. When stealth is required, however, members of Abbathor's clergy prefer the garb and tools of rogues. In all cases, however, the Hands of Greed keep the signs of their calling—including their scarlet underclothes and their holy symbols—concealed, as it is considered an affront to Abbathor to proclaim his name or his symbol openly.

Specialty Priests (Aetharnor)

REQUIREMENTS:	Dexterity 11, Wisdom 9
PRIME REQ.:	Dexterity, Wisdom
ALIGNMENT:	LE, NE, CE
WEAPONS:	Club, dagger, dart, hand crossbow, knife, lasso, short bow, sling, broad sword, long sword, short sword, and staff
ARMOR:	Any
MAJOR SPHERES:	All, charm, combat, divination, guardian, summoning, wards
MINOR SPHERES:	Creation, healing, necromantic, protection, summoning, sun
MAGICAL ITEMS:	Same as clerics and thieves
REQ. PROFS:	Mining
BONUS PROFS:	Appraising, gem cutting

- Most aetharnor (the plural form of aetharnar) are either gold dwarves or shield dwarves, but dwarves of nearly every subrace are called to be specialty priests of Abbathor.
- Aetharnor are not allowed to multiclass.
- Aetharnor may select nonweapon proficiencies from both the priest and rogue groups with no crossover penalty.
- Aetharnor understand and use thieves' cant.
- Aetharnor have some thieving skills as defined in the Limited Thieving Skills section of "Appendix 1: Demihuman Priests."
- Aetharnor can cast *detect metals and minerals* (as the 1st-level priest spell detailed in *Powers & Pantheons*) once per day.
- At 3rd level, aetharnor can cast *maskstone* (as the 2nd-level priest spell) once per day.
- At 5th level, aetharnor can cast *darkness, 15´ radius* (as the 2nd-level wizard spell) once per day.
- At 7th level, aetharnor can detect illusions at will in a path 10 feet wide and 60 feet long in front of them. They must concentrate to use this ability.
- At 10th level, aetharnor can cast *conceal riches* (as the 4th-level priest spell) once per day.
- At 13th level, aetharnor can cast *Von Gasik's refusal* (as the 5th-level wizard spell) and *knock* (as the 2nd-level wizard spell) once each per day.
- At 15th level, aetharnor can cast *steal enchantment* (as the 7th-level wizard spell) or *Gunther's kaleidoscopic strike* (as the 8th-level wizard spell).
- At 20th level, aetharnor can cast *glorious transformation* (as the 9th-level wizard spell) once per month. Note that aetharnor still require a *philospher's stone* to do this.

Specialty Priests (Noroghor)

REQUIREMENTS:	Constitution 9, Wisdom 9
PRIME REQ.:	Constitution, Wisdom
ALIGNMENT:	CN, CE
WEAPONS:	Any bludgeoning (wholly Type B) weapon
ARMOR:	Any
MAJOR SPHERES:	All, animal, combat, guardian, protection, summoning, wards
MINOR SPHERES:	Elemental, healing, plant, travelers
MAGICAL ITEMS:	Same as clerics
REQ. PROFS:	Animal training
BONUS PROFS:	Animal lore, modern languages (choose one monstrous tongue, such as Auld Wyrmish or beholder)

- While most noroghor (the plural form of noroghar) are either gold dwarves or shield dwarves, dwarves of nearly every subrace are called to be priests of the Wyrm Cult.
- Noroghor are not allowed to multiclass.
- At 3rd level, noroghor are immune to the fear auras of young adult dragons of all species. For every two levels above 3rd, the maximum age category of dragon to whose aura noroghor are immune increases by one. For example, at 5th level, noroghor are immune to the fear auras of adult or younger dragons. This immunity applies equally to all types of dragons, including gem dragons, but it is affected by spells or magical items that increase or decrease a dragon's effective age category with regard to its fear aura.
- At 5th level, noroghor can cast *efficacious monster ward* (as the 3rd-level priest spell) once per day.
- At 7th level, noroghor can cast *shape change* (as the 9th-level wizard spell) three times per day for a period of up to 1 turn, but can only take the shapes of creatures and other living things they have seen personally. Their favorite shapes include snakes, wyverns, dragons, boars, bears, and various large cats (tigers, panthers, mountain lions, and so on).
- At 7th level, noroghor detect illusions at will in a path 10 feet wide and 60 feet long in front of them. They must concentrate to use this ability.
- At 10th level, noroghor can cast *polymorph other* (as the 4th-level wizard spell) once per day on willing recipients only. (Typically this granted power is employed only on devout cultists.) Recipients receive a +25% bonus to all system shock rolls incurred as a result of this change.
- At 13th level, noroghor become immune to the effects of one type of dragon breath weapon.
- At 15th level, noroghor can cast *age dragon* (as the 7th-level priest spell) once per day on willing recipients only or *flame strike* (as the 5th-level priest spell) once per day.

Abbathoran Spells

In addition to the spells listed below, priests of the Trove Lord may cast the 1st-level priest spell *detect metals and minerals*, detailed in *Powers & Pantheons* in the entry for Geb.

2nd Level

Maskstone (Pr 2; Illusion/Phantasm) *Reversible*

Sphere:	Elemental Earth
Range:	Touch
Components:	V, S, M
Duration:	1 year/level
Casting Time:	5
Area of Effect:	A square that is 1 foot/level on a side
Saving Throw:	None

This spell alters the appearance of stone to hide seams, openings, traps, runes, doors, and so on. The priest touches the central point of the area to be masked and visualizes what appearance is desired (in other words, hue, fissures, shape, and general appearance). The spell cloaks the stone with a long-term illusion matching the caster's visualization. A caster of at least 6th level can cloak a second section of stone of similar dimensions, and a caster of at least 9th level, a third section.

Features of the stone under the *maskstone* spell remain physically unchanged. A known door can be felt for and located in 1d3 rounds. Unless it has been used by the searcher before, determining its method and direction of opening and the location of any locks or catches is extremely difficult without a *dispel magic* to end the cloaking effect. Only characters with thieving skills have the necessary expertise, and they find catches, locks, and traps on such doors at a –15% penalty to their find traps rolls, unlock locks at a –10% penalty to their open locks rolls, and remove found traps at a –10% penalty to their remove traps rolls.

A dwarf, duergar, gnome, xorn, or other subterranean dweller can tell by examination that the stone's surface has been magically masked but not what its true appearance is. Features affixed to the stone's surface (such as maps or inscriptions) are hidden by this magic. *True seeing* penetrates the spell.

The reverse of this spell, *reveal stone*, negates *maskstone*. If not used for this purpose, it clearly indicates secret or hidden doors, panels, cavities, storage niches, catches, locks, and other deliberately hidden features by momentarily illuminating them with a glowing outline. These features are revealed if the stone has a *maskstone* spell on it or if it is simply in poorly lit or confusing natural conditions.

The material components are an eyelash (from any creature) and a pinch of dust or sand. The reverse of the spell requires a scrap of gauze and a piece of phosphorous or a handful of iron filings.

3rd Level

Abbathor's Greed (Pr 3; Divination)

Sphere:	Divination
Range:	0
Components:	V, S
Duration:	Instantaneous
Casting Time:	6
Area of Effect:	10-foot-wide path, 10 feet long/level
Saving Throw:	None

The priest who casts this spell can determine the single most valuable item within the spell's area of effect. Note, however, that the information gained involves an item's monetary value only. Magical items are revealed to be only as valuable as the materials from which they are made. This aside, the caster learns the item's exact value (in terms of gold pieces).

This use of this spell is not without risks. For every 1,000 gp value of an item, there is a 1% cumulative chance that Abbathor takes notice of the item and desires it for himself. If this occurs, there is an equal chance that Abbathor sends an avatar to retrieve the object. The total chance will not exceed 95%.

The avatar's sole purpose is to retrieve the desired item and return with it to the Gray Wastes. Under no circumstances does the avatar of Abbathor become involved in the affairs of the priest. Any attempt to prevent the avatar from carrying out its duty is dealt with accordingly.

4th Level

Conceal Riches (Pr 4; Illusion/Phantasm)

Sphere:	Charm
Range:	Touch
Components:	V, S
Duration:	Permanent
Casting Time:	7
Area of Effect:	1 person or an area up to 20 × 20 × 20 feet
Saving Throw:	None

Conceal riches makes all the items worn or carried by one person or within an area up to 20 × 20 × 20 feet look worthless, fine clothes look shabby, and new, expensive, or luxurious items appear old and worn. This illusion is used by priests of Abbathor to disguise themselves or their treasure hoards and abodes (or those of others, for a fee) to thwart robbery attempts. They also use this spell to decrease the chance that they are detained or molested when traveling from one locale to another while carrying great wealth or dressed in the finery they admire. The effect is permanent until dispelled or dismissed by the caster.

Berronar Truesilver

(The Revered Mother; the Mother Goddess;
Matron of Home and Hearth;
Mother of Safety, Truth, and Home)

Intermediate Power of Mount Celestia, LG

PORTFOLIO:	Safety, truth, home, healing, dwarven home life, records, traditional clan life, marriage, familial love, faithfulness/loyalty, honesty, obligations, oaths, the family, protector of dwarven children
ALIASES:	None
DOMAIN NAME:	Solania/Erackinor
SUPERIOR:	Moradin
ALLIES:	Angharradh, Cyrrollalee, Hathor, Isis, the Morndinsamman (except Abbathor, Deep Duerra, Laduguer), Yondalla
FOES:	Abbathor, Deep Duerra, Laduguer, Urdlen, the goblinkin and evil giant pantheons
SYMBOL:	Two silver rings
WOR. ALIGN.:	Any

Berronar Truesilver (BAIR-roe-nahr TROO-sihl-vur) is the bride of Moradin. She dwells with him at the Soul Forge beneath the mountains in Solania (fourth of the Seven Heavens, called *Khynnduum* in the oldest dwarven writings). The Revered Mother is the defender and protector of the home—not a passive homebody. She is seen as the patron of marriage and love, and her name is often invoked in small home rituals for protection against thieves and duplicity. Berronar is also the goddess of healing. Lawful good dwarves who value their families, clans, and the common strength and security of dwarven society revere her for her caring and loving service to the entire race. All dwarves of any alignment who seek a safe refuge or who want their loved ones or relatives kept safe offer her appeasement as well.

Although Berronar's avatar is rarely seen in the Realms, the Revered Mother works ceaselessly to preserve and protect dwarven culture and civilization. Her favorite techniques involve manifesting her powers in dwarven mortals on occasions crucial to the survival of a clan, people, or lore records. She does so either to guide and empower them to protective feats of arms or to lead them to the discovery of forgotten records, facts, and truths.

If a braid of Berronar's beard is cut off, it regrows in a single day. At the end of that day, the lock that was cut off turns to gold (worth 10,000-40,000 gold pieces). Both the goddess herself and her avatar form in the Realms have this ability. On very rare occasions, when the most powerful priest of Berronar in a community makes humble supplication to the goddess, Berronar gives such locks of hair to mortal dwarves. This gold is given only to dwarven communities that are exceptionally poor or hard-pressed and unable to recover economically otherwise.

Berronar is the powerful matron who, along with Moradin, has held the sometimes fractious dwarven pantheon united during an extended period of slow decline in the dwarven population of the Realms. She works hand-in-hand with Sharindlar, guiding dwarves into and through the lasting bonds of marriage once the Lady of Life brings them together. The Mother of Hearth and Home also works closely with Moradin, Clangeddin, and Gorm to ensure the safety of dwarven holds. Berronar views the antics of Dugmaren, Haela, and Marthammor with patient humor, foreseeing the day when they and their followers settle down and join in the traditional clan life of the Stout Folk. The Revered Mother is the tireless foe of Abbathor, viewing his all-consuming greed as the greatest threat to dwarven unity at a time when a united front may be all that keeps the Stout Folk from being overrun by orcs and their kin.

The Revered Mother is a kind and caring goddess with a strong motherly love for all dwarves and their allies who value compassion, fidelity, simplicity, tradition, the home, and family. Berronar has a ready, hearty laugh and a merry disposition, but she never wavers in the face of adversity or despairs in times of great loss. She can be strict or even fierce, if the situation so warrants, but the indomitable Mother Goddess of the dwarves is ever forgiving of her children, be they mortal or divine. Berronar settles many disagreements among the Morndinsamman, and her skills at persuasion are such that she can usually make two foes understand each other and set aside their differences. Berronar often sends an avatar to defend threatened dwarven clans, especially small ones threatened by events beyond their control.

Berronar's Avatar (Cleric 35, Paladin 25, Wizard 18)

Berronar appears as either a tallish or a huge dwarf, fearless of aspect but gentle in speech, whose brown beard is braided into four rows. She favors spells from the spheres of all, combat, creation, divination, guardian, healing, law, protection, and wards, plus the schools of abjuration and divination, although she can cast spells from any sphere or school.

AC –4; MV 12 or 15; HP 219; THAC0 –4; #AT 2/1
Dmg 6d6+11 (huge *mace* +4, +7 STR)
MR 80%; SZ M (6 feet tall) or H (19 feet tall)

Str 19, Dex 18, Con 22, Int 19, Wis 24, Cha 24
Spells P: 15/14/13/13/13/12/9, W: 5/5/5/5/5/3/3/2/1
Saves* PPDM 1, RSW 1**, PP 2, BW 2, Sp 4

*Includes +2 bonus to saving throws to a minimum of 1. **Includes dwarf +6 Con save bonus to a minimum of 1. The Con save bonus also applies to saves vs. poison to a minimum of 1.

Special Att/Def: Berronar wields *Wrath of Righteousness*, a huge *mace +4* of steel chased with gold. This weapon slays on contact all evil thieves and anyone currently engaged in killing for a living (for example, mercenary warriors, hired murderers, and priests or other officials knowingly on a mission that involves deliberately causing the death of another). This property fails if the target struck succeeds at a saving throw vs. death magic at a –4 penalty; one successful saving throw means that the being is forever immune to this power of *Wrath of Righteousness*.

The Revered Mother also wears two silver rings of great power. One prevents anyone from knowingly telling a falsehood within 100 feet of her; the other prevents mortals from using any thieving abilities within 100 feet of her. A thief may avoid this if she or he succeeds at a saving throw vs. spell with a penalty of –2 every round in which an attempt to use any thief skill is made. If either of these rings is removed from Berronar's possession, it crumbles into nothingness in 2d6 days. Its magic becomes only 33% reliable in the last 2 days before it falls apart.

Berronar has the power to take the shape of an aged dwarf of either sex, or even a short, stooped human crone—and when in such a form, no god or mortal can detect anything of her divine nature or powers (although she retains full use of them). Berronar often uses this lesser form to watch and judge dwarves, walking among them to see what treatment she receives.

Berronar wears *everbright* silver *chain mail +5* that cannot be harmed by fire. It protects its wearer from all fire, heat, and electrical (lightning) attacks. Berronar can be struck only by +2 or better magical weapons. She is immune to all illusion/phantasm spells and magical effects.

Other Manifestations

Berronar can, at a range of one mile or less, use *suggestion* on any intelligent creature. The saving throw is made at a –7 penalty if the creature is lawful good, a –5 penalty if of another good alignment, a –3 penalty if of a neutral alignment, and a –1 penalty if evil. Berronar employs this power to guide chosen dwarves into performing specific actions (opening certain chests, going to certain locations, and so on) that lead to the discovery of secrets she wants known again. These secrets are usually about the past glories of the dwarven civilizations.

In more pressing conditions, Berronar can empower an individual dwarf with her favor, which appears as an aura or radiance of bright silver. While so imbued (a condition typically lasting 1 or 2 turns), a favored dwarf has the Armor Class of Berronar's avatar, –4. Next she or he is affected as if by a *haste* spell for which no aging occurs. Finally, the dwarf receives attack and damage bonuses of +2. This direct and unsubtle form of aid is granted only in emergencies.

Berronar prefers to work through lawful good dwarven fighters, using *suggestion* to encourage appeals to her. If such a warrior appeals to the Revered Mother for specific aid and makes an appropriately large sacrifice, there is a 5% chance that Berronar imbues the warrior with power. The sacrifice should consist mainly of the dwarf's wealth, which Berronar causes to vanish from her temple altars. She then personally distributes it to the poorest dwarves throughout the Realms. (DMs might want to raise this chance to around 45% for NPCs.) Only dwarves of exceptionally pure heart are considered for this honor, and Berronar grants it at most only once in every 10 years to the same individual.

Berronar is served by aasimon, archons, earth elementals, einheriar, galeb duhr, guardian nagas, hammer golems, hollyphants, incarnates (of charity, faith, and justice), ki-rin, maruts, noctrals, pers, shedu, sunflies, and t'uen-rin. Her omens are often suggestion effects to her priests and illusions that dissolve to reveal a truth (a revealed area, an item of symbolic meaning, etc.). Certain gems, including octel, shandon, and sphene, are said by dwarves to be the hardened tears of Berronar. Rock crystal also qualifies, but only when clear within and found naturally smoothed by ice or water. The discovery of such jewels is believed to be a sign of Berronar's favor, and no other dwarven faith—including that of Dumathoin—incorporates any

of these stones in either its rituals or its sacred lore. Other signs of her favor include the sudden blossoming of white flowers and the discovery of freshwater springs. The Revered Mother indicates her displeasure by shattering the crude clay statuettes crafted in her image that adorn the hearth mantles of most dwarven homes, by causing hearth flames to turn black in color and be extinguished, and by unleashing small, localized tremors that do little damage aside from knocking the being that has garnered the Revered Mother's displeasure to the ground and leaving small cracks in the floor and nearby walls.

The Church

CLERGY:	Clerics, crusaders, specialty priests
CLERGY'S ALIGN.:	LG
TURN UNDEAD:	C: Yes, Cru: No, SP: Yes, at priest level –2
CMND. UNDEAD:	C: No, Cru: No, SP: No

All clerics (including fighter/clerics), crusaders, and specialty priests of Berronar receive religion (dwarven) and reading/writing (Dethek runes) as bonus nonweapon proficiencies. Clerics of Berronar (as well as fighter/clerics) cannot turn undead before 7th level, but they always strike at +2 on all attack and damage rolls against undead creatures. At 7th level and above, clerics (including multiclassed clerics) can turn undead as other clerics do, but as a cleric of four levels less than their current level. These modifications apply only to the cleric class and not to crusaders or specialty priests. All priests of Berronar were female until the Time of Troubles; a few males have joined the priesthood since then.

Berronar and her followers are widely respected throughout dwarven culture as well as among other human and demihuman societies. None would question the dedication to duty, compassion, or goodness of the Revered Mother's priests. Only among the younger dwarven Wanderers is there a hint of dissent, for some hold that the clergies of Berronar and Moradin cling too tightly to the old ways in the face of new and ever-expanding threats to the Stout Folk.

Temples of the Revered Mother may be found both above and below the surface. A temple to Berronar aboveground consists of a circle of stones, usually in a wooded area, in which small fires are kindled in a random pattern. Gems and metal sculptures are set up among them on metal poles to sparkle and reflect back the firelight during worship. Actual sparkler fireworks are used on the two main holy days to mark the ending of each unison prayer. An underground temple to Berronar is a cavern in which the priests have carefully arranged mosses, lichens, fungi, and the like brought by the hands of faithful. They keep these watered and nourished to form a lush carpet all over the floor; this covering also climbs the walls as high as possible. Luminescent fungi are favored, to give the cavern as much natural light as possible. Magical items with the power to create *dancing lights* are highly valued, and nondwarven wielders of such items are sometimes even hired to illuminate such a temple by this means. Such "lighters" must come to the temple naked and blindfolded, but they are treated with the utmost care and courtesy. When the ceremony is over, they are taken safely back to the surface under guard, in such a way as to maintain their dignity but keep the location of and route to the temple hidden from them.

Novices of Berronar are known as the Daughters/Sons of Berronar. Full priests of the Revered Mother are known as Revered Sisters/Brothers. In ascending order of rank, the titles used by Berronan priests are Hearthmistress/Headmaster, Homesteader, Lorekeeper, Faithkeeper, Fidelite, and Sacred Heart. High Old Ones have unique individual titles but are collectively known as the Keepers of the Truesilver. Specialty priests are known as faernor, a dwarvish word that can be loosely translated as *those of the home*. The clergy of Berronar includes gold dwarves (54%), shield dwarves (45%), and a handful (1%) of jungle dwarves and gray dwarves. Berronar's clergy is composed primarily of specialty priests (42%) and clerics (38%), plus a handful of fighter/clerics (5%) and crusaders (5%). Female dwarves still constitute most of the priesthood (98%).

Dogma: The Children of Moradin are shaped on the Soul Forge and ever warmed by the embrace of the Revered Mother. Tend the hearth and home, drawing strength and safety from truth, tradition, and the rule of law. Join with friends, kin, and clan in common purpose. Do not succumb to the misery of greed or the evils of strife, but always bring hope, health, and cheer to those in need. Once an oath is made, Berronar watches over its keeping—to break it is to grieve her sorely. Children must be cherished and guarded well from harm, for they are future of the race.

Day-to-Day Activities: Berronar's priests serve as the guardians and protectors of dwarven clans; they also maintain lore records and family histories. The members of Berronar's clergy strive to further the good health and good character of all dwarves. They heal the sick and injured, attempt to treat, eradicate, and stop the spread of disease, develop antidotes to dwarfsbane and other poisons that can affect dwarves, and encourage truthfulness, obedience to law, peaceful harmony, and governance of greed and goldlust. Priests of Berronar never ignore a dwarf in need of aid, and they always help to the best of their ability. If a Revered Sister/Brother lacks magical means of curing, she or he finds someone who can heal or provide all the nonmagical care possible. The duty of a priest of Berronar is to keep every dwarf alive, whatever the cost.

In many respects, Berronar's priests are the pillars on which dwarven society is built. Revered Sisters/Brothers are instrumental in maintaining traditional dwarven culture, in knitting together families, in educating and nurturing young dwarves, and in maintaining the orderly governance of dwarven society. While rarely holding formal positions of leadership, the senior priest of Berronar in a dwarven hold or clan usually holds a position of great influence that rivals, if not exceeds, that of the titular ruler of the hold or clan.

Holy Days/Important Ceremonies: Priests of Berronar worship the Mother Goddess by kneeling, closing their eyes, picturing the Revered Mother, and whispering prayers that begin and end with her name. They typically do this when asking for her guidance or when they are about to heal in her name. Her guidance is often given via an inner feeling or decision.

Annual offerings of silver are made to Berronar in the form of coins, jewelry, drinking vessels, or trade-bars (a dwarven invention). White flowers sometimes adorn the offerings in token of dwarven love and affection for the Mother Goddess.

Midwinter day and Midsummer night are celebrated by Berronar's faithful as holy days of the Revered Mother, although monthly observances are common in the larger temples. More elaborate rituals to Berronar take place aboveground on Midsummer Night and underground the rest of the time. Rituals honoring Berronar typically begin with a chanted prayer and continue with an address from the Keepers of the Truesilver. This ends in a responsive prayer led by a High Old One or chosen priest. Next comes a report of the good works and successes of the priesthood and an identification of failures and problems still to be overcome. Another responsive prayer follows, then a rising, spirit-lifting unison prayer. If a very sick dwarf or dwarves are present, unison healing then takes place. The entire assembled clergy lays hands on the afflicted ones and calls on Berronar. Healing does not always occur, although the deadening of pain (for 1d4+1 days) always does—the assembled priests take the pain upon themselves. If healing does take place, it is a manifestation of the goddess, not a cast spell. Berronar's Touch, as this is known, has in the past cured blindness, insanity, lycanthropy, poisonings, life energy loss, bodily transformations due to parasitic or symbiotic plant life, tissue corrosion, and the like, in addition to more simple wounds and diseases.

As betrothal and married life are the province of Berronar, lawful good dwarves follow her custom of exchanging rings with those for whom they feel deep, mutual trust and love, a ceremony that is never entered into lightly. The rings are often silver, matching the Revered Mother's symbol, and are treated by dwarven smiths to be *everbright* (never to tarnish), then blessed by priests of Berronar. If one of the parties participates with deceit in his or her heart, Berronar's power makes one of the rings crumble during the blessing (or both rings, if both are false).

Major Centers of Worship: Araufaern Caurak, the Abbey of Earthhearth, is a great subterranean fortress atop a low plateau that dominates the eastern reaches of the Firecaverns of the Deep Realm. The Firecaverns include a long, narrow rift, warmed by nearby lava flows that stretch for miles in the depths, and many side caverns linked to the rift. The Firecaverns are lit by (and named for) a distinctive fungus that grows thickly on the rift's wall and floor and gives off a strong, steady amber hue. The abbey resembles the bottom half of a white marble pyramid capped by a gleaming, gilded dome. Earthhearth is accessed by a broad, slowly ascending ramp leading up from the cavern floor below to a great gate in the center of the abbey's western wall. Both the abbey and the Firecaverns are ruled by High Princess Royal Rathauna Forgesilver, and the easy-going, tolerant settlement embodies the principles of Berronar's faith. Earthhearth serves as the governmental, militant, medical, educational, cultural, and social heart of the Firecaverns.

The abbey serves as the chapter house of the Legion of Silver Helms, a military order composed predominantly of crusaders and fighter/clerics dedicated to the Revered Mother. This militia defends the great cavern complex's borders. The Grand Hearth, as the vast central hall of the abbey is known, houses a wide variety of activities, including exhibits of dwarven craftsmanship, royal marriages, storytelling, balls, feasts, and the like.

Affiliated Orders: Berronar's Valkyries are crusaders and fighter/clerics who operate as small bands of elite dwarven female warriors. The role of the order is to ensure that dwarven warriors (who are predominantly male) return to their hold and clan alive after going to war. As such, the Valkyries accompany dwarven armies to battle, but instead of immediately joining in the fray, they choose a high vantage point from which to observe. If and when small pockets of dwarven warriors are in danger of being overrun, or when a dwarf is too badly wounded to withdraw, the Valkyries charge to the rescue.

The Order of the Silver Knightingale is a loosely structured order composed primarily of physicians, medics, clerics, and specialty priests skilled in the art of healing. Silver Knightingales, most of whom are female, accompany dwarven warriors into battle but do not fight except to defend themselves. Their role is to minister to the dead and dying and minimize the number of dwarven casualties using their healing skills. In peacetime, members of the order disperse to their individual clans and holds where they continue their roles as healers.

Priestly Vestments: The ceremonial garb of members of Berronar's clergy includes white underrobes with cloth-of-silver overtunics. The Revered Mother's priests remain bareheaded. The holy symbol of the faith is twin, interlocking, large silver rings worn on a steel or silver chain hung around the neck. Many Revered Sisters/Brothers add twin silver rings to their vestments, one on each ring finger.

Adventuring Garb: In combat situations, Revered Sisters/Brothers favor silver chain mail with silvered (*everbright*–treated) helms. Many priests of the Mother Goddess are reluctant to shed blood or spread violence and thus restrict themselves to blunt, bludgeoning weapons such as maces, flails, and warhammers.

Specialty Priests (Faernor)

REQUIREMENTS:	Strength 9, Wisdom 12
PRIME REQ.:	Strength, Wisdom
ALIGNMENT:	LG
WEAPONS:	Battle axe, club, crossbow, flail, hand axe, mace, morning star
ARMOR:	Any
MAJOR SPHERES:	All, charm, combat, creation, divination, guardian, healing, law, plant, protection, sun, wards
MINOR SPHERES:	Animal, astral, elemental (earth), necromantic
MAGICAL ITEMS:	Same as clerics
REQ. PROFS:	Endurance
BONUS PROFS:	Healing, herbalism

- While most faernor (the plural form of faernar) are shield dwarves or gold dwarves, dwarves of nearly every subrace are called to be specialty priests of Berronar's clergy.
- Faernor are not allowed to multiclass.
- Faernor cast spells from the sphere of protection as if they were priests of four levels higher.
- Faernor can cast *cure light wounds* (as the 1st-level priest spell) or *cantrip* (as the 1st-level wizard spell) once per day.
- At 3rd level, faernor can cast *aid* or *spiritual hammer* (as the 2nd-level priest spells) once per day.
- At 5th level, faernor can cast *cure disease* (as the 3rd-level priest spell) or *detect lie* (as the 4th-level priest spell) once per day.
- At 7th level, faernor can cast *cure serious wounds* or *neutralize poison* (as the 4th-level priest spells) or *fortify* (as the 4th-level priest spell) once per day.
- At 10th level, faernor can cast *cure critical wounds* or *succor of Berronar* (as the 5th-level priest spells) once per day.
- At 13th level, faernor can cast *wall of force*, *wall of iron*, or *wall of stone* (as the 5th-level wizard spells) once per day.
- At 15th level, faernor can cast *gate* (as the 7th-level priest spell) twice per tenday.

Berronan Spells

4th Level

Guardian Hammer (Pr 4; Invocation)

Sphere:	Guardian
Range:	Touch (of area to be guarded)
Components:	V, S, M
Duration:	Special
Casting Time:	7
Area of Effect:	Special
Saving Throw:	None

This spell creates a *guardian hammer*: an invisible, hammer-shaped field of force activated when a guarded door or other area is disturbed (even years after the spell was cast). When activated, it charges through the air to strike the living thing nearest to the disturbed guardian area or any being in the area. (If there are more than one, determine the target randomly.) A *guardian hammer* strikes only once but does not miss. When it hits, it appears momentarily as a glowing, translucent hammer and then fades away into nothingness. Its strike does 4d12 damage and stuns (no voluntary actions possible) its victim for 1d4+1 rounds. Struck beings must succeed at a saving throw vs. paralyzation to avoid being knocked down, forcing possible item saving throws vs. fall for fragile carried items.

Guardian hammers can be destroyed before activation by casting a *dispel magic* on the guarded area or by totally destroying (for example, by *disintegration*) the guarded area without entering it. Once activated, a *guardian hammer* can dodge all magical and physical barriers (by phasing in and out of the ethereal plane, if necessary) and cannot be destroyed or diverted to another target by physical means.

The material components for this spell are a drop of sweat or spittle or a tear from the caster; a hair from a dwarven stonemason; and a pebble or lump of ice.

5th Level

Berronar's Favor (Pr 5; Conjuration/Summoning)

Sphere:	Summoning
Range:	Special
Components:	V, S, M
Duration:	Instantaneous
Casting Time:	1 hour
Area of Effect:	Special
Saving Throw:	Special

When dwarven enclaves fall on economic hard times, this effect can be used to help put the community back on its feet. The spell summons a lock of Berronar's hair that turns into gold within 24 hours of its arrival. The golden lock is worth between 2,000 and 8,000 gp. It does not radiate magic nor can it be dispelled or negated.

Despite the usefulness of this spell, it has two important restrictions: First, the caster must be Berronar's high priest in the enclave and of lawful good alignment. Second, the spell must be cast on behalf of a suffering dwarven enclave, and the acquired gold must be used to help the enclave through its difficult times. If the gold is used for any other purpose, especially an evil or selfish purpose (for example, personal gain), it is forfeit and vanishes immediately.

If these two conditions are not met, Berronar simply refuses to grant the spell. Obviously, Berronar's adventuring priests are unlikely to receive this while away from their enclaves.

The material component for this spell is the caster's holy symbol. The casting time accounts for other factors in the spell's casting, such as prayer, meditation, and the like.

Succor of Berronar (Pr 5; Necromancy)

Sphere:	Healing
Range:	Touch
Components:	V, S, M
Duration:	Instantaneous
Casting Time:	1 round
Area of Effect:	One creature
Saving Throw:	None

This spell gives aid in whatever fashion the recipient requires, whether the affliction be due to injury, poison, disease, or the like. While casting *succor of Berronar*, the priest duplicates the following spell effects: *cure disease*, *cure serious wounds*, *cure blindness or deafness*, *neutralize poison*, and *repair injury* (this last if critical hit optional rules are being used).

In addition, for the next 24-hour period, curses (including lycanthropy) and addictions are held in abeyance, sanity is restored, and the recipient's spirit receives a great boost.

This spell can be effectively used only once a month on any given recipient.

The material components of this spell are the priest's holy symbol and a drop of holy water.

Clangeddin Silverbeard

(The Father of Battle, Lord of the Twin Axes, the Giantkiller, the Goblinbane, the Wyrmslayer, the Rock of Battle)

Intermediate Power of Arcadia, LG

PORTFOLIO:	Battle, war, valor, bravery, honor in battle
ALIASES:	Clanggedin (shield dwarves), Clanggendin
DOMAIN NAME:	Abellio/Mount Clangeddin
SUPERIOR:	Moradin
ALLIES:	Arvoreen, Cyrrollalee, Helm, the gnome pantheon (except Urdlen), the Morndinsamman (except Abbathor, Deep Duerra, Laduguer), Tempus, Torm, Tyr, the Red Knight
FOES:	Abbathor, Deep Duerra, Garagos, Laduguer, Surtr, Thrym, Urdlen, Vaprak, the goblinkin and evil giant pantheons
SYMBOL:	Two crossed battle axes
WOR. ALIGN.:	LG, NG, CG, LN, N, CN

Clangeddin Silverbeard (CLAN-gehd-din SIHL-vur-beerd) is the Father of Battle and primary dwarven war god. All dwarves who must fight, especially dwarves who are warriors by profession, worship Clangeddin, their patron and exultant leader in war. The Father of Battle is the deity of choice among lawful neutral dwarven warriors.

Clangeddin watches over the battle-skills and performances of dwarves from his mountain fortress in Arcadia. He encourages valor in battle, weapon-mastery and training, and wisdom in war, and most often manifests his powers to further these aims. Clangeddin is concerned with war as a way of life and is very different from Moradin in this respect. The aptly named Father of Battle especially hates giants and has taught the dwarves—and the gnomes, through their gods—special ways of fighting giant-type creatures.

Clangeddin maintains good relations with the other members of the Morndinsamman, with the notable exceptions of Abbathor and the duergar deities. He works closely with Moradin, Gorm, and Marthammor, and regards Haela as both a daughter and a protégé. The Father of Battle works closely with the gods of the gnome pantheon, particularly Gaerdal Ironhand, and he has forged strong alliances with Arvoreen, the Red Knight, Torm, and Tyr. The most hated enemies of the Father of Battle are Grolantor and his hill giant followers, followed closely by Karontor, Memnor, Kostchtchie, Vaprak, Surtr, and Thrym, plus the various evil giant races that revere them. Since the Time of Troubles, Clangeddin has nursed a grudge against Labelas Enoreth, elven god of time and longevity, for destroying his avatar form in a battle that raged across the isle of Ruathym.

Clangeddin is a resolute warrior who never backs down from danger and who refuses to surrender even when all seems lost. He is a strict and ethical deity who brooks no treachery or deceit and who never negotiates or compromises. Triumph must be obtained through valor and bravery, and Clangeddin is swift to humble and humiliate any who overcome by cowardly or deceitful means. The Father of Battle is known for often snatching victory from the narrowest of margins in battle. Clangeddin uses his magic only to influence events indirectly, never in battle. He only resorts to influencing a battle when the very existence of his avatar in the Realms is threatened. He always prefers force of arms to spells. Clangeddin is merry in battle, roaring appreciation of shrewd strategies, bravery, and feats of skill even when such are directed against him. He often sings (both stirring battle-ballads and taunting little ditties to unnerve enemies) in the midst of a fight, and dwarves have learned to listen for hints, cues, and warnings in his lyrics. He is a master at turning the tables on enemy armies by anticipating their movements on the battlefield and singing directions to dwarves fighting with him. Like most dwarves, Clangeddin admires most those who help themselves. He typically appears at a battle only to right hopeless odds against dwarves, to balance treachery and punish the treasonous, and to aid the weak of all races against evil, especially the acts of giants.

Clangeddin's Avatar (Fighter 35, Bard 25, Cleric 20)

Clangeddin appears as a tall, burly dwarf, fierce and indomitable in his battered, bloodstained, and rusty chain mail. Bald and silver-bearded, he is always alert, his eyes darting here and there, his gaze as sharp as that of a hunting hawk, and his smile ever-present. When the use of magic cannot be avoided, he favors spells from the spheres of all, combat, law, protection, and war, and from the schools of invocation/evocation and alteration, although he can cast spells from any sphere or school.

AC –6; MV 12 or 15; HP 231; THAC0 –10; #AT 7/2
Dmg 1d8+18 (*battle axe* +4, +12 STR, +2 spec. bonus in battle axe) and 1d8+18 (*battle axe* +4, +12 STR, +2 spec. bonus in battle axe)
MR 55%; SZ M (6 feet tall) or H (17 feet tall)
STR 24, DEX 17, CON 23, INT 18, WIS 19, CHA 22
Spells P: 12/11/11/9/7/5/2, W: 5/5/5/5/4/4/1
Saves PPDM 2, RSW 1*, PP 4, BW 4, Sp 5
    *Includes dwarf +6 CON save bonus to a minimum of 1. The CON save bonus also applies to saves vs. poison to a minimum of 1.

Special Att/Def: He wields two mithral *battle axes* +4. He can throw these up to 100 yards, and both strike with full bonuses, as though he were swinging them directly. After striking, each *axe* magically returns to Clangeddin's hand at the end of the round.

Clangeddin inflicts double damage against giant-class creatures, which attack him at –4. His touch can, at will, *mend* any metal weapon or armor as though it had never been broken, even restoring missing pieces. Any nonmagical weapon that the Father of Battle touches strikes at a +9 bonus to attack rolls (normal damage) for 7 rounds thereafter, a power Clangeddin typically uses to aid dwarves he is fighting alongside. In the heat of battle, Clangeddin is fond of singing, with the intent of both unnerving his opponents (who suffer a morale penalty of –2) and uplifting his allies (who receive a morale bonus of +4).

The Father of Battle wears steel *chain mail* +5. He can be struck only by +2 or better magical weapons.

If slain, Clangeddin becomes an entity akin to a ghost. The Father of Battle's ghostlike anima form cannot be turned and can become invisible at will. He can work magic and employ a ghost's attacks, and he has half his normal hit points.

Other Manifestations

Clangeddin's favor is usually seen as a flickering amber, red, or white radiance around a dwarf or weapon that is temporarily imbued with the god's power.

This power typically gives any or all of the following aids to affected beings for 1 turn: (1) first strike in any combat round; (2) an increase in Armor Class of 8; (3) a temporary increase for warriors of 7 levels, with resultant saving throw and THAC0 changes and temporary hit points—all damage taken is subtracted from these points first; (4) the immediate breaking of any *charms* or other magical controls, recognizing them for what they are; (5) the ability to stand upright and unmoving against any charge, force, magical effect, or blow—damage is suffered, but falling or overbearing is impossible.

This power typically gives any or all of the following benefits to a weapon: (1) +9 bonus to attack, not damage, with nonmagical weapons for seven rounds thereafter; (2) double damage, or triple to giant-type creatures; (3) immunity to breakage or other damage (automatic successful item saving throws).

Clangeddin sometimes takes away especially brave dwarves who sacrifice themselves to ensure a dwarven victory, cloaking them in a bright radiance before they vanish. Dwarves believe that the dying servant is restored by Clangeddin and taken to serve the god as a guardian. Such individuals sometimes appear again briefly in the Realms as "ghost dwarves" to guide lost or defend weak dwarves in the wilds. These ghosts are easily recognized by those who knew them in life.

Clangeddin is served by agathinon, aurumvorae, cave bears, earth elementals, einheriar, galeb duhr, hammer golems, incarnates (of courage, justice, and faith), juggernauts, ki-rin, leomarhs, living steel, maruts, mountain lions, per, shedu, silver dragons, stone golems, stone guardians, and t'uen-rin. Clangeddin rarely bothers with the subtlety of omens, but if he does, these are usually gut-level events such as earth tremors, rockfalls, and earthblood (seeping red liquid from newly exposed veins of ore).

The Church

CLERGY:	Clerics, crusaders, specialty priests, fighters
CLERGY'S ALIGN.:	LG, LN
TURN UNDEAD:	C: Yes, Cru: No, SP: No
CMND. UNDEAD:	C: No, Cru: No, SP: No

All clerics (including fighter/clerics), crusaders, and specialty priests (including fighter/specialty priests) of Clangeddin receive religion (dwarven) and reading/writing (Dethek runes) as bonus nonweapon proficiencies. Clerics of Clangeddin can use any weapons, not just bludgeoning (wholly Type B) weapons. Clerics of Clangeddin (as well as fighter/clerics) cannot turn undead before 7th level, but they always strike at +2 on all attack and damage rolls against undead creatures. At 7th level and above, clerics (including multiclassed clerics) can turn undead as other clerics do, but as a cleric of four levels less than their current level. These modifications apply only to the cleric class. All of Clangeddin's clergy members were male until the Time of Troubles, but since then the church has begun to accept females.

The Father of Battle, one of the senior members of the Morndinsamman, and his followers are widely revered throughout dwarven culture for their dedication and martial skill. More pacifistic members of dwarven society may wish Clangeddin's priests were less belligerent, but none question their crucial role in the continued survival of the dwarven race. Among other races, Clangeddin and his followers are often perceived as little more than bloodthirsty berserkers, but those who fight alongside the Father of Battle's followers quickly learn of their principled approach to warfare and the lengths to which they will go to defend their fellow dwarves and allies.

Clangeddin's most sacred shrines are dwarven cairns erected on the fields of past battles, whether they be on the surface or in the tunnels of the Underdark. Sometimes a cavern in which the followers of Clangeddin won a great victory is dedicated as a great temple to the Father of Battle. (Many times when a new clanhold or kingdom is being carved out of hostile territory, a temple of Clangeddin is dedicated in the cavern where the climatic battle was won, thus firmly establishing the dwarven presence.) Such temples are dominated by great stone statues of dwarven heroes past, armor and weapons worn by Clangeddin's greatest warriors, and huge granite blocks stained blood-red that serve as altars on which weapons are offered up to the god.

Novices of Clangeddin, like novices of Haela, are known as the Unblooded. Full priests of the Father of Battle are known as Axebrothers/Axesisters. In ascending order of rank, the titles used by Clangeddite priests are Axecutter, Squire, Knight of the Third Rank, Knight of the Second Rank, Knight of the First Rank, and Knight Commander—but these are often superseded by titles that go with a position. High Old Ones have unique individual titles but are collectively known as War Princes/Princesses. Specialty priests are known as alaghor, a dwarvish word that can be loosely translated as *those who demonstrate valor in battle*. The clergy of Clangeddin is evenly divided between gold dwarves (50%) and shield dwarves (50%), with a rare jungle dwarf or gray dwarf as well. Clangeddin's clergy is numerically dominated by its most martial members, including crusaders (25%), fighters (23%), specialty priests (20%), fighter/specialty priests (11%), fighter/clerics (11%), and clerics (10%). Most priests of the Father of Battle are male (90%).

Dogma: War is the finest hour of dwarvenkind. Seize the opportunity to defend the Stout Folk and ensure their victory wherever conflict does erupt. Revel in the challenge of a good fight, and never waver in the face of adversity, no matter how ominous. When not fighting, prepare for the next conflict physically, tactically, and by acquiring resources. Attack hill giants whenever possible and other evil giants when necessary.

Death on the field of battle is never welcomed and lives should never be thrown away foolishly. However, if necessary for victory, the highest service that followers of the Father of Battle can perform is to sacrifice themselves for the cause on the field of battle by protecting as many other dwarves as possible.

Day-to-Day Activities: The members of Clangeddin's clergy form an elite warrior caste in many clans, maintaining their positions by training hard physically every day. They are always preparing for war, physically, tactically, and by acquiring resources. To ensure dwarven victory in every open fray, priests of Clangeddin try to further the weapon training, tactical training, and battle skills of every living dwarf. Weaponcrafting and training are required for all worshipers of the god, and priests of the god pass on their battle knowledge at an almost frantic rate to all dwarves who will lend an ear. Priests of Clangeddin seek to make the dwarves ever stronger on the battlefield and are always alert for new tactics, traps, and weapons. For instance, they take great interest in the items devised by the Lantanna and other worshipers of the human god Gond.

Holy Days/Important Ceremonies: Clangeddin's faithful honor the anniversaries of past battles, whether they were won or lost, as holy days. Individual temples mark particular days more than others, as the entire year-long calendar is overfilled with anniversaries of past battles. Conflicts whose importance and heroes have faded into the mists of time are commemorated every decade, century, or millennium, as appropriate.

On holy days or during battle, always on a known (past, present, or immediately pending) battlefield, priests of Clangeddin chant, pray, and break weapons that they have anointed with their own blood. The god often manifests as a glowing radiance to consume the weapons, and this radiance may extend to worshipers as a temporary protective aura in battle. Offered weapons not consumed by the god are either twisted and shattered (whereupon they must be melted down and used for other things) or left untouched (whereupon they may be used again, with the god's approval).

The Father of Battle is often worshiped by frantic prayers in the midst of the fray. At such times, the god preferentially answers those who fight on fearlessly. When time permits, however, either on the evening before an anticipated battle or at the burial of a great dwarven warrior, the rituals of worship include a procession of the faithful onto the battlefield or gravesite. Clangeddin's priests lead the participants in a mournful dirge, a wordless rising and falling chant. The sound rises slowly into an exultant roaring and ends in a single, high, clear singing note—an odd, eerie contrast to the rough-voiced bloodsong that has preceded it. The slow-marching procession is always accompanied by slow, steady drumbeats (from drums carried by lesser priests) and consists of dwarves wearing their most battered armor (freshly used, if possible). These faithful are led and followed by chain mail-armored priests, who may echo the drumbeat by crashing weapons against shields. When the procession reaches its goal, the priests cast down their shields, hold their weapons high, and begin to whisper the god's name. They then close their eyes and continue whispering, concentrating on whatever image each one has of Clangeddin. (This is always the appearance of the avatar or manifestation if the dwarf has witnessed the direct acts of the god.) The priests then begin to move toward wherever they feel the god's presence is strongest and so blindly draw together until they collide. At that spot, they make the weapon sacrifice, speak the names of the valiant fallen that they wish the god to remember and hold in esteem, then kneel to await a sign. And an answer is often given—anything from a roll of thunder to a shield speaking a blessing, command, or answer. If the ritual was a burial, it is concluded with the interment and a solemn march away. If, instead, it was a preparation for a battle, it is concluded with a war chant and a "wild run," in which the participants wave weapons and emit whoops and war-cries.

Major Centers of Worship: Alagh Rorncaurak, the Battlecavern of Unquenched Valor, is a vast natural chasm deep beneath the Earthfast Mountains that tower over neighboring Impiltur. Located in what was once the heart of the dwarven city of Earthfast, Clangeddin's great natural cathedral is now located on the western periphery of the embattled dwarf-held caverns. It is the subject of frequent assaults by orcish armies intent on overrunning the dwarven kingdom. Cindarm mac Faern, grandnephew of Torg mac Cei, the late Ironlord of Earthfast, leads the elite (but badly outnumbered) Clangeddites against wave after wave of orcish assaults. Only the recent arrival of dwarven mercenaries of Clan Hammerhand has given the temple's defenders enough breathing room to fortify their defenses. While the temple's central sanctuary and the entrance to the remaining dwarf-held districts of Earthfast are still inviolate, the temple's shattered western barracks are the site of countless skirmishes between wandering orcish patrols and dwarven defenders.

Affiliated Orders: Scores of military orders and countless dwarven brotherhoods have been dedicated to the Father of Battle, beginning with the earliest, long-forgotten kingdoms of the dwarves. The followers of Clangeddin in each clanhold or kingdom tend to organize themselves into one or more fighting companies, and each band has its own name and famous exploits. Legendary companies of past millennia include the Knights of the Ninth Axe, the Valorous Harts of High Shanatar, the Order of the Crescent Moon (jointly dedicated to Clangeddin and Selûne), the Fellowship of the Bleeding Axe, the Sailors of the Mountainous Waves (the Madbeard marines of fabled Haunghdannar), the Shining Blades of Iltkazar, the Glory of Gauntlegrym, and the Company of the Last Kuldjargh.

Because magic seems to go awry in their hands, and they can never control real power of the Art like human wizards, dwarves have always been fascinated by magic and the capturing of magical powers within an item that a dwarf has created and can wield. Down through the ages, there have been over a thousand thousand dwarven smiths of skill in working with magic. They have always been among the wealthiest, most powerful, and most respected dwarves. Some have gone further than that, looking beyond dwarven skill to the inspiration that guided them and seeing in it a divine presence—a presence that, they believe, lives in the magical items themselves.

Centuries ago, the Father of Battle embraced some of these cults of Axe Dwarves—for they most commonly worship sentient axes—in a bid to fold sentient magic weapons into his portfolio and to join such battle-loving dwarves with the more orthodox branches of his faith. While Clangeddin has exhibited little patience or tolerance for dwarves who revere weapons controlled by malevolent or insane spirits, he has been willing to grant spellcasting powers to those few cults that adhere to the principles, if not the ritual practices, of his faith. Despite the efforts of the Father of Battle, however, the majority of such cults stray far from the principles of Clangeddin's faith and are supported by other divine powers. Such cults have gone to war to extend the rule of these sacred items over other dwarves, and even over small communities of humans, halflings, and gnomes.

The most fearsome relic around which a dwarven axe cult is based is the *Living Axe*, an animated, bronzed, adamantite, double-bladed battle axe of great size that is neutral evil in alignment and delights in killing, periodically flying amok among orcs or whatever creatures it chances upon (including dwarves who worship it). The *Living Axe* does 2d6 points of damage per strike, attacks twice a round, flies at MV 18 (A), is known to be immune to all enchantment/charm spells, and has all the powers of a *watch axe* (see below). This legendary *watch axe* has been known to hunt beings across the Realms, capriciously sparing some who openly defy it and butchering others whom it surprises before they even realize what is happening. The *Living Axe* is said to be very old, and most believe it was once wielded by an avatar of the Father of Battle before the collapse of the great cavern of Bhaerynden (now the Great Rift). While its precise powers are unknown, the War Princes/Princesses of Clangeddin suspect that the intelligence within the *Living Axe* has been driven insane by the twisted dreams of Diinkarazan, the mad derro demipower, and that the Mad God may be the power behind many of the most depraved dwarven axe cults.

Priestly Vestments: Clangeddin's priests wear silver chain mail armor, war helms, and tabards depicting the symbol of the Father of Battle as their ceremonial garb. Priests of Clangeddin seldom take off their helms, although there is no prohibition against doing so. The holy symbol of the faith is a pair of miniature steel battle axes welded together in a cross; this is typically suspended on a chain and worn around the neck.

Adventuring Garb: In combat situations, priests of the Father of Battle favor the most effective armor available, often replacing their ceremonial silver chain mail with suits of dwarven plate mail (base AC 2). They never like to fight with shields, but they will do so to protect other dwarves. While Clangeddin's priests employ a wide range of weaponry, they prefer weapons that cleave, crush, or bludgeon, such as axes, maces, and flails. They rarely employ missile weapons (other than throwing axes or the occasional heavy crossbow) or swords. The magical weapon of choice among the members of Clangeddin's clergy is magical axe.

Whether they are supported by Clangeddin or not, Axe Dwarven priests—who are all members of the crusader class—are always armed with multiple throwing axes and a variety of other weapons, and they wear high, spired, and spiked helms of fantastic design. Devout Axe Dwarves also seek to create more magical weapons.

Specialty Priests (Alaghor)

REQUIREMENTS:	Strength 15, Wisdom 9
PRIME REQ.:	Strength, Wisdom
ALIGNMENT:	LG, LN
WEAPONS:	Any
ARMOR:	Any
MAJOR SPHERES:	All, combat, guardian, law, protection, sun, war
MINOR SPHERES:	Charm, creation, divination, elemental (earth), healing, necromantic, travelers, wards
MAGICAL ITEMS:	Same as clerics
REQ. PROFS:	Battle axe; armorer or weaponsmithing
BONUS PROFS:	Blindfighting, one weapon style specialization

- While most alaghor (the plural form of alaghar) are shield dwarves or gold dwarves, members of nearly every dwarven subrace are called to be specialty priests of Clangeddin's clergy.
- Alaghor may multiclass as alaghar/fighters, and if the DM allows kits for multiclassed characters, they may take any allowed fighter/cleric kit for dwarves.
- Alaghor may select nonweapon proficiencies from the warrior group and fighting style specializations normally available only to warriors without penalty if the DM is using fighting style specializations from the *Complete Fighter's Handbook* or PLAYER'S OPTION: *Combat & Tactics*. Such fighting style specializations include weapon and shield style, two-handed weapon style, two weapon style, etc.
- Alaghor can cast *command* (as the 1st-level priest spell) in combat situations twice per day.
- At 3rd level, alaghor can cast *spiritual hammer* or *rockburst* (as the 2nd-level priest spells) once per day.
- At 5th level, alaghor can cast *strength* (as the 2nd-level wizard spell) on themselves once per day, receiving the benefit as if they were warriors, or they can cast *strength of one* (as the 3rd-level priest spell) once per day.
- At 7th level, alaghor can cast *axe storm of Clangeddin* (as the 4th-level priest spell) or *defensive harmony* (as the 4th-level priest spell) once per day.
- At 7th level, alaghor who are not multiclassed can make three melee attacks every two rounds.
- At 10th level, alaghor can cast *detect magic* (as the 1st-level priest spell) at will.
- At 13th level, alaghor can inflict a triple-damage battle axe blow once per day. (The attack must be selected after a successful hit, but before the damage is rolled.)
- At 13th level, alaghor who are not multiclassed can make two melee attacks per round.
- At 15th level, alaghor can cast *blade barrier* (as the 6th-level priest spell) once per day.

Clangeddite Spells

1st Level

Silverbeard (Pr 1; Alteration)

Sphere:	Combat
Range:	0
Components:	V, S, M
Duration:	1 turn+1 round/level
Casting Time:	4
Area of Effect:	The caster
Saving Throw:	None

By means of this spell, the priest temporarily transforms his or her beard into refined silver. In addition to the stunning visual impact of this spell effect, a *silverbeard* serves as an unusual shield in combat situations.

If the priest is unarmored, *silverbeard* confers a base AC of 8 (7 if a shield is also borne) for the duration of the spell. If armor of any sort is worn, this spell confers a +1 AC bonus for the duration of the spell. Repeated use of this spell gradually transforms the color of the priest's beard to silver.

The material component is the priest's holy symbol.

2nd Level

Rockburst (Pr 2; Alteration)

Sphere:	Combat
Range:	10 yards/level
Components:	V, S
Duration:	1 round
Casting Time:	5
Area of Effect:	1 cubic foot/level
Saving Throw:	Special

This spell allows the caster to make a boulder or rockpile explode suddenly, propelling jagged shards in all directions. If the pile or area of rock targeted is larger than the volume the priest can affect, only part of it flies about.

Shrapnel endangers all beings within 20 feet of the center of the effected rock. Those beings within 10 feet must succeed at a saving throw vs. spell for half damage. Those beings between 10 and 20 feet distant who succeed at a saving throw are allowed a second saving throw. If both rolls are successful, they avoid all damage (due to luck, dodging, and cover). If only one roll is successful, they suffer half damage. The presence of cover or armor does not automatically lessen damage due to the unpredictability of ricochets, bounces, and the like.

The shrapnel does a base damage of 1d4+1 points per level of the caster (in other words, 1d4+1 points per cubic foot of rock) to a maximum of 10d4+10. In rare cases, the explosion removes enough rock to cause an avalanche or cave-in, but the DM decides the likelihood of this event.

4th Level

Axe Storm of Clangeddin (Pr 4; Alteration)

Sphere:	Combat
Range:	0
Components:	V, S, M
Duration:	3 rounds
Casting Time:	7
Area of Effect:	40 foot cube, 1 dwarf/2 levels of caster
Saving Throw:	None

When this spell is cast, each affected dwarf gains an additional attack per round with every axe wielded in melee combat or hurled at an opponent. Movement, spellcasting, spell effects, or attacks with weapons other than axes are not hastened. For the purposes of this spell, axes include battle axes, hand axes, hatchets, throwing axes, and two-handed battle axes; these may be nonmagical or magical.

This spell is not cumulative with itself or with other similar magic. A *slow* spell negates the effects of an *axe storm of Clangeddin*, but otherwise has no effect.

The material components of this spell are the priest's holy symbol and a small sealed glass vial of air capped in the midst of a thunderstorm.

Deep Duerra
(Queen of the Invisible Art, Axe Princess of Conquest, Daul of Laduguer)

Demipower of Acheron, LE

PORTFOLIO:	Psionics (the Invisible Art), conquest, expansion, duergar warriors, duergar psionicists
ALIASES:	None
DOMAIN NAME:	Thuldanin/Citadel of Thought
SUPERIOR:	Laduguer
ALLIES:	Laduguer
FOES:	Blibdoolpoolp, Blood Queen, Callarduran Smoothhands, Diinkarazan, Diirinka, Great Mother, Gzemnid, Ilsensine, Ilxendren, Laogzed, Maanzecorian (dead), Orcus (dead)/Tenebrous (undead), Psilofyr, the drow pantheon, the Morndinsamman (except Dugmaren Brightmantle, Laduguer, and Sharindlar), Shevarash, Urdlen, the drow pantheon (except Eilistraee)
SYMBOL:	Shattered skull (the exact race of which varies, but usually illithid, drow, or dwarven)
WOR. ALIGN.:	LN, N, LE, NE

Deep Duerra (DEEP DWAIR-uh) is the duergar demigoddess of psionics, conquest, and expansion. She is venerated by gray dwarves skilled in the Invisible Art as well as duergar warriors who seek to conquer much of the Underdark and chafe at the defensive mindset of Laduguer's priests. A few rare surface dwellers with wild talents have begun to call on the Queen of the Invisible Art as well for aid in understanding (and more importantly, concealing) their powers, which are viewed with suspicion and fear by most of the populace. (It is assumed that the Invisible Art (psionics), as detailed in PLAYER'S OPTION: *Skills & Powers*, is permitted in the campaign if Deep Duerra is included in the dwarven pantheon. If the DM has only the *Complete Psionics Handbook*, appropriate adjustments will need to be made to the statistics given for Duerra's avatar below.)

The legends of the duergar tell of the gray dwarves' greatest queen, a warrior queen named Duerra, who led her grim troops to numerous victories against the surface dwarves, the drow, the illithids, and other Underdark races. During her centuries-long reign, the empire of the gray dwarves expanded to include vast reaches of the Underdark, including much of the territory that once composed Deep Shanatar, bringing the duergar to the pinnacle of their power. Tales of dubious authenticity also relate how Deep Duerra overran a city of mind flayers and wrested from them numerous powers of the mind. Supposedly Duerra's victory allowed the duergar to gain their current ability in psionics and enabled them to hold their own against the spells of the drow and the psionics of the illithids. Although much of Deep Duerra's empire has since fragmented and contracted, the gray dwarves still revere her uncompromising drive to expand duergar power throughout the Underdark.

Duerra has been estranged from the Morndinsamman since her ascension, and notwithstanding her immediate banishment by Moradin after her apotheosis, she has no interest in ending her supposed exile. Duerra's only ally is Laduguer, who is said to be her father. While she obeys and respects her patron, at least for now, Duerra secretly chafes at Laduguer's bitterness and resentment. She feels that for centuries he has squandered every opportunity to help the gray dwarves conquer the endless tunnels of the Underdark that are their patrimony. In truth, the Queen of the Invisible Art sees the duergar as a unique race with a manifest destiny to conquer the Underdark, and she feels that the gray dwarves' distant kinship with shield, gold, and wild dwarves is irrelevant and best forgotten. The actions of Duerra and her worshipers, like those of Laduguer and his followers, have fostered bitter rivalries with the other races of the Underdark and their gods. The enmity between Duerra and the illithid gods is particularly fierce, as she is rumored to have stolen many secrets of the Invisible Art from Ilsensine, the Great Brain of the illithids.

Duerra is bombastic, arrogant, and imperious. She expects her every whim to be attended to instantly, and she is firmly convinced of her own inalienable right to rule. The Queen of the Invisible Art is dismissive of wizardly magic, considering it inferior to the power of the mind. Duerra is always plotting, planning, and strategizing her next conquest. She is never satisfied with what she has already acquired, as it is the conquest, not the holding, that she enjoys. The Axe Princess is ruthless in her drive to ensure victory, and she has absolutely no tolerance for any being, mortal or divine, who does not live up to her standards. Likewise, Duerra considers no sacrifice too great if it offers greater benefits down the road. The Queen of the Invisible Art occasionally dispatches her avatar to aid in conflicts between the duergar and other psionic races, particularly aboleth and illithids. Duerra also dispatches an avatar when a city of gray dwarves has a golden opportunity to expand its territorial holdings at the expense of other races of the Underdark, but for whatever reason, the duergar rulership is reluctant to act on it.

Duerra's Avatar (Psionicist 25, Fighter 23, Priest 18)

Duerra appears as a stocky, powerful gray dwarf clad in ornate, gleaming chain mail and bearing a huge battle axe. Her beard and most of her head are shaved, her only hair a monk's tonsured cut and a tightly wound braid hanging down her back. Duerra favors spells from the spheres of all, combat, divination, elemental, guardian, healing, law, thought, and war, although she can cast spells from any sphere. Duerra has access to all attack and defense forms, as well as all disciplines, devotions, and sciences.

AC –2; MV 12; HP 181; THAC0 –2; #AT 5/2
Dmg 1d8+12 (*battle axe +3*, +7 STR, +2 spec. bonus in battle axe)
MR 45%; SZ M (6 feet tall)
STR 19, DEX 16, CON 20, INT 22, WIS 21, CHA 18
Spells P: 11/11/11/10/7/4/2
Psionic Summary: Mental #AT: 2; Mental THAC0 –7; Mental AC –10; Dis all/Sci all/Dev all; PSPs: 360; Att: all; Def all.
Saves** PPDM 3, RSW 1*, PP 4, BW 4, Sp 6
  *Includes dwarf +5 CON save bonus to a minimum of 1. The CON save bonus also applies to saves vs. poison to a minimum of 1. **Because she is a psionicist, an additional +2 bonus to all saving throws vs. enchantment/charm spells should be applied as needed.

Special Att/Def: Duerra wields *Mindshatter*, a *battle axe +3* that can *steal psionic strength* (as the 1st-level priest spell cast at the 10th level of ability) on any successful attack and transfer them to its bearer. She can cast *deflect psionics* (as the 4th-level priest spell) at will once per round. The Queen of the Invisible Art continuously broadcasts a mental *chant* (as the 2nd-level priest spell) at all times. Allied gray dwarves within 30 yards of Duerra need never check morale and are immune to the effects of magical *fear* (including dragon fear).

Duerra can be struck only by +1 or better magical weapons. She wears *everbright*-treated *chain mail +3*. She is completely immune to any mind-affecting power, spell, or psionic effect.

If slain, the Queen of the Invisible Art becomes an entity akin to a ghost. Duerra's ghostlike anima form cannot be turned and can become invisible at will. She can work magic, use psionics, and employ a ghost's attacks, and she has half her normal hit points while in this form.

Other Manifestations

Duerra manifests as a nimbus of silver light that surrounds a creature's head like a crown. This power typically gives one or all of the following aids to affected beings, for 1 turn: (1) quadruples PSP total; (2) bestows aa psionic defense—*intellect fortress*, *mental barrier*, *mind blank*, *thought shield*, or *tower of iron will*—with no PSP cost; (3) grants complete immunity to any mind-affecting power, spell, or psionic effect.

Like her patron, Duerra is served by ash mephits, azer, baatezu, baku Dark Ones, banelar, bone nagas, brain moles, cerebral parasites, chaggrin, dark nagas, demaraxes, earth elementals, earth elemental vermin (crawlers), earth mephits, earth weirds, fhorges, gray oozes with psionic ability, hammer golems, helmed horrors, hook spiders, intellect devourers, ironmaws, imps, incarnates (of anger and pride), living steel, maelephants, meenlocks, mineral mephits, observers, razorvine, reaves, rust dragons, rust monsters, sandmen, shadowdrakes, steeders, stone wolves, sword spirits, su-monsters, tso, werebadgers, xavers, and yugoloths. She demonstrates her favor through the discovery of greenstones, sapphires, silver rings (reminiscent of crowns), and small pools of absolutely still, fresh water. She indicates her displeasure by afflicting the subject of her annoyance with a *feeblemind* spell (no saving throw allowed).

The Church

CLERGY:	Clerics, crusaders, psionicists, specialty priests
CLERGY'S ALIGN.:	LN, LE
TURN UNDEAD:	C: Yes, Cru: No, Psi: No, SP: No
CMND. UNDEAD:	C: No, Cru: No, Psi: No, SP: No

All clerics, crusaders, and specialty priests (including multiclassed combinations of all three) of Duerra receive religion (dwarven) and reading/writing (Dethek runes) as bonus nonweapon proficiencies. Priests of Duerra (any type, including clerics, crusaders, specialty priests, cleric/thieves, and fighter/clerics) may multiclass the psionicist class as well, allowing, in certain cases, dwarven clergy of Duerra to multiclass in three classes (cleric/thief/psionicist and fighter/cleric/psionicist). Clerics of Duerra (as well as multiclassed clerics) cannot turn undead before 7th level, but they always strike at +2 on all attack and damage rolls against undead creatures. At 7th level and above, clerics can turn undead as other clerics do, but as a cleric of four levels less than their current level. These modifications apply only to the cleric class and not to crusaders or specialty priests, unless specifically noted. Until the Time of Troubles, all priests of Duerra were female, but since then some males have joined the clergy.

Within gray dwarven communities, perceptions of Duerra's church vary widely. Younger duergar admire the brashness and assertiveness her priests display. Older gray dwarves view Duerra's priests as impertinent upstarts who are likely to bring the combined wrath of the aboleth, drow, illithids, and other races of the Underdark down upon their heads.

The followers of Duerra are little known outside the Underdark. Even shield and gold dwarves are unlikely to have heard of the Queen of the Invisible Art. Other Underdark races perceive the emergence of Duerra's faith as an increasing threat to their own territories, and illithids in particular loathe the dwarven adepts who dare employ the Invisible Art against its rightful masters.

Temples of Duerra are hewn from solid rock and are always constructed in symmetric patterns designed to be architecturally pleasing to the observer and to muffle sound. An empty throne sits atop an elevated dais in the central chancel, but it is never occupied except by an avatar of the goddess. Duerra's houses of worship serve as armories, barracks, and command centers for the senior priests who lead the temple army. Most are extensively fortified and well stocked with emergency supplies, weapons, and armor.

Novices of Duerra are known as the Close-minded. Full priests of the Queen of the Invisible Art are known as Mindaxes. In ascending order of rank, the titles used by Duerran priests are Psionic Blaster, Mind Thruster, Ego Whipper, Id Insinuator, Psychic Crusher, and Thought Conqueror. High Old Ones have unique individual titles but are collectively known as Axe Princesses/Princes of the Invisible Art. Specialty priests are known as norothor, a dwarvish word that can be loosely translated as *those who seize enemy land.* The clergy of Duerra consists primarily of gray dwarves (99%), but a handful of gold dwarves, shield dwarves, and wild dwarves skilled in the Invisible Art secretly serve the Daul of Laduguer as well while remaining in or near their own communities. Duerra's clergy consists of specialty priests (25%), psionicists (22%), crusaders (18%), clerics (11%), fighter/specialty priests (9%), fighter/clerics (8%), and cleric/thieves (7%). Fully three-quarters of each group of priests multiclass the psionicist class as well. Duerra's clergy is predominantly female (97%).

Dogma: The children of Laduguer shall conquer the earth and stone from which they sprang and the voids in which they dwell. The seizing of new lands, new wealth and new servitors is the manifest destiny of those who mine the Night Below. Magic is weak, unreliable, and unsubtle when compared to the powers of the mind unless bequeathed and steadied by the will of the gods. By means of the Invisible Art, the duergar shall destroy or enslave all who rely on their petty magics to survive. One day all will bow to the power of the duergar and the brilliance of the Invisible Art.

Day-to-Day Activities: Duerra expects her priests to be capable leaders who use cunning strategy to defeat their enemies in an endless quest for increased power. Unlike the Laduguran clergy, who are typically responsible for the defense of duergar cities, homelands, and mines, senior Mindaxes command elite strike forces composed of duergar warriors, junior Laduguran priests, and Duerran priests. These teams are responsible for the scouting and seizing of new tunnels. Within duergar society, Axe Princesses/Princes of the Invisible Art monitor the very thoughts of both slaves and their gray dwarven masters, alert for any sign of disloyalty, and eliminate troublesome elements as necessary. Duerran priests instruct young gray dwarves in developing their natural psionic talents and teach the art of war and survival techniques in the wilds of the Underdark.

Holy Days/Important Ceremonies: The Duerran church celebrates two holy days annually. The first, known as the Rallying, is celebrated on Midwinter eve. On this night, the followers of Duerra assemble to commemorate the triumphs and conquests of the previous year and to proclaim their intentions to seize new territory. Grim chants of war and the pounding of hammers against stone echo through the tunnels as the duergar work themselves into a grim fury. The culmination of such martial exaltations is the display of the newly seized skull of an enemy from another race whose territory will be besieged in the coming year. The other holy day of the Duerran faith is celebrated on the 5th of Mirtul. On this day, skilled practitioners of the Invisible Art assemble in Duerran temples to join in the Melding, a psionic ritual in which the assembled minds of the gray dwarves contact Duerra herself. The duergar temporarily form a common mind that rivals that of the great Elder Brains of the illithids. It is from such Meldings that many insights leading to great advances in duergar technology and psionics have come. Offerings to the Queen of the Invisible Art are made at both ceremonies; these typically include dirt or stone carried back from the borders of newly conquered territory, the brains of psionic individuals, or shattered skulls from members of any intelligent race.

Major Centers of Worship: The duergar city of Underspires is located deep below the Osraun Mountains of northern Turmish, suspended above a gigantic rift in the earth. The entire city is constructed from gigantic stalactites dangling above a chasm whose bottom has never been plumbed, and its structures are linked by numerous stone causeways. The royal palace and great Duerran temple of Underspires is known as Ultokolor, the Worldthrone. Underspires is ruled by War King Olorn Ridaugaur (a fighter/psionicist), son of Deep Duerra and grandson of Laduguer. His wife, War Queen Ovdana Xothcorlar (a specialty priest of Duerra/psionicist), daul of Cathbara, blood of Llaemna, and the high priest of Duerra in Underspires, rules at his side. The militaristic, subterranean city-state has long been ruled by its preeminent generals, drawn from the ranks of Duerra's followers, and the rulers of Underspires have waged many bloody wars with their neighbors. There is continuous strife between the armies of Underspires and the drow of Undraeth, a city deep beneath the Aphrunn Mountains, which has been ruled for centuries by the hated foe of the duergar, Queen Nathglaryst. Likewise, in the late 1200s DR, the gray dwarves of Underspires waged a five-decade-long and ultimately inconclusive war with their surface kin in Ironfang Keep among the Mountains of the Alaoreum. (This is not to be confused with the mysterious fortress of the same name on the shores of the Moonsea.) That conflict, known to the dwarves of the Alaoreum as the Campaign of Darkness, has continued fitfully to the current day.

In the Year of Shadows (1358 DR), during the Fall of the Gods, Duerra's avatar appeared in Underspires in the form of the Queen Mother, who was serving as regent of the duergar city until War King Olorn reached his maturity. Duerra began assembling and training an army of elite duergar warriors. Initial forays against the outlying dwarven and drow settlements of Ironfang and Undraeth served to shape the army of Underspires into its highest level of readiness in centuries. Under the leadership of their divine regent, the duergar extended their holdings to the Underdark tunnels deep beneath the Cloven Mountains, reaching the deepest mines of long-fallen Tathtar. Duerra then disappeared into the southernmost reaches of the Underdark, and the young War King ascended to the Underthrone.

Since the Time of Troubles, the duergar king, a dark-skinned dwarf nearly 12 feet in height, has sent his armies against the illithids of Oryndoll to the west beneath the Shining Plains and against the drow, dwarves, and svirfneblin beneath the Dragonreach lands to the North. In twelve years of war, the gray dwarves have overrun the outlying territories of their enemies, but the quick conquests won under Duerra's leadership have been few and far between. The emerging empire of the gray dwarves has quickly amassed a wide number of enemies and rivals, and it may be vulnerable to a concerted attack by its foes.

Affiliated Orders: The Mindstalkers of the Invisible Art are a secretive group of Duerran psionicist/priests with cells in most northern gray dwarven settlements. The Mindstalkers seek to unite the disparate duergar realms of the Northdark into a great empire ruled by the collective consciousness of the order. While the Mindstalkers are centuries from accomplishing their goal, they have begun to extend their invisible tendrils into most duergar settlements beneath the Savage Frontier, and much of the trade conducted by gray dwarven merchants in the region is at their direction. In recent decades, the Mindstalkers have established a cell in the subterranean city of Skullport in the dungeons of Undermountain beneath Waterdeep. They seek to purchase surface-dwellers with unusual psionic talents to breed into the gray dwarven race, and they have been actively culling wild talents from Skullport's slave bazaars for years.

Priestly Vestments: The ceremonial garb of Duerra's priests includes ornate, gleaming chain mail (often treated with *everbright* or *blueshine*) and dark blue velvet robes trimmed with the fur of surface animals. No headgear of any sort is worn, but a beautiful weapon, often bejeweled, is always borne. The holy symbol of the faith is a two-inch diameter silver orb, carved to resemble the skull of an illithid, with a large crack running across the top. A steel chain is usually threaded through the skull's ear holes so that it can be worn around the neck.

Adventuring Garb: Outside of ceremonial functions, Duerran priests eschew their glittering mail for the drab chain or dwarven plate mail (base AC 2) common to the duergar and a hooded, ankle-length gray-blue robe. The primary weapon of most Mindaxes is the battle axe, in deliberate imitation of their goddess, but Duerra's priests are also skilled in the use of weapons favored by most gray dwarves, including heavy and light crossbows, picks, short swords, spears, and war hammers.

Specialty Priests (Norothor)

REQUIREMENTS:	Constitution 11, Intelligence 12, Wisdom 15, Charisma 12
PRIME REQ.:	Wisdom, Charisma
ALIGNMENT:	LN, LE
WEAPONS:	Any
ARMOR:	Chain mail or dwarven plate mail
MAJOR SPHERES:	All, combat, divination, elemental (earth), guardian, healing, law, thought, war
MINOR SPHERES:	Necromantic, numbers, protection, summoning, sun (reversed only), travelers
MAGICAL ITEMS:	Same as clerics and psionicists and warriors
REQ. PROFS:	Blindfighting; mental armor (from PLAYER'S OPTION: *Skills & Powers*)
BONUS PROFS:	Land-based riding (steeders); contact, harness subconscious, rejuvenation (from PLAYER'S OPTION: *Skills & Powers*)

- Although most norothor (the plural form of norothar) are gray dwarves, dwarves of any subrace can become specialty priests of Duerra.
- Norothor are allowed to multiclass as norothor/psionicists and as norothar/fighters.
- Norothor may select nonweapon proficiencies from the psionicist and warrior groups without penalty.
- Norothor suffer no penalty to their psionic abilities if they wear metal armor. Helms, however, cannot be worn while using psionics unless such headgear is psionically active or features magical enchantments that affect or stimulate psionic powers.
- Norothor can cast *morale* or *thought capture* (as the 1st-level priest spells) once per day.
- At 3rd level, norothor can cast *detect psionics* (as the 1st-level wizard spell detailed in *Pages from the Mages* or *Wizard's Spell Compendium, Volume 1*) at will when concentrating. No other action except slow (one-half or slower) movement can be undertaken while using this ability.
- At 3rd level, norothor can cast *augment psionics* or *spiritual hammer* (as the 2nd-level priest spell) once per day. The *spiritual hammer* created by this ability looks like an axe but otherwise functions as the hammer of

the spell. This *spiritual axe* does not require concentration to maintain. The priest assigns it a target and then may take other actions, including spellcasting. The *spiritual axe* continues to attack the specified target until the target dies, the effect expires, or the priest spends one round redirecting the *axe* to another target. If the *spiritual axe's* target dies, it hangs in the air above the corpse until redirected to a new target or the effect expires.

- At 5th level, norothor can cast *deflect psionics* (as the 3rd-level priest spell) or *rigid thinking* (as the 4th-level priest spell) once per day.
- At 7th level, norothor can cast *augment psionics* (as the 2nd-level priest spell) or *cure critical wounds* (as the 5th-level priest spell) once per day.
- At 10th level, norothor can cast *mind blank* (as the 8th-level wizard spell) once per day.
- At 13th level, norothor can cast *lower resistance* (as the 5th-level wizard spell) twice per day.
- At 15th level, norothor can cast *mindshatter* (as the 5th-level priest spell) once per day.

Duerran Spells

1st Level

Steal Psionic Strength (Pr 1; Alteration)

Sphere:	Thought
Range:	10 yards/level
Components:	V, S, M
Duration:	Instantaneous
Casting Time:	4
Area of Effect:	One creature
Saving Throw:	Neg.

This spell steals 1d8 PSPs per two levels of the caster (to a maximum of 10d8 PSPs) from a being with psionic abilities and transfers them to the priest casting the spell. The target receives a saving throw vs. spell to avoid the effect. If the target has fewer PSPs than the priest rolls to steal, the priest receives all the target's remaining PSPs. The bonus PSPs are used up first when the recipient engages in psionic activity, whether it be a psionic attack, defense, or power. If for some reason stolen PSPs are not used up before this spell expires, the stolen PSPs dissipate.

This spell dissipates without effect if the target and/or the caster has no psionic ability or if the target has 0 (zero) PSPs. Psionic defense modes are ineffective in blocking the theft of PSPs by use of this spell, but magical defenses such as a *ring of mind shielding* or certain spells granting impervious mind shielding block the effect.

The material component is the priest's holy symbol.

2nd Level

Augment Psionics (Pr 2; Alteration)

Sphere:	Thought
Range:	Touch
Components:	V, S, M
Duration:	1 round+1 round/level
Casting Time:	5
Area of Effect:	1 psionic creature
Saving Throw:	None

The recipient of this spell receives a special bonus of 3d8 additional PSPs for the duration of the spell. The *augment psionics* spell enables the recipient to actually have more PSPs than his or her full normal total. The bonus PSPs are used up first when the recipient engages in psionic activity, whether it be a psionic attack, defense, or power.

This spell has no effect on individuals without any psionic ability and is wasted if used on them.

The material component is the priest's holy symbol.

4th Level

Deflect Psionics (Pr 4; Abjuration)

Sphere:	Thought
Range:	0
Components:	S, M
Duration:	7 rounds
Casting Time:	7
Area of Effect:	Special
Saving Throw:	Special

This spell employs magic to deflect psionic attacks against the priest. For the duration of the spell, any being directing a psionic attack at the caster must first roll a saving throw vs. spell to proceed. If the attacker succeeds in his or her saving throw, the psionic attack proceeds normally, and the priest can defend himself or herself psionically. However, if the psionic attacker fails his or her saving throw, the attack is shifted to take effect against another being within 10 yards of the priest.

If there is no other individual within the area of effect aside from the priest and the attacker, the attack proceeds normally against the priest. If there is more than one individual within the area of effect aside from the priest and the attacker, the being with the most PSPs suffers the attack instead. If there is more than one individual within the area of effect aside from the priest and the attacker, but no individual has any PSPs, the being with the highest Intelligence score suffers the attack instead. Ties are resolved randomly by the DM. The attacker can never become the target of his or her own psionic attack. Neither the priest nor the attacker has any control over the target of the deflected attack.

The material component is the priest's holy symbol.

Dugmaren Brightmantle

(The Gleam in the Eye, the Wandering Tinker, the Errant Explorer)

Lesser Power of the Outlands, CG

Portfolio:	Scholarship, invention, discovery
Aliases:	None
Domain Name:	Outlands/Dwarvish Mountain (Soot Hall)
Superior:	Moradin
Allies:	Brandobaris, Cyrrollalee, Deneir, Erevan Ilesere, Garl Glittergold, the Morndinsamman (except Abbathor, Deep Duerra, Laduguer), Nebelun/Gond, Oghma, Shaundakul, Thoth, Tymora, Urogalan
Foes:	Gargauth, Ilsensine, Maanzecorian (dead), Urdlen
Symbol:	Open book
Wor. Align.:	LG, NG, CG, LN, N, CN

Dugmaren Brightmantle (DUHG-mah-ren BRITE-man-tuhl) is the patron of dwarven scholars and the embodiment of the chaotic and exploratory spirit that consumes some of the Stout Folk. He is venerated by dwarves and a few gnomes, all of whom are scholars, inventors, engineers, tinkers, and fiddlers. His worshipers are consumed with the acquiring of knowledge simply for its own sake rather than for any practical purpose. Whereas Moradin draws smiths and other craftsfolk to his forge, Dugmaren attracts those free-thinkers who want to create something truly new, not a variation on an old theme.

Dugmaren is thought to be a child of Moradin—a chaotic element split off from his father's stern lawfulness and nurtured by the favor of his mother Berronar. In fact the All-Father relates well to Dugmaren's creative and explorative instincts, but the Wandering Tinker often drifts away from projects before they are completed and usually before he has found a use for the knowledge he has gathered—a trait that irritates Moradin to no end. Dugmaren is always getting himself enmeshed in one exploit or another, and his regular accomplices include Haela or Marthammor of the Morndinsamman and Brandobaris, Erevan Ilesere,

Nebelun/Gond, or Shaundakul from the other human or demihuman pantheons. Aside from Gargauth, who embodies everything corruptive and malevolent in the discovery of lost or undiscovered knowledge, the gods of the illithids, who seek to hoard knowledge for themselves, and Urdlen, who hates everyone and everything, the Wandering Tinker has no true foes. However, Dugmaren finds the company of Abbathor, Deep Duerra, Laduguer, and the goblin and evil giant gods trying at best. The Wandering Tinker is tolerated by the lawful members of the dwarven pantheon because his inventions and innovations have proven to have had beneficial aspects.

Dugmaren is a benign, inquisitive, cheerful, and optimistic deity concerned with discovering the unknown. He is an inveterate acquirer of trivia and little-used knowledge, an experimenter and a fiddler. Although he dwells within the Dwarvish Mountain in the Outlands, he often ventures into the planes of Arborea, Elysium, and Bytopia. The Wandering Tinker sometimes dispatches an avatar to act as an unseen guide for dwarven scholars and travelers, protecting them in their searches and providing hints on where to look for knowledge.

Dugmaren's Avatar (Bard 28, Thief 21, Fighter 18, Cleric 18)

Dugmaren appears as an old dwarf with twinkling blue eyes, slightly hunched and wearing a bright blue cloak. He always carries a collection of books with him. He can cast spells from all spheres and schools, but does so in an experimental (and often haphazard) way.

AC –1 (–3); MV 12 or 15; HP 180; THAC0 3; #AT 5/2
Dmg 2d4+6 (*broad sword +4*, +2 spec. bonus in broad sword)
MR 60%; SZ M (6 feet tall) or L (8 feet tall)
Str 15, Dex 20, Con 18, Int 22, Wis 21, Cha 18
Spells P: 11/11/11/10/7/4/2, W: 6/5/5/5/5/1
Saves PPDM 3, RSW 1*, PP 4, BW 4, Sp 5
   *Includes dwarf +5 Con save bonus to a minimum of 1. The Con save bonus also applies to saves vs. poison to a minimum of 1.

Special Att/Def: Dugmaren wields *Sharptack*, a *broad sword +4* with the power to cast *feeblemind* twice per day. He wears a bright blue *cloak of displacement*, resulting in the Armor Class given in parentheses above. He can be struck only by +1 or better magical weapons.

Dugmaren is immune to all mind-affecting spells and abilities. Each round, he can avoid any three attacks directed solely at himself (chosen at the beginning of the round before determining whether they succeed) by intuiting how they will unfold and simply avoiding them. He can also determine how to use any mechanical or magical object simply by handling it for one or more rounds. The Wandering Tinker can cast *blink*, *dimension door*, and *teleport without error* once per turn each.

Other Manifestations

Dugmaren rarely manifests in an obvious or direct fashion. Instead, the Wandering Tinker prefers to guide his followers to new discoveries as subtly as possible. For example, he might manifest by causing a book to open to a page of particular interest or by causing a secret door to shift slightly, revealing its existence to a determined seeker.

When he does find it necessary to manifest his presence directly, Dugmaren typically envelops a worshiper or object in a bright nimbus of blue-tinted light. The effect of such an aura varies according to the situation. Dugmaren typically manifests through the actions of sentient creatures by giving them the ability to use a single divination spell, such as *detect magic*, *ESP*, *identify*, *legend lore*, or *true seeing*, or a single defensive spell, such as *anti-magic shell*, *ironguard*, *magical vestment*, *minor globe of invulnerability*, *protection from evil*, or *shield*. The Wandering Tinker sometimes manifests by transforming a follower's mental picture into a physical object in a fashion similar to the effects of the spell *major creation*.

Dugmaren is served by archons, aasimon, einheriar, electrum dragons, feystags, and gynosphinxes. He demonstrates his favor through the discovery of king's tears, pearls, unlooked-for scraps of lore of any sort, and faint, long-forgotten melodies with no apparent source. The Wandering Tinker indicates his displeasure by temporarily preventing a tome from opening, by causing a device to seize up and stop working, or by blocking one or more forms of sensory input (usually hearing) for a time. He also provides cryptic omens in the form of riddles, puzzles, and impossible objects.

The Church

CLERGY:	Clerics, specialty priests
CLERGY'S ALIGN.:	NG, CG, N, CN
TURN UNDEAD:	C: Yes, SP: No
CMND. UNDEAD:	C: No, SP: No

All clerics (including fighter/clerics) and specialty priests of Dugmaren receive religion (dwarven) and reading/writing (Dethek runes) as bonus nonweapon proficiencies. Clerics of Dugmaren (as well as multiclassed clerics) cannot turn undead before 7th level, but they always strike at +2 on all attack and damage rolls against undead creatures. At 7th level and above, clerics can turn undead as other clerics do, but as a cleric of four levels less than their current level. These modifications apply only to the cleric class. Until the Time of Troubles, all priests of Dugmaren were male dwarves or male gnomes, but females of both races are now accepted into the clergy.

The followers of Dugmaren are viewed with a certain measure of distrust and suspicion by most dwarves. While Dugmaren's apostles are well regarded for their learning and inventiveness, few dwarves are willing to spend a great deal of time in the company of the Wandering Tinker's faithful. There are two reasons for such reticence: the fear of getting caught up in the spectacular failure of yet another experiment, and the fact that the quixotic behavior of Dugmaren's followers is tiring to the orderly mindset common to the children of Moradin. Other human and demihuman races tend to be more tolerant of Dugmaren's followers than their fellow dwarves are.

Temples of Dugmaren are found both above ground and below. They are usually sprawling complexes crammed full of the detritus of countless experiments as well as artifacts collected on extended sojourns to distant locales. At the center of each such house of worship is a huge library housing a large collection of rune stones plus the tomes and scrolls of other races. Altars of Dugmaren consist of a simple block of granite (or some other hard stone) upon which sits a single ever-burning candle symbolizing the quest for knowledge.

Novices of Dugmaren are known as the Curious. Full priests of the Wandering Tinker are known as Seekers of Truth and Mystery. In ascending order of rank, the titles used by Dugmarenite priests are Questing Wanderer, Avid Fiddler, Philosophical Tinker, Seeking Scholar, Searching Sage, and Errant Philosopher. High Old Ones have unique individual titles but are collectively known as the High Savants. Specialty priests are known as xothor, a dwarvish word that can be loosely translated as *those who seek knowledge*. The clergy of Dugmaren includes shield dwarves (53%), gold dwarves (46%), and a handful (1%) of gray dwarves, jungle dwarves, and gnomes. Dugmaren's clergy is dominated by specialty priests (85%), but does include a few clerics (12%) and fighter/clerics (3%) as well. The priesthood is unevenly divided by gender: 96% male and 4% female.

Dogma: The secrets of the world are waiting to be revealed. Travel widely, broaden your mind at every opportunity, and pursue the life of a scholar. Cultivate the spirit of inquiry among the young and be a teacher to all. Seek to recover the lost and/or arcane knowledge of ages past and apply it in the world of today. Try new methods of doing things just for the joy of experimenting. Learn a little of everything, for you never know what might be of use down the road.

Day-to-Day Activities: Priests of the Wandering Tinker spend their days in scholarly pursuits, seeking to learn, teach, and advance nearly every field of knowledge even marginally interesting to the dwarven race. Many Seekers of Truth and Mystery serve as instructors to the young, while others record and archive current dwarven practices for future generations. Dugmaren's clergy members travel widely, seeking new experiences, new ideas, and the recovery of lost dwarven lore.

Holy Days/Important Ceremonies: The church of Dugmaren has little in the way of formal ritual or ceremony. Priests of the Wandering Tinker whisper a prayer of thankfulness to Dugmaren when they discover a piece of forgotten lore or whenever they make a significant discovery of any sort.

Greengrass and Highharvestide are the only holy days regularly celebrated by Dugmaren's faithful. Such days begin with several hours of private early-morning introspection, usually spent staring into the heart of a single lit candle. These personal meditations are followed by a day-long convocation of scholars in which the results of scholarly investigations since the last such symposium are presented, defended, and discussed.

Major Centers of Worship: With the founding of Luruar in the Year of the Gauntlet (1369 DR) and the elevation of Alustriel to rule it, Silverymoon's role as the preeminent center of learning within the Moonlands of the North has continued to expand. With the blessing and encouragement of King Harbromm and the Bright Lady, 40 dwarven scholars from Citadel Adbar, under the direction of Savant of Mysteries Daurant Tomescribe, emigrated to Silverymoon in the first few months of the Year of the Tankard (1370 DR). There they founded a temple of Dugmaren alongside the other colleges, temples, and libraries of the Gem of the North. Both rulers saw this development as a way to ensure that the dwarves of the emerging nation of Luruar contributed to and benefited from the scholarly work and intellectual ferment already underway in the capitol city.

Since its inception, the Athenaeum of Philosophy, located east of the Market and northwest of Alustriel's Palace, between Fortune Hall and the Temple of Silver Stars, has been the home of invention, experimentation, philosophical and scholarly debate, and seminars on a wide range of topics—this last being open to the general public. Although the worshipers of Tymora and Selûne have uttered more than a few fervent prayers to their goddesses after alarming explosions emanating from the experimental laboratories beneath Dugmaren's house of worship, the introduction of two score dwarven inventors and sages to Silverymoon's scholarly circles has been a great success and is starting to draw more dwarves from the lands of fallen Delzoun, as well as scholars of other races based in Silverymoon, to share in the intellectual ferment.

The Athenaeum itself once served as a training facility for the Knights of Silver based in the nearby palace, and halls that were once employed for dining, sleeping, and weapons training are now occupied by sprawling laboratories and great libraries filled with obscure knowledge of questionable usefulness. The temple is always ablaze with light as its residents experiment, tinker, and invent night and day. Visiting scholars of any race are welcome to reside in the temple for a night or even a tenday, but few find the ever-present chaos conducive to a good night's sleep.

Affiliated Orders: The Order of the Lost Tome is a loosely structured fellowship of errant dwarven scholars dedicated to the recovery of lost dwarven lore for the benefit of kingdoms and clan holds throughout the Realms. Individual Knights of the Lost Tome usually work alone or in the company of dwarven and nondwarven adventurers unaffiliated with the order. They combine their passion for knowledge and investigative abilities with the martial skills necessary to defeat the current occupants of fallen dwarven strongholds thought to contain examples of and treatises on lost dwarven lore.

Priestly Vestments: Dugmaren's priests tend to eschew formal religious garb aside from plain, homespun white garments with vibrant sashes the width of a hand. High Old Ones of the faith wear simple silver circlets to denote their status. The holy symbol of the faith is a silver locket crafted to resemble an open book. Many of Dugmaren's followers keep small bits of lore—riddles, puzzles, command words, etc.—inside such lockets in homage to the god—and also to keep them readily available in unexpected situations.

Adventuring Garb: Members of Dugmaren's clergy dress practically when exploring dangerous or unknown territories. Most favor light armor and weapons, preferring maneuverability over defense. Many carry unique weapons; most also have items with defensive capabilities of widely varying usefulness and reliability, which they have invented and wish to field-test.

Specialty Priests (Xothor)

REQUIREMENTS:	Intelligence 10, Wisdom 13
PRIME REQ.:	Intelligence, Wisdom
ALIGNMENT:	NG, CG
WEAPONS:	Any
ARMOR:	All armor types up to and including chain mail; no shield
MAJOR SPHERES:	All, astral, charm, divination, guardian, numbers, protection, thought, travelers, wards
MINOR SPHERES:	Chaos, creation, healing
MAGICAL ITEMS:	Any
REQ. PROFS:	Engineering

Bonus Profs: Ancient or modern languages (pick any two), ancient history, two skills from: artistic ability, brewing, carpentry, cobbling, fishing, leatherworking, pottery, rope use, seamanship, seamstress/tailor, stonemasonry, weaving, blacksmithing

- While most xothor (the plural form of xothar) are shield dwarves or gold dwarves, members of nearly every subrace are called to be specialty priests of Dugmaren's clergy.
- Xothor are not allowed to multiclass.
- Xothor may select nonweapon proficiencies from the rogue group without penalty.
- In addition to the bonus proficiencies for ancient or modern languages listed above, xothor gain an additional language every two levels (that is at 3rd level, 5th level, etc.). This ability tops out at 20th level.
- Xothor have a limited ability to use magical wizard scrolls and priest scrolls containing spells beyond their current ability. A xothar's understanding of magical writings is far from complete, however. The xothar has a percentage chance (equal to 100 − 5 × [level of the priest − level of the spell to be read]) to read the scroll incorrectly and alter (which sometimes involves reversing) the spell's effect. This sort of malfunction is not always detrimental to the xothar and his or her party, but it never functions exactly the way the xothar intended. For example, if a xothar reads a *fireball* scroll incorrectly, it might have a burst radius of 3 inches, igniting an opponent's shirt or an ally's beard, or it might become a *frostball*, coating everyone within the normal area of effect in ice. The exact effect of any flubbed scroll reading is up to the DM, but roughly one-third of the time it is helpful in an unexpected way, one-third of the time it is harmful in an unexpected way, and one-third of the time it is relatively neutral in its impact.
- Xothor can cast *mending* (as the 1st-level priest spell) or *brightmantle* (as the 2nd-level priest spell) once per day.
- At 3rd level, xothor can cast *augury* (as the 2nd-level priest spell) or *idea* (as the 2nd-level priest spell) once per day.
- At 5th level, xothor can cast *Alimir's fundamental breakdown* (as the 3rd-level wizard spell) or *tongues* (as the 3rd-level wizard spell) once per day.
- At 7th level, xothor can cast *divination* (as the 4th-level priest spell) once per day.
- At 10th level, xothor can cast *commune* (as the 5th-level priest spell) or *magic missile* (as the 1st-level wizard spell) once per day.
- At 13th level, xothor can cast *legend lore* (as the 6th-level wizard spell) once per day.
- At 15th level, xothor can cast *teleport without error* (as the 7th-level wizard spell) once per day.

Dugmarenite Spells

1st Level

Mending (Pr 1; Alteration)
Sphere:	Creation
Range:	30 yards
Components:	V, S, M
Duration:	Permanent
Casting Time:	4
Area of Effect:	1 object
Saving Throw:	None

This spell repairs small breaks or tears in objects. It will weld a broken ring, chain link, medallion, or slender dagger providing but one break exists. Ceramic or wooden objects with multiple breaks can be invisibly rejoined to be as strong as new. A hole in a leather sack or wineskin is completely healed over by a mending spell. This spell does not, by itself, repair magical items of any type. One turn after the spell is cast, the magic of the joining fades, and the effect cannot be magically dispelled. The maximum volume of material the caster can mend is 1 cubic foot per level.

The material components of this spell are two small magnets of any type (usually lodestones) or two burrs.

2nd Level

Brightmantle (Pr 2; Abjuration)
Sphere:	Protection
Range:	Touch
Components:	V, S, M
Duration:	Special
Casting Time:	5
Area of Effect:	Creature touched
Saving Throw:	None

This spell envelops the recipient's head in a nimbus of faint, flickering blue light. While under the influence of a *brightmantle*, the target can think perfectly clearly with no impairment. Intelligence checks are made with a +2 bonus. Alcohol, drugs, and poisons are not removed from the recipient's system, but their side effects, which muddle the brain, temporarily abate. Spells from the school of enchantment/charm and the spheres of charm and thought that impede the ability of the target to think clearly, such as *chaos, charm monster, charm person, command, confusion, delude, feeblemind, friends, forget, magic jar, mental domination, scare,* or *suggestion,* have no effect while the target is protected by a *brightmantle*. It may, at the DM's option, provide a lucid period for an individual afflicted with insanity. The duration is 1 hour per caster level when cast on dwarves; otherwise, it is 1 turn per caster level.

The material components of this spell are the priest's holy symbol and a pinch of smelling salts (or any restorative whose preparation is based on spirits of ammonia).

Dwarven Powers: Dugmaren Brightmantle

7th Level

Guardian Mantle (Pr 7; Abjuration, Invocation)

Sphere:	Protection
Range:	0
Components:	V, S, M
Duration:	1 turn+1 round/level
Casting Time:	1 round
Area of Effect:	The caster
Saving Throw:	None

The *guardian mantle* spell creates a blanket of translucent bluish energy that encases the priest's body as protection from melee and missile attacks. Those attempting to attack the priest must roll a successful saving thow vs. spell at a –4 penalty or find the attack foiled by the mantle. Attackers using magical weapons can add the weapon bonuses to the saving throw. Maintaining this defensive enchantment requires no concentraion on the part of the caster, who can cast spells or choose to ignore attackers. The mantle does not protect against spells or spell-like powers and cannot be made permanent. While the mantle is in effect, it suppresses all the priest's protective magics for its duration *except* armor (including armor, shields, and helms). For example, neither *bracers of defense* nor an *amulet of life protection* will operate while this spell is in effect, but *leather armor +2* is not affected.

The material components are the priest's holy symbol, a piece of blue velvet, and a gem of at least 500 gp value.

Dumathoin

(Keeper of Secrets under the Mountain, the Silent Keeper, the Mountain Shield)

Intermediate Power of the Outlands, N

Portfolio:	Keeper of metals and other buried wealth (secrets under the earth), the earth's riches, ores, gems, minerals, mining, exploration, the shield dwarf race, guardian of the dead
Aliases:	None
Domain Name:	Outlands/Dwarvish Mountain (Deepshaft Hall)
Superior:	Moradin
Allies:	Callarduran Smoothhands, Cyrrollalee, Geb, Gond, Grumbar, Flandal Steelskin, the Morndinsamman (except Abbathor, Deep Duerra, Laduguer), Segojan Earthcaller, Sehanine Moonbow, Skoraeus Stonebones
Foes:	Abbathor, Deep Duerra, Kiaransalee, Laduguer, Urdlen, the goblinkin and evil giant pantheons
Symbol:	A cut, faceted gem inside a mountain (silhouette)
Wor. Align.:	Any

Dumathoin (DOO-muh-THOE-in) is the Keeper of Secrets Under the Mountain, and he hides the secrets of the earth until deserving and diligent dwarves are ready to be guided to them. He lays veins of iron, copper, gold, silver, and mithral where he feels they will best benefit his followers. He watches over the safety and security of miners of all races and has a special role as the protector of shield dwarves and the creator of the urdunnirin.

Dumathoin created a paradise under the mountains for the shield dwarves when Moradin named him their protector. He shaped natural caverns of great beauty, studded with rich and beautiful deposits of shining metals and glittering outcroppings of crystalline gems. He was angered when the dwarves began to mine the mountains, destroying the beauty he had created. Dumathoin was pleased, flattered, and a little awed, however, when he saw the finely crafted items the dwarves produced from the ores they had mined. He no longer objects to tunneling, mining, or the collecting of treasures underground.

The Silent Keeper frowns, however, on clumsy or crude rock-cutting that does not smooth the earth, follow the natural flows, and highlight the individual features of the rocks. Cutting that causes cavern collapses and

floodings are even less to his liking, and he is openly angered by those who pillage. Pillagers, in Dumathoin's eyes, are beings of all races who take the earth's riches away (in other words, to the surface) for unfair or selfish purposes, taking more than their share and leaving rubble and other messes in their wake.

Dumathoin is friendly with Geb, Flandal Steelskin, Segojan Earthcaller, and other nondwarven gods of the earth and smithcraft. He supplies nondwarven gods of blacksmiths with adamantite ore and sometimes does business with the other gods (through his and their priests) for metals and ores as well. Dumathoin has a nonhostile relationship of some sort with Ilsensine, god of illithids. But aside from the close proximity of their outer planar realms, the exact nature of the relationship is unknown to any other powers, and no such détente exists between the two gods' followers in the Realms.

The Silent Keeper never speaks, communicating instead with gestures. He has never been known to do more than grunt or sigh (in exertion or pain) in the presence of mortals. Dumathoin may also set subtle clues as to his purposes and the nature of the world beneath the surface, such that only those with keen eyes and wits can perceive them. The Keeper has a stolid patience and tolerance (particularly of nondwarves and hasty behavior) lacking in most other dwarven deities. However, he is just as patient and implacable an enemy when angered. Most who offend Dumathoin and realize what they have done set at once to loudly and fervently praying for his forgiveness. They frequently offer to make amends by bringing back gems and metal treasures to the place where they offended him—immediately, if possible, or by a specified time otherwise. If they keep this promise, Dumathoin is usually appeased. If they seem forgetful, they had better not ever go near a mountain or cave again!

Although Dumathoin spends much of his time in the Outlands, he uses his *stone seeing* ability (unlimited range) to keep underground and mountainous areas of Toril under almost constant surveillance.

Dumathoin's Avatar

(Fighter 34, Earth Elementalist 30, Cleric 25, Thief 12)

Dumathoin appears as a barrel-chested male dwarf with hair and beard of sculpted gray stone, earth-brown skin, and eyes of silver fire. His shoulders are as broad as most barn doors, and his arms are knotted and bulging with corded muscles. He casts priest spells from the spheres of all, combat, creation, divination, elemental (earth, fire), healing, protection, travelers, and wards. He can only cast wizard spells from the school of elemental earth and those spells that involve earth, stone, or metal. (The fact that he grunts and gestures rather than verbalizes does not affect his spellcasting capabilities.)

AC –6; MV 12 or 15, Br 12 or 15; HP 238; THAC0 –10; #AT 5/2
Dmg 5d6+18 (*mattock +5*, +11 Str, +2 spec. bonus in broad sword)
MR 70%; SZ M (6 feet tall) or H (18 feet tall)
Str 23, Dex 17, Con 24, Int 19, Wis 21, Cha 17
Spells P: 12/12/12/11/10/8/4, W: 8/8/8/8/8/8/8/7/7*
Saves PPDM 2, RSW 1**, PP 4, BW 4, Sp 4
   *Numbers assume one extra elemental earth spell per spell level. **Includes dwarf +6 Con save bonus to a minimum of 1. The Con save bonus also applies to saves vs. poison to a minimum of 1.

Special Att/Def: Dumathoin wields *Magmammer*, a *mattock +5* made of solidified magma with all of the powers of a *mattock of the titans* and a *maul of the titans.*

Dumathoin is immune to all earth, stone, metal, and fire-based spells. He is also immune to psionics, as well as any spell from the schools of divination or enchantment/charm. Dumathoin can see through solid rock to a range of 120 feet, and he employs *stone seeing* at all times, allowing him to scry anywhere on or beneath the surface of Toril. Once per day he can summon 3d6 16-HD earth elementals to do his bidding for 12 turns; they will fight to the death for him. If encountered underground, Dumathoin has the power to attack opponents by localized rockfall the same way he manifests (see below). He can cause such a fall once per round by a simple gesture, unerringly doing 4d8 damage to all in a 20-foot-diameter area. When in physical contact with the earth, Dumathoin *regenerates* at 3 points of damage per round.

A magical weapon enchanted to +2 or better is required to hit Dumathoin. He is completely immune to any elemental earth sphere or school spell, effect, or ability that he does not wish to be affected by. He is immune to all dragon breath weapons that create fire, lightning, cold, or acid.

Other Manifestations

The Keeper of Secrets commonly manifests in two helpful ways and two harmful ways, treating dwarves and nondwarves equally.

Often when miners or other creatures are lost underground, particularly when their light sources are all gone, the power of Dumathoin guides them to safety by causing rock crystals exposed in the stone walls to sparkle or wink in sequence, beckoning and outlining a route. Where crystals are lacking, areas of bare rock may glow for a time.

Many miners pray to Dumathoin in thanks for another underearth phenomenon: the sudden, spontaneous shifting of wedged boulders or rubble blockages that have trapped miners or prevented their further exploration.

In the same way, they call rumblings in the deep and other earth tremors "the warnings of Dumathoin" and heed them whenever they occur, particularly as a cavern is first entered or a rockface first struck with pick or hammer. If warning tremors are ignored, or Dumathoin's anger is severe, a cave-in occurs above the offenders—typically a minor one doing 4d8 points of damage (a successful saving throw vs. petrification reduces this damage to 2d8 points). Dumathoin also uses this technique to punish individuals whose actions offend him. In such cases, the Keeper typically causes a localized rockfall (in other words, down on the head of one offending character) from either a rock ceiling overhead, or if on the outside of a mountain, from a peak or ledge above. The damage is the same as that of a cave-in, but no saving throw to reduce it is allowed, and there is no chance of other characters being hit or a further collapse occurring—Dumathoin's power is precise.

Dumathoin is served by azer, earth and fire elementals, galeb duhr, undead dwarves, and urdunnirin. He demonstrates his favor through the discovery of veins of precious ore and gems of all types (except octel, shandon, sphene, and rock crystal, all of which are sacred to Berronar). The Silent Keeper indicates his displeasure by making rich veins play out quickly, leading miners to discover pyrite (also known as fool's gold) or causing uncut gems to shatter into worthless fragments upon the first touch of a gemcutter's tools.

The Church

CLERGY:	Clerics, crusaders, specialty priests
CLERGY'S ALIGN.:	LG, NG, LN, N
TURN UNDEAD:	C: Yes, Cru: No, SP: No
CMND. UNDEAD:	C: No, Cru: No, SP: No

All clerics (including fighter/clerics), crusaders, and specialty priests of Dumathoin receive religion (dwarven) and reading/writing (Dethek runes) as bonus nonweapon proficiencies. Clerics of Dumathoin (as well as multiclassed clerics) cannot turn undead before 7th level, but they always strike at +2 on all attack and damage rolls against undead creatures. At 7th level and above, clerics can turn undead as other clerics do, but as a cleric of four levels less than their current level. These modifications apply only to the cleric class. All priests of Dumathoin were male until the Time of Troubles; recently, however, females have been permitted in the clergy.

All dwarves who live in (or venture into) subterranean areas or mountains, or those who work directly with the riches of the earth, worship the Silent Keeper. All dwarven miners and many nondwarven ones at least appease him, even if they do not fully support him. Miners in the North and dwarves throughout the Realms often carry a small diamond, agate, or other gemstone (of about 10 gp value, but not including octel, shandon, sphene, or rock crystals, for reasons noted above) with them to attract his favor.

Temples and shrines of Dumathoin are commonly found across the North, in dwarven holds such as Adbarrim, Felbarr, Hillsafar Hall, Ironmaster, Mithral Hall, Tethyamar, and the Far Hills. There are also temples in the lands that were once held by the realms of High and Deep Shanatar (now the kingdoms of Amn, Erlkazar, Tethyr, and Calimshan). While shrines and temples of Dumathoin are typically found in the holds of the shield dwarves, they are extremely rare among the other dwarven subraces, except for the gold dwarves—in whose realms they are merely uncommon. But the gold dwarves have constructed at least two grand Dumathan houses of worship in the cities of the Deep Realm. Temples of Dumathoin are constructed in the deepest and best-hidden natural caverns, which may be opened up or improved by dwarves without disqualifying them for use. Such caverns are commonly chosen for their veins of precious ores and/or the presence of many gems in the surrounding rock, although the presence of Dumathoin's hidden gifts is not strictly necessary. At the heart of such temples are simple altars consisting of natural boulders or large stone blocks. Statues of the Silent Keeper, depicting him in his many aspects, line the walls.

Novices of Dumathoin are known as the Uncut. Upon taking the Silent Vow, they become full priests and are known as Keepers of the Shield. In ascending order of rank, the titles used by the Keepers of the Shield are Agate, Onyx, Amethyst, Jargoon, Garnet, Topaz, Opal, Sapphire, and Diamond. The highest ranking priests of Dumathoin are collectively known as Beljurils, but most have unique individual titles as well. Specialty priests are known as delvesonns, a dwarvish word that can be loosely translated at *Dumathoin's hidden gifts*. The clergy of Dumathoin is composed primarily of shield dwarves (80%), gold dwarves (18%), and gray dwarves (1%). Nondwarves, such as humans, rock gnomes, stout halflings, and svirfneblin, make up the remainder of the clergy and must be clerics, crusaders, or (if normally permissible to the race in question) fighter/clerics. Dumathoin's clergy is nearly evenly split between specialty priests (45%) and clerics (44%). The remainder of the clergy members are fighter/clerics (6%) or crusaders (5%). The priesthood is still predominantly (97%) male.

Dogma: Walk the deep and silent ways of Dumathoin. Seek out the hidden gifts of the Keeper of Secrets Under the Mountain. That which is hidden is precious, and that which is precious shall stay hidden. Seek to enhance the natural beauty of Dumathoin's gifts and go with, not against, the contours of the deeps. Beauty is in the discovery and the crafting, not the holding. Keep the places of our dead inviolate and well tended; the noble ancestor of our race will neither be robbed nor mocked through the actions of thieves and defilers. Abide not undead creatures, especialty those that take the form of dwarves, thus mocking the creation of Moradin.

Day-to-Day Activities: Priests of Dumathoin seek always to uncover the buried wealth of the earth without marring the beauty of the ways beneath the surface or being overly greedy. They often supervise mining operations and maintain underground safety and security. They work to clean up the rubble of mining, to grow and put in place luminous fungi and edible deep-mosses, and to direct water through the earth to best serve the underlife that includes, of course, dwarves. Priests of this faith are always hunting for new veins of ore, new sources and species of useful fungi, and new delves or underways never explored before. They try to identify encountered dangers and determine strategies to deal with these menaces of the deep places appropriately. They also bargain with other (nonhostile) underground races to avoid over-exploitation of resources.

A priest of Dumathoin is always learning the tiniest details of conditions and life underground. Most priests are therefore invaluable in leading companions through the underways in darkness (for example, when all torches have been used). They can also find water, veins of ore, and cracks or fissures that provide ways out, or can be mined to yield a way from one cavern to another.

As Keeper of Secrets Under the Mountain, Dumathoin is the dwarves' protector in death. While it may have been otherwise in the early days of dwarven civilization, Dumathoin's priests have been the primary morticians and tomb protectors since the latter days of Ammarindar, the lost dwarven realm that existed as a contemporary of Netheril. In fact, priests of Dumathoin do their god justice as Keeper of Secrets, for it is incredibly difficult to find dwarven tombs at all, let alone plumb their mysteries.

Holy Days/Important Ceremonies: Nights of new moons and the days to either side of each such a night are considered holy days. They are known collectively as the Deepstone Triad, for the moon is considered to be hidden deep beneath the surface during this time. Also, special holy days known as Splendarrsonn can be decreed by a High Old One of the faith, usually when dwarves discover a major new lode, lost subterranean treasure cache or delve, or something of the sort.

Gems and jewelry are sacrificed to Dumathoin at each celebration of the Deepstone Triad and on all other holy days. Such precious stones are offered up on altars dedicated to the god. Gems sacrificed to the Keeper are pulverized and mixed with certain herbs and fungal secretions to derive a paste that serves to make rock porous, help plant material adhere to it, and provide nourishment for plants in contact with it. With buckets of this acrid, purple-and-green fibrous paste, priests of Dumathoin creep about the underways painting and planting fungi and other plant life to improve the underground environment. These improvements include not only beautification of the underground ways, but also concealment of stone dwarven doors, redirection of watercourses to turn water-wheels or fill reservoirs, and so on.

Among the various burial practices used by priests of Dumathoin, there are only three set precepts that must be met. First, the body must be washed, and three or more stone burial tokens—the corpse's personal mark, the clan's mark, and Dumathoin's mark—must be braided into the deceased's beard. Second, the corpse is clothed in his or her own armor or a light suit of mail burial armor. (No matter what trade a dwarf plied in life, none enters the afterlife unarmored and unreadied.) Finally, the priest presiding over the burial must create a song honoring the dead dwarf's life and deeds; the song is carved into the lid of the coffin or sarcophagus (or when in a large clan tomb with numerous niches for fallen dwarves, onto the back of a mausoleum seal, a plaque, or a marker covering the recess where the deceased is buried).

The song is never sung out loud in honor of the ever-silent Dumathoin. If someone finds it and speaks or sings it aloud, it is believed that a curse will settle on the one who committed the sacrilege. (Some suggest that the corpse itself might reanimate and smite the offender.)

Burial practices may change slightly to suit particular clans, but a number of alterations in typical burial practices occur upon the passing of a dwarf deserving of special status. In general, there are simply more ceremonies, and more attention is paid to the construction of the tomb. The following are some specific variations that might be found in the burials of important dwarves:

- The burial of a priest is a more convoluted and lengthy process, incorporating aspects of Dumathoin's worship and that of the god whom the priest served. Priests therefore tend to be buried within well-guarded tombs, and their sarcophagi are surrounded by (if not buried under) tokens and offerings from the priest's friends and faithful. Priests of Clangeddin or Moradin are often interred with the remains of their greatest conquered adversary, ensuring a grand afterlife of battle against dwarf-foes. Unlike many other dwarven tombs, priests' spells are used heavily in the interment of a priest to protect the remains and offerings (and, some hint, to prevent the gods from calling on their servants after their time has passed).
- Clan allies of any race can be interred within dwarven tombs, but only if they fell in battle defending the allied clan, the tomb, or a place sacred to Dumathoin.
- While others are buried with standard ceremony and accouterments, wizards are always clad in robes made of woven silver and sealed in solid silver sarcophagi (or a burial crèche lined with silver); this is due to a superstition born of an old dwarven myth that Dumathoin paid Mystra his weight in silver to garner his faithful protection from the magics that disturb the sleep of the dead. While there is believed to be little truth in this legend, the custom still prevails.
- Clan outcasts (assuming a priest of Dumathoin willing to officiate over their burials can even be found) are buried without a clan mark in their beards, and their coffins or burial place markers often depict the broken or marred symbols of their former clans.

Major Centers of Worship: Aecaurak Splendarrsonn, the Gilded Hall of Glittering Gems, is a vast natural cavern deep in the heart of Mirabar's mines, on the level known as the Third Below. The Gilded Hall was first consecrated as a temple of Dumathoin millennia ago by King Anarok of the Royal House of the Helm in the dwarven realm of Gharraghaur. The original cavern, located at the nexus of several veins of gold, was expanded centuries ago by the followers of Dumathoin so as to reveal the beauty and brightness of the golden ore without actually extracting it. This gives the impression that the entire cavern is gilded with gold leaf. In addition, thousands of gems have been enchanted so as to float about the chamber, and a few of them serve as the focus of *continual light* spells, creating a brilliant rainbow of colors throughout the cavern. The current high priest of the Gilded Hall is Voice of the Mountain Agrathan Hardhammer, a prominent Councilor of Mirabar's elected Council of Sparkling Stones. Both human and dwarven miners attend worship services at Aecaurak Splendarrsonn.

A long-sealed temple of Dumathoin, the Vault of Hidden Silences, still exists on the Lost Level in the depths of Undermountain beneath the city of Waterdeep. A single priest, Bandaerl Dumatheir, son of Rykos, blood of Melair, High Old One of Dumathoin, and protector of Melairbode's essence (an archlich specialty priest), guards the temple and adjoining crypts of Clan Melairkyn from unwanted interlopers and Halaster's mischief. (Further details of this temple may be found in *Undermountain: The Lost Level*.)

Corundumdelve, the Hidden Gem of the Depths, is a legendary temple of Dumathoin constructed by the urdunnirin tens of miles below the surface of Faerûn. Located deep beneath the Alimir mountains of the Almraiven peninsula in eastern Calimshan, this temple remains hidden. Its location has never been revealed, even to the dwarves of Deep Shanatar when that realm was at its height. Unlike conventional temples, the Hidden Gem is not composed of walls, passages, and chambers, but it is actually a vast dodecahedron composed entirely of tightly packed amethysts, rubies, and sapphires, each larger than a dwarven helm. Navigating (or even simply abiding in) the temple requires the ability to pass through stone as if it did not exist, an ability of the urdunnirin and a few High Old Ones of Dumathoin who are capable of casting *earth walk*.

Affiliated Orders: The Knights of the Mithral Shield, based in Citadel Adbar, is an order of 300 Dumathan crusaders and multiclassed delvesonn/fighters. These elite dwarven warrior priests serve as the honor guard of King Harbromm of Adbarrim and, as of the fall of the orc-held Citadel of Many Arrows, King Emerus Warcrown of Felbarr. Each Dumathan knight is sworn to serve the Mountain Shield as protector of the shield dwarves, whom Dumathoin is forever pledged to protect.

Priestly Vestments: Dumathoin's clergy favor leather garments, whether they be armor or mining gear. They keep their heads bare and wear earth-brown cloaks and over-robes. Like all dwarves, they grow their hair and beards long, but none of the Silent Keeper's generally hirsute priests braid or trim their hair. The holy symbol of the faith is a miniature silver pick.

Adventuring Garb: In times of likely strife, Dumathoin's priests garb themselves in the most effective armor and weapons available. The Silent Keeper's clergy members typically favor picks, hammers, and other mining tools in combat, but they are usually proficient in the use of a wide range of weapons.

Specialty Priests (Delvesonns)

REQUIREMENTS:	Constitution 12, Wisdom 9
PRIME REQ.:	Constitution, Wisdom
ALIGNMENT:	LG, LN, N
WEAPONS:	Any
ARMOR:	Any
MAJOR SPHERES:	All, creation, combat, elemental (earth, fire), healing, necromancy, protection, wards
MINOR SPHERES:	Divination, guardian, travelers
MAGICAL ITEMS:	Same as clerics
REQ. PROFS:	Blacksmithing; pick one: armorer or weaponsmithing
BONUS PROFS:	Mining, mountaineering, survival (mountains, Underdark)

- While most delvesonns are shield dwarves or urdunnirin, dwarves of nearly every subrace are called to be specialty priests of Dumathoin.
- Delvesonns are not allowed to multiclass.
- Delvesonns may select nonweapon proficiencies from the warrior group without penalty.
- Delvesonns are protected at all times as if by a *ring of mind shielding* and are completely immune to *ESP*, *detect lie*, and *know alignment*, as well as comparable psionic powers.
- Delvesonns can cast *detect metals and minerals* (as the 1st-level priest spell detailed in *Powers & Pantheons*) or *fist of stone* (as the 1st-level wizard spell) once per day.
- At 5th level, delvesonns can cast *meld into stone* or *stone shape* (as the 3rd-level priest spells) once per day.
- At 7th level, delvesonns can cast *identify* (as the 1st-level wizard spell) as a wizard of the same level at will.
- At 10th level, delvesonns can cast *stoneskin* (as the 4th-level wizard spell) once per day.

- At 13th level, delvesonns can cast *passwall* (as the 5th-level wizard spell) once per day.
- At 15th level, delvesonns can speak with stones (as the *stone tell* 6th-level priest spell) three times a day.
- In extremely rare circumstances, single-classed delvesonns who are particularly favored by the Silent Keeper are selected as the Chosen of Dumathoin and may continue to advance beyond 14th level without having to earn triple normal experience points. (These normally become NPCs under the control of the DM.) After 14th level is exceeded, the delvesonn's physical body begins to calcify slowly. When the petrification process is complete (usually within a decade), the Chosen of Dumathoin is composed entirely of rock, with skin of light gray hue, a beard composed of a cluster of stalactites, and normal eyes—except for the irises, which sparkle like deep green emeralds. Thereafter, the Chosen of Dumathoin is considered to be a priestly archlich, with all the attendant abilities and restrictions. Despite the strictures of the new form, the delvesonn retains full mobility and moves, sounds, and acts like a normal dwarven priest.

Dumathan Spells

In addition to the spells listed below, priests of the Silent Keeper may cast the 1st-level priest spell *detect metals and minerals*, detailed in *Powers & Pantheons* in the entry for Geb.

2nd Level

Dumathoin's Rest (Pr 2; Abjuration, Necromancy)
Sphere: Necromantic, Wards
Range: 10 yards/level
Components: V, S, M
Duration: Instantaneous
Casting Time: 5
Area of Effect: 30-foot radius
Saving Throw: None

This spell causes animated skeletons and zombies to collapse. Such remains cannot be reactivated or reanimated for a minimum of 24 hours, during which time they will presumably be properly interred. This affects 2d6 Hit Dice of animated skeletons and/or zombies, 3d6 Hit Dice if the remains are of dwarves.

The material component is the priest's holy symbol.

4th Level

Crypt Ward (Pr 4; Abjuration, Enchantment/Charm) *Reversible*
Sphere: Guardian
Range: Special
Components: V, S, M
Duration: Permanent
Casting Time: 1 hour
Area of Effect: 100 square feet
Saving Throw: None

This spell is cast over a dwarven tomb or crypt. If the tomb is larger than the spell's area of effect, additional castings can ensure that the entire crypt complex benefits from the spell. Otherwise, it is effective only within its 100-square-foot area.

Once a *crypt ward* is in place, it causes the dwarven remains interred therein to animate temporarily in order to protect the tomb from grave robbers. Whenever an intruder enters the area of effect, the dwarven bones contained therein rise and attack. The bones attack as fighters equal to one-third of the caster's level at the time the *crypt ward* is set up (fractions dropped) and possess 5 hit points per one-third level of the caster. Thus, a *crypt ward* cast by a 12th-level priest produces 4th-level bones that possess 20 hit points each. Note, however, that the animated bones are not undead creatures; rather, the effect is similar animates weapons. The dwarven bones do not animate and attack if the intruders are other dwarves, so long as the visitors do not attempt to plunder the tomb. Other races will be attacked if not accompanied by a dwarf.

In any case, the dwarven bones animated by this spell cannot leave the area of effect. If intruders flee the area, the dwarven bones return to their resting places until the next intrusion. If the animated dwarves are slain, the remains have been destroyed.

Dispel magic cannot negate a *crypt ward*, but a *limited wish*, *wish*, or *remove crypt ward* can. The destruction of all the dwarven bones in the tomb complex also negates the spell.

The reverse of this spell, *remove crypt ward*, enables the caster to negate a *crypt ward*. In most dwarven enclaves, *remove crypt ward* is reserved for rare times when dwarven remains must be transported to a new site. A priest attempting to remove the *crypt ward* must be of equal or greater level than the caster who set the spell in place.

This spell is available to priests of all dwarven religions, but its use is typically reserved for the priests of Dumathoin, who are generally regarded as the keepers of the dead. It is said that dwarven priests of old were far stronger than those of today, so it is likely that, in truly ancient dwarven strongholds, there are *crypt wards* that cannot be removed by modern priests.

The material components for both versions of this spell are the caster's holy symbol and the ritual sacrifice of 10,000 gp worth of precious metals and minerals.

Stonefall (Pr 4; Alteration, Elemental Earth)
Sphere: Elemental Earth
Range: 120 yards
Components: V, S, M
Duration: 1 round
Casting Time: 7
Area of Effect: 3 cubic feet/level or creates one stone
Saving Throw: Special

This spell causes rocky materials present in an area to fall suddenly in one of four fashions. If this spell is cast within 3 rounds after a *stonefire* spell has been cast by a priest of Moradin, the fiery damage of that spell is added to the striking damage of this one.

(1) If cast underground, it causes stalactites to fall or starts a cave-in. A fall of stalactites forces the intended target to roll 1d6 Dexterity ability checks. This simulates the number of stalactites that fall; if fewer stalactites are available, lessen the number of checks. Each failed check equals one hit for 2d6 points of damage. Fragile items may well have to roll item saving throws vs. crushing blow if carried by a being that is struck or underneath an area where the stalactites fall. This sort of attack is relatively unlikely (roll of 1 on 1d6) to cause a more general cave-in. If it does, the effect under option 2 occurs as well.

(2) A deliberate cave-in causes 4d8 points of damage to all below it (succeed at a saving throw vs. petrification for half damage). If the situation makes it possible for a cave-in to miss the intended targets, the priest must make a successful attack roll (at a +5 bonus to attack) as if attacking directly. A miss means that the target scrambled adroitly enough away to avoid all damage.

(3) If cast indoors, it causes a ceiling collapse. An indoor ceiling collapse causes only 3d8 damage (succeed at a saving throw vs. petrification for half damage) to all below the area of effect, but damage to breakable items in the room and the space above the ceiling must be considered. Beings that fall down from or with the ceiling suffer 3d6 points of damage (minimum; a successful saving throw vs. spell lowers this damage to half) or more falling damage if directed by the distance fallen, at 1d6 per 10 feet fallen (save for half).

(4) If cast in open air, it causes one fist-sized stone to fall rapidly out of the sky and strike the intended target, causing 3d8 points of damage. The target is allowed a saving throw vs. spell to avoid the missile and all damage.

The material component of this spell is a handful (at least three) of fingerjoint-sized or larger stones or pebbles.

5th Level

Stone Seeing (Pr 5; Divination, Elemental Earth)

Sphere:	Divination, Elemental Earth
Range:	Unlimited
Components:	V, S, M
Duration:	1 round/level
Casting Time:	8
Area of Effect:	Special
Saving Throw:	None

Similar to the wizard spells *clairvoyance* and *wizard eye*, *stone seeing* enables the caster to scry whatever is within sight range of the priest from the spell locale chosen. Distance from the priest is not a factor, but, unlike the aforementioned wizards spells, the selected locale must be entirely contained within solid rock.

Stone seeing enables the caster to see through the enveloping rock to a range of 100 yards per level of the caster or as far as the rock itself extends, whichever is less. The caster can only see in one direction at a time, but by turning his or her head, she or he can adjust the direction of the *stone seeing* in any direction desired. The spell enables the caster to see various veins and inclusions in solid rock, including creatures that can move through rock, such as xorn. The spell enables sight beyond the rock surface only as dwarves do, in other words, as if the caster were peering out from a cavern floor, wall, or ceiling.

The material components are the priest's holy symbol and a small stone chip of the type of rock on which the spell is centered.

6th Level

Earth Walk (Pr 6; Alteration)

Sphere:	Elemental Earth
Range:	0
Components:	V, S
Duration:	1 turn/level
Casting Time:	1 round
Area of Effect:	Caster only
Saving Throw:	Special

This spell enables the priest to pass into and through stone and earth as if she or he were a xorn with a movement rate of 6. This ability adapts well to ambush tactics, and opponents have a –3 penalty to their surprise rolls.

The spellcaster can carry objects that weight up to twice the priest's body weight (total) through the stone as well. For the spellcaster to use this ability offensively, the priest must make a successful attack roll to grab the subject, who is then allowed a saving throw vs. petrification to break free. If the saving throw fails, the spellcaster imprisons the caught being (as effects of the 9th-level wizard spell *imprisonment*). A *freedom* spell releases the trapped being (as the reverse of *imprisonment*).

A *phase door* cast on a earth walking priest instantly kills the dwarf.

Gorm Gulthyn

(Fire Eyes, the Golden Guardian, the Sentinel,
Lord of the Bronze Mask, the Eternally Vigilant)

Lesser Power of Bytopia, LG

Portfolio:	Guardian and protector of all dwarves, dwarven guardians, defense, watchfulness, vigilance, duty
Aliases:	None
Domain Name:	Shurrock/Watchkeep
Superior:	Moradin
Allies:	Arvoreen, Cyrrollalee, Garl Glittergold, Gaerdal Ironhand, Helm, the Morndinsamman (except Abbathor, Deep Duerra, Laduguer)
Foes:	Abbathor, Deep Duerra, Laduguer, Urdlen, the goblinkin and evil giant pantheons
Symbol:	A shining bronze or brass metal mask with two eyeholes of flame
Wor. Align.:	LG, NG, CG, LN, N

Gorm Gulthyn (GORM GULL-thin) is the guardian and protector of dwarvenkind throughout the Realms as well as the god of all Stout Folk who serve as guardians. Those dwarves who require protection or armed aid pay tribute in appeasement to the Lord of the Bronze Mask. Lawful neutral and lawful good dwarves in particular turn to Fire Eyes.

Gorm is closely allied with Clanggedin, Marthammor, and Moradin, and he has excellent relations with the other nonchaotic and nonevil dwarven deities. Gorm is ever vigilant against Abbathor's suspected betrayals, although he has never proven the Trove Lord's treachery. The Lord of the Bronze Mask has established good relations with the powers of other pantheons who view the world much as he does, such as Arvoreen, Gaerdal Ironhand, and Helm, but he has little patience for those he distrusts, including Baervan Wildwanderer, Brandobaris, and Mask. While Gorm regularly contests with the goblinkin and evil giant pantheons, he reserves his greatest hatred for the orcish god Shargaas, as the Night Lord is the only power to have ever successfully stolen an object the Sentinel was actively guarding.

Gorm says little, but has a stern, booming voice when he does speak. He is consumed by the demands of his role as protector and has little interest in or tolerance for foolish activities that might detract from his readiness or sentimentality that might interfere with his dispassion. The Sentinel is ever on the alert for threats to dwarves, and he is a tireless defender of the Stout Folk, even coming to the defense of gray dwarves when they are beset by foes whose evil makes that of the duergar pale in comparison.

While Gorm can dispatch up to two avatars simultaneously, there are always so many battles in which his intercession is critical that the Sentinel can rarely afford for his avatars to remain in any single location for more than a turn. As a result, each avatar is nearly always resident in the Realms, *teleporting* from place to place to aid dwarves in withstanding armed attacks or powerful monsters, and they return to Watchkeep only when in need of the armory amassed there or to use his *Seat of Healing*. Gorm acts only when dwarves are already engaged in combat and need his aid. At such times he appears, engages in a frenzied, all-out attack, seeking to do the most damage to the enemies of the dwarves as he possibly can, and then vanishes again. He cannot return to a given locale in avatar form twice in a 24-hour period, but he can manifest himself between his avatar appearances in a continuing battle.

Gorm's Avatar (Paladin 29, Cleric 22, Diviner 18)

Gorm appears as a dwarf clad in full plate armor of golden-brown hue, chased and decorated with red, crawling, ever-changing runes. He favors spells from the spheres of all, combat, guardian, protection, war, and wards and from the schools of divination, although he can cast spells from any sphere or school except the school of conjuration/summoning.

AC –4; MV 12 or 15; HP 211; THAC0 –8; #AT 2/1
Dmg 1d10+13 (*two-handed battle axe +4*, +9 Str)
MR 70%; SZ M (6 feet high) or L (11 feet high)
Str 21, Dex 17, Con 22, Int 19, Wis 20, Cha 21
Spells P: 12/12/11/11/9/6/3, W: 6/6/6/6/6/4/4/3/2*
Saves** PPDM 2, RSW 1†, PP 4, BW 4, Sp 6

*Numbers assume one extra divination spell per spell level. *Includes +2 bonus to saving throws to a minimum of 1. †Includes dwarf +5 Con save bonus to a minimum of 1. The Con save bonus also applies to saves vs. poison to a minimum of 1.

Special Att/Def: In battle, he wields *Axegard*, a *two-handed battle axe +4* that confers the powers of a *robe of eyes* upon its bearer. The runes inscribed on his *full plate armor +4* act as a *ring of spell turning*. Gorm's magical *Seat of Healing* at his home in Watchkeep can restore all damage inflicted on the god or any being he allows to sit on it. The *Seat* also *regenerates* extensive damage in 1d4+1 turns.

Gorm can cast *fire eyes of Gorm* every other round in combination with physical attacks and ongoing magical effects. His touch is equivalent to either a *heat metal* attack or serves to restore a living recipient to full alertness, eliminating any negative effects of fatigue due to exertion or lack of sleep.

Gorm is protected by a permanent *protection from normal missiles* effect natural to his body. He can be struck only by +2 or better magical weapons. It cannot be dispelled or temporarily negated and operates constantly and independently of the god's magical activity. The Lord of the Bronze Mask is never surprised. He is immune to both magical and nonmagical heat and fire attacks of all kinds and to mind-affecting spells, affects, abilities, psionics, and illusions. He can detect the presence of living or undead creatures within 100 yards with pinpoint accuracy. Once per turn, Gorm can by silent act of will use *spell turning*. In Gorm's case, however, he can reflect back the effects of any spells, spell-like magical powers, or magical items directed at him back on the casters or wielders. *Spell turning* counts as Gorm's spellcasting activity for the round, but it cannot be stopped by physical restraints or attacks, it operates instantaneously, and it can deal with any number of simultaneous attacks launched at the god.

If slain, Gorm becomes an entity akin to a ghost. The Sentinel's ghostlike anima form cannot be turned and can become invisible at will. He can work magic and employ a ghost's attacks, and he has half his normal hit points.

Other Manifestations

Gorm prefers to act directly, husbanding his power for personal combat. He therefore manifests seldom, except to imbue dwarven individuals with temporary combat powers. This usually involves conferring a temporary +3 *protection from good/evil aura*, as well as immunity from a specific attack form (for example, fire) or spell. Sometimes Fire Eyes temporarily enchants a weapon, conferring a +3 attack and damage bonus until the conclusion of the current or next battle.

On occasion, Gorm rouses sleeping dwarves or otherwise warns of intruders or impending attack by causing a disembodied metal gauntlet to appear and strike any handy metal shield or breastplate. The struck metal rings with a terrific rolling, gonglike noise and sports two burning eyes for the next turn. When the eyes fade, two eyeholes will have been burned in the metal. Dwarves treasure such damaged shields and armor and always display them as trophies, rather than melting them down to make a whole item again.

If Gorm must leave a battle knowing the dwarves there still face a grave challenge, he manifests later as a glowing hand. His hand breaks ropes, hurls back siege ladders, and strikes blows (one a round, for 1d6+11 points of damage). It operates with Gorm's full strength and sees by means of two burning eyes in its palm.

Gorm is served by agathinon, azer, earth and fire elementals, einheriar, galeb duhr, guardian nagas, hammer golems, helmed horrors, incarnates of courage and faith, maruts, noctrals, per, sapphire dragons, shedu, silver dragons, and spectators. He demonstrates his favor through the discovery of alestones, amaratha, azurites, fire agates, fire opals, flamedance, jacinths, rubies, and scapras. The Sentinel indicates his displeasure through the discovery of shattered shields, upside-down helms, and ephemeral footprints that quickly fade away if followed.

The Church

CLERGY:	Clerics, crusaders, specialty priests
CLERGY'S ALIGN.:	LG, NG, LN
TURN UNDEAD:	C: Yes, Cru: No, SP: Yes, at priest level –4
CMND. UNDEAD:	C: No, Cru: No, SP: No

All clerics (including fighter/clerics), crusaders, and specialty priests of Gorm receive religion (dwarven) and reading/writing (Dethek runes) as bonus nonweapon proficiencies. Clerics of Gorm can use any weapons, not just bludgeoning (wholly Type B) weapons. Clerics of Gorm (as well as multiclassed clerics) cannot turn undead before 7th level, but they always strike at +2 on all attack and damage rolls against undead creatures. At 7th level and above, clerics can turn undead as other clerics do, but as a cleric of four levels less than their current level. These modifications apply only to the cleric class. Until the Time of Troubles, the priesthood of Gorm was all male; since then a few females have joined the church.

Gorm is well regarded by the children of Moradin for his unswerving dedication to the defense of the Stout Folk. While most dwarves regard Fire Eyes as stern and humorless, few discount his role in ensuring the continued survival of those dwarven strongholds that have not fallen. Among the other gnome, halfling, and human races, Gorm is well regarded by those of similar disposition who tend to follow deities such as Arvoreen, Gaerdal Ironhand, and Helm, but he is written off as the archetypal dour dwarf by most elves and others of a more chaotic bent.

Temples of Gorm are always plain, unadorned stone caverns or rooms quarried from solid rock. The altar is a stone bench in front of a closed, locked door of massive construction, representing a location that a dwarf might have to guard. Instead of a stone bench, a temple might use an old tomb casket; if occupied, it must be by a fallen, not undead, priest of Gorm. Such chambers are often adorned with visored helms, or if particularly blessed, a shield or breastplate with twin eyeholes burned through, as discussed above under Other Manifestations. The Sentinel's chapels are typically adjacent to an armory, a training hall, and barracks, and most such houses of worship are located amidst fortifications that guard entrances to the halls of the Stout Folk.

The clergy of Gorm are collectively known as Guardians or Guardian-Priests. Novices of Gorm are known as the Watchful Guards. Full priests of Fire Eyes are known as the Vigilant Host. In ascending order of rank, the titles used by Gormite priests are Lookout of the First Rank, Scout of the Second Rank, Sentry of the Third Rank, Sentinel of the Fourth Rank, Defender of the Fifth Rank, and Guardian of the Sixth Rank. High Old Ones have unique titles but are collectively known as Lord/Lady Protectors. Specialty priests are known as barakor, a dwarvish word that can be loosely translated as *those who shield*. The clergy of Gorm includes both shield dwarves (48%) and gold dwarves (52%). While there are no formal barriers to either gray dwarves or jungle dwarves joining the ranks of Gorm's clergy, none are known to have done so in recent history. The Sentinel's clergy is dominated by specialty priests (41%), with the remainder nearly balanced between clerics (22%), crusaders (20%), and fighter/clerics (17%). The clergy of Fire Eyes is 95% male.

Dogma: Never waver in your duty to Gorm's sacred charges. Defend, protect, and keep safe the children of the Morndinsamman from the hostile forces of the outside world. Be always vigilant and ever alert so that you are never surprised. If need be, be prepared to pay the greatest price so that the clan and the community survive, and your name will be honored for generations.

Day-to-Day Activities: The Vigilant Host guards most clan-hold entries, the Gates on the borders of The Deep Realm, as well as all temples of Gorm. Priests of Gorm serve as protectors and bodyguards for all dwarves, especially the young and child-rearing parents of both sexes. They instruct dwarven warriors fulfilling such roles in the arts of alertness, blindfighting, and weapons-skills (in other words, in campaigns using proficiencies, the priests of Gorm can tutor dwarves in all proficiencies useful to guardians). The foremost aim of any lesser priest of Gorm is to protect the dwarves assigned to him. Veteran priests of higher rank may choose whom they protect. If this involves sacrificing one's life, so be it; that is "Gorm's greatest price," as every priest of Gorm knows.

Holy Days/Important Ceremonies: Every festival in the Calendar of Harptos is sacred to the priesthood of Gorm. On such holy days, guardians of Gorm gather for a salute, a ritual involving the rhythmic grounding of weapons, and a responsively chanted prayer. Offerings to Gorm are of weapons used, even broken, in the service of guardianship anointed with tears, sweat, and drops of blood of the dwarf making the offering. Rituals involve silent vigils, muttered prayers, and answering visions from the god. At the height of a salute, if the ritual is performed in the chancel of one of Gorm's temples, the door behind the altar sometimes opens by the power of the god and through it may come instructive phantom images, scrolls or potions, weapons, pieces of armor, or even maps—small aids from the god, to help his faithful fulfill their duties. When this happens, the morale of a worshiper of Gorm who is wearing or using any gift from the god increases by a bonus of +4.

Major Centers of Worship: At the bottom of the Great Rift, guarding the entrance to the Deep Lands, are the Gates, a pair of titanic metal doors that bar the entrance of outsiders from the Guardcavern immediately behind them, the great city of Underhome, and the Deep Realm of the gold dwarves beyond. Over fifty priests of Gorm garrison the Gates at all times, with two hundred more available at a moment's notice. The Keepers of the Gate are based in Araubarak Gulthyn, the Great Shieldhall of Eternal Vigilance, a soaring subterranean vault adjoining the great Guardcavern in which dwarven caravans muster for trips to the surface Realms. The task of securing the entrance to the last great dwarven kingdom in Faerûn is led by

Prince Protector of the Golden Realm Starag Crownshield, son of Vorn, blood of Pyradar. The Great Shieldhall is itself an invulnerable fortress whose defenses have never been breached. Twin adult sapphire dragons lair in the Great Shieldhall's narthex under the direction of specially trained dwarven riders. A series of nine double doors, each a miniature replica of the great hizagkuur Gates, bar entrance to the temple's innermost sanctum. A pair of hammer golems and seven priests of Gorm defend each set of portals. The chancel doubles as a well-stocked armory, and from its stores an army of five thousand dwarven warriors can be—and has been, on several occasions in centuries past—outfitted to sally forth against great armies seeking to plunder the wealth of the gold dwarves. Above the altar floats the greatest relic of the Gormite faith, a massive bronze mask with eyeholes alight with fire, known as the *Face of the Guardian*. Aspirants in the Deep Realm seeking to join the ranks of Gorm's guardians stand before the *Face* during their initiations and are seared by twin beams of fire that erupt from the ever-dancing flames. If accepted by the Golden Guardian, they emerge unscathed, but those found wanting are reduced to piles of ash.

Affiliated Orders: Numerous knightly orders large and small have been founded in Gorm's name and affiliated with his church over the centuries. Numbered among the legendary Gormite orders of times past and present are the Twin-Bladed Axes of Fire, the Silent Sentinels, the Guardian-Knights of Gorm, the Vigilant Halberdiers, the Company of the Scarlet Moon, the Fellowship of the Stern Gauntlet, and the Order of the Smoking Shield. One of the oldest and most revered knightly orders of Gorm, the Sacred Shields of Berronar's Blessed, may be found in nearly every clanhold and kingdom guarding nurseries full of dwarven children and their parents. Knights of the Sacred Shield are also charged with recovering kidnapped dwarven youths who are to be sold as slaves on the surface or in the Underdark. At least two dwarven clans owe their continued free existence to the rescue of an entire generation of dwarven youth from the clutches of the Spider Queen's priests by the Knights of the Sacred Shield.

Priestly Vestments: The clergy of Gorm favor red and black cloaks and helms, worn over armor of the finest metal and type available. The holy symbol of the faith is a miniature bronze shield that is usually worn around the neck on a burnished steel chain as a medallion.

Adventuring Garb: When adventuring or on guard duty, Gorm's priests always wear and wield the best armor and weapons available. Members of Gorm's clergy never remove all their armor or lay aside all their weapons unless sorely wounded or in need of care. Members of the Vigilant Host often mark their status with red and black armbands on the left and right arms, respectively.

Specialty Priests (Barakor)

REQUIREMENTS:	Strength 9, Constitution 10, Wisdom 9
PRIME REQ.:	Strength, Constitution, Wisdom
ALIGNMENT:	LG, LN
WEAPONS:	Any
ARMOR:	Any
MAJOR SPHERES:	All, combat, divination, guardian, healing, law, protection, sun, war, wards
MINOR SPHERES:	Animal, charm, creation, elemental (earth), necromantic, summoning
MAGICAL ITEMS:	Same as clerics
REQ. PROFS:	Armorer or weaponsmithing
BONUS PROFS:	Alertness, blindfighting

- While most barakor are shield dwarves or gold dwarves, dwarves of nearly every subrace are called to be specialty priests of Gorm's clergy.
- Barakor are not allowed to multiclass.
- Barakor may select nonweapon proficiencies from the warrior group without penalty.
- Barakor who are serving as guardians are never surprised and are able to interpret noises, half-seen movements, and other symptoms of approach and movement correctly with an accuracy of 10% per level. For instance, a barakar might hear a faint scuffling and identify it as studded leather worn by a crawling man against a particular stone she or he noticed earlier. A barakor always checks around his or her feet and overhead often and takes care to know the distance and exact direction of features in his or her surroundings. The guardian-priest described above,

for instance, would know exactly where, and how far away, the unseen intruder in studded leather was—and just where to throw an axe in order to hit him or her. These carefully developed skills give barakor an attack bonus of +5 with missiles of any sort, against any target within 60 feet of their guardpost. If they have not had time to examine the surroundings, this bonus drops to +2. In addition, barakor always win initiative rolls when on active guard duty, even when they are charged by multiple opponents coming out of the darkness.

- Barakor can cast *sentry of Gorm* (as the 1st-level priest spell detailed in *Faiths & Avatars* under the name *sentry of Helm*) or *blessed watchfulness* (as the 1st-level priest spell) once per day.
- At 3rd level, barakor can cast *iron vigil* (as the 2nd-level priest spell) or *sacred guardian* (as the 1st-level priest spell) once per day.
- At 3rd level, barakor become immune to attack forms, spells, spell-like abilities, and psionics that would put them to sleep. They still need natural sleep, however.
- At 5th level, barakor can cast *spike stones* (as the 5th-level priest spell) or *shield* (as the 1st-level wizard spell) once per day.
- At 7th level, barakor can cast *fire eyes* (as the 4th-level priest spell) once per day.
- At 7th level, barakor can make three melee attacks every two rounds.
- At 10th level, barakor can cast *unceasing vigilance of the holy sentinel* (as the 5th-level priest spell) or *wall of stone* (as the 5th-level wizard spell) once per day.
- At 10th level, barakor need only have half the normal amount of natural sleep per night to function as if fully rested and to naturally heal damage.
- At 13th level, barakor can cast *know alignment* (as the 2nd-level priest spell) at will. Unlike the priest spell, however, this granted power is unerring, overriding even the strongest magical concealments and misdirections. Spellcasting is not possible while exercising this granted power, but a barakor doing so need not remain stationary and can even participate in strenuous, acrobatic combat.
- At 13th level, barakor can make two melee attacks per round.
- At 15th level, barakor can cast *true seeing* (as the 5th-level priest spell) twice per day.

Gormite Spells

In addition to the spells listed below, priests of Gorm may cast the 1st-level priest spell *sentry of Helm* (known to dwarves as *sentry of Gorm*), which is detailed in *Faiths & Avatars* in the entry for Helm.

1st Level

Blessed Watchfulness (Pr 1; Alteration)

Sphere:	Guardian
Range:	Touch
Components:	V, S
Duration:	4 hours+1 hour/level
Casting Time:	4
Area of Effect:	Creature touched
Saving Throw:	None

By casting this spell, the caster confers exceptional powers of observation and alertness to one creature for the duration of the spell. While *blessed watchfulness* is in effect, the designated sentinel remains alert, awake, and vigilant for the duration of the spell. In fact, it takes a roll of 1 to surprise someone under this effect. Those under the effect of this spell resist *sleep* spells and similar magic as if they were 4 levels or Hit Dice higher than their actual level, and they gain a +2 bonus to saving throws against other spells or effects that could lower their guards or force them to abandon their watches, including *charm, beguiling, fear, emotion,* and similar mind-affecting spells. However, if the effect normally allows no saving throw, watchers who have *blessed watchfulness* in effect on them gain no special benefit.

2nd Level

Alert Allies (Pr 2; Divination, Alteration)

Sphere:	Thought
Range:	Touch
Components:	V, S
Duration:	Special
Casting Time:	1 round+1 round per creature touched
Area of Effect:	30 yard radius
Saving Throw:	None

This spell enables the priest to send an instantaneous mental missive to his or her comrades alerting them to a dangerous situation. It is not possible to send any message other than "Alert" by means of this spell, nor is two-way communication of any sort possible, but the true meaning of the mental missive, other than the fact that a dangerous situation exists, can be pre-arranged if so desired.

Alert allies can only be cast on awake, living, and sentient (animal [1] intelligence or higher) creatures. The somatic component of the spell involves the priest physically touching foreheads for one full round with each recipient. One ally, up to a maximum of 10 such individuals, can be linked by means of this spell per level of the spellcaster.

Once cast, the mental links forged by means of this spell last until the *alert* is broadcast or for at most 8 hours. An *alert* has a maximum range of 30 yards around the priest. Anyone beyond that range does not hear the alert, although the spell effect (and the mental link) ends nonetheless. Likewise, anyone maintaining a psionic defense shield, wearing a *ring of mind shielding*, or employing similar magics also does not receive the mental warning. However, if a recipient is asleep and that condition is not maintained by chemical or magical means (although it may have been induced by such), she or he immediately awakens and is aware that an *alert* has been issued.

It is possible to issue a mental missive and then perform another action aside from casting a spell in the same round. The *alert* broadcast effectively imposes an initiative penalty of 1 on any other course of action attempted in the same round.

Iron Vigil (Pr 2; Alteration)

Sphere:	Guardian
Range:	0
Components:	V, S
Duration:	1 week (seven days)+1 day/level
Casting Time:	1 turn
Area of Effect:	The caster
Saving Throw:	None

This spell allows the caster to ignore hunger, thirst, and extremes of climate for an extended period of time. While the spell is in effect, the priest requires no food or drink. She or he is effectively immune to exposure, dehydration, and heat or cold injury, since no naturally occurring climatic condition can cause him or her harm. (Lightning, floods, tornadoes, earthquakes, and other such hazardous phenomena can still cause physical injury, of course.)

Iron vigil allows the caster to ignore the need to sleep by choosing to mediate instead. While meditating, the caster can keep watch on his or her surroundings but suffers a +1 penalty to any surprise checks. If the character wishes to memorize spells, she or he must sleep normally.

At the spell's end, the priest must eat and drink; if no food or water is available, the character must make a Constitution check once every 4 hours with a cumulative –1 penalty or fall into a coma and perish within 1d3 days if she or he receives no aid. The caster also requires at least 4 hours of rest for each day that she or he did not eat, drink, or sleep during the vigil.

4th Level

Fire Eyes of Gorm (Pr 4; Evocation)

Sphere:	Combat
Range:	0
Components:	V, S, M
Duration:	1 round/level
Casting Time:	7
Area of Effect:	Ray, 1 foot long/level
Saving Throw:	½

This spell causes the priest's eyes to emit twin rays of fire. These thin, ruby-red beams are hot enough to burn holes in plate armor in 1 round and in most stone walls in 2 rounds. The eye beams cause 2d8 points of damage per round to any creature they touch except the caster (including items worn or carried). Creatures struck who succeed at a saving throw vs. spell sustain only half damage.

The caster can train his or her eye beams on a maximum of two creatures per round, attacking with the priest's normal THAC0. Beings struck by one beam in a round take the above damage. Beings struck by two beams in the same round take the above damage twice unless they are wearing armor, in which case they take the same damage as being struck by one beam and their armor must succeed at a saving throw vs. lightning or be destroyed. Magical items gain saving throw bonuses equal to any magical "plus" bonuses they possess. If the priest desires, she or he can forgo attacking a person and try to strike a particular item, attacking with the priest's normal THAC0 if two strikes are made or with a –4 penalty for a called shot if only one attack is made. Items other than magical armor must succeed at item saving throws vs. magical fire if they are struck or be destroyed. (Magical items, including magical armor, gain saving throw bonuses equal to any magical "plus" bonuses they possess. Artifacts and relics are not affected by this spell.) If the priest focuses on a stationary object (such as a wall), striking it is automatic, and the DM must adjudicate what degree of structural damage occurs within the amount of time the priest focuses the eye beams on the stationary object.

While the caster's eyes are emitting fire, she or he can see normally but cannot cast or wield any other magic. The caster can end the spell at will before it would expire normally. Emitting the beams can also be interrupted temporarily so that the priest can look at creatures and things without burning them. The spell does not stop the priest from engaging in physical activities (including combat) while it is active.

The caster is immune to the direct effects of his or her eye beams (or their reflection), but not to the effects of any fires they might start. Creatures immune to flame damage are unharmed by *fire eyes*.

The material component is the priest's holy symbol.

Haela Brightaxe
(Lady of the Fray, Luckmaiden, the Hard)

Demipower of the Beastlands, CG

PORTFOLIO:	Luck in battle, patron of dwarves who love to fight and who battle monsters, love of/joy of battle, dwarven monster kills, dwarven fighter adventurers
ALIASES:	None
DOMAIN NAME:	Brux/Findar Endar
SUPERIOR:	Moradin
ALLIES:	Arvoreen, Brandobaris, Cyrrollalee, Eilistraee, the Morndinsamman (except Abbathor, Deep Duerra, Laduguer), Tempus, Tymora
FOES:	Abbathor, Beshaba, Deep Duerra, Laduguer, Urdlen, the goblinkin and evil giant pantheons
SYMBOL:	An unsheathed sword encircled by a flaming bolt (a two-ended spiral of flame)
WOR. ALIGN.:	Any

Haela Brightaxe (HUH-ae-la BRITE-ax) is the patron of dwarves who love the fray, who wander the surface lands (especially in the North), who face unknown dangers, and who battle monsters. Although dwarves of all alignments venerate the Lady of the Fray, those Stout Folk of chaotic or neutral good alignment who love battle or exhibit berserker tendencies tend to actively embrace the worship of the Luckmaiden.

Haela dwells in a simple cave in the Beastlands, but she bothers none of the animals that dwell there, keeping to herself, hidden by everpresent mists in the depths of a forest. Findar Endar, as the grotto is known, is protected by her Guardians. Rarely at home, the Luckmaiden is usually to be found in wildspace or on a world such as Toril, wherever dwarves are enjoying battle but in need of aid.

Haela is well known among dwarves for her ready laugh, her booming voice, and her ever-cheerful nature. The Luckmaiden is charming, resourceful, and delivers gallows witticisms with a broad grin.

Although she recognizes no superior save Moradin, Haela is the only widely recognized dwarven demipower active in the Realms today, and as such, the Luckmaiden is ever-mindful of the wishes of the more established and more powerful members of the Morndinsamman. As a goddess of dwarven warriors, particularly those who travel far afield, Haela's portfolio overlaps with that of the Marthammor Duin, and she works closely with the Finder-of-Trails. Likewise, the Lady of the Fray maintains good relations with Clangeddin Silverbeard, the Father of Battles, into whose sphere of influence she also crosses.

Haela's Avatar (Fighter 25, Cleric 18, Wizard 16)

Haela appears as a powerfully muscled female dwarf. Sometimes she appears clad in fine dwarven scale mail or plate mail, and sometimes she manifests in naught but her long, flowing silver hair and beard. She dances and twirls about constantly, wielding a two-handed sword that cannot cut her. She often hurls it into the air and catches it by the blade, vaults up to a high ledge or balcony with a hand upon the sword's point, or slides down it exuberantly, in play. She casts spells from the spheres of all, combat, creation, guardian, healing, necromantic, protection, and sun. She favors spells from the schools of abjuration and invocation/evocation, although she can cast spells from any school.

AC 0; MV 24; HP 189; THAC0 –4; #AT 5/2 or 1
Dmg 2d12+13 (oversized *two-handed sword* +3, +8 Str, +2 spec. bonus in two-handed sword) or 1d10+8 (touch, +8 Str)
MR 40%; SZ M (6 feet high)
Str 20, Dex 21, Con 19, Int 17, Wis 18, Cha 22
Spells P: 10/10/9/9/6/4/2, W: 5/5/5/5/5/3/2/1
Saves PPDM 3, RSW 1*, PP 4, BW 4, Sp 6
  *Includes dwarf +5 Con save bonus to a minimum of 1. The Con save bonus also applies to saves vs. poison to a minimum of 1.

Special Att/Def: She wields *Flamebolt*, an over-sized (for her height) *two-handed sword* +3 (2d12 points of base damage) that is always encircled by tongues of spiraling, but harmless, flame while she fights. Haela can will the blade to vanish or reappear freely and it does so instantly, but *Flamebolt* cannot reappear on the same round in which it vanishes. Haela can parry just as well when weaponless as when she bears a weapon. She can be struck only by +1 or better magical weapons.

Once per turn Haela can call into being her *Brightaxe*, a shining silver throwing axe as tall as a man. It appears in midair in 1 round and flashes through the air in accordance to her will in the next round. *Brightaxe* flies up to 140 feet and deals any creature struck by it 3d12 points of damage (no saving throw allowed), and (if mortal) *stunning* them (no voluntary activities, including spellcasting or magical activations of any kind) for the following round.

Once per day Haela can cast *ironguard* (as the 5th-level wizard spell detailed in *Pages from the Mages*) upon herself, a power that lasts for nine rounds with all the attendant drawbacks such as the inability to wield a metal weapon. After invoking *ironguard*, Haela can, by touch, transfer this protection to another creature at any time while it is active.

Once per day, Haela can employ *resurrection* (as the 7th-level priest spell) on any one being without penalty. Creatures so restored to life automatically succeed at their resurrection survival checks. Haela customarily only *resurrects* dwarves who died valiantly in battle, although if dwarves beg her to, she uses this power to aid nondwarven companions and allies of the dwarves.

Haela usually appears in a spectacular blue-white burst of flames that blossom from nowhere and do no damage. Once present, she engages the fiercest foe of, or the creature offering the most pressing danger to, the dwarves that she can find. She battles it for 4 rounds, and if it is slain, attacks a second opponent of the dwarves for the remaining round or rounds. The Luckmaiden then empowers a dwarf and/or a weapon (see Other Manifestations, below) and disappears with a hand held high. Haela's presence causes such exultation in dwarves that they fight with a +1 bonus on all attack rolls while they can see her. In cases where Haela aids beleaguered dwarves, she usually dances in front of their enemies, engaging and parrying rather than striking to do damage, allowing the dwarves time to regroup and drag their wounded to safety. Then she *heals* 2d4 dwarves (again see Other Manifestations, below), strikes one blow in earnest, and vanishes, hurrying on to the next conflict.

In such cases, consider Haela able to engage 1d8 creatures while parrying their attacks in her battle dance. She cannot stop magical attacks, but automatically ruins all spellcasting, and lessens/thwarts physical attacks upon her or the dwarves she is protecting as follows:

- If Haela faces one or two opponents, all attacks are automatically thwarted, and the creatures cannot advance against her.
- If Haela faces three, four, or five opponents, all their attack rolls are made at a penalty of –3, and they receive a –1 penalty to damage.
- If Haela faces six, seven, or eight opponents, all their attack rolls are made at a penalty of –1, but there is no effect on damage they inflict.
- Creatures in excess of eight are unaffected by Haela's dance of battle: they get through to attack normally. Count flying creatures as two opponents when using these totals. If Haela deems it necessary to *heal* (once per round) while dancing, her healing action lessens her parrying ability by 2 opponents.
- Any successful attacks on Haela while she is parrying do half damage if she is armed and full damage if she is unarmed.

Haela is seldom in any one place for long, and almost never returns to the same fray or dwarven individuals twice in a day. However, she favors especially bold or valiant dwarves, and may, in the course of their lives, aid them repeatedly. It is said that she appears when her favorites die, to carry their souls away to become her Guardians, and to avenge their deaths by pursuing and slaying their killers, however long it takes and no matter how powerful they are. If such killers are subsequently *raised*, Haela takes no further action against them.

Other Manifestations

Haela manifests only rarely, preferring to appear directly instead. When she does manifest, it is either in cases where she will not be otherwise needed or to help dwarves hold on until she can arrive later to help.

Haela's manifestations always involve an aura of silvery flames, shot through with blue-white and amber sparks. These are images only, not true flames or sparks, and cannot ignite anything.

If Haela's aura surrounds a dwarf, her power *heals* the dwarf of all injuries and allows the dwarf to strike at a +4 bonus to attack for 1d4+1 rounds. This imbues the dwarf with power enough to consider any weapons wielded to be silver and equivalent to +4 magical weapons, for purposes of what can be hit by the empowered dwarf.

If Haela's aura surrounds a weapon, it is rendered supreme for 1d4+1 rounds: Any attacks made with it during this time cannot miss, and do full normal damage. If a weapon empowered by Haela is already magical, its magical properties are suspended by Haela's magic and cannot operate (or be harmed or drained): The weapon does only physical damage until Haela's power fades.

Haela is served primarily by the spirits of fallen dwarven warriors who become her Guardians (einheriar), but on occasion other creatures of the Upper Planes, including aasimon (particularly agathinon), asuras, bariaurs, courage incarnates, hollyphants, quesar, and warden beasts act on her behalf. She manifests her pleasure with the discovery of bloodstones, carnelians, jacinths, jargoons, red-hued jaspers, red-hued orls, red tears, crimson-hued rubies, red spinels, and red-hued ziose stones. She manifests her displeasure when such gems dissolve into tiny puddles of blood when touched.

The Church

Clergy:	Clerics, crusaders, specialty priests
Clergy's Align.:	NG, CG, N, CN
Turn Undead:	C: Yes, Cru: No, SP: No
Cmnd. Undead:	C: No, Cru: No, SP: Yes

All clerics (including fighter/clerics), crusaders, and specialty priests (including fighter/specialty priests) of Haela receive religion (dwarven) and reading/writing (Dethek runes) as bonus nonweapon proficiencies. Clerics of Haela can use any weapons, not just bludgeoning (wholly Type B) weapons. Clerics of Haela (as well as fighter/clerics) cannot turn undead before 7th level, but they always strike at +2 on all attack and damage rolls against undead creatures. At 7th level and above, clerics (including multiclassed clerics) can turn undead as other clerics do, but as a cleric of four levels less than their current level. These modifications apply only to the cleric class. Before the Time of Troubles, the priesthood of Haela was all female; since then, some males have joined the clergy.

Haela is well regarded by shield dwarves, particularly wanderers, and her cult is slowly growing among the younger gold dwarves of the South. The Luckmaiden is well known and well regarded among nondwarven adventurers of the North through the near-legendary deeds of her followers, but she is commonly seen as nothing more than a dwarven god of berserkers—akin to bloodthirsty Garagos—by the more sedentary inhabitants of human and elven cities.

Temples of Haela are caves or underground rooms, sometimes in old abandoned holds or the cellars of human ruins. They are typically storehouses of food, small smithies, and armories crammed with odd weapons and armor, and are never guarded by less than a dozen priests (more often, 16 to 20 are in residence). There is always a highly destructive trap set somewhere in such a temple: If the dwarves are slain or forced out, no enemy of the dwarves will get the store of weapons without taking heavy losses. One famous temple of Haela, overrun by orcs near Amphail, proved to have a trap of six separate *blade barriers* that came into being one after another and used the cached weapons of the temple as the whirling weapons.

Novices of Haela, like novices of Clangeddin, are known as the Unblooded. Full priests are known as Blades of the Brightaxe. In ascending order of rank, the titles used by Haelan priests are First Blood, Deadly Dirk, Stout Spear, Sharp Axe, Shining Sword, Flamebolt, and Brightaxe. High Old Ones have individual titles but are collectively known as the Hallowed Crimson. Specialty priests are known as luckmaidens. The clergy of Haela includes shield dwarves (70%), gold dwarves (28%), and gray dwarves (2%). Haela's clergy is evenly divided between specialty priests (34%), clerics (33%), and crusaders (33%). Fully one-half of the specialty priests and clerics are fighter/specialty priests and fighter/clerics, respectively. The gender mix of Haela's clergy is about 85% female and 15% male, though only females can be luckmaidens.

Dogma: Through battle there is validation, liberation, and exultation. Trust in Haela to see you through the fray, and the monsters of the world shall fall to the sharp blades of your axes, regardless of their apparent strength and numbers. The Luckmaiden blesses those dwarves who believe in her beneficence, and she, through her faithful, will always be there for the beleaguered and the besieged. Rejoice the power of your swing in battle, the sound of your weapon smiting a worthy foe, and the challenge of the fray. If asked, show mercy on a noble foe who abides by a code of honor, but hold not your hand against the treacherous, the liars, and the honorless.

Day-to-Day Activities: Priests of Haela wander throughout the Realms, aiding dwarves in battle. They wander because no priest knows where or when she or he will be needed—each relies upon Haela's guiding hand to position him or her as necessary.

Blades of the Brightaxe aid beleaguered dwarves (and known allies and companions of dwarves) against creatures of all sorts by healing, casting spells, and fighting alongside them. Their objectives are to achieve victory for the dwarven side and to allow the maximum possible number of dwarves to survive. The priests wish also to make all dwarves comfortable with their own skills in combat—to Haela's worshipers, battle-skills are needed to guide the hands of all dwarves if the Stout Folk are to survive.

Priests of Haela are always heavily armed and are often skilled at weapon and armor repair. They freely give away the weapons they carry to dwarves in need but always keep at least one weapon for themselves, although it may be well hidden. They practice throwing weapons in a variety of ways, such as onto ledges, to cut ropes, and to land upright, points buried in the turf, beside those needing them. Priests of Haela who attempt to deliver a weapon in such a manner gain a +3 bonus to their Dexterity checks.

The senior priests of Haela teach their juniors much concerning tactics, secrets, and hints for fighting specific monsters, and knowledge of their habits, lairs, and weaknesses. A DM can impart detailed information from the MONSTROUS MANUAL tome to PCs who ask a priest of Haela the right questions. All individuals or groups aided by a priest of Haela are expected to pay for the aid with a spare weapon that the priest can give to some other

needy band. Failing that, a shield, pair of gauntlets, or other armor or useful gear can be substituted. It is considered bad form to give the priest back a weapon she or he just gave you.

Holy Days/Important Ceremonies: The followers of the Luckmaiden celebrate three holy days of note. The first such day of the year, celebrated annually on Greengrass, is known as the Time of the Spawning. On this day Haela's clergy prepare for the next wave of orcs and other monsters to pour forth from the occupied holds of long-fallen dwarves to threaten the remaining Stout Folk once again. The Time of Spawning is marked by grim ceremonies of preparation for the coming onslaught and includes endless choruses of battle hymns, rhythmic chanting to the beat of endless drumming, and the ritual shattering of weapons and armor seized from previous opponents.

The second major holy day of the Haelan faith is known as the Axe Held High, a day that glorifies the valor of the Lady of the Fray and her role in defending the Stout Folk against their ancient foes. On this day of joyous celebration, ceremonies are held at midday, outdoors in the full embrace of the sun. The followers of the Luckmaiden hold that an unsheathed sword appears momentarily in the center of the solar orb at high noon. While no other faith has ever reported such an apparition, every member of the Blades of the Brightaxe in good standing with Haela who participates in the proscribed rituals receives the benefits of her enveloping aura (see Other Manifestations above) for the next twenty-four hours.

Finally, the Feast of the Moon is celebrated by the followers of Haela as the Commemoration of the Fallen. On this day, those dwarves and nondwarves alike who fell in the defense of the Stout Folk while battling monstrous opponents are remembered by the recounting of their battles and the consecration of new armor and weapons in their memory.

On all such holy days, Haela's devout followers are expected to offer several drops of their own blood (one per level of the follower) as well as the blood of enemies of the dwarves they have defeated since the previous holy day (one drop of blood per foe, and one foe per level of the follower).

Major Centers of Worship: Endar Aglandtor, the Sword Grotto, is an abbey of the Luckmaiden hidden in a series of dwarf-dug caverns hewn from the base of a granite uprising known as the Tor of Swords. Located north-northwest of the Hill of Lost Souls, the Tor of Swords stands just east of the most northerly of the easternmost loops that the ever-twisting Winding Water makes. The hill once marked the northernmost border of the Helbryn, the great hunting preserve of the long-fallen dwarven kingdom of Oghrann. Today the Tor of Swords serves as the chapter house of Haela's Host (see below) under the able leadership of Blade of the Crimson Axe Aglaya Rockfist, daul of Rorrina, blood of Helmma. From their isolated redoubt, the priests of the militant order keep watch over the Hill of Lost Souls, the Battle of Bones, and other unnamed battlefields in the region where dwarven warriors fell long ago. The clerics, crusaders, and specialty priests of Haela's Host clash frequently with the monsters of the Serpent Hills, the Marsh of Chelimber, and the Forest of Wyrms, and they are very effective in keeping monstrous population of the region in check. The Tor of Swords is named for the quintet of sentient magical swords said to have been entombed within the hill before the erection of the Standing Stone. Since most tales confuse the Tor of Swords with the nearby Dungeon of Swords, located to the northwest in the Serpent Hills, few adventuring bands have ever explored the isolated knoll, and none have found the legendary blades. Assuming the sentient swords are more than myth, it is likely they are now wielded by the ablest swordswomen of Haela's Host.

Torstultok, the Hall of Grand Hunts, is a temple-fortress of Haela well known among the Stout Folk of the North for the numerous all-dwarven and mixed-race adventuring companies it sponsors to reclaim long-lost dwarven relics from orc-held halls. Torstultok is located in the Forlorn Hills, a region best known for its two most famous ruins: the Crumbling Stair and the House of Stone. The temple is located in a sprawling complex of tunnels and grand halls beneath the eastern end of the Watchers of the North, the line of hills that mark the northern edge of the Forlorn Hills. Torstultok was known as Firehammer Hold before the Fallen Kingdom fell, and much treasure is still ascribed to the latter name in the tales of the North. Although those same tales claim that the dwarves of Firehammer Hold perished in a plague that ravaged the hold shortly after the founding of the Kingdom of Man, in truth, the dwarves' numbers dwindled over time, and the leaders of the hold staged the evidence of a deadly plague in order to increase the security of those dwarves who remained.

An unexpected consequence of this action was the arrival in subsequent centuries of treasure-hungry adventurers seeking long-lost dwarven hordes of gold. To assuage the anger of such would-be-plunderers, the dwarves began a practice of hiring such wanderers to seek out other dwarven holds that they knew to be occupied by orcs. From this tradition evolved the hold's current role as a clearinghouse for battle-loving dwarves and adventurers of other races seeking glory amidst the ruins of long-fallen dwarven kingdoms. Haela's clergy have even begun to lure adventurers to the temple by means of ancient-looking, incomplete maps and other enticing lures. One such example may be found on the walls of a not-so-secret hidden room in the Singing Sprite, a slate-shingled, many-gabled stone inn located in the bowl between the three hills that the village of Secomber is built upon.

Affiliated Orders: Numerous religious and military orders have been founded by the followers of the Luckmaiden in past centuries, but few ever survive longer than a generation or two. Some of the most famous orders in existence today include Haela's Host (see above), the Dauls of the Luckmaiden, the Shining Host of the Underdeeps, the Dancing Damsels of the Brightaxe, and the hippogriff-mounted Skyriders of Aglandar (as the Great Rift is known in dwarvish). Most orders are known for the valor and daring of their members, and such bands typically focus their efforts on reducing the population of evil monsters in the region in which they are based.

Priestly Vestments: Haela's clergy favor either armor or plain steel-gray robes, with an overcloak of scarlet and crimson footwear, as ceremonial vestments. An open-faced helm is always worn. The holy symbol of the faith is a steel medallion embossed with Haela's symbol.

Adventuring Garb: When adventuring, the Luckmaiden's clergy garb themselves in the best armor available—chain mail is preferred—and always seek to wield weapons of the finest quality. Helms are always worn, but they need not be open-faced.

In honor of an ancient custom, priests of Haela are forever toting large sacks of caltrops around, hoping to get a chance to use them. (About 35 to 75 caltrops can fit in a large sack, depending on the size of the caltrops and the sack. Caltrops are covered in the *Arms and Equipment Guide.*) As Ardeep crumbled and the Fallen Kingdom splintered centuries ago, Haela's priests, along with many others, fought valiantly, if ultimately futilely, to preserve what remained of the Realm of Three Crowns along the banks of the River Delimbiyr. At that time, numerous halfling farmers made their homes in the verdant farmland surrounding Secomber under the protective aegis of the allied priests of Haela based in the nearby Firehammer Hold. In thanks for the vigilant axes of the Luckmaiden's clergy and the ready supply of weapons they shared, the Little Folk continually repaid Haela's valiant priests with bags of caltrops—typically three at a time. This practice is now both a joke and an affectionate tradition for both groups.

Specialty Priests (Luckmaidens)

REQUIREMENTS:	Strength 11, Dexterity 10, Wisdom 9
PRIME REQ.:	Strength, Dexterity, Wisdom
ALIGNMENT:	CG, NG
WEAPONS:	Any
ARMOR:	Any
MAJOR SPHERES:	All, combat, guardian, healing, protection, travelers, war
MINOR SPHERES:	Creation, divination, necromantic, summoning, sun
MAGICAL ITEMS:	Same as clerics
REQ. PROFS:	Weaponsmithing
BONUS PROFS:	Blind-fighting, tumbling

- Luckmaidens must be female dwarves. While most luckmaidens are shield dwarves and many of the rest are gold dwarves, dwarves of nearly every subrace are called to be specialty priests of Haela's clergy.
- Luckmaidens are allowed to multiclass as fighter/luckmaidens, and if the DM allows kits for multiclassed characters, they may take any allowed fighter/cleric kit for dwarves.
- Luckmaidens may select nonweapon proficiencies from the warrior group without penalty.
- Luckmaidens have a +2 bonus on all saving throws when actively participating in melee combat.

- Luckmaidens can cast *armor*, on themselves only, or *shield* (as the 1st-level wizard spells) once per day.
- At 3rd level, luckmaidens can cast *aid* (as the 2nd-level priest spell) or *strength* (as the 2nd-level wizard spell) on themselves only, once per day.
- At 5th level, luckmaidens can cast *draw upon holy might* or *lighten load* (as the 2nd-level priest spells) once per day.
- At 7th level, luckmaidens can cast *detect weapons* (as the 1st-level priest spell) at will.
- At 7th level, luckmaidens who are not multiclassed can make three melee attacks every two rounds.
- At 10th level, luckmaidens can cast *prayer* (as the 6th-level priest spell) or *flame strike* (as the 5th-level priest spell) once per day.
- At 13th level, luckmaidens who are not multiclassed can make two melee attacks per round.
- At 15th level, luckmaidens can cast *heal* or *heroes' feast* (as the 6th-level priest spells) once per day.

Haelan Spells

1st Level

Detect Weapons (Pr 1; Divination)

Sphere:	Divination
Range:	0
Components:	V, S, M
Duration:	1 turn
Casting Time:	1 round
Area of Effect:	10 feet × 90 feet
Saving Throw:	None

When the *detect weapons* spell is cast, the priest detects weapons in a path 10 feet wide and up to 90 feet long in the direction she or he is facing. The caster can turn, scanning a 60° arc per round. The spell is blocked by solid stone at least 1 foot thick, solid metal at least 1 inch thick, or solid wood at least 1 yard thick. In addition, the caster has a 10% chance per level to determine if a specific type of weapon is present. One type of weapon can be checked for each round.

The spell detects concealed, *invisible*, and improvised weapons that have been used to harm or are carried with intent to harm. Broken weapons are detected only if still usable (for example, a spear with its shaft snapped in half). In some old ruins, the sheer number of abandoned weapons renders this spell ineffective except to search for particular types of weapons, as all checking in most directions will reveal the presence of weapons.

The spell requires the use of the priest's holy symbol.

2nd Level

Haela's Battle Blessing (Pr 2; Alteration)

Sphere:	Combat
Range:	Touch
Components:	V, S, M
Duration:	2 rounds+1 round/level
Casting Time:	5
Area of Effect:	Creature touched
Saving Throw:	None

Haela's battle blessing aids the recipient in battle. Normally a roll of a 20 on an attack roll is always a hit. When this spell is used by the priest or an ally, the chances of an automatic hit are improved. If cast by a priest of 8th level or less, both a 19 or a 20 are always hits on an attack roll by the spell recipient. If cast by a priest of 9th level or greater, an 18 is also always a hit on an attack roll by the recipient. This spell does not, by itself, allow damage to be inflicted on creatures vulnerable only to magical weapons.

The spell requires the use of the priest's holy symbol.

Hurl Rock (Pr 2; Alteration) *Reversible*

Sphere:	Combat
Range:	10 yards/level
Components:	V, S, M
Duration:	1 round
Casting Time:	1
Area of Effect:	One rock (see below)
Saving Throw:	None

This spell allows a dwarf to suddenly and violently use *telekinesis* on a loose rock, hurling it as a missile. Only stone can be used, either natural stone or petrified objects. The stone must be loose; it cannot be part of a wall, rock face, or ceiling. The projectile strikes with the caster's THAC0. The range of this spell refers to the distance between the priest and the stone missile. The projectile can leap up to 30 feet vertically and up to 30 feet horizontally. Misses use "Table 45: Grenade-Like Missile Effects" in the Dungeon Master *Guide*.

The caster can move up to 2 cubic feet/level. Rocks that are too large are detected as such; the priest can choose another rock in the same round, but if it is also too large, the spell is wasted.

At times, it may be important to know what damage the missile itself sustains after being hurled; for instance, if it is a fragile, valuable object or ,say, a petrified companion. The missile suffers 2d4 points of damage from its use in this spell and double that damage if it falls more than 50 feet in the process. This shatters the missile if it is brought to 0 hit points. Assume rocky missiles to have an average hit point total of 6 per 2 cubic feet, so that a rock of the maximum size that a 3rd-level priest can move (6 cubic feet) has 18 hit points.

Rocky missiles that shatter spray shrapnel; all creatures within 10 feet of the landing site of a shattering missile must succeed at a saving throw vs. spell or suffer 1d4+1 points of damage.

Any item struck by the missile or its shrapnel (see above) must succeed at an item saving throw vs. crushing blow. A being struck by the missile is hurt as follows:

Rock Volume (in Cubic Feet)	Damage
1–2	2d4
3–4	2d8
5–6	2d10
7–8	3d8
9–10	3d10
More than 10	4d12

Note that a typical man-sized statue is 12 cubic feet.

The reverse of this spell, *rock shield*, allows the caster to deflect rocky missiles of all types and from all sources. The shield remains in effect for 1 round/level, infallible against all missiles whose edges contain or are made of stone. Once cast, it does not require continued concentration or further action. The deflections are in directions uncontrollable by the user of the shield. Use "Table 45: Grenade-Like Missile Effects" in the Dungeon Master *Guide* to determine their destination, noting that deflections may hit companions of the *shield*-user or his or her enemies. *Rock shield* is incompatible with *protection from normal missiles*.

The material component of this spell is a tiny pebble held in the priest's hand and not consumed during casting. The reverse of the spell requires two small pebbles (which are not consumed) and a translucent piece of glass, mica, ice, crystal, or a gem.

Laduguer

(The Exile, the Gray Protector, Master of Crafts,
the Slave Driver, the Taskmaster, the Harsh)

Intermediate Power of Acheron, LE

Portfolio:	Magical weapon creation, skilled artisans, magic, the gray dwarf race, protector of gray dwarves
Aliases:	None
Domain Name:	Thuldanin/Hammergrim
Superior:	Moradin (estranged)
Allies:	Deep Duerra, Grumbar
Foes:	Blibdoolpoolp, Blood Queen, Callarduran Smoothhands, Diinkarazan, Diirinka, Great Mother, Gzemnid, Ilsensine, Ilxendren, Laogzed, Maanzecorian (dead), the Morndinsamman (except Deep Duerra, Dugmaren Brightmantle, and Sharindlar), Orcus (dead)/Tenebrous (undead), Psilofyr, Shevarash, Urdlen, the drow pantheon

Symbol:	Shield with broken crossbow bolt motif
Wor. Align.:	LN, N, LE, NE

Laduguer (LAA-duh-gwur) is the patron of the duergar, or gray dwarves, a malevolent breed of dwarves who dwell in the dark reaches of the Underdark and who withdrew from the rest of dwarven society long ago along with their god. The Exile is venerated by most gray dwarves as the protector of the race who defends them from the countless other creatures of the Underdark who wish to enslave them and seize their tunnels, mines, and crafts. Duergar craftsmen, particularly those who seek to create magical weapons, pay particular homage to Laduguer.

Laduguer has long been estranged from the other members of the Morndinsamman, and he regards them as lazy, indolent, and feckless. The reasons behind the Gray Protector's exile vary according to the perspective of the speaker: The Morndinsamman, as well as most gold and shield dwarves, hold that Laduguer was banished by Moradin for his crimes, while Laduguer, as well as most gray dwarves, asserts that he took a stand on principle against the other dwarven gods, and that his exile is self-imposed. The Exile particularly loathes Moradin, his nominal superior, and the personal animosity between the two accounts for much of Laduguer's enmity against the rest of the dwarven pantheon. In fact, Laduguer's only ally is Deep Duerra, a once-mortal demipower he elevated to the rank of divinity.

The withdrawal of Laduguer's followers to the Underdark and their subsequent territorial conflicts with races such as aboleth, beholders, derro, drow, illithids, ixzan, kuo-toa, myconids, svirfneblin, and troglodytes has created a great deal of strife and enmity between the Exile and other powers with an interest in the Night Below. Although he once managed to win hegemony over the giant tarantulas known as steeders during a brief alliance with Lolth, the Spider Queen and the Gray Protector have long feuded as their followers battled. Likewise Ilsensine, the Great Brain of the illithid race, has long sought revenge against Laduguer for some ancient slight. The Abyssal Lord once known as Orcus is also a target of Laduguer's wrath, for the Prince of the Undead once subverted the worship of the duergar of the Galenas beneath the Mines of Bloodstone.

Laduguer is habitually grim, gloomy, and joyless. The Exile's nature is certainly evilly inclined, but much of this is the evil of a being turned in on itself and bitter at what he sees as being unvalued and rejected by the other dwarven powers. Laduguer is supremely lawful, unbending and harsh, and he demands constant toil under harsh conditions from the duergar. He does reward hard work by teaching the crafting of magical items (especially weapons) and by extending his protection. The Exile sends an avatar to defend a hardworking and oppressed duergar community by use of protective and warding magic, rarely entering into open battle. (It is assumed that the Invisible Art (psionics), as detailed in Player's Option: *Skills & Powers* is permitted in the campaign if Laduguer is included in the dwarven pantheon. If the DM has only the *Complete Psionics Handbook*, appropriate adjustments will need to be made to the statistics given for Laduguer's avatar, below.)

Laduguer's Avatar

(Fighter 33, Cleric 25, Thief 25, Psionicist 23, Wizard 20)

Laduguer appears as a tall, gaunt duergar with skin coloring that can change from gray to brown shades to match his environment. The Exile is bald and always wears a frown. He favors spells from the spheres of all, creation, elemental (earth), guardian, protection, war, and wards and from the schools of abjuration and invocation/evocation, although he can cast spells from any sphere or school. If the Invisible Art (psionics) is permitted in the campaign, Laduguer has access to all attack and defense form, as well as all disciplines, devotions, and sciences.

AC –5; MV 12 or 15; HP 225; THAC0 –10; #AT 5/2
Dmg 1d4+17 (*war hammer +4*, +10 Str, +2 spec. bonus in war hammer)
MR 75%; SZ M (6 feet high) or Huge (13 feet high)
Str 22, Dex 20, Con 21, Int 20, Wis 18, Cha 19
Spells P: 11/11/10/10/9/8/4, W: 5/5/5/5/4/4/4/2
Psionic Summary: Mental #AT: 2; Mental THAC0 –2; Mental AC –10;

Dis all/Sci all/Dev all; PSPs: 265; Att: all; Def all.
Saves** PPDM 2, RSW 1*, PP 4, BW 4, Sp 5

*Includes dwarf +6 Con save bonus to a minimum of 1. The Con save bonus also applies to saves vs. poison to a minimum of 1. **Because he is a psionicist, an additional +2 bonus to all saving throws vs. enchantment/charm spells should be applied as needed.

Special Att/Def: Laduguer wields *Grimhammer*, a *war hammer +4* that engenders *hopelessness* (as the 4th-level wizard spell *emotion*) on any successful hit if the target fails a saving throw vs. spell. He wears *chain mail +4* and carries a *shield +1*, a bulwark that also gives him immunity to normal missiles. He wears a magical ring that can be changed to any protective type (*feather falling*, *fire resistance*, *free action*, *mind shielding*, *protection +5*, *regeneration*, or *spell turning*) once per day per function for up to 6 turns each.

The Exile can cast *protection from good, 10-foot radius*, and *wall of force* three times per day each. Laduguer can cast *fool's gold*, *dig*, *enchanted weapon*, *stoneskin*, *conjure (earth) elemental*, *fabricate*, *passwall*, *stone shape*, *wall of stone*, and *enchant an item* once per day each. He is permanently protected from attack by animated or living mineral creatures (golems, galeb duhr, earth elementals, etc.), and he is also completely immune to all mind-affecting spell, power, or psionic effect. He can be struck only by +2 or better magical weapons.

If slain, Laduguer becomes an entity akin to a ghost. The Exile's ghostlike anima form cannot be turned and can become invisible at will. He can work magic and employ a ghost's attacks, and he has half his normal hit points.

Other Manifestations

Laduguer's power is usually seen as a flickering dark radiance enveloping an area, weapon, or person that is temporarily imbued with the god's power. An empowered area gains one of the following effects for 1 hour: *guards and wards* (as the 6th-level wizard spell); *wardmist* (as the 7th-level wizard spell detailed in *Volo's Guide to the North*, *Volo's Guide to the Sword Coast*, and *Wizard's Spell Compendium, Volume 4*). An empowered weapon gains one of the following effects for 1 turn: *bladethirst* (as the 2nd-level wizard spell detailed in *Pages from the Mages*); *enchanted weapon* (as the 4th-level wizard spell); *flame tongue*, temporarily imbuing the powers of the magic sword of the same name (as detailed in the DUNGEON MASTER Guide). An empowered being gains one of the following effects for 1 turn: *magical vestment* (as the 3rd-level priest spell); *fire shield* (as the 4th-level wizard spell); *protection from normal missiles* (as the 3rd-level wizard spell); *globe of invulnerability* (as the 6th-level wizard spell).

Dwarven Powers: Deep Duerra and Laduguer

Laduguer is served by ash mephits, azer, baatezu, baku, Dark Ones, banelar, bone nagas, brain moles, cerebral parasites, chaggrin, dark nagas, demaraxes, earth elementals, earth elemental vermin (crawlers), earth mephits, earth weirds, fhorges, gray oozes with psionic ability, hammer golems, helmed horrors, hook spiders, intellect devourers, ironmaws, imps, incarnates of anger and pride, living steel, maelephants, meenlocks, mineral mephits, observers, razorvine, reaves, rust dragons, rust monsters, sandmen, shadowdrakes, steeders, stone wolves, sword spirits, su-monsters, tso, werebadgers, xavers, and yugoloths. He demonstrates his favor through the discovery of adamant, black sapphires, bloodstones, diamonds, hizagkuur, mithral, and silver, but does not otherwise send omens to his priests.

Steeder: AC 4; MV 12; HD 4; THAC0 17; #AT 1; Dmg 1d8 (bite); SA cling, leap; SW suffers double damage leaping onto a set spear or spike; SZ L (4′ high, 8′ long); ML Avg (11); Int low (5–7); AL N; XP 270.

Notes: Steeders lack a poisonous bite, attacking with sharp mandibles. Gray dwarves ride steeders using leather saddles. The dwarves use a complex series of prods and straps to control the steeders. Only steeders with 20 or more hit points are used as mounts. Steeders can move on walls or ceilings at half their normal movement rate thanks to a sticky secretion exuded by their feet and can cling to a surface with only a single foot. Steeder saddles are constructed to allow for this. Steeders do not spin webs, nor can they move in them.

SA—There is a 50% chance a steeder tries to cling to its prey. This requires an attack roll against AC 10, modified by Dexterity and magical adjustments. After clinging to a victim, a steeder can automatically bite. A victim can escape by rolling a successful Dexterity or Strength check (player's choice which) with a –10 penalty. While held, victims suffer a –2 penalty to attack and damage rolls. Once every 3 rounds steeders can leap 240 feet in any direction, even when mounted. This is considered a charging attack.

The Church

CLERGY: Clerics, crusaders, specialty priests
CLERGY'S ALIGN.: LN, LE
TURN UNDEAD: C: Yes, Cru: No, SP: No
CMND. UNDEAD: C: No, Cru: No, SP: No

All clerics (including multiclassed cleric combinations), crusaders, and specialty priests (including specialty priest/psionicists) of Laduguer receive religion (dwarven) and reading/writing (Dethek runes) as bonus nonweapon proficiencies. If the Invisible Art (psionics) is permitted in the campaign, priests of Laduguer of any type, including clerics, crusaders, specialty priests, cleric/thieves, and fighter/clerics, may multiclass with the psionicist class as well, allowing dwarven clergy of Laduguer in certain cases to multiclass in three classes (cleric/ thief/psionicist or fighter/cleric/ psionicist). Clerics of Laduguer (including multiclassed clerics) cannot turn undead before 7th level, but they always strike at +2 on all attack and damage rolls against undead creatures. At 7th level and above, clerics can turn undead as other clerics do, but as a cleric of four levels less than their current level. These modifications apply only to the cleric class. Before the Time of Troubles, Laduguer's priesthood was exclusively male. Since that time, some females have joined the clergy.

Within gray dwarven communities, Laduguer and his clergy are considered strict taskmasters whose strengths and mandates ensure the very survival of the duergar. Few gray dwarves resent the Exile's mercilessly high standards, and most duergar respect him for his principled stand against the lazy and weak Morndinsamman and their shield and gold dwarven followers. Shield dwarves, gold dwarves, and svirfneblin regard Laduguer and his followers as embittered fools deserving of their fates who have done much to undermine the strength of the dwarven race in both their absence and their assaults on nonduergar dwarven holds. Other races in the Underdark have little sympathy for the gray dwarves or their embittered god and seek only to destroy or subjugate them.

Temples of Laduguer are grim, smoke-filled halls hewn from solid rock and bereft of adornment, aside from weapons and armor demonstrating the skilled craftsmanship of the Exile's priests. Laduguer's houses of worship are filled with armories, barracks, smithies, storerooms, and steeder stables.

Many are built directly atop mine shafts from which the raw materials are extracted. Great coal-burning forges provide the only warmth, and their ashen exhaust covers ever surface in dark soot. Clerical guards, many of them mounted on steeders, are everywhere, overseeing the skilled smith-work that proceeds without pause.

Novices of Laduguer are known as the Untempered. Full priests of the Exile are known as Grimcloaks. In ascending order of rank, the titles used by Ladugueran priests are Deep Adept, Dark Craftsman, Invisible Artisan, Rune Weaver, Grim Guardian, and Doom Knight. High Old Ones have individual titles but are collectively known as the Ardukes of the Gray Gloom. Specialty priests are known as thuldor, a dwarvish word that can be loosely translated as *those who endure*. The clergy of Laduguer consists primarily of gray dwarves (99%), but a handful of embittered and/or exiled gold dwarves, shield dwarves, and wild dwarves serve the Exile as well. Laduguer's clergy consists primarily of specialty priests (55%), but includes clerics (16%), crusaders (14%), fighter/clerics (8%), and cleric/thieves (7%). If the Invisible Art (psionics) is permitted in the campaign, two-thirds of each group of priests multiclass the psionicist class as well. The overwhelming majority of the clergy (95%) is male.

Dogma: The children of Laduguer have rejected the indolent and feeble gods of their forefathers and withdrawn from their lazy once-kin so as not to be tainted by their weaknesses. Strict obedience to superiors, dedication to one's craft, and endless toil are necessary to achieve wealth, security, and power. The hands of a craftsman are his tools, and a master craftsman always uses the most appropriate tools available. Nothing is ever easy, nor should it be. Suffer pain stoically and remain aloof, for to show or even feel emotion is to demonstrate weakness. Those who are weak are undeserving and will suffer an appropriate fate. Adversity is Laduguer's forge, and the harsh trials through which the duergar must pass are his hammer blows—endure all and become stronger than adamantite.

Day-to-Day Activities: Laduguer's priests serve as the leaders, defenders, and elite artisans of gray dwarven society. As reflected in the title given to High Old Ones—*arduke* being a dwarven title for clan leader—Laduguer's clergy derive their spiritual and temporal authority from the role the Exile's early priests played in leading the ancestors of the gray dwarves away from the rest of dwarven society. Unlike gold and shield dwarven cultures where religious and clan leadership are usually distinct, the duergar make no distinction between the two roles. As the protectors of duergar enclaves, members of Laduguer's clergy command and serve in the military and are ultimately responsible for the care, feeding, and training of steeders. They are responsible for the brewing of poisons, the infliction of torture, and the exploitation of slaves. To ensure the safety of the gray dwarves as a whole, Laduguer's priests forcefully repel contacts from other races, permitting trade only under very controlled circumstances far removed from duergar strongholds. The Exile's clergy are also expected to be skilled craftsmen, particularly of magical weapons, and the older and more frail priests are typically the elite artisans of any gray dwarven community.

Holy Days/Important Ceremonies: As befits their grim lives, gray dwarves are a race almost without joy who reserve their celebrations for victories over enemies and for the grim pleasure of inflicting pain on those unlucky enough to fall into their clutches.

The only regular holy day is celebrated annually at Midwinter and is known as Grimtidings. On this day only, the duergar lay down their hammers and gather to hear their priests recount the trials the duergar have suffered since their voluntary exile and the weaknesses of the other dwarven subraces and their gods. Laduguer is extolled for his artistry and craftsmanship, and a litany of those who have given insult to the god and the gray dwarves and against whom a promised, deadly revenge is recited.

The Ardukes of the Gray Gloom also declare holy days, known as Guerdon Revels, after major victories and when prisoners—particularly gold and shield dwarves—are captured. While the work does not stop during such festivals, most gray dwarves are given a few moments off from their labors to observe the recounting of heroics by duergar warriors, to examine plundered loot, and to participate in the torture and painful deaths of any prisoners.

Major Centers of Worship: Dunglorrin Torune, Overlake Hold, is located far beneath the surface in Gracklstugh, the largest city of gray dwarves in the Northdark. Deeper even then Menzoberranzan and Blingdinstone, Gracklstugh is a teeming city on the shore of the Darklake, renowned for the steel blades crafted in its forges. The temple itself is carved into the heart of a massive stalagmite formed from the exodus of a nearly vertical stream that winds downward for miles from the surface lands of the North to rain down on the subterranean tor and drain into the adjoining Darklake. Dunglorrin Torune bristles with chimneys from which billows forth the smoke of the temple's forges and ledges from which balls of burning pitch can be hurled from stone catapults at any invaders attempting a waterborne invasion of the surrounding city. Priest-guards mounted on steeders patrol the stalagmite's steep, slick slopes, and they ferry the raw materials from the mines to the temple's foundries and finished goods to the merchants in the city below. The high priest of Overlake Hold is Morndin Gloomstorm, son of Kildor, blood of Balgor, of Shimmergloom's Run. Morndin is one of the few surviving duergar of Clan Bukbukken, a clan that once occupied the undercity of Mithral Hall and served the great shadow wyrm Shimmergloom, the Drake of Darkness, before the shield dwarves of Clan Battlehammer reclaimed their ancestral home and drove the gray dwarves back to Gracklstugh.

Affiliated Orders: The Gray Lances of the Snarling Steeder are a mounted order of duergar crusaders and fighter/priests. The Gray Lances serve as the elite cavalry of gray dwarven armies, and their most common opponents are drow mounted on riding lizards. Individual duergar knights and their steeder mounts are well schooled in subterranean warfare techniques for battles that unfold across cave floors, walls, and ceilings.

Priestly Vestments: The clerical vestments of Laduguer's priests consist of utilitarian metal armor and the gray, hooded mantles for which the Grimcloaks are named. The holy symbol of the faith is a gem of any type, split nearly in twain by a large crack, one half of which is deeply flawed and the other half of which is perfect. For the duergar, such gems symbolize their split from the rest of the dwarven race and their superiority over those they have forsaken.

Adventuring Garb: Laduguer's priests favor weapons commonly employed by gray dwarves including heavy and light crossbows, picks, short swords, spears, and war hammers. When stealth is required, Grimcloaks prefer leather and studded leather armor. In situations requiring direct melee combat, the Exile's priests favor the heaviest armor available, usually a medium shield and chain mail or dwarven plate mail (base AC 2).

Specialty Priests (Thuldor)

REQUIREMENTS:	Strength 15, Dexterity 12, Wisdom 9 or Strength 12, Dexterity 15, Wisdom 9
PRIME REQ.:	Strength, Dexterity, Wisdom
ALIGNMENT:	LN, LE
WEAPONS:	Any
ARMOR:	Any
MAJOR SPHERES:	All, combat, divination, elemental (earth), guardian, healing, law, protection, sun (reversed only), thought, war, wards
MINOR SPHERES:	Animal, creation, necromantic
MAGICAL ITEMS:	Same as clerics
REQ. PROFS:	Land-based riding (steeders) and pick one: animal training (steeders), blacksmithing, mining, armorer, weaponsmithing
BONUS PROFS:	Animal handling (steeders), herbalism

- While most thuldor (the plural form of thuldar) are gray dwarves, dwarves of any subrace can become specialty priests of Laduguer.
- If psionics are permitted in the campaign, thuldor are allowed to multiclass as thuldor/psionicists.
- If psionics are permitted in the campaign, thuldor may select nonweapon proficiencies from the psionicist group without penalty.
- Thuldor gain a +1 bonus to their Armor Class.
- Thuldor can cast *darkness* (as the reversed form of the 1st-level priest spell *light*) or *strength of stone* (as the 1st-level priest spell detailed in the Moradin entry) once per day.
- At 3rd level, thuldor can cast *meld into stone* (as the 3rd-level priest spell) or *slow poison* (as the 2nd-level priest spell) once per day.
- At 5th level, thuldor can cast *stone shape* (as the 3rd-level priest spell) once per day.
- At 7th level, thuldor can cast *find traps* (as the 2nd-level priest spell) at will.
- At 7th level, thuldor gain a +1 bonus to all saving throws.

- At 10th level, thuldor can cast *stoneskin* (as the 4th-level wizard spell) once per day.
- At 13th level, thuldor can cast *wall of stone* (as the 5th-level wizard spell) or *stone tell* (as the 6th-level priest spell) once per day.
- At 15th level, thuldor can cast *turn pebble to boulder* or its reverse, *turn boulder to pebble*, (as the 4th-level wizard spells) twice per day.

Laduguerean Spells

In addition to the spells listed below, priests of Laduguer may cast the 1st-level priest spell *strength of stone* detailed in the entry for Moradin.

1st Level

Stoneblend (Pr 1; Illusion/Phantasm)

Sphere: Elemental Earth
Range: Touch
Components: V, S, M
Duration: Special
Casting Time: 4
Area of Effect: Creature touched
Saving Throw: None

This spell enables the recipient to blend against stone walls so as to be effectively invisible for as long as she or he holds still. The creature must press its body against the stone surface when the spell is cast.

Careful observation of the exact area in which a stoneblended being stands allows a 5% chance for visual detection. Tactile or other physical inspection of the specific region immediately reveals the presence of the stoneblended being and ends the spell effect. While breathing and small shifts do not end the spell, any sudden movement or large shift in position immediately ends the effect.

The material components of this spell are the priest's holy symbol and a pinch of dust. This spell also requires that the recipient be dressed in dull or drab colors (browns, blacks, and/or grays) that do not violently clash with the surrounding environment.

3rd Level

Blessed Craftsmanship (Pr 3; Enchantment/Charm)

Sphere: Creation
Range: Touch
Components: V, S, M
Duration: Special
Casting Time: 1 turn
Area of Effect: One craftsperson and one item
Saving Throw: None

This spell taps into Laduguer's skills and insights as a master craftsman to augment the recipient's skills while working on a particular project. While the *blessed craftsmanship* is temporary, the item worked on is permanently enhanced.

The recipient of this spell can work only on the object selected a minimum of 8 hours per day with no significant interruption. The spell adds a +3 bonus to the nonweapon proficiency check for any artisan nonweapon proficiency. This bonus also increases the chance that an object of quality is created. A roll of 20 still indicates a failure, however. Examples of applicable nonweapon proficiencies include armorer, blacksmithing, carpentry, gem cutting, leatherworking, pottery, stonemasonry, weaponsmithing, and weaving.

The material components of this spell are the priest's holy symbol and the materials and tools to be used in the craft project, all of which must be touched by the priest during the casting.

Enchanted Hammer (Pr 3; Enchantment)

Sphere: Creation
Range: Special
Components: V, S, M
Duration: 5 rounds/level
Casting Time: 1 turn
Area of Effect: Metal or weapons touched
Saving Throw: None

This spell enchants a hammer of silver or mithral to confer magical properties upon a metal weapon or suit of armor. The affected metal receives a bonus of +1. Metal weapons become the equivalent of a +1 weapon. Metal armor becomes the equivalent of +1 armor. Metal sufficient to make one suit of metal armor, two large weapons (axe, hammer, sword, etc.), or four small weapons (bolts, daggers, etc.) can be affected by this spell. The spell functions on existing magical weapons and armor as long as the total combined bonus is +3 or less.

Missile weapons enchanted in this way lose their enchantment when used, but otherwise the spell lasts for its full duration. This spell is often used in combination with other spells to create magical metal weapons and suits of metal armor, with this spell being cast once per desired plus of the bonus per item to be formed.

The material component is the priest's holy symbol. A small silver or mithral hammer to be struck against the armor, weapon, or metal to be enchanted is required.

Marthammor Duin

(Finder-of-Trails, the Watcher over Wanderers,
the Watchful Eye, the Hammer, the Finder, the Wanderer)
Lesser Power of Ysgard, NG

PORTFOLIO:	Guide and protector to dwarven adventurers, explorers, expatriates, travelers, and wanderers, lightning
ALIASES:	Muamman Duathal
DOMAIN NAME:	Nidavellir/Cavern of Rest
SUPERIOR:	Moradin
ALLIES:	Baervan Wildwanderer, Cyrrollalee, Gwaeron Windstrom, Lathander, Mielikki, the Morndinsamman (except Abbathor, Deep Duerra, Laduguer), Shaundakul, Stronmaus, Tapann, Tymora, Waukeen
FOES:	Deep Duerra, Laduguer, Urdlen, the goblinkin and evil giant pantheons
SYMBOL:	An upright mace, over a single leather boot trimmed with fur, toe to the right or a mace in gauntlets
WOR. ALIGN.:	LG, NG, CG, LN, N, CN

Marthammor Duin (Mar-THAM-more DOO-ihn), known on other worlds as Muamman Duathal (Moo-AM-man Doo-AH-thuhl), is the protector of dwarves who make their lives in human society in the North, rather than keeping to mountain or deep-delve enclaves. Commonly known as Wanderers, all such dwarves make offerings to him in appeasement for good fortune.

Marthammor is the patron of adventurers and explorers and all those dwarves who travel or live far from the dwarven homelands, allowing them to find routes to escape or to victory in their travels. He also watches over dwarven craftsfolk of any good alignment, keeping their homes and persons safe. His secondary aspect as god of lightning is unique among dwarves. The Finder-of-Trails is a growing cult in the North, and he may be evolving into an intermediate power.

Marthammor is seldom at home in his Cavern of Rest, which is guarded by the souls of those dwarves who perished while traveling aboveground and by boars and war dogs trained by the god himself. The Cavern lies in the ever-shifting underways of Nidavellir, third layer of Ysgard. Marthammor spends most of his time wandering the northern reaches of Faerûn in his avatar form. Marthammor sometimes sends his avatar to act as a guide or to warn urban dwarves of trouble brewing in their homelands. More often, he sends omens in the form of lightning, subsidence on trails, sudden rockfalls, or priestly divination through stone-flinging (the pattern of a fist is a common sign).

Marthammor is almost gnomelike in his approach to life; he's open and friendly, and he's definitely curious what lies over the next horizon. He has a keen interest in the doings of the multiverse as a whole, and he is far less xenophobic than most dwarves or their deities.

Marthammor is one of the youngest powers of the Morndinsamman, and as such the other members tolerate what they call his antics. Moradin hopes Marthammor will settle down in a few millennia and gives thanks, at least, that he is not as chaotic as Dugmaren Brightmantle. Marthammor is on good terms with Dugmaren, as the theme of traveling to gain knowledge is a shared concern of these gods, and the Finder-of-Trails is welcome in Dugmaren's Soot Hall. While he hates all goblinkin and evil giant gods, Marthammor harbors a particular loathing for Grolantor.

Marthammor's Avatar (Ranger 30, Cleric 20)

Marthammor appears as a thin, raven-bearded dwarf dressed in leather armor and furs, and cloaked in natural colors (usually green). He sometimes carries a walking stick of rough wood. He casts spells from the spheres of all, animal, charm, combat, creation, divination, elemental, guardian, healing, necromantic, plant, protection, summoning, sun, travelers, war, wards, and weather.

AC –4; MV 12 or 15; HP 207; THAC0 –9; #AT 2
Dmg 2d10+13 (*mace +4*, +9 STR) or 1d6+10 (*quarterstaff +1*, +9 STR)
MR 70%; SZ M (6 feet high) or L (12 feet high)
STR 21, DEX 19, CON 20, INT 20, WIS 19, CHA 20
Spells P: 12/11/11/9/7/5/2
Saves PPDM 2, RSW 1*, PP 4, BW 4, Sp 6
*Includes dwarf +5 CON save bonus to a minimum of 1. The CON save bonus also applies to saves vs. poison to a minimum of 1.

Special Att/Def: Marthammor wields *Glowhammer*, a huge *mace +4* of steel that glows and pulses as if still red-hot from the forge. It is not in fact hot and does 2d10 base damage by its impact only, not through heat or flame. Marthammor can swing this weapon, or another, in a combat round and also employ one of his magical powers every second round, without affecting his physical activity.

Marthammor's walking stick, which he often leaves behind (supposedly by accident) after encountering dwarves, serves as a *quarterstaff +1*. When in the hands of a dwarf, it furnishes one *limited wish* if that wish is spoken aloud as the stick is broken. The walking stick then crumbles to dust as the magic is expended, accompanied by the ringing tone of a mace crashing against metal in the distance. A nondwarf who breaks one of Marthammor's staves merely destroys its magic, ending up with two or more splintered pieces of wood. Marthammor can create one such walking stick at the end of every 6 turns. The creation requires a physical staff be cut from a tree (a physical activity), and then enchanted (the Finder-of-Trail's magical activity for that round; it requires continual grasping of the staff and concentration but does not preclude other physical activity). Marthammor can use the staff himself, including its *limited wish*.

Marthammor can *blink, dimension door, pass without trace, passwall,* or *water walk* at will, one power per round. He can *call lightning* and cast a 10d6 *lightning bolt* twice per turn, even if there is no storm of any sort in the area. There must be a round between each round in which he uses these magical powers.

Marthammor can cast *freedom* (the reverse of *imprisonment*), at will, by touching the ground. He is at all times himself immune to the effects of petrification and polymorph spells cast by others, as he is to *charm, entangle, maze,* and *trap the soul* effects. In addition to his conscious powers, he has continuous, natural *free action* (as the ring). The Finder can be struck only by +2 or better magical weapons. Finally, Marthammor is immune to lightning and electrical effects of any sort, and he can always direct the direction of reflection of any bolt of lightning cast within 100 yards of his location.

Other Manifestations

The Finder-of-Trails almost always manifests himself in one of four ways helpful to dwarves and to their companions and friends.

In the wilds, Marthammor indicates to troubled dwarves the safest or best way to proceed by appearing as a glowing upright mace, floating in midair. His image is a bright, blue-white translucent mace that has no tangible existence, but which is not destroyed by being passed through. It is unaffected by *dispel magic* or other magical attacks and effects. The *Mace of Marthammor* gives enough light to read by and floats along in front of dwarves, patiently guiding them along a route.

In situations where precipices, pit-traps, or other dangers lurk, or when a wrong choice of route has been made, Marthammor manifests as a glowing, blue-white, disembodied hand. The hand will signal "stop" by appearing fingers together and palm open in warning; it then points back or in other directions to outline traps or to indicate a better way. The hand can even trace clan symbols or dwarven runes to establish its identity or to communicate messages.

In the homes of dwarves, Marthammor manifests as a mace of pulsing light that strikes unseen surfaces in midair to make a ringing, crashing sound audible only to dwarves. This alarm warns of thieves or other intruders and strikes one blow against an intruder (normal footman's mace damage, automatic hit) before vanishing. Such a blow is typically delivered at a key moment, in other words, against a first intruder readying a rope ladder for others or to disrupt spellcasting or missile fire directed at the residents Marthammor is protecting.

In cases of imminent invasion or other natural disaster that dwarven residents cannot hope to defeat, Marthammor can appear in the dreams of dwarves to warn them to move away in haste. If no dwarf is asleep, Marthammor manifests as a glowing *magic mouth* floating above the image of his symbol, and warns the residents directly. Any wizard who attempts to duplicate Marthammor's *magic mouth* symbol invites an immediate personal attack by the god. If such an impostor has a trap planned for the god, Marthammor senses it and bring several other dwarven deities—such as his friends Clanggedin and Gorm—with him.

Marthammor is served by bariaurs, blink dogs, galeb duhr, hawks, hunting dogs, firestars, owls, phoenixes, pseudodragons, and storm giants. He occasionally rewards dwarves with the courage to emerge from their isolated communities with precious stones polished by mountain streams that flow down to human communities. He shows his disfavor by causing folk to get lost or through the whining and growling of animals (especially dogs) that only those in disfavor can seem to hear.

The Church

CLERGY:	Clerics, crusaders, specialty priests
CLERGY'S ALIGN.:	LG, NG, CG, LN, N, CN
TURN UNDEAD:	C: Yes, Cru: No, SP: No
CMND. UNDEAD:	C: No, Cru: No, SP: No

All clerics (including fighter/clerics), crusaders, and specialty priests of Marthammor receive religion (dwarven) and reading/writing (Dethek runes) as bonus nonweapon proficiencies. Clerics of Marthammor (as well as fighter/clerics) cannot turn undead before 7th level, but they always strike at +2 on all attack and damage rolls against undead creatures. At 7th level and above, clerics (including multiclassed clerics) can turn undead as other clerics do, but as a cleric of four levels less than their current level. These modifications apply only to the cleric class. Marthammor's priesthood broke with the dwarven tradition of having priests be the same gender as their deity long before the Time of Troubles, so Marthammor's clergy today is approximately 19% female, a very progressive figure for the dwarven pantheon.

Marthammor is well regarded by wanderers, shield dwarves who seek the company of humans in their towns and cities. The Watcher's advocacy of racial integration, exploration, and adventure is little understood by the hidden, shield dwarves who remain cloistered in isolated dwarven holds deep in the northern mountains, but they evince only incomprehension, not antipathy, toward the Finder-of-Trails and his priests. Dwarves of other races have little awareness of the faith of the Watcher over Wanderers.

Marthammor is worshiped on the bare heights of stony tors on moonless nights, or on holy days and for important rituals, in underground caverns. The caverns must always be natural, unaltered by the hands of intelligent beings. Underground or on tor-top, an altar to Marthammor is always a simple stone cairn or wooden tripod, supporting a stone hammer, head uppermost. Priests of Marthammor stand looking at the hammer, praying to their god for guidance as to where they are needed and what they have done wrong or poorly. The god places visions in their minds, choosing which priests will guard temples, which explore particular areas, and so on. Temples of the Finder-of-Trails are scattered across the northlands, typically in the foothills midway between the traditional mountain territories of the dwarves and the human cities of the plains.

Novices of Marthammor are known as the Lost. Full priests are known as Watchful Eyes. In ascending order of rank, the titles used by Marthammoran priests are Sun Seeker, Far Wanderer, Trail Finder, Vigilant Guardian, Stalwart Protector, and Valiant Hammer. High Old Ones have unique individual titles. Specialty priests are known as trailblazers. The clergy of Marthammor includes shield dwarves (96%), gold dwarves (2%), gray dwarves (1%), and wild dwarves (1%). The dramatic shift in composition by the clergies of most human deities of the Faerûnian pantheon toward increased numbers of specialty priests has been enthusiastically embraced by the Watcher. As a result, Marthammor's clergy is now composed primarily of specialty priests (85%), with the remainder even split between clerics (5%), fighter/clerics (5%), and crusaders (5%). The majority of Marthammor's priests are male (81%), but the number of female priests is growing rapidly.

Dogma: If the Children of Moradin are to survive as a race, they must adapt, grow, and learn to dwell in harmony with other good races, particularly humans. The Stout Folk must be encouraged to emerge from the illusory safety of their hidden delves and find true security in fellowship with humankind and demihumankind. Help fellow wanders and sojourners in the world, giving all that is needful. Guide those who are lost and guard those who are defenseless. Seek out new ways and new paths, and discover the wide world in your wanderings. Herald the way of newfound hope.

Day-to-Day Activities: Priests of Marthammor make marked trails in the wilderness northlands of the Realms, from Uttersea to the Great Ice Sea. They also establish way-caches of food and supplies (spare boots, clothing, weapons, drinking-water, bandages and splints, firemaking supplies, and the like) along these trails.

Priests of Marthammor patrol these ways, healing and guiding dwarves they meet, providing a warm fire, a hot meal, and friendly companionship to exhausted, lonely, lost or hurt dwarves—of any faith or race.

Priests of Marthammor work with healers and priests of all races to help dwarves, allies, and companions of dwarves. While they do not accompany adventurers, they are in a sense adventurers themselves, often fighting monsters, discovering ruins, and facing the same perils that adventurers do. Travelers in the North—especially the northern Sword Coast region—often encounter small bands of 3d4 dwarven priests of Marthammor. Such bands do not reveal their clerical status unless they are dealing with dwarves or known dwarven allies or companions.

The ghosts of diligent servants of Marthammor are said to haunt certain trails, old abandoned delves, and mountain passes. When dwarves or dwarven allies or companions are lost in such places, particularly in blizzards or storms, the phantom priests appear, gesturing silently, and guide the travelers along a safe route to refuge or their destination.

Holy Days/Important Ceremonies: Followers of Marthammor celebrate numerous holy days during the year. Each festival day in the Calendar of Harptos and nine days after each festival day is considered holy to Marthammor. In years when Shieldmeet occurs, the holy day follows it nine days later; there are not two adjacent days, one following Midsummer and one Shieldmeet. On most holy days, and at least once a year for each worshiper, followers of the Finder-of-Trails must burn used ironwork and dwarf-made footwear in homage to the Watcher.

Midwinter and the ninth of Alturiak are known to the faithful as the Rooting and the Rebirth respectively. The former holy day celebrates the reforging ties to the mountain homelands, and the latter celebrates the reemergence of dwarven wanderers from their mountain fastnesses.

Greengrass and the ninth of Mirtul are known to the faithful as the Wind and the Wayfaring respectively. The former celebrates new discoveries and the latter celebrates extended sojourns in the homelands of other races.

Midsummer and the ninth of Eleasias are known to the faithful as the Hammer and the Anvil. These holy days celebrate dwarven craftsmanship and creativity. Shieldmeet is celebrated as the Shepherding, a day when dwarven wanderers are expected to introduce the hidden to their human and demihuman neighbors.

Highharvestide and the ninth of Leafall are celebrated as the Thunderbolt and the Fulmination. On these days followers of the Finder-of-Trails pray for guidance in any upcoming battles of the Stout Folk.

Finally, The Feast of the Moon and the ninth of Nightal are celebrated as the Beacon and the Runestone respectively. These holy days celebrate the path revealed by Marthammor and the knowledge learned by interacting with other cultures.

Major Centers of Worship: In the Year of the Crown (1351 DR), nearly fifty priests of the Finder-of-Trails established the Vault of the Lost Wayfarer in a great natural cavern at the heart of Berun's Hill that had once been the crypt of Maegar, son of Relavir, grandson of Anarok, of the Royal House of the Helm of Gharraghaur. The existence of a dwarven tomb beneath the tor has long been the talk of legends in the North, but the Marthammoran priests who finally found the cavernous vault discovered that it had been plundered long ago by duergar who had tunneled up from below. Berun's Hill and Twilight Tor—Mrinolor and Anaurdahyn in the tongue of the dwarves—are the southernmost and northernmost tors respectively, of the Starmetal Hills, a range of knolls that runs parallel to the Long Road west of Longsaddle and has been the target of several meteor showers in recent millennia. Berun's Hill and, to a lesser extent, Twilight Tor command a splendid view of the Dessarin valley to the north and east, and both hilltops have long been employed by the followers of Marthammor both to worship the Watcher Over Wanderers on moonless nights and to observe passing travelers and caravans on the Long Road. Under the leadership of Immar Mistwalker, High Old One of Marthammor, son of Gadlyn, blood of Dorn, the Watchful Eyes have gradually extended their aegis over a region stretching from Wyvern Tor in the foothills of the Sword Mountains to Twilight Tor and from the town of Triboar to the Neverwinter Woods. Thanks to the regular patrols and ready assistance of the Watchful Eyes, small dwarven holds in the area have been able to reestablish long-sundered trade links with the neighboring human communities along the Long Road and the River Dessarin.

The Hospice of Deadsnows is a dual-faith religious stronghold located on the northern slopes of Mount Sabras in the Nether Mountains along the Fork Road, approximately halfway between Sundabar and the Fork. The fortified abbey was once the keep of a human lord whose dream of establishing a kingdom here was shattered by relentless orc attacks. Deadsnows is named for the battle that killed its lord, a winter skirmish that left orc and human bodies strewn over several miles of snow-covered ground. Deadsnows is now home to 450 dwarves dedicated to Marthammor Finder-of-Trails who dwell in harmony with 30 priests of Lathander. The humans serve Lathander in the promotion of growth and beginnings. To this end, they have a walled garden and shop for experimentation that is crammed with odd pieces of apparatus and failed experiments. The walls of Deadsnows are studded with watchtowers and covered with climbing roses inside and on top. The priests of Lathander tend the flowers and they help to provide cover for the defenders looking over the top of the wall. The dwarves serve Marthammor by providing a safe redoubt for isolated dwarven holds in the region and by maintaining contact between them and the emerging nation of Luruar. Under the leadership of Kerrilla Gemstar, a founding member of the Council of 12 Peers of Luruar, the dwarven followers of Marthammor worship in a natural cavern beneath a tor rising at the center of the walled community. In troubled times, everyone retreats to the cavern and the entrances are walled off. The cavern has two secret paths into the Underdark, but traps to keep drow and other creatures from ascending into the dwarven halls guard them. In keeping with the dictates of their respective deities, the folk of Deadsnows make any travelers other than armed orcs and evil beings welcome at an inn called the Rose and Hammer, located in the abbey forecourt. The hospice provides desperate travelers refuge from winter weather and orcs. The priests of Marthammor and Lathander heal visitors in exchange for service, typically time on a fighting patrol scouring the mountain slopes near Deadsnows. Patrols drive out trolls, orcs, and predators attracted to the sheep and ponies kept in two high, fenced meadows.

Affiliated Orders: While Marthammor's clergy regularly assists adventuring dwarves, few priests actually become adventurers. The Knights of the North Star are a widely dispersed order of Marthammoran priests who individually join adventuring companies based in the North composed primarily of humans and demihumans of other races. Members of the order seek to learn more of their companions' cultures, so as to ease the integration of Wanderer dwarves into other societies, and to direct the efforts of such adventuring companies toward activities consistent with the goals of dwarves in general. At least once per year each knight must deliver an oral or written report to the most convenient Marthammoran enclave.

Priestly Vestments: Priests of Marthammor garb themselves in gray robes and maroon overtunics emblazoned on both the front and back with a Watchful Eye beneath the symbol of Marthammor. The holy symbol of the faith is a miniature electrum hammer.

Adventuring Garb: Priests of Marthammor favor cloaks of gray or mottled green, brown, and gray over any sort of armor, including a helm if desired. While Watchful Eyes may employ any sort of bludgeoning weapon, they prefer hammers and staves, both weapons associated with the Finder. *Glowstones* are much prized the Marthammoran clergy, and it is not unusual for the Finder-of-Trail's priests to possess one or two. (*Glowstones* are described in *Dwarves Deep* and in the ENCYCLOPEDIA MAGICA™ *Volume 4 & Index* tome.)

Specialty Priests (Trailblazers)

REQUIREMENTS:	Constitution 11, Wisdom 9
PRIME REQ.:	Constitution, Wisdom
ALIGNMENT:	NG
WEAPONS:	Any bludgeoning (wholly Type B) weapon
ARMOR:	Any
MAJOR SPHERES:	All, astral, combat, creation, divination, guardian, healing, protection, sun, travelers, weather
MINOR SPHERES:	Animal, charm, elemental (earth), necromantic, plant, summoning
MAGICAL ITEMS:	Same as clerics
REQ. PROFS:	Endurance or mountaineering or survival (mountains)
BONUS PROFS:	Direction sense, tracking, local history (neighboring human communities)

- Trailblazers must be dwarves. While trailblazers are almost exclusively shield dwarves, a few dwarves of nearly every subrace are called to be specialty priests of Marthammor's clergy.
- Trailblazers are not allowed to multiclass.
- Trailblazers may select only the required nonweapon proficiencies listed above from the warrior group without penalty.
- Trailblazers are immune to all electrical and lightning attacks.
- Trailblazers can cast *free action* (as the 4th-level priest spell) or *pass without trace* (as the 1st-level priest spell) once per day.
- At 3rd level, trailblazers can cast *spiritual hammer* (as the 2nd-level priest spell) or *call lightning* (as the 3rd-level priest spell) once per day.
- At 5th level, trailblazers can cast *lightning bolt* (as the 3rd-level wizard spell) once per day. They gain a second use of this ability per day at 10th level.
- At 7th level, trailblazers can cast *haste* (as the 3rd-level wizard spell) once per day on themselves only without the normal aging penalty.
- At 10th level, trailblazers can cast *find the path* (as the 6th-level priest spell) at will.
- At 13th level, trailblazers can cast *clear path* (as the 5th-level priest spell) once a day.
- At 15th level, trailblazers can cast *hovering road* (as the 7th-level priest spell) once a day.

Marthammoran Spells

2nd Level

Marthammor's Intuition (Pr 2; Divination)

Sphere:	Divination
Range:	0
Components:	V, S, M
Duration:	Special
Casting Time:	1 turn
Area of Effect:	1-mile radius
Saving Throw:	None

This spell enables the caster to divine the approximate location—up to 1 mile away in any direction, including up and down—of the nearest dwarf or dwarves in immediate or imminent need of aid. Such emergencies might include a battle against more powerful foes, a life-threatening medical emergency, a broken wagon wheel, or the like, but in no case is the priest made aware of more than the general nature of the emergency. There is no guarantee that the situation revealed is one that the caster is capable of addressing or that the caster can reach the location revealed by the spell in time to be of assistance.

If no dwarf in need of assistance is within 1 mile of the caster, the spell ends and the priest is aware of the result. If multiple groups are in need of aid, *Marthammor's intuition* reveals only the nearest emergency, not necessarily the most pressing.

If the priest heads toward the dwarf or dwarves in need within 1 turn of the casting, moving as fast as safely possible, *Marthammor's intuition* guides him or her along the most efficient route to the scene.

On rare occasions, at Marthammor's discretion, this spell foreshadows an imminent event rather than revealing an ongoing situation. In such circumstances, the caster can usually reach the scene in time to prevent an imminent disaster.

The material components are the priest's holy symbol and a strand of the priest's beard hair.

3rd Level

Marthammor's Thunderbolts (Pr 3; Evocation)

Sphere:	Combat
Range:	40 yards+10 yards/level
Components:	V, M
Duration:	Instantaneous
Casting Time:	6
Area of Effect:	Special
Saving Throw:	Special

This spell enables the caster to simultaneously unleash twin *thunderbolts* either from both hands or both eyes. Each *thunderbolt* can be directed at a different target within range and can either be directed to cure 1d8 points of damage or cause 3d6 points of damage. Targets of the latter usage suffer only half damage if they succeed at a saving throw vs. spell.

The twin *thunderbolts* begin at the caster and streak outward as far as the target selected by the caster, assuming she or he is within range. Unlike the 3rd-level wizard spell *lightning bolt*, *Marthammor's thunderbolts* has no effect on objects and is blocked by interposing barriers. The thunderbolts do not reflect or rebound and cannot be forked.

The material component is the priest's holy symbol.

Glowglory (Pr 3; Invocation/Evocation)

Sphere:	Combat, Creation
Range:	Touch
Components:	V, S, M
Duration:	Special
Casting Time:	6
Area of Effect:	1 *glowstone* or 1 square foot/caster level of normal stone
Saving Throw:	None

This spell allows priests to unleash a *beam of power* from a *glowstone* or to make normal stone (in a surface area of up to 1 square foot per level of the caster) radiate a *continual light* radiance for 1 turn/level. (*Glowstones* are described in *Dwarves Deep* and in the ENCYCLOPEDIA MAGICA™ *Volume 4 & Index* tome.) If the priest desires, the radiance of normal stone can be modified to a gentle release of heat that is enough to warm chilled beings to prevent frostbite, death from exposure, and to ensure comfortable sleeping and activity in exposed or icy cold conditions.

When used on a *glowstone* touched by the caster, this magic unleashes a *beam of power*. A *beam of power* is a cutting beam of radiant force that rends stone, wood, and flesh alike. It is typically used as a weapon or a tool, to quarry stone or open passages in solid rock.

A *beam of power* inflicts the same damage as a heavy catapult hit to wood or stone objects or surfaces. It deals 6d6 points of damage per contact to living things. In either case, a *beam of power* is mentally aimed with the same THAC0 as if the priest were attacking directly. It lashes out to its furthest extent (30 feet) in a single round. Other spellcasting, death, or unconsciousness on the part of the caster ends the *beam of power* and the spell instantly. *Beams of power* can be tracked in any direction while cutting or to follow a moving target (at MV 15). A *beam of power* lasts for as long as the caster concentrates, up to 1 round per level.

The material components are a pinch of gold dust or gem dust.

Moradin

(The Soul Forger, Dwarffather, the All-Father, the Creator)

Greater Power of Mount Celestia, LG

PORTFOLIO:
: Dwarves (survival, renewal, and advancement), creation, smithing of all sorts, craftsmanship, war, the dwarven race, protection, metalcraft, stonework (stonemasonry, tunneling, construction), engineering, dwarven engineers, protection

ALIASES:
: None

DOMAIN NAME:
: Solania/Erackinor

SUPERIOR:
: None

ALLIES:
: Corellon Larethian, Cyrrollalee, Flandal Steelskin, Garl Glittergold, Geb, Gond, Helm, Kossuth, the Morndinsamman (except Abbathor, Deep Duerra, and Laduguer), Torm, Tyr, Yondalla

FOES:
: Abbathor, Deep Duerra, Laduguer, the goblinkin and evil giant pantheons

SYMBOL:
: Hammer and anvil

WOR. ALIGN.:
: LG, NG, CG, LN, N, CN

Moradin (MOAR-uh-din) is the creator god of the dwarven race and leader of the Morndinsamman. He is said to have created all dwarves, forging them from metals and gems in the fires that lie at the "heart of the world," and breathing life—the first dwarven souls—into the cooling forms. All dwarves appease Moradin, even if they do not wholeheartedly support him. Lawful good dwarves support and work openly to serve the Soul Forger, even if they also worship another deity. His name is invoked by dwarves involved in smithwork or craftsmanship of any sort, and they give him homage by doing their best work and seeking to emulate his stonework and craftsmanship. Moradin is said to inspire dwarven inventions and seeks constantly to improve the race—increasing dwarven good nature, intelligence, and ability to exist in harmony with other living things. At the same time, he battles the pride and isolationist tendencies that occur naturally in his elite creations.

Moradin is held by many dwarven creation myths to have been incarnated from rock, stone, and metal, with his soul eternally present in the form of fire. That same fire fueled the forge in which Moradin created the Stout Folk and, in some myths, Moradin breathes fire over the first dwarves to bring them to life.

The Soul Forger rules the other dwarven deities sternly, and only his wife, Berronar Truesilver, can regularly bring a smile to his face. In some dwarven realms, the Soul Forger is said to be the father of Dumathoin, Abbathor, Laduguer, Clangeddin, Sharindlar, Diirinka, Vergadain, Thard Harr, Gorm Gulthyn, Marthammor Duin, and Dugmaren Brightmantle, but the exact relationships and ordering vary from culture to culture. It is the All-Father who banished Deep Duerra, Laduguer, Diirinka, Diinkarazan, and their followers, smiting them with his hammer and driving them forth. If Abbathor is ever banished, it will be at the Soul Forger's command. Moradin loathes Gruumsh, Maglubiyet, and the other goblinkin deities (those of the orcs, goblins, hobgoblins, bugbears, kobolds, and urds), and he detests the evil giant deities as well. His gruff and uncompromising nature wins him few friends outside the dwarven pantheon, but he is said to be close with Cyrrollalee, Garl Glittergold, Flandal Steelskin, Gond, Helm, Kossuth, Tyr, and Torm, and enjoys a strategic alliance with Yondalla and Corellon Larethian. Moradin has little patience for the elven powers, but he has worked effectively with them in the past when it was necessary.

Moradin is a stern and uncompromising defender of the dwarven people and of the principles of law and good. Moradin is a harsh but fair judge. He judges dwarves on their achievements and the success of their endeavors, not just on their good hearts. The Soul Forger is strength and force of will embodied; his weapons, armor, and tools are virtual extensions of his own incarnate being. Moradin seldom appears in the Realms, preferring to work through manifestations rather than avatars. His usual reason for intervention in either form is to encourage dwarves to follow the correct path or make the best decision at a critical time. He also intervenes to aid or inspire dwarves who may serve the race in the future, or to aid or encourage nondwarves who aid the dwarves.

Moradin's Avatar

(Fighter 37, Cleric 33, Earth Elementalist 25, Fire Elementalist 25, Bard 18)

Moradin appears as a stern-faced, 20-foot-tall male dwarf with a powerful musculature, especially in the upper body, with flowing white (or black) hair and beard that reaches his knees. He is plainly dressed, wearing furs and a smith's leather leggings and aprons, plus bracers of pure gold on his forearms. The Soul Forger exudes an aura of power that is visible as a faint white radiance, though he can cloak this if he wishes. When entering combat, Moradin's garb transforms into dwarven plate mail and a large shield. The Soul Forger favors spells from the spheres of all, combat, creation, divination, elemental, guardian, healing, law, protection, sun, and war, although he can cast spells from any sphere. He can cast spells from the schools of elemental air, earth, fire, and water.

AC –7; MV 12 or 15; HP 247; THAC0 –10; #AT 5/2
Dmg 4d10+21 (huge *war hammer* +5, +14 STR, +2 spec. bonus in war hammer)
MR 70%; SZ M (6 feet high) or L (20 feet high)
STR 25, DEX 20, CON 24, INT 21, WIS 20, CHA 22
Spells P: 13/13/12/12/9/9/9, W: 7/7/7/7/7/7/7/6*
Saves PPDM 2, RSW 1**, PP 4, BW 4, Sp 4
*Numbers assume one extra elemental earth and fire spell per spell level.
**Includes dwarf +6 CON save bonus to a minimum of 1. The CON save bonus also applies to saves vs. poison to a minimum of 1.

Special Att/Def: Moradin wields *Soulhammer*, a huge, glowing *war hammer* +5. The Soul Forger wears magical *dwarven plate mail* +5 and a *shield* +5 of his own making that many believe is part of the god himself. Any weapon striking his bracers transmits an energy discharge causing 2d6 points of damage to the wielder. Any frontal attack roll that misses by 1, 2 or 3 points is deemed to have been parried by Moradin's bracers. If Moradin is slain, his weapon, bracers, and armor vanish and reappear on the *Soul Forge* within Mount Celestia.

Once per day, Moradin can work *imprisonment* (as the 9th-level wizard spell) on a being by touch. By the same means, he can *banish* (as the 7th-level wizard spell, but effective on the Prime Material Plane and not requiring naming or components) three times per day. When Moradin himself leaves a plane or *teleports*, he can at will leave a *fire storm* and/or a *stone storm* (as the 7th-level priest spells) behind him, centered on his last location. Either effect inflicts 2d8+33 points of damage.

Moradin cannot be harmed by forged weapons of any type or source. He is immune to petrification and paralyzation attacks, and to elemental fire and elemental earth sphere and school spells, abilities, and effects. He is also immune to illusion/phantasm school spells, abilities, and effects from other than divine sources. The Soul Forger moves through solid rock at will. He can be struck only by +3 or better magical weapons.

If slain, Moradin becomes an entity akin to a ghost. The Soul Forger's ghostlike anima form cannot be turned and can become invisible at will. He can work magic and employ a ghost's attacks and has half his normal hit points.

Other Manifestations

Moradin commonly manifests as a white radiance. This envelops either a being or an object. An enveloped being (nearly always a dwarf) is temporarily imbued by Moradin with one of his avatar spell abilities. An enveloped object (a war hammer, if available) is animated by Moradin's will, and may serve as a weapon, as a battering ram (to free imprisoned Folk or to reveal a hidden way), or as a guide (floating along to show a route).

Moradin is served by aasimon, archons, aurumvorae, azer, baku, einheriar, elementals of all varieties, fire beetles, galeb duhr, gold dragons, guardian naga, hammer golems, hollyphants, incarnates of faith, living steel, maruts, noctrals, per, sapphire dragons, shedu, silver dragons, urdun-

nirin, and xavers. The Soul Forger demonstrates his favor through the revelation of rare metals, by the appearance of his symbol on an anvil after a hammer blow or on an item after it is removed from the forge, or by a nimbus of fire that envelops (without burning) an item of great workmanship immediately after it is completed. The Soul Forger indicates his displeasure by the sudden breaking of an item in its crafting (usually a weapon), by suddenly extinguishing a forge fire, or by causing an anvil to shatter into hundreds of pieces when struck.

The Church

CLERGY:	Clerics, crusaders, specialty priests
CLERGY'S ALIGN.:	LG
TURN UNDEAD:	C: Yes, Cru: No, SP: Yes
CMND. UNDEAD:	C: No, Cru: No, SP: No

All clerics (including fighter/clerics), crusaders, and specialty priests of Moradin receive religion (dwarven) and reading/writing (Dethek runes) as bonus nonweapon proficiencies. clerics of Moradin (as well as fighter/clerics) cannot turn undead before 7th level, but they always strike at +2 on all attack and damage rolls against undead creatures. At 7th level and above, clerics (including multiclassed clerics) can turn undead as other clerics do, but as a cleric of four levels less than their current level. These modifications apply only to the cleric class. Until the Time of Troubles, Moradin's priests were all male. Since then, females have begun entering the priesthood at a fairly rapid rate.

Moradin and his mortal servants are very highly regarded in dwarven society, and his priests often serve as leaders in dwarven communities. Dwarven daily life is consumed with mining, smithcraft, engineering, and creative endeavors, and the Soul Forger's assistance is frequently acknowledged by most dwarven artisans. The only criticism of the Soul Forger's clergy, as expressed by younger dwarves who prefer the teachings of Dugmaren, Haela, and Marthammor, is that Moradin's Forgesmiths are too set in their traditional ways and too slow to adapt to the changing world around them. Among the other human and demihuman races, Moradin's priests are perceived as prototypical dwarves and as the mortal manifestations of their god, and how this is interpreted depends on the viewer's general perception of and regard for dwarves.

Temples of Moradin are located underground and carved out of solid rock. They are never set in natural caverns. Moradin's temples usually resemble vast smithies dominated by one or more grand halls of hardworking dwarven craftsmen. Hammers and anvils, the signs of the god, are the dominant decorative themes, as are statues of the All-Father and the other gods of the dwarven pantheon. The center of the Soul Forger's shrine or temple is a great ever-burning hearth and a forge of the finest equipage. Should the fire be extinguished (something the Soul Forger's priests will go to any length to prevent), the temple is abandoned or torn down stone by stone. Usually another temple is built on a new site, but occasionally a temple is entirely rebuilt and reconsecrated.

Novices of Moradin are known as the Unworked. Full priests of the Soul Forger are known as Forgesmiths and as the Tempered. In ascending order of rank, the titles used by Moradite priests are Adept of the Anvil, Hammer of War, Artisan of the Forge, Craftsman of Runes, Artificer of Discoveries, and Smith of Souls. High Old Ones have unique individual titles but are collectively known as the High Forgesmiths. Specialty priests are known as *sonnlinor,* a dwarvish word that can be loosely translated as *those who work stone.* The clergy of Moradin includes gold dwarves (50%), shield dwarves (48%), jungle dwarves (1%), and even gray dwarves (1%). Moradin's clergy is nearly evenly divided between specialty priests (47%) and clerics (43%), and includes a handful of crusaders (5%) and fighter/clerics (5%). Most priests of Moradin are male (94%).

Dogma: The Soul Forger is the father and creator of the dwarven race. By seeking to emulate both his principles and his workmanship in smithcraft, stoneworking, and other tasks, the Children of Moradin honor the All-Father. Wisdom is derived from life tempered with experience. Advance the dwarven race in all areas of life. Innovate with new processes and skills, and test and work them until they are refined and pure. Found new kingdoms and clan lands, defending those that already exist from internal and external threats. Lead the Stout Folk in the traditional ways laid down by the Soul Forger. Honor your clan leaders as you honor Moradin.

Day-to-Day Activities: Priests of Moradin strive to restore the dwarven races to strong numbers and a position of influence in Faerûn, by founding new dwarven kingdoms and increasing the status of dwarves within the wider human-dominated society prevalent in the Realms today. They preside over a wide range of formal ceremonies (consecrations of forges, temples, and other buildings, crowning of monarchs, etc.) and the education of the young, especially in the teaching of history. They maintain genealogies and historical archives, cooperating with Berronar's priests. Adventuring is encouraged in the priesthood, but only adventuring that directly serves the interests of the dwarven race.

Holy Days/Important Ceremonies: Those who worship the Soul Forger gather monthly around the forge to celebrate the All-Father and to make offerings. In some dwarven cultures, Moradin is worshiped at the time of the full moon, while in others the Soul Forger is venerated beneath the crescent moon. In addition, any High Forgesmith can declare a holy day at any time and often does so as a way of celebrating a local event. Offerings of common or precious metals—especially those already worked by dwarven hands into items of beauty or practical use, such as tools or ornamented hardware—are made on the monthly holy days. Sacrifices of common or precious metals are melted down at the forge and reformed into shapes usable by the clergy. Rituals are performed while making such offerings, which involve chanting, kneeling, and reaching bare-handed into the flames of the forge (Moradin prevents harm to the truly faithful) to handle red- and white-hot objects directly.

Priests entering a temple of Moradin bow to the forge and surrender any weapons (in times of peace). Priests of Moradin strike the anvil standing by the entry once with their hammers before surrendering them to faithful dwarven warriors. At least seven warriors are usual at any shrine, but four will always be there. Priests of another faith, without permission of a High Old One or the avatar of Moradin, cannot advance beyond the *wall of fire,* a knee-high, permanent magical effect surrounding the central forge. Priests of Moradin engage in humble, verbal prayer and in open, earnest discussion of current dwarven problems and issues, more so than any other priesthood. Such discussion is considered to be between equals (even if nondwarves participate), save that the ranking priest of Moradin has the sole authority to open and close discussion on a particular topic.

Worship usually ends with a rising, quickening chant in unison of: "The dwarves shall prevail, the dwarves shall endure, the dwarves shall grow!" This is repeated, ever more loudly, until the plain, massive, battered smith's hammer on the largest of the forge rises from the anvil of its own volition (moved by the power of the listening god). It may (or may not) move about or glow to denote the god's will, marked pleasure, or agreement. It descends gently to the anvil, though it comes to rest with a thunderous ring, as if brought down with all the strength of a powerful dwarf.

Major Centers of Worship: Thuulurn, the Foundry of Stout Souls, is a fortified monastic enclave of priests dedicated to Moradin, located in the heart of the Deep Realms, east of the Great Rift. Thuulurn is both a temple and a city, with over 5,600 inhabitants. The temple-city is carved from solid rock. It resembles a large dungeon like Undermountain far more than it does a surface city set in a large cavern. Huge forges burn continuously throughout the enclave, leaving the air heavy with smoke and most chambers stifling hot (at least to surface-dwellers and nondwarves). Keeping aloof from most other gold dwarves of the Deep Realms, the Forgesmiths of Thuulurn (under the able leadership of Thungalos Truetemper, First Hammer of Moradin) work continuously to influence events in the Deeps and surface lands, to the betterment of all dwarves. They have been known to hire adventurers of other races to carry out their aims. Often, a mission for the dwarves is demanded as a payment for healing badly beaten adventurers or *raising* one or more slain individuals. Typical missions include a strike against the duergar, freeing dwarves from drow slavery in the Depths Below, slaying an aboleth at a certain underground lake, finding and slaying the latest cloaker overlord with designs on the Deep Realm, and so on.

The temple-city is self-sufficient. Whatever it lacks is brought in from elsewhere by its priests or worshipers. Dwarven offerings have made Thuulurn very rich, but this wealth is seen only as a means to bringing about the Soul Forger's ends. Of late, tales have begun to spread that the Forgesmiths of Thuulurn have dispatched a great army of gold dwarves westward through the Underdark. Whether this tale is true or not, and where such an army might be headed, is still unknown.

In the North, the most visible monument to the Soul Forger is the Stone Bridge, a massive stone arch that spans the broadest imaginable spring flood of the River Dessarin. The Stone Bridge, built long ago to link the two halves of the ancient dwarven kingdom of Besilmer, rises in a great arc, without supporting pillars, its span two miles long and 400 feet above the water. The Bridge is built of weathered granite, six paces broad and so skillfully fitted that it seems of one piece. It has no parapet or railing on either side. Dwarves explain the awesome size and continued survival of the Bridge to the fact that it is also a temple to Moradin. Lawful good dwarves still make pilgrimages to the Bridge, said to be one of the Soul Forger's favorite spots on Faerûn. On at least one occasion, Moradin's avatar appeared on the Bridge and destroyed a horde of orcs harrying the remaining members of the Ironstar clan as they fled southward to valley of the River Delimbiyr.

Affiliated Orders: The Hammers of Moradin are an elite military order dominated by crusaders and fighter/clerics with chapters in nearly every dwarven stronghold and members drawn from every dwarven clan. The Hammers serve both as commanders of dwarven armies and as an elite strike force skilled in dealing with anything from large groups of orcs to great wyrms to malevolent fiends from the Lower Planes. The order is dedicated to the defense of existing dwarven holdings and the carving out of new dwarven territories. Individual chapters have a great deal of local autonomy but, in times of great crisis, a Grand Council (the reigning monarchs and senior Hammers of the affected region) assemble to plot strategy and divine Moradin's will.

Priestly Vestments: Ceremonial vestments for priests of Moradin include flowing, shining robes of woven wire of electrum treated with *blueshine*. Other ceremonial garb includes silvered (*everbright*) helms, silver-plated war hammers, and earth-brown leather boots. The holy symbol of the faith is a miniature electrum war hammer, treated with *blueshine*.

Adventuring Garb: In combat, Moradin's clergymembers favors chain mail or dwarven plate mail, a helm, and a medium or large shield. Priests of the Soul Forger are skilled in the use of the war hammer, but many favor other weapons as well, such as battles axes, broad swords, and hand axes.

Specialty Priests (Sonnlinor)

REQUIREMENTS:	Strength 10, Wisdom 11
PRIME REQ.:	Strength, Wisdom
ALIGNMENT:	LG, LN
WEAPONS:	Any
ARMOR:	Any
MAJOR SPHERES:	All, combat, creation, divination, elemental, guardian, healing, law, protection, sun, war
MINOR SPHERES:	Astral, necromantic, wards
MAGICAL ITEMS:	Same as clerics
REQ. PROFS:	War hammer; armorer or weaponsmithing
BONUS PROFS:	Blacksmithing, stonemasonry

- While most sonnlinor are shield dwarves or gold dwarves, dwarves of nearly every dwarven subrace are called to be specialty priests of Moradin's clergy.
- Sonnlinor are not allowed to multiclass.
- Sonnlinor can select nonweapon proficiencies from the warrior group without penalty.
- Sonnlinor can cast *animate weapon*, *command* or *strength of stone* (as the 1st-level priest spells) once per day.
- At 3rd level, sonnlinor can cast *protection from paralysis* (as the 2nd-level wizard spell) or *spiritual hammer* (as the 2nd-level priest spell) once per day.
- At 5th level, sonnlinor can cast *dispel magic* or *stone shape* (as the 3rd-level priest spells) once per day.
- At 7th level, sonnlinor can cast *stonefire* (as the 4th-level priest spell) once per day.
- At 10th level, sonnlinor can cast *true seeing* (as the 5th-level priest spell) four times a day.
- At 10th level, sonnlinor can cast *flame strike* (as the 5th-level priest spell) once a day.
- At 13th level, sonnlinor can cast *defensive harmony* (as the 5th-level priest spell) or *soul forge* (as the 5th-level priest spell) once per day.
- At 15th level, sonnlinor can cast *elemental aura* (as the 9th-level wizard spell) five times per tenday.

Moradite Spells

1st Level

Strength of Stone (Pr 1; Invocation/Evocation)

Sphere:	Elemental Earth
Range:	Touch
Components:	V, S, M
Duration:	3 rounds+1 round/level
Casting Time:	4
Area of Effect:	1 creature
Saving Throw:	None

This spell grants supernatural strength to the recipient by raising his or her Strength score by 1d4 points or to a minimum of 16, whichever is higher. Each 10% of exceptional Strength counts at 1 point, so a character with a Strength of 17 could be raised a high as an 18/30, but no higher. Both the caster and the recipient must be in contact with solid stone or earth when the spell is cast—standing on the ground will do nicely, but flying or swimming will not. The spell lasts until the duration expires or until the subject loses contact with the earth. Obviously, this can happen in a number of ways, including being picked up or grappled by a larger creature, being knocked through the air by an impact or explosion, or even being magically moved in some fashion.

The material components are a chip of granite and a hair from a giant.

4th Level

Stonefire (Pr 4; Alteration)

Sphere:	Elemental Earth, Elemental Fire
Range:	Touch
Components:	V, S, M
Duration:	1 round/level
Casting Time:	7
Area of Effect:	1 cubic foot/level
Saving Throw:	None

This spell allows the caster to ignite stone into roaring flames. The stone blackens, stretches to reveal holes, burns away from the edges of these holes in ever-widening cavities until large amounts of stone have actually been burnt away, and then smolders into quiescence again, creaking as it cools.

The *stonefire* gives off an acrid, billowing white smoke, an earthy, metallic stink, and flames that cause 2d6 points of fire and heat damage (per round) to creatures within 10 feet. Actual contact with *stonefire* causes 4d4 points of damage and forces a system shock check to avoid collapsing, unconscious, from the pain.

Creatures especially susceptible to fire damage may suffer as much as double these effects. Creatures made of stone take 4d4 points of damage in the first round and a like amount each round until a successful saving throw vs. spell is made, checking each round. Creatures resistant to fire may suffer as little as 1d2 points of damage from contact with *stonefire*. (They suffer some damage due to the corrosive effects of the burning.) Stone burned away by this spell is consumed, forever gone.

If key areas of stonework (such as pillars) or natural stone walls, ceilings, or supporting floors are burned away, collapses and cave-ins may occur. The effects of cave-ins are detailed in the spell description for *stonefall* in the entry for Dumathoin. Collapses entail the same damage, plus falling damage (and item saving throws) for beings and things that fall as a result of the spell. This spell cannot be precisely controlled, even with long practice; it is unsuitable for stone carving or decorating uses. The caster can affect 1 cubic foot of stone per level; a man-sized statue is roughly 12 cubic feet.

The material components of this spell are a few grains of saltpeter and a piece of stone that are rubbed together.

5th Level

Soul Forge (Pr 5; Enchantment/Charm)

Sphere:	Creation, Law
Range:	Touch
Components:	V, S, M
Duration:	1 hr./level
Casting Time:	1 turn
Area of Effect:	Creature touched
Saving Throw:	None

By means of this spell, the priest strengthens and tempers the moral fiber of a willing recipient. A creature tempered by a *soul forge* spell is immune to all *fear* effects (including dragon *awe*) and need never check morale. Further, the creature cannot be taken over by an outside intelligence against its will and receives a +1 bonus to its Armor Class and saving throws when attacked by evil creatures.

It is rumored that a longer, ceremonial version of this spell exists that can extend this protection to 1 day per level of the caster.

Soul forge is effective only when cast on lawful good beings. There is a 25% chance this spell fails when cast on nondwarves.

The material component is the priest's holy symbol.

7th Level

Stone Storm (Pr 7; Evocation) *Reversible*

Sphere:	Elemental Earth
Range:	10 yards/level
Components:	V, S, M
Duration:	1 round
Casting Time:	1 round
Area of Effect:	Special
Saving Throw:	½

When a *stone storm* spell is cast, the whole area is enmeshed in a vortex of swirling, battering rock and stone. Creatures within the area of hurtling stone suffer 2d8 points of damage plus 1 additional point of damage per caster level (thus, a 14th-level priest inflicts 2d8+14 points of damage). Creatures that make a successful saving throw vs. spell suffer only one-half damage. The area of effect is selected by the caster at the instant of casting from two options. The first is a circle of 60-foot radius with a 10-foot radius "eye" in the center that is not affected. The second is a cloud whose total dimensions do not exceed 120 in feet (for example, a cloud might be 40 feet wide, 20 feet tall, and 60 feet long).

The reverse of this spell, *stone quench*, clears twice the area of effect of a *stone storm* of dust, dirt, and other particles suspended in the air. Thus, a dusty haze that obscures vision and impedes breathing, such as that generated in battle or caused by an avalanche, is cleared instantly. Magic of 6th level or less that creates such effects is instantly ended (*dust devil, wall of sand, sandstorm,* and so on). Creatures from the Elemental Plane of Earth of less than demigod status can be returned to that plane by *stone quench* cast for this purpose. The base chance is a roll of 6 or better on 1d20. The caster's level is added to the roll and the creature's Hit Dice or level is subtracted from the roll.

The material components of this spell are the priest's holy symbol and a handful of pebbles, sand, or dirt that must be thrown into the air.

Sharindlar

(Lady of Life, Lady of Mercy, the Merciful, the Bountiful, the Shining Dancer)

Intermediate Power of Ysgard, CG

PORTFOLIO:	Healing, mercy, romantic love, fertility, dancing, courtship, the moon
ALIASES:	None
DOMAIN NAME:	Nidavellir/The Merciful Court
SUPERIOR:	Moradin
ALLIES:	Angharradh, Chauntea, Cyrrollalee, Eldath, Hanali Celanil, Hathor, Ilmater, the Morndinsamman (except Abbathor, Deep Duerra, Laduguer), Sheela Peryroyl, Shiallia, Tapann, Yondalla, various Animal Lords
FOES:	Urdlen
SYMBOL:	A flame rising from a steel needle
WOR. ALIGN.:	LG, NG, CG, LN, N, CN, LE, NE, CE

Sharindlar (Sha-RIHN-dlar) the Merciful is widely known as the dwarven goddess of healing and mercy. Dwarves wounded in battle are often healed in her name. Sick dwarves, dwarven healers, midwives, physics, and lovers pray to the Lady of Life. However, her aspect kept secret from nondwarves is her most important modern role: her patronage of romantic love, courtship, and fertility. Dwarves of all alignments and races who are courting appease her, as do those who sentence others in the cause of justice. When dwarves dance, they pray to Sharindlar to guide their feet, for she is said to be the greatest dancer the dwarves have ever known.

Sharindlar is on excellent terms with most of the other members of the Morndinsamman. She has forged working relationships with those whose principles she abhors—Abbathor, Deep Duerra, and Laduguer—to facilitate her efforts for the benefit of the dwarven race. The Lady of Life has served as an emissary between Laduguer of the gray dwarves and Moradin on the rare occasions they must communicate. Sharindlar has little tolerance for hatreds or rivalries that interfere with her efforts to dispense healing and mercy to the wounded and distressed. She has made strong friendships with the deities of the korreds, and some myths claim that Shiallia, the Dancer in the Glades, is the offspring of Sharindlar's brief dalliance with Tapann.

Sharindlar is invariably warm and caring with a kind word for all, both mortal and divine. She is given to shouts of joy, impromptu dances, and gales of uncontrollable laughter. The Lady of Life is an inveterate matchmaker and true romantic who seeks to conjoin star-crossed lovers no matter what the odds. More than one favored dwarven bachelor or maiden has been swept up in a series of whirlwind affairs, thanks to the unceasing efforts of the Shining Dancer to provide the perfect mate.

Sharindlar's Avatar (Cleric 35, Wizard 23)

Sharindlar appears as a slim, spirited, full-bearded and flame-haired dwarven maiden. She possesses arresting eyes that seem to change color often—different observers down the centuries have reported them as being of differing hues. To observers of races whose females do not grow beards (such as humans), Sharindlar's beard may seem to vanish, or appear and reappear like a flickering flame. Sharindlar never wears armor and is usually barefoot and clad in diaphanous gowns. Occasionally, she appears at parties wildly garbed in boots or high-heeled shoes, with rich gowns and ornate accoutrements. If Sharindlar is attacked, flames rise around her body to armor her in flame. Her clothing vanishes, reappearing unharmed as the flames die. She favors spells from the spheres of all, animal, charm, creation, healing, necromantic (regular or reversed), plant, sun, and time and the schools of alteration, divination, and enchantment/charm, although she can cast spells from any sphere or school.

AC −2 (−4); MV 12 or 15; HP 178; THAC0 −2; #AT 2
Dmg 1d2+15 (*whip +6, +9* Str) and 1d6+12 (*footman's mace +2, +9* Str)
MR 70%; SZ M (6 feet high) or H (13 feet high)
Str 21, Dex 20, Con 19, Int 19, Wis 18, Cha 25
Spells P: 13/13/11/11/10/10/9, W: 5/5/5/5/5/5/5/5/3
Saves PPDM 2, RSW 1*, PP 5, BW 8, Sp 6
*Includes dwarf +5 Con save bonus to a minimum of 1. The Con save bonus also applies to saves vs. poison to a minimum of 1.

Special Att/Def: Sharindlar fights with a *whip +6* that is studded with adamantine barbs (chaotic good-aligned) and a *mace +2* that never makes any sound when it strikes. The mace forces ethereal and invisible creatures into full presence and visibility on the Prime Material Plane for at least two rounds, by touch.

Sharindlar can enact the effects of *forget, friends,* and *charm person* on other beings (saving throws at −6 penalty) by touch. She may use each of these three abilities seven times per day.

At will (in addition to *regeneration* and magical or physical attacks in the same round), Sharindlar can cloak her body in flames. These affect flammable materials as normal flames do, deal 2d8 damage per round of contact to any creature entering them (such damage is gained by the goddess through her regenerative ability), and improve her Armor Class by 2.

Sharindlar cannot be *charmed* or fooled by magic that works on the mind or senses. Her touch is said to *neutralize poison*, which she can do three times a day. Sharindlar herself is said to be immune to all known poisons. She can be struck only by +2 or better magical weapons.

If slain, Sharindlar becomes a ghostlike entity. This form cannot be turned and can become invisible at will. She can work magic, employ a ghost's attacks, and has half her normal hit points.

Other Manifestations

Sharindlar rarely appears in avatar form in the Realms, but quite often aids dwarves by manifesting as an amber or rosy radiance and warmth. If healing herbs or plant antidotes are required and exist nearby, Sharindlar illuminates them with her radiance, to mark them for searching dwarves. If a sick dwarf seeks shelter or water, Sharindlar's radiance guides them. If dwarves are cold and lack shelter, Sharindlar's warmth and light can keep them comfortable while they rest, even on glaciers or rock ledges in blizzards. Her light is bright enough for wizards to study by and for maps and books to be read.

At dances, moots, and other meetings when dwarves may be conceived, Sharindlar often attempts to sway the thoughts and actions of dwarves by her warmth and radiance. Dwarven sages still argue over whether this is purely the result of her presence, serving as a hint and sign of approval, or if she can manifest subtle aphrodisiac powers.

Sharindlar is served by dryads, (Ysgardian) dwarves of Nidavellir, einheriar, foo dogs, galeb duhr, hollyphants, incarnates of hope, temperance, and wisdom, korred, lillendi, linnorm dragons, slyphs, and sunflies. She manifests her favor through the discovery of emeralds, moonstones, and round silver coins and her displeasure through the discovery of worn, mateless boots, shattered egg shells, and curdled milk.

The Church

CLERGY:	Clerics, specialty priests
CLERGY'S ALIGN.:	LG, NG, CG
TURN UNDEAD:	C: Yes, SP: No
CMND. UNDEAD:	C: No, SP: No

All clerics and specialty priests of Sharindlar receive religion (dwarven) and reading/writing (Dethek runes) as bonus nonweapon proficiencies. Clerics of Sharindlar cannot turn undead before 7th level, but they always strike at +2 on all attack and damage rolls against undead creatures. At 7th level and above, clerics can turn undead as other clerics do, but as a cleric of four levels less than their current level. These modifications apply only to the cleric class. All priests of Sharindlar were female before the Time of Troubles, but some males have joined the priesthood since then.

Sharindlar is universally well regarded by dwarves and held in high esteem by those who share her beliefs among other races. Even the most xenophobic elves and the most supercilious humans are impressed by her devotion to the downtrodden and her kind and unassuming nature, despite their deep-held prejudices.

Temples to the Lady of Life are great halls, free of pillars or other architectural features. Serving as both chancels and grand ballrooms, they are well lit, often above ground or partially open to the sky, and typically hold fountains, pools, and formal gardens. The goddess's temples have numerous small guest chambers for visitors, of which there are many. Most of the

Dwarven Powers: Sharindlar

Shining Dancer's temples have a small library that serves as a repository of runestones inscribed with dwarven genealogies, clan records, courting rites, descriptions of formal dances, astronomy charts, medicinal practices, herbal brews, agricultural and husbandry records, and the like.

Novices of Sharindlar are known as the Chaste. Full priests are known as Merciful Maidens/Youths. In ascending order of rank, the titles used by Sharindlaran priests are Dancing Tresses, Golden Allure, Healing Touch, Merciful Smile, Loving Heart, and Fruitful Mother/Father. High Old Ones have unique individual titles but are collectively known as the Sons/Daughters (Dauls) of Sharindlar. Specialty priests are known as *thalornor*, a dwarvish word that can be loosely translated as *those who are merciful*. The clergy of Sharindlar includes gold dwarves (49%), shield dwarves (48%), jungle dwarves (2%), and even gray dwarves (1%). Sharindlar's clergy is nearly evenly divided between specialty priests (58%) and clerics (42%). The priesthood is still nearly all female (99%).

Dogma: Be merciful in speech and deed. Bring relief and healing where needful. Temper anger and hostility with constructive and charitable endeavor. The children of Moradin must live in safety and propagate. Maintain and encourage the traditional rites of courting and marriage. Celebrate the endless, joyous dance of life by living it to the fullest. Sharindlar restores the fertile seed of dwarven life, while Berronar protects the fruit.

Day-to-Day Activities: The traditional duties of Sharindlar's clergy include dispensing healing and mercy to dwarves and other individuals in need. This role requires both hospices in dwarven strongholds and travel to isolated dwarven holds scattered throughout surface and subterranean wildernesses. As dwarven birthrates slowly decline and the ranks of the Stout Folk shrink, particularly among the shield dwarves of the North, priests in Sharindlar's service devote most of their energy to reverse these trends, with the assistance of Berronar's clergy. The Merciful Maidens/Youths have focused on maintaining and teaching dwarven courting rites: traditional dances, ritual forms of address, and the like. They strive to bring young dwarves together, engendering likely matches, particularly outside the traditional clans, hoping to increase the number of prolific unions. Sharindlar's oversight of fertility has been extended in many dwarven cultures (particularly in surface-dwelling cultures such as High Shanatar and Besilmer) to include agriculture and animal husbandry. A particular emphasis has been placed on developing new strains of crops—wheat, barley, mushrooms, lichens, etc.—and hardier breeds of beasts—donkeys, sheep, etc.

Holy Days/Important Ceremonies: The worship of Sharindlar has been kept secret from outsiders, especially her fertility aspect. Dwarves in general refer to her as the Lady of Mercy whenever they know nondwarves to be listening. Dwarven priests of any faith who care for the wounded or sick often pray briefly for Sharindlar's favor.

When the moon begins to wax (the night after the new moon), at Greengrass, at Midsummer Night, and whenever the moon is full, Sharindlar's clergy gather to pray to the Lady of Life. The more secret rituals of Sharindlar take place in hidden caverns, wherever there is a pool of water. Such ceremonies involve dancing, prayers for the Lady's mercy and guidance, and the sacrifice of gold. Gold is heated until molten, and dwarves let blood from their own forearms into the mixture, which is then poured into the water, as Sharindlar's name is chanted and the dwarves dance about the pool in a frenzy, armor and weapons near at hand but not worn or carried.

In the Deep Realm, Sharindlar's rituals take place around the Lake of Gold, a subterranean lake whose rocky bottom is streaked with gleaming veins of gold. The Lady of Life's dwarven faithful never take gold from the lake, whose bottom is now carpeted with the sparkling gold dust of long ages of worship resulting from rituals performed in an effort to raise the low birthrate of the race. Rituals in honor of Sharindlar's fertility aspect celebrated here always end with splendid feasts and courting chases through the underways of the Deeps. Rituals invoking Sharindlar's healing strength enacted by two or more priests of the goddess involve their gathering over injured or sick beings. The Lady of Life's priests sprinkle the ill from a vial of water from the Lake of Gold, while whispering secret names and descriptions of the goddess. This ritual has a 20% chance of aiding healing per priest taking part, increased by 10% if water from the Lake of Gold is used, and another 20% if the injured being is favored by Sharindlar (a DM decision: Sharindlar has been known to favor nondwarves, pack animals, and even monsters). The aid increases of healing spells and potions to their maximum possible effect, doubles the at-rest healing rate, and halts the spread or effect of parasites (including rot grubs), diseases, and poisons completely for 1d4+1 days. The DM chooses the beneficial effect according to the circumstances. Even Sharindlar's name, whispered or repeated silently in the mind by the faithful, has a calming effect on upset or pain-wracked dwarves of all faiths, allowing them to sleep.

Major Centers of Worship: Tyn'rrin Wurlur, the Vale of Dancing Water, is a sprawling temple complex built among the ruins of the long-fallen summer palace of King Torhild Flametonguee of Besilmer. Nestled amidst the rolling Sumber Hills—the modern name for the hills bisected by the River Dessarin, which lie just south of the Stone Bridge—the Rook of Torhild, as it is also known, is located on the western bank of the River Dessarin east of the abandoned, monster-haunted, adventurers' keeps along the Larch Path. If dwarven legends are true, the temple's catacombs contain the lost riches of fallen Besilmer, as yet unplundered, and access to subterranean tunnels that stretch from the Sword Mountains to the Unicorn Run.

The very existence of Sharindlar's temple in the Sumber Hills is a closely guarded secret among the Stout Folk of the North, a practice in keeping with the general reticence among dwarves to even discuss the beliefs and role of the Lady of Life with nondwarves. Passersby on the swift-flowing current below the hidden vale can see naught but three tiny creek-fed waterfalls that rush over the 30-foot-high cliff in an endless cascade of water and shimmering light. The aboveground structures of the temple complex are nearly invisible to anyone flying overhead, appearing as little more than boulder-strewn hillocks. Few travelers make the dangerous trek overland from the village of Red Larch to the western bank of the River Dessarin—even fewer stumble into the isolated dell, as the few footpaths in the region are cunningly constructed so as to lead travelers away from the elevated valley.

The fortified hospice of Tyn'rrin Wurlur is ably led by the aging matriarch, Dame of the Dessarin March Gwythiir, daul of Zarna. Gwythiir is assisted by a council of the eight highest-ranking priests residing in the abbey, collectively known as the Ladies of Merciful Life. When not roaming the North healing those in need, the temple's clergy—whose ranks include nearly two hundred dwarven priests who have received the call of the Lady of Life—spend their days at the temple tending small vineyards, making wine, and cultivating mushrooms on the shaded banks of the small creeks that wind through the valley. The wine presses of Tyn'rrin Wurlur are renowned in dwarven societies throughout the North for producing tuber nectar, a grape and mushroom wine legendary for its aphrodisiac properties. The Vale of Dancing Water is nearly as well known among the Stout Folk for its instruction of young dwarves, both male and female, in the rites of courting and the formal dances that have been passed down for centuries. In recent decades, successful dwarves—particularly those who have earned both wealth and honor by adventuring—have been returning to Tyn'rrin Wurlur when they are ready to settle down to enlist the Dame of the Dessarin March in finding them a suitable mate. Finally, the Vale of Dancing Water serves always-welcoming hospice to wounded or sick dwarves who seek sanctuary in order to finish out their days, or if possible, until they recover. Aging dwarves, particularly those whose careers developed their fighting prowess, often retire to Tyn'rrin Wurlur where they serve as seasoned, if aging, defenders of the vale.

Affiliated Orders: While Sharindlar has no martial orders dedicated to her name, about one in five of her priests serve small dwarven communities as midwives, independent of the faith's more organized temple hierarchies. Members of this informal sorority are known collectively as the Maidens of Midwifery, and often extend their roles to include that of physician, matchmaker, and brewer of both aphrodisiacs and elixirs said to increase fertility.

Priestly Vestments: For ceremonial functions, Sharindlar's priests wear red robes with a blue girdle. The head is left bare except for a robin's egg blue scarf. The holy symbol of the faith is a silver disk embossed on both sides with the symbol of the goddess. It is often hung from an argent chain placed around the neck.

Adventuring Garb: Sharindlar's priests avoid violence if possible, but they defend themselves or their charges against obviously hostile and violent opponents. While they prefer regular dwarven garb, the Maidens of Mercy gird themselves with armor when appropriate. A blue scarf, tied around the brow, upper arm, wrist, or ankle, is worn as an adornment. Although they rarely advertise it, members of Sharindlar's clergy usually carry a small knife so that they can mercifully end the suffering of creatures whose pain cannot otherwise be alleviated and whose demise is imminent.

Specialty Priests (Thalornor)

REQUIREMENTS:	Constitution 9, Wisdom 11
PRIME REQ.:	Constitution, Wisdom
ALIGNMENT:	CG
WEAPONS:	Any bludgeoning (wholly Type B) weapon, plus knives
ARMOR:	Any
MAJOR SPHERES:	All, animal, charm, creation, healing, necromantic, plant, sun, time
MINOR SPHERES:	Elemental, guardian, protection
MAGICAL ITEMS:	Same as clerics
REQ. PROFS:	Herbalism
BONUS PROFS:	Dancing, etiquette, healing

- While most thalornor (the plural form of thalornar) are either gold dwarves or shield dwarves, dwarves of nearly every subrace are called to be specialty priests of the Lady of Life.
- Thalornor are not allowed to multiclass.
- Thalornor can cast *cure light wounds* (as the 1st-level priest spell) once per day.
- At 3rd level, thalornor can cast *aid* (as the 2nd-level priest spell) once per day.
- At 3rd level, thalornor can cast *detect dwarves* (as the 1st-level priest spell) at will.
- At 5th level, thalornor can cast *merciful touch* (as the 3rd-level priest spell) once per day.
- At 7th level, thalornor can cast *cure serious wounds* (as the 4th-level priest spell) once per day.
- At 10th level, thalornor can cast *cure critical wounds* (as the 5th-level priest spell) once per day.
- At 13th level, thalornor can cast *heal* (as the 6th-level priest spell) once per day.
- At 15th level, thalornor can cast *flowstone* (as the 5th-level priest spell) once per day.
- At 20th level, thalornor can cast *word of recall* (as the 6th-level priest spell) once per day.
- At 20th level, thalornor can cast *gate* (as the 7th-level priest spell) twice per tenday.

Sharindlaran Spells

In addition to the spells listed below, priests of the Lady of Life can cast the 3rd-level priest spell *ease labor* and the 4th-level priest spell *fertility*, both of which are detailed in *Powers & Pantheons* in the entry for Shiallia.

1st Level

Detect Dwarves (Pr 1; Divination)

Sphere:	Divination
Range:	0
Components:	V, S, M
Duration:	1 turn
Casting Time:	1 round
Area of Effect:	10 feet × 90 feet
Saving Throw:	None

When the *detect dwarves* spell is cast, the priest detects living dwarves, dead dwarves, azer, duergar, derro, half-dwarves, and spilled dwarven blood, even if they are invisible, shapechanged, concealed by illusions, and so on, in a path 10 feet wide and up to 90 feet long in the direction she or he is facing. The approximate number of dwarves present within the area of effect can also be determined within 10%. The caster has a 5% chance per level to determine the subrace and gender of dwarves detected, to a maximum of 75%. The caster can turn, scanning a 60° arc per round. The spell is blocked by solid metal at least 1 inch thick, solid stone at least 1 foot thick, or solid wood at least 1 yard thick.

The material component is the priest's holy symbol.

3rd Level

Merciful Touch (Pr 3; Alteration)

Sphere:	Healing
Range:	Touch
Components:	V, S, M
Duration:	Special
Casting Time:	6
Area of Effect:	Creature touched
Saving Throw:	None

By means of this spell, the priest can both heal and relieve suffering. *Merciful touch* cures 1d12 points of damage. The dweomer also alleviates conditions not otherwise removed by the curative aspect of this spell for up to 24 hours. For example, the discomfort caused by a disease is held in abeyance, although the disease itself is neither cured nor placed in remission. Likewise, the excruciating pain of an injury such as a broken ankle is masked for the duration; however, it is still not possible for the creature to put weight on the ankle. Spells such as *irritation* can be effectively negated if the duration of the *merciful touch* exceeds the duration of the spell that inflicts the suffering. *Merciful touch* only affects conditions in existence at the time it is cast.

The material component is the priest's holy symbol.

5th Level

Flowstone (Pr 5; Alteration)

Sphere:	Elemental Earth
Range:	10 yards
Components:	V, S, M
Duration:	1 round
Casting Time:	8
Area of Effect:	3 cubic feet/level
Saving Throw:	Special

This spell makes stone flow like syrup and then harden. The stone flows in response to gravity but may be directed by beings (such as skilled dwarves) wielding wooden paddles or erecting temporary dams. The flowing stone is not heated or altered in hue. The spell does not affect worked stone.

Dwarves often use this spell to shape stone conduits, by flowing stone around logs that are later burnt away, and to sculpt stone into smooth door surrounds, covering or shielding embedded locks and the like.

Its most deadly use is to trap beings by entombing them or encasing their feet or other body parts in the hardening stone. A creature in contact with flowing stone is allowed a saving throw vs. poison. If successful, the creature entirely avoids entrapment, winning free of the affected area without harm. (Those entering the area again must make another saving

throw.) Failure means the creature is partially encrusted, slowed to half movement, and suffers a 2-point Dexterity penalty until the stone is washed off (within 2 rounds) or shattered and scraped off (thereafter). If an encrusted being is rendered immobile or in the center of a flowing area more than 10 feet across, a saving throw vs. spell is required to avoid entrapment.

A creature struggling against hardening stone is allowed a Strength check. If successful, it reaches the edge of the flow area and emerges with one or more limbs encased in immobilizing blobs of stone. Failure means the creature is entrapped in the hardening stone. If stone covers a creature's breathing orifices (in most beings, the head), death occurs in 1d4+1 rounds. If stone merely prevents movement, death by starvation occurs in 1d10+10 days or when the creature is overcome by rising water, attacking beasts, or the like.

Attacks on the stone transmit half damage directly to the trapped creature. An encased limb can be freed either by amputation (lose 25% of full hit points and an immediate system shock roll against death), or by inflicting 20 points of crushing or piercing damage on the stone (10 points on the trapped creature). A second *flowstone* spell can free trapped beings without harm.

The material components of this spell are a drop of water, a daub of mud, a grain of sand, and a pebble.

Thard Harr
(Lord of the Jungle Deeps, Disentangler)

Lesser Power of the Beastlands, CG

PORTFOLIO:	The wild dwarven race, jungle survival, hunting
ALIASES:	None
DOMAIN NAME:	Krigala/The Forbidden Plateau
SUPERIOR:	Moradin
ALLIES:	Baervan Wildwanderer, Cyrrollalee, Jazirian, the Morndinsamman (except Abbathor, Deep Duerra, and Laduguer), Nobanion, Ubtao, various Animal Lords
FOES:	Deep Duerra, Eshowdow, Laduguer, Sseth, Urdlen, the goblin pantheon
SYMBOL:	Two crossed, metal gauntlets of silvery-blue, luminous metal, ending in claws and covered with lapped scales
WOR. ALIGN.:	Any

Thard Harr (THARD HAHRR) is the protector of wild dwarves (also known as *jungle dwarves*), aiding them against intruders and marauding beasts. The Lord of the Jungle Deeps is revered only by *dur Authalar* (*the People*) as the wild dwarves of the jungles of Faerûn refer to themselves. Some hunters of other races and alignments operating in jungle areas look to the Disentangler for guidance as well, but they have little to do with the mainstream of Thard's faith or with wild dwarven society.

The Lord of the Jungle Deeps maintains friendly, but distant, relations with most of the other members of the Morndinsamman, but he is far removed from the concerns of dwarven life, at least as expressed by the gold and shield dwarf cultures of Faerûn. Sharindlar and Dumathoin are probably the only dwarven powers to interact with Thard on a regular basis, the former for her interest in the rampant fertility of the jungle and the latter for his oversight of the albino shield dwarves of Chult who come into occasional contact with their wild kinfolk. Thard has forged alliances and developed hatreds for many of the other powers whose worshipers dwell or have dwelt in the jungles of southern Faerûn. Notable allies include Jazirian, lord of the couatl, and Ubtao, Father of the Dinosaurs, Founder of Mezro, and god of the Tabaxi. The Disentangler's most notable foes include Eshowdow the Shadow Giant, Ubtao's antithesis and lord of the Eshowe (jungle humans), Sseth the Great Snake, god of the yuan-ti, and Kuro (Khurgorbaeyag), the most widely worshiped god of the Batiri (jungle goblins). Finally, although they are not true powers in their own right, Thard has forged close relationships with many of the Animal Lords who also dwell in the Beastlands.

Thard seldom speaks, but he has been known to purr, growl, snarl, and roar like a great cat. He is given to great swings of emotion and grand gestures. The Disentangler has no tolerance for pretentious behavior, civilization, or social constraints of any sort. He seldom appears in the Realms, preferring to roam the Beastlands, aiding his worshipers by manifestations instead. The Lord of the Jungle Deeps lives on the Forbidden Plateau, where Ubtao has his secondary realm, but he also loves to wander the three layers of the Beastlands, constantly stalking the beasts that dwell there and frolicking with them, running as one of them rather than preying upon them.

Thard's Avatar (Ranger 29, Druid 24)

Thard appears as a dark-skinned, potbellied dwarf covered with tattoos and tufts of long, matted hair. The Disentangler is naked except for his long beard, the thick growth of hair that covers his torso, and an ornate copper helm that conceals his face. His helm is fashioned in the shape of a crocodile's head, festooned with a fringe of dangling teeth, reportedly torn from creatures the god has slain. Thard can cast spells from the spheres of all, animal, chaos, charm, creation, divination, elemental, healing, plant, sun, travelers, and weather.

AC −2; MV 15; Cl 12; HP 204; THAC0 −8; #AT 2
Dmg 2d8+10 (claw, +10 Str) and 2d8+10 (claw, +10 Str)
MR 50%; SZ M (6 feet high)
Str 22, Dex 19, Con 21, Int 17, Wis 18, Cha 20
Spells P: 11/11/10/10/9/8/3
Saves PPDM 2, RSW 1*, PP 4, BW 4, Sp 6
   *Includes dwarf +6 Con save bonus to a minimum of 1. The Con save bonus also applies to saves vs. poison to a minimum of 1.

Special Att/Def: Thard wears scaled, adamantine gauntlets strapped to his forearms at the elbow (as high as they reach). These gauntlets end in jointed, razor-sharp claws that can rake or thrust for 2d8 damage each and are reputedly unbreakable. Jungle dwarves speak of opponents or natural forces so powerful and dangerous that they might well blunt the claws of Harr himself, but they never allude to the breaking of any claw or the defeat of their god in any fight.

The Lord of the Jungle Deeps can breathe out a spicy, greenish-blue gas once per day, in a cone 5 feet wide at its base and 20 feet wide at its furthest extent (20 feet away). Creatures in this cloud when it is released and on the round following must make a successful saving throw vs. breath weapon, or be unable to unleash or activate any spells or magical items for the next nine rounds. Currently operating magic continues to function, but cannot be altered in target, power level, or attitude, as the DM judges appropriate.

Thard has a special empathy with jungle animals, and they never attack him. He can command any of them not controlled by an outside force within 100 yards of him to obey him by mental commands, and they understand his intent perfectly. Thard is immune to *charm* effects, *hold* effects, illusions, and poisons of any sort. He cannot be caught in any web, shrubbery, vines, jaws, or glues (of monsters or plants), and he can *feather fall* any distance. He is fearless, oblivious to pain and its effects, and he can reattach severed limbs or torn body parts just as a troll does. His touch can empower any dwarf to do this (including *regeneration* of 1d4+1 points per round) for three rounds. He can be struck only by +1 or better magical weapons.

Other Manifestations

Thard's manifestations involve low, continuous thudding and snarling sounds that apparently emanate from the empowered beings. The sounds are unstoppable and have no special effect. Empowered beings begin to glow with a crawling, pulsing nimbus of cherry-red light, and they are imbued with power from the god for up to 1 turn.

Thard empowers only one being at a time, either a wild dwarf or a jungle beast. A beast simply uses its natural attacks and abilities to fight for the jungle dwarves to the death. It is rendered immune to natural or magical *entanglement*, including snares, any form of *charm* or mental influences, including illusions. It becomes fearless, attacking despite fire, spells, or opponents of large size or demonstrated ferocity.

An empowered dwarf gains a temporary bonus of four levels (affecting THAC0, all saving throws, and hit points). Temporary hit points gained in this way are lost with the withdrawal of Thard's power, but any damage suffered by an empowered dwarf is taken first from these. Empowered dwarves also gain *claws of Thard Harr*.

Thard often manifests in one dwarf after another in the same conflict, so that intruders may face one empowered dwarf for a turn, another for the next turn, and so on. The god never aids the same dwarf for more than 6 turns in a day, but he may grant aid in separate visits (either actual, or in manifestations), to this limit, if danger persists.

Thard is served by alligators, asuras, baku, bats, boalisks, buraq, crocodiles, dinosaurs (children of Ubtao), dryads, earth and water elementals, einheriar, elephants, emerald dragons, giant beetles, grippli, hollyphants, insect swarms, jaculi, jaguars, leomarhs, leopards, mist dragons, normal and giant animals, spitting snakes, strangleweed, sunflies, tigers, treants, triflower fronds, and warden beasts. He demonstrates his favor through the discovery of calantra wood carvings, diamonds, emeralds, gold, green spinels, metal weapons, and zalantar wood rods. The Lord of the Jungle Deeps indicates his displeasure by causing the recipient of his wrath to become tangled in a vine and trip, by shattering precious gems with the roar of some great beast hidden by the surrounding jungle, or by causing metal to rust, wood to rot, and leather to rapidly decay.

The Church

CLERGY:	Clerics, specialty priests
CLERGY'S ALIGN.:	NG, CG, N, CN
TURN UNDEAD:	C: Yes, SP: No
CMND. UNDEAD:	C: No, SP: No

All clerics and specialty priests of Thard receive religion (dwarven) and reading/writing (Dethek runes) as bonus nonweapon proficiencies. Clerics of Thard Harr can use any weapons, not just bludgeoning (wholly Type B) weapons. Clerics of Thard Harr cannot turn undead before 7th level, but they always strike at +2 on all attack and damage rolls against undead creatures. At 7th level and above, clerics can turn undead as other clerics do, but as a cleric of four levels less than their current level. These modifications apply only to the cleric class. The church of Thard Har ceased following the dwarven traditions about clergy and gender long ago, so the numbers of females in the formerly male-exclusive priesthood are relatively large.

Like the Tabaxi and Ubtao, the wild dwarves of the Jungles of Chult and the Mhair Jungles are nearly monotheistic in outlook, and the worship of the Lord of the Jungle Deeps is so firmly embedded in their culture it is nearly impossible, regardless of alignment, for them to conceive of any alternative faith. Outside of the human and demihuman cultures of the Chultan peninsula, however, Thard and his followers are little more than legend, even among the gold dwarves of the South. Ancient dwarven tradition holds that Thard was once revered as a dwarven god of nature by the other dwarven subraces, but High Shanatar, the last dwarven culture to revere him as such, has long since fallen.

Temples of Thard rarely incorporate artificial structures like buildings or dwarf-carved caves. The Disentangler is worshiped in isolated sanctuaries of incredible natural beauty rich in animal and plant life. Soaring cliffs, great waterfalls, vast gorges, hot springs, natural caverns, and volcanic mud flats deep in the heart of the jungles of the Chultan peninsula are common places for Thard's worshipers to gather. Like the great druid groves of the North, such sites are strong in faith magic and can often serve as a source for mystic rituals of great power. Usually up to a dozen priests of the Lord of the Jungle Deeps watch over such holy sites, and they can call on the beasts of the surrounding jungle as well as nearby tribes of wild dwarves to defend these sanctuaries.

Priests of the Lord of the Jungle Deeps are known as shamans (although they are not actually members of that class) and eschew the use of a formal hierarchy of titles. High Old Ones are collectively known as the Lords/Ladies of the Jungle. Each priest receives a personal title in a dream on the night the individual is initiated into the clergy. Such titles typically include the name of a great beast of the jungle over which the priest is then believed to have a small amount of supernatural control. Specialty priests are known as *vuddor*, a dwarvish word that can be loosely translated as *those of the jungle*. The clergy of Thard consists primarily of jungle dwarves (99%), plus a small handful of gold, gray, and shield dwarves (1%). Most of the Disentangler's priests are male (60%), but in recent centuries increasing numbers of females (40%) have been admitted to the priesthood as well. Thard's clergy is nearly evenly divided between specialty priests (53%) and clerics (47%).

Dogma: The jungle is the fullest expression of the earth, the wind, the sun, and the rains. Live in harmony with nature under the wise and benevolent protection of the Lord of the Jungle Deeps. Outsiders seek to pillage and destroy, and their unnatural ways bring misery. Like the great tigers of the jungle, be strong and wary of beasts, whether they walk on two legs or four. Seek to understand that which you do not, but be wary of bringing unknown gifts into your lair. Be one with nature—live neither against it nor apart from it. Honor the ways of your people, but assume not that Thard's way is the only way—just the best way for his children.

Day-to-Day Activities: Priests of Thard represent the Lord of the Jungle Deeps, protecting dur Authalar with powers given to them by the god and leading them on prosperous hunts and careful explorations. They are the leaders and generals of, and speakers for, their people.

The responsibility for eliminating persistent intruders (unless dwarven) into wild dwarven territory falls to the Disentangler's priests, and they are expected to lead such attacks as fearlessly and diligently as Thard himself. If a foe is too strong, a priest tries to mentally call Thard himself to the scene, and the Lord of the Jungle Deeps often responds by either sending a manifestation, or in very rare situations, by dispatching an avatar to deal with the threat directly.

Thard's wisdom teaches that one can best defeat an enemy that one knows well. Seasoned wild dwarves try to capture at least one intruder alive for questioning, before sacrificial use. If sparing the intruder seems likely to bring possible future benefits to the dwarves, they do so. Jungle dwarves are interested in trade—metal, glass objects, and tools—in return for pelts, meat, or even live beasts. They conduct trade so long as they can conduct it on territory of their choosing, to set up traps and ambushes to guard against treachery under the direction of priests of Thard.

Holy Days/Important Ceremonies: Ceremonies venerating the Lord of the Jungle Deeps are held on nights of the full and new moon. On such occasions, several hunting bands come together under the direction of one or more priests of Thard. The drums and chants of the wild dwarves then echo throughout the jungle, striking terror in the hearts of intelligent beings and beasts alike. Whenever the moon is full, and often when the moon is new, blood sacrifices of beasts and/or intruders are offered up to the Lord of the Jungle Deeps. Although they are not cannibals and do not usually eat intelligent beings, the assembled wild dwarves then often eat the still-warm sacrifice, regardless of its species.

Major Centers of Worship: Morndin Vertesplendarrorn, the Emerald Crater, is located high above the Jungles of Chult in the truncated cone of a shattered volcano left by the eruption of what was once the northwesternmost of the Peaks of Flame centuries ago. The crater is now totally overgrown by the jungle and rife with such animal and plant life as is little seen in the rest of Chultan peninsula, let alone Faerûn. The Emerald Crater has long been a place of pilgrimage for the wild dwarves of the surrounding jungles. Thard is said to have appeared here on more than one occasion, so great is the beauty of the region. However, there is little physical evidence that the wild dwarves visit the mountain valley on a regular basis, for their stories teach that it is a crime to hunt or otherwise despoil the riotous life that dwells within. However, interlopers find themselves quickly confronted and driven off by elite bands of wild dwarves if they even approach, let alone enter, the Emerald Crater.

One reason Morndin Vertesplendarrorn has its preeminent position among the wild dwarven culture (the dur Authalar tend to abandon such locales after a generation or two), is the presence of Esmerandanna, an emerald great wyrm who has dwelt within the volcanic crater since its violent creation in the Year of the Quivering Mountains (77 DR). The Resplendent Queen, as the sage dragon is known, has long been fascinated by the customs and history of the wild dwarves of the surrounding region. Over the centuries, her paranoia that the roving bands of wild dwarves who venerate the Lord of the Jungle Deeps wish to steal her treasure has slowly subsided. In fact, the great wyrm has forged a bond of friendship with the disparate priests of the Thardite faith and agreed to guard their most sacred runestones. As a result, the wild dwarves of Chult return to the Emerald Crater to venerate their god and to record and store their most sacred carvings. The draconic guardian who resides therein has become firmly woven into the mythology of the wild dwarves as the Daul (daughter) of Thard.

Affiliated Orders: The Thardite faith has no formal military orders. However, on rare occasions, Thard's clergy collectively determine that it is in the best interest of dur Authalar to go to war. At such times, the best warriors of the widely scattered hunting bands come together to form the Pack. The Pack includes *bloods* (warriors of 2nd through 4th level), war leaders (warriors of 5th through 7th level), and priests of demonstrable fighting skill. Once assembled, not unlike the barbarian and orc hordes of the North, the Pack is a nearly unstoppable juggernaut that drives beasts and beings, great and small, from its path. Once the Pack's objective is achieved—the destruction of a yuan-ti enclave or a Batiri village, for example—the Pack quickly disperses and its surviving participants return to their small hunting bands.

Priestly Vestments: Priests of Thard bear the god's crossed-gauntlets sign as a tattoo, usually on one shoulder or on the scalp, overgrown by their hair. Priests of Thard never cut their beards (even the females), but instead braid them into ropes that they tie around their waists or shoulders. If an enemy or beast cuts a priest's beard, there is no penalty; if it is done by the priest himself or herself, it is a sign that she or he is turning away from Thard's service and can no longer expect aid from the god. The skull of a large jungle beast, such as a rhinoceros, great cat, or giant crocodile is worn as a helm. For ceremonial purposes, the pelts or skins of jungle monsters are worn as robes. The holy symbol of the faith is the tattoo of the Disentangler's symbol each priest bears. When a ritual would normally require a priest to present his holy symbol, it is sufficient for a priest of Thard to simply cross his forearms at the wrists several inches in front of his chest.

Adventuring Garb: Like other wild dwarves, the Disentangler's priests rarely don clothing, with the exception of their beast helms, as their long, woven hair serves as adequate garb. They cover their bodies with tattoos and grease. The grease serves to keep off insects and makes them hard to hold (AC 8). When going to war, priests of the Disentangler plaster their hair and bodies with mud that, when combined with the grease they normally coat their bodies in, forms a crude but effective armor (AC 7). Thard's priests favor metal weapons and tools, if available, but otherwise they employ their fists, clubs, and the *claws of Thard Harr* (see below).

Specialty Priests (Vuddor)

REQUIREMENTS:	Dexterity 9, Wisdom 9
PRIME REQ.:	Dexterity, Wisdom
ALIGNMENT:	NG, CG
WEAPONS:	Any
ARMOR:	Grease, caked mud, and beast helm
MAJOR SPHERES:	All, animal, combat, elemental, guardian, healing, plant, protection, weather
MINOR SPHERES:	Chaos, charm, creation, divination, necromantic, sun, travelers
MAGICAL ITEMS:	Same as clerics
REQ. PROFS:	Herbalism
BONUS PROFS:	Animal lore, survival (jungle)

- While most vuddor (the plural form of vuddar) are jungle dwarves, dwarves of any subrace can become specialty priests of Thard.
- Vuddor are not allowed to multiclass.
- Vuddor can cast *entangle*, *invisibility to animals*, or *pass without trace* (as the 1st-level priest spells) once per day.
- At 3rd level, vuddor can cast *barkskin*, *goodberry*, or *snake charm* (as the 2nd-level priest spells) once per day.
- At 5th level, vuddor can cast *hold animal*, *snare*, or *summon insects* (as the 3rd-level priest spells) once per day.
- At 7th level, vuddor can cast *call woodland beings* or *repel insects* (as the 4th-level priest spells) once per day.
- At 7th level, vuddor can cast *detect snares and pits* (as the 2nd-level priest spell) at will.
- At 10th level, vuddor can cast *commune with nature* or *animal summoning II* (as the 5th-level priest spells) once per day.
- At 13th level, vuddor can cast *wall of thorns* or *anti-animal shell* or *animal summoning III* (as the 6th-level priest spells) once per day.
- At 15th level, vuddor can cast *creeping doom* or *changestaff* (as the 7th-level priest spell) once per day.

Thardite Spells

1st Level

Claws of Thard Harr (Pr 1; Alteration)

Sphere:	Combat
Range:	Touch
Components:	V, S, M
Duration:	3 rounds+1 round/level
Casting Time:	4
Area of Effect:	Dwarf touched
Saving Throw:	None

This spell transforms the hands of a willing recipient into rending talons known as the *claws of Thard Harr*. Each talon inflicts 1d4+2 points of damage on a successful attack and up to two attacks are possible per round (one with each claw). It is not possible to wield a weapon while under the effects of this spell.

The material component is the priest's holy symbol. A preserved talon of a wild beast that the caster has personally slain is also required, but is not consumed by the spell.

2nd Level

Disentangle (Pr 2; Alteration)

Sphere:	Protection
Range:	80 yards
Components:	V
Duration:	1 round/level
Casting Time:	5
Area of Effect:	One creature
Saving Throw:	None

This spell enables the recipient to escape any rope, web, plant, jaws, glues (of monsters or plants), or wrestling hold, as long as the binding is caused by a physical effect. *Disentangle* does not enable the recipient to alter shape, so it is not possible to squeeze through a far-too-small opening whose distance is firmly fixed, such as wooden stocks or metal shackles or the bars of a cage, nor does it aid a creature that has been swallowed.

This spell is effective against both magical and nonmagical restraints. *Disentangle* allows immediate escape from effects such as *bind*, *entangle*, *Evard's black tentacles*, or a *rope of entanglement*, but it has no effect on effects such as a *hold person* spell or a ghoul's paralyzation ability.

3rd Level

Lesser Guardian Hammer (Pr 3; Alteration)

Sphere:	Guardian
Range:	Touch (of area to be guarded)
Components:	V, S, M
Duration:	Instantaneous, when triggered
Casting Time:	1 turn
Area of Effect:	Special
Saving Throw:	None

A *lesser guardian hammer* is an invisible, hammer-shaped field of force that appears when a guarded door, lock, threshold, or area is disturbed (even years after the spell was cast). When activated, it flies through the air to strike the nearest living thing (if more than one target is available, determine the one struck randomly). A *guardian hammer* strikes only once, but it does not miss. When striking, it appears momentarily as a glowing, translucent hammer, and then fades away into nothingness. Its unavoidable strike inflicts 2d12 points of damage. In addition, the creature struck must make a successful saving throw vs. petrification or be knocked down.

A *lesser guardian hammer* can be destroyed before activation by a successful *dispel magic* cast on the guarded area or by totally destroying the guarded area without entering it (for example, by *disintegration*). Once activated, a *lesser guardian hammer* bypasses magical and physical barriers; it cannot be destroyed, reflected, or diverted by any means.

The material components for this spell are a drop of sweat or spittle or a tear from the caster, a hair from any creature, and a pebble.

Vergadain

(God of Wealth and Luck, the Merchant King, the Trickster, the Laughing Dwarf, the Short Father)

Intermediate Power of the Outlands, N

PORTFOLIO:	Wealth, luck, chance, nonevil thieves, entrepreneurial skills such as suspicion, trickery, negotiation, sly cleverness
ALIASES:	Bes
DOMAIN NAME:	Outlands/Dwarvish Mountain (Strongale Hall)
SUPERIOR:	Moradin
ALLIES:	Brandobaris, Gond, the gnome pantheon (except Urdlen), the Morndinsamman (except Deep Duerra, and Laduguer), Lliira, Nephthys, Shaundakul, Tyche (dead), Tymora, Mask, Waukeen
FOES:	Beshaba, Deep Duerra, Laduguer, Urdlen, the goblinkin and evil giant pantheons
SYMBOL:	A gold piece (always a circular coin), or a dwarf wearing a panther skin and tail (Bes)
WOR. ALIGN.:	Any

Vergadain (VUR-guh-dane), the Master Merchant, is the patron of dwarven merchants and most nonevil dwarven thieves. A schemer and a rogue, Vergadain is venerated by dwarves of any neutral alignment engaged in commerce and concerned with wealth. Vergadain is sometimes called the Trickster, though not by dwarves who worship him, and the Laughing Dwarf, though a dwarf would never use such a term.

Long ago Vergadain assumed the Realms-based aspect of Bes, the Short Father, a lesser power of the Mulhorandi pantheon. While Bes's cult has long since sunk into obscurity, a few human merchants in the city of Skuld still call on Vergadain's aspect as the Mulhorandi god of luck and chance.

Vergadain is on good terms with most members of the Morndinsamman, having forged a particularly close relationship with Dugmaren Brightmantle, and the Master Merchant even maintains an uneasy truce with Abbathor, the Great Master of Greed. Vergadain trades with a great number of other mortals and powers, and as a result, he has forged solid relationships with a wide range of beings, far more than the other, relatively insular, members of the dwarven pantheon. In his aspect as Bes, Vergadain has forged a strong relationship with Nephthys, though she frowns heavily on his patronage of nonevil thieves and trickery.

Vergadain's home plane is that of the Outlands, but he seems to spend little time there. Instead, he restlessly roams wildspace and the worlds that can be found in it. He concentrates his efforts wherever there are humans, giants, demihumans, and humanoids to be bilked of their belongings by his tricks, and dwarves to appreciate his cleverness and daring—and to profit by it. Vergadain delights in showing up at desperate dwarven settlements with exactly the unique, rare, or hard-to-find object or substances they are lacking. If the dwarves are not in dire straits, the treasure granted by Vergadain is hidden, and clues to its location are often hidden in the lyrics of a song or rhyme.

Vergadain can appraise the exact material, historical, and cultural value of any treasure, and he knows the maximum price a customer is willing to pay. He delights in his magnificent collection of art objects and jewelry in Strongale Hall. The Master Merchant has a great singing voice and is a master of disguise and mimicry. He is said to be a great poet as well, and he dispenses clues to his worshipers, hidden in a verse or rhyme, to the locations of great treasures. Vergadain smiles more than any other dwarven deity—or sane living dwarf! His eyes are actually seen to twinkle enigmatically more often than he shows his smile to the world. Vergadain delights in and excels at con games, even simple tavern-tricks, and admires someone who bests him rather than punishing them or trying to get even. He is always looking for new techniques, and when he detects a con artist, he often watches and follow for a time to see what he can. Most of Vergadain's adventures concern the elaborate con games he has played on many humans, demihumans, humanoids, and giants in order to win their every belonging of worth. He is not above using any sort of harmless trick to accomplish his ends, and he is eternally suspicious of potential adversaries who might try to trick him in return.

Vergadain's Avatar (Thief 33, Bard 28, Ranger 20, Cleric 18)

Vergadain appears as a tall dwarf clad in brown and yellow merchant's clothing, which is often tattered or dusty. Underneath these garments, he wears armor and often carries musical instruments, disguises, and treasure (such as gems) in sacks. He guards these sacks by thrusting poisonous snakes and similar creatures into them with his valued belongings. His footwear contains concealed weapons (such as knives or garrotes), or hiding places (such as hollow heels), or both. He favors spells from the spheres of all, charm, creation, divination, guardian, numbers, travelers, wards, and weather and from the schools of abjuration, divination, enchantment/charm, and illusion/phantasm, although he can cast spells from any sphere or school.

AC –4; MV 15 or 18; HP 192; THAC0 1; #AT 2
Dmg 2d4+12 (*broad sword +4, +8* Str)
MR 70%; M (6 feet high) or SZ L (10 feet high)
Str 20, Dex 24, Con 18, Int 19, Wis 19, Cha 23
Spells P: 11/10/10/9/6/4/2, W: 6/5/5/5/5/5/1
Saves PPDM 3, RSW 1*, PP 4, BW 4, Sp 5
  *Includes dwarf +5 Con save bonus to a minimum of 1. The Con save bonus also applies to saves vs. poison to a minimum of 1.

Special Att/Def: Vergadain can be struck only by +2 or better magical weapons. He wields a *broad sword +4* named *Goldseeker* that detects monetary treasure within 20 feet of his person when grasped. It has a common, well-used appearance and communicates the precise location and rough size of treasures telepathically. The weapon can be used by anyone, but Vergadain is very attached to it and seeks to regain it from anyone who takes it from him. Vergadain wears a concealed suit of golden *chain mail +5*.

The Merchant King also has a *necklace of enlargement* that allows any wearer to assume any height at will between 1 foot and 15 feet. Vergadain can tell where this necklace is, even several planes distant (he helped enchant it, and it is linked to him), and he can override the control of any other being wearing it when he is within a mile of the necklace. The necklace is of nondescript appearance, apparently limitless powers, and changes size to fit the wearer. It cannot power or enact any other magical effect, nor does it alter the wearer's appearance, or the size of any clothing or gear. Vergadain usually shrinks any thief who steals the necklace to 1 foot in height, which instantly entangles the rogue in his or her clothing or even pin the unlucky robber under his or her own falling equipment (dagger, belt, boots, etc.). At that point, Vergadain instantly forces the thief to 15 feet in height, ruining the clothing as she or he shoots up through it (and inflicting minor damage), attracting the god's and everyone else's attention to his or her exact location, and braining the battered thief (1d2 points of damage and 1d2 rounds stunned) on any normal ceiling present. If a thief is smart enough not to wear the necklace or allow it to touch his or her bare skin anywhere, only the necklace changes size. This is still attention-getting and harmful to any clothing concealing it, of course, and Vergadain can track the thief by the necklace until the thief gets rid of it.

Vergadain can use *improved invisibility* at will. He can *mislead* once a day. He can also *see invisible creatures* at will, but only if they are living (not dead or undead) and within 40 feet. Vergadain can *spider climb* at will. Nine times a day, he can, at will, create *silence* in a 20-foot-radius or smaller area, altering the size of the area at will. Such silence remains in effect for 1 turn (or less if dispelled by the avatar; it resist all mortal *dispel magic* spells and abilities).

Other Manifestations

Vergadain likes to appear in avatar form in the Realms. He manifests only rarely, and in one of four ways: (1) Vergadain may appear as an unseen dwarven singer or musician, whose song, drumming, or piping leads lost dwarves to refuge, safety, an escape route, or treasure. (2) He may appear more subtly, seizing control of a singer, prophet, or sage for his own purposes. That person utters, speaks, or sings words to leave clues or directions to the whereabouts of great treasure. At times, Vergadain signals his presence by animating a gold piece, his symbol, to orbit the head of the possessed being; he does this particularly when the being is not a dwarf, and he wants only dwarves to notice the message. (3) Vergadain can appear as an animated, endlessly rolling gold coin that travels along the floor or ground. The coin can travel uphill, or even bound up steps, to lead beings to treasure; the coin settles only to mark a hiding place or the route onward (a loose flagstone leading to a tunnel, for instance). It gives no warning of guardian monsters or traps. (4) Finally, he can appear as a long rope that comes to hand unexpectedly when a dwarf needs it most (for example, to escape down a cliff or castle wall, or to rescue a fallen companion). The rope later vanishes.

Vergadain is served by arcane, aurumvorae, copper dragons, crystal dragons, ghost dragons, gold-colored cats, gynosphinxes, kenku, leprechauns, messenger snakes, and plumachs. He demonstrates his favor through the unexpected discovery of gold dice, jewels, precious metals (particularly gold), rare spices, other prized trade goods, and the receiving of exactly nine coins (of any mintage) during a business transaction. The Merchant King indicates his displeasure through a run of bad luck, a snake left in a sack (a symbol of Vergadain's own wiliest con tricks), the presence of lock lurkers and luck eaters, the discovery of pyrite (also known as fool's gold), and the receiving of exactly five coins (of any mintage) during a business transaction.

The Church

Clergy:	Clerics, specialty priests, thieves
Clergy's Align.:	N, CN
Turn Undead:	C: Yes, SP: No, T: No
Cmnd. Undead:	C: No, SP: No, T: No

All clerics (including cleric/thieves, a multiclassed combination allowed to dwarven priests of Vergadain) and specialty priests of Vergadain receive religion (dwarven) and reading/writing (Dethek runes) as bonus nonweapon proficiencies. Clerics of Vergadain (as well as cleric/thieves) cannot turn undead before 7th level, but they always strike at +2 on all attack and damage rolls against undead creatures. At 7th level and above, clerics (including multiclassed clerics) can turn undead as other clerics do, but as a cleric of four levels less than their current level. These modifications apply only to the cleric class. Vergadain's clergy were all male before the Time of Troubles. Since then, females have begun entering the clergy.

Followers of Vergadain are usually seen as suspicious characters, particularly outside dwarven society, and the Merchant King's faithful are viewed with a mixture of respect and envy for their commercial success and distrust of their principles and practices. Thus, few dwarves willingly admit that Vergadain is their deity. If a follower of the Master Merchant denies to others that Vergadain is that person's true deity, the god is not offended, so long as the proper sacrifices are made. Priests and followers are allowed to hide their reverence on occasion, since few people knowledgeable about this cult are very happy at conducing transactions and deals with them.

Temples of Vergadain are windowless chambers located either in underground complexes or on the surface in fortresslike, near impregnable vaults. They are filled with countless coins, jewels, and other treasures, whose collective value usually rivals that of most dragon's hoards, with appropriate magical and nonmagical traps to guard them. The central chapel is always dominated by huge stone cauldrons that serve as altars. Huge gold coins, fully 5 feet across, hang above each altar. These coins are guardian anators that emit *lightning bolts* and *magic missiles* at unauthorized beings who take things from an altar (where the offerings of Vergadain's faithful are placed). A being of neutral or chaotic neutral alignment can avoid this magical wrath by whispering the anator's password prior to removing an item from the cauldron. Note that the password to each anator is usually known only to the seniormost priest of the temple and to Vergadain himself, and such passwords can be quickly changed by those knowing the old password.

Novices of Vergadain are known as the Impoverished. Full priests of the Merchant King are known as Gilded Merchants. In ascending order of rank, the titles used by Vergadainan priests are Alloyn, Copprak, Argentle, Electrol, Aurak, and High Aurak. High Old Ones have unique individual titles but are collectively known as Merchant Princes. Specialty priests are known as *hurndor*, a dwarvish word that can be loosely translated as *those who trade*. The clergy of Vergadain includes gold dwarves (60%), shield dwarves (39%), gray dwarves (1%), and a handful of jungle dwarves. Vergadain's clergy is nearly evenly divided between specialty priests (37%), clerics (33%), and thieves (30%). The majority of Vergadain's priests are male (93%).

Dogma: The truly blessed are those whose enterprise and zeal brings both wealth and good luck. Dwarves are well suited to earn their fortunes by the effort of both their hands and their minds; use both to pry wealth out of others. Work hard, be clever, seek the best bargain, and the Merchant King will shower you with gold. Live life to its fullest; save, tithe, and spend your riches and thus encourage more trade. Treat others with respect, but shirk not your responsibilty to try to strike a deal better for you than for them—to not try would be to leave the gifts that Vergadain gives you idle.

Day-to-Day Activities: Vergadain's priests are dedicated to furthering the success of dwarven merchant commerce with other races, especially humans, but always to the benefit of dwarves. The priesthood is expected to be personally wealthy and to maintain the Merchant King's temples in excellent style. Their role is to increase general dwarven influence and prosperity and thus help the dwarves to further their craftwork, weapons-mastery, and inventions. Gold donated on Vergadain's altars is spent or traded shrewdly, to support dwarven merchants. Vergadain's clergy use it to bail dwarven merchants out of debt where possible, place bribes to help dwarven trade and commerce with other lands and races of Faerûn, and so on. Through these means the priests of Vergadain hope to increase dwarven importance in the Realms, and they often work with priests of the other dwarven gods (particularly Dumathoin and sometimes even Abbathor) to do so.

Holy Days/Important Ceremonies: Priests of Vergadain work tirelessly to support and promote dwarven merchants and craftsfolk throughout Faerûn. Whenever they render aid or handle material wealth of any sort, they mutter Vergadain's name in homage. Most of Vergadain's faithful also do so, and this makes up the bulk of Vergadain's daily worship. It is said that Vergadain can see into the mind of any creature within 10 feet wherever his name is uttered. He sometimes warns a dwarf of treachery by means of a vision or a preventative manifestation.

Holy days of the Vergadainan faith are known as *coin festivals* to the faithful and as *trade moots* to those cynics who would purchase their wares, for Vergadain's followers typically seek to earn as much coin as they can before such ceremonies—and thus last-minute bargains are to be had—so as to earn status among their fellows by garish displays of personal wealth and large tithes. Coin Festivals are held on the days before and after a full moon, on Greengrass, and any day proclaimed holy by a Merchant Prince. Offerings of gold are made to Vergadain once a month at such coin festivals by placing them on an altar dedicated to the Merchant King.

The proper rituals of worship to the god consist of meeting in windowless rooms or underground, around torches, braziers, or other flames. The rituals call for dancing in slow, stately shiftings around the flame, wearing and displaying gold and other objects of worth. Every dwarf who worships the god throws at least one gold piece into the flame as the dance continues. The flame consumes valuables placed in it utterly, sometimes dying away to reveal a map, clue, scroll, potion, or other sending of the god. These sendings are rare, and although helpful, they are rarely powerful. The appearance of a weapon is known but extremely rare. Perhaps the most common sending of Vergadain is a duplicate key to a strongbox, vault, or barrier that prevents dwarves from reaching wealth rightfully belonging to them, or stolen by cheating them over a period of time.

The dance ends when the flame flares upward, signifying the god's attention and thanks. The priests light candles or conjure light, and then discuss business (usually current projects to further dwarven wealth). Transfers of necessary fees, bribes, aid, or other funds from one dwarf to another occurs next, usually from priests to the faithful they have called to worship. Finally, the ranking priest passes his hand through the flame, which slowly diminishes. At this time, any dwarf present kisses a gold coin as a gesture of farewell, and then departs.

Major Centers of Worship: Aefindar Ultokhurnden, the Trademoot of Golden Fortune, is a fortresslike cathedral at the center of the dwarven city of Eartheart on the rim of the Great Rift. The exterior granite walls of the Trademoot are plated in gold and polished regularly, making the temple shine so bright that it is almost difficult to look at when the sun is at its highest. The great hall of the Merchant King's temple serves the city as its central market place, and its upper chambers houses the ministry of trade and commerce. The lower levels of the Trademoot house much of the city's

wealth as well as three grand chapels of Vergadain. This center of bustling commerce is presided over by Merchant Prince Royal Ghaern Goldthumb, son of Cael, blood of Lambryn. The temple houses well over two hundred priests at any time, and is the home base of hundreds of dwarven merchants whose caravan networks span much of Faerûn. If rumors are to be believed, three adult or mature adult dragons serve as guardians of the Trademoot's treasure vaults, in addition to countless traps that riddle the lower levels.

Affiliated Orders: The Golden Hands of Vergadain is a widely scattered order of priests and thieves found in most major cities where dwarves live and trade, as well as along the major trading routes used by the dwarves. In exchange for a small percentage of any recovered wealth, members of the Golden Hands seek to secure the safety of dwarven merchants and deal with those who would cheat the Stout Folk. In cities, the Golden Hands organization is often structured like a thieves' guild, employing many rogues. They raid warehouses of merchants of other races believed to contain goods stolen from dwarven merchants by force or fraud. Along trade routes, the Golden Hands resemble roving mercenary companies composed largely of fighting clerics and specialty priests. They often seek out and destroy monsters or brigands threatening trade routes, ransom kidnapped dwarven merchants, and recover goods from plundered dwarven caravans.

Priestly Vestments: Vergadain's clergy favor rich robes of obvious cost studded with gems and trimmed with furs. A string of linked gold coins is draped over the shoulders and around the neck. While the colors used for clerical vestments vary widely, gold and deep purple are preferred in lands where their use is not banned by sumptuary laws. Ceremonial armor includes ornate chain mail, a gem-studded gorget bearing the god's symbol, and an elaborately decorated helm. Senior priests (5th level and higher) are expected to have their ceremonial armor plated in gold, and it is a mark of great status within the church for junior priests to do so as well.

The holy symbol of the faith is a round gold coin. Such coins must be acquired in payment for trade goods and cannot be minted specifically for this purpose. Whenever another gold coin of similar value catches the priest's eye, which usually happens least once a month, the priest is expected to exchange the current holy symbol for the new coin, which then becomes the new holy symbol.

Adventuring Garb: Vergadain's clergy favor leather armor underneath their normal clothing. This provides some measure of protection yet is unlikely to give offense to trading partners by implying that the Gilded Merchant's safety is in question in the other's company. In dangerous situations, members of Vergadain's clergy favor chain mail, with a helm and a gorget bearing the god's symbol, seeing it as a necessary compromise between the need for both protection and maneuverability. Most priests of the Merchant King favor small weapons that are easily concealed, such as daggers, knives, and short swords.

Specialty Priests (Hurndor)

REQUIREMENTS:	Dexterity 12 or Intelligence 12, Wisdom 9
PRIME REQ.:	Dexterity or Intelligence, Wisdom
ALIGNMENT:	N, CN
WEAPONS:	Club, dagger, dart, hand crossbow, knife, lasso, short bow, sling, broad sword, long sword, short sword, and staff
ARMOR:	Leather or chain mail
MAJOR SPHERES:	All, astral, charm, creation, divination, guardian, healing, numbers, travelers, wards, weather
MINOR SPHERES:	Animal, combat, healing, protection, sun, time
MAGICAL ITEMS:	Same as clerics
REQ. PROFS:	Etiquette, gaming
BONUS PROFS:	Appraising, modern languages (common, or a language used by a common trading partner of the dwarves), reading/writing (common)

- While most hurndor (the plural form of hurndar) are shield dwarves or gold dwarves, dwarves of nearly every subrace are called to be specialty priests of Vergadain's clergy.
- Hurndor are not allowed to multiclass.
- Hurndor can select nonweapon proficiencies from both the priest and rogue groups with no crossover penalty.
- Hurndor understand and use thieves' cant.
- Hurndor have limited thieving skills as defined in the Limited Thieving Skills section of "Appendix 1: Demihuman Priests."
- Hurndor receive an effective +2 bonus to their Charisma when dealing with other dwarves.
- Hurndor can cast *cure light wounds* (as the 1st-level priest spell) or *weighty chest* (as the 1st-level priest spell) once per day.
- At 3rd level, hurndor can cast *frisky chest* or *wyvern watch* or (as the 2nd-level priest spells) or *fool's gold* (as the 2nd-level wizard spell) once per day.
- At 5th level, hurndor can cast *friends* (as the 1st-level wizard spell) or *invisibility* (as the 2nd-level wizard spell) once per day.
- At 7th level, hurndor can cast *detect enemies* (as the 2nd-level priest spell) at will.
- At 7th level, hurndor can cast *taunt* (as the 1st-level wizard spell) on a lawful creature or *free action* (as the 4th-level priest spell) once per day.
- At 10th level, hurndor can appraise the value of any goods within 5% of their true value.
- At 10th level, hurndor can cast *know customs* (as the 3rd-level priest spell) at will.
- At 13th level, hurndor can cast *detect lie* or its reverse, *undetectable lie* (as the 4th-level priest spells), two times per day.
- At 15th level, hurndor can cast *confusion* (as the 7th-level priest spell) twice a day.

Vergadainan Spells

2nd Level

Detect Enemies (Pr 2; Divination)
Sphere:	Divination
Range:	0
Components:	V, M
Duration:	1 turn
Casting Time:	1 round
Area of Effect:	60-foot radius
Saving Throw:	None

This spell detects the presence and direction of any creature within a 60-foot radius that has immediately hostile intentions toward the caster. The creature or creatures can be invisible, ethereal, astral, out of phase, hidden, disguised, or in plain sight. The priest feels a compulsion to face each individual enemy in range. The priest need not turn to face each, but she or he unerringly recognizes as hostile any such creature that the priest sees as she or he turns to face it. Unseen enemies are sufficiently detected to negate surprise attack rounds, and a thief positioning for a backstab against the priest has his or her relevant skill score halved (usually hide in shadows or move silently). The caster also has a 5% chance per level to detect longer-term hostility toward himself or herself, even if no direct attack is imminent.

The material component of this spell is the priest's holy symbol, which need not be displayed in an obvious fashion, allowing the priest a reasonable chance to cast this spell without alerting opponents.

Merchant's Glamer (Pr 2; Illusion/Phantasm)
Sphere:	Charm
Range:	10 feet
Components:	V, S, M
Duration:	Special
Casting Time:	5
Area of Effect:	One cubic foot/level
Saving Throw:	None

Material goods affected by this spell appear to be much finer than they actually are. Old, rusty weapons can be made to look new, goods of ordinary quality can be made to appear fine, and a common sword can be made to appear as a weapon of quality. For all purposes, the ensorcelled goods appear to be genuine, unless tested with magics that specifically penetrate illusions, such *detect illusion* and *true seeing*.

The spell lasts up to 24 hours, or until the goods are sold, at which time the dweomer unravels. The actual quality of the goods is revealed after a time equal to 1 turn per caster level after the magic starts to fall apart.

Priests of Vergadain do not generally sell goods affected by this spell to other dwarves. If confronted by an irate customer, their usual tactic is either to claim that the customer switched the goods after purchase (and intimate that they have connections with dwarven priests able to use *detect lie*) or to claim that their goods are sold "as is" and the inability of the customer to pick quality goods is not their problem.

The material components are the priest's holy symbol and a tuft of wool.

4th Level

Stone Trap (Pr 4; Alteration)
Sphere:	Guardian
Range:	10 yards/level
Components:	V, S, M
Duration:	Permanent until discharged
Casting Time:	1 turn
Area of Effect:	1 cubic foot/level
Saving Throw:	Special

This spell renders stone invisible and moves it to a mid-air location (within range) chosen by the caster. It levitates in place, sometimes for years, until the spell is released either by will of the caster or by the caster's death. Release can be accomplished by the utterance of a word or phrase (often a phrase spoken in the original spellcasting). The spell might also be keyed to specific conditions like the 1st-level wizard spell *magic mouth* (in other words, "when the lock on the door is broken or picked" and so on).

When the *stonetrap* is triggered, the stone turns visible as it falls. This spell is often used to hold boulders as deadfalls above archways (including castle or delve entrances), vault doors, thrones, bathtubs, beds, or other strategic areas.

Creatures in the area are allowed a saving throw vs. spell. Failure inflicts full damage (2d4 points of damage per level of the caster). A successful saving throw allows a Dexterity check. Success allows escape without damage; failure inflicts half damage.

Skilled dwarves often fashion false stone ceilings of smooth-finished stones and raise them overhead to serve as *stone traps*. *True seeing* reveals the levitating stone clearly, but if the caster has prepared it with enough skill (using shaped stone blocks or carved ornaments such as gargoyle heads or vault arches), the viewer may not recognize the viewed stone as any sort of trap. The levitating stone does faintly radiate magic, but then many dwarven delves might radiate magic if spells have been used in their shaping or subsequent use. A suspicious thief can find the trap at half his or her normal find trap thieving skill chance, and successful removal (also at half the usual chance) can bring the stone down without harm to the thief.

The material components of this spell are a speck of grit, a drop of water, an eyelash from any creature, and a pebble.

ELVEN PANTHEON

The Fair Folk of the Realms worship a pantheon of deities known as the Seldarine, a complex term that can be roughly translated as *the fellowship of brothers and sisters of the wood*, implying the wide diversity in interests that exists among the gods of the elven pantheon and their desire for cooperation. They act independently of one another, but the elven powers are drawn together by love, curiosity, and friendship to combine their strengths, to accomplish a task, or in the face of outside threats. Corellon Larethian, the acknowledged ruler of the Seldarine—sometimes joined by his consort, who is either identified as Sehanine or Angharradh—reinforces this freedom of action and compels none of the Seldarine to perform any task. Instead, the gods of the elven pantheon seem to sense when something needs doing, and they simply gather when necessary. With the exception of Fenmarel Mestarine, the Seldarine reside in the realm of Arvandor—a term that means the *high forest* in elvish—on the plane of Arborea on the layer known as Olympus.

Relations ascribed to the various powers of the Seldarine vary widely from culture to culture; some legends hold them all to be brothers and sisters, others believe Corellon (and sometimes Sehanine or Angharradh) created the other powers from the natural environment of Arvandor. Other sages link the Seldarine in various romantic relationships. In most representations, the elven pantheon includes more gods than goddesses, but every member of the Seldarine can appear as either male or female. The androgynous nature of the Seldarine reflects the gender equality found in most elven societies.

Aside from disagreement over the nature of Angharradh, there is general agreement among the elves of Faerûn as to which powers make up the Seldarine. Each elven realm and subrace places its own emphasis on the relative importance of various powers to the point where some members of the Seldarine fade from memory in some isolated elven cultures.

Formal membership in the Seldarine is determined by Corellon (or by Corellon and Angharradh, according to some myths). Unlike the dwarves, who still count Laduguer as a member of the Morndinsamman despite his banishment by Moradin, the Fair Folk do not include banished members of the elven pantheon when they use the term *Seldarine*. The good and neutral elven gods, including Corellon, Angharradh, Aerdrie Faenya, Deep Sashelas, Erevan Ilesere, Fenmarel Mestarine, Hanali Celanil, Labelas Enoreth, Rillifane Rallathil, Sehanine Moonbow, Shevarash, and Solonor Thelandira, have always been members of the Seldarine in good standing, although Fenmarel has withdrawn from active involvement in the pantheon. Many of the drow powers, including Araushnee (now Lolth), Eilistraee, and Vhaeraun, were once considered part of the Seldarine. They were exiled from Arvandor by Corellon's decree following an invasion of Arvandor by the anti-Seldarine, a coalition of evil gods assembled by the traitorous Araushnee and her complicitous son. Of the drow pantheon, only Eilistraee might someday formally rejoin the Seldarine, but it is more likely she will simply remain a close ally of the pantheon to which she once belonged. The Dark Maiden did not intentionally participate in Araushnee's schemes, but she willingly accepted banishment nonetheless, foreseeing the day her role as an outsider would be needed to guide those drow who spurned the self-destructive dogma of the Spider Queen.

The Seldarine are closely linked with the gods of the Seelie Court and other sylvan deities, and the Fair Folk often include prayers to other faerie powers when worshiping the Seldarine. All faiths that venerate one or more members of the Seldarine practice tolerance for followers of the other elven gods as well as for religions of closely allied nature (the cult of Skerrit the Forester being a prime example). The Seelie Court is more or less assumed to include the deities of the sprites, sea sprites, pixies, nixies, atomies, grigs, satyrs, korred, nymphs, brownies, leprechauns, dryads (and hamadryads), unicorns, pegasi, centaurs, swanmays, killmoulis, treants, pseudodragons and faerie dragons, seelie faeries, faerie fiddlers, and gorse faeries. It is ruled by Titania and Oberon, and certain of the previously listed creatures are considered more tightly a part of the Court than others. (The enemy of the Seelie Court is the Unseelie Court, ruled by the Queen of Air and Darkness, who is served by unseelie faeries, quicklings, and bramble faeries, among others.) While such powers have close ties to the elves, they are not counted as part of the Seldarine.

While the gods of the elven pantheon are actively involved in the collective lives of their worshipers, few intervene directly in events affecting a particular individual or even a small group of elves. Like the Fair Folk, the Seldarine tend to have very long-range perspectives, and they never intervene directly in the unfolding history of the Realms without a great deal of consideration and discussion. Notable instances of intervention by the Seldarine have resulted in the creation and settlement of Evermeet, the Descent of the drow, the decision to summon representatives of the elves to the Elven Court of Cormanthyr, the founding of Myth Drannor under the guiding principles it embodied, the creation of the Harpers, the initiation of the Retreat that began in the Year of Moonfall (1344 DR), and the defense of Evermeet in the Year of the Unstrung Harp (1371 DR).

Elven mythology holds that the Fair Folk were born of the blood which Corellon shed in his battles with Gruumsh and bathed in the tears of Sehanine (or Angharradh). (Most members of the pantheon have an enmity for or at least a dislike of the goblinkin pantheons: those of the orcs, goblins, hobgoblins, bugbears, kobolds, and urds.) Some legends state that the first elves appeared in the Realms fully formed and shaped in Corellon's image, woven by magic from sunbeams, moonbeams, forests, clouds, seas, and shadows. Other myths claim that at least some of the elven subraces—the gold elves and moon elves, in particular—migrated to Abeir-Toril through magical *gates* from one or more other worlds, most commonly identified as "Faerie." Myths discussing the natural origins of the Fair Folk are closely tied to the ability of many members of the Seldarine to assume nonelven, natural forms far greater in size than is common for their avatars. For example, Rillifane Rallathil has appeared as a massive oak tree, Deep Sashelas has appeared as a giant, towering (vaguely humaniform) wave of sea water, Aerdrie Faenya has appeared as a white cloud, and Corellon Larethian has appeared as an azure crescent moon or star.

One is struck in elven theology by the close relationships between the Fair Folk, magic, and the natural world. Most of elven faiths emphasize elven unity with life and nature, and they tend to blend the distinction between elves and their environment, much as the Seldarine are held to be spirits of Arvandor. For example, the Fair Folk have spirits, not souls, and many elves believe they will be reincarnated as animals, plants, faerie folk, or even elves once again. Similarly, elves are creatures of the Weave, tightly bound to and part of the web of magic that envelops Abeir-Toril.

The Fair Folk refer to themselves as Tel'Quessir, an elvish term meaning *the people*. They refer to all other beings as N'Tel'Quess, a less-than-diplomatic elvish expression meaning *not-people*. The Tel'Quessir originally included seven known subraces of elves, each of which is believed to have appeared in the Realms over 25 millennia ago and all of which have interbred with humans to form half-elves. The earliest elven inhabitants of Abeir-Toril were the Sy-Tel'Quessir, commonly known as green elves, forest elves, sylvan elves, or wood elves, the Ly'Tel'Quessir, commonly known as lythari, and the avariel, also called winged elves. While the Sy-Tel'Quessir may still be found in many of the great forests of the Realms, the avariel and the Ly'Tel'Quessir have all but vanished from Faerûn and today many believe them to be creatures of legend only.

The Ssri-Tel'Quessir—also known as dark elves or Ilythiiri, the name of the most successful tribe—emerged from the southern jungles of Faerûn around the same time that the Ar-Tel'Quessir, commonly called gold elves, sun elves, sunrise elves, or high elves, and the Teu-Tel'Quessir, known variously as moon elves, silver elves, or gray elves, appeared in the northern reaches of Faerûn. The Alu-Tel'Quessir, commonly known as aquatic elves, sea elves, or water elves, appeared in both the Great Sea and the Sea of Fallen Stars sometime thereafter. Although the two geographically isolated populations of sea elves have since diverged in skin tone, they are still interfertile and considered a single subrace. Finally, elven crossbreeds, incredibly rare for most of elven history, have slowly emerged as a small but distinct population in the Realms. While most half-elves are of mixed human and elven heritage, legends speak of halfling-elf and dwarf-elf crosses as well. Only in Deepingdale, Loudwater, Dambrath, and the Yuirwood are half-elf populations even relatively stable, however, for their offspring are invariably the same race as the other parent if both parents are not half-elves. In keeping with the generally tolerant natures of the Seldarine, elven churches, particularly that of Hanali Celanil, are far more welcoming and accepting of half-elves than elven society in general.

The First Flowering of the Fair Folk occurred as the Time of Dragons came to an end. The elves settled into five major civilizations along the western coast and southern reaches of Faerûn. From north to south along the lands now known as the Sword Coast were Aryvandaar (gold elves), Illefarn (green elves), Miyeritar (dark and green elves), Shantel Othreier (gold and moon elves), and Keltormir (moon and green elves). In the southern realms were three smaller realms in the major forest south of what is now known as the Vilhon Reach—Thearnytaar, Eiellûr, and Syòpiir (green elves)—and two realms in the forests that once covered the Shaar—Orishaar (moon elves) and Ilythiir (dark elves). The relentless aggression of the expansionistic Vyshaantar Empire (Aryvandaar) and the unbridled cruelty of destructive Ilythiir played out over the course of five Crown Wars that eventually shattered elven power in Faerûn.

After the fourth Crown War, the Seldarine were forced to intervene, and the Ssri-Tel'Quessir, found only in Ilythiir after the destruction of Miyeritar, were transformed into the obsidian-skinned, white-haired beings they are today. Named *dhaeraow*—an elvish term for *traitor*, since corrupted into *drow*—these elves were banished to the sunless reaches of the Underdark. After the Descent, at Corellon's insistence, the elders of the elven race assembled in the great forest to the east to debate the cause of the divisiveness and strife at a place of decision and judgment that became the Elven Court. After much debate, the Vyshaan were found to be culpable and the Vyshaantar Empire was destroyed in the fifth Crown War that followed the verdict. In the ten millennia since the last Crown War, elven civilizations have risen, and in some cases fallen, on Evermeet the Green Isle, in the Vale of Evereska, in the High Forest, in the great forest of Cormanthor, and in distant woodlands of the Yuirwood, but the destructive intraelven strife of the Crown Wars has never been repeated on such a wide scale. The Fair Folk have never recovered in population, however, and the age when the elves ruled Faerûn has long since passed. In fact, with inception of the Retreat in the Year of Moonfall (1344 DR), the elven presence on the mainland of Faerûn has fallen to its lowest levels in 25 millennia.

The diversity of the elven pantheon reflects the wide range of elven subraces, for each subrace is closely associated with a subset of the Seldarine and each elven power is closely associated with one or more of the subraces. In particular, Corellon Larethian, Hanali Celanil, and Labelas Enoreth are closely associated with the Ar-Tel'Quessir and Hanali Celanil, Sehanine Moonbow (or Angharradh), and Solonor Thelandira are closely associated with the Teu-Tel'Quessir. Similarly, Rillifane Rallathil, Shevarash, and Solonor Thelandira are closely associated with both the Sy-Tel'Quessir and (with the exception of Shevarash) the Ly Tel'Quessir, while Deep Sashelas is closely associated with the Alu-Tel'Quessir. Before the Descent, the Ssri-Tel'Quessir were closely associated with Araushnee (now Lolth), Eilistraee, Vhaeraun, a relationship that still exists between the drow and the dark gods they worship. The deep schism between the drow and the other elven subraces is also reflected in the divisions between the Seldarine and Araushnee and her brood, just as the deific battles between the Seldarine and the anti-Seldarine reflect the strife of the Crown Wars.

By some measures, the Seldarine contain a pantheon within a pantheon. In centuries past, before the Cha-Tel'Quessir (half-green elves of the Yuirwood) appeared in Aglarond, the Sy-Tel'Quessir of the Yuirwood adopted and co-opted ancient powers previously venerated by primitive humans who had preceded even the elven settlement of the forest. Little remains to mark the worship of these ancient powers, although their legends are still retold in the oral tradition of the Cha-Tel'Quessir. At the heart of the Yuirwood is the Sunglade, dominated by two concentric rings of stone menhirs. While each stone of the outer ring bears an inscription to a different member of the Seldarine, each stone of the inner ring is inscribed with the symbol of one of the gods of the Yuir. Of those ten stones, only four symbols are still legible: Relkath of the Infinite Branches, Magnar the Bear, Elikarashae, and Zandilar the Dancer. A fifth menhir is believed to have once held the sign of the Simbul, the goddess of the edge and the moment of choice, from whom Alassra Shentrantra's common appellation is derived. All but one of the gods of the Yuir, weakened by the long absence of their faithful, were absorbed by the Seldarine when the Fair Folk first arrived in the Yuirwood, and they are now simply wild, primitive aspects of Rillifane Rallathil, Shevarash, Labelas Enoreth, and the other elven powers. Only Zandilar the Dancer retained any degree of independence after the coming of the Sy-Tel'Quessir. However, she too declined in power and was forced to merge with the Mulhorandi goddess Bast (now known as Sharess) after an unsuccessful gambit against Vhaeraun the Masked Lord that she initiated in the hope of averting the defeat of her adopted worshipers by the drow. Details of those aspects of the gods of the Yuir that are still remembered may be found in the entries for the corresponding powers of the Seldarine or, in the case of Zandilar the Dancer, in the entry for Sharess found in *Powers & Pantheons*.

General Elven and Half-elven Priest Abilities: The general abilities and restrictions of elven and half-elven priests, aside from the specific changes noted later in this section for each elven faith, are summarized in the discussions of elven priests and half-elven priests in "Appendix 1: Demihuman Priests."

Aerdrie Faenya

(The Winged Mother, Lady of Air and Wind,
Queen of the Avariel, She of the Azure Plumage,
Bringer of Rain and Storms)

Intermediate Power of Arborea and Ysgard, CG

PORTFOLIO:	Air, weather, avians, rain, fertility, avariel
ALIASES:	Angharradh
DOMAIN NAME:	Olympus/Arvandor and Ysgard/Alfheim
SUPERIOR:	Corellon Larethian
ALLIES:	Akadi, Cyrrollalee, Eachthighern, Eilistraee, Fionnghuala, Isis, Koriel, Lurue, Remnis, Shaundakul, Sheela Peryroyl, Syranita, Stillsong, the Seldarine, various Animal Lords
FOES:	Auril, Talos and the Gods of Fury (Auril, Malar, and Umberlee), the drow pantheon (except Eilistraee)
SYMBOL:	Cloud with the silhouette of a bird
WOR. ALIGN.:	NG, CG, N, CN

Aerdrie Faenya (AIR-dree FAH-ane-yuh) is the elven goddess of the air, weather, and birds. As the bringer of rain, she is the closest the Fair Folk have to a fertility goddess. At one time, the Winged Mother's followers were composed largely of the avariel, much like Deep Sashelas was and is worshiped primarily by sea elves. However, unlike their aquatic kin, the winged elves were nearly wiped out by the dragons before the First Flowering, and what was believed to be the last of their race in Faerûn flew westward before the start of the Crown Wars. Today, gold, moon, and wild elves who desire certain weather conditions make the most frequent sacrifices to Aerdrie. Her small church is also popular with elves who possess flying mounts, such as asperii, dragons, giant eagles, griffons, hippogriffs, and pegasi. The Lady of Air and Wind is revered by all nonevil birds, particularly aarakocra and other sentient avians, but their numbers are small and declining as well. She is also called on by elves oppressed by overly lawful creatures.

Aerdrie is both an aspect of Angharradh and one of the three elven goddesses—the other two being Hanali Celanil and Sehanine Moonbow—who collectively form the Triune Goddess. This duality tightly binds Aerdrie with the two other senior elven goddesses, and the three collectively serve alongside Corellon in leading the Seldarine. Aerdrie maintains close relations only with those powers of the air who share a love of birds and freedom as deeply held as the Lady of Air and Wind. Aerdrie is particularly close with Syranita, the gentle goddess of the aarakocra, and some theologians speculate the two may eventually merge if the bird-men continue their steady decline. Aerdrie is also close with the avian lords of the Beastlands, particularly the hawk lord. Since the Time of Troubles, Aerdrie has been romantically linked with her long-time ally, the human god Shaundakul, the Rider of the Winds, but this new twist in their relationship is undoubtedly little more than a passing fancy, at least on the Winged Mother's part. Aerdrie contests with Talos and the Gods of Fury, for they challenge her control of the winds and seek to wield them for purely destructive purposes. The deep antipathy between the Winged Mother and the Frostmaiden stems from the war in Arvandor between the Seldarine and the anti-Seldarine forces who were arrayed against them. Aerdrie soundly defeated Auril in that battle, forever banishing the Frostmaiden from Olympus, and the two goddesses continue their eternal war on the myriad worlds of the Prime.

Aerdrie is the elven expression of freedom and impulse, and she dislikes being tied down to any one place for too long. Her realm is so close to the philosophical border between Arborea and Ysgard that it moves back and forth, sometimes part of Arvandor and sometimes part of Alfheim. Aerdrie delights in the sound of wind instruments and in creating unpredictable atmospheric conditions, including fairly severe or violent thunderstorms on occasion, but her primary joy is simply feeling the air rush past her with the ground far below. The Winged Mother is a somewhat distant goddess who rarely involves herself in elven culture, and she is far more chaotic than the rest of the Seldarine. Of all the elven races, only Aerdrie takes a keen interest in the avariel, and few of them remain in the Realms.

Aerdrie's Avatar (Air Elementalist 35, Cleric 29, Fighter 21)

Aerdrie appears as a tall, slim elflike female with sky-blue skin, feathered, flowing white hair and eyebrows, and large birdlike wings whose feathers seem constantly to change color—blue, green, yellow, and white. The lower half of her body from the hips down vanishes into swirling mist, so she seems never to touch the ground. She favors wizard and priest spells involving air, weather, flight, electricity, and gas, although she can cast spells from any sphere or school except elemental earth and fire.

AC –5; MV Fl 48; HP 199; THAC0 0; #AT 5/2
Dmg 1d6+6 (*quarterstaff +3*, +1 STR, +2 spec. bonus in quarterstaff)
MR 80%; SZ M (6 feet tall)
STR 16, DEX 24, CON 20, INT 24, WIS 21, CHA 20
Spells P: 12/12/12/12/11/10/7, W: 9/9/9/9/9/9/9/8/8*
Saves PPDM 2, RSW 3, PP 4, BW 4, Sp 4
  *Numbers assume one extra elemental air spell per spell level.

Special Att/Def: Aerdrie wields *Thunderbolt*, an electrically charged *quarterstaff +3* in combat. Targets struck by the weapon also suffer 4d6 points of electrical damage. A successful saving throw vs. spell reduces the damage by half.

The Winged Mother may cast *call aerial beings* (summoning quadruple the normal number of respondents, who always obey her call and are willing to serve her unto death), *call lightning*, *control winds*, *control weather*, *flight of Remnis*, or *wind walk* once per round at will. Once per round she can unleash twin *lightning bolts* or twin *wind blasts*, the latter inflicting twice the normal damage of the spell. At will, the Lady of Air and Wind can negate the power to fly or levitate of any creature within 120 feet of her. She can summon 2d6 16-HD or 1d8 24-HD air elementals once per day.

Aerdrie is immune to missile fire, and no avians will attack her. She is also immune to all spells, effects, and abilities from the elemental air sphere or school that she does not wish to be affected by. She can be struck only by +2 or better magical weapons.

Other Manifestations

Aerdrie rarely manifests in the Realms, except through natural processes such as strong winds, rain showers, and even powerful storms. The Lady of Air and Wind manifests around Evermeet as great storms, vast cyclones, and winds of hurricane force that affect only nonelven ships. Her efforts also ensure that no ill wind or weather can ever destroy the Green Isle.

The Winged Mother does watch over those Fair Folk who take flight into her domain, whether it be through magic or their own wings. If an elf or worshiper of any race somehow falls from a great height, whether it be off a cliff or out of the sky, the Winged Mother may manifest as a deep blue nimbus of flickering light that envelops the plummeting creature and enables him or her to slow his or her descent and make a gentle landing, similar to the effects of a *feather fall* spell. If a worshiper in flight is targeted by a land-bound archer, the enveloping nimbus of Aerdrie's manifestation confers a defensive shield equivalent to a *protection from normal missiles* effect. While the Lady of Air and Wind rarely grants omens to her priests, when she does they manifest as *whispering winds*.

The Seldarine call on agathinon, asuras, and ancient treants as their preferred servants, but Aerdrie is also served by aarakocra, aasimar, aasimon, air elementals, aerial servants, androsphinxes, asperii, atomies, avorels, azmyths, birds of all nonevil species (particularly eagles, falcons, hawks, kingfishers, and owls), cloud dragons, cloud giants, crystal dragons, djinn, eladrin (particularly bralani), faerie dragons, firetails, fremlins, frosts, griffons, gorse, hippogriffs, hollyphants, kenku, kholiathra, ki-rin, lammasu, lillendi, noctrals, opinicus, pegasi, pegataurs, phoenixes, pixies, reverend ones, rocs, seelie faeries, shedu, silver dragons, sylphs, spirits of the air, sprites, storm giants, sunflies, swanmays, swarms of grasshoppers or locusts, sword archons, talking owls, tempests, tressym, t'uen-rin, vortexes, windghosts, and wind walkers. She demonstrates her favor through the discovery of feathers of any sort, hornbill ivory carved in the form of an avian species, psaedros, raindrops (a common name for cassiterite crystals), sapphires, turquoise, weirwood birdpipes, and wind instruments of any sort. The Winged Mother indicates her displeasure by suddenly transforming a gentle zephyr or little rain shower into a lashing storm, by causing flocks of birds to suddenly dissolve, each bird going its separate way, and by causing the offender's plumage—whether it be natural or a form of adornment—to suddenly molt.

The Church

CLERGY: Clerics, mystics, specialty priests, air elementalists
CLERGY'S ALIGN.:   CG, CN
TURN UNDEAD: C: Yes, Mys: No, SP: No, AEle: No
CMND. UNDEAD: C: No, Mys: No, SP: No, AEle: No

All clerics (including multiclassed half-elven clerics), mystics, and specialty priests of Aerdrie receive religion (elf) and reading/writing (Espruar) as bonus nonweapon proficiencies. Most priests of Aerdrie have a strong fear of being confined or trapped bordering on claustrophobia. They suffer a −1 penalty on initiative, attack rolls, and saving throws under such conditions (this includes nearly all underground areas). Aerdrie's priests must sleep outdoors except during winter or times of bad weather.

Like all the Seldarine, Aerdrie is venerated by all elves save the drow. However, aside from those winged elves who remain, very few of the Fair Folk primarily worship the Lady of Air and Wind. The Queen of the Avariel is seen as flighty, even for the chaotic Seldarine, and somewhat distant, and the inclusion of the aarakocra and other avian races slightly diminishes the strength of elven devotion to her.

Aerdrie's temples, known as aeries, are usually located on high hilltops or mountain slopes having a good view of the land around them and the open sky. While the Winged Mother's shrines are little more than alpine ledges, accessible only to those creatures capable of flight, Aerdrie's temples are delicate crystalline spires bedecked with glass chimes whose ringing tones peal across mountain valleys, borne by swirling winds. Small open-mouthed caves, connected by short tunnels that honeycomb the peaks on which the goddess's temples rest, allow access to Aerdrie's glass-enclosed chapels and permit the wind to whistle through the heart of the peak.

Novices of Aerdrie are known as Eaglets or the Tethered. Full priests of the Winged Mother are known as Winged Brothers or Sisters. Titles used by Aerdrian priests vary widely from temple to temple, with many high-ranking priests having unique individual titles. Among the priest caste of the winged elves of Mount Sundabar, commonly employed titles include Aquiline Hunter, Cloud Walker, Feathered Dancer, Rain Bringer, Rising Thermal, Silent Screech, Sky Diver, Soaring Spirit, and Wind Chaser. Specialty priests are known as halcyons. At one time, the clergy of Aerdrie was dominated by winged elves (90%), but her church today consists primarily of moon elves (40%), gold elves (38%), aarakocra (10%), and elves and half-elves of other subraces (8%). A handful (4%) of winged elves (including half a dozen or so half-winged elves whose wings are strong enough only for gliding) compose the remainder of her clergy, scattered across the most distant and inaccessible reaches of the Realms. Although specialty priests compose only a small fraction of Aerdrie's clergy (20%), they occupy nearly all of the high positions within the Wind Mother's church. The remainder of Aerdrie's priests are either clerics (42%), including multiclassed half-elven clerics, air elementalists (30%), or mystics (8%). About 59% of Aerdrie's clergy members are female, the remainder are male.

Dogma: The ever-changing reaches of the sky are the great gift of the Winged Mother. Take flight into her windswept embrace, and gambol amidst the everchanging clouds. Honor those who dwell with the Lady of Air and Wind and cherish the birds who dance on her tresses. In change there is beauty and in chaos there is the birth of new life. Ascend, soar, glide, dive, and ascend again and relish in the freedom that the Winged Mother bequeaths. The air is the breath of life.

Day-to-Day Activities: Aerdrie's priesthood is primarily concerned with exploration and maintaining good relations with sentient avian races (for example, giant eagles and aarakocra). With the decline of the avariel, few elven priests of the Winged Mother are capable of flight without magical aid. As a result, many Winged Siblings work to create new spells and items by which magical flight is possible, and a not a few of their more adventuresome brethren seek lost relics of yore that permit the same. Similarly, members of Aerdrie's clergy raise winged steeds employed by the aerial cavalries of elven realms and tend cotes of fanciful birds from far-off lands to dwell in formal elven gardens and to supply the molted plumage employed in elven fashions. As servants of the Bringer of Rain and Storms, Aerdrie's priests work closely with elves involved in agriculture and horticulture to ensure favorable weather systems for their crops. Winged Brothers and Sisters are also charged with destroying evil avians, such as eblis, perytons, and simpathetics, as the Lady of Air and Wind considers them perversions of nature.

Holy Days/Important Ceremonies: The Dance of Swirling Winds is a semiannual festival held on the vernal and autumnal equinoxes to celebrate the changing seasons and to honor the Winged Mother. The winds are always strong on such days no matter where Aerdrie's followers gather. Celebrants make offerings of beautiful feathers and join in an aerial ballet danced to the music of wind instruments played by some of the participants. Those who lack wings or magical means of flight may *ride the wind* (as the 2nd-level wizard spell) as a gift of the goddess herself. For the duration of the formal ceremony, recipients of Aerdrie's blessing are usually tethered by long ropes to others who can command their own aerial movements. Once the dance breaks up, however, wind dancers, as they are known, are swept across the forest canopy for miles in a breathtaking flight before settling gently in a sylvan glade not too far from home.

Major Centers of Worship: According to legend, great aeries of the avariel may be found in undiscovered lands far to the west of Faerûn, whose inhabitants are descended from winged elves who fled the relentless annihilation of their race by the great wyrms of the North during the Time of Flowers. Before they fled, the center of Aerdrie's faith was the Aerie, a great temple-city said to have been located amidst the Star Mounts at the heart of the High Forest. While some claim that the Aerie's last remnants are now inhabited by the great red wyrm known to humans as Inferno, more credible tales hold that Elaacrimalicros, an ancient green dragon who has savaged the surviving population of aarakocra in the region, has claimed the legacy of the avariel.

The Aerie of the Snow Eagles is a crystalline citadel built atop the peak of Mount Sundabar in the distant land of Sossal, north and east of Pelvuria, the Great Glacier. The last redoubt of the avariel in Faerûn, Aerdrie's preeminent temple has long been forgotten, even by the Fair Folk of Cormanthyr, Evereska, and Evermeet. From the steep, icy slopes of Mount Sundabar, the Children of the Winged Mother take flight across the frigid skies of the Cold Lands, fishing in the freezing waters of Sossar Bay, hunting across the icy reaches of the Great Glacier, and engaging in aerial acrobatics across the northern sky. The temple itself resembles an inverted glass cone built to replace the sheared-off mountain top of Mount Sundabar. (The avariel believe the peak was removed by a Netherese archmage seeking to create his own floating sky city before the fall of Netheril, but in truth it may have been destroyed when white wyrms destroyed the remnants of the dwarven kingdom of Dareth.) The crystalline, conical temple is nearly 3,000 feet in diameter at its base and 3,000 feet high at its peak.

Within the temple's *glassteeled* walls, endless zephyrs dance hither and yon and tiny rain showers erupt out of thin air, a never-ending manifestation of the power of the Lady of Air and Wind. The temple floor is overgrown with tropical plants nurtured by the brilliant sunshine and regular rainfall to create a jungle paradise. Rare birds from the farthest reaches of Abeir-Toril gambol and caw while young winged elves test out their wings overhead. The avariel community of Mount Sundabar, including the crystalline temple on the mountain top and winged elven nests on the mountain's flanks, is loosely governed by Winged Father Aquilan Greatspan, an avariel. Aquilan has led the last remaining major enclave of winged elves in Faerûn for nearly five centuries, and his wise leadership has seen the avariel survive, if not exactly prosper, amidst the ruins of the Ice Kingdom of Dareth. Like the Stout Folk who preceded them, the greatest threat to the avariel is Hoarfaern, the realm of white dragons and their bestial servant creatures who dwell in the dwarf-carved halls of the northern Mountains of Dareth.

Affiliated Orders: The Wing of Plumed Kingfishers is an aerial military order composed primarily of moon and gold elven crusaders and rangers. The order is subdivided into aerial cavalry divisions by the species of their mounts, with asperii-, giant eagle-, griffon-, hippogriff-, and pegasi-mounted Plumed Kingfishers predominating. Before the power of elven civilization began to ebb in Faerûn, this order patrolled the skies above most forests of the Realms, protecting land-bound elves below from threats above. Today only two major branches of the ancient order of Plumed Kingfishers survive, one based in Evermeet and the other based in Evereska. The Wing of the Green Isle includes a division of moon elves mounted on giant eagles, a division of gold elves mounted on pegasi, and a handful of moon and gold elven dragon riders mounted on gold, silver, and bronze dragons. The Wing of the Evereskan Eyrie includes a large division of moon elves mounted on giant eagles and a smaller division of the Teu-Tel'Quessir mounted on asperii.

Priestly Vestments: Ceremonial garb for priests of Aerdrie consists of sky-blue robes, with those of high rank wearing the darkest shades. Feathers are used in decorating their clothing and armor, and at least one feather is worn in the hair. The holy symbol of the faith is a feather of great beauty, willingly given after molting by a sentient avian who venerates the Winged Mother. A new feather must be found at least once per year.

Adventuring Garb: When adventuring, Aerdrie's priests prefer light, flexible armor that maximizes maneuverability and minimizes weight and drag. Streamlined helms, carved to resemble stylized bird heads and padded to reduce concussions, are secured with leather chin straps. Missile weapons—particularly javelins and elven bows with flight arrows—are commonly employed in combat. If at all possible, priests of Aerdrie who lack wings of their own obtain *wings of flying* or similar magical means of flight. At the very least, they seek to train a steed capable of flight, such as an asperii, dragon, giant eagle, griffon, hippogriff, or pegasus.

Specialty Priests (Halcyons)

REQUIREMENTS:	Dexterity 13, Wisdom 13
PRIME REQ.:	Dexterity, Wisdom
ALIGNMENT:	CG, CN
WEAPONS:	Blowgun, bow with flight arrows, dagger, dart, javelin, horseman's mace, quarterstaff, spear, staff-sling
ARMOR:	Leather, elven chain
MAJOR SPHERES:	All, animal, chaos, creation, divination, elemental (air, water), protection, sun, travelers, weather
MINOR SPHERES:	Charm, combat, healing, summoning
MAGICAL ITEMS:	Same as clerics
REQ. PROFS:	Animal training (avians), bowyer/fletcher
BONUS PROFS:	Animal lore (avians), musical instrument (wind instrument), weather sense

- Halcyons must be elves, half-elves, aarakocra, or kenku. While in earlier eras most elven halcyons were winged elves, elves and half-elves of every subrace are called to be specialty priests of Aerdrie's clergy.
- Halcyons are not allowed to multiclass.
- Halcyons may cast wizard spells from the elemental air school as defined in the Limited Wizard Spellcasting section of "Appendix 1: Demihuman Priests."
- Halcyons gain a +2 bonus on reaction rolls when dealing with avian and semiavian creatures such as pegasi and giant eagles.
- Halcyons can cast *feather fall* (as the 1st-level wizard spell) or *Murdock's feathery flyer* (as the 1st-level wizard spell) once per day.
- At 3rd level, halcyons can cast *ride the wind* (as the 2nd-level wizard spell) or *whispering wind* (as the 2nd-level wizard spell) once per day.
- At 5th level, halcyons can cast *fly* or *gust of wind* or *protection from normal missiles* (as the 3rd-level wizard spells) once per day.
- At 7th level, halcyons can shapechange into a bird up to three times per day like a druid. Each avian form assumed in a single day must be of a different species of bird. This size can vary from that of a hummingbird to as large as an ostrich. Upon assuming a new form, the halcyon heals 10–60% (1d6×10%) of all damage she or he has suffered (round fractions down). The halcyon can only assume the form of a normal (real world) bird in its normal proportions, but by doing so he takes on all of that creature's characteristics—its movement rate and abilities, its Armor Class, number of attacks, and damage per attack. The halcyon's clothing and one item held in each hand also become part of the new body; these reappear when the halcyon resumes his normal shape. The items cannot be used while the halcyon is in animal form.

- At 10th level, halcyons can cast *air walk* or *control winds* (as the 5th-level priest spells) or *flight of Remnis* (as the 4th-level priest spell) once per day.
- At 13th level, halcyons can cast *control weather* or *wind walk* (as the 7th-level priest spells) once per day.
- At 15th level, halcyons can summon one 16-HD air elemental once a tenday. This elemental remains under the control of the halcyon for one hour and cannot be taken control of by another creature. If the summoner is killed or struck unconscious, the summoned elemental goes on a rampage, attacking everyone in sight except its summoner until its one hour time limit on the Prime Material has elapsed. It is important to note that the elemental summoned is not a servant of the halcyon but rather is looked upon as an agent of Aerdrie that is to be respected. The ability to summon an elemental is granted once each day when halcyons receive their normal complement of spells.

Aerdrian Spells

In addition to the spells listed below, priests of the Winged Mother may cast the 4th-level priest spell *calm winds* and the 7th-level priest spells *conjure air elemental* and *whirlwind*, all of which are detailed in *Faiths & Avatars* in the entry for Akadi.

1st Level

Speak with Avians (Pr 1; Alteration)
Sphere:	Animal, Divination
Range:	0
Components:	V, S
Duration:	2 rounds/level
Casting Time:	4
Area of Effect:	1 avian within 30 feet
Saving Throw:	None

This spell empowers the priest to comprehend and communicate with any normal or giant avian that is not mindless. The priest is able to ask questions of and receive answers from the creature, although friendliness and cooperation are by no means assured. Furthermore, terseness and evasiveness are likely in basically wary and cunning creatures, while the more stupid ones will make inane comments. If the animal is friendly or of the same general alignment as the priest, it may do some favor or service for the priest (as determined by the DM). This spell differs from *speak with animals* and *speak with monsters* in that it allows conversation only with normal or giant nonfantastic avians such as cardinals, doves, giant eagles, jays, ravens, and so on.

3rd Level

Wind Blast (Pr 3; Alteration)
Sphere:	Elemental Air
Range:	0
Components:	V, S, M
Duration:	Instantaneous
Casting Time:	6
Area of Effect:	Special
Saving Throw:	None

When this spell is cast, it causes a powerful cone-shaped wind gust originating at the priest's hand and extending outward in a cone 5 feet long and 1 foot in diameter at its base per level of the caster (up to a maximum of 50 feet long and 10 feet in diameter). The force of the *wind blast* inflicts 4d4 points of damage on man-sized and larger creatures. Small and tiny creatures suffer the damage noted above and must also succeed at a saving throw vs. spell or be thrown as far as 25 feet backward. If they smash into any hard object, such as a wall or a large tree, they must succeed at a saving throw vs. petrification or be stunned for 1d4 rounds and suffer 1d6 points of additional damage from the force of the impact.

The material components are the priest's holy symbol and a small paper fan.

4th Level

Flight of Remnis (Pr 4; Conjuration/Summoning)

Sphere:	Animal, Summoning
Range:	1 mile
Components:	V, S
Duration:	Special
Casting Time:	7
Area of Effect:	Special
Saving Throw:	None

This spell is a specialized variant of *animal summoning*. This spell allows the caster to call a number of birds of prey (including blood hawks, condors, eagles, falcons, fire falcons, giant eagles, giant owls, giant vultures, hawks, kingfishers, owls, rocs, talking owls, vultures, and zygraats, among others), up to a maximum total of 32 Hit Dice. Only carnivorous birds within 1 mile of the spellcaster at the time of the casting answer the call. If there are giant eagles within range, up to 48 total Hit Dice of them can be summoned. The caster can make only one call and does not get to choose what form of avian shows up, if any. (If more than one species is available, the race with greater Hit Dice is summoned. Eagles and giant eagles are always summoned to the exclusion of other birds if they are within range.) The avians aid the caster by whatever means they possess, staying until a fight is over, a specific mission is finished, the caster is safe, or she or he sends them away.

Note: In most cases avians are readily available. Eagles and giant eagles are most common in the mountains.

Angharradh

(The Triune Goddess, the One and the Three,
the Union of the Three, Queen of Arvandor)

Greater Power of Arborea, CG

PORTFOLIO:	Spring, fertility, planting, birth, defense, wisdom
ALIASES:	Aerdrie Faenya, Hanali Celanil, Sehanine Moonbow
DOMAIN NAME:	Olympus/Arvandor
SUPERIOR:	Corellon Larethian
ALLIES:	Berronar Truesilver, Chauntea, Cyrrollalee, Eilistraee, Lurue, Mielikki, Milil, Mystra, Oberon, Selûne, Sharindlar, Sheela Peryroyl, Silvanus, Sune, Titania, Yondalla, the Seldarine
FOES:	Auril, Malar, the Queen of Air and Darkness, Talos, Umberlee, the drow pantheon (except Eilistraee), the goblinkin pantheons
SYMBOL:	Three interconnecting circles laid out in a triangle that points down
WOR. ALIGN.:	LG, NG, CG, LN, N, CN

Angharradh (ON-gahr-rath) is the face of the power who is both three separate goddesses—Aerdrie Faenya, Hanali Celanil, and Sehanine Moonbow who are collectively known as the Three—as well as a single goddess—the One—who subsumes their separate aspects. The Triune Goddess presents many different faces, depending upon circumstances. In spring and during harvest time she is a fertility goddess. She watches over the planting of crops, blesses births, and keeps the land green and growing. In wartime, she is a grim warrior deity who wields a red sword and mercilessly slays the enemies of the elves. When wisdom is required, the One and the Three is a source of guidance and council. Among the Fair Folk, Angharradh is worshiped nearly exclusively by moon elves and a handful of half-moon elves. The other elven subraces worship Angharradh's aspects as separate goddesses, but they rarely give homage to the Union of the Three. Whether Angharradh is truly a combination of the three goddesses or a separate deity in her own right actually lies in the hearts of her individual worshipers.

According to silver elven mythology, Angharradh was born from the essence of the three greatest goddesses of the Seldarine before the first of the Fair Folk walked the forests of Faerûn. The Triune Goddess arose in the aftermath of a great battle between the Seldarine and the anti-Seldarine, a host of evil powers who had invaded Arvandor at the bequest of Araushnee (now Lolth), Corellon's traitorous consort. When an arrow launched by Elistraee at an onrushing ogrish god was subtly warped by the magic of the treacherous Araushnee and felled the Protector instead, Aerdrie struck down the Dark Maiden in revenge. The Seldarine assumed the unconscious daughter of Araushnee and Corellon was to blame for her father's collapse. Sehanine's timely escape from Vhaeraun's prison allowed the Goddess of Moonlight to expose Araushnee's crimes and the Masked Lord's complicity, but the Weaver of Destiny defiantly rejected the collective authority of the assembled Seldarine to convene a council to investigate her actions. In response, Aerdrie, Hanali, and Sehanine drew together and merged into a luminous cloud before coalescing in the form of the Triune Goddess. Angharradh then restored Corellon to health, taking her place by the Protector's side and declaring her intention to prevent treachery from ever entering the heart of a goddess of Arvandor again.

As the consort of Corellon and co-ruler of the Seldarine, Angharradh is on excellent terms with the other members of the elven pantheon. The Triune Goddess has a strong, motherly interest in both Eilistraee and Mielikki, and, more so than Corellon, maintains strong ties with the paramount goddesses of other human and demihuman pantheons. Angharradh strongly opposes the destructive efforts of Talos and the Gods of Fury (particularly Malar, for it was the Beastlord who unleashed the Elf-Eater on Evermeet in the Year of the Unstrung Harp (1371 DR)). The Triune Goddess reserves her strongest hatred for Lolth, as the Spider Queen has never ceased her efforts to undermine Corellon or to destroy his progeny, the Fair Folk.

As the One and the Three, Angharradh is both three distinct goddesses and a goddess in her own right. While some Teu-Tel'Quessir assume that the aspect of Sehanine is Angharradh's primary facet—a point of confusion due in part to the belief by other subraces of the Fair Folk that Sehanine, not Aerdrie or Hanali, is Corellon's consort—in truth all three goddesses are equal and each reflects the duality that is their individual nature and that of the Triune Goddess. As such, Angharradh's nature reflects the personality traits of each of the Three, including the impulsive and whimsical nature of the Winged Mother, the romantic and affectionate nature of the Heart of Gold, and the serene and ephemeral nature of the Daughter of the Night Skies. The fusion of the Three was born of Araushnee's betrayal and the collective threat to Arvandor and the Seldarine. As such, the Triune Goddess exhibits the fierce protectiveness and unbending resolve of the Queen of Arvandor.

Angharradh's Avatar (Ranger 34, Cleric 34, Mage 34)

Angharradh appears as a female elf of unearthly beauty and grace who is gloriously gowned and shining with gems the color of starlight. In times of war she appears in a suit of gleaming silver elven plate mail. The Triune Goddess favors spells from the spheres of all, combat, guardian, plant, protection, war, and wards and from the schools of abjuration, enchantment/charm, illusion/phantasm, and invocation/evocation, although she can cast spells from any sphere or school.

AC –5; MV 15; HP 226; THAC0 –10; #AT 2/1
Dmg 1d8+13 (*long sword +5*, +8 Str) or 1d8+11 (*spear +3*, +8 Str) or 1d6+12 (*footman's flail +3*, +8 Str)
MR 90%; SZ M (7 feet tall)
Str 20, Dex 21, Con 21, Int 23, Wis 24, Cha 24
Spells P: 15/14/13/13/11/10/9, W: 8/8/8/8/8/7/7/7/7
Saves PPDM 2, RSW 3, PP 4, BW 4, Sp 4

Special Att/Def: Angharradh wields a variety of weapons depending on the situation. The *Blade of Red Tears* is a crimson-hued *long sword of quickness +5*. *Duskshaft* is a great duskwood *spear +3* that requires any creature struck by it to succeed at a saving throw vs. spell or be *held* (as the 5th-level wizard spell *hold monster*). *Tremorflail* is a *footman's flail +3* that inflicts 6d10+3 points of damage to chaotic evil opponents and can be used to shatter walls and buildings (as a *horn of blasting*). The *Net of Stars* is a gossamer netting that envelops creatures in a silvery web of magic four times as strong as *iron bands of Bilarro* (in other words, requiring a successful bend bars attempt with one-quarter the normal chance of success).

Angharradh is immune to all gaze and breath attacks. Her gaze can cause any mortal being to *sleep* for 1d6 days (no saving throw). She can employ any of the special attacks or defenses of Aerdrie Faenya, Hanali Celanil, or Sehanine Moonbow, and she has all of their innate immunities. She can be struck only by +3 or better magical weapons.

Other Manifestations

Angharradh may manifest in any of the ways detailed in the descriptions of Aerdrie Faenya, Hanali Celanil, and Sehanine Moonbow. The Triune Goddess is served by the same creatures as the Three and demonstrates her favor or disfavor in ways identical to those of the Three.

The Church

CLERGY:	Clerics, crusaders, druids, mystics, specialty priests
CLERGY'S ALIGN.:	NG, CG, N, CN
TURN UNDEAD:	C: Yes, Cru: No, D: No, Mys: No, SP: Circle singers as the other deity followed; totem sisters no
CMND. UNDEAD:	C: No, Cru: No, D: No, Mys: No, SP: No

All clerics (including multiclassed half-elven clerics), crusaders, druids, mystics, and specialty priests of Angharradh receive religion (elf) and reading/writing (Espruar) as bonus nonweapon proficiencies.

The Teu-Tel'Quessir view the Three as separate aspects of the One and consider the Triune Goddess to be as powerful and influential as Corellon Larethian and who presides, alongside her consort, with equal authority over the Seldarine and the Fair Folk. Gold elves generally do not know what to make of Angharradh. Most consider her to be either a separate goddess or a typical silver elf misinterpretation of Sehanine Moonbow, consort to Corellon Larethian. They generally do not object to the silver elves' veneration of the tripartite deity, however, and even pay her homage themselves on rare occasions. Dark elves, green elves, sea elves, winged elves, and most half-elves do not worship Angharradh, nor is her nature and existence even debated, as is the case among the Ar-Tel'Quessir.

Angharradh's temples resemble the houses of worship dedicated to the Three, either emphasizing the characteristics of the temples of one of the three goddesses, or blending all three styles of temple equally. The Triune Goddess's temples always display the symbol of the One and the Three as well as the symbols of the individual goddesses.

Novices of Angharradh are known as Triune Seekers. Full priests of the Triune Goddess are known as Trimorphs. Angharradhan priests use titles as appropriate for the aspect they primarily venerate. Specialty priests are known as either circle singers or totem sisters (druids). The clergy of Angharradh includes moon elves (93%), half-moon elves (5%), and elves and half-elves of other subraces (2%). Angharradh's clergy is composed primarily of clerics, crusaders, mystics, and specialty priests of Aerdrie Faenya (15%), Hanali Celanil (35%), and Sehanine Moonbow (40%). The remainder (10%) are totem sisters, a type of druid. Perhaps 33% of the specialty priests of the three affiliated with the faith of Angharradh are actually circle singers. The clergy of Angharradh is pretty evenly split between male (48%) and female (52%).

Dogma: Through unity and diversity there is strength. Be ever vigilant against She Who Was Banished and work together in defending the lands of the Fair Folk from those who would work evil. Celebrate the One and the Three for their collective purpose and individual expressions of life. Through the melding of widely different skills and interests, creativity, life, and artistry are nurtured and new ideas are discovered.

Day-to-Day Activities: Priests of Angharradh serve the Triune Goddess much like the clergies of Aerdrie Faenya, Hanali Celanil, and Sehanine Moonbow. Most priests of the Triune Goddess are affiliated with one aspect of the Three, and their activities reflect their association with that particular aspect. A handful of female silver elven priests are practitioners of the ancient secrets of totemic magic. These mysterious elves create small wood or stone charms inscribed with pictorial symbols that can pass special magical abilities on to their owners. Totem-sisters are also considered wise women and sages and are often consulted on important issues.

They also serve as priests of Aerdrie Faenya, Hanali Celanil, and Sehanine Moonbow, as well as their single embodiment, Angharradh. Totem-sisters craft beneficial totemic images for their tribe and are considered great sources of wisdom and comfort. They attend births, bless young children, help with planting and harvest, and bless warriors going into battle. Particularly successful totem sisters are sought out by other tribes and aspiring totemic practitioners for advice and counsel.

Holy Days/Important Ceremonies: Members of Angharradh's priesthood celebrate the holy days and important ceremonies of one of the Three, depending upon which aspect of the Triune Goddess they particularly venerate. The only holy day celebrated exclusively by those who pray to Angharradh is the Melding of the Three, held quadrennially on *Cinnaelos'Cor (the Day of Corellon's Peace)*, more commonly known in the Calendar of Harptos as Shieldmeet. While this holy day is more generally observed by elves in honor of the Protector, the Teu-Tel'Quessir celebrate the tripartite aspects of Angharradh and the unification of the Three that have led to centuries of peace in Arvandor and elven realms in Faerûn. In addition to singing great hymns to the Triune Goddess, Angharradh's faithful often assemble to invoke great feats of cooperative magic on this day.

Major Centers of Worship: The Hall of Trifold Harmony is a soaring temple of green and white marble in the elven city of Taltempla on the eastern shore of the Green Isle. Angharradh's house of worship is located amidst neighboring temples of Aerdrie Faenya, Hanali Celanil, and Sehanine Moonbow in the temple district of Evermeet's second-largest city, and the ranks of the Triune Goddess's priesthood are drawn from silver elves who serve in the temples of both the One and the Three. The temple of Angharradh is jointly administered by a triumvirate of the seniormost silver elven priests of the three elven goddesses resident in the city. They are Faranni Omberdawn, Blythswana Iliathor, and Renestrae Narlbeth, respectively the fourth, second, and first-ranking priests in their individual temples. The Hall of Trifold Harmony serves as the center of silver elven culture in Taltempla, and the Triumvirate of Angharradh assists the informal ruler of the city, High Mage Gaelira, in ameliorating the infrequent disputes that arise among the temples of the various Seldarine powers venerated in the city.

Affiliated Orders: The Angharradhan church has no knightly orders specifically affiliated with the Triune Goddess. However, some members of orders affiliated with either Aerdrie Faenya, Hanali Celanil, or Sehanine Moonbow worship their order's patron as an aspect of Angharradh.

Priestly Vestments: Angharradh's priests wear the ceremonial garb of the clergies of the Three. Some priests wear the garb of one aspect of the Triune Goddess, while other priests incorporate pieces of each fashion into their holy vestments. The holy symbol of the faith is an inverted silver triangle inscribed on both faces with the symbol of the Triune Goddess.

Adventuring Garb: In combat situations, clerics, crusaders, and specialty priests of the One and the Three favor ornate, gleaming suits of elven chain mail or, in rare situations, elven plate mail. Their preferred weapons include long and short bows, long and short swords, and spears, although most are trained in a wide range of weapons. Shields emblazoned with the symbol of the Triune Goddess are common among the faithful, as are heraldic charges per pall (parted in three, as the letter "Y") with the symbol of Sehanine on top, the symbol of Aerdrie in the lower left, and the symbol of Hanali in the lower right as viewed by the shield-bearer. Totem-sisters favor long bows and spears and use only nonmetallic armors.

Specialty Priests (Circle Singers)

REQUIREMENTS:	Wisdom 16, Charisma 16
PRIME REQ.:	Wisdom, Charisma
ALIGNMENT:	CG
WEAPONS:	Varies
ARMOR:	Varies
MAJOR SPHERES:	Varies
MINOR SPHERES:	Varies
MAGICAL ITEMS:	Same as clerics
REQ. PROFS:	Varies
BONUS PROFS:	Singing, otherwise varies

Circle singers receive all the benefits of and must abide by the restrictions governing specialty priests of either Aerdrie Faenya, Hanali Celanil, or

Sehanine Moonbow. Even among moon elves, specialty priests of the Three are considered to be members of the clergy of one of Angharradh's three aspects as well as priests of the Triune Goddess herself.

- Circle singers must be elves or half-elves. While most circle singers are moon elves or half-moon elves, elves and half-elves of every subrace are called to be circle singers, even if they venerate only the Three and not the One.
- Circle singers are not allowed to multiclass.
- Circle singers may cast cooperative magic with other priests of Angharradh, Aerdrie Faenya, Hanali Celanil, or Sehanine Moonbow.
- Circle singers can cast *ring of hands* (as the 1st-level priest spell) once per tenday.
- At 3rd level, circle singers can cast *mystic transfer* or *sanctify* (as the 2nd-level priest spells) once per tenday.
- At 5th level, circle singers can cast *line of protection* or *unearthly choir* (as the 3rd-level priest spells) once per tenday.
- At 7th level, circle singers can cast *focus* or *fortify* or *uplift* (as the 4th-level priest spells) once per tenday.
- At 10th level, circle singers can cast *meld* or *thoughtwave* (as the 5th-level priest spells) once per tenday.
- At 13th level, circle singers can cast *the great circle* or *spiritual wrath* (as the 6th-level priest spells) once per tenday.
- At 15th level, circle singers can cast *spirit of power* (as the 7th-level priest spell) once per tenday.

Specialty Priests (Totem Sisters)

REQUIREMENTS:	Wisdom 12, Charisma 15
PRIME REQ.:	Wisdom, Charisma
ALIGNMENT:	NG, CG, N, CN
WEAPONS:	Any
ARMOR:	Hide, leather, padded, studded leather, or chain mail, shield
MAJOR SPHERES:	All, animal, charm, elemental, healing, plant, weather, sun
MINOR SPHERES:	None
MAGICAL ITEMS:	Same as clerics
REQ. PROFS:	Long bow, spear
BONUS PROFS:	Artistic ability (general)

Totem sisters of Angharradh are effectively druids. The abilities and restrictions of totem sisters, aside from the changes noted above and later in this section, are summarized in the discussion of elven priests in "Appendix 1: Demihuman Priests" and detailed in full in the entry for druids in *Faiths & Avatars* and in the *Player's Handbook*.

- Totem sisters must be female moon elves.
- Totem sisters are not allowed to multiclass.
- Totem sisters can use totemic magic, a type of magic similar to rune magic. (Totemic magic is discussed in *Elves of Evermeet*.)

Angharradhan Spells

Priests of the Triune Goddess may cast all unique spells permitted to priests of Aerdrie Faenya, Hanali Celanil, and Sehanine Moonbow.

Avachel

For more information on Avachel (AH-vah-chel), see the entry for Hlal in the draconic pantheon discussion in *Cult of the Dragon* and the *Draconomicon*, and see the entry for Aasterinian in the draconic pantheon discussion in *Monstrous Mythology* and in *On Hallowed Ground*.

Avachel is a male aspect of the draconic goddess Hlal (also known as Aasterinian) who is venerated by the Fair Folk as the boon companion of Erevan Ilesere. Although Quicksilver, as Avachel is commonly titled, is in some respects an interloper power of the elven pantheon, he is more commonly and correctly seen as an ally of the Seldarine. In some elven myths, Avachel is said to have been a great mercury wyrm who underwent apotheosis after sacrificing himself to defeat an invasion by evil humans who

threatened a band of green elves. Other legends speak of an avatar of Hlal in the guise of a mortal mercury dragon who joins with the Trickster in a similar series of events. Regardless of the truth behind his ascension, Avachel is nearly Erevan's equal in his ability to get into trouble, but he is a tireless defender of the Fair Folk, particularly green elves. Quicksilver is a good-natured, impulsive deity, with a fondness for dispatching avatars to Evermeet and the other woodlands of Toril in the guise of a silver or green elf armed only with an enchanted staff that requires all who are hit by it to succeed at a saving throw vs. spell or fall asleep, or in the guise of a great mercury wyrm, with all the attendant powers thereof.

Corellon Larethian

(Creator of the Elves, the Protector, First of the Seldarine, Protector and Preserver of Life, Ruler of All Elves, Coronal of Arvandor)
Greater Power of Arborea, CG

PORTFOLIO:	Magic and elven magic (especially elven High Magic), music, arts, crafts, war, the elven race (especially gold elves), poets, poetry, bards, warriors
ALIASES:	None
DOMAIN NAME:	Olympus/Arvandor
SUPERIOR:	None
ALLIES:	Chauntea, Cyrrollalee, Eilistraee, Emmantiensien, Garl Glittergold, Horus-Re, Lathander, Lurue, Mielikki, Milil, Moradin, Mystra, Oberon, Selûne, Shiallia, Skerrit, Silvanus, Sune, Tapann, Titania, Tyr, Ubtao, Yondalla, the Seldarine
FOES:	Cyric, Talos, Malar, Moander, the Queen of Air and Darkness, the drow pantheon (except Eilistraee), the orc and goblinkin pantheons
SYMBOL:	Crescent moon
WOR. ALIGN.:	LG, NG, CG, LN, N, CN

The leader of the elven pantheon, Corellon Larethian (CORE-eh-lon Lah-RETH-ee-yen), is said to have given birth to the entire elven race, although sometimes Sehanine (or Angharradh) is given credit as well. Elven lore states that the Fair Folk sprang from drops of blood Corellon shed in epic battles with Gruumsh mingled with Sehanine's (or Angharradh's) tears. The Creator of the Elves embodies the highest ideals of elvenkind, and he is the patron of most aesthetic endeavors, including art, magic, music, poetry, and warfare. He is venerated by all the Fair Folk, except the drow and those who have turned to Lolth, Ghaunadaur, Vhaeraun, and other dark powers. Corellon is especially popular with elf and half-elf mages, musicians, and poets.

As ruler of the Seldarine, Corellon has a strong relationship with almost all the other elven powers, including Eilistraee, his daughter by Araushnee (Lolth), whom he reluctantly banished from Arvandor along with her mother at the Dark Maiden's insistence. Either Sehanine or Angharradh is now said to be Corellon's consort, depending on the subrace of the speaker, and the Protector works closely with the Goddess of Moonlight and the Triune Goddess in their dual aspects. Only Fenmarel Mestarine is somewhat estranged from the Coronal of Arvandor, and the Lone Wolf's differences with Corellon are not all that great. The Creator of the Elves has forged strong alliances with the leaders of the other demihuman pantheons in the face of the seemingly endless waves of human expansion and the ever-present threat of the monstrous populations and their dark powers, as well as with the good- and neutral-aligned powers of the humans. The Protector works closely with Mystra, the Mother of All Magic. Whereas the Lady of Mysteries governs the Weave, Corellon oversees elven magic, particularly elven High Magic, and the intimate connection between the Fair Folk and the mantle of magic that envelops the world. (More information on elven High Magic is found in the *Cormanthyr: Empire of the Elves* sourcebook.) Corellon's epic battle with Gruumsh One-Eye, leader of the orc pantheon, is legendary, and the pair of pantheistic patriarchs have never reached a lasting truce in their never-ending battle over territory. Malar's relentless attacks on the Seldarine and the Fair Folk have likewise earned him Corellon's eternal enmity. The rift between Corellon and his former lover Araushnee, now known as Lolth, is still as bitter as the day he banished the Spider Queen to the Abyss and named her *tanar'ri*. The Protector's rift with his errant son Vhaeraun is nearly as deep, and the Protector has despaired of the Masked Lord ever repenting of his evil ways. In his vigilant defense of elves and their homelands, Corellon has earned the enmity of countless powers whose worshipers seek to seize the forests, magic, or wealth of the Fair Folk.

Corellon is a powerful warrior god whose hands protect his creations with the gentleness of a sculptor and the unspeakable power of a master swordswinger. While other deities may reflect the joy, delights, and accomplishments of the Fair Folk, Corellon stands as an ever-vigilant watcher over them. His life spirit flows from and into the elves and their lands, and while mortal elves daydream and enter the reverie, Corellon never abandons his watchfulness. Only when it is time for the Fair Folk to pass from Faerûn to Arvandor does he finally cease watching over each elf and allows Sehanine to take a larger role in caring for them. Corellon frequently wanders the elven lands and borders in disguise (often in the form of one of the diminutive sylvan race), observing the actions of priests and craftsfolk and defending elven homelands from interlopers. Though his martial might is swift and terrible, the soft-spoken Creator of the Elves is ever humble and always open to learning something new, one of his sources of might. He enjoys discovering new philosophies of thought and new methods of action, even from mortals, and he has a keen interest in other cultures.

Corellon's primary servitors are identical twin spirits, Lashrael and Felarathael. Held by some of the Fair Folk, particularly gold elves, to be demipowers in their own right, Corellon's messengers are solars who resemble tall, shining, androgynous elves clad in gleaming white robes. They are most often seen delivering messages for the Protector in the Realms, and they are also dispatched to defend elves if they are threatened. The two have distinctive personalities, however. Lashrael is given to emotional extremes. When delivering a message, Lashrael speaks with great conviction, and depending upon the message, enormous joy or sorrow. In battle, Lashrael is ferocious, neither asking nor giving quarter. Felarathael, on the other hand, is the very image of rational detachment, treating all situations with logic and calm reason. Felarathael always speaks in a slow, measured, but immensely reassuring voice, and fights with unhurried skill. When Lashrael or Felarathael strike a victim in combat, they may inflict one of the following effects in lieu of damage: victim *sleeps* (no saving throw allowed), victim is randomly teleported 1d10 miles, victim is polymorphed into a woodland animal, or victim suffers from amnesia.

Corellon's Avatar (Fighter 36, Mage 35, Bard 29, Cleric 25)

Corellon usually appears as an androgynous male elf of truly unearthly beauty and grace, although he can assume the form of either sex. Despite his obvious strength, the primary impression the Creator of the Elves radiates is that of litheness and swiftness, and he is possessed of incredible speed and reflex. He always wears a sky-blue cloak, a large amulet about his neck with a crescent moon motif within a large circle, and a pair of dazzling battle gauntlets. Corellon draws his spells from all spheres (although he never employs reversed forms) and schools.

AC –6; MV 15; HP 224; THAC0 –10; #AT 5/2
Dmg 3d10+18 (great *long sword* +6, +10 Str, +2 spec. bonus in any sword) or 2d10+15 (*long bow* +5, +10 Str)
MR 90%; SZ M (7 feet tall)
Str 22, Dex 24, Con 20, Int 23, Wis 22, Cha 24
Spells P: 12/12/12/12/11/8/4, W: 8/8/8/8/8/8/8/7/7
Saves PPDM 2, RSW 3, PP 4, BW 4, Sp 4

Special Att/Def: Corellon wields *Sahandrian*, a great glittering *long sword* +6 that causes 4d10 points of damage per round to anyone else aside from a member of the Seldarine who dares to hold or wield it (double damage to goblinkin). He also employs *Amlath'hana*, a *long bow* +5 that never misses to a range of 1 mile (if the target is within his line of sight) and whose arrows, drawn from a quiver with an infinite supply, each deals 2d10 points of damage. Corellon's amulet serves as a *talisman of pure good*, and he has a slender wand with all of the powers of a *staff of power*, a *staff of the magi*, and a *wand of frost*, as well as unlimited charges available if necessary.

In lieu of casting a wizard or priest spell, once per round Corellon can cast any elven High Magic ritual at will, whether it be a *ritual of solitude*, a *ritual of complement*, or a *ritual of myriad*, without penalty. In addition, he can summon 1d4 16-HD air elementals to do his bidding once per turn that serve him unquestioningly until no longer needed.

Corellon is immune to any magic that prevents his free movement (*hold*, *paralyzation*, *web*, etc.), causes wounds or energy drains, or exercises any form of mind control (*charm person*, *magic jar*, *domination*, etc.). He is immune to all spells from the illusion/phantasm school of magic that he does not wish to be affected by. He can be struck only by +3 or better magical weapons.

Other Manifestations

Corellon manifests as an azure nimbus that envelops a living creature, weapon, or natural geological formation in an aura of flickering sky blue flame.

This power typically gives any or all of the following aids to affected beings, for 13 rounds: *idea* (as the 2nd-level priest spell); *sixth sense* (as the 1st-level priest spell); *strength* (as the 2nd-level wizard spell) and a temporary 1d6-point boost to the being's Dexterity (maximum of 20).

This power typically gives any or all of the following aids to a weapon, for 13 rounds: *bladethirst* (as the 2nd-level wizard spell detailed in *Pages from the Mages*); the heat and burning effects of a *flame tongue* weapon or the cold effects of a *frostbrand* weapon; *quickness*, as a *short sword of quickness*.

This power typically affects a geological formation in any or all of the following ways: *earthquake* (as the 7th-level priest spell); *soften earth and stone* (as the 2nd-level priest spell); *stone shape* (as the 3rd-level priest spell); or *glassee* (as the 6th-level wizard spell).

The Seldarine call on agathinon, asuras, and ancient treants as their preferred servants, but Corellon is also served by aasimar, aasimon (such as the twin solars described above), baelnorn, buraq, cath shee, centaurs, cooshee, disenchanters, dryads, einheriar, eladrins (particularly firres and ghaeles), elven cats, feystags, firestars, firetails, gold dragons, hamadryads, hollyphants, hybsils, incarnates of charity, courage, faith, hope, justice, temperance, and wisdom, ki-rin, kholiathra, lillendi, lythari, maruts, moon dogs, moon-horses, noctrals, nymphs, oreads, pers, phoenixes, reverend ones, seelie faeries, sharn, silver dogs, silver dragons, sylphs, spectral wizards, spellhaunts, sprites, sunflies, t'uen-rin, unicorns, weredragons, and wizshades. He demonstrates his favor through the discovery of beljurils, crescent-shaped stones, diamonds, moonstars, moonstones, star rubies, and star sapphires, the sighting of a fallen star, the rising of an azure-tinted crescent moon, or the sighting of an azure-hued star. The Protector indicates his displeasure through the appearance of a falling star that seems to fall from the upper tip to the lower tip of the crescent moon like a heavenly tear, the premature appearance of fall colors in a single tree, or the sound of three twigs snapping in rapid succession.

The Church

CLERGY:	Clerics, crusaders, specialty priests, wizards
CLERGY'S ALIGN.:	LG, NG, CG
TURN UNDEAD:	C: Yes, Cru: No, SP: Yes
CMND. UNDEAD:	C: No, Cru: No, SP: No

All clerics (including multiclassed half-elven clerics and elven fighter/clerics, a multiclassed combination allowed to elven priests of Corellon), crusaders, and specialty priests of Corellon receive religion (elf) and reading/writing (Espruar) as bonus nonweapon proficiencies.

Corellon is venerated by all the Tel'Quessir who have not turned to dark powers, even those who do not specifically worship him, for the Fair

Folk were born of his blood, and they do not forget their debt to the Creator. Likewise, Corellon's role in banishing Lolth and the drow from the surface, thus ending the madness of the Crown Wars, has earned him the eternal, if largely unspoken, gratitude of elves across Faerûn. Curiously, the clergy Corellon's church is somewhat removed from elven society, and the Protector's priesthood is less involved in the governance of elven realms than a N'Tel'Quess might imagine. While the Protector's followers are held in high esteem for their unflagging contribution to the defense of elven realms and the breathtaking beauty of their artistry, in general their place in elven society reflects the guardian and creative aspects of Corellon's nature far more than his position as Coronal of Arvandor and Ruler of All Elves. Some theologians suggest the warriors and wizards who predominate in positions of authority in elven society in a sense comprise the priesthood of Corellon in his leadership aspect, but this view is not widely accepted.

Corellon is venerated in rocky areas of natural beauty, always with a special place for viewing the moon and stars. Temples of the Protector are rare, however, since the elves are individualistic when it comes to his worship. Shrines are more common, but they are little more than clearings with a good view of the sky. His temples are shaped from great natural geological formations, including shallow caves entered from above, natural amphitheaters, and great rock spires. Trees and other plants are woven into such edifices, resulting in great natural cathedrals woven of stone and plants.

Novices of Corellon are known as the Faerna. Full priests of the Protector are known as the Faernsuora. In ascending order of rank, the titles used by Corellite priests are Aegisess (Protector), Adoness (Peacekeeper), Kerynsuoress (Holy Warrior), Ivae'ess (Lightbringer), Avae'ess (Joybringer), Syolkiir (Wildstar), Lateu'suoress (Crescent-Moonblessed), Araegisess (Great Protector), Aradoness (Great Peacekeeper), and Arkerynsuoress (Great Holy Warrior). High-ranking priests have unique individual titles but are collectively known as the Cormiira (Blessings of Corellon). Specialty priests are known as feywardens. The clergy of Corellon includes gold elves (33%), moon elves (30%), wild elves (15%), sea elves (10%), half-elves of various ancestries (12%) and even a handful of dark elves. Corellon's clergy is nearly evenly divided between clerics (38%), including fighter/clerics, specialty priests (30%), crusaders (28%) and a handful of wizards (4%), including mages, specialist wizards, and multiclassed mages. The clergy of Corellon contains a few more males (55%) than females (45%).

Dogma: The Tel'Quessir are both wardens and sculptors of magic's endless mysteries. Through Art and Craft, bring forth the beauty that envelops and let the spirit gambol unfettered. The song of joy and the dance of freedom shall ever soar on the wings of those who dare take flight. Guard against the slow death of stultifying sameness by seeking out new experiences and new ways. Ward against those who seek only to destroy in their inability to create and commune with the natural and mystical world. Be ever vigilant in force of arms and might of magic against any return of the banished darkness, and also be strong in heart against the corruption from within which allowed the Spider Queen to foment the chaos and evil of the Crown Wars.

Day-to-Day Activities: Priests of Corellon are expected to serve actively in the defense and artistic development of elven communities and to work to mediate disputes that arise among the Fair Folk or between the elves and other sylvan deities. In service to the Protector, many Corellite priests serve in the armed forces of their homeland, defending elf-claimed territories from the relentless expansion of other races and training their fellow elves in combat skills and magic. Others work closely with elven artisans and craftsfolk instructing them in the skills they need to create works of wondrous beauty, as well as using their own creative talents in similar pursuits. Finally, members of Corellon's priesthood are often called upon to act as diplomats and arbitrators between the various clergies, the various subraces of elves, the various classes of elven society, and even between elven communities. While few priests of the Coronal of Arvandor actually serve as rulers or councilors, many work behind the scenes to ensure the smooth functioning of government.

Holy Days/Important Ceremonies: Corellon's faithful celebrate a great number of holy days, most of which are tied to astronomical events and occur only once every few years (such as Shieldmeet) or decades. Of particular import, once per lunar month, when the crescent moon softly illuminates the night sky, Corellon's faithful gather in moonlit glades to celebrate the gifts of their deity in a festival known as Lateu'quor, the Forest

Communion of the Crescent Moon. Devotees of the Protector offer up their praises through music, song, dance, and the offering up of their most beautiful creations. True works of art are sometimes brought up to Arvandor so as to be appreciated by the spirits of those elves who dwell among the Seldarine, while others are kept within Corellon's shrines and temples so that the Fair Folk of Faerûn may wonder at the fruits of Corellon's greatest gift: creativity. On rare occasions such revels spontaneously unleash a glorious magical ceremony whose results are guided only by the Creator of the Elves. Sometimes the landscape is reshaped, and the site is thereafter considered sacred to the Protector. At other times, the communal magic coalesces into an item—usually a sword, long bow, set of cloak and boots, suit of elven mail, or musical instrument—of unearthly beauty. Such items are then enchanted by Corellon's seniormost priests and are thereafter considered holy relics of the faith.

Major Centers of Worship: Corellon's Grove, located near the center of the northern half of Evermeet at the heart of the great forest that blankets the Green Isle, is held to be the site closest to Arvandor in all of the Realms. Many Tel'Quessir claim to have seen Corellon Larethian himself, as well as other members of the Seldarine, wandering amidst this oasis of unearthly beauty. Corellon's Grove is visited by the Fair Folk of Evermeet for solemn ceremonies, private worship, or simple private meditation.

The trees that surround Corellon's Grove magically weave their branches together, preventing entrance to the shrine. Treants sometimes join the guardian trees in watching over the shrine, as do the countless sylvan creatures who roam the Green Isle. Wrought iron gates entwined with ivy and blooming roses year-round permit passage only to Tel'Quessir who approach wishing to worship Corellon and the Seldarine.

Gleaming white marble walkways flanked by tall columns adorned with ivy and roses, like the entrance gates, lead through the heart of the Grove and connect the numerous shrines found within. Magical fountains are scattered throughout the grove, and their enchanted waters are said to confer one or more effects similar to those of *potions of healing, elixirs of health, potions of heroism, potions of invulnerability, potions of extra-healing,* and *potions of vitality.* Within the Grove may be found shrines to Aerdrie Faenya, Hanali Celanil, Labelas Enoreth, Rillifane Rallathil, Sehanine Moonbow, and even the king and queen of faerie, Oberon and Titania. Each shrine contains a white marble statue depicting one of the Seldarine or faerie monarchs, and elves who pray before them are said to sometimes receive magical blessings from the power so depicted. The Ar-Tel'Quessir who constructed Corellon's Grove chose not to include shrines to the rogue powers of the Seldarine—such as Erevan Ilesere, Fenmarel Mestarine, Shevarash, or Solonor Thelandira—or to aspects of the Seldarine worshiped by the other subraces—such as Angharradh, Bear, Eagle, Raven, or Wolf, but all such powers and aspects of powers are nonetheless venerated in Corellon's Grove by the Fair Folk. Corellon's shrine is the largest by far found within the Grove, a great dome of green marble woven into the forest canopy. The First of the Seldarine and Creator of the Elves is portrayed traditionally as a tall, unnaturally thin, androgynous elven figure with a thin face, high cheekbones, and narrow, slanted eyes. The figure is clad in scale armor and carries a long, slim sword. A delicate coronet graces the brow of the Coronal of Arvandor, and a sense of peace and contentment radiates from the statue itself. Any of the Fair Folk who pray here may receive a special blessing from Corellon, although at most one such favor is granted per year. Corellon may manifest as discussed above, or he may grant the ability to cast *cure light wounds* or *cure serious wounds* once at some future time. Some elves report after praying at the shrine that the Protector gifted them with an item of magic (usually a weapon or article of clothing), while others have found woodland animal companions or mounts such as giant eagles, moon-horses, or pegasi awaiting them as they completed their supplications.

In the aftermath of the destruction of the Grove caused by the rampage of the Elf-Eater in the Year of the Unstrung Harp (1371 DR), Corellon's Grove is rebuilt by all the Fair Folk and expanded and changed considerably. When completed, the reconsecrated Grove contains shrines of all the known powers and distinct aspects of the Seldarine, and its design better represents the diverse architectural styles employed by the various elven subraces.

Affiliated Orders: Corellon is the divine patron of many knightly orders, many of which claim to trace their heritage and membership back to the Time of Flowers. Such orders are typically composed largely of crusaders, warriors, and wizards (particularly fighter-mages), but their composition has varied widely over the millennia and from culture to culture.

Notable orders in ages past have included the Knights of the Golden Wyrm, the Blade of Sahandrian, the Fey Staghorns, and the Swords of the Seldarine. On Evermeet, the Wings of Yathaghera, the Knights of the Alicorn, the Weavers of Bladesong, and the Vassals of the Reverend Ones are all pledged to support the Protector in the defense of the Green Isle. Few orders have remained on the mainland of Faerûn since the Retreat began in the Year of Moonfall (1344 DR), but of those that remain, the Swords of Evereska are the most notable for their unwavering defense of that alpine vale. Outside of elven homelands, the most frequently encountered agents of an elven knightly order belong to the Fellowship of the Forgotten Flower, a loosely structured organization dedicated to the recovery of lost elven relics from long-abandoned elven realms.

Priestly Vestments: Ceremonial vestments for priests of Corellon—often worn in normal situations by choice, although such attire is not required—consist of azure robes made of gossamer and embroidered with silver quarter moons. Silver circlets engraved with the Protector's symbol are worn on the brow. The holy symbol of the faith is a silver or mithral lunate pendant worn on an slender chain hung from the neck.

Adventuring Garb: When adventuring, Corellon's priests generally favor sky blue cloaks, elven chain mail, long swords, and long bows in conscious imitation of their divine patron. Clerics, restricted to bludgeoning weapons, favor clubs, slings, staff slings, and staves, although maces and flails are employed as well. Leather, studded leather armor, or elven chain mail is favored in situations requiring stealth, in addition to *elven cloaks* and *boots*, whereas elven chain mail or elven plate mail (or N'Tel'Quess approximations) are favored in situations requiring direct melee combat.

Specialty Priests (Feywardens)

REQUIREMENTS:	Strength 11, Intelligence 11, Wisdom 9
PRIME REQ.:	Strength, Intelligence, Wisdom
ALIGNMENT:	CG
WEAPONS:	Any
ARMOR:	Any
MAJOR SPHERES:	All, astral, charm, combat, creation, divination, guardian, healing, necromantic, protection, sun, war, wards
MINOR SPHERES:	Animal, chaos, summoning, plant, thought
MAGICAL ITEMS:	Same as clerics
REQ. PROFS:	Long sword, long bow, artistic ability, spellcraft
BONUS PROFS:	Musical instrument, singing

- Feywardens must be elves or half-elves. Most feywardens are gold elves or moon elves. They cannot be drow.
- Feywardens are not allowed to multiclass.
- Feywardens may select nonweapon proficiencies from the warrior group without penalty.
- Feywardens gain a +2 bonus to Charisma with respect to elves.
- Feywardens are immune to the paralyzing touch of ghasts as well as ghouls. They gain a +1 bonus to saving throws vs. other forms of paralysis as well, such as the touch of a lich or the various *hold* spells.
- Feywardens can cast *sixth sense* (as the 1st-level priest spell) once per day.
- Feywardens gain a +2 bonus to their nonweapon proficiency check when crafting any item, including weapons and armor, or when inventing a new song or poem. When they are of sufficient level, feywardens gain bonuses adjudicated by the DM when constructing magical items or helping others to do so.
- At 3rd level, feywardens can cast *faerie fire* (as the 1st-level priest spell) or *idea* (as the 2nd-level priest spell) once per day.
- At 5th level, feywardens can cast *strength* (as the 2nd-level wizard spell) or employ a variant of *strength* that increases Dexterity instead of Strength once per day.
- At 5th level, feywardens gain a +2 bonus to saving throws vs. poison and automatically save against spider venoms.
- At 7th level, feywardens can cast *abjure* (as the 4th-level priest spell) or *minor creation* (as the 4th-level wizard spell) once per day.
- At 10th level, feywardens can cast *enchanted weapon* (as the 4th-level wizard spell) or *major creation* (as the 5th-level wizard spell) once per day.

- At 10th level, goblinkin (goblinoids) have a −2 penalty to saving throws they roll against the priest spells of feywardens.
- At 13th level, feywardens can cast *banishment* or *prismatic spray* (as the 7th-level wizard spells) once per day.
- At 15th level, feywardens can cast *holy word* or *sunray* (as the 7th-level priest spells) once per day.

Corellite Spells

1st Level

Augment Artistry (Pr 1; Alteration)

Sphere:	Creation
Range:	0
Components:	V, S, M
Duration:	Special
Casting Time:	1 round
Area of Effect:	One creature
Saving Throw:	None

This spell combines magic with the act of creation to enhance the artistry of any work created by the recipient of this spell. For every three levels of experience of the priest (round up), the recipient of this spell receives a +1 bonus, to a maximum of +3, to his or her next nonweapon proficiency check against an ability requiring artistic ability. While the effects of this spell last only until the next such nonweapon proficiency check, the results of the augmented artistry are permanent.

In addition to the nonweapon proficiency artistic ability, this spell usually augments a proficiency check for dancing, gem cutting, singing, or any other skill that is traditionally considered an artistic endeavor. This spell does not affect traditional crafts where functionality is emphasized over artistry, including nonweapon proficiencies such as armorer, blacksmithing, leatherworking, seamstress/tailor, weaving, or weaponsmithing, unless the proficiency check is specifically for the esthetic appeal of the finished product. In all cases, the applicability of this enchantment to a particular endeavor is adjudicated by the DM.

The material components of this spell are the priest's holy symbol and a scroll bearing a piece of epic poetry (not necessarily the original work).

Sixth Sense (Pr 1; Abjuration)

Sphere:	Protection
Range:	0
Components:	V, S, M
Duration:	1 hour
Casting Time:	1 round
Area of Effect:	The Caster
Saving Throw:	None

This spell imbues the priest with a sixth sense, alerting him or her of unexpected danger (to himself or herself or an ally) within 10 feet of the caster's current position. Although the exact nature of the threat is never revealed, the priest does realize that something dangerous is about to occur a moment before the event unfolds. While so protected, the priest receives a +3 bonus to all surprise checks, and any ability check made to determine the success of an immediate reaction to a dangerous situation is made with a +3 bonus. For example, if the priest is deftly moving along a high mountain ledge, the magic of this spell might warn of a powerful gust of wind in time for him or her to grab onto an outcropping of rock, also granting a +3 bonus to the Strength check to hold on to the rock spur. Likewise, if an ally steps out on to a hidden pit trap, the priest would realize the friend's danger in time to make a desperate grab for his or her arm and receive a +3 bonus to the Strength check to hold on. In addition, sixth sense provides a +3 bonus to saving throws made to avoid natural phenomena, such as rockfalls, avalanches, etc.

The material components are the priest's holy symbol and a drop of sweat.

4th Level

Sylvan Creature Form (Pr 4; Alteration)

Sphere:	Animal
Range:	0
Components:	V, S, M
Duration:	2 turns/level
Casting Time:	7
Area of Effect:	The caster
Saving Throw:	None

When this spell is cast, the priest is able to assume the form of any nonevil humaniform sylvan creature, as adjudicated by the DM, from as small as a gorse (3 inches tall) to as large as a voadkyn (9 ½ feet tall). Other commonly assumed forms include those of an atomie, brownie, dobie, dryad, grig, hamadryad, killmoulis, korred, leprechaun, nixie, nymph, pixie, satyr, sylph, sprite, or sea sprite. It is not possible to assume nonhumaniform guises, such as that of a centaur or unicorn, nor that of an evil sylvan creature, such as a bramble faerie or quickling. Furthermore, the priest also gains the assumed form's physical mode of locomotion and breathing. No system shock roll is required. The spell does not give the new form's other abilities (attack, magic, special movement, etc.), nor does it run the risk of the priest changing personality and mentality.

When the new form is assumed, the caster's equipment, if any, melds into the new form (in particularly challenging campaigns, the DM may allow protective devices, such as a *ring of protection*, to continue operating effectively). The caster retains all mental abilities, including spell use, assuming the new form allows completion of the proper verbal and somatic components and the material components are available. A caster not used to a new form might be penalized at the DM's option (for example, a –2 penalty to attack rolls) until she or he practices sufficiently to master it.

Thus, a priest changed into a sylph could fly, but his or her magic resistance would be unaffected, and she or he could not summon an air elemental or turn *invisible* at will. A change to a korred would provide an 18/76 Strength and the ability to hurl boulders but not the ability to *laugh* or to participate without risk in a korred dance.

Naturally, the strength of the new form is sufficient to enable movement. The priest retains his or her own hit points, attack rolls, and saving throws. Only one form may be assumed by means of this spell, although the priest can revert to normal form at any time, immediately ending the spell. When voluntarily returning to his or her own form and ending the spell, she or he heals 1d12 points of damage. The priest also returns to his or her own form when slain or when the effect is dispelled, but no damage is healed in these cases.

The material component is the priest's holy symbol.

5th Level

Crystallomancy (Pr 5; Alteration)

Sphere:	Divination
Range:	Touch
Components:	V, S, M
Duration:	Special
Casting Time:	1 round
Area of Effect:	1 gemstone
Saving Throw:	None

This spell causes a clear or translucent crystalline gemstone to serve as a scrying device. The spell does not function unless the priest is in good standing with Corellon Larethian. The gemstone becomes similar to a *crystal ball*. For every 1,000 gp value of the gemstone, the priest may scry for 1 round, up to a maximum of 1 hour.

For every three levels of the priest above 7th, it is possible to cast a single divination spell of 4th level or less into the area under observation (thus, one at 10th, two at 13th, three at 16th, etc.). Only detection spells, such as *detect magic* and *detect evil/good*, may be so cast, as adjudicated by the DM.

The material components are the priest's holy symbol and the crystalline gemstone, which must be of at least 1,000 gp value. Neither is consumed in the casting of this spell.

Deep Sashelas
(Lord of the Undersea, the Dolphin Prince, the Knowledgeable One, Sailor's Friend, the Creator)

Intermediate Power of Arborea, CG

PORTFOLIO:	Oceans, sea elves, creation, knowledge, underwater and sea elven beauty, water magic
ALIASES:	None
DOMAIN NAME:	Olympus/Arvandor and Ossa (Aquallor)/Elavandor
SUPERIOR:	Corellon Larethian
ALLIES:	Cyrrollalee, Eadro, Eilistraee, Istishia, Persana, the Seldarine, Surminare, Syranita, Trishina, Valkur, Water Lion, various Animal Lords
FOES:	Blibdoolpoolp, Demogorgon, Sekolah, Panzuriel, Umberlee, the drow pantheon (except Eilistraee)
SYMBOL:	Dolphin
WOR. ALIGN.:	LG, NG, CG, LN, N, CN

Deep Sashelas (DEEP SA-sheh-lahs) is the Lord of the Undersea and the patron of sea elves, whom he created long ago by modifying Corellon's land-bound creations. Sashelas is a powerfully creative deity who is forever changing the environments below the sea, creating islands and reefs by altering continental rifts, tinkering with undersea volcanoes, and the like. He is also said to create the deep undersea caverns that the sea elves can use for air-breathing when they wish. Sashelas is known as the Knowledgeable One, for he provides advice as to where food can be found or the enemies are hidden. The sea elves also claim that Deep Sashelas is the author of the *Chambeeleon*, a resplendent spell tome held in the royal vaults of Thunderfoam an age ago but since lost. Followers of other aquatic gods make similar claims.

Deep Sashelas is a member of the Seldarine and remains on good terms with the other elven deities, but he directs most of his efforts toward maintaining an alliance of nonhuman sea powers known as the *asathalfinare*. While he does not explicitly lead the group, the Lord of the Undersea occupies a pivotal role and mediates many potential conflicts and disagreements. Other members of the *asathalfinare* include Trishina, the dolphin goddess (who is Sashelas's consort), Surminare, goddess of the selkies, Syranita, goddess of the aarakocra (whose membership is somewhat of an anomaly), Persana, god of the tritons, Eadro, leader of the merfolk and locathah, and the enigmatic Water Lion.

The Lord of the Undersea opposes the machinations of all evil powers of the seas, including Abyssal lords such as Demogorgon and Dagon, as well as those whose followers long ago retreated to the Underdark, such as Blibdoolpoolp. Sashelas has a special enmity for Sekolah the Great Shark, the sahuagin god, and for Panzuriel the Enslaver, a dark power worshiped by kraken and other sentient, evil denizens of the ocean depths. The Lord of the Undersea helped banish and weaken Panzuriel long ago. Sashelas respects Panzuriel's growing power, and the Lord of the Undersea considers carefully what steps can be taken to restrain and bind that evil power of the sea bed. Likewise, Sashelas works to contain the evil of the human sea goddess Umberlee, and of late has lent his aid to the human god of sailors, Valkur, as a natural counterweight to Umberlee's burgeoning influence over the seas of Abeir-Toril.

The Lord of the Undersea is a charismatic leader and an inspired creator whose art is everchanging. Unlike the other Seldarine, Deep Sashelas is rarely satisfied with what he's done and always seeks to improve it. Deep Sashelas can be fickle and flighty, and there are many myths that involve his amorous exploits with such creatures as mermaids, selkies, mortal sea elven maids, human females, and even one demigoddess, it is rumored. Trishina has some tolerance for such straying, but not too much. Sashelas's fellow Seldarine derive great amusement from Trishina's ability to spot Sashelas's wandering attentions and stymie him, usually by warning off the object of his desire.

Deep Sashelas is very active on Abeir-Toril. His avatars often terraform the undersea environment, although he does not undertake such actions without first consulting other deities with an interest in such matters. He does not overinvolve himself by dispatching avatars to help sea elves in battles, but he will do so if he scents any involvement by Sekolah, and his avatars keep a watchful eye on any unexplained activities that might involve Panzuriel (unusually organized raids by merrow or koalinths, for example). His avatar is 50% likely to be accompanied by an avatar of Trishina unless the avatar has been sent to woo or seduce some pretty female who has attracted his eye. Rarely the avatar may accompany an avatar of another member of the *asathalfinare*.

Deep Sashelas's Avatar

(Water Elementalist 33, Cleric 32, Fighter 21)

Deep Sashelas appears as a handsome, androgynous sea elf male with sea-green skin, blue-green eyes, and free-flowing blue-green hair. He casts spells from all spheres and schools, except for those incantations involving open flames, but he favors spells from the spheres of creation, elemental (water), and weather and the schools of alchemy, alteration, elemental (water), and invocation/evocation.

AC –3; MV 15, Sw 36; HP 190; THAC0 0; #AT 2 or 5/2 or 2
Dmg 1d8+12 (*long sword +4*, +8 Str) or 1d6+14 (*trident +4*, +8 Str, +2 spec. bonus in trident) or 4d10×2 (watery fists)
MR 40% (90% underwater); SZ M (7 feet tall)
Str 20, Dex 20, Con 18, Int 23, Wis 21, Cha 23
Spells P: 13/13/13/11/10/9/8, M: 8/8/8/8/8/8/8/8*
Saves PPDM 2, RSW 3, PP 4, BW 4, Sp 4
   *Numbers assume one extra elemental water spell pe spell level.

Special Att/Def: Deep Sashelas wields *Dolphin's Tooth*, a *long sword +4* that inflicts double damage on sahuagin and ixitxachitl and that can create a 20d6 *lightning bolt* once per day, and the *Trifork of the Deeps*, a *trident +4* with all the powers of a *trident of fish command*, a *trident of submission*, and a *trident of warning*.

The Dolphin Prince can cast *cetacean form* at will, but without restriction on the form assumed. Sashelas can employ the following spells, once per day each, while underwater: *dig* (affects coral and rock as well as earth or clay), *earthquake*, *coral shape*, and *transmute rock to mud*. He can also cast *weather summoning* once per day while above the surface. The Lord of the Undersea can summon 1d10+10 dolphins to serve him for up to 12 hours once per day. At will, Sashelas can assume the form of a giant, towering wave of sea water up to 100 feet high and wide. In this form, the Lord of the Undersea attacks as a monstrous water elemental, with two pummeling attacks per round, but cannot use his spell abilities.

Sashelas is immune to nonmagical weapons and all elemental water school or sphere spells, spell-like effects, and abilities. He cannot be affected by caused wounds, energy drains, or death magic while any part of his body is in contact with pure sea water. He can be struck only by +2 or better magical weapons.

Other Manifestations

The Lord of the Undersea almost always manifests in one of three ways helpful to aquatic elves. In the wilds of the Undersea, Sashelas appears to his followers in distress as a far-off light that never seems to move closer or draw farther away. Followers of the Dolphin Prince who follow the beacon are led to safety, but any foes in the surrounding region—particularly sharks or sahuagin—who also spy the light and attempt to

Elven Powers: Deep Sashelas and Trishina

head toward Sashelas's manifestation find themselves led astray, oftentimes into a dangerous situation they have little chance of escaping (such as directly in the path of a pod of hungry killer whales).

Secondarily, Sashelas sometimes manifests in sea elven communities to warn of imminent attack, particularly when such raids involve Sekolah's followers. Such manifestations involve the opening of a small rent in the sea floor that allows a large air bubble to escape. Instead of dissipating or immediately floating to the surface, such air bubbles dance about the general vicinity of the rift for several minutes. Such bubbles act in a fashion similar to a *crystal ball*: Any follower of Sashelas who stares into the bubble is able to scry on the immediate threat, giving members of the threatened community time to prepare defenses, retreat, or otherwise react to the imminent attack. Once the threat is recognized by the community, the manifestation ends as the bubble rises to the surface and dissipates.

In situations where Sashelas needs to communicate with members of his faith, he manifests in a third manner as a distinctly dolphin-shaped region of water, differentiated from the surrounding sea water by the nimbus of silver light that envelops it. Such a manifestation playfully dashes and darts about, much like a true dolphin, except that it never surfaces. Any sentient sea creature Sashelas allows to come into physical contact with the manifestation receives a momentary vision through which the Dolphin Prince communicates the reason for his appearance.

The Seldarine call on agathinon, asuras, and ancient treants as their preferred servants, but Sashelas is also served by aballins, asrai, balaenas, delphons, dolphins, einheriar, eladrins (particularly novieres), nereids, porpoises, reverend ones, water elementals, whales (particularly narwhals), and zoveri. He demonstrates his favor through the discovery of ambergris, aquamarines, Angelar's skin, beljurils, blue-green chrysocollas, pink and crimson coral, horn coral, hydrophanes, lumachellas, blue-green microclines, blue-green mykaros, pearls, beautiful shells of any sort, water opals, and waterstars. The Lord of the Undersea indicates his displeasure by the discovery of dead, floating fish, tridents with broken tines, and unexpected contact with water-logged driftwood floating beneath the surface.

The Church

CLERGY:	Clerics, crusaders, druids, specialty priests
CLERGY'S ALIGN.:	NG, CG, N (druids only), CN
TURN UNDEAD:	C: Yes, Cru: No, D: No, SP: Yes
CMND. UNDEAD:	C: No, Cru: No, D: No, SP: No

All clerics, crusaders, druids, and specialty priests of Deep Sashelas receive religion (elf, aquatic) and reading/writing (Espruar) as bonus nonweapon proficiencies. Priests of Deep Sashelas must be aquatic elves, aquatic half-elves, or malenti. The DM is encouraged to allow Deep Sashelas's clergy access to the underwater spells detailed in *Of Ships and the Sea*.

As Lord of the Undersea and de facto leader of the *asathalfinare*, Deep Sashelas is well regarded by most nonevil races who reside beneath the surface of Toril's oceans. Whereas aquatic elves generally venerate Sashelas to the near exclusion of the other members of the Seldarine, elves of other races view him simply as one god of the pantheon of nature- and magic-oriented deities who compose the Seldarine. Some sailors (particularly land elves) sacrifice to Sashelas for their safety and aquatic elven clerics take these offerings and trade with other mortals for the gain of the entire race.

Temples of Deep Sashelas are found in most aquatic elven communities, including Iumathiashae, off the coast of Evermeet, Fhaoralusyolkiir, located near the mouth of the Vilhon Reach, and Adoivaealumanth, located off the coast of Telflamm in the Easting Reach. The Dolphin Prince's temples usually serve as the spiritual, physical, and social centers of aquatic elven communities. Those found in the Sea of Fallen Stars are typically undersea coral temples, carefully grown and tended, while those found in the Great Sea are typically sprawling constructs of natural stone and sea materials resembling spiraling shells. Inside all such temples are a network of small and medium-sized caves and passages lit by *continual light* magics of varying shades and intensities. Some chambers are air-filled and are used to examine items plundered from the sunken ships of air-breathers, but most are filled with sea water and artwork crafted by sea elves. A wide variety of stone statues, mosaics made of shells, scrimshaw, air fountains, and a motley collection of artifacts from the Waterless Void above are scattered throughout Sashelas's temples for the use and enjoyment of the inhabitants of the surrounding community. Central chapels are usually grand vaults characterized by three-dimensional radial or spiral symmetries.

Sashelas's numerous temples are managed by an organized clerical hierarchy collectively known as Delphions. The clergy of each temple are locally autonomous, but they provide each other with information about the movement of the sahuagin and other enemies. Novices of the faith are known as the Impure, while acolytes of the faith are known as the Bathed. Titles employed in most temples of the Great Sea include Sea Otter, Seal, Walrus, Sea Lion, Delphinus, Narwhal, and Balaenas. Titles employed in most temples of the Inner Sea include Clam, Oyster, Nautilus, Argonaut, Trophon, Cowrie, Abalone, Conch, and Pearl. High priests of the faith are collectively known as Delphites but always have unique individual titles. Almost all Delphions are aquatic elves (99%), with the remainder (1%) aquatic half-elves. According to legend, a handful of malenti—a type of sahuagin that is externally identical to an aquatic elf—have renounced their evil heritage in ages past and become priests of Deep Sashelas. Specialty priests come into two varieties: sea druids and aquarians. Aquarians (50%) and clerics (35%) make up the large majority of the clergy and are strongly affiliated with a single community. Crusaders (10%) make up the militant arm of the faith and tend to migrate from community to community in response to increasing tensions with neighboring communities of sahuagin. Sea druids (5%) have little to do with their kin, tending to the vast unsettled reaches of the Undersea and leading largely solitary lives. They are organized into at least two druidic domain hierarchies, the Circle of the Great Sea and the Circle of Fallen Stars. The clergy of Shashelas is pretty evenly split between male (51%) and female (49%) members.

Dogma: Swim the great currents and the shallow seas. Exult in the everchanging beauty and life of the bounteous Undersea. Revel in the joy of creation and increase its myriad aspects. Seek not to hold that which is everchanging, but instead love the change itself. Seek out fellow swimmers who honor the ways of the Lord of the Undersea, and ally with them against those who see only the darkness of the deeps. Follow the way of the dolphin. Promote the use of the seas by all reasonable folk for all time to come; fight those who would hoard its riches or pollute its depths.

Day-to-Day Activities: The clergy of Deep Sashelas are more organized than most elven priesthoods because of their role as mediators and befrienders of nonaquatic races. Delphions interact regularly with dolphins who inhabit the region surrounding their home communities, and senior priests are almost always accompanied by their dolphin companions. Sashelan priests establish and maintain contacts with land-dwelling elves, if feasible. As a result of their extensive networks of contacts, Sashelas's priests have prevented many sahuagin incursions from succeeding, gaining the latter's undying hatred. Delphions also conduct ritual shark hunts and attack sahuagin communities.

Delphions expend a great deal of effort on the creation of beautiful works of art in homage to the Creator. Individual priests of Deep Sashelas create fabulous sculptures of living coral in and around their homes and in their communities. Others sculpt extraordinary jeweled and pearled living coral works of art or train fish to perform spectacular and delightful maneuvers and dances.

Holy Days/Important Ceremonies: Deep Sashelas is honored individually through the creation of works of art and other wonders, and prayers are given to the Lord of the Undersea upon initiating and after completing such projects. Daily observances by Sashelas's clergy thank Deep Sashelas for his benevolence and the beauty of the undersea world, but the most important rituals are timed to coincide with especially high and low tides, known as the High Flow and the Deep Ebb, respectively. During such ceremonies, the Delphions make offerings of precious natural objects and items of great artistry. Meanwhile, acolytes swim in complex patterns accompanied by dolphins, and sing deep, reverberating songs of praise to the Lord of the Undersea and his creations. While both ceremonies are similar in form, the High Flow is a joyous celebration emphasizing beauty, creativity, and artistry, while the Deep Ebb is a grim, martial ceremony emphasizing the remembrance of those who are lost and vigilance against the everpresent enemies of the Undersea.

Major Centers of Worship: The great city of Thunderfoam is located beneath the waves of the Trackless Sea atop a submerged plateau due north of Evermeet and due west of Uttersea. Steam from great rents in the sea floor warms the frigid waters, rendering the region habitable to the Alu-Tel'Quessir. The scions of Alaer have long ruled the aquatic elves of Aluchambolsunvae from the Dolphin Throne at the heart of the submerged capitol city under the benevolent aegis of Deep Sashelas and his clergy. The Caldera of the Dancing Dolphin is a natural amphitheater located atop Mount Delphion on the eastern outskirts of Thunderfoam. On the northern slope of the great crater is the Dome of the Dancing Dolphin, a massive volcanic dome that has been transformed by the clergy of Sashelas into an aquatic cathedral of stunning beauty and size. From the Dolphin Dome, as the temple is commonly known, Sashelas's priests oversee the spiritual, artistic, and martial needs of the aquatic kingdom's populace.

The clergy of the Dome of the Dancing Dolphin have grown particularly concerned of late by the emergence of the Kraken Society as a power in the Trackless Sea. Despite reports that Slarkrethel serves Umberlee, the priests of Aluchambolsunvae fear that the kraken secretly serves the banished Panzuriel as well as Umberlee by aiding that dark power's efforts to reestablish his malign influence in Abeir-Toril's seas. In response to this perceived threat, Delphions of the Dolphin Dome have extended their network of allied beings as far east as the shores of Faerûn, and they are said to be recruiting agents among the land-dwellers to extend their influence into the cities of the North where the Kraken Society has established a presence.

Affiliated Orders: The Knights of the Killer Whale are an order of Sashelan crusaders dedicated to the destruction of the evil races of the sea, including ixitxachitl, koalinth, krakens, merrow, scrags, and sahuagin. The order is based in the Citadel of the Seven Seas, a great hollowed-out undersea volcanic plug encircled by the Mintarn archipelago in the Sea of Swords

The Lances of the Sea Unicorn are an order of clerics, crusaders, and aquarians who garrison a series of nine undersea citadels and numerous smaller redoubts that stretch across the floor of the Sea of Fallen Stars from Delthuntle to Airspur. The order seeks to largely contain the sahuagin of the Alamber Sea to the eastern reaches of the Inner Sea, as most sea elven communities of the Sea of Fallen Stars are located to the west of that border.

Deep Sashelas also sponsors several loosely affiliated pods of sea elven rangers, but they are not considered part of his clergy (that is, the church's hierarchy).

Priestly Vestments: Priests of Deep Sashelas wear either loose-fitting sea green robes or armor created entirely from shells but eschew any form of headdress. Shell mail, as it is known, effectively serves only an ornamental role for sea elves, as it provides a base Armor Class of 9. The holy symbol of the faith is a lustrous pearl at least one half inch in diameter.

Adventuring Garb: Sashelas's clergy generally eschew armor, even when entering dangerous situations as they find it impedes their underwater movements and adds little to their defenses. Only a few Sashelan priests possess sea elven scale mail (described below), but those who do generally employ it in combat situations. Clergy of Deep Sashelas favor the traditional weapons of the sea elves—nets, spears, and tridents—and rare is the Delphion who is proficient in anything else (aside from underwater crossbows).

The most intricately constructed demihuman scale mail is found in the undersea kingdoms of the sea elves. More as a matter of appearance and ceremony than for additional protection—it provides protection equal to that of normal scale mail, the sea elves adapted the idea of scale mail to their own peculiar designs. Their armor can be worn underwater, as it is made of metals that do not rust, and the scales are affixed to the backing of eel-skin, which does not disintegrate as leather does in salt water. Brought forth only in times of war or great ceremony, this expensive armor is worn only by the noble elven elite. This scale mail is unique among others for its beautiful silver coating. Some surface armorers wonder whether this coating is silver, platinum, or even mithral. It is generally agreed that the rare scale mail of the sea elves is nearly as valuable as elven chain mail.

Specialty Priests (Sea Druids)

REQUIREMENTS:	Wisdom 12, Charisma 15
PRIME REQ.:	Wisdom, Charisma
ALIGNMENT:	N
WEAPONS:	Net, trident, spear, dagger, knife
ARMOR:	Sea elven scale mail, sea elven shell mail
MAJOR SPHERES:	All, animal, elemental (air, earth, water), healing, plant, sun, weather
MINOR SPHERES:	Creation, divination
MAGICAL ITEMS:	Same as druids
REQ. PROFS:	Herbalism
BONUS PROFS:	Modern languages (pick one from: dolphin, dragon turtle, koalinth, locathah, merman, morkoth, sahuagin, sea elvish, sea sprite, triton, wereshark, whale), sea lore, swimming, survival (underwater)

The abilities and restrictions of sea druids, aside from the changes noted above and below, are summarized in the discussion of elven priests in "Appendix 1: Demihuman Priests" and detailed in full in the *Player's Handbook*.

- Sea druids may be aquatic elves, aquatic half-elves, or malenti.
- Sea druids are allowed to multiclass, if multiclass druid combinations are normally allowed by race.
- Sea druids receive a +2 bonus to all saving throws vs. electrical attacks.
- Sea druids learn the languages of aquatic creatures (dolphin, dragon turtle, koalinth, locathah, merman, morkoth, sahuagin, sea elvish, sea sprite, triton, wereshark, whale), gaining one extra proficiency slot for this purpose every three levels (at 3rd, 6th, etc.).
- At 3rd level, sea druids pass through aquatic vegetation, such as seaweed and kelp beds, without leaving a trail and at full movement rate.
- At 3rd level, sea druids can identify aquatic plants, animals, and untainted fresh and salt water with perfect accuracy.
- At 7th level, sea druids are immune to *charm* spells cast by aquatic creatures such as kelpies, nixies, and sirines.
- At 7th level, sea druids can shapechange into a normal (not giant) reptile, fish, or mammal up to three times per day. The sea druid can use each animal form (reptile, fish, or mammal) only once per day and can choose from only those animals that make their normal habitat beneath the surface of the ocean. Mammal forms allowed include dolphins, porpoises, seals, sea otters, and other small mammals.

Specialty Priests (Aquarians)

REQUIREMENTS:	Strength 9, Dexterity 9, Wisdom 13
PRIME REQ.:	Dexterity, Wisdom
ALIGNMENT:	CG
WEAPONS:	Net, trident, spear, dagger, knife, underwater crossbow
ARMOR:	Sea elven scale mail, sea elven shell mail
MAJOR SPHERES:	All, animal, chaos, creation, divination, elemental (water), guardian, healing, necromantic, protection, wards, weather
MINOR SPHERES:	Combat, elemental (air, earth), summoning, sun
MAGICAL ITEMS:	Same as clerics
REQ. PROFS:	Artistic ability, swimming
BONUS PROFS:	Modern languages (dolphin), sea lore

- Aquarians may be aquatic elves, aquatic half-elves, or malenti.
- Aquarians are not allowed to multiclass.
- Aquarians can turn aquatic undead creatures—such as lacedons and sea zombies—as clerics, but turn other types of undead creatures as a cleric three levels lower than their actual level.
- Aquarians have a +1 bonus to attack and damage rolls against sahuagin (and malenti, if known as such).
- Aquarians can speak to and understand the language of dolphins, despite the higher sounds employed.
- Aquarians may cast wizard spells from the elemental water school as defined in the Limited Wizard Spellcasting section of "Appendix 1: Demihuman Priests."

- Aquarians can cast *surface sojourn* once per day.
- At 3rd level, aquarians can cast *charm person* (as the 1st-level wizard spell) once per day.
- At 5th level, aquarians can cast *summon cetacean* once per day. This spell may be cast once more per day for every three additional experience levels of the caster.
- At 10th level, aquarians can cast *divination* (as the 4th-level priest spell) once per day.
- At 13th level, aquarians can cast *conjure water elemental* (as the 6th-level priest spell detailed in *Faiths & Avatars*) twice per tenday.
- At 15th level, aquarians can cast *cetacean form* (as the 7th-level priest spell) twice per day.

Sashelan Spells

In addition to the spells listed below, priests of the Lord of the Undersea may cast the 6th-level priest spell *conjure water elemental* detailed in *Faiths & Avatars* in the entry for Istishia.

1st Level

Surface Sojourn (Pr 1; Alteration)

Sphere:	Elemental Water
Range:	Touch
Components:	V, S, M
Duration:	3 hours/level
Casting Time:	1 round
Area of Effect:	One creature
Saving Throw:	None

Surface sojourn affects only water-dwelling beings who are capable of existing on land for short periods of time but who favor aquatic environments. Examples of eligible races include aquatic elves, aquatic half-elves, malenti, merfolk, and sahuagin.

For the duration of this spell, the recipient may exist on land without the attendant discomfort, penalties, restrictions, or the like that doing so normally entails. During such sojourns, the recipient is enveloped in a thin mantle of water that keeps his, her, or its skin moist.

The material components of this spell are the priest's holy symbol and a snail shell.

2nd Level

Shark Charm (Pr 2; Enchantment/Charm)

Sphere:	Animal, Charm
Range:	30 yards
Components:	V, S
Duration:	Special
Casting Time:	5
Area of Effect:	30-foot cube
Saving Throw:	None

When this spell is cast, a hypnotic pattern is set up that causes one or more sharks to cease all activity except a side-to-side swaying movement. If the sharks are charmed while simply swimming about, the duration of the spell is 1d4+2 turns; if the sharks are aroused and angry or can scent blood in the water, the charm lasts 1d3 turns; if the sharks are angry or attacking or if a sahuagin is present within 30 yards, the spell lasts 1d4+4 rounds. The priest casting the spell can charm sharks whose total hit points are less than or equal to his or her own. On average, a 1st-level priest could charm sharks with a total of 4 or 5 hit points; a 2nd-level priest could charm 9 hit points' worth, etc. The hit points can be those of a single shark or those of an entire school, but the total hit points cannot exceed those of the priest casting the spell. A 23-hit point caster charming a dozen 2-hit point sharks would charm 11 of them. This spell is also effective against any shark-related monster, such as a bunyip or wereshark, subject to magic resistance, hit points, and so forth.

3rd Level

Summon Cetacean (Pr 3; Conjuration/Summoning)

Sphere:	Summoning, Elemental Water
Range:	1-mile radius
Components:	V, S
Duration:	Special
Casting Time:	6
Area of Effect:	Special
Saving Throw:	None

This spell is a specialized variant of the 4th-level priest spell *animal summoning I*. By means of this spell, the caster calls a number of cetaceans, such as dolphins, porpoises, or whales, whose combined Hit Dice total 32 or less. If more than one species is available, the race with greater Hit Dice is summoned. Dolphins are always summoned to the exclusion of all other cetaceans if they are available. Only cetaceans within 1 mile of the spellcaster at the time of the casting respond.

Unlike the *animal summoning I* spell, the caster can make only one call and does not get to choose what form of cetacean shows up, if any. The cetaceans summoned aid the caster by whatever means they possess, staying until the fight is over, a specific mission is finished, the caster is safe, they are sent away, etc.

7th Level

Cetacean Form (Pr 7; Alteration)

Sphere:	Combat
Range:	0
Components:	V, S, M
Duration:	1 hour/level
Casting Time:	1 round
Area of Effect:	The caster
Saving Throw:	None

This spell is similar to the 9th-level wizard spell *shapechange*, but it only allows the caster to assume the form of a cetacean or partial cetacean of any species except giant whales or leviathans. Commonly assumed forms include that of a dolphin or narwhal. The caster gains all of the chosen creature's abilities except for innate magical abilities, magic resistance, and those abilities dependent upon Intelligence.

The caster also adopts the form's vulnerabilities. For example, a priest who becomes a dolphin still cannot breathe out of the water for more than 24 hours. Like the *shapechange* spell, a priest who is killed while in another form does not revert to his or her original shape, which may disallow certain types of revivification.

The caster can change forms as many times as desired within the duration of the spell. She or he can change into a dolphin while swimming in shallow seas and then into a sperm whale to dive to great depths. The first form adopted has whatever hit points the casting priest had at the time of the casting of the *cetacean form* spell, and subsequent forms carry the current total hit points with them. Each alteration in form takes only one second, and no system shock survival roll is required.

The material component for this spell is a small pinch of ambergris and the priest's holy symbol.

Erevan Ilesere

(The Trickster, the Chameleon, the Green Changeling, the Ever-shifting Shapechanger, the Fey Jester, the Jack of the Seelie Court)

Intermediate Power of Arborea, CN

PORTFOLIO:	Mischief, change, rogues
ALIASES:	None
DOMAIN NAME:	Olympus/Arvandor
SUPERIOR:	Corellon Larethian
ALLIES:	Avachel, Baravar Cloakshadow, Brandobaris, Dugmaren Brightmantle, Eilistraee, Garl Glittergold, Milil, Nathair Sgiathach, Oberon, Shaundakul, Squelaiche, Tapann, Titania, Tymora, the Seldarine
FOES:	Beshaba, Mask, the Queen of Air and Darkness, the drow pantheon (except Eilistraee)
SYMBOL:	Nova star with asymmetrical rays
WOR. ALIGN.:	NG, CG, N, CN

Erevan Ilesere (AIR-eh-van ILL-eh-seer) is the elven god of mischief and change and the patron of elven and half-elven rogues. The Trickster's following is not as large as most of his fellow elven gods for Erevan is too unpredictable for most elves. Nevertheless, he commands his share of attention from the Fair Folk, particularly by those engaged in thievery or other forms of knavery, those who seek excitement so as to alleviate the boredom of near-immortality, as well as many young elves who seek a life of adventure and danger. Erevan is also revered by some members of the small sylvan races, such as pixies, sprites, and leprechauns, but most such fey beings revere the deities of the Seelie Court.

The Trickster often seeks the company of similarly inclined powers of other pantheons, for the patience of his fellow elven powers has been worn thin by eons of endless pranks at their expense. Despite his fickle nature, however, Erevan is fiercely devoted to the Seldarine, and the other elven powers know that they can count on him to come to their aid should they require it. Erevan is part of an informal group of mischiefmakers that includes Brandobaris, Garl Glittergold, and Tymora. He likes to play pranks with them (and on them), and as a result, he has made a few enemies among the more serious and sober of powers of many pantheons—Helm being a notable example—although the Trickster does not much care as long as he is having a great time. The Trickster's boon companion is Avachel, an aspect of the draconic power Hlal, also known as Aasterinian or Quicksilver. The Trickster and Quicksilver are almost never separated and their adventures are legendary among younger elves who dream of emulating the mythic duo's daring exploits.

Erevan has long-standing rivalries with other rogue powers, including Beshaba and Mask, for their cruelty and greed offends the Trickster's light-hearted nature.

Erevan is a fickle, utterly unpredictable power who can change his appearance at will. He is one of the most fun-loving powers in the multiverse, and he seems incapable of remaining still or concentrating on a single task for any extended period of time. The Trickster enjoys causing trouble for its own sake, but his pranks are rarely either helpful or deadly. However, Erevan becomes very dangerous if sylvan races or weak elven groups are threatened, and he is always championing the underdog.

Erevan rarely fights another being directly, preferring to escape and possibly catch his opponent off guard at a later time. His favorite tactic is to change his height to any size from between 1 inch to 6 feet and alter his appearance to reflect one of his innumerable guises. Regardless of how he appears at any given time, Erevan always wears green somewhere upon his person, a sign of his love of the woodlands the Fair Folk call home. The Trickster's weakness for fine wine has gotten him into trouble on more than one occasion, but his vows to swear off the grape only last long enough to refill his glass. Erevan's fancies are as fleeting as a desert rain, and he is attracted to mortals who make their own luck. He does not appreciate those who constantly rely on his favor to get by, and he abandons those who persistently rely on his unwavering assistance. Mortals who rely on themselves, however, are often granted a helping hand by the fickle Trickster.

Erevan's Avatar (Thief 33, Ranger 26, Mage 21, Bard 18)

Erevan appears as an elf, brownie, faerie, pixie, sprite, or other sylvan creature of widely varying appearance and size. He favors spells from the spheres of all, chaos, charm, creation, guardian, healing, plant, protection, summoning, thought, and travelers and from the schools of alteration, enchantment/charm, and illusion/phantasm, although he can cast spells from any sphere or school.

AC –3; MV 24; HP 208; THAC0 –5; #AT 2 and 1
Dmg 1d8+5 (*long sword +4, +1 Str*) and 1d6+5 (*short sword of quickness +4, +1 Str*)
MR 85%; SZ T to M (1 inch to 6 feet tall)
Str 17, Dex 24, Con 19, Int 20, Wis 18, Cha 20
Spells W: 5/5/5/5/5/4/4/2
Saves PPDM 3, RSW 4, PP 4, BW 4, Sp 4

Special Att/Def: Erevan wields *Mischief*, a *long sword +4* that *knocks* open all barriers, doors, and locks with but a touch, and *Quickstrike*, a *short sword of quickness +4*. The Trickster always carries disruptive magical items such as a *chimes of hunger* or *horns of blasting*. Erevan can cast *call woodland beings*, *chaos*, *polymorph any object*, *shapechange*, or *tree* at will, once per round, and he makes extensive use of these magics prior to entering combat.

Erevan can be struck only by +2 or better magical weapons. He cannot be harmed by anyone who he can make smile or laugh.

Other Manifestations

Erevan rarely manifests, preferring to dispatch an avatar to any unfolding event that catches his attention. When he does manifest, the Trickster's influence is as often disruptive as it is helpful. Typical manifestations include the gradual appearance of a green haze that creates a temporary wild magic zone or unleashes the effects of a spell such as *chaos* or *chaotic combat* or a wand such as a *wand of endless repetition* or a *wand of wonder*.

The Seldarine call on agathinon, asuras, and ancient treants as their preferred servants, but Erevan is also served by aasimar, asrai, atomies, bacchae, bariaurs, cath shee, centaurs, change cats, chaos beasts, chaos imps, cooshee, copper dragons, crystal dragons, dopplegangers, dryads, einheriar, eladrins (particularly coures), elven cats, ethyks, faerie dragons, faerie fiddlers, feystags, firestars, firetails, frosts, grigs, gorse, hamadryads, hybsils, kenku, kholiathra, korred, leprechauns, luck eaters, magebanes, mercury dragons, monkey spiders, nixies, nymphs, ooze sprites, oreads, pixies, pseudodragons, raccoons, ratatosk, reverend ones, satyrs, sea sprites, seelie faeries, sprites, sunflies, sylphs, tressyms, vortexes, and weredragons. He demonstrates his favor through lucky coincidences, playful pranks, and discovery of good luck charms such as alexandrites, amber, azurite, carnelians, frost agates, jade, rubies, turquoises, and electrum coins. The Trickster indicates his displeasure through a sequence of minor misfortunes such as the loss and recovery of valued small items and the like.

The Church

CLERGY:	Clerics, specialty priests, thieves
CLERGY'S ALIGN.:	CG, CN
TURN UNDEAD:	C: Yes, SP: No, T: No
CMND. UNDEAD:	C: No, SP: No, T: No

Priests of Erevan include multiclassed half-elven clerics, elven cleric/thieves, and elven fighter/cleric/thieves. Erevan's specialty priests include elven specialty priest/thieves. All clerics and specialty priests of Erevan receive religion (elf) and reading/writing (Espruar) as bonus nonweapon proficiencies.

For the Fair Folk, Erevan represents all that is chaotic and free in the elven psyche and the spirit of mischievous fun they share with many other sylvan beings. The Trickster's church is regarded as little more than a loose fellowship of adventuresome rogues and pranksters, and most elves find Erevan to be too unpredictable for their tastes to actually venerate the god.

Tales of the priesthood's various exploits are widely enjoyed by elf youths and commoners, for they often are at the expense of their elders and those of noble blood and highbrowed attitudes. Despite the general appreciation for anecdotes about the exploits of Erevan's followers, individuals are often rightly regarded with a great deal of suspicion in person. Members of other races regard the followers of Erevan as archetypal examples of the flighty behavior ascribed to all elves (who can never be safely trusted).

Erevan may never be worshiped in the same location twice, and few of his followers remain in at any location for any length of time. As such, only a handful of temples of the Trickster exist, and they are carefully hidden. For the most part, Erevan's houses of worship are little more than permanent shrines by the standards of other faiths and they are reserved for meetings and the like. The handful of priests who tend such shrines of necessity must go elsewhere to pray to their god.

Novices of Erevan are known as the Gullible. Full priests of the Trickster are known as Quicksilvers. Priests of Erevan of all ranks create their own titles and most change their titles frequently. Specialty priests are known as mischiefmakers. Priests of the faith typically associate themselves with one or more regional branches of the faith, but such ties are voluntary and typically quite fluid. Contact between the various branches of the faith is infrequent at best. The clergy of Erevan includes moon elves (45%), green elves (30%), half-elves of various ancestries (15%), gold elves (9%), and a handful of elves of other races (1%). Erevan's clergy includes specialty priests (40%), specialty priest/thieves (20%), thieves (16%), cleric/thieves (14%), and clerics (10%). The clergy of Erevan has slightly more males (53%) than females (47%).

Dogma: Change and excitement are the spice of life. Live on the edge, unbound by the conventions of society in a spirit of constant self-reinvention. Puncture the self-righteousness, sanctimony, and pretension that pervades orderly society with mischievous pranks that both amuse and enlighten. Inspire laughter and happiness, giddy silliness, and welcome release from care so that the routine of day-to-day existence does not become worn so deep that it grinds all the joy from life. Celebrate the spontaneous, and practice random acts of helpfulness.

Day-to-Day Activities: Priests of Erevan are wild, mischievous, independent, and utterly unpredictable, playing tricks on others for the sheer

Elven Powers: Avachel and Erevan Ilesere

joy of it. They oppose settled interests of all sorts and delight in upsetting both the rule of law and powerful people and in generally creating mayhem. They have little in the way of formal duties, and minister to the faithful primarily through example and instruction in the skills required of mischievous rogues.

Holy Days/Important Ceremonies: Followers of Erevan gather monthly for a Midnight Gambol, which is held in a sylvan glade beneath the light of the full moon. The exact location of each Midnight Gambol is a secret that is passed among the faithful by word of mouth in the days leading up to the event. Anyone who manages to discover the festivities through his or her own ingenuity is welcome to participate. Erevan's followers are often joined in their revels by the mischief-loving subjects of the Seelie Court, particularly sprites and pixies. Each Midnight Gambol includes the sacrifice of beautiful objects (most of which are borrowed), dancing, wine-drinking, tale-telling, and endless prank-playing.

Major Centers of Worship: Given the faith's restriction prohibiting followers of the Trickster from ever worshiping their god in the same place twice, it is not surprising that few temples of Erevan of any note exist in the Realms. However, a few sacred sites, scattered throughout Faerûn, serve as the foci of pilgrimages by Erevan's most daring followers.

Overlooking the head of the Arglander River in the heart of the High Peaks (the mountain range due south of the Deepwash) lies a hidden cavern complex known as Quicksilver's Lair. Said to have once been the abode of Avachel, Erevan's boon companion, the legendary site is now the home of a clutch of mercury dragons, believed to be the descendants of Avachel. The caverns house a vast store of beautiful objects, most of which were brought there by followers of the Trickster. The resident wyrms guard the objects with care. If the tales of the Fair Folk are to be believed, the greatest collection of relics from the ancient elven realms of Eiellûr, Syòrpiir, Orishaar, and Thearnytaar is hidden here as well, assembled as those realms crumbled before the armies of Ilythiir. All priests of the Trickster aspire to pray to their god once in their lives at Quicksilver's Lair, but the route to the site is a secret that each petitioner must discover separately. The High Peaks are said to be strewn with the lost treasures brought as offerings by those who failed to find the lair.

Affiliated Orders: While no formal military orders are associated with Erevan's church, countless bands and guilds of elven and half-elven rogues have been founded in honor of the Trickster. A notable example is the Knaves of the Missing Page, a fellowship of elven spellfilchers (mage/thieves) based in the Vale of Evereska but active throughout Faerûn. Knaves specialize in the recovery of elven magical artifacts, spell scrolls, and spell tomes that have been acquired by other races, particularly humans.

Priestly Vestments: The ceremonial garb of the Trickster's priesthood emphasizes the practical over the ornamental. Erevan's priests wear black leather armor and black leather caps, though their armor is often concealed by clothing or cloaks. The holy symbol of the faith is a stolen trinket of some sort that has been *blessed* by a priest of Erevan. Each such holy symbol must be replaced by another purloined token at least once every ten days, more frequently if at all possible. Note that the spell *create holy symbol* is never granted to priests of Erevan as the god expects them to provide for themselves.

Adventuring Garb: Priests of Erevan outfit themselves as is common for rogues, favoring black leather armor or silenced elven chain mail for protection and weapons such as clubs, daggers, darts, knives, lassos, long swords, short bows, slings, short swords, and staffs. Magical items that facilitate thieving skills as well as those that allow the wearer to alter his appearance or form are highly prized.

Silenced elven chain mail has each link of chain armor wrapped in thin leather or light cloth bunting. This to some extent silences the armor, at the cost of increasing its encumbrance by one-third and increasing its price significantly as well. Of course, it is even rarer than ordinary elven chain mail itself. Silenced elven chain mail has the following modifiers to thief skills: pick pockets (–25%), open locks (–5%), find/remove traps (–5%), hide in shadows (–10%), and climb walls (–25%).

Specialty Priests (Mischiefmaker)

REQUIREMENTS:	Dexterity 13, Intelligence 10, Wisdom 9
PRIME REQ.:	Dexterity, Intelligence, Wisdom
ALIGNMENT:	CN
WEAPONS:	Any
ARMOR:	Leather armor, padded armor, studded leather armor, silenced elven chain mail
MAJOR SPHERES:	All, chaos, charm, creation, guardian, healing, protection, travelers
MINOR SPHERES:	Divination, plant, summoning, thought
MAGICAL ITEMS:	Same as clerics or thieves
REQ. PROFS:	None
BONUS PROFS:	Disguise

- Mischiefmakers must be elves, half-elves, leprechauns, sprites, or pixies. While most mischiefmakers are moon elves, green elves, or half-elves, elves and half-elves of every subrace are called to be specialty priests of Erevan's clergy.
- Mischiefmakers are allowed to multiclass as mischiefmaker/thieves.
- Mischiefmakers may select nonweapon proficiencies from the rogue group without penalty.
- Mischiefmakers understand and use thieves' cant.
- Single-class mischiefmakers have limited thieving skills as defined in the Limited Thieving Skills section of "Appendix 1: Demihuman Priests." Multiclassed mischiefmaker/thieves receive no extra thieving skill points or bonuses for their mischiefmaker class; their thieving skills are based solely on their thief levels.
- Mischiefmakers receive a +2 bonus to all saving throws that are the result of magic cast by lawful creatures and to all saving throws against priest spells from the sphere of law.
- Mischiefmakers can cast *faerie fire* (as the 1st-level priest spell) on one or more opponents or *reduce* (as the reverse of the 1st-level wizard spell *enlarge*) on themselves only, once per day.
- Mischiefmakers love *wands of wonder* and other magical items that generate random effects. For such items, they can pick the result they get from a spread of one effect to either side of the effect randomly rolled for on the item's effects table, chart, or list. (Essentially, they get to pick from the result rolled, the result one line higher on the chart, or the result one line lower on the chart. For purposes of this determination, pretend that the top of a chart or list wraps to the bottom and vice versa.)
- At 3rd level, mischiefmakers can cast *change self* (as the 1st-level wizard spell) or *knock* (as the 2nd-level wizard spell) once per day.
- At 5th level, mischiefmakers can cast *alter self* (as the 2nd-level wizard spell) or *tree* (as the 3rd-level priest spell) once per day.
- At 7th level, mischiefmakers can cast *chaos* (as the 5th-level wizard spell) or *invisibility* (as the 2nd-level wizard spell) once per day.
- At 10th level, mischiefmakers can cast *misdirection* (as the 2nd-level wizard spell) or *nondetection* (as the 3rd-level wizard spell) either once each or twice for one or the other per day.
- At 13th level, mischiefmakers can cast *polymorph any object* (as the 8th-level wizard spell) once per day.
- At 15th level, mischiefmakers can cast *shapechange* (as the 9th-level wizard spell) once per day.

Erevanian Spells

3rd Level

Sprite Venom (Pr 3; Alteration)

Sphere:	Combat
Range:	Touch
Components:	V, S, M
Duration:	1 round/level
Casting Time:	5
Area of Effect:	One arrow/level
Saving Throw:	None

By means of this spell, the caster can create an ointment similar to that employed by sprites to coat the tips of their arrows. For every level of the caster, she or he can create enough *sprite venom* to coat the tip of a single arrow, dart, needle, or quarrel. (Sling bullets and other missile weapons that inflict bludgeoning damage do not benefit from the application of *sprite venom*.)

Any creature struck by an arrow treated with *sprite venom* must make a successful saving throw vs. poison or fall into a deep sleep for 1d6 turns. Unlike the ointment created by sprites, magic resistance protects against the ointment created by this spell.

The material components of this spell are the priest's holy symbol and a pinch of sand from a sandman, a type of elemental from the Elemental Plane of Earth.

5th Level

Pixie Dust (Pr 5; Alteration) *Reversible*

Sphere:	Combat
Range:	0
Components:	V, S, M
Duration:	2 rounds/level
Casting Time:	1 round
Area of Effect:	10 foot radius
Saving Throw:	None

This spell creates a single handful of fine powder that can coat all creatures within a 10-foot radius, making them invisible. Creatures coated with *pixie dust* cannot be seen with normal sight, normal detection, or even magical means (such as the *detect invisibility* spell). However, *dust of appearance* and the *true seeing* spell do reveal beings and objects made invisible by *pixie dust*.

Pixie dust must be used immediately after the spell is cast, or the magic is wasted. A handful tossed into the air can cover a radius of 10 feet from the user.

Invisibility bestowed by *pixie dust* lasts for 2 rounds/level. Attack while thus invisible is possible, always by surprise if the opponent fails to note the invisible creature and always by an Armor Class 4 better than normal (while invisibility lasts). *Pixie dust* remains effective even after an attack is made.

The reverse of *pixie dust*, *revealing dust*, makes invisible objects become visible.

The material components of this spell are the priest's holy symbol and a pinch of dirt from the bower of the Seelie Court. The latter can usually be obtained a pinch at a time only by careful negotiation with one of the faerie races, and payment involving participation in some mischievous prank of the sylvan being's devising is usually required.

7th Level

Faerie Form (Pr 7; Alteration)

Sphere:	Animal
Range:	0
Components:	V, S, M
Duration:	1 hour/level
Casting Time:	1 round
Area of Effect:	The caster
Saving Throw:	None

This spell is similar to the 9th-level wizard spell *shapechange*, but it only allows the caster to assume the form of any type of faerie, brownie, or sprite (including atomies, brambles, brownies, dobies, faerie fiddlers, gorse, grigs, killmoulis, nixies, pixies, quicklings, sea sprites, sprites, squeakers, stwingers, and other similar sylvan creatures). The caster adopts the form of the chosen creature, gaining all of that form's abilities except for innate magical abilities, magic resistance, and those abilities dependent upon Intelligence.

The caster also adopts the form's vulnerabilities and weaknesses. For example, a priest who becomes a sprite will have a great deal of difficulty in opening a normal-sized door. Like the *shapechange* spell, a priest who is killed while in another form does not revert to his or her original shape, which may disallow certain types of revivification.

The caster can change forms as many times as desired, within the duration of the spell. She or he can change into a sprite and fly away and then to a nixie to dive into a lake. The first form adopted has one-quarter of the hit points the casting priest had at the time of the casting of the *faerie form* spell (round up). Subsequent forms carry the current total hit points with them until the original form is resumed. Each alteration in form takes only one second, and no system shock survival roll is required.

The material components for this spell are locks of hair from three different species of sprite.

Felarathael

See the entry for Corellon Larethian for details on Felarathael (FEH-leh-RAH-thay-ehl), a servitor of the Protector who is sometimes mistakenly referred to as a demipower.

Fenmarel Mestarine

(The Lone Wolf)

Lesser Power of Limbo, CN

PORTFOLIO:	Feral elves, outcasts, scapegoats, isolation and isolationists
ALIASES:	None
DOMAIN NAME:	Limbo/Fennimar
SUPERIOR:	Corellon Larethian
ALLIES:	Eilistraee, Gwaeron Windstrom, the Seldarine, various Animal Lords
FOES:	The drow pantheon (except Eilistraee)
SYMBOL:	Pair of elven eyes in the darkness
WOR. ALIGN.:	LG, NG, CG, LN, N, CN

Fenmarel Mestarine (FEHN-muh-rehl MESS-tuh-reen) is the eternal outsider, the solitary god who holds himself aloof from his fellows. He is venerated by outcasts from elven society, many of whom have withdrawn voluntarily in response to perceived slights, as well as by elves who have been isolated from the main body of their race and who live in wild, relatively uncivilized rural groups. Although he does not actively seek the worship of mortals, Fenmarel serves as the teacher and protector of those who turn to him, one who is silent and subtle, instructing his people in survival, spying, camouflage, deception, and secrecy.

Fenmarel dislikes the company of other powers, and he avoids relationships of any sort—whether they be alliances or mutual enmities—whenever possible. The Lone Wolf is even somewhat of an outcast among the Seldarine, his nominal allies, although he supports them in their endless war with the Spider Queen and her followers. He has removed himself to Limbo voluntarily, although he has a home in Arvandor when he so chooses. Fenmarel was once Lolth's lover, one of the first to be seduced by her power and promises, but he turned away from her before completely slipping over to the dark side, for which she has never forgiven him. Neither has Fenmarel forgiven Lolth for her breach of faith with the elven race, and thus he hates drow. The Lone Wolf gets along well enough with Solonor Thelandira (said to be his brother) and Shevarash, both of whom join him in actively combating the plots of the Spider Queen and defending the Fair Folk against her depredations. However, Fenmarel's relations with Corellon Larethian are somewhat strained by his perception that the Protector still somehow holds the younger god at fault for succumbing to Lolth's entreaties long ago. Only the kindheartedness of Sehanine Moonbow draws the Lone Wolf back to Arvandor on rare occasions.

Fenmarel is eternally sullen and serious, a perfect counterbalance to fun-loving Erevan Ilesere. He has no interest in communicating with members of other pantheons or N'Tel'Quess unless absolutely necessary, and when he does speak he is usually bitter and cynical. Although he tries to avoid commitments of any sort, the Lone Wolf always abides by his word, no matter how reluctantly it is given. Fenmarel frequently dispatches his avatar to patrol the elven borders in disappearing woodlands, jungles, and similar environments, not unlike Corellon in more sizable homelands.

Fenmarel's Avatar (Ranger 27, Thief 25, Cleric 18, Illusionist 16)

Fenmarel appears as an elf clad in leaves and scraps of clothing, with a skin color appropriate to that environment (usually green-brown), bearing extensive tattoos. He favors spells from the spheres of all, animal, chaos, charm, elemental, guardian, healing, necromantic, plant, protection, summoning, sun, and weather and from the school of illusion/phantasm, although he can cast spells from any sphere or any school except necromancy, invocation/evocation, and abjuration.

AC –1; MV 15, Fl 24, Sw 18; HP 187; THAC0 –6; #AT 2 and 1
Dmg 1d4+12 (*dagger of venom* +4, +8 STR) and 1d4+12 (*dagger of throwing* +4, +8 STR)
MR 65%; SZ M (5 feet tall)
STR 20, DEX 23, CON 18, INT 21, WIS 20, CHA 16

Spells P: 11/11/10/10/6/4/2, W: 6/6/6/6/6/4/3/2*
Saves PPDM 3, RSW 4, PP 4, BW 4, Sp 5
    *Numbers assume one extra illusion/phantasm spell per spell level.

Special Att/Def: Fenmarel wields *Aspfang*, a *dagger of venom +4*, and *Thornbite* (a *dagger of throwing +4*). He wears a *necklace of missiles* that automatically replenishes its missiles 1 turn after they are hurled. Once per round he can cast *entangle*, *plant door*, or *plant growth* at will.

Fenmarel always *passes without trace* and can use *improved invisibility* at will. He is permanently cloaked in a mantle of *nondetection*. Fenmarel can be struck only by +1 or better magical weapons.

Other Manifestations

Fenmarel manifests in subtle and secretive ways that are easy even for his followers to miss. He often provides his faithful followers with elusive clues that assist them in finding sustenance or in defeating those who would disturb them. For example, the Lone Wolf might cause a small gust of wind to disturb some leaves that have recently fallen to the ground just as a follower was looking in that direction, thus both drawing attention to the spot and enabling the worshiper to spot the footprint that was previously hidden beneath the leaves.

Fenmarel does not work through the actions of mortal creatures, except to direct predators away from elves under his protection and toward the borders to deter intruders. He conveys omens and warnings of threats to his priests through their divinatory rituals (using leaves, animal bones, sticks, and the like).

The Church

CLERGY:	Specialty priests
CLERGY'S ALIGN.:	CN
TURN UNDEAD:	SP: No
CMND. UNDEAD:	SP: No

All specialty priests of Fenmarel receive religion (elf) and reading/writing (Espruar) as bonus nonweapon proficiencies.

The church of Fenmarel is regarded with a great deal of suspicion and hostility in most elven societies, for many of his followers in such areas are considered to be little better than outlaws, even if their exile is voluntary. Only in isolated tribes that actively venerate the Lone Wolf (usually to the exclusion of all other deities) are his faithful accorded respect for the practical lessons of survival that they teach. Among other races, Fenmarel and his followers are either unknown or spoken of as primitive followers of a savage god, both of whom are better left undisturbed.

The followers of the Lone Wolf can be loosely divided into two camps, neither of which constructs temples to the god. Elven outcasts, who either remove themselves or are forcibly banished from elven society, are loners by nature who rarely even seek out other members of their faith, let alone join with them in formal worship. Similarly, isolated, primitive tribes of elves are unlikely to construct edifices of any sort, let alone a temple. However both types of worshiper construct personal

shrines to the god, the location of which is always kept secret, even from fellow worshipers. The composition of such shrines varies widely from individual to individual and from tribe to tribe, but most shrines of Fenmarel include some common elements. Typically located in a hidden hollow or niche of some sort, shrines often contain bones, teeth, or claws representing the savagery of the world as well as sticks and leaves representing the environment in which both protection and sustenance may be found. Exiles often include a personal token symbolizing the reasons for their separation from elven society.

Novices of Fenmarel are known as the Lost. Full priests of the Lone Wolf are known as the Unbowed. Fenmarel's priests create their own individual titles or forgo them altogether. Specialty priests, known as lone wolves, are comprised of green elves (53%), moon elves (22%), half-elves (10%), lythari (8%), gold elves (6%), and a handful of elves of other ancestries (1%). Fenmarel's clergy includes only specialty priests (100%). The clergy of Fenmarel has a slightly higher number of male members (56%) than female members (44%).

Dogma: The world is a harsh and unforgiving place, with uncompromising demands on those who would forge their own path. Rely not on others for protection, for betrayal comes easily, but on you own skills and those taught to you by the Lone Wolf: the skills of camouflage, deception, and secrecy. Follow the way of the Lone Wolf, for his is the path of self-sufficiency. Fear not hard work, for the fruits of your labor prove your worth to yourself.

Day-to-Day Activities: For the most part, members of Fenmarel's clergy are found only among bands of feral elves in the wilderness. Outcasts from elven society who make their way among other cultures are typically lay followers and not priests. Members of Fenmarel's clergy instruct their fellows in the skills first taught by the god, including how to spy, survive on their own, engage in deceptions and guerrilla tactics, and use poisons to take down enemies with subtlety, but otherwise they have few formal responsibilities aside from ensuring their personal survival.

Holy Days/Important Ceremonies: The church of Fenmarel does not celebrate widely recognized holy days. Instead, each individual or band venerates the Lone Wolf in personal worship services of their own devising. Many outcasts mark the day of their personal banishment with private contemplation, while tribes of feral elves mark anniversaries of important events in the group's oral history, many of which are correlated with astronomical events easily noted by the naked eye.

Major Centers of Worship: The Misty Vale is a largely unexplored, thickly overgrown, stiflingly hot jungle tucked between the Dun Hills, the Cliffs of Talar, and the Bandit Wastes, due east of Lapaliiya and the Shining Sea. In the courts of the High Suihk of Ormpur and the Overking of Lapaliiya, records dating back to the founding of both realms speak of a race of feral elves dwelling in the steaming forest who hunt down and kill any intruders into their ancient homeland. To the other races of the region, these legendary denizens of the Misty Vale are known as the grugach. This term's origin has been variously ascribed to an archaic elvish term meaning *feral ones*, a green elven clan name, and a word coined

Elven Powers: Fenmarel Mestarine

by a traveler from another world who saw similarities between the tales told in Lapaliiya and the most reclusive wild elves of his own land. In truth, the Fair Folk of the Misty Vale are simply a primitive and highly xenophobic clan of green elves, albeit with a significant amount of moon elven and dark elven blood, who have been isolated from the outside world for centuries. The term *grugach* is indeed a misnomer dating back to the visit of a sorcerer from a world known as Oerth, but the name has stuck in the popular imagination of the region.

The Misty Vale has been continuously occupied by the Fair Folk since the Second Crown War was fought approximately 13,000 years ago. First, the moon elven realm of Orishaar (located in the forests that now make up the Duskwood and the plains of the Shaar) fell swiftly to the brutal surprise attack of the dark elves of Ilythiir. Then the green elven realms of Syòrpiir, Eiellûr, and Thearnytaar (located in the woodlands that stretched from what is today the Thornwood to the Chondalwood) fell in the five centuries that followed. The fall of Eiellûr was aided in part by traitorous green elves who thought their appeasement actions could help restore the peace. After each defeat at the hands of the dark elves, the surviving populace was enslaved by the Ilythiiri. In most cases, the enslaved moon elves and green elves were absorbed into the general population by the genetically dominant dark elves within a generation or two. The betrayers of Eiellûr were rewarded by the Ilythiiri with an untamed, tangled tract of jungle on a plateau overlooking the River Talar. While few survived the horrors that had been previously unleashed in the woodlands by dark elven sorcerers and still lurked therein, a small band, reduced to a barbaric way of life, managed to survive with the protection of Fenmarel and took to calling themselves the Or-Tel'Quessir or *people of the woods*. Over time their feral descendants were joined by escaped moon elven and green elven slaves fleeing conscription and life on the Ilythiiri slave farms, and the population grew. Although the Ilythiiri would have undoubtedly hunted the Misty Vale tribe to extinction eventually, the Descent of the Drow spared the Or-Tel'Quessir from that horrific fate.

Of all the Seldarine, the Fair Folk of the Misty Vale venerate only Fenmarel, for they turned away from the rest of the elven pantheon millennia ago out of feelings of both personal guilt and abandonment by their gods. Tales of the Lone Wolf's own betrayal by the Spider Queen have been incorporated into the ancient tales of betrayal at the hands of the hated Ilythiiri that still dominate the oral tradition of the Or-Tel'Quessir. Some myths claim that Fenmarel personally led the tribe out of bondage. Other legends claim the Lone Wolf dwelt alone among the beasts of the Misty Vale until the Or-Tel'Quessir arrived and that for many years he taught them the skills of camouflage, deception, and secrecy they would need to survive. While the feral Or-Tel'Quessir have built no temples to their god, Fenmarel's shrines are found wherever the jungle is thickest and most tangled. In turn, the Lone Wolf acts through the fearsome predators of the forest, descended from the castoffs of unholy experiments of Ilythiiri sorcerers, causing them to hunt down intruders but ignore the Fair Folk who dwell among them.

Affiliated Orders: The Fenmaren church has no affiliated knightly orders for obvious reasons. Among the Or-Tel'Quessir, every able-bodied adult of the tribe fights for the Lone Wolf. Thus, in a sense the entire tribe acts as the militant arm of the faith.

Priestly Vestments: The ceremonial garb of Fenmaren priests in primitive bands deep in the wilderness consists of bodies plastered in mud and covered with leaves and sticks. Among more civilized groups, Fenmaren priests garb themselves in hide armor adorned with bones, teeth, and crude drawings of wild beasts. The holy symbol of the faith is a talon or fang of a wild beast slain without any assistance by the priest who bears it.

Adventuring Garb: When adventuring, priests of Fenmarel prefer weapons and armor constructed through the use of skills taught by their god, although they employ the best armor and weapons available if need be.

Specialty Priests (Lone Wolves)

REQUIREMENTS:	Constitution 11, Wisdom 9
PRIME REQ.:	Constitution, Wisdom
ALIGNMENT:	CN
WEAPONS:	Blow gun, club, dagger, dart, hand axe, knife, quarterstaff, short bow, sling, spear, staff-sling
ARMOR:	Hide armor, leather armor, wooden shield
MAJOR SPHERES:	All, animal, chaos, combat, creation, healing, plant, protection, summoning, travelers
MINOR SPHERES:	Divination, elemental, sun, weather
MAGICAL ITEMS:	Same as clerics
REQ. PROFS:	Herbalism, hunting
BONUS PROFS:	Animal lore, survival (pick one type)

- Lone wolves must be elves or half-elves. While most lone wolves are green elves or half-elves of Sy-Tel'Quessir ancestry, elves and half-elves of every subrace are called to be specialty priests of Fenmarel's clergy.
- Lone wolves are not allowed to multiclass.
- Lone wolves may select nonweapon proficiencies from the warrior group without penalty.
- Lone wolves can cast *entangle* or *pass without trace* (as the 1st-level priest spells) once per day.
- At 3rd level, lone wolves can cast *blur* (as the 2nd-level wizard spell) or *obscurement* (as the 2nd-level priest spells) once per day.
- At 3rd level, lone wolves can cast *barkskin* (as the 2nd-level priest spell) once per day.
- At 5th level, lone wolves can cast *spike growth* or *tree* (as the 3rd-level priest spells) once per day.
- At 7th level, lone wolves can cast *hallucinatory forest* or *plant door* (as the 4th-level priest spells) or *charm monster* (as the 4th-level wizard spell) once per day.
- At 10th level, lone wolves can cast *commune with nature* (as the 5th-level priest spell) once per day.
- At 13th level, lone wolves can cast *wall of thorns* (as the 6th-level priest spell) once per day.
- At 15th level, lone wolves can cast *transport via plants* or *creeping doom* (as the 7th-level priest spells) or *acid storm* (as the 7th-level wizard spell) once per day.

Fenmaren Spells

1st Level

Beast Tattoo (Pr 1; Enchantment)

Sphere:	All
Range:	0
Components:	V, S, M
Duration:	1 hour/level
Casting Time:	1 round
Area of Effect:	The caster
Saving Throw:	None

This spell augments any one ability score that corresponds to a creature tattooed on the caster's body. The affected ability must relate to an attribute the creature supposedly represents. For example, cats are often associated with agility, foxes with cunning, etc. The exact characteristic that corresponds with a given species may vary from culture to culture, however.

In game terms, this spell augments one ability score (the one most closely associated with the animal depicted) by 1 point, up to a maximum of 19. Thus, if bears are associated with strength in the caster's culture, she or he can use a bear tattoo to increase his or her Strength by 1 point (or 10% for characters with exceptional Strength).

The material component of this spell is the priest's holy symbol. A tattoo on the caster's skin is also required to cast the spell.

3rd Level

Find Sustenance (Pr 3; Divination)

Sphere:	Divination
Range:	0
Components:	V, S
Duration:	1 day
Casting Time:	1 round
Area of Effect:	The caster
Saving Throw:	None

By means of this spell, the caster can find food and water as if she or he has the survival proficiency. After the spell is cast, the priest develops a sixth sense as to where to look for food and water; this lasts until sufficient food is found. For every level of experience above 4th, the priest can find sufficient sustenance for one human or demihuman for one day. Thus a 7th-level priest could find sufficient food and water for three people.

While food and water found by means of this spell may vary widely in taste, nutritional value, and safety, continued use of this spell allows the priest to locate a sufficiently diverse assortment of food to support life. Thus, it results in a fairly healthy and balanced diet without excessive risk of disease.

Find sustenance fails if there is absolutely no food or water to be found, a scenario that almost never occurs if the priest has unrestricted access to the natural world.

4th Level

Solitude (Pr 4; Enchantment)

Sphere:	Wards
Range:	0
Components:	V, S, M
Duration:	Special
Casting Time:	1 turn
Area of Effect:	10 foot/level radius
Saving Throw:	Special

By means of this spell, the caster significantly reduces the possibility that she or he might be disturbed by other sentient beings (defined as beings of low intelligence or greater). As long as the priest remains within a fixed radius of the point where the spell is cast, there is a reduced chance that anyone will intrude purely through happenstance. Should a chance encounter be indicated, the caster can make a saving throw vs. spell to avoid it.

The radius of *solitude*, beyond which the priest cannot pass without ending the spell, is 10 feet per level of the caster. If the priest moves beyond the perimeter set when the spell is cast, the spell ends immediately, and the normal probability of random encounters resumes (although there is no implication that an encounter will necessarily happen immediately thereafter). This spell also ends whenever the priest's presence is discovered by a sentient being or when another sentient being enters the radius of the spell effect, whether she or he is aware of the presence of the caster or not. Obviously, this spell has no effect if cast in the presence of other sentient beings.

For example, if the priest casts this spell in the middle of a forest, far away from any settlement or road, there is little chance of a random encounter disturbing his or her *solitude*. Still, someone specifically following clues to the priest's location (whether or not the tracker is aware of exactly whom she or he is seeking) would be totally unaffected by this spell. If, however, the priest cast this spell within visual range of a road or other location with regular traffic, while the spell would ensure that no one would simply stumble across the caster as they traveled through the woods, it would provide no isolation from discovery by those who use the thoroughfare as a matter of course. Of course, the DM always has the option of inserting necessary encounters, despite this spell.

The material component of this spell is a handful of earth sprinkled along the perimeter of the region of enforced *solitude*.

Hanali Celanil

(The Heart of Gold, Winsome Rose, Archer of Love, Kiss of Romance, Lady Goldheart)

Intermediate Power of Arborea, CG

PORTFOLIO:	Love, romance, beauty, fine art and artists
ALIASES:	Angharradh
DOMAIN NAME:	Olympus/Arvandor
SUPERIOR:	Corellon Larethian
ALLIES:	Eachthighern, Eilistraee, Cyrrollalee, Isis, Lliira, Lurue, Milil, Sharess, Sharindlar, Sheela Peryroyl, Sune, Tymora, Verenestra, the Seldarine
FOES:	Bane (dead), Cyric, Eshebala, Moander (dead), Shar, Talona, Talos and the gods of fury (Auril, Malar, and Umberlee), the drow pantheon (except Eilistraee)
SYMBOL:	Heart of gold
WOR. ALIGN.:	LG, NG, CG, LN, N, CN

Hanali Celanil (HAN-uh-lee SELL-uh-nihl) is the elven goddess of love, romance, and beauty. Lady Goldheart is predominantly depicted as female, although on rare occasions it is said that she has taken male form. Hanali is revered especially by gold elves and moon elves. Her followers also include elven artisans (particularly sculptors), lovers, performers (particularly bards and dancers), and nobles. Lady Goldheart is also widely revered by half-elves born of joyous unions, in honor of the love that brought their parents together. Hanali is closely associated with Evergold, a sacred crystal fountain and pool found within her crystal palace in Arvandor. She keeps watch over her followers by using the placid waters of Evergold as an immense crystal ball, and *philters of love* created by elves are said to contain drafts of this fountain's waters.

Hanali is both an aspect of Angharradh and one of the three elven goddesses—the other two being Aerdrie Faenya and Sehanine Moonbow—who collectively form the Triune Goddess. This duality tightly binds Hanali with the two other senior elven goddesses, and the three collectively serve alongside Corellon in leading the Seldarine. Hanali has been romantically involved with nearly every member of the Seldarine, particularly Erevan Ilesere, yet she remains amicable with nearly all of her current and former suitors alike. The only notable exception is Fenmarel Mestarine, although he and Lady Goldheart are still formally allied. The Lone Wolf resents the fact that Hanali spurned him long ago in favor of Erevan Ilesere, and some believe that Hanali's fickleness was what drove Fenmarel into the embrace of Lolth (Araushnee).

Hanali shares the waters of Evergold with the human goddess Sune, as well as the demipower Sharess and several other goddesses of pantheons not worshiped in the Realms. A friendly but intense rivalry exists between Lady Firehair and Lady Goldheart over the innate superiority of human vs. elven beauty. Hanali is close to the human goddess Sharess, particularly in her aspect as Zandilar, as the Dancer was once an elven demigoddess of the Yuir elves whose energy was directed toward passionate, physical love that burns hot and quickly but eventually dies out. While Verenestra (the patron goddess of dryads, nymphs, and sylphs) is rather jealous and snobbishly avoids contact with other goddesses of beauty, love, or romance, Hanali's kind nature and joyous celebration of life have finally won over the Oak Princess, making the two fast friends. Lady Goldheart actively opposes the efforts of those powers who would destroy beauty and love (such as Lolth and Talos) or who nurture bitterness and heartache (such as Shar). Hanali's deep enmity for Eshebala, the Queen of the Foxwomen, is rooted in the latter's exploitation of both beauty and love for her own self-serving, vain, and hedonistic reasons.

Hanali is a being of timeless beauty and benign nature, who always forgives minor transgressions and delights in rewarding her followers with the bliss of unexpected love and affection. She embodies romance, beauty, love, and joy in elven spirits, her only flaws being her own mild vanity and flighty nature. Although she rarely appears to her faithful, Hanali delights in seeing the growth of love among elves, and her avatar often acts in secret to protect young lovers.

Hanali's Avatar (Mage 33, Cleric 30)

Hanali appears as a beautiful elven maiden, clad in a short dress or gown of white and gold. She is always barefoot and wears gold anklets and toe rings. She favors spells from the spheres of all, animal, chaos, charm, creation, plant, and sun and from the schools of abjuration, enchantment/charm, and illusion/phantasm, although she can cast spells from any sphere or school.

AC –4; MV 15; HP 169; THAC0 2; #AT 1
Dmg 1d10+1 (touch, +1 Str)
MR 85%; SZ M (5 ½ feet tall)
Str 16, Dex 22, Con 19, Int 21, Wis 20, Cha 25
Spells P: 12/12/11/11/9/9/8, W: 7/7/7/7/7/7/7/7/7
Saves PPDM 2, RSW 3, PP 5, BW 7, Sp 4

Special Att/Def: While she wields no physical weapons, Hanali's beauty serves as both her primary weapon and her defense. Like a nymph,

Lady Goldheart's beauty can blind or even kill. In any round she so chooses, Hanali can manifest a *nymph's beauty* (see the spell section below). Likewise, whether she chooses to manifest a *nymph's beauty* or not, any being within 60 feet of Hanali must make a successful saving throw vs. spell with a –4 penalty each round (a –8 penalty for beings of the opposite gender) or be permanently charmed, unable to attack her. If Lady Goldheart has bathed in the waters of Evergold within the past day, these saving throw penalties increase to –6 and –12, respectively. Hanali's charm abilities are so powerful that even other avatars and creatures normally immune to charm are subject to their effects (but they do receive a saving throw).

Hanali can be struck only by +2 or better magical weapons, and she can cast *dimension door* or *plant door* at will. In a round that she makes no melee attacks, she can cast any two spells she has memorized. She wears a *ring of invisibility* and a *ring of free action*. At will, once per round, Lady Goldheart can create a bejeweled golden chalice (5000 gp value) filled with two drafts of a *philter of love*.

Other Manifestations

Hanali can also manifest as a soft rose-hued nimbus of light that envelops a creature or object. When Hanali's aura envelops an elf, half-elf, or faerie or creature of the Seelie Court, his or her Charisma increases by 2 points with respect to members of the opposite gender. The radiant glow also acts as a *friends* spell, affecting any who behold the favored being's beauteous visage. While Hanali's glow usually fades with the coming of dusk or dawn, an elven worshiper may, no more than once during his or her lifetime, receive a permanent increase in Charisma, often as a reward for creating or preserving a beautiful object, making a great sacrifice, or completing a great quest for the benefit of a loved one. Hanali's manifestation also allows the recipient to *detect romantic interest* for the duration of the effect.

Hanali manifests in common items by transforming them into works of art discreetly marked by her symbol. An item so blessed by Lady Goldheart is notable for its grace, beauty, and artistry. Such transformations are permanent unless the item is question is stolen, defaced, or sold for less than honorable reasons, in which case the transformed object reverts to its normal form. Acceptable reasons for selling such an object include raising money to feed and clothe one's family, trading the work of art in exchange for a person's life or freedom, or similar noble pursuits. Also, if the buyer does not meet Lady Goldheart's approval, the prize may transform back into the original, worthless object at some point after the seller has departed. If the transformed object is a chalice or container for liquids of any sort, the first vial of holy water poured into it transforms into a single draft of a *philter of love*.

The Seldarine call on agathinon, asuras, and ancient treants as their preferred servants, but Hanali is also served by aasimar, aasimon, asrai, atomies, cath shee, cooshee, dryads, einheriar, eladrins, electrum dragons, elven cats, faerie dragons, firestars, frosts, gorse, hamadryads, hollyphants, kholiathra, lillendi, mercury dragons, nereids, nixies, nymphs, oreads, pixies, reverend ones, satyrs, sea sprites, seelie faeries, sirines, sylphs, sprites, stwingers, sunflies, titans, and tressym. She demonstrates her favor through the tinkling chimes of bellflowers, the heat of a lover's flush, sun showers, the sudden appearance of a rainbow, sudden spectacular blooming of flowers, an abundance of natural fertility, or by guiding followers to areas of unspoiled natural beauty. The Heart of Gold indicates her displeasure by briefly casting a shadow over an item of beauty or by creating a fleeting vision of the face of a lost love or an item of great beauty that has been lost.

The Church

CLERGY: Clerics, mystics, specialty priests
CLERGY'S ALIGN.:   NG, CG, CN
TURN UNDEAD: C: Yes, Mys: No, SP: Yes, at priest level –2
CMND. UNDEAD: C: No, Mys: No, SP: No

All clerics (including multiclassed half-elven clerics), mystics, and specialty priests of Hanali receive religion (elf) and reading/writing (Espruar) as bonus nonweapon proficiencies. Although it is not an absolute requirement, very few clerics of Hanali have a Charisma score below 15.

Hanali's church is widely regarded among all elven races, with the notable exception of the drow. Her church is very popular among gold elves, particularly young nobles, and Lady Goldheart is believed to oversee their endless galas, revels, and romances. Among moon elves, Hanali is seen as the most beautiful face of Angharradh in her guise as guardian of romantic love and cherished beauty. While Hanali's cult is small among green and winged elves, they see her as the embodiment of natural beauty found in the forest and atop the mountains. Likewise, while Lady Goldheart's church in aquatic elven communities is small, Hanali is given praise for the beauty of the undersea, with shrines dedicated to her in undersea grottoes and in shallow, crystal-clear seas among coral reefs. Although Hanali is not widely known outside of elven society, there is an intense rivalry between the followers of Lady Goldheart and those of Sune.

Temples of Hanali are bright and beautiful, with fountains and springs throughout and great gardens encircling the central chapel. Most of Lady Goldheart's houses of worship are designed with young lovers in mind, providing endless mazes of shady paths, babbling brooks, quiet pools, leafy bowers, and flowering hedgerows, so as to facilitate amorous trysts and romantic rendezvous. Interior chambers are designed so as to permit the entrance of the sun, moon, and gentle breezes. Many chambers display beautiful works of art, serving the local community as museums, while others are designed as great concert halls from which strains of music spill out into the surrounding gardens.

Novices of Hanali are known as the Beauteous. Full priests of the Heart of Gold are known as Paramours. In ascending order of rank, the titles used by Hanalian priests are Dove, Suitor, Lover, Libertine, Soft Caress, Heart's Desire, and Fiery Ardor. High-ranking priests have unique individual titles. Specialty priests are known as goldhearts. The clergy of Hanali includes gold elves (30%), moon elves (28%), half-gold elves (17%), half-moon elves (15%), wild elves (7%), half-wild elves (2%), and a handful (1%) of dark elves, sea elves, winged elves, and half-elves of those ancestries. Hanali's clergy includes specialty priests (38%), mystics (32%), and clerics (including multiclassed half-elven clerics) (30%) and is nearly evenly split between females (54%) and males (46%).

Dogma: Life is worth living because of the beauty found in the world and the love that draws twin hearts together. Nurture what is beautiful in life, and let beauty's glow enliven and brighten the lives of those around you. The greatest joy is the rapture of newfound love and the tide of romance that sweeps over those wrapped in its embrace. Seek out and care fore love wherever it takes root and bring it to its fullest bloom so that all may share in the joy and beauty it creates. Always give shelter and succor to young lovers, for their hearts are the truest guides to life's proper course.

Day-to-Day Activities: Hanali's priests are flighty and somewhat vain, given to dancing and wild celebrations. The hierarchy is loosely organized, and priests are free to join or leave the church as they wish. Paramours preside over marriage and rites of passage ceremonies for young elves, although they are not required to marry, for Hanali's concern is love, not necessarily marriage. Members of Hanali's clergy spend their days cultivating beauty and love in all their myriad forms. Many of Lady Goldheart's priests tend fine gardens, while others amass personal or temple-based collections of gems, crystal sculptures, and other fine works of art. While things of gold and crystal, particularly jewelry and statues, are favored, beautiful art in any form is admired, collected, and displayed. Hanali's priests must always be finely dressed, and displaying one's personal beauty to its best advantage is a requirement of every priest of the Heart of Gold.

Holy Days/Important Ceremonies: While Hanali's priests are given to frequent impromptu revels, their greatest celebrations are held every month beneath the bright light of the full moon. Such holy days are known as Secrets of the Heart, for romantically involved participants are said to experience the full bloom of their affections on such nights, allowing them to evaluate the strength of their feelings. Likewise, the inner beauty of celebrants visibly manifests as a rosy glow in their cheeks and eyes for days thereafter. Offerings of objects of great beauty are made to Lady Goldheart during such holy festivals, some of which are swept into Arvandor while others are returned to be shared among all of Hanali's followers. It is not uncommon for artists to unveil their latest work at such holy days, nor is it rare for young lovers to either pledge their troth secretly or proclaim it to all assembled, for doing so is said to invite Hanali's favor.

Major Centers of Worship: The Vale of Evereska is located amidst the Shaeradim, a small mountain range on the western edge of Anauroch, due north of the Battle of Bones. (Humans sometimes employ the nomenclature Graycloak Hills for the mountains surrounding Evereska, but that is more properly applied to the next set of hills to the north, also known as the Tomb

Hills.) The Vale is a wide alpine valley with an inner ring of knolls surrounding the center of the valley. The three highest hills, known as the Sisters, form a fairly even triangle around the walled city of Evereska. The highest hill of the three, Bellcrest, is the site of Hanali's temple, an enormous structure of white marble and moonstone, surrounded by gardens that bloom year-round with rare flowers and exotic fruit. The Fountainheart of Shimmering Gold is led by the stunningly beautiful moon elf, Hamalitia Everlove, whose beauty has continued to increase over the centuries. The temple has housed countless Evereskan weddings, revels, and dances, and in addition to displaying works of Evereska's greatest artisans, holds many greatest artistic treasures from Ascalhorn, Eaerlann, Illefarn, Myth Drannor, and Sharrven.

On a low pedestal at the center of the gardens, accessed through a maze of rose-entwined boxwood, stands a statue of the goddess carved from rare white stone. The sculpture depicts Lady Goldheart with angular, delicate features, exquisite lips curved in a knowing smile, and almond-shaped lips. One long-fingered hand rests over her heart, and the other touches a pointed ear, a traditional portrayal of the goddess showing that she is ever receptive to the prayers of lovers. The love of Amnestria (moon elven daughter of Queen Amlaruil Moonflower of Evermeet) and Bron Skorlsun (a human ranger and Harper), combined with the magic of Amnestria's *moonblade*, created a *gate* from the base of the garden statue to the island of Evermeet. In the Year of Maidens (1361 DR), however, the *gate's* mainland terminus was moved to Blackstaff Tower in Waterdeep by Danilo Thann after the Waterdhavian dandy and Arilyn Moonblade, half-elf daughter of Amnestria and Bron, solved a series of murders by the Harper Assassin.

Affiliated Orders: The Chaperones of the Moonlight Tryst are a fellowship of romantically inclined rogues and rangers who discretely safeguard young elven lovers from those who would take advantage of their distraction and/or innocence. Members of this merry band are also called on occasionally to facilitate secret meetings between lovers of rival houses or to aid them in eloping against their family's wishes. Chaperones of the Moonlight Tryst usually work closely with the priests of the local temple of Hanali, as those who serve Lady Goldheart often receive the confidences of those struck by the arrows of the Archer of Love.

Priestly Vestments: Hanali's priesthood pride themselves on the stunning beauty of their clerical vestments. Paramours wear golden robes sprinkled with gold dust, and they wear their hair long and unbound without any covering. Gold rings, necklaces, bracelets, anklets, and earrings are common adornments. The holy symbol of the faith is either a miniature gold rose or a miniature gold stylized heart. Both forms of Hanali's holy symbol are often worn as a brooch or necklace.

Adventuring Garb: Hanali's priests are drawn to romantic quests like moths to a flame, and thus they take to adventuring more than one might otherwise expect. In dangerous situations, Hanali's followers must strike a balance between beauty and pragmatism. Paramours favor weapons and armor that are a beauty to behold, emphasizing the natural elven grace of their bearer, yet that also guard against any weapon strike or spell that might mar their natural beauty. As such, Hanali's priesthood prefer chainmail (of elven make if available), shields, and weapons unlikely to bring them into melee combat or to disfigure the appearance of an opponent.

Specialty Priests (Goldhearts)

REQUIREMENTS:	Charisma 16, Wisdom 12
PRIME REQ.:	Charisma, Wisdom
ALIGNMENT:	CG
WEAPONS:	Club, dart, flail, lasso, mace, mancatcher, net, quarterstaff, sling, short bow
ARMOR:	Leather, chain mail, elven chain mail, and shield
MAJOR SPHERES:	All, animal, chaos, charm, creation, guardian, healing, necromantic, plant, protection, sun
MINOR SPHERES:	Divination, wards, weather
MAGICAL ITEMS:	Same as clerics
REQ. PROFS:	Etiquette, herbalism
BONUS PROFS:	Artistic ability, dancing, singing

- Goldhearts must be elves or half-elves. While most goldhearts are gold elves, moon elves, half-gold elves, and half-moon elves, elves and half-elves of every subrace are called to be specialty priests of Hanali's clergy.

- Goldhearts are not allowed to multiclass.
- Goldhearts can cast *friends* (as the 1st-level wizard spell) once per day.
- At 3rd level, goldhearts can cast *charm person* (as the 1st-level wizard spell) on someone of the opposite gender once per day. The target receives a –1 penalty on his or her saving throw for every point of Charisma the goldheart has above 16 (–1 at 17, –2 at 18, etc.).
- At 5th level, goldhearts can cast *enthrall* (as the 2nd-level priest spell) once per day.
- At 7th level, goldhearts receive a +1 bonus to their Charisma scores. They receive another +1 bonus at 15th level, and a third +1 bonus at 20th level. Their Charisma scores cannot exceed 25 by this method.
- At 7th level, goldhearts can cast *Otiluke's resilient sphere* or *rainbow pattern* (as the 4th-level wizard spells) once a day.
- At 10th level, goldhearts can cast *charm monster* (as the 4th-level wizard spell) or *magic font* (as the 5th-level priest spell) once per day.
- At 13th level, goldhearts can make a *philter of love* once per tenday.
- At 15th level, goldhearts can cast *prismatic spray* (as the 7th-level wizard spell) or *heal* (as the 6th-level priest spell) once per tenday.

Hanalian Spells

1st Level

Divine Romantic Interest (Pr 1; Divination)

Sphere:	Divination
Range:	Touch
Components:	S
Duration:	Special
Casting Time:	1 round
Area of Effect:	Creature touched
Saving Throw:	Neg.

This spell enables the priest to divine the existence and subject (or subjects) of the unspoken love, crush, or romantic interest of the first creature touched by the caster. A successful saving throw vs. spell by an unwilling target prevents the caster from learning the identity of the romantic interest, but conveys to the caster whether or not the target harbors any such secret affections at the time of the spell is cast.

Curiously, this spell does not reveal whether or not any other creature harbors romantic interest toward the caster. Theologians postulate that Lady Goldheart wishes to surprise even her most faithful followers with unexpected love.

5th Level

Hamatree (Pr 5; Alteration)

Sphere:	Plant
Range:	Touch
Components:	V, S
Duration:	Permanent
Casting Time:	24 hours
Area of Effect:	The caster
Saving Throw:	None

This spell creates a permanent link between the caster and a very old oak tree (at least 100 years of age), much like the bond between a dryad (or hamadryad) and her tree. The casting of the spell invests a portion of the caster's spirit within the tree and permanently bonds his or her life force with that of the tree. The link created by a *hamatree* spell can be severed only by means of a *limited wish* or *wish*.

Once cast, the caster can literally step through any living, healthy tree and *dimension door* to the oak tree with which she or he is bound. Likewise, she or he can use *speak with plants* to communicate with her tree whenever in physical contact with it.

The caster can choose to transfer any damage she or he suffers to the great oak with which the priest is linked if desired, up to the number of hit points the caster had when casting the spell. However, any fire damage inflicts double the damage to the tree that would have affected the caster. It takes the tree two days to regenerate 1 point of damage, and this process can be hastened only by means of a *plant growth* or *heal* spell, either of which speeds the recovery process up to 1 point of damage per day. Depending upon the age and size of the oak, the tree may have between 7 and 12 Hit Dice, as determined by the DM.

The great drawback of this spell is that any damage inflicted on the oak with which the caster is bound is suffered equally by the caster (except for damage transferred by the caster), no matter where she or he may be. Upon the death of the caster, the tree dies immediately. Upon the death of the oak, the caster must immediately make a successful system shock roll or die.

The verbal and somatic components of this spell require the caster to spend the entire casting time in contact with the chosen tree while singing to awaken its slumbering spirit. This spell can be cast only once in the lifetime of the caster.

7th Level

Nymph's Beauty (Pr 7; Enchantment/Charm)

Sphere:	Charm
Range:	Special
Components:	V, S, M
Duration:	2 turns
Casting Time:	1 round
Area of Effect:	Special
Saving Throw:	Neg.

This spell grants the caster the beauty of a nymph and its attendant dangers. Both male and female casters can employ this spell, each able to affect both genders equally.

Observers gazing upon the caster during the spell's duration are permanently blinded unless they make successful saving throws vs. spell. (This blindness can be cured by a *heal* spell, *limited wish*, or *wish*, but not by *cure blindness or deafness*.) If the caster is already nude or disrobes during the casting, she or he can choose between the following two alternative effects: unconsciousness (4d6 rounds) or death. Observers must make successful saving throws vs. spell or succumb to the effect chosen by the priest upon casting the spell.

This spell functions effectively in any lighting conditions except near or total darkness.

The material components are the priest's holy symbol and the tear of a nymph that is placed on the tongue during casting and vanishes upon completion.

Khalreshaar

Although Khalreshaar (Kal-REH-shay-are) is not listed in *Faiths & Avatars* as an alias of Our Lady of the Forest, Khalreshaar is the name by which Mielikki is known on Evermeet, the Green Isle. In this aspect, Mielikki is said to serve Rillifane Rallathil, not Silvanus, delivering messages and doing errands for the Leaflord when speed is of the essence. While Khalreshaar/Mielikki is in some respects an interloper god in the elven pantheon, the Fair Folk speak of a female human druid who was elevated to the ranks of the divine by the Seldarine when she was slain by soldiers of a human warlord as she attempted to defend elven woodlands from the encroachment of civilization.

Since the Time of Troubles, a growing cult, composed primarily of half-elves, has begun to give more credence to myths which claim that Mielikki is the daughter of Silvanus and Hanali Celanil. They have begun to venerate Khalreshaar as the first truly half-elven power, much to the dismay of many full-blooded elves. See the entry for Mielikki in *Faiths & Avatars* for more information about Khalreshaar.

Labelas Enoreth

(The Lifegiver, Lord of the Continuum, the One-Eyed God, the Philosopher, the Sage at Sunset)

Intermediate Power of Arborea, CG

PORTFOLIO:	Time, longevity, the moment of choice, history
ALIASES:	Chronos, Karonis, Kronus, the Simbul
DOMAIN NAME:	Olympus/Arvandor
SUPERIOR:	Corellon Larethian
ALLIES:	Deneir, Cyrrollalee, Eilistraee, Milil, Mystra, Null, Oghma, Savras, Shekinester, the Seldarine
FOES:	Myrkul (dead), Orcus (dead)/Tenebrous (undead), Yeenoghu, Velsharoon, the drow pantheon (except Eilistraee)
SYMBOL:	Setting sun
WOR. ALIGN.:	LG, NG, CG, LN, N, CN

Labelas Enoreth (LAH-bay-lahs EHN-or-eth) is the elven god of longevity and time. At the creation of the Fair Folk, Labelas blessed the elves with long lifespans and decreed that their appearances would not be marked by the passage of time. The Lifegiver cooperates with Sehanine in overseeing the lifespan of elves and their growth away from and beyond mortal realms. He measures the lives of the Fair Folk and decrees when they should be ended, allowing passage to Arvandor. As Lord of the Continuum, Labelas governs the orderly passage of time and guards against those who would alter the path of history. Labelas confers wisdom and teachings on young and old alike, and although he is rarely invoked, the Lifegiver is often praised. The Lifegiver knows the future and past of every elf, faerie, or sylvan creature. Labelas is worshiped by sages, historians, philosophers, librarians, and all those who measure the changes wrought by the passing of years.

Labelas has also been venerated in other guises at various places and times in history. When the Sy-Tel'Quessir settled the Yuirwood, the Seldarine merged with the ancient gods of the Yuir, transforming them into aspects of the various powers of the elven pantheon. The Simbul was the Yuir goddess of the moment of choice, the edge, the space between the now and the future, what is and is not, the power of balance embodied in the point of decision where fate is determined intuitively without reason or knowledge. When the Seldarine and the Yuir elven deities merged, the Simbul had to chose between Labelas Enoreth (the Seldarine power of time and philosophy) and Erevan Ilesere (the elven god of change) to ally with, and eventually she became an aspect of Labelas and then faded into near oblivion. Even the Cha-Tel'Quessir of the Yuirwood have long forgotten this goddess, and the Simbul, Queen of Aglarond, only discovered the divine ancestry of her name in the Year of the Banner (1368 DR). Likewise, a long forgotten-aspect of Labelas, known as Chronos, Karonis, or Kronus, was worshiped centuries ago in the tiny realm of Orva, now sunk beneath the waters of the Vast Swamp of eastern Cormyr.

Labelas gets on well with the rest of the Seldarine, although his relationship with Erevan Ilesere is sorely tested by the other's antics on occasion, but the Lifegiver makes allies of few other powers. In ancient times, when Mystryl was venerated as the human goddess of time, Labelas was closely allied with the Lady of Mysteries, and that close relationship has continued with the current incarnation of Mystra. Labelas and the Guardian of the Lost, an aspect of the draconic deity Null also known as Chronepsis, have an understanding, and it is said that Labelas and Shekinester, Queen of the Nagas, are slowly building an alliance. Since the Time of Troubles, Clangeddin Silverbeard, dwarven god of battle and war, has nursed a grudge against Labelas for defeating him in battle on the isle of Ruathym. While the Lifegiver has attempted to apologize for his actions, the Father of Battle is slow to forgive, as is typical of the Stout Folk. The Lifegiver strongly opposes the powers of entropy and undeath, particularly Tenebrous and Yeenoghu.

Labelas is also a philosopher-god, a patient teacher and instructor. His demeanor is calm and meditative, and he is not given to sudden action or hasty speech. According to legend, he traded an eye for the ability to peer through time. Labelas concerns himself with transgenerational changes and the growth of learning and wisdom among elves, and thus rarely involves himself directly in the lives of individuals.

Vartan Hai Sylvar is a gold elf who served as the avatar of Labelas during the Time of Troubles. While in mortal form, Labelas inflicted a great deal of pain and destruction on the isle of Ruathym and Vartan's companions, the crew of the *Realms Master,* causing Vartan to reject his god for a time. Eventually, Labelas and Vartan reconciled, but not before the gold elf had taught his deity a great deal about the proper exercise of his power and value of trust and friendship. The Chosen of Labelas has served for a brief period as Vartan's proxy in the plane of Arvandor, but he has left that service to return to the Realms. He continues to serve his god, and both god and elf have grown from this relationship.

Labelas's Avatar (Mage 32, Cleric 31, Bard 25)

Labelas appears as an androgynous elf with silver hair and misty gray eyes, one of which is always covered by an eye-patch. He wears pale-colored robes of green, blue, white, and gray. He favors spells from the spheres of all, animal, astral, charm, divination, elemental, healing, necromantic, numbers, plant, protection, sun, thought, time, and weather and from the schools of abjuration, divination, and enchantment/charm, although he can cast spells from any sphere or school (including the optional school of chronomancy, if that school is used).

AC –3; MV 15; HP 171; THAC0 0; #AT 1
Dmg 1d6+5 (*quarterstaff +4, +1 Str*)
MR 90%; SZ M (6 feet tall)
Str 16, Dex 21, Con 20, Int 23, Wis 24, Cha 20
Spells P: 14/13/12/12/12/11/8, W: 7/7/7/7/7/7/7/7/7
Saves PPDM 2, RSW 3, PP 5, BW 7, Sp 4

Special Att/Def: He wields the *Timestave*, a *quarterstaff +4* that can *age plant, age object, age creature, age dragon*, or the reversed forms of those spells on any successful hit, as determined by the wielder. Once per round, Labelas can cast any spell from the sphere of time (or from the school of chronomancy, if that optional school is used).

Labelas's gaze can place one being per round in *temporal stasis* for as long as Labelas wishes. (Targets must make successful saving throws vs. spell at a –4 penalty to negate.) His touch restores youth or prematurely ages beings up to 100 years. (No saving throw is allowed, and no being can be affected more than once in its lifetime by either form of Labelas's touch.) It also sends any creature that has moved by any means to another point in time back to its normal time. All creatures hostile to the Lifegiver and within 120 feet of his form are automatically slowed (no saving throw allowed), and all allies within the same radius are automatically *hasted*, but without the normal aging penalty.

Labelas can be struck only by +2 or better magical weapons. The Lifegiver is immune to all spells that would slow his movement (*slow, hold, paralyzation, time stop*, etc.), all spells from the sphere of time, and all unnatural aging.

Other Manifestations

Labelas rarely manifests, preferring to work through subtle signs and careful guidance of the flow of history. Nevertheless, on occasion he manifests as a faint mist that envelops a creature or object and visits upon it the effects of an *age creature* or *age object* spell or the corresponding reverse. Typically such manifestations undo the effects of aging, but the reverse has been observed on rare occasions as well.

The Seldarine call on agathinon, asuras, and ancient treants as their preferred servants, but Labelas is also served by aasimar, aasimon (particularly lights), baelnorn, einheriar, eladrin, electrum dragons, feystags, firestars, gold dragons, hollyphants, hybsils, incarnates of hope, faith, justice, and wisdom, kholiathra, ki-rin, lillendi, lythlyx, memory webs, moonhorses, opinicus, radiance quasielementals, reverend ones, scile, seelie faeries, silver dragons, sunflies, talking owls, temporal dogs, temporal gliders, time dimensionals, t'uen-rin, and unicorns. He demonstrates his favor through the discovery of black sapphires, ghost stone (a faded form of kunzite, also known as spodumene), king's tears, rubies, star rubies, sunstones, and tomb jade. Labelas's omens are given in the form of subtle, hidden, or ambivalent events and signs, challenging his priests to understand the god's signals. The Lifegiver indicates his displeasure by inflicting the ravages of time on an object, causing it to crumble to dust.

The White Stag of Labelas is the special servant of the elven god of longevity that has been observed only on Evermeet. Physically, it is a huge, snow white animal, with massive muscles and red, glowing eyes. Observers say the creature's divine aura is literally tangible and felt by all those who see it. The stag's appearance is considered to be an omen of great events, for it invariably leads any who follow it to a place where a vision or direct divine message is given. As a divine being, the stag is in no danger on the Green Isle, but should the unthinkable every happen and the beast be pursued by enemies, it is fully capable of defending itself. The White Stag appears wherever elves are in need of guidance and wisdom. Some claim that its spends the remainder of its time in Arvandor and is sent to Faerûn only when elves are in danger or require its services.

The White Stag: AC 5; MV 36; HD 6; hp 48; THAC0 14; #AT 3; Dmg 2d4 (horns)/1d4 (hoof)/1d4 (hoof); SD mislead; MR 10%; SZ L (7 ½' tall); ML fearless (20); Int high (14); AL CG; XP 650.

Mislead: The stag usually leads those who follow it to a divine message. However, when defending itself against those who follow it with ill intent, it can lead pursuers on a wild goose chase with the same effect as if it had cast *lose the path* (the reverse of *find the path*) on all who view it. This causes them to become lost and allows the stag to escape as soon as they lose sight of it. The *lose the path* effect lasts for a day.

The Church

CLERGY:	Clerics, mystics, specialty priests, chronomancers
CLERGY'S ALIGN.:	LG, NG, CG, LN, N, CN
TURN UNDEAD:	C: Yes, Mys: No, SP: No, Chr: No
CMND. UNDEAD:	C: No, Mys: No, SP: No, Chr: No

All clerics, mystics, and specialty priests of Labelas receive religion (elf) and reading/writing (Espruar) as bonus nonweapon proficiencies. If chronomancers, as detailed in the *Chronomancer* supplement, are permitted in the campaign, then elven and half-elven chronomancers may be members of Labelas's clergy.

The church of Labelas has a small, but dedicated, following in most elven cultures, and its teachings are widely heralded throughout the realms of the Tel'Quessir. The counsel of the Lifegiver's priests is always sought when far-reaching decisions must be made. Although Labelas is venerated by members of all the elven subraces, the Ar-Tel'Quessir in particular revere the Lifegiver and follow the teachings of his clergy for the philosophical nature and farseeing perspective of both the god and his priests is in close harmony with their natural perspective on the course of life. The faithful of Labelas are on good terms with the cult of Hanali Celanil, for the followers of the Heart of Gold give thanks to the Lifegiver for preserving the beauty that Lady Goldheart bequeaths.

Temples of the Lifegiver are monuments unbowed by the passage of time, whether they be built amidst the branches of a venerable forest giant or constructed from weathered stone carved from the slopes of an ancient mountain range. The central chapel of each temple is dominated by a massive golden sundial inlaid in the floor, and windows are placed or limbs trimmed back so as to allow the direct rays of the setting sun to bathe the massive time pieces in colorful hues. Each house of worship has a library of some sort associated with it, and many such temples house some of the greatest collections of elven lore assembled in the Realms.

Novices of Labelas are known as Tyros. Full priests of the Lifegiver are known as Time Sentinels. In ascending order of rank, the titles used by Labelasan priests are Observer, Recorder, Librarian, Lorist, Scholar, Historian, Sage, and Philosopher. High-ranking priests have unique individual titles but are collectively known as the Wizened. Specialty priests are known as chronologians. The clergy of Labelas includes gold elves (40%), moon elves (30%), wood elves (12%), sea elves (10)%, half-elves of those ancestries (7%), and a handful of elves and half-elves of other stock (1%). Labelas's clergy is divided between clerics (77%), specialty priests (20%), and a handful of mystics (2%) and chronomancers (1%). (If chronomancers are not permitted in the campaign, then the percentage of mystics in the clergy should be raised to 3%.) The clergy of Labelas has many more women (61%) than men (39%).

Dogma: The march of time is inexorable, but the blessings of the Lifegiver enable the children of Corellon to live long and fruitful lives, unmarked by the passage of years. Record and preserve the lessons of history, and draw lessons from that which has unfolded. In the end, the sun always sets before the next day dawns anew. When you follow Labelas's teachings, time is on your side.

Day-to-Day Activities: Priests of Labelas are the keepers of elven history and lore, and they are charged with searching for hidden facts of the past. They compile and protect such sacred knowledge and record it for the instruction of future generations. Members of Labelas's clergy are also philosophers and teachers, responsible for educating the young and promoting and acquiring knowledge.

Holy Days/Important Ceremonies: The faithful of Labelas do not celebrate individual holy days, for the passage of time is uniform, independent of the events that unfold in each regular interval. Instead, the Lifegiver's followers gather each day in small groves near his temples as the sun sets to mark the passage of another day, a daily ritual known as the Marking of Time. They utter prayers to Labelas and recite all that they have learned in the past day to be recorded by the lorekeepers of Arvandor who serve the One-Eyed God.

It is considered a great honor if a priest of Labelas attends a birth, as it is a sign that the child will live a long and fruitful life. Such visitations always occur at the first sunset after the birth and involve casting a *bless* spell on the infant as prayers to Labelas are exclaimed to the heavens. A priest of the Lifegiver does not perform such a ceremony unless she or he receives a vision in advance from the god giving such instructions.

Major Centers of Worship: The ruins of the elven city of Mhiilamniir lay at the heart of the High Forest, less than two days' travel from the west end of the Old Road and three days' travel east from the Lost Peaks. At the height of Eaerlann's civilization, Mhiilamniir was the site of a number of major temples and seats of power for elven clergies in the North. While Mhiilamniir's largest building is a now-ruined temple dedicated to Corellon Larethian, the city's oldest temple has always been the Temple Beyond Time, a soaring tower shaped like an elongated hourglass consecrated in the name of the Lifegiver. Labelasan religious texts suggest that the Temple Beyond Time existed as far back as the early days of Aryvandaar, nearly 25 millennia ago. Mhiilamniir is no longer safe enough for elven pilgrims to visit due to the tenancy of a rabidly paranoid green dragon, Choloracridara, who lairs in Corellon's ruined house of worship and claims the entire temple city and its environs as her domain. Nonetheless, Labelas's temple and its inhabitants survive unmolested due in part to the temple's peculiar relationship with the time stream. The Temple Beyond Time can be seen or entered for a few moments at widely varying intervals. The only permanent inhabitants of the Temple Beyond Time are a trio of Siluvanedenn baelnorn, known collectively as the Timespinners: Susklahava Orbryn, Roanmara Neirdre, and Phantyni Evanara. In life, each of the Timespinners was a gold elven priestess of Labelas, and they have served the Lifegiver for millennia as historians, sages, and oracles. The faithful of the Lifegiver interpret the god's omens as to when the Temple Beyond Time can be reached and then travel to the site in order to consult with the eternal seers who dwell within. Those petitioners who enter the tower bear the risk that when they emerge many years may have passed, even though the interval seemed like little more than a few hours to those within.

The dark, calm waters of Lake Eredruie, a large pond at the headwaters of the Glaemril in the forests of northwestern Deepingdale, have long been held to be sacred to Labelas by the Fair Folk. Elves who immerse themselves in the lake's waters can add 3d20 years to their lifespan, although the magic of the waters works only once. A flask of Lake Eredruie water acts as a *potion of healing* on elves and half-elves only, but loses its potency if mixed with any other liquid or substance. The Teu-Tel'Quessir of the neighboring village of Velethuil, known to humans as Bristar, have long venerated the Lifegiver at the Treespring of Eredruie, a natural spring that bubbles forth from a hollow in the upper trunk of a hiexel and runs down the side of the tree to feed the neighboring Lake Eredruie. The Treespring is tended by an aged moon elf, Sorsasta Fernsong, rumored to have enchanted numerous *elixirs of health*, *elixirs of youth*, and *potions of longevity* from the potent waters.

Affiliated Orders: The Order of the Setting Sun is a fellowship of elf and half-elf archeologists, bards, historians, lorekeepers, scholars, sages, and the like who seek to preserve and/or rediscover the relics and knowledge of elven cultures that have passed into history. The Knights Paradoxical are an elite order of warriors, wizards, and priests who seek to preserve the integrity of the time stream and prevent significant alterations to history by chronomancers and their ilk. Members of this ancient order may be found guarding legendary *time gates* and tracking down copies of *time conduit* spells (as detailed in the various *Arcane Age* products) to keep them out of the hands of those who would meddle with history either deliberately or through carelessness.

Priestly Vestments: Priests of Labelas wear light gray robes of wispy, gossamer construction. When a small light source is viewed through the robes, such vestments shine with the deep reds, purples, and oranges of the sunset. The holy symbol of the faith is a semicircular gold disk carved to resemble the setting sun.

Adventuring Garb: Servants of Labelas eschew heavy armor or sophisticated weaponry. For most priests of the Lifegiver, simple light gray robes (of more durable construction than their ceremonial vestments) and a staff

or dagger serve as adequate protection. When available, *elven cloaks*, *elven boots*, and other items that allow the wearer to pass unnoticed are employed by members of Labelas's clergy.

Specialty Priests (Chronologian)

REQUIREMENTS:	Intelligence 11, Wisdom 12
PRIME REQ.:	Intelligence, Wisdom
ALIGNMENT:	CG
WEAPONS:	Club, dagger, knife, quarterstaff, sling, staff-sling
ARMOR:	Leather armor or elven chain mail
MAJOR SPHERES:	All, animal, astral, charm, divination, necromantic, numbers, plant, protection, sun, thought, time
MINOR SPHERES:	Healing, weather
MAGICAL ITEMS:	Same as clerics
REQ. PROFS:	Reading/writing (Common)
BONUS PROFS:	Astrology, ancient history (elves)

- Chronologians must be elves or half-elves. While most chronologians are gold elves or moon elves, elves and half-elves of every subrace are called to be specialty priests of Labelas's clergy.
- Chronologians are not allowed to multiclass.
- Chronologians may select nonweapon proficiencies from the wizard group without penalty.
- Chronologians receive a +2 bonus to saving throws against spells that affect their perception of time, including *haste*, *slow*, *temporal stasis*, and all spells from the sphere of time (or the school of chronomancy, if such a school is in use), as well as all aging attacks, such as that of a ghost. If no saving throw is normally allowed, chronologians receive a saving throw vs. spell anyway, albeit without the above-mentioned bonus.
- Chronologians can cast *know time* (as the 1st-level priest spell) at will.
- Chronologians can cast *know age* (as the 1st-level priest spell) or *withdraw* (as the 2nd-level priest spell) once per day.
- At 3rd level, chronologians can cast *choose future* (as the 3rd-level priest spell) or *nap* (as the 2nd-level priest spell) once per day.
- At 5th level, chronologians can cast *haste* or *slow* (as the 3rd-level wizard spells) once per day. They do not age due to the activation of this ability.
- At 7th level, chronologians can cast *age plant* or *body clock* (as the 4th-level priest spells) once per day.
- At 10th level, chronologians can cast *age object* or *time pool* (as the 5th-level priest spells) once per day.
- At 10th level, chronologians gain a +1 bonus to their Wisdom score. They gain an additional +1 bonus at 20th level. This cannot raise their Wisdom above 25.
- At 13th level, chronologians can cast *age creature* (as the 6th-level priest spell) or *legend lore* (as the 6th-level wizard spell) once per day.
- At 13th level, chronologians age at only half the normal rate, whether naturally or due to a magical effect.
- At 15th level, chronologians can cast *temporal stasis* or *time stop* (as the 9th-level wizard spells) once per day.

Labelasan Spells

2nd Level

Protection from Aging (Pr 2; Abjuration)

Sphere:	Protection, Time
Range:	Touch
Components:	V, S, M
Duration:	3 rounds/level
Casting Time:	5
Area of Effect:	One creature
Saving Throw:	None

While protected by the effects of this spell, the recipient is immune to unnatural aging and aging attack forms, such as the sight of a ghost. The spell does not protect against natural aging or willingly accepted aging affects, such as that inflicted by a *haste* spell.

The material components of this spell are the priest's holy symbol and a powdered black sapphire worth at least 50 gp.

3rd Level

Renewed Youth (Pr 3; Alteration) *Reversible*

Sphere:	Healing, Time
Range:	10 yards
Components:	V, S, M
Duration:	1 round/level
Casting Time:	6
Area of Effect:	One creature
Saving Throw:	Neg.

This spell temporarily restores a middle-aged or older recipient to the peak of physical health enjoyed in his or her prime. The game effect of this spell is to temporarily reverse any penalties to ability scores suffered due to aging, as detailed in Table 12: Aging Effects in the *Player's Handbook*. For example, a 250-year-old elf would temporarily receive a +3 bonus to Strength, a +2 bonus to Dexterity, and a +2 bonus to Constitution thanks to the effects of this spell but would not suffer a corresponding penalty to Intelligence or Wisdom. Willing recipients can, of course, forgo the saving throw.

While this spell does not ameliorate any damage suffered, it might increase the recipient's tolerance for pain. If a temporary boost in Constitution results in increased hit points (due to a modified hit point adjustment), those phantom hit points are lost first, as is the case with the 2nd-level priest spell *aid*.

The reverse of this spell, *weight of years*, temporarily ages the target. The priest must touch the target to affect it. If the caster is 5th-level or lower, she or he can temporarily impose the physical ability score penalties of middle age if the target fails a saving throw vs. spell. If the caster is 6th to 9th, she or he can impose the penalties of old age, and if 14th level or higher, the caster can impose the penalties of venerable age. The caster can choose to age the target by fewer categories than possible for his or her level if desired. The temporary aging inflicted by *weight of years* cannot force a creature to die of old age, nor can it make an old creature middle-aged, effectively aiding it.

Neither *renewed youth* nor *weight of years* has any effect on dragons or extraplanar or conjured beings.

The material components are the priest's holy symbol and a freshly cut (or magically preserved) flower, or for the reverse, the priest's holy symbol and crushed air-dried flower petals or a shriveled, dried fruit.

5th Level

Speak with Ancient Dead (Pr 5; Necromancy)

Sphere:	Divination
Range:	1
Components:	V, S, M
Duration:	Special
Casting Time:	1 turn
Area of Effect:	1 creature
Saving Throw:	Special

This spell is a more potent version of the 3rd-level priest spell *speak with dead* that allows the priest to speak with spirits who have long ago departed from the mortal world. Except as noted in the table below, this spell is otherwise identical to the less powerful but more common version of this spell.

Caster's Level of Experience	Max. Length of Time Dead	Time Questioned	No. of Questions
9	10 years	1 turn	4
10–14	100 years	2 turns	5
15–20	1,000 years	3 turns	6
21–25	10,000 years	1 hour	7
26+	Unlimited	1 day	9

7th Level

Temporal Anomaly (Pr 7; Alteration)

Sphere:	Time
Range:	10 yards
Components:	V, S, M
Duration:	2d4 rounds
Casting Time:	1 round
Area of Effect:	Special
Saving Throw:	None

By means of this spell, the priest can create a ripple in the timestream so that a physical effect occurs without the physical cause occurring. For example, the priest can cause a dart to appear in an opponent's neck without actually appearing to throw anything.

During the casting of this spell, the priest enters an alternate timestream for up to 1 round per level of the caster. During that time interval, the priest can attempt to carry out any action normally open to him or her, and other creatures can react accordingly. When the casting is complete, the priest returns from the alternate time stream, although to observers it appears as if she or he spent only a single round casting a spell, and the effects of any action caused in the alternate time stream suddenly become apparent without obvious cause or any memory of such events by other participants. Any spells cast, charges employed, or other magical effects employed in the alternate reality are not used up when the priest returns to his or her true timestream.

For example, a 14th-level priest casts *temporal anomaly*. For the next 2d4 rounds, she or he can interact with the current situation as normal. The caster could try to hit an opponent with darts, but to do so would require a successful attack roll, and the opponent could react accordingly. She or he could also bind the wounds of an ally and cast *cure light wounds*. When the priest returns to his or her normal time stream, observers will believe that the caster spent a single round casting a spell. Upon completion of the spell, however, the foe would suddenly sport a dart in the neck and the ally would suddenly be bandaged and *cured*.

The material components of this spell are the priest's holy symbol and a powdered ruby worth at least 1,000 gp.

Lashrael

See the entry for Corellon Larethian for details on Lashrael (LASH-ray-ehl), a servitor of the Protector who is sometimes mistakenly referred to as a demipower.

Rillifane Rallathil

(The Leaflord, the Wild One, the Great Oak,
the Many-Branched, the Many-Limbed,
Old Man of the Yuirwood)

Intermediate Power of Arborea, CG

PORTFOLIO:	Woodlands, nature, wild elves, druids
ALIASES:	Bear, Eagle, Raven, Wolf, Relkath of the Infinite Branches, Magnar the Bear
DOMAIN NAME:	Olympus/Arvandor or Seelie Court
SUPERIOR:	Corellon Larethian
ALLIES:	Baervan Wildwanderer, Cyrrollalee, Eilistraee, Eldath, Emmantiensien, Mielikki, Sheela Peryroyl, Silvanus, Skerrit, Oberon, Osiris, Titania, Verenestra, the Seldarine, various Animal Lords
FOES:	Malar, Moander (dead), Talos, the Queen of Air and Darkness, the drow pantheon (except Eilistraee)
SYMBOL:	Oak tree
WOR. ALIGN.:	LG, NG, CG, LN, N, CN

Rillifane Rallathil (RILL-ih-fane RALL-uh-thihl) is protector of the woodlands and guardian of the harmony of nature. He is often likened by his priests to a giant ethereal oak tree, so huge that its roots mingle with the roots of every other plant in the Realms, that stands at the heart of Arvandor, the High Forest of Olympus. The great tree draws into itself all the ebb and flow of seasons and lives within the woodlands of the green elves. At the same time, it defends and sustains those lands against disease, predation, and assaults of all kinds. The Leaflord is the patron of the Sy-Tel'Quessir and revered by many voadkyn.

When the Sy-Tel'Quessir settled the Yuirwood, the Seldarine merged with the ancient gods of the Yuir, transforming them into aspects of the various powers of the elven pantheon. Both Magnar the Bear and Relkath

of the Infinite Branches, also known as Many-Limbed, Many-Branched, and the Old Man of the Yuirwood, became aspects of the Leaflord. Relkath easily merged with and slowly reinvigorated a primitive facet of the Leaflord's nature that had been slowly overshadowed over the ages by the increasingly tamed way of life of the Fair Folk, even among the Sy-Tel'Quessir. As a result of this subtle change of heart, in the centuries since absorbing Relkath, Rillifane's primordial spirit has returned to the fore to great effect. Concurrently, the Sy-Tel'Quessir and Cha-Tel'Quessir (half-elves of the Yuirwood) have rediscovered the ways of their most primitive ancestors and reforged their tribal cultures, eschewing the formation of successors to the great green elven civilizations such as Illefarn, Thearnytaar, Eiellûr, and Syòrpiir. In contrast to the obvious impact of the absorption of Relkath by the Leaflord, Magnar the Bear was almost totally subsumed after being absorbed, and this aspect of Rillifane is little remembered even among Cha-Tel'Quessir. The half-elves of the Yuirwood speak only of Magnar's Great Sleep, a centuries-long hibernation from which the Bear has yet to emerge.

Much like Ubtao, Ulutiu, and Uthgar, Rillifane is served by a host of great spirits including the primeval Bear (comingled with Magnar the Bear by the Cha-Tel'Quessir), Eagle, Raven, and Wolf, among others. These aspects of the Leaflord are recognized only by the Sy-Tel'Quessir and a few Cha-Tel'Quessir and not by the other elven or half-elven subraces. Unlike those other powers' worshipers, however, Rillifane's followers do not venerate any one great spirit exclusively, although they may have done so in the distant past. Instead, the Leaflord's faithful call upon one or more spirits associated with their god as appropriate for the situation at hand.

Rillifane is on good terms with all the Seldarine, as well as most sylvan and faerie powers. The Leaflord's primary concern is that all creatures have the opportunity to act out their roles in nature without abusing them, a concern Rillifane shares with Corellon Larethian, the great creator and protector of the Fair Folk. Solonor Thelandira and Rillifane work together closely to preserve and protect the natural world, but they do differ fundamentally on the issue of hunting. In the spirit of the alliance that binds the Great Archer and the Leaflord, Solonor does not permit his priests and followers to hunt within the woods where Rillifane's brooding, forbidding presence cautions against this, unless their need is great. While Rillifane permits hunting for food by hungry folk, he detests hunting for sport. Rillifane is closely allied with Emmantiensien the Treant-King and Silvanus the Oak Father. The trio's conversations are many and seemingly endless to others, as none of the three is given to hasty thought or expression. Rillifane is always a respected guest at the Seelie Court, and aside from Emmantiensien, he is friendliest with Skerrit the Forester and often romantically linked with Verenestra the Oak Princess.

Rillifane is quiet, reflective, and enduring over eons unchanged. He is the least flighty of all the Seldarine, the least likely to act on a whim, and often grave and self-absorbed. The Leaflord rarely sends an avatar to the Prime, disliking direct action and preferring that his priests carry out his wishes. Rillifane's avatar appears only when major destruction of a Tel'Quessir (usually Sy-Tel'Quessir) habitat is threatened. The appearance of such an avatar is heralded by sudden gusts of wind shaking leaves from the trees, a sign unmistakable to his priests.

Rillifane's Avatar (Druid 34, Ranger 33, Bard 23, Mage 18)

Rillifane appears as a green-skinned male elf clad in armor of living bark, armed with a great greenwood staff or long bow. He makes no sound as he moves, speaks very rarely, and fires his bow in silence. He favors spells from the spheres of all, animal, elemental, healing, plant, sun, weather, thought, and time and from the elemental schools, although he can cast spells from any sphere or school.

AC –3; MV 15; HP 227; THAC0 –10; #AT 2
Dmg 1d6+15 (quarterstaff +5, +8 Str, +2 spec. bonus in quarterstaff) or
1d6+13 (long bow +5, +8 Str)
MR 50%; SZ M (6 feet tall)
Str 20, Dex 21, Con 22, Int 20, Wis 23, Cha 19
Spells P: 15/14/13/13/11/10/9, W: 5/5/5/5/5/3/3/2/1
Saves PPDM 2, RSW 4, PP 4, BW 4, Sp 5

Special Att/Def: Rillifane wields the Oakstaff, a quarterstaff +5 with all the powers of a staff of the woodlands, a staff of swarming insects, and a staff of thunder and lightning. At will, the Leaflord can cause the Oakstaff to transform into a long bow +5. Any arrow shot from Rillifane's bow can damage any type of being, even those affected only by weapons of a certain magical bonus. Any creature struck by an arrow fired from this bow by the avatar must make a successful saving throw vs. spell or die instantly. Otherwise, flight arrow damage, as noted above, is sustained. Rillifane usually carries 1d3 other miscellaneous magical items of a kind suitable to his nature as a woodland or elemental power with him as well (such as a ring of elemental (earth) command, wand of flame extinguishing, Quaal's feather token, etc.).

Similar to the 4th-level priest spell call woodland beings, the Leaflord may summon up to 100 Hit Dice of sylvan or natural woodland creatures to do his bidding each day. With a wave of his hand, the avatar can cast each of the following effects three times per day: charm person or mammal, fire quench, turn wood, wall of thorns, and warp wood. At will, he may cast tree (oak) or employ transport via plants in woodlands and speak with plants. The Leaflord's movements in woodlands are 99% likely to be absolutely silent.

Rillifane cannot be harmed by caused wounds, diseases, poisons, gas attacks, or energy drains. Rillifane can be struck only by +2 or better magical weapons.

Other Manifestations

Rillifane manifests infrequently, but when he does it takes the form of a green or amber nimbus that envelops a creature or tree. Any creature so enveloped gains the power to cast a single priest spell from the spheres of animal or plant. Typical powers granted to creatures include animal friendship, goodberry, locate animal or plant, pass without trace, speak with animals, speak with plants, or tree, all of which are cast as if the caster were a 7th-level priest (if she or he is not already higher). Any tree enveloped by the Leaflord's aura animates as a treant at maximum hit points. Sometimes such changes are permanent, and other times the tree reverts to its original form after serving Rillifane for a period of time.

The Seldarine call on agathinon, asuras, and ancient treants as their preferred servants, but Rillifane is also served by aasimar, aasimon, alaghi, amber dragons, atomies, badgers, bariaurs, bears, belabra, bhaergala, bombardier beetles, buraq, cantobeles, cath shee, centaurs, cooshee, dryads, earth elementals, einheriar, eladrins, elven cats, ethyks, faerie dragons, feystags, foo dogs, forest spirits, giant lynxes, giant sundews, grigs, hamadryads, hollyphants, hybsils, jaguars, jungle giants, jungle snakes, kholiathra, leopards, leprechauns, lythari, mist dragons, mold men, monkey spiders, moon-horses, nature elementals, norans, sprites, swanmays, mountain lions, nymphs, oreads, owls, pixies, porcupines, pseudodragons, quickwood, ratatosk, reverend ones, seelie faeries, silver dogs, singing trees, skunks, small forest mammals, stag beetles, sunflies, sylphs, talking owls, thornies, thylacines, tigers, unicorns, vampire moss, warden beasts of the forests, werebears, wereboars, weretigers, wild boars, wild stags, wolverines, wolves, and wood giants. He demonstrates his favor through the discovery of amber, emeralds, microline, the sudden changing of colors of a single leaf or an entire tree, the budding and rapid growth of a new tree limb, or the sudden appearance of a forest animal that approaches to be petted without fear. The Leaflord indicates his displeasure by causing the leaves of an entire branch to suddenly fall off in front of the offending individual's feet, creating the sound of twigs repeatedly snapping in a rapid succession, or causing an object such as an acorn to fall out of the sky and strike the offending individual on the head.

The Church

CLERGY:	Clerics, druids, mystics
CLERGY'S ALIGN.:	NG, CG, N, CN
TURN UNDEAD:	C: Yes, D: No, Mys: No
CMND. UNDEAD:	C: No, D: No, Mys: No

All clerics (including multiclassed half-elven clerics), mystics, and specialty priests (including multiclassed half-elven specialty priests) of Rillifane receive religion (elf) and reading/writing (Espruar) as bonus nonweapon proficiencies.

Rillifane is venerated by nearly all the Sy-Tel'Quessir, and his priests serve as the spiritual and moral leaders of most green elven tribes and communities. The Leaflord's church is greatly admired by the other subraces of the Fair Folk for its principled stand in favor of the preeminence of nature, and the faith's priests are widely respected wherever they travel. Nevertheless, the uncompromising stance of some members of Rillifane's clergy sometimes leads to conflicts over both tactics and degree with the leaders of the Ar-Tel'Quessir, the Teu-Tel'Quessir, and other churches of the Seldarine. Halflings, particularly tallfellows, gnomes, particularly forest gnomes, centaurs, and hybsils all pay homage to the Leaflord if they live in or on the border of elven woodlands. Dwarves rarely come into contact or conflict with the forest-dwelling followers of Rillifane, and humans tend to view the Leaflord as simply an even more primitive and wild aspect of Silvanus the Oak Father.

Rillifane's temples are actually huge oak trees with platforms built among the branches and vine bridges connecting them to each other and platforms in adjoining trees. Shrines of the Leaflord, always a grand oak tree deep within the depths of a forest but too small to serve as a temple of the Leaflord, are chosen by members of Rillifane's clergy after receiving a dream or vision directing them to particular tree. Such shrines are marked by the priest with a carving of a small canary in the trunk about 2 feet from the ground. With the cutting back of forests and the subsequent growth of trees selected as shrines, it is not unheard of for such symbols to be discovered high above the ground and/or on the edge of a much-shrunken woods. Should a shrine be defiled in any way, the dedicating druid (or nearest worshiper of Rillifane if the druid is dead) instantly knows of the action and is expected to do everything possible to bring about the defiler's death.

Novices of Rillifane are known as Acorns. Full priests of the Leaflord are known as Oakhearts. In ascending order of rank, the titles used by Rillifanean priests are Felsul, Silverbark, Laspar, Hiexel, Blueleaf, Phandar, Duskwood, Shadowtop, and Weirwood. High-ranking priests have unique individual titles, and druids have titles reflecting their place in the hierarchy of that branch of the faith as well. Specialty priests are known as druids (or skinwalkers). The clergy of Rillifane includes green elves (52%), moon elves (26%), lythari (8%), gold elves (6%), half-elves of various ancestries (4%), voadkyn (3%), and a handful of other elven races as well (1%). Rillifane's clergy is dominated by specialty priests (75%), including multiclassed half-elven specialty priests, but includes clerics (20%), including multiclassed half-elven clerics, and mystics (5%) as well. The clergy of Rillifane contains a pretty even number of male (51%) and female (49%) members.

Dogma: The Great Oak draws energy from all the living creatures of the world and nourishes, sustains, and protects them from outside threats. Live in harmony with the natural world, allowing each living being the opportunity to serve out its natural purpose in life. As the Leaflord's countless branches, his faithful are to serve as his mortal agents in the natural world. Defend the great forests from those who would ravage their riches, leaving only destruction in their path. Contest both the quick and the slow death of Rillifane's bounty and hold strong like the great oaks in the face of those who can see only their own immediate needs.

Day-to-Day Activities: The church of the Leaflord generally keeps to itself, extending itself only to help fellow elves and other sylvan beings. The church hierarchy is organized regionally and divided into branches, as each type of priest serves a specific role. The druids who compose the bulk of Rillifane's clergy tend to the health of the forests and those who dwell within, fiercely contesting any attempt to further reduce those forests that remain. Many clerics serve as ambassadors of the faith, working outside the communities of the Sy-Tel'Quessir to educate other races and even other elven subraces how to better dwell in harmony with nature. The few mystics found within the clergy act much as individual druids do, eschewing the formal organization of the circles. In times of war, however, the leaders of each region unite the branches of the faith and the Sy-Tel'Quessir warriors into a single force.

Rillifane's priests are deadly enemies of those who hunt for sport or those who harm trees maliciously or unnecessarily. In particular, all priests of Rillifane have a great hatred for the priests of Malar, since the followers of the Beastlord often make elves the object of their hunts and their ethos is anathema to those who serve the Leaflord. Rillifane's priesthood is charged with rooting out and destroying sentient plants whose nature has been twisted by external forces into a warped perversion of nature. In particular, they seek to destroy hangman trees, obliviax, death's head trees, black willows, serpent vines, and any form of evil treant, including dark trees.

Holy Days/Important Ceremonies: Rillifane's faithful gather twice yearly at the vernal and autumnal equinoxes to hold fey dances in large groves of oak trees deep in the heart of great forests. The Budding is a joyful celebration of new life celebrated through dance and song and preceded by an extended period of fasting. A ritual hunt of an ancient and noble hart is undertaken on this day, from which the venison serves to break the fast of the Leaflord's faithful. This ritual honors Rillifane's bounty and reminds his followers of the natural cycle of life that plays out beneath the Leaflord's boughs. The Transformation marks the arrival of autumn and the vibrant hues that bedeck the canopies of the Leaflord around this time. The Sy-Tel'Quessir and elves of other subraces who seek a form of spiritual rebirth or a major change in their lives gather to celebrate Rillifane's eternal promise that the trees will bloom again and that life is a process of continual renewal.

Major Centers of Worship: Moontouch Oak is the name of both a gargantuan oak tree over 300 feet tall and the temple of the Leaflord nestled amidst the forest giant's boughs. Located at the heart of the Tangled Trees region of Cormanthor on the northern bank of the Elvenflow where Moontouch Creek joins the River Duathamper, the temple tree is believed to be the largest living oak in Faerûn. Some elven legends claim that the tree is actually the still-living remnants of an avatar of the Leaflord that led several clans of the Sy-Tel'Quessir eastward, away from the devastation of the Crown Wars, many centuries ago. Moontouch Oak has housed approximately two score green elven druids of the Circle of Emerald Leaves in its branches since the early days of the Sy-Tel'Quessir settlement of Arcorar, as the Elven Woods were then known. From –982 DR, with the coming of Venominhandar to the Emerald Vale, until –206 DR, when the great green wyrm was finally slain, the druids of Moontouch Oak were sorely besieged, as were their kin, but the temple-tree was never abandoned, despite numerous attacks by the wyrm and its minions. With the death of Venom, as the dragon was known, the Sy-Tel'Quessir set about reclaiming the woodlands, now known as the Tangled Vale, under the direction of the druids of Moontouch Oak. Nine centuries later, when the Army of Darkness ravaged Cormanthyr and eventually destroyed Myth Drannor, the druids of Moontouch Oak again stood firm in the face of the nycaloth-led assault, and the temple tree of Rillifane was never violated. Nine millennia after the conclusion of the Crown Wars, Moontouch Oak stands unbowed. The temple consists of a network of platforms sculpted from the tree's branches and hollows cultivated in the great oak's trunk, all of which are linked by bridges of woven vines. *Hallucinatory terrain* spells and the thick leaf coverage mask the religious community's very existence from the outside world, but the influence of the Circle of Emerald Leaves is felt throughout the Tangled Vale and beyond. The aged green elf who leads the Circle is Great Druid of the Tangled Vale Katar Oakstaff, who was a child in the final years of Coronal Eltargrim's reign before Myth Drannor fell.

Affiliated Orders: While rangers are not included in the church hierarchy of Rillifane, many such elven warriors do serve in loose fellowships affiliated with individual druid circles as the militant arm of the faith. Each such band of rangers has its own name, but collectively they are known as the Order of the Oakstaff.

Priestly Vestments: The ceremonial garb of the Leaflord's priests includes a laurel wreath worn on the head and armor fashioned of tree bark. Dark green dyes are rubbed into the armor to show rank within the church, with the darkest hue reserved for the high priests of the faith. Tree bark armor provides protection equivalent to leather armor, but the wearer incurs a –1 penalty for all saving throws against fire. The holy symbol of the faith is an acorn enclosed in amber.

Adventuring Garb: When adventuring, members of Rillifane's clergy favor armor and weapons made from natural materials such as wood and animal parts, including those with magical enhancements.

Specialty Priests (Druids)

REQUIREMENTS:	Wisdom 12, Charisma 15
PRIME REQ.:	Wisdom, Charisma
ALIGNMENT:	N
WEAPONS:	Club, dagger, dart, long bow, scimitar, short bow, sickle, sling, spear, staff
ARMOR:	Leather, hide, or tree bark armor, wooden shield
MAJOR SPHERES:	All, animal, elemental, healing, plant, sun, weather
MINOR SPHERES:	Divination, thought, time
MAGICAL ITEMS:	Same as druids
REQ. PROFS:	Animal lore
BONUS PROFS:	Herbalism

All of Rillifane's specialty priests are druids. Their abilities and restrictions, aside from the changes noted above and later in this section, are summarized in the discussion of elven priests in "Appendix 1: Demihuman Priests" and detailed in full in the *Player's Handbook*.

- Druids of Rillifane must be elves, half-elves, or wood giants (voadkyn). While most of Rillifane's druids are green elves, elves and half-elves of every subrace are called to be specialty priests of Rillifane's clergy.
- Elven druids of Rillifane are not allowed to multiclass. Half-elven druids of Rillifane are allowed to multiclass as fighter/druids, druid/mages, or fighter/mage/druids, but not as druid/rangers.
- At any time prior to reaching 7th level, green elven druids of Rillifane, sometimes known as skinwalkers, can seek out a totem animal in a ritual involving fasting and meditation for 1d4 days followed by 1d4 days of following the animal that appears. Once a green elven druid gains enlightenment and wisdom from the totem animal, she or he can thereafter shapechange into that animal form (and only that form). At 1st level, she or he can assume the totem animal form once every three days for 2d6 hours. At 2nd or 3rd level, she or he can assume the totem animal form once every two days for 2d10 hours. At 4th, 5th, or 6th level, she or he can assume the totem animal form once per day for 2d20 hours. Between 7th and 10th level, she or he can assume the totem animal form once per day for 3d20 hours. At 11th level and above, a skinwalker can assume the totem animal form at will for as long as she or he wishes. Such transformations receive the same benefits and are governed by the same restrictions as the shapechange ability of druids as detailed in the *Player's Handbook*. This skinwalking ability replaces the normal ability of a druid of 7th level or greater to shapechange into any reptile, bird, or mammal form. Once a totem animal is chosen, it cannot be changed nor can the druid renounce the skinwalking ability so as to increase the number of forms she or he can assume.

The type of totem animal is determined randomly or selected by the DM. Examples of totem animals include crows, hawks, cooshee, coyotes, foxes, otters, raccoons, rabbits, lynxes, mountain lions, cath shee, and bears, but never wolves. Some myths claim that the lythari were once green elven druids of Rillifane who had wolves as their totem animals. The bond forged between those priests and the spirit of the wolf was so strong that they became the Ly-Tel'Quessir. It is unclear why the Sy-Tel'Quessir can no longer receive wolves as totem animals, but no such union has resulted from a skinwalker ritual in millennia.

Rillifanean Spells

In addition to the spells listed below, priests of the Protector may cast the 2nd-level priest spell *banish blight*, the 5th-level priest spell *tree healing*, and the 7th-level priest spell *create treant*, all of which are detailed in the entry for Mielikki in *Faiths & Avatars*, as well as the 4th-level priest spell *oakheart*, detailed in the entry for Silvanus in *Faiths & Avatars*. For over a century, the Leaflord has not granted the 7th-level spell *conjure nature elemental*, detailed in the entry for Chauntea in *Faiths & Avatars*, for reasons unknown.

1st Level

Sap (Pr 1; Conjuration)

Sphere:	Plant
Range:	10 yards
Components:	V, S, M
Duration:	3 rounds+1 round/level
Casting Time:	4
Area of Effect:	10 foot×10 foot area
Saving Throw:	Special

A *sap* spell coats everything within the area of effect in tree sap. After the spell is cast, any creature entering the area of effect slows to half its movement rate while in the affected region. Any creature caught within the area of effect when the spell is cast must make a successful saving throw vs. spell or be covered in the sticky substance. Those who succeed can reach the nearest unaffected surface by the end of the round, although their movement rate is also reduced to half normal while within the area of effect. Those who fail their saving throws have their movement rate reduced to 1 and have their Dexterity reduced by half. Casting spells, employing magical items requiring any sort of movement, or launching any sort of physical attack is impossible while under the effects of this spell. In addition to any lost bonuses (because of lower Dexterity), the creature incurs a +2 Armor Class penalty (to a maximum of AC 10). Winged creatures and those employing magical items such as *wings of flying* cannot fly while within the affected area.

A *free action* spell or ring or similar effect negates the effects of a *sap* spell for the affected individual only. Thoroughly dousing an individual covered in *sap* with wine also ends the effect.

The material components of this spell are the priest's holy symbol and a drop of tree sap.

2nd Level

Acorn Barrage (Pr 2; Enchantment)

Sphere:	Combat, Plant
Range:	10 yards
Components:	V, S, M
Duration:	1 round
Casting Time:	5
Area of Effect:	1 acorn/level
Saving Throw:	None

By means of this spell, the priest can cause a barrage of acorns, either naturally or magically created, to launch from his or her hand, from the ground, or from an oak tree within 10 yards. The acorns can fly up to 40 yards, striking as many targets as the priest wishes (up to the number of acorns the priest can animate). The priest may direct the acorns in any combination at any living or nonliving targets that she or he can see. The priest can animate a maximum of one acorn per experience level.

Each acorn requires a successful attack roll to hit a target. The attack roll is made as though the acorns were missile weapons hurled by the priest with a sling. Range penalties do apply. Dexterity modifiers apply only if the acorns are held in the hand. The acorns inflict 1d2 points of damage each.

This spell is ineffective under water, and acorns hurled by this target have no magical ability to follow a moving target beyond the accuracy of the priest's targeting.

The material components of this spell are the priest's holy symbol and as many acorns as needed.

4th Level

Amber Prison (Pr 4; Conjuration)

Sphere:	Plant
Range:	Touch
Components:	V, S, M
Duration:	Special
Casting Time:	7
Area of Effect:	One creature
Saving Throw:	Neg.

This spell encases the target in a hard, translucent coating of fossil resin in a yellow, orange, or brownish-yellow hue. However, if the target makes a successful saving throw vs. spell, this spell dissipates without effect. A creature targeted by this spell who is already covered in tree sap, such as the result of a *sap* spell, receives a –4 penalty to the saving throw vs. spell when attempting to avoid the effects of an *amber prison*. The caster can choose to have a part of the target remain free from the amber when the spell is cast. If the priest attempts to leave a significant part of the subject's anatomy free, such as the head or a hand, the target receives a +2 bonus to the saving throw to avoid the effect. (Pinpoint accuracy, such as leaving just a nose or a finger free, is not possible when using this spell.)

An *amber prison* takes some time to harden, and during that period it is possible for the target to break free or be broken free from the solidifying resin. Every round after the spell is cast, the target can make an attempt to bend bars/lift gates, success indicating that the *amber prison* shatters. The percentage chance of success drops by 1% every round, to a minimum of 0. Creatures of huge size or larger can automatically shatter the *amber prison* in one round. An *amber prison* is considered to be AC 0 for purposes of attempting to shatter it with a weapon. For every 3 points of physical damage inflicted on an *amber prison*, the imprisoned target of the spell suffers 1 point of damage, but his or her chance to bend bars/lift gates increases by 3%. If 30 or more total points of physical damage are inflicted on an *amber prison*, it immediately shatters, freeing the subject trapped within. A *shatter* spell causes an *amber prison* to crumble completely if it fails a saving throw vs. crushing blow.

If the target's air passages are covered by the *amber prison*, the prisoner still receives some air flow through the semipermeable encasement as it hardens. As such, suffocation occurs much slower than might be imagined. Every round in which the target is encased, she or he must roll a successful Constitution check. Every failure indicates that the target's effective Constitution drops by 1 point. When the target's effective Constitution score reaches 0, she or he dies from suffocation. If freed before suffocation occurs, the subject's Constitution rises to the original value at a rate of 1 point per round.

When the effects of an *amber prison* end, no matter how the subject is freed (even after death), all remaining shards of amber melt into worthless, nonmagical tree sap.

The material components of this spell are the priest's holy symbol, a chunk of amber worth at least 100 gp, and a drop of sap.

Sehanine Moonbow

(Daughter of the Night Skies, Goddess of Moonlight, the Lunar Lady, Moonlit Mystery, the Mystic Seer, the Luminous Cloud, Lady of Dreams)

Intermediate Power of Arborea, CG

PORTFOLIO:	Mysticism, dreams, death, journeys, transcendence, the moon, the stars, the heavens, moon elves
ALIASES:	Angharradh
DOMAIN NAME:	Olympus/Arvandor
SUPERIOR:	Corellon Larethian
ALLIES:	Baravar Cloakshadow, Cyrrollalee, Dumathoin, Eilistraee, Kelemvor, Leira (dead), Lurue, Milil, Mystra, Oberon, Savras, Segojan Earthcaller, Shaundakul, Selûne, Titania, Urogalan, the Seldarine
FOES:	Cyric, Gruumsh, Malar, Myrkul (dead), the Queen of Air and Darkness, Shar, Talos and the Gods of Fury (Auril, Umberlee, and Malar), Velsharoon, the drow pantheon (except Eilistraee)
SYMBOL:	Full moon with moonbow (opaque milky crescent)
WOR. ALIGN.:	LG, NG, CG, LN, N, CN

Whereas Corellon's symbol is the crescent moon, Sehanine Moonbow (SEH-ha-neen MOON-boe) is the elven goddess of the moon or, more specifically, the full moon. She governs divinations, omens, and subtle magics and protects against madness. She watches over the dreams of the elves, keeping them from harm while in reverie and sending omens to protect them from future dangers. Sehanine watches over the passage of elven spirits from the world, and she is protectress of the dead. The Daughter of the Night Skies is also a guardian and guide to those elves whose days in the mundane world of mortals are done and who seek to travel from the lands they know and love to distant refuges such as Evermeet. She also watches over such refuges and ensures they are kept safe from intrusion. Sehanine governs long journeys, both physical and spiritual, and in elven cultures that proclaim the reality of reincarnation, Sehanine and Corellon work together to guide the spirit to its best subsequent incarnation as it works its way toward perfection. Although Sehanine is venerated by all the Fair Folk (including half-elves and a handful of gnome illusionists), she is particularly revered by moon elves, who view her as their protector, and gold elves, who are the most withdrawn from the world of all the elven subraces. Tel'Quessir seeking to explore transcendental mysteries, awaiting passage to Evermeet or Arvandor, or undergoing physical or spiritual journeys pray to the Goddess of Moonlight, as do mystics, seers, diviners, and weavers of illusions.

Alternately called the wife and daughter of Corellon, Sehanine is the mightiest of the female powers in the elven pantheon. Identified with the mystic power of the moon, Sehanine's tears are said to have mingled with Corellon's blood and given life to the elven race. The elves do not forget this. Sehanine is both the primary aspect of Angharradh and one of the three elven goddesses—the other two being Hanali Celanil Aerdrie Faenya and Hanali Celanil—who collectively form the Triune Goddess. This duality tightly binds Sehanine with the two other senior elven goddesses, and the three collectively serve alongside Corellon in leading the Seldarine, just as the Goddess of Moonlight is said to do in other myths. Sehanine has excellent relations with all of the Seldarine, and it is her kind-heartedness that soothes the anger of Shevarash in his darkest fury and her welcoming nature that brings Fenmarel back to Arvandor on occasion. The Luminous Cloud has few strong relationships outside of the Seldarine, for her otherworldliness is beyond even most other deities. Sehanine works closely with Selûne, for the two share similar concerns, and the Goddess of Moonlight is a strong ally of Eilistraee, whom she considers an adopted daughter of sorts. Sehanine has also forged alliances with some of the other human and demihuman powers who oversee death, but she has no tolerance for those who practice in the black arts of necromancy. (Sehanine does tolerate careful experimentation in white necromancy, and it is said that she vigilantly oversees the creation of baelnorn as a necessary, if undesirable, practice.) Sehanine's antipathy for Lolth has existed since the latter was Araushnee, consort of Corellon and the mastermind who nearly engineered the death of the Protector and the defeat of the Seldarine. The Lady of Dreams actively opposes the nefarious schemes of the Spider Queen and the other drow powers. With the rise of humanity and its rapacious expansion into traditional elven homelands, Sehanine has found her energies increasingly occupied by thwarting the destructive ravages of gods such as Auril, Cyric, Malar, Talos, and Umberlee.

Sehanine rarely concerns herself directly with events in the Realms, aside from weaving illusions around secret elven retreats such as Evermeet, Synnoria, Rucien-Xan, and Myth Dyraalis and guiding elves coming to those lands. Her power waxes and wanes with the phases of the moon, growing strongest when the moon is full. As befits the elven goddess of mysteries, Sehanine is cloaked in secrets and illusions and rarely speaks her mind directly, preferring to communicate through a process of dreams, visions, and other mystic experiences. The Goddess of Moonlight is truly spiritual and ephemeral being who evades any attempt to define her and whose serenity surrounds her like a mantle of moondust.

Sehanine's Avatar (Illusionist 34, Diviner 34, Mystic 28, Ranger 20)

Sehanine appears as an elven female who is simultaneously youthful and ageless, wearing a diaphanous flowing gown formed of semi-solid gossamer moonbeams. She favors spells from the spheres of all, astral, charm, divination, guardian, healing, necromantic, protection, summoning, sun, and travelers and from the schools of alteration, divination, elemental (air), and illusion/phantasm, although she can cast spells from any sphere or school.

AC –4; MV 15, Fl 24; HP 186; THAC0 1; #AT 2
Dmg 1d6+3 (*quarterstaff +2*, +1 Str)
MR 90%; SZ M (5 feet tall)
Str 17, Dex 20, Con 18, Int 22, Wis 24, Cha 22
Spells P: 13/12/12/12/12/11/6, W: 8/8/8/8/8/7/7/7*
Saves PPDM 2, RSW 3, PP 4, BW 4, Sp 4
   *Numbers assume one extra divination or illusion/phantasm spell per spell level.

Special Att/Def: Sehanine wields *Moonshaft*, a *quarterstaff +2* with all the powers of a *staff of the moonglow* and a *staff of night* (both described in the Encyclopedia Magica™, *Volume 4 & Index* tome), but she prefers to employ spells, wands, and innate abilities to disable enemies if forced to fight. Her gown has the powers of a *cloak of displacement*, and she carries *wands of polymorphing* and *paralyzation*. Drops of light that fall from Sehanine's gown form tiny pools on the earth. At most one such drop falls per turn. If swiftly bottled, it serves the imbiber as a *potion of invisibility* (one dose).

Sehanine's power as a spellcaster varies with the phase of the moon. While neither the number of spells she can cast nor her saving throws, hit points, or her THAC0 change, the spell level at which all spells and spell-like powers are cast varies from +5 (when the moon is full) to –5 (when the moon is new or fully eclipsed). Sehanine can cast *sleep* three times per day. She can cast *false seeing* (the reverse of *true seeing*) at will at any single creature within 120 feet who fails a saving throw vs. spell with a –4 penalty. She trails *motes of moonlight* as she walks and can send forth a beam of them in any direction she points. She can communicate through *dream* spells at will without entering a trance state. She can create a *moonbow* or *moonbridge*, once per round, at will. All saving throws made against Sehanine's illusion/phantasm spells are made with a penalty of –2, cumulative with any other saving throw penalties that might apply to individual spells. Anyone looking at the Daughter of the Night Sky must make a successful saving throw vs. spell with a –2 penalty or fall into a deep sleep for 1d4 turns.

Sehanine herself is wholly immune to all illusion/phantasm spells and mind-affecting or mind-altering spells or abilities, including psionics, and her infravision extends as far as her normal vision. She is immune to any spell that causes blindness. Sehanine can be struck only by +2 or better magical weapons.

Other Manifestations

Sehanine manifests through dreams and waking visions. She grants boons only to worshipers who enter an altered state of awareness, whether it be through meditation, dance, or trance.

The Mystic Seer's most common manifestations grant the recipients the ability to call on Sehanine's wisdom (as the 7th-level wizard spell *vision*), enable them to communicate through dreams to other beings (as the 5th-level wizard spell *dream*), or allow them to view truths otherwise unseen (as the 5th-level priest spell *true seeing*). Sehanine sometimes manifests in drugged, drunken, unconscious, or sleeping beings and causes them to ramble on about random topics in all languages known (as the 1st-level wizard spell *dreamspeak*, also known as *Detho's delirium*, from *Pages from the Mages* or the *Wizard's Spell Compendium, Volume 1*). The foci of such a manifestation's need not be worshipers or even elves, although the Luminous Cloud manifests as such only if at least one worshiper is present. The Goddess of the Moon sometimes manifests in enspelled worshipers when they are sleeping or in a trance state so as to unravel spell effects (as the 6th-level wizard spell *greater spelldream* from the *Wizard's Spell Compendium, Volume 2*) or to utter cryptic prophecies to those in attendance.

The Seldarine call on agathinon, asuras, and ancient treants as their preferred servants, but Sehanine is also served by aasimar, aasimon (particularly lights), azmyths, baelnorn, buraq, cath shee, cooshee, einheriar, eladrins,

electrum dragons, elven cats, feystags, firestars (known as moondancers to the faithful), firetails, frosts, hollyphants, incarnates of faith and hope, kholiathra, ki-rin, lythari, mist dragons, moon dogs, moon-horses, mortai, nic'Epona, pixies, radiance quasielementals, reverend ones, seelie faeries, silver dogs, silver dragons, sprites, sunflies, t'uen-rin, and even a tiefling or two. She demonstrates her favor through the discovery of mithral, moonbars, moonstones, silver, sunstones and the occurrence of a meteor shower or single fallen star. The Daughter of the Night Skies indicates her displeasure by causing the moon to appear to wink at the target of her wrath.

The Church

Clergy:	Clerics, crusaders, mystics, specialty priests
Clergy's Align.:	NG, CG, N, CN
Turn Undead:	C: Yes, Cru: No, Mys: No, SP: Yes
Cmnd. Undead:	C: No, Cru: No, Mys: No, SP: No

All clerics (including multiclassed half-elven clerics), crusaders, mystics, and specialty priests of Sehanine receive religion (elf) and reading/writing (Espruar) as bonus nonweapon proficiencies. All priests of Sehanine may pray for and receive the 1st-level wizard spell *sleep* as one of their 1st-level spells if they desire. Their casting time for this spell is 4, not 1. All other aspects of the spell remain the same.

The church of Sehanine is generally perceived as removed from the daily concerns and outward expression of everyday life. As such, little is known of the Lady of Dreams and her clergy members by the N'Tel'Quess. Among elves, Sehanine's faith is closely held and deeply cherished, for the Luminous Cloud envelops and binds together all the Tel'Quessir. For the Fair Folk, Sehanine embodies the joy at the heart of the elven spirit, and her priests serve as guides to the next world or life that one may achieve through transcendence.

Sehanine's temples are soaring monuments open only to elves and a few pious half-elves. Most such temples are constructed of white stone (often marble) and shaped so as to suggest imminent flight. Symmetry and circles are highly prized by the faith, reflected in the architecture of Sehanine's houses of worship. The central chapel is always perfectly circular and is usually open to the night sky or covered by a retractable or transparent dome. Great gardens and hedgerow mazes often encircle the main structure, their formations imitating the paths of the heavenly bodies in the night sky above. Near long-standing temples, megaliths form great stone circles for use in tracking the position of the moon, fixed stars, and wandering stars by elven astrologers.

Novices of Sehanine are known as the Mooncalled. Full priests of the Daughter of the Night Skies are known as the Heavenly. In ascending order of rank, the titles used by Sehanite priests are Stargazer, Moondancer, Sky Seer, Vision Seeker, Omen Teller, Dream Walker, Transcendentalist and Reverent Dreamer. High-ranking priests have unique individual titles. Specialty priests are known as starsingers. The clergy of Sehanine includes moon elves (54%), gold elves (34%), wild elves (5%), half-moon elves (4%), half-gold elves (1%), and half-wild elves (1%), and a handful (1%) of dark elves, sea elves, winged elves, and half-elves of those ancestries. Sehanine's clergy includes specialty priests (40%), mystics (35%), clerics (20%), including multiclassed half-elven clerics, and crusaders (5%) and the priesthood is nearly evenly split between females (52%) and males (48%).

Dogma: Life is series of mysteries whose secrets are veiled by the Luminous Cloud. As the spirit transcends its mortal bounds and new mysteries are uncovered, a higher form is achieved and the cycle of life continues. Through contemplation and meditation, communion with the Lady of Dreams is achieved. Through dreams, visions, and omens revealed in sleep or the reverie, the Daughter of the Night Sky unveils the next step along the path and the next destination on the endless journey of mystic wonder that is life and death and life. Revere the mysterious moon, who draws forth tides of being from us all.

Day-to-Day Activities: Sehanine's priests are the seers and mystics of elven society. They serve as the spiritual counselors to elves and half-elves who seek to embark on journeys in search of enlightenment so as to transcend their current state of being. As shepherds and protectors of the dead, Sehanine's priests organize and administer funeral rites and guard the remains of the fallen. They seek out and destroy undead creatures, for Sehanine holds such creatures—with the notable exceptions of baelnorn and other good-aligned undead beings who voluntarily prolong their existence in order to serve their kin—to be blasphemous. As defenders of elven homelands, Sehanine's clergy are responsible for weaving and maintaining the illusions that guard those sanctuaries that remain and for divining potential threats to their continued existence. The prime task of adventuring priests is the retrieval of lost arcane and magical knowledge, especially if it pertains to illusions and/or divinations. Other seek out isolated elven enclaves, bringing them news of the Retreat and practical assistance in preparing for such a journey if they so choose. (Sehanine's priests do not provide any guidance along the journey itself, as this is done through direct intuitive revelation by the Lady of Dreams herself.)

Holy Days/Important Ceremonies: Sehanine's faithful celebrate a wide variety of holy days, all of which are tied to the position of various heavenly bodies, particularly the phase of the moon and various types of eclipses. Many of these celebrations occur once per decade, once per century, or even once per millennium. The most frequent celebrations of Sehanine's faithful are held monthly beneath the light of the full moon. Lunar Hallowings, as such holy days are known, are marked with personal meditation and collective entrance into a communal trance. On occasion, Sehanine manifests through her assembled worshipers, knitting together their spirits in a true sharing of minds. Such holy days are concluded with a joyous freeform dance beneath the most visible manifestation of the Goddess of Moonlight (the moon) that lasts until the first rays of dawn. Once per year, Sehanine's faithful gather on the night of the Feast of the Moon for the Mystic Rites of the Luminous Cloud. Similar in many ways to the monthly Lunar Hallowings, the Mystic Rites of the Luminous Cloud are notable for the visible manifestation of the Lady of Dreams whereby the assembled worshipers are enveloped in a mantle of shimmering, silvery light that then rises up and darts across the heavens. During such mystical flights across the sky, the sacred mysteries of Sehanine are revealed to the participants, with each participant learning secrets appropriate to his current level of spiritual development. The ceremony concludes when the nimbus of light returns to the earth and the forms of Sehanine's worshipers coalesce.

When the time comes for an elf to leave the ordinary lands of mortals and pass on to Arvanaith, it is common for the individual elf to spend several days in vivid daydreams and waking reverie. Exactly when this happens is unknown to any elf, even to Sehanine's own priests. It is usually obvious to other elves when one of the Tel'Quessir is undergoing this change, but two marker events are definitive indicating that the Transcendence has begun. First, Sehanine sends the elf a vision where she or he must go to begin this journey from the world. Second, within the lens of the elf's eye appears a telltale opaque milky crescent, the moonbow of Sehanine's honorific name. When the time comes for an elf great in wisdom and accomplishment to depart, an accompanying full moon may display the moonbow as an event in nature. On rare occasions at such a time, other elves join with the one about to depart in a shared trance state, sharing memories and knowledge in a direct telepathic communion known as the Circle of Transcendence. In some elven cultures this departure is a physical one, that is the elf walks off alone into the wilderness and his or her body is never found. In other societies, the elf's spirit departs its material body, leaving behind a lifeless husk.

In cases of violent or accidental death where the spirit is not utterly destroyed, Sehanine's priests serve in the stead of the departed spirit in the ritual of Transcendence. A Ceremony of Recovery involves one or more days of meditation and mystic communion with the natural and spiritual worlds. If successful, the priest channels the lost spirit through his or her own link with Sehanine, enabling the spirit to transcend to Arvanaith. During such ceremonies, after contacting the lost spirit, Sehanine's priests display the characteristic moonbow within the lens of their eyes, but such manifestations of the Lady of Dreams vanish immediately upon the ritual's conclusion.

Elven funeral rites vary widely from community to community and from individual to individual, reflecting the nature of the departed spirit. If the elf has simply answered Sehanine's call, as opposed to death by accident or violence, death rituals are more often a celebration that the elf has achieved the joys of Arvanaith than a time of mourning. In either case, if the body remains, the method of disposal varies as well. In some communities, the assembled mourners gather with great pomp to watch the body be interred in the ground, with examples of the late elf's artistry and passions displayed and speakers expounding on the merits of the deceased. Other elven societies bury the body immediately, regarding it as a mere husk from which the life force has departed. After disposing of the shell, they cele-

brate the spirit of the elf who once resided there. Still other elves believe that burning is the only way to truly rid the spirit of its earthly ties. Not only does it free the spirit for Arvanaith, it also prevents anyone from using the body for nefarious purposes.

Elven cultures that bury the bodies of the fallen with great ceremony leave the most durable archeological evidence of their funeral rites, and thus the practice of interring the bodies of elven dead in formal tombs is less widespread than commonly perceived. Of all the elven subraces resident in Faerûn, the remains of gold elves, and to a lesser extent moon elves, are most commonly interred within burial vaults, but that practice is by no means universal within those subraces, nor is it restricted to them alone. Elven tombs are typically hewn from bedrock and warded by powerful magic. Whereas the Stout Folk typically trust in mechanical traps to ensure the sanctity of their fallen kin, the Fair Folk weave protective mantles into the construction of tombs and eschew false tombs and extended gauntlets of traps. The Luminous Cloud is said to gather elven tombs to her bosom, and most are cloaked in enduring illusions designed to obfuscate their location and to mislead grave robbers who would violate the sanctity of the elves interred within. Elven tombs are typically subdivided into three chambers, each of which is of circular or rectangular shape with an arching dome-shaped or semicylindrical ceiling, respectively. The first such chamber represents the world from which the elf has departed and is dominated by carvings of the natural world including plants and animals from sylvan settings. Commonly a pool of crystalline water, enspelled so as to prevent evaporation or stagnation, is set in the center of the first chamber. The second chamber is dominated by a stone bier on which rests the body of the fallen elf. The Fair Folk rarely place their dead within a sarcophagus unless the body is badly mauled, as they feel to do so restricts the freedom of the spirit in Arvanaith. The walls of the second chamber are adorned with examples of the fallen elf's gifts, and the ceiling is carved with a depiction of the heavens as they were at the time of the elf's death. (By analyzing such records, sages are sometimes able to date the age of a particular elven tomb.) The third chamber represents Arvanaith, the destination of the elf's spirit. The walls of the chamber are carved with depictions of the Seldarine (as the pantheon is perceived in the culture that created the tomb). The ceiling is carved with a stylized depiction of a crescent moon within a full moon, symbolizing the combined role of Corellon and Sehanine (or Angharradh) in overseeing the passage of the spirit to Arvanaith. The third chamber is otherwise empty, but all who enter are overwhelmed with a feeling of great peace. This is not a magical effect but a collective manifestation of the Seldarine. Violent action or thought is impossible within the third chamber of an elven tomb. Items of magic and other riches are rarely entombed within an elven tomb when they could be better used by those elves who have not yet journeyed to Arvanaith. Nevertheless, ancient elven tombs are sometimes filled with artifacts of elven artistry, including examples of magical items or spells developed by the elf interred within the tomb. Sometimes the elves of a single house are interred within the same crypt. In such cases the first chamber may be shared by the individual tombs, with the second and third chamber housing the body of the fallen and representing the destination of the spirit.

Major Centers of Worship: While the largest temples of Sehanine are found on the Green Isle, in the Vale of Evereska, and in the woods of the Elven Court, the site most sacred to the Lady of Dreams is the Tears of Aloevan. This is an otherworldly cloud of magic accessed through a mystical pool of water found in an unearthly sylvan glen at the heart of Ardeep Forest. Much like the dark elf Qilué Veladorn serves both Mystra and Eilistraee today, Aloevan was once the Chosen of both Sehanine and the Lady of Mysteries. The moon elven queen's descent into madness and her eventual death was a tragic loss for both the Fair Folk and the other human and demihuman races of the region caused by her inability to control the silver fire that raged within her. Upon her death, Aloevan's spirit was unable to pass on to Arvanaith and was instead enmeshed within a nimbus of silver fire that hovered between Faerûn and Arvandor. To assuage the madness of their queen who had sacrificed so much, seven priests of Sehanine created a link between the natural world and the spiritual limbo in which Aloevan's spirit was trapped. For centuries, Sehanine's priests have labored to ease the torment of the mad queen and in the process have recreated the long-lost court of Ardeep within the pocket dimension formed from the silver fire Aloevan could no longer control. Aloevan's spirit is now capable of manifesting in a form similar to that of a spectral harpist within the Court of Silver Fire, as the mystic temple is known, but her laughter and tears are tinged with madness and only the beneficence of the seven priests enables her to hold on to the vestiges of her sanity. During times of a solar eclipse, passage between the glen in Ardeep Forest and the Court of Silver Fire is possible. At such times a priest of Sehanine may make his or her way to Aloevan's mystical court at Sehanine's request to replace one of the seven priests who is ready to pass on to Arvanaith. Although many others have sought entrance to Aloevan's court, none have returned to tell the tale, so it is unknown if any who were not called there by Sehanine have ever succeeded.

Affiliated Orders: The Knights of the Seven Sacred Mysteries are well known for their service in defense of elven homelands from N'Tel'Quess invaders as well as their ongoing efforts to retrieve tomes of long-lost elvish lore and items of elven artistry from the ruins of fallen realms. The order is composed of elves and a few half-elves, most of whom are of moon elven or gold elven ancestry, and it includes many crusaders, as well as a handful of clerics, fighters, and rangers, in its ranks. The order's entrance requirements are kept secret from nonmembers, but it is generally known that there are seven tiers in the order's hierarchy and that it can take a century or more of faithful service to Sehanine before the next mystery is revealed. Knights of the First Mystery are the lowest ranking members of the order, while Knights of the Seventh Mystery are some of the most powerful agents of Sehanine in the Realms. No half-elf has ever risen higher than the rank of Knight of the Fourth Mystery, but it is not known if that fact indicates the difficulty of ascending the order's rarefied ranks and the small representation of half-elves in the order or if it is a manifestation of a bias against those who have some degree of N'Tel'Quess ancestry. The order's preeminent chapter houses are found in the city of Ruith on Evermeet, the Vale of Evereska, and amidst the Tangled Trees settlement of the Elven Woods.

The Sentinels of the Moonbow are a small fellowship of rangers pledged to the service of the Goddess of Moonlight. Sentinels watch over animals that may hold the reincarnated spirits of elves of ages past and that may once again assume elven form. These rangers in the service of Sehanine are also pledged to the tracking and destruction of undead creatures whose existence is a blight upon the land.

The Veiled Choir is a mysterious sisterhood of elven mystics whose very existence is obscured by a veil of legend, mystery, and rumor. Sisters of the Veiled Choir are renowned for their prophetic ability, and their visions are revealed in an unending chorus of song. Only a handful of these ancient elven seers are believed to exist, residing in ancient temples of the Lady of Dreams whose very existence has long been forgotten by even the Fair Folk. Young elves in search of adventure often attempt to find the sisterhood's oracular redoubts of which, curiously, none are located on the Green Isle. On rare occasions a lucky and persistent elf discovers a Veiled Cantoria, but those who seek to simply follow in their footsteps always fail in their quest. The reward for reaching a sanctuary of the Veiled Choir is always the blessing of the Luminous Cloud and a mysterious prophecy, the unraveling of which may consume the rest of the recipient's life.

Priestly Vestments: Members of Sehanine's clergy favor silvery-white diaphanous gowns (for the priestesses) and togas (for the priests). A silver diadem is worn on the head, oftentimes with a moonstone pendant dangling above the brow. Simple sandals are worn on the feet, and a silver lace sash is worn around the waist. The holy symbol of the faith is a moonbar crystal carved in the shape of a small flat disk (approximately three inches in diameter), and such devices are often worn around the neck on a delicate-looking silver or mithral chain.

Adventuring Garb: Priests of the Daughter of the Night Skies favor mail over leather armor, and most carry round shields whose unadorned, reflective fronts are polished mirror bright. Such armor is typically fancifully adorned, emphasizing the grace and bearing of the wearer. Senior priests are well known for the elaborate suits of elven chain mail or elven plate mail they favor, although many such suits were lost with the fall of Myth Drannor. Sehanine's clergy favor missile weapons, particularly short and longbows, and staves. *Staffs of the moonlight* and *rings of shooting stars* are particularly prized.

Specialty Priests (Starsinger)

REQUIREMENTS:	Intelligence 9, Wisdom 13
PRIME REQ.:	Intelligence, Wisdom
ALIGNMENT:	CG
WEAPONS:	Bow, javelin, quarterstaff, sickle, sling, staff-sling
ARMOR:	Any
MAJOR SPHERES:	All, astral, charm, divination, guardian, healing, necromantic, protection, summoning, sun, travelers
MINOR SPHERES:	Numbers, thought, wards
MAGICAL ITEMS:	Same as clerics
REQ. PROFS:	Bow, bowyer/fletcher
BONUS PROFS:	Astrology, navigation

- Starsingers must be elves or half-elves. While most starsingers are moon elves or gold elves, elves and half-elves of every subrace are called to be specialty priests of Sehanine's clergy.
- Starsingers are not allowed to multiclass.
- Starsingers receive a +2 bonus to their saving throws vs. death magic. This bonus improves to +4 on the night before, during, and after the full moon. It drops to +0 on the night before, during, and after the new moon.
- On nights before, during, and after the full moon, opponents' saving throws against spells and granted powers employed by starsingers suffer a −2 penalty. On the night before, during, and after the new moon, this becomes a +2 bonus for the opponent of the starsinger.
- Starsingers may cast wizard spells from either the divination school or illusion/phantasm school as defined in the Limited Wizard Spellcasting section of "Appendix 1: Demihuman Priests." At 1st level, each starsinger must choose one school or the other, and the choice of study is irrevocable thereafter.
- Starsingers can cast *motes of moonlight* (as the 1st-level priest spell) or *sleep* (as the 1st-level wizard spell) once per day.
- At 3rd level, starsingers can cast *mirror image* (as the 2nd-level wizard spell) or *infravision* (as the 3rd-level wizard spell) once per day. If latter effect is cast upon an elf or half-elf who naturally possesses infravision, the use of this granted power increases his or her infravision to 120 feet.
- At 5th level, starsingers can cast *detect spirits* or *starshine* (as the 3rd-level priest spells) once per day.
- At 7th level, starsingers can cast *commune* or *moonbeam* (as the 5th-level priest spells) once per day.
- At 10th level, starsingers can cast *dream* (as the 5th-level wizard spell) or *true seeing* (as the 5th-level priest spell) once per day.
- At 13th level, starsingers can cast *greater spelldream* (as the 4th-level wizard spell detailed the *Wizard's Spell Compendium, Volume 2*) or *Presper's moonbow* (as the 5th-level wizard spell detailed in *Pages from the Mages* or the *Wizard's Spell Compendium, Volume 3*) or *vision* (as the 7th-level wizard spell) once per day.
- At 15th level, starsingers can cast *heal* (as the 6th-level priest spell) or *gate* or *holy word* (as the 7th-level priest spells) once per day.

Sehanite Spells

In addition to the spells listed below, priests of the Lunar Lady may cast the 2nd-level priest spell *Eilistraee's moonfire*, detailed in the entry for Eilistraee, the 3rd-level priest spell *moon blade*, detailed in the entry for Selûne in *Faiths & Avatars*, and the 2nd-level priest spell *moon shield*, detailed in the entry for *The Moonweb*, a holy tome of Selûne, in *Prayers from the Faithful*.

1st Level

Motes of Moonlight (Pr 1; Alteration)

Sphere:	Sun
Range:	0
Components:	V, S
Duration:	1 hour+1 turn/level
Casting Time:	4
Area of Effect:	10 feet/level
Saving Throw:	None

This spell creates a trail of shimmering, silvery lights in the direction pointed by the caster. The beam of light thus caused is equal in brightness to a shaft of moonlight, and any priest of Sehanine standing among the *motes of moonlight* is treated as if they were bathed in the light of a full moon. Objects in darkness beyond this beam can be seen, at best, as vague and shadowy shapes. The spell is targeted at any fixed point within range of the beam's terminus, 10 feet per level of the caster, and she or he must have a line of sight or unobstructed path to that point when the spell is cast. The beam starts at the caster's holy symbol. Once cast, *motes of moonlight* hang in place, even if the target or holy symbol is then moved. The caster can dismiss the motes on command.

This spell is often used in conjunction with a *moonbridge* incantation in regions where the moon's light does not reach and on nights of the new moon.

3rd Level

Detect Spirits (Pr 3; Divination)

Sphere:	Divination
Range:	0
Components:	V, S, M
Duration:	10-foot × 60-foot path
Casting Time:	6
Area of Effect:	Special
Saving Throw:	None

This divination reveals the presence of disembodied or noncorporeal spirits of all types, including wraiths, ghosts, spectres, astrally projecting creatures, characters or monsters employing *magic jar* or possession, and animal and nature spirits. Characters or monsters who are simply invisible, phased, or ethereal do not count as spirits, since they are physically present in the flesh despite their unusual status. The caster detects spirits in a path 10 feet wide and 60 feet long; any spirits of the type described above in the area of effect are revealed in their preferred form or appearance for all to see. Simply detecting a spirit does not give the caster any special ability to communicate with or attack the entity.

The material component for this spell is a small pendant of copper wire worth at least 20 gp.

4th Level

Moonbow (Pr 4; Alteration)

Sphere:	Sun
Range:	0
Components:	V, S, M
Duration:	1 round/2 levels
Casting Time:	7
Area of Effect:	Special
Saving Throw:	None

This spell creates a crystalline bow the size and strength of a long bow or short bow, as chosen by the caster during the casting. A thin beam of silvery light serves as the bowstring and, when it is drawn back causes a shimmering, silver arrow to magically appear in the proper position.

Only the caster can employ the crystalline bow created by means of this spell, and it fades into a luminous cloud that dances about for 1d4+1 rounds and then vanishes into nothingness if released for any reason. At most, two shafts from the bow can be fired per round at any target within range. Each shaft trails a stream of *motes of moonlight* (as the 1st-level spell of the same name but lasting only 1d4+1 rounds) delineating the path of flight. A successful attack roll is required to hit an opponent with a shaft fired by the *moonbow*. After any attack, whether it hits or misses, the arrow fired vanishes in a fashion similar to the crystalline bow, as described above.

The effects of a successful hit with a *moonbow* vary depending the type of the target. If shot into a region of magical *darkness*, the arrow negates the effect but otherwise does nothing but trail the aforementioned *motes of moonlight*. Against a living creature, a *moonshaft* acts as a bolt of energy from the Positive Material Plane, inflicting 7d4 points of damage. Against undead creatures who draw their power from the Negative Material Plane and rare natives of that Inner Plane, a *moonshaft* inflicts 14d4 points of damage and bathes the target in silvery *faerie fire* for 1d4+1 rounds. (Multiple successful attacks against a single undead creature do not double the effectiveness of the *faerie fire* effect, but instead simply extend the effect if the

additional period ends later than the first.) Against undead creatures who draw their power from the Positive Material Plane (such as mummies) and rare natives of that Inner Plane, a *moonshaft* cures 7d4 points of damage per level, but otherwise has no effect.

The material components of this spell are the priest's holy symbol and the silken thread of a cobweb coated in dew gathered beneath the light of the full moon.

Moonbridge (Pr 4; Alteration)

Sphere:	Sun
Range:	120 yards
Components:	V, S, M
Duration:	1 round/level
Casting Time:	7
Area of Effect:	Special
Saving Throw:	None

This spell transforms a shaft of moonlight, whether it be naturally occurring or magically created (such as by a *motes of moonlight* spell), into a translucent bridge capable of supporting beings of good alignment. Beings of neutral alignment can also walk atop a *moonbridge* as long as they stay in direct physical contact with the caster (or form part of a chain, of which at least one member must be in physical contact with the priest). Evilly aligned beings find *moonbridges* as insubstantial as moonlight. In areas bathed in moonlight with no distinctive shafts of light, the caster can create a *moonbridge* from his or her location at the time in any direction, as long as the entire length of the *moonbridge* is bathed in moonlight without interruption.

A *moonbridge* is at most 3 feet wide and at least 20 feet long, although it can extend as far as 120 yards, according to the caster's desire. It lasts as long as the spell's duration or until ordered out of existence by the caster. The angle of inclination and direction of the *moonbridge* varies as noted above.

The material components of this spell are the priest's holy symbol and a vial of holy water that has been bathed in the light of the last full moon for at least 6 consecutive hours.

Shevarash
(The Black Archer, the Night Hunter, the Arrow Bringer)

Demipower of Arborea and Limbo, CN

PORTFOLIO:	Hatred of the drow, vengeance, military crusades, loss, revenge
ALIASES:	Elikarashae
DOMAIN NAME:	Olympus/Arvandor and Limbo/Fennimar
SUPERIOR:	Corellon Larethian, Fenmarel Mestarine
ALLIES:	Callarduran Smoothhands, Hoar, Psilofyr, Shar, Shaundakul, the Seldarine
FOES:	Blibdoolpoolp, the Blood Queen (of the aboleth), Deep Duerra, Diinkarazan, Diirinka, Great Mother, Gzemnid, Ilsensine, Ilxendren (of the ixzan, freshwater Underdark relatives of the ixitxachitl), Laduguer, Maanzecorian (dead), the drow pantheon (except Eilistraee)
SYMBOL:	Broken arrow above a tear drop
WOR. ALIGN.:	LG, NG, CG, LN, N, CN

Shevarash (SHEV-uh-rash), who embodies the hatred the Fair Folk hold for the drow, is the elven god of vengeance and military crusades. He is venerated by elves and half-elves who have suffered the loss of loved ones through violence, particularly those who burn with revenge against the drow, and by those who have sworn to destroy the Spider Queen and the other evil gods of the dark elves. Some elven theologians speculate that Shevarash serves to gather in the bitterness and hatred that has riven the elven race since the Crown Wars, thus keeping the contagious evil of the Spider Queen from spreading to the elven population at large.

Nearly 6,000 years ago, circa –4400 DR, on Midwinter night— the longest, darkest night of the year—an army of duergar and drow poured forth from the Underdark and overran both the dwarven realm of Sarphil on the southern shore of the Moonsea and the Elven Court at the heart of the great forest of Arcorar. The Dark Court Slaughter claimed the lives of countless elves and dwarves, including most of the assembled leaders of the Fair Folk and the Stout Folk who had come to the Elven Court to reestablish their long-standing alliance. Among the fallen was the family of the archer-guard Shevarash, once a carefree hunter of the Elven Court. In an anger-tinged prayer to Corellon, Shevarash vowed to become the Seldarine's hand against the drow to extract revenge for the loss of his family. The grief-stricken warrior swore a grim oath neither to laugh nor smile until the drow goddess Lolth and her foul followers were destroyed. It was a tall order, but for the remainder of his life, Shevarash became the deadliest nemesis of the drow, raiding their underground cities, slaying their priests, and destroying shrines to their foul gods. Shevarash was finally slain by a horde of myrlochar (soul spiders) after killing the high priestess Darthiir'elgg Aleanrahel and six of her consorts, circa –4070 DR. Upon his death and with the assistance of Fenmarel Mestarine, Shevarash the Black Archer underwent apotheosis to become the Night Hunter and the Arrow Bringer.

When the Sy-Tel'Quessir settled the Yuirwood, the Seldarine merged with the ancient gods of the Yuir, transforming them into aspects of the various powers of the elven pantheon. Of the Seldarine, Shevarash absorbed the aspect of Elikarashae, the youngest of the Yuir gods, as Elikarashae had only recently undergone apotheosis. The Sy-Tel'Quessir settlers of the Yuirwood incorporated the legends of Elikarashae into their own myths of Shevarash, and in the folklore of the elves of the Yuirwood, the god's aspect as Elikarashae became a mighty elven warrior who bore three great weapons: the spear Shama, which could speak to elf warriors of pure heart and noble mind; the sling Ukava, which never missed; and the club Maelat, which could only be wielded in the defense of the Yuir. Elikarashae was credited with defeating many of the Yuir's enemies, particularly the mountain trolls and drow, for which the great warrior had been lifted up to Arvandor and made a god, or so the myths held.

Shevarash maintains no permanent realm in the Outer Planes, although he visits both Arvandor and Fennimar frequently. The Black Archer is closely allied with the Seldarine, particularly the more militant powers, although none of the elven gods are as consumed with hatred and vengeance as he is. Although Shevarash considers Fenmarel his superior, the Lone Wolf and the Black Archer share little in common aside from their mutual hatred of the drow. Of the rest of the Seldarine, Shevarash works closely with Corellon and Solonor in particular, but the other two powers are more concerned with defending elven realms than bringing the war into the tunnels of the drow, much to the Black Archer's frustration. As consumed by his hatred of the dark elven powers now as he was during the night of the Dark Court Slaughter, the Black Archer now hunts Lolth, Ghaunadaur, Vhaeraun and the other dark gods of the drow directly, often venturing into the Abyss to do so. Shevarash has moderated his hatred toward Eilistraee and the good-aligned drow who worship the Dark Maiden. He does not kill them out of hand, but he still dislikes them thoroughly. In life, the Black Archer's extended forays into the Underdark nurtured his antipathy for the other evil denizens of the Night Below, and as a god he battles their divine patrons as well. Shevarash's all-consuming crusade is such that the only long-standing divine allies he has garnered since his apotheosis are those such as Callarduran Smoothhands and Psilofyr who share his hatred of the drow and their pantheon of dark gods. As humanity has begun to venture ever deeper into the Underdark, Shevarash has begun to work more with human gods such as Shaundakul and Hoar. To the great distress of the other members of the Seldarine, the Black Archer's bitterness is such that he has recently begun to find solace in the soothing embrace of Shar.

Shevarash is taciturn, violent, and consumed by thoughts of bitterness and revenge. He never displays any emotion aside from anger and a brief exultation or triumph after each victory. The Black Archer has no patience for those who do not share his zeal for vengeance, and he has no interest in moderating his crusade in the interests of peace. The Black Archer often dispatches his avatar in anticipation of an attack by the drow on a relatively undefended elven settlement, or if he appears too late to prevent a repeat of the slaughter that still haunts him, Shevarash pursues the dark elves back into the Underdark and hunts them down until all are dead.

Shevarash's Avatar (Ranger 25, Cleric 18)

Shevarash appears as a tall, muscular green elf clad in elven chain mail and a shadowy cloak. He favors spells from the spheres of all, chaos, combat, elemental (earth), guardian, healing, necromantic, protection, summoning, sun, travelers, and war, although he can cast spells from any sphere.

AC –3; MV 15; HP 174; THAC0 –4; #AT 2
Dmg 2d4+10 (+13 vs. drow) (*broad sword +3/+6 vs. drow*, +5 Str, +2 spec. bonus in broad sword) or 1d8+10 (*long bow +5*, +5 Str)
MR 75%; SZ M (6 feet tall)
Str 20, Dex 21, Con 18, Int 18, Wis 19, Cha 20
Spells P: 11/10/10/9/6/4/2
Saves PPDM 3, RSW 5, PP 4, BW 4, Sp 6

Special Att/Def: Shevarash wields two principle weapons. The Black Archer's *Black Bow* is a *long bow +5*, and any arrow shot from it acts as an *arrow of slaying drow* if it hits. In melee combat, Shevarash wields *Traitorbane*, a *broad sword +3/+6 vs. drow*. In addition to any bonuses Shevarash normally receives, he also receives a +4 bonus to all melee or missile damage rolls against drow opponents.

When Shevarash appears as Elikarashe to the Yuir, he wields three principle weapons: *Shama*, a *spear +3* of chaotic good alignment (Dmg 1d10+13 [*spear +3*, +10 Str]); *Ukava*, a *sling +1* that is constantly loaded with *bullets +1* and never misses (Dmg 1d4+12 [*sling +1* and *bullets +1*, +10 Str]); and *Maelat*, a *club +4* that causes all those who try to wield it for any reason other than defending the Yuir or the Yuirwood 1d20 points of damage during each round they touch or grasp the club (Dmg 1d8 +14 [*club +4*, +10 Str]).

Once per round, at will, Shevarash may cast *dispel magic*, *light*, *lower resistance*, or *nondetection*. *Faerie fire* is ineffective against him. and he can see perfectly even in absolute darkness (such as that created by a *darkness* spell). He can be struck only by +1 or better magical weapons.

Elven Powers: Shevarash

Other Manifestations

Shevarash commonly manifests as a bright white flame that envelops a being to be aided or weapon to be wielded. In the former case, the Black Archer's manifestation typically confers the benefits of an *armor*, *haste*, *ironguard*, *protection from normal missiles*, or *shield* spell. In the latter case, Shevarash's power imbues the weapon with an additional +1 attack bonus and +2 damage bonus vs. chitines, driders, drow, myrlochar, and yochlol above any beyond all magical bonuses (if any) the weapon already possesses (to a maximum attack or damage bonus of +6).

The Seldarine call on agathinon, asuras, and ancient treants as their preferred servants, but Shevarash is also served by aasimar, eladrin (particularly ghaeles), and reverend ones. He demonstrates his favor through the discovery of webstone engraved with his symbol, spider webs that have been torn apart, and crushed (normal-sized) spiders. The Black Archer indicates his displeasure by manifesting as twin red flames that appear in the darkness like the eyes of a malevolent beast.

The Church

CLERGY:	Crusaders, specialty priests, rangers
CLERGY'S ALIGN.:	CG, CN
TURN UNDEAD:	Cru: No, SP: No, R: No
CMND. UNDEAD:	Cru: No, SP: No, R: No

All crusaders and specialty priests of Shevarash receive religion (elf) and reading/writing (Espruar) as bonus nonweapon proficiencies.

The cult of Shevarash is little known, even among the Fair Folk, except in communities where attacks by drow raiders are fairly common. Although the dedication and passion with which Shevarashan priests pursue their hated quarry is much appreciated by their kin, few elves can understand the intense, all-consuming hatred that consumes members of this faith. To the Fair Folk, the all-consuming hunger for vengeance exhibited by Shevarashan avengers has more in common with the wars waged by the N'Tel'Quess than it does with elven sensibilities. As such, there is a measure of pity among elves for the sad fate of those who join this cult out of grief, and many elven theologians doubt that the spirits of those who follow the Black Archer are able to ascend to Arvanaith when they inexorably fall to the overwhelming spells and blades of the drow. Among other surface races, the cult of Shevarash is almost unknown. In the Underdark, however, the reign of terror waged against the drow and the other evil-aligned races by the fanatic warriors of Shevarash is much appreciated by those few good-aligned races that dwell in the deep tunnels. Deep-dwelling dwarves, deep gnomes, and myconids in particular give succor to followers of the Black Archer and greatly appreciate their tireless crusade.

Temples of Shevarash are located in cave mouths that connect elf-occupied forests with the deep tunnels of the Underdark and from which drow raiders have emerged (or might emerge). The Black Archer's temples are constructed to serve first and foremost as nigh-impregnable forts blocking access in either direction that can be held by a handful of defenders. Most are designed to withstand long-term sieges and include well-stocked armories, storerooms, and cisterns of fresh water. The walls of Shevarash's houses of worship are typically adorned only with trophies seized from fallen drow. Shevarash's followers sometimes construct shrines to their god in the Underdark, but such monuments are makeshift at best, quickly built in caves that serve as a temporary base of operations. Fallen warriors of the cult are brought back to the surface to be interred or, if absolutely necessary, buried in unmarked cairns in the Underdark so as to hide them from the drow.

Novices of Shevarash are known as the Haunted. Full priests of the Black Archer are known as Dark Avengers. Shevarashan priests have unique individual titles, most of which include a litany of the foes they have slain. Specialty priests are known as dhaeraowathila, an elvish word that can be loosely translated as *drowbane*. The clergy of Shevarash includes green elves (33%), moon elves (32%), gold elves (29%), and half-elves of those subraces (6%). Shevarash's clergy is evenly divided between specialty priests (34%), crusaders (33%), and rangers (33%), and has equal numbers of males (50%) and females (50%).

Dogma: The greatest enemy of the Seldarine is Lolth, who sought the corruption of Arvandor and the overthrow of the Creator. The greatest enemy of the Fair Folk is the drow, the debased followers of the Spider Queen who long ago were enmeshed in her dark web. Redemption and revenge may be achieved through the utter destruction of the drow and the dark powers they serve. Only then may the joy of life begin anew. Hunt fearlessly!

Day-to-Day Activities: The followers of Shevarash are consumed with their quest to root out and destroy the drow and the sources of power of their dark gods. As such, since its founding by the lieutenants of Shevarash after their leader's death and apotheosis, the church of the Black Archer has been totally focused on its military campaign against the drow. Individual priests spend their days drilling, designing tactics for warfare in the Underdark, guarding known entrances to the Underdark, and participating in hit-and-run raids and major assaults on drow-held territories in the Underdark. Not a few members of the Black Archer's clergy join adventuring bands that intend to explore the Underdark, for the cult of Shevarash is small and additional swords in the battle against the drow are always welcomed.

Holy Days/Important Ceremonies: Midwinter Night is observed by the cult of Shevarash in memory of the Dark Court Slaughter. On this holy day, those who wish to join the ranks of the clergy are inducted into the faith and vows of unceasing vengeance are shouted into the night. In honor of their god's original vow, each new priest swears to never again laugh or smile until the Spider Queen and the other dark gods of the drow are slain and their followers are destroyed.

Major Centers of Worship: The Vault of Unquenched Vengeance lies beneath a great jet black oak on the outskirts of the Elven Court in the great forest of Cormanthor. This natural cavern is located amidst the roots of the ancient tree and housed the body of Shevarash for a day before his apotheosis. Since the Black Archer's ascension, the tree has turned jet black, stopped growing, and never produced any leaves, yet it is apparently still alive. The faithful of Shevarash have transformed his temporary burial vault into a fortified redoubt, for the cave serves as the terminus of the last remaining entrance to the Underdark, or so it is believed, in the vicinity of the Elven Court. The temple also serves as the starting point for many crusades against the drow who still dwell below, and all followers of the Black Archer aspire to complete a pilgrimage to the temple before their deaths.

Affiliated Orders: The church of Shevarash is essentially a military cult, and as such, the priesthood is the martial arm of the faith and there are no affiliated orders outside of the faith. Not every member of the church's disparate army is a member of the clergy, however. Individual bands often adopt their own monikers, much as military units do across the Realms, and based on their successes, achieve varying degrees of renown.

Priestly Vestments: The ceremonial garb of the faith consists of silver chain mail, a blood-red half-cloak, and a silver helm with a fixed half-visor that covers only the upper half of the face. The holy symbol of the faith is a broken arrowshaft that has been dipped in drow blood and *blessed* by a priest of Shevarash.

Adventuring Garb: Priests of Shevarash favor bows and swords, but they employ a wide variety of weapons in their unceasing quest for vengeance. For armor, most Dark Avengers favor chain mail (elven chain mail if available) as a good balance between protection and maneuverability. Followers of the Black Archer have no compunction against seizing the armor and weapons of the drow for their own use.

Specialty Priests (Dhaeraowathila)

REQUIREMENTS:	Strength 11, Dexterity 11, Wisdom 9
PRIME REQ.:	Strength, Dexterity, Wisdom
ALIGNMENT:	CG, CN
WEAPONS:	Any
ARMOR:	Any
MAJOR SPHERES:	All, chaos, combat, elemental (earth), guardian, healing, necromantic, protection, summoning, sun, travelers, war
MINOR SPHERES:	Animal, charm, creation, divination
MAGICAL ITEMS:	Same as clerics
REQ. PROFS:	Bow (any), local history (drow), modern languages (low drow/Undercommon)
BONUS PROFS:	Blind-fighting, tracking, modern languages (drow silent speech)

- Dhaeraowathila must be gold elves, moon elves, green elves, or half-elves. Dark elves and half-dark elves are never called to be specialty priests of Shevarash's clergy, and aquatic elves are effectively barred by their inability to pursue the drow into their homelands in the Underdark.
- Dhaeraowathila can multiclass as dhaeraowathila/fighters.
- Dhaeraowathila may select nonweapon proficiencies from the warrior group without penalty.
- Dhaeraowathila are immune to spells cast by drow spellcasters from the sphere of charm or the school of enchantment/charm.
- Dhaeraowathila are immune to spider venom.
- Dhaeraowathila are considered to have selected drow as their species enemy, much like rangers, and as such receive the corresponding bonuses and penalties. Whenever a dhaeraowathila encounters a drow, she or he gains a +4 bonus to his or her attack rolls. This enmity can be concealed only with great difficulty, so the priest suffers a –4 penalty on all encounter reactions with drow, even those of nonevil alignment. Furthermore, dhaeraowathila actively seek out this enemy in combat in preference to all other foes unless someone else presents a much greater danger.

- Dhaeraowathila can cast *light* (as the 1st-level priest spell) or *spider climb* (as the 1st-level wizard spell) a total of twice per day.
- At 3rd-level, dhaeraowathila can cast *change self* (as the 1st-level wizard spell) or *misdirection* (as the 2nd-level wizard spell) or *undetectable alignment* (as the reverse of the 2nd-level priest spell *know alignment*) once per day.
- At 5th level, dhaeraowathila can cast *dispel magic* (as the 3rd-level priest spell) or *obscurement* (as the 2nd-level priest spell) once per day.
- At 7th level, dhaeraowathila can cast *fly* (as the 3rd-level wizard spell) and *feather fall* (as the 1st-level wizard spell) once per day each.
- At 7th level, dhaeraowathila who are not multiclassed can make three melee attacks every two rounds.
- At 10th level, dhaeraowathila can cast *free action* (as the 4th-level priest spell) or *lower resistance* (as the 5th-level wizard spell) once per day.
- At 13th level, dhaeraowathila are immune to the effects of a *whip of fangs* or a *wand of viscid globs*.
- At 13th level, dhaeraowathila who are not multiclassed can make two melee attacks per round.
- At 15th level, dhaeraowathila can create one *arrow of slaying* keyed to kill drow per month that they devote to the task. They can create no other types of *arrows of slaying*.

Shevarashan Spells

2nd Level

Infrainvisible (Pr 2; Alteration)

Sphere:	Sun
Range:	Touch
Components:	V, S, M
Duration:	24 hours maximum
Casting Time:	5
Area of Effect:	Creature touched
Saving Throw:	None

This spell masks the heat signature of the creature touched, causing it to be undetectable to infravision, although still visible to normal sight. Of course, the *infrainvisible* creature is not magically silenced, and certain other conditions (including *detect invisibility* spells and similar magics) can render the creature detectable. Even allies cannot see the *infrainvisible* creature or his or her gear with infravision unless these allies can normally see invisible things or they employ magic to do so. Items dropped or put down by the *infrainvisible* creature become visible to infravision; items picked up disappear only if tucked into the clothing or pouches worn by the creature. Note however that light and very hot heat sources (such as fire) never become *infrainvisible*, although a source of light or heat can become so (thus, in effect creating a light or heat signature with no visible source).

The spell remains in effect until it is magically broken or dispelled, until the priest or recipient cancels it, until the recipient attacks any creature, or until 24 hours have passed. Thus the *infrainvisible* being can open doors, talk, eat, climb stairs, etc., but if she or he attacks, she or he immediately becomes visible to infravision, although the *infrainvisibility* allows him to attack first if the target is relying solely on infravision and not normal vision. All highly Intelligent (Intelligence of 13 or more) creatures with 10 or more Hit Dice or levels of experience have a chance to detect *infrainvisible* beings. They roll a saving throw vs. spell; success means they noticed the *infrainvisible* being.

The material components of this spell are the priest's holy symbol and a drop of fire beetle ichor.

3rd Level

Shevarash's Infravision (Pr 3; Alteration)

Sphere:	Sun
Range:	Touch
Components:	V, S, M
Duration:	2 hours+1 hour/level
Casting Time:	1 round
Area of Effect:	Creature touched
Saving Throw:	None

By means of this spell, the priest enables the recipient to see in normal darkness up to 120 feet without light. Note that strong sources of light (fire, lanterns, torches, etc.) tend to blind this vision, so the spell's effect does not function efficiently in the presence of such light sources. Invisible creatures are not detectable by infravision.

The material components of this spell are the priest's holy symbol and either a pinch of dried carrot or an agate.

Depress Resistance (Pr 3; Abjuration, Alteration)

Sphere:	Combat
Range:	60 yards
Components:	V, S, M
Duration:	1 turn
Casting Time:	6
Area of Effect:	One creature
Saving Throw:	None

Using this spell, a priest can temporarily reduce the magic resistance of a target creature. The magic resistance of the creature works against the *depress resistance* spell at half its normal value. No saving throw is allowed.

A creature that does not resist the effects of this spell has its magic resistance reduced by 10% for 1 turn. Against drow, the base is 50% plus 2% per level. This spell has no effect on creatures that have no magic resistance.

The material components of this spell are the priest's holy symbol and a broken iron rod.

Solonor Thelandira

(Keen-Eye, the Great Archer, the Forest Hunter)

Intermediate Power of Arborea, CG

PORTFOLIO:	Archery, hunting, wilderness survival
ALIASES:	None
DOMAIN NAME:	Olympus/Arvandor
SUPERIOR:	Corellon Larethian
ALLIES:	Chauntea, Cyrrollalee, Emmantiensien, Eldath, Eilistraee, Ferrix, Fionnghuala, Gwaeron Windstrom, Oberon, Mielikki, Nobanion, Shaundakul, Silvanus, Skerrit, Titania, the Seldarine, various Animal Lords
FOES:	Bhaal (dead), Gorellik, Grankhul, Grolantor, Malar, Moander, the Queen of Air and Darkness, Talos, the drow pantheon (except Eilistraee)
SYMBOL:	Silver arrow with green fletching
WOR. ALIGN.:	LG, NG, CG, LN, N, CN

Solonor Thelandira (SOE-loe-nohr Theh-LAN-dih-ruh) is the elven god of hunting, archery, and survival in wild and harsh places. The Great Archer's prowess with the bow is unmatched by any other power venerated in the Realms. Solonor is concerned with the integrity of nature and the balance between exploitation and agriculture on one hand and fallow, wild terrains on the other. Like Corellon Larethian and Fenmarel Mestarine, the Great Archer watches over the boundaries of elven lands. He instructs the Fair Folk in the art of hiding in and moving through natural foliage so as not to be detected as well as the art of archery and hunting. Solonor is primarily revered by elven and half-elven rangers, hunters, woodsmen, and fighters. In particular, elven hunters appeal to him for better catches of game and elven warriors trapped in hostile territory call on him for aid. In recent centuries a few humans, primarily hunters, have joined his faith as well.

Solonor is allied with all the powers who collectively compose the Seldarine. In particular, the Great Archer works closely with Corellon Larethian, Fenmarel Mestarine, and Shevarash to defend the borders of elven homelands. In many tales, Fenmarel is said to be the brother of Solonor, and despite the former's estrangement from the Seldarine for which Solonor holds Lolth responsible, the Lone Wolf and the Great Archer are still close allies. Solonor has served as Shevarash's mentor since the green elf's apotheosis, and the two are united in their hatred of the Spider Queen and her followers, the drow, although the Great Archer is not as consumed with vengeance as the Night Hunter. Solonor and Rillifane Rallathil work closely to preserve and protect the natural world. Although the Great Archer is more tolerant of the slow growth of civilization than the Leaflord, a philosophical difference that sometimes spills over into the relations between their two faiths, they are united in their efforts to preserve the great forests of the Fair Folk from the relentless expansion of humankind. Solonor and Eilistraee are true kindred spirits, with some myths depicting them as half-siblings and other myths suggesting a burgeoning romantic relationship (much to the dismay of both Shevarash and Fenmarel). Among the nonelven powers, Solonor is closely allied with other powers concerned with the natural world, including Mielikki, Lady of Forests, another goddess with which he has been romantically linked, Silvanus the Oakfather, Skerrit the Forester, and the various Animals Lords, particularly those concerned with hunting such as the Cat Lord and Wolf Lord. Solonor despises powers that favor despoliation over nature, and actively opposes the efforts of such gods and their followers. Solonor's greatest foes are Malar and Talos, followed closely by Lolth and members of the Unseelie Court. The Beastlord's eternal, unquenchable bloodlust is a vile perversion of every principle Solonor holds dear. Likewise, the Destroyer's hunger for destruction works to tear apart the delicate balance the Greater Archer has striven to forge and maintain. The Queen of Air and Darkness, much like the Spider Queen, embodies the corruption that can take root even in the hearts of even those of fey ancestry and against which the Great Archer stands ever vigilant.

Solonor is always in pursuit of quarry, and he rarely remains in one location for very long. Unlike many hunters, the Great Archer stalks prey only out of concern for the overall balance between the species and to destroy evil-doers, particularly the drow. His serious, sometimes grim, demeanor reflects the difficulty he faces in forging a workable compromise between the competing forces of civilization and wilderness, instinct and knowledge, and savagery and domesticity. Solonor's word is his bond, and his pledge is never given lightly. Solonor does not close to do battle with an enemy, but tracks and pursues instead, firing arrows from a never-empty quiver. The favorite tactic of this deity, should he anticipate battling a particularly dangerous foe, is to physically touch that being and then retreat. Once by himself again, he can then manufacture a special *arrow of slaying* designed especially to kill that one opponent, should it strike home. He then hunts his quarry relentlessly, hoping to bring him down in a single shot. Many fiends from the Lower Planes have felt the bite of Solonor's deadly arrows.

Solonor's Avatar (Ranger 34, Druid 29, Bard 19)

Solonor appears as a strong, sinuous male elf clad in a great cloak of living leaves. He casts spells from the spheres of all, animal, combat, divination, elemental, healing, plant, sun, travelers, and weather and favors spells from the schools of alteration, enchantment/charm, and illusion/phantasm, although he can cast spells from any school.

AC –3; MV 15; HP 228; THAC0 –10; #AT 2 (elven long bow—melee) or 3 (bow)
Dmg 1d6+14 (*elven long bow +5*, +9 Str) or 1d8+17 (*long bow +5* and *arrow +3*, +9 Str)
MR 80%; SZ M (6 ½ feet tall)
Str 21, Dex 24, Con 22, Int 20, Wis 20, Cha 19
Spells P: 12/12/11/11/9/9/7, W: 4/4/4/4/4/3/2
Saves PPDM 2, RSW 5, PP 4, BW 4, Sp 6

Special Att/Def: Solonor wields *Longshot*, an *elven long bow +5* (see below under the Adventuring Garb subsection of The Church section) that can shoot as far as the horizon without penalty, and carries the *Quiver of Endless Arrows*, a magical quiver that can supply two *arrows +3* of any type (flight, sheaf, silver, or cold-wrought iron) per round. Twice per day he can draw forth an *arrow of slaying* for any type of creature as desired. If he takes three rounds to enhance the enchantment of a particular *arrow of slaying* after physically touching his intended quarry, Solonor can make it effective against any such individual being of less than demipower status. The Great Archer wears a *necklace of adaptation* and *boots of varied tracks*. In forest and sylvan settings, Solonor can use *improved invisibility*, *pass without trace*, and move without making a sound at will.

Keen-Eye cannot be surprised by any creature within 500 yards of his person, is immune to missiles of any sort, and can bend the flight path of any arrow shot at him so that it turns back around and targets the archer who launched it. He can be struck only by +2 or better magical weapons.

Other Manifestations

Solonor most commonly manifests in one of three ways. Beings are enveloped in a nimbus of silver-green light that confers upon them the benefits of a *protection from normal missiles* spell for the next 7 rounds. Bows engulfed in the same ambient radiance receive a +3 attack bonus on their next three shots. Arrows in flight engulfed in the silver-green fire of Solonor may deliver a spell effect such as *faerie fire*, *flame arrow*, *hold monster*, *shocking grasp*, or the like as if cast by priest of the same level or Hit Dice as the archer. On very rare occasions, such arrows act as an *arrow of slaying* for a particular species or an individual.

The Seldarine call on agathinon, asuras, and ancient treants as their preferred servants, but Solonor is also served by aasimon, androsphinxes, azmyths, bariaurs, black bears, brown bears, bhaerghalas, buraq, cath shee, centaurs, cooshee, dryads, einheriar, eladrin, elven cats, faerie dragons, firbolgs, firestars, firetails, foo creatures, frosts, great cats, griffons, guardinals, hamadryads, hollyphants, hybsils, incarnates of courage, kholiathra, korred, lammasu, lillendi, lythari, moon dogs, moon-horses, oreads, pers, pixies, reverend ones, seelie faeries, silver dogs, sprites, swanmays, sunflies, unicorns, wemics, wolves, and wood giants. He demonstrates his favor through the discovery of bloodstones, obsidian, variscite, or phandar wood, the tinkling of chime oaks in winter, the splitting of an arrow embedded in a target by the next arrow, and the discovery of game in a time of need. Omens granted by the god take the form of natural phenomena, such as unusual flights of birds or strange behavior by wild animals. Keen-Eye indicates his displeasure by causing bowstrings to snap, arrowheads to chip, shatter, or fall off, bows and arrow shafts to warp, or twigs to snap.

The Church

CLERGY:	Clerics, rangers
CLERGY'S ALIGN.:	NG, CG, CN
TURN UNDEAD:	C: Yes, R: No
CMND. UNDEAD:	C: No, R: No

All clerics (including multiclassed half-elven clerics and elven cleric/rangers, a multiclassed combination allowed to elven priests of Solonor) and rangers of Solonor receive religion (elf) and reading/writing (Espruar) as bonus nonweapon proficiencies. Single-classed clerics of Solonor must select a weapon proficiency in either the long bow or short bow, at twice the regular cost.

While Solonor is well regarded throughout elven society, most of his worshipers are drawn from those Fair Folk who live outside the great cities in small forest communities. His worship is particularly prevalent among green elves and moon elven commoners involved in the day-to-day realities of living in harmony with nature and preserving the environment in the face of the destructive impulses of other races. While some gold elves drawn to the simple appeal of living in direct harmony with the woods may be found in Solonor's church, for the most part the Ar-Tel'Quessir and even the haughtiest Teu-Tel'Quessir nobility romanticize the teachings of the Great Archer while contemptuously dismissing those who compose the ranks of the Great Archer's faithful as base and worthy of a small measure of scorn.

Temples of Solonor can be found at the heart of deep forests, only accessible via carefully hidden and guarded woodland paths. The Great Archer's houses of worship are a mixture of natural and carefully sculpted features emphasizing the competing principles that Solonor tries to balance. Most temples are cultivated in a grove of trees carefully tended from seedlings to form two or more concentric rings of forest giants. Each tree is grown so as to form one or more natural hollows within its trunk at various elevations, and vine rope bridges are threaded through each tightly packed grove to connect the chambers in the heart of each tree. At ground level, roots, rocks, earth, plants are woven into near impregnable defensive fortifications to ensure the sanctity of the temple perimeter. Earthen chambers are hewn from the dirt beneath the grove, nestled among the tightly woven root structures. In the surrounding woods, trees are carefully planted so as to create narrow, spokelike paths radiating outward from the central grove. Although not immediately obvious to casual observation, the plant growth along such paths is cultivated so as to impede movement but permit the flight of arrows, thus forming natural shooting galleries in which invaders are easily targeted. Solonor's temples contain both ceremonial chambers adorned with hunting trophies and hollows with more practical applications such as crafting and repairing bows and arrows, the curing of venison and other meats, the tanning of hides, and the carving of bones to form tools and figurines.

Novices of Solonor are known as Fledglings. Full priests of Keen-Eye are known as Hawkeyes. In ascending order of rank, the titles used by Solonoran priests are Fletcher, Bowyer, Archer, Gray Wolf, Snow Tiger, Grizzly Bear, Blood Hawk, Fire Falcon, and Gold Eagle. High-ranking priests have unique individual titles. Specialty priests are known as rangers. The clergy of Solonor includes moon elves (33%), green elves (28%), gold elves (22%), half-moon elves (8%), half-green elves (3%), half-gold elves (2%), lythari (3%), and a handful (1%) of elves and half-elves of other ancestries. Solonor's clergy includes rangers (36%), cleric/rangers (33%), and clerics (31%), including half-elven multiclassed clerics other than cleric/rangers. The clergy is almost equally divided among males (52%) and females (48%).

Dogma: Walk in harmony with nature and oppose the efforts of those who would disturb her delicate balance. Preserve the wild places from excessive encroachment, and work with those who would settle the land to preserve the beauty that first attracted them. Hunt only for sustenance, culling the old and the weak from the herd so that all species may prosper. Like an arrow in flight, it is difficult to arrest the consequences of an action. Choose your targets carefully, for an ill-considered action can have a long-reaching impact.

Day-to-Day Activities: Solonor's priests serve as scouts and archers in elven armies, as bowyers, fletchers, and archery instructors in elven settlements, and as hunters and providers for far-flung rural communities. Among those Fair Folk who largely eschew the trappings of civilization, members of Solonor's priesthood preside over initiation ceremonies into adulthood. Hawkeyes serve the Great Archer by working to maintain the balance of nature. Solonor's priests are deadly enemies of those who worship Malar, Talos, or Moander, and they often join forces with those who serve the Leaflord in order to exterminate followers of those evil gods whenever they make their presence known.

Holy Days/Important Ceremonies: Solonor's faithful generally eschew frivolous celebrations, considering them unnecessary distractions to the tasks at hand. Once per lunar month, under the soft light of the full moon, the Great Archer's faithful assemble to give thanks for the skills Solonor has taught and the bounty thus provided. Hunters sacrifice hunting trophies that cannot otherwise be employed, and unbroken arrows engraved with the symbol of Solonor are fired into the sky to poke holes in the firmament and allow the light of Solonor's teachings to shine forth on his people (these arrows are never fired in a direction that would cause them to fall where they might hurt someone, including straight up). Each Shieldmeet, known to the Fair Folk as *Cinnaelos'Cor* (*the Day of Corellon's Peace*), the followers of Solonor assemble to compete in great archery meets. The winners of such contests are said to receive the Keen-Eye mark of the Great Archer, a blessing that confers a +1 attack bonus on all attacks made with a bow until the next Shieldmeet.

Major Centers of Worship: Moondark Hill is located in the Vale of Evereska—discussed in greater detail in the entry for Hanali Celanil—on the eastern fringes of the moon elven city at the base of one of the greatest peaks of the Shaeradim. Eastpeak's shadow cloaks the low knoll in darkness for much of the night when the moon is full, giving rise to the hill's name. The Great Archer's faithful gather to worship their god when the full moon rises above the top of Eastpeak and its light washes over the hilltop like a

wave of silver. Built into the steep western slope of Moondark Hill is the Hall of the High Hunt, a great open-air pavilion encircled by a tightly packed colonnade of ancient shadowtops. A pure mountain spring rises in the heart of the hill and winds through a series of natural caverns before exiting at the heart of the Shadowtop Glade. When in residence, Solonor's clergy dwell in the caves of Moondark Hill amidst the great hunting trophies of the faithful. The leader of the priesthood is High Huntsman Pleufan Trueshot, an ancient moon elf who is said to have hunted in the Far Horns forest that once covered much of the Backlands. Much to the dismay of much of the Evereskan moon elven nobility, Pleufan has invited human and half-elven followers of the Great Archer—most of whom are Harpers or Heralds—to worship at the Hall of the High Hunt during the monthly ceremonies whenever they wish. Some haughty Teu-Tel'Quessir have gone as far as to move their estates to the far side of the valley in response.

The moon elven village of Ssrenshen, known to humans as Moonrise Hill, is located in the northern reaches of Deepingdale between Lake Sember and the Glaemril at the foot of Moonrise Crag in an old, thickly grown stand of ash, duskwood, and oak trees. Like the elven village of Velethuil (Bristar) to the southwest, it is the source of many skilled elven archers in the army of the Dale. The archers of Moonrise Hill are known for their amazing feats with the bow—such as hitting the eye of a bird in flight a mile away—and the Fair Folk attribute the prowess at archery of the village's inhabitants to the blessings of Solonor and an ancient tradition dating back before the fall of Myth Drannor. In the Year of Old Crowns (−91 DR), the Moonshadows, a company of rangers, fighters, fighter/mages, and even a few wizards known for their skill at archery, were formed to guard the forests of Semberholme and its environs. While the elven presence in the woods enveloping Lake Sember is much reduced today, the ancient traditions of the Moonshadows are continued by the elven archers of Ssrenshen and they continue to patrol the region. In the center of the village is the petrified stump of an ancient oak tree nearly 50 feet in diameter whose branches once towered over both the village and bald-topped crag millennia ago. A great hollow has been carved out of the heart of the tree, and it serves as both the chapter-house of the Moonshadows and as a sacred temple of Solonor. Moonrise Hollow, as the temple and hall is known, consists of both the hollowed out stump and the earthen cellars dug amidst its ancient roots. Many of the greatest hunting trophies and tombs of the greatest archers of Cormanthor may be found in these earthen catacombs, as can the Greenshaft, a holy relic of the Solonoran faith said to be the first arrow shot from the bow of the Forest Hunter in the Elven Woods in a time before the Fair Folk walked beneath the endless forest canopy.

Affiliated Orders: Solonor's church is affiliated with a large number of military orders, few of which number more than several score warriors. The Stag Hunters, the Fellowship of the Fleeting Hart, the Wolves of Dawn, the Shadowsheafs, the Knights of the Green Bow, the Keen-eyed Hunters, and the Archer Knights are particularly famous examples of bands of elven rangers, fighters, and/or priests dedicated to serving the Great Archer. Many less renowned bands stalk the shadowed forest paths of Faerûn as well, guarding the woodlands, the Fair Folk, and their allies who dwell within.

Priestly Vestments: The ceremonial garb of Solonor's clergy consists of suits of silvered chain mail—elven chain mail, if available—with silver cloaks and leaf green hoods. The holy symbol of the faith is either an oversized arrowhead at least three inches in length embossed on both faces with Solonor's symbol, a silver medallion embossed with the head of a stag, or three feathers attached to a leather disk hung from a leather cord.

Adventuring Garb: The silver cloaks with green hoods are exchanged outside of ceremonial occasions for leaf green hooded cloaks and leather boots (or *elven cloaks* and *boots*, if available). Solonor's followers favor bows of any sort (except crossbows), daggers, knives, and long swords, spears. Elven bows are particularly prized, as are magical bows and arrows, *bracers of archery*, and *quivers of Ehlonna* (known as *quivers of Mielikki* or as *quivers of Solonor* in the Realms). Most members of Solonor's priesthood wear leather armor, studded leather armor, or silenced elven chain mail. (The last is detailed in the entry for Erevan Ilesere under the heading Adventuring Garb.)

During their years of experience, elves have found that often archers are attacked without much chance to defend themselves. They have therefore created the elven bow (either a long bow, short bow, or composite long or short bow), designed to fire with the same rate and accuracy of a normal bow of its type, and yet the elves can use it to fend off attacks until they can defend themselves with a better weapon or spell. The elven bow is a beautiful piece of work, carved mostly from wood, highly decorated and polished, with substantial metal inlays. These inlays enable the bow to be used as a parrying weapon until the elf can draw a more suitable weapon. Meanwhile, the elf's bow is not damaged by the attack and can be used again. If used as an offensive weapon, the elven bow acts as a club, causing 1d6 points of damage to S- or M-sized creatures, 1d3 to L-sized or larger creatures. Elven bows weigh 8 pounds and typically cost 150 gp.

Specialty Priests (Rangers)

REQUIREMENTS:	Strength 13, Dexterity 13, Constitution 14, Wisdom 14
PRIME REQ.:	Strength, Dexterity, Wisdom
ALIGNMENT:	NG, CG
WEAPONS:	Any
ARMOR:	Any (penalties to some special abilities accrue if wearing heavier armor than studded leather)
MINOR SPHERES:	Animal, combat, plant, travelers
MAGICAL ITEMS:	Same as rangers
REQ. PROFS:	Long, short, or composite bow (including elven bows); animal lore, set snares, survival (woodland)
BONUS PROFS:	Bowyer/fletcher, hunting, tracking, weapon specialization in long or short bow

All of Solonor's specialty priests are rangers. Their abilities and restrictions, aside from the changes noted above and later in this section, are summarized in the discussion of elven priests in "Appendix 1: Demihuman Priests" and detailed in full in the *Player's Handbook*.

- Rangers dedicated to Solonor must be elves or half-elves. While most rangers in Solonor's service are green elves or moon elves, elves and half-elves of every subrace are called to be specialty priests of Solonor's clergy.
- Rangers in Solonor's service, whether they are elves or half-elves, are allowed to multiclass as cleric/rangers.
- Rangers in Solonor's service may select any available weapon specialization or group proficiency in the long, short, or composite bow (including elven bows). For example, if the weapon mastery rules given in PLAYER'S OPTION: *Combat & Tactics* are permitted in the campaign, Solonor's ranger clergy are permitted to become weapon masters in the long, short, or composite bow (including elven bows), but not crossbows or other types of bows.

Solonoran Spells

2nd Level

Keen Eye (Pr 2; Alteration)

Sphere:	Combat
Range:	0
Components:	V, S, M
Duration:	1 round/level (3 shots maximum)
Casting Time:	5
Area of Effect:	The caster
Saving Throw:	None

Also known as *bull's eye*, this spell assists the recipient in making called shots with a missile weapon. While gifted with a *keen eye*, all called shots are made without the normal –4 attack penalty, and the recipient does not suffer the normal +1 penalty to initiative. This spell provides no bonuses to missile attacks that are not called shots or to attacks of any sort made with melee weapons. Also, it does not provide a bonus of any sort if the normal penalties assessed for attempting a called shot are mitigated by other factors.

The material components of this spell are the priest's holy symbol and a hawk feather.

3rd Level

Archer's Redoubt (Pr 3; Evocation)

Sphere:	Protection
Range:	0
Components:	V, S, M
Duration:	5 rounds/level
Casting Time:	6
Area of Effect:	Special
Saving Throw:	None

When this spell is cast, an invisible barrier, pierced only by a narrow arrow slit, comes into being and totally encompasses the caster. This shield provides the equivalent protection of AC 2 against all frontal attacks and AC 0 against all other attacks. The barrier also adds a +1 bonus to the priest's saving throws.

It is not possible to move an *archer's redoubt*, and voluntarily exiting its confines ends the spell effect immediately. However, the placement of the arrow slit can move as mentally directed by the caster. Although it is not possible to effectively employ a melee weapon or hurled weapon while within an *archer's redoubt*, it is possible to fire a crossbow or any sort of bow without hindrance.

The material component of this spell is the priest's holy symbol.

Everfull Quiver (Pr 3; Alteration)

Sphere:	Combat
Range:	Touch
Components:	V, S, M
Duration:	1 round/level
Casting Time:	6
Area of Effect:	One quiver and two arrows
Saving Throw:	None

This spell enchants a quiver that contains at least two arrows. In every round thereafter, the caster can withdraw up to two arrows per round without depleting the total number of arrows found within the quiver. If more than two arrows are ever withdrawn in 1 round, the spell effect ends immediately, and only the first two arrows withdrawn do not deplete the real supply. If anyone aside from the caster attempts to withdraw an arrow from an *endless quiver*, the spell effect ends immediately as well.

The caster can withdraw any type of arrow that was found within the *everfull quiver* when the spell was cast. Thus, if the priest casts *endless quiver* on a quiver containing one flight arrow, one sheaf arrow, and one silver arrow, he could then withdraw two silver arrows, one silver arrow and one flight arrow, etc., per round. No arrow drawn from an *endless quiver* while the spell effect lasts is ever magical, even if the one or more arrows in the *endless quiver* are magical. An arrow drawn from an *endless quiver* fades into nothingness in two rounds.

The material components of this spell are the priest's holy symbol, a quiver, and two or more arrows, none of which are consumed in the casting.

Zandilar

Zandilar (ZAN-dih-lahr) is the only god of the Yuir that was not absorbed as an aspect of one of the Seldarine. See the entry for Sharess in the "Faerûnian Pantheon (Demipowers)" chapter in *Powers & Pantheons* for more information.

GNOME PANTHEON

The Forgotten Folk of the Realms worship a pantheon of deities known collectively as the Lords of the Golden Hills. They are so named for the region of Bytopia where most dwell. The powers included in the pantheon varies from gnome clan to clan (and even more so from world to world), but those presented hereafter are venerated or at least acknowledged in most gnome settlements in the Realms. Urdlen, the Crawler Below, dwells in the Abyss, but he has tunneled into Bytopia on more than one occasion only to be driven back each time.

While Garl Glittergold is clearly acknowledged as the leader of the gnome pantheon, he has never banished any god from that pantheon, even Urdlen, despite relentless attacks by the Evil One against its fellow powers and the Forgotten Folk. The Lords of the Golden Hills include Baervan Wildwanderer the Masked Leaf, Baravar Cloakshadow the Sly One, Callarduran Smoothhands the Deep Brother, Flandal Steelskin the Master of Metal, Gaerdal Ironhand the Shield of the Golden Hills, Garl Glittergold the Watchful Protector, Nebelun the Meddler, Segojan Earthcaller the Lord of the Burrow, and—by nature of the threat he embodies—Urdlen. As noted later in this chapter, Nebelun is a special case. Although the Meddler is a deity and is venerated as such on other worlds, in the Realms, Gond the Wonderbringer has assumed Nebelun's aspect and is venerated by the Forgotten Folk in his stead. It remains to be seen whether or not the followers of Nebelun will eventually separate from the church of the Wonderbringer. This seems unlikely for the foreseeable future given Gond's widely heralded appearance in the form of a gnome on the shores of Lantan during the Time of Troubles. As such, Gond/Nebelun is currently counted as a member of both the gnome pantheon and the human Faerûnian pantheon.

Several of the Lords of the Golden Hills have a boon companion that accompanies them wherever they may go. Some examples include *Arumdina*, the sentient battle axe of Garl Glittergold, Chiktikka Fastpaws, an intelligent giant raccoon who accompanies Baervan Wildwanderer everywhere, and the intelligent stone golem that accompanies Segojan Earthcaller. Other gnome deities typically travel together or in the company of a nongnome deity of a related portfolio. Mythic tales almost always involve the gnome hero being accompanied by one faithful companion or receiving significant aid from a deity (often in the form of hints and riddles) presented by well-disposed creatures as the adventure unfolds. This reflects the value the Forgotten Folk place on companionship and sharing with trusted fellows, whether they are gnomes or of other races.

The gnome deities, it is said, were born as gems or veins of rich ore in the heart of the world. The gentle erosion of underground waters eventually released them. Some members of the pantheon are still associated in myth with the gems or metal from which myth says they were birthed—Baervan with emeralds, Callarduran with rubies, Flandal with the magical ore, arandur, Garl with gold, and Segojan with diamonds. Other deities have lost this association. Little in the way of familial relations has ever been ascribed to the Lords of the Golden Hills, although some legends refer to gods of the pantheon as brothers. Some myths claim that there were once female gnome deities, but their fate, assuming they ever existed, has long been forgotten. Members of the all-male pantheon have nothing to say on the matter except to betray a hint of ancient sadness. Notwithstanding, it is an ancient tradition of the Forgotten Folk that when a young gnome wishes to leave the close bonds of his or her community, even for a short period of time, that she or he avoid engendering a feeling of rejection in family and friends by attributing his or her wanderlust to a divine vision to search for the missing sister gods.

The Lords of the Golden Hills are actively involved in the lives of the Forgotten Folk. Compared to the gods of other pantheons, they frequently dispatch avatars to intercede on behalf of their worshipers. However, instead of appearing to their worshipers on a regular basis, the gnome gods typically dispatch avatars only to undertake adventures that will indirectly benefit the Forgotten Folk. A subtle but important aspect of such exploits, as chronicled by gnome legends, is that they encourage small groups of worshipers to settle new lands that they might not otherwise explore. While the Forgotten Folk are not in decline like the dwarves and the elves, their numbers are no longer increasing significantly. The out-of-the-way, relatively untrammeled corners of the Realms that gnomes prefer to inhabit have become less and less remote as the years unfold. This has lead to increased competition for living space with both allies and foes.

While some nongnome sages claim that Forgotten Folk are the creation of Netherese arcanists seeking to create a race of perfect servants, more cautious scholars note the existence of gnome artifacts dating back long before the appearance of the Forgotten Folk during the Silver Age of Netheril. Gnome folklore holds that the first gnomes were born from gems discovered by Garl and

Arumdina in a fashion similar to that ascribed to the gods. The Watchful Protector discovered a sealed cavern whose walls and ceiling were studded with countless gems embedded in veins of valuable ore. When Garl polished the gems and breathed on them, the jewels opened like a blossom to release the first gnomes. Before leading them into the world, Garl bequeathed laughter and a spirit of mischievousness to the newly born race by telling them a joke. Those who were born of diamonds chose to dwell beneath the land and became the rock gnomes, those born of emeralds chose to dwell amidst the great trees and became the forest gnomes, and those born of rubies wandered deep into the heart of the earth and became the deep gnomes (or svirfneblin).

One is struck, in the study of gnome theology, by the relationship between the Forgotten Folk, particularly their heroes, and the Lords of the Golden Hills. In general, gnomes are not a tremendously devout folk, yet they have a rich oral tradition that shows the tales of gods blending with those of mortal heroes. The gods embody the sense of mischievous fun and enduring community that characterizes gnome society, coupled with a strong sense of wanderlust and desire for adventure that is less common among the Forgotten Folk. The relationship between the gods, the people, and the gems and ores with which they work is tightly intertwined.

It is unknown where or when the Forgotten Folk first appeared in the Realms, for gnomes have little in the way of recorded history. Since the Forgotten Folk are rarely referred to in other races' historical texts, there is a dearth of information concerning the emergence and migration of the gnomes across Faerûn. What is known is that a large population of the Forgotten Folk were enslaved by the wizards of Netheril several millennia ago, until the Fair Folk of Illefarn and Eaerlann began to assist small groups to escape their Netherese masters. The elves hid the gnomes in the frontier garrisons they had built to defend their forests. They taught them the art of weaving illusions, so they could hide from those who might try to recapture them. A wave of escapes inspired a series of revolts, and after several ill-fated attempts to magically bind gnome artisans to their will, the Netherese arcanists freed their gnome slaves in –2387 DR. The great dispersion of rock and forest gnomes that followed scattered scores of gnome communities throughout the quiet backwaters of the Realms, predominantly to the south and east of what is now Anauroch. Although they were not part of the main wave of emigration, those gnomes who dwell in the Backlands and Sunset Vale of the western Heartlands—particularly forest gnomes who dwell in the Forgotten Forest, a small remnant of the Far Horns forest, and rock gnomes who dwell in and around the Trielta Hills—have preserved a large stock of stories that tell of their flight from the mad Netherese arcanists and the resulting trials they endured while forging their own communities. Of particular note, it was in these communities that the first spriggans appeared, a legacy of Netherese magical tinkering.

The diversity of the gnome pantheon reflects in part the differences between the gnome subraces. But the interlocking aspects of the various gods' portfolios and the same powers' close cooperation reflects the close ties the various gnome subraces retain. While Segojan is predominantly identified with rock gnomes, Baervan is identified with forest gnomes, and Callarduran is identified with deep gnomes, each is venerated in communities of all three subraces, as are the other gods that constitute the rest of the pantheon. (See "Appendix 1: Demihuman Priests" for more about forest gnomes.) While duergar and derro share a mutual enmity with surface dwarves and drow are implacable foes of the surface elves, deep gnomes entered the Underdark voluntarily, and they maintain good relations with their surface kin. The only evil branch of gnomes in Faerûn are spriggans, but while Urdlen has adopted them in part, they are more of a nuisance than a major threat, and their numbers are limited.

General Gnome Priest Abilities: The general abilities and restrictions of gnome priests (including spriggans), aside from the specific changes noted later in this section for each gnome faith, are summarized in the discussion of gnome priests in "Appendix 1: Demihuman Priests."

Baervan Wildwanderer
(The Masked Leaf, the Forest Gnome, Father of Fish and Fungus)

Intermediate Power of Bytopia, NG

PORTFOLIO: Forests, travel, nature, forest gnomes
ALIASES: None
DOMAIN NAME: Dothion/the Golden Hills (Whisperleaf)
SUPERIOR: Garl Glittergold
ALLIES: Brandobaris, Clangeddin Silverbeard, Cyrrollalee, Damh, Emmantiensien, Fionnghuala, Gwaeron Windstrom, Marthammor Duin, Mielikki, Nathair Sgiathach, Rillifane Rallathil, Shaundakul, Sheela Peryroyl, Shiallia, Silvanus, Skerrit, Tapann, Thard Harr, Verenestra, various Animal Lords, the gnome pantheon (except Urdlen)
FOES: Abbathor, Gaknulak, Kuraulyek, Kurtulmak, Laogzed, Malar, Urdlen, the goblinkin pantheons (orc, goblin, hobgoblin, bugbear, kobold, and urd deities, among others)
SYMBOL: Raccoon's face
WOR. ALIGN.:   LG, NG, CG, LN, N, CN

Baervan Wildwanderer (BAY-ur-van WILD-wander-er) is the god of forest-dwelling gnomes and their communities, travel, and the outdoors. He loves oak trees and all forest animals and is a guardian of the wild. Baervan gifted forest gnomes with the ability to communicate with forest animals, and taught them to how to hide in and move through wooded environments without being detected. The Masked Leaf is the patron god of forest gnomes, but he is well loved by all of the gnome subraces. He is even revered by the svirfneblin as the Father of Fish and Fungus. Baervan is worshiped by those who love the woodlands, as well as many wanderers, thieves, fighter/thieves, and fighters, particularly those who prefer living in the outdoors rather than in a city all the time.

Baervan's friend and constant companion in his escapades is a giant raccoon named Chiktikka Fastpaws, who is highly intelligent but prone to act before he thinks. Many stories are told of the adventures that this duo has shared, often started by Chiktikka's humorous ability to get into trouble by borrowing something valuable, such as a minor artifact. Baervan is closely allied with the other gods of the gnome pantheon, with the notable exception of Urdlen. He works closely with Segojan Earthcaller, for both gods are concerned with the natural world. Traditionally, their portfolios are divided between caring for forest animals and plants for Baervan, and burrowing animals for Segojan. Baervan sometimes accompanies Garl, or even Baravar, on their mischievous escapades, and the trio's shared interest in mischief embodies and encourages this aspect of the gnome psyche. Baervan's carefree nature and penchant for jests strains the patience of Gaerdal Ironhand, albeit not to the extent that the pranks of Baravar Cloakshadow do. Baervan is closely allied with many of the sylvan poweres of the Seelie Court. His passion for oak trees has led to his endless, if so far fruitless, pursuit of Verenestra's affections. The Masked Leaf is a frequent participant in the councils of Emmantiensien, Rillifane Rallathil, and Silvanus, though he rarely has the patience to sit through an entire discussion with these slow-speaking woodland giants. Baervan has few foes aside from Urdlen, although the Beastlord has earned his ire for hunting forest gnomes under the Masked Leaf's protection.

Baervan is gentle, good-natured, and mischievous. His penchant for good-natured pranks rivals Garl Glittergold. Except for Chiktikka's company, he tends to keep to himself. Though Baervan sometimes plays jokes on others, it is hard not to like him. The Masked Leaf's tricks are often designed to serve some purpose, unlike the mischief typical of Forgotten Folk. If Baervan wants to send someone a message, he does so in the form of a joke. Baervan dispatches avatars to help repair severe damage to nature, though sometimes just to create mischief.

Baervan's Avatar (Thief 33, Druid 30, Ranger 25, Illusionist 25)

Baervan frequently appears as a middle-aged male forest gnome with nut-brown skin and dull gray hair. He wears clothes of wood-brown hues. His raccoon friend always accompanies him. He favors spells from the spheres of all, animal, charm, elemental (earth, water), healing, plant, summoning, sun, travelers, and weather and from the school of illusion/phantasm, though he can cast spells from any sphere or school except the wizard schools of abjuration, invocation/evocation, and necromancy.

AC –4; MV 15; HP 207; THAC0 –4; #AT 5/2
Dmg 1d8+12 (spear +3, +7 Str, +2 spec. bonus in spear)
MR 60%; SZ M (4 feet tall)
Str 19, Dex 23, Con 20, Int 21, Wis 22, Cha 19
Spells P: 12/12/12/12/11/9/8, W: 6/6/6/6/6/6/6/5*
Saves PPDM 2, RSW 1**, PP 4, BW 4, Sp 1**

*Numbers assume one extra illusion/phantasm spell per spell level. **Includes gnome +5 Con save bonus to a minimum of 1.

Special Att/Def: Baervan wields *Whisperleaf*, a *spear +3* whose shaft was cut (with the tree's permission) from an ancient oak tree of the same name found in Bytopia near the Masked Leaf's home. (Baervan is specialized in the use of spears, but he is considered merely proficient in all other melee and missile weapons.) If this spear is destroyed, Baervan may make another from the wood of the tree Whisperleaf in a single day. Only Baervan may safely approach this tree; it attacks all others (treat as a treant of maximum size and hit points). Whisperleaf regenerates all wood loss within an hour.

In battle Baervan may animate any ordinary tree as a treant of 12 Hit Dice by touching it with his special spear. The animation lasts for 5d4 turns. Animated trees obey all of Baervan's orders and no one else's for the duration of their animation. Baervan may do this as often as he likes, animating one tree per round.

The Masked Leaf can *pass without trace*, *speak with animals*, or *speak with plants* at will. Once per round, he may cast *animal summoning III*, *call woodland beings*, *entangle*, *locate animals or plants*, *plant growth*, *transport via plants*, or *warp wood*. He can be struck only by +2 or better magical weapons.

Baervan is always accompanied by an avatar of Chiktikka Fastpaws.

Chiktikka Fastpaws (Giant Racoon): AC 5; MV 15; HD 12; hp 96; THAC0 9; #AT 3; Dmg 2d6 (claw)/2d6 (claw)/2d10 (bite); SD thieving skills; SZ S (3 ½′ long); ML fearless (19–20); Int high (14); AL NG; XP 9,000.

Thieving Skills: Chiktikka can pick pockets, hide in shadows, and move silently as a master thief (99% chance of success in each).

Other Manifestations

The Masked Leaf may manifest as an amber radiance to settle over a worshiper or any type of plant. This manifestation can confer upon a favored worshiper the benefits of a spell such as *barkskin*, *locate plants and animals*, *pass without trace*, *plant door*, *speak with plants*, or *tree* or coalesce into a handful of *goodberries*. Baervan's manifestation can animate a tree as a treant for up to seven rounds, create a *spike growth* effect, or act as combined *entangle* and *plant growth* spells.

Baervan is served by forest animals of all types (particularly raccoons and giant raccoons), amber dragons, dryads, earth elementals, faerie dragons, feystags, hamadryads, hybsils, leprechauns, nature elementals, singing trees, sprites, swanmays, treants, wild stags, and wood giants. He demonstrates his favor by permitting his faithful to discover acorns, pieces of amber, emeralds, oak leaves or the sudden growth of plants on a well-trodden trail where such would seem out of place. The Masked Leaf indicates his displeasure by causing a tree branch to gently strike the target of his disaffection or by causing small animals to behave oddly (like pelting a gnome with acorns).

The Church

CLERGY:	Clerics, specialty priests
CLERGY'S ALIGN.:	LG, NG, CG
TURN UNDEAD:	C: Yes, SP: Yes, at priest level –4
CMND. UNDEAD:	C: No, SP: No

All clerics of Baervan (including fighter/clerics, cleric/illusionists, and cleric/thieves) and specialty priests receive religion (gnome) as a bonus nonweapon proficiency.

The church of the Masked Leaf is well regarded among most gnome communities, particularly forest gnomes, for Baervan and his followers are a likable bunch. Baervan's penchant for getting into trouble has long been a source of amusement and pride for the Forgotten Folk, and they generally embrace his mischievous nature as portrayed in the behavior of his clergy. Among other races, the church of Baervan is little known save among other elven and sylvan deities. The Fair Folk, particularly the Sy-Tel'Quessir, view the cult of the forest gnomes with great affection, as they do the followers of the Seelie Court.

Baervan's worshipers assemble in forest clearings to venerate their god, preferably sylvan glades ringed by a circle of ancient oaks, although such arboreal menhirs are not required. Long-standing shrines of the Masked Leaf are transformed into woodland chapels with the circle of broad trunks growing closer together and the canopy of intertwined limbs and leaves forming a natural roof.

Novices of Baervan are known as Acorns. Full priests of the Masked Leaf are known as Wildwanderers. In ascending order of rank, the titles used by Baervanian priests are Chipmunk, Squirrel, Opossum, Hedgehog, Marten, Red Fox, Lynx, and Wolf. High-ranking priests have unique individual titles. Specialty priests are known as fastpaws. The clergy of Baervan includes forest gnomes (65%), rock gnomes (33%), and deep gnomes (2%). His priesthood is split almost evenly between males (55%) and females (45%). Baervan's clergy includes specialty priests (45%), cleric/thieves (35%), clerics (12%), cleric/illusionists (6%), and fighter/clerics (2%).

Dogma: The great forests of the outdoors await those Forgotten Folk daring enough to venture forth from their burrows. Wander the great woodlands in search of excitement and sylvan sites of incredible beauty. Befriend and protect the creatures of the forest. Care for and nurture the woodlands where you live. Be ever curious, and follow life wherever it may lead. Defend your community and yourself against the incursions of goblinkin and other brutish races.

Day-to-Day Activities: Members of Baervan's priesthood are found mostly in aboveground gnome communities in the great forests of the Realms. Individual priests often wander far afield, typically accompanied by a raccoon (or giant raccoon) companion. All members of the Masked Leaf's clergy are concerned with the protection of nature (and the gnomes who dwell in harmony with it). They are actively involved in driving off evil creatures, particularly spriggans.

Holy Days/Important Ceremonies: Baervan's priests gather monthly in sylvan glens under the light of the full moon to dance, hurl acorns at each other, and sacrifice magical trinkets or other treasures to the god. If a follower has been unable to acquire any magical gift to offer to Baervan over the course of the last three tendays, a knickknack of some value temporarily enchanted by means of some minor magic (often a *light* spell) is commonly offered up to Baervan.

Major Centers of Worship: The Forgotten Forest is a mature wood filled with huge oak, walnut, and shadowtop trees. Nestled between the Greypeak Mountains, the Lonely Moor, and the Marsh of Chelimber, few travelers have even circumnavigated the edges of this mysterious and overgrown forest. The woods are known primarily as the home of Fuorn, the legendary treant king of the Forgotten Forest spoken of in the few bard's tales that discuss this land. A large and thriving nation of forest gnomes is hidden beneath the forest canopy, reveling in the arboreal isolation of their sylvan home. Only the Fair Folk of the Vale of Evereska and the Greycloak Hills are welcomed as visitors, and it is through these frequent guests that this greatest concentration of followers of Baervan in the Realms conduct a limited trade with the outside world.

At the heart of the Forgotten Forest, near Fuorn's favorite place, stands a circle of twelve great chime oaks (transplanted centuries ago from the eastern starwood of the great forest of Cormanthor) whose trunks have grown so close together that only a Small-sized creature can pass between them. Oaksong Tower, so named for the melodies of the chime oaks and the towerlike natural cathedral formed by the ring of trees, is the central chapel for a community of 100 or more priests of the Masked Leaf who dwell in the surrounding forest. Baervan's followers work closely with their kin throughout the forest as well as the great treant-priests of Emmantiensien to nurture and protect the forest and defend its borders against interlopers from

the surrounding dangerous regions. While leadership roles in the temple are shared by the senior priests of the faith, the current high priest is Briar Farwalker, a venerable forest gnome who recently returned from a decades-long trip to the Chondalwood.

Affiliated Orders: The Wild Wayfarers are a loosely organized band of rogues, priests, and cleric/thieves found in both city and sylvan settings. Members of this fellowship share a love of travel, new experiences, adventure, and good times. Many serve their communities as far-ranging scouts who keep tabs on emerging threats in the region, while others bend their talents to a life of adventuring. Their experiences with the world at large encountered during their travels serve both to entertain and enlighten their home communities of the Forgotten Folk.

Priestly Vestments: The clerical garb of Baervan's priests includes a green cap (always worn at a jaunty angle), and wood brown clothing (leather armor will do in a pinch). The holy symbol of the faith is an over-sized acorn, carefully tended so it achieves triple the normal dimensions before is it ritually harvested by asking the tree that bore it for its use in Baervan's name.

Adventuring Garb: When adventuring, members of Baervan's priesthood favor woodland armor, such as leather armor and wooden shields, and weapons of the forest, such as clubs, slings, spears, and staves.

Specialty Priests (Fastpaws)

REQUIREMENTS:	Constitution 10, Wisdom 9
PRIME REQ.:	Constitution, Wisdom
ALIGNMENT:	NG, CG
WEAPONS:	Club, crossbow, dagger, hand/throwing axe, knife, sling, spear, short bow
ARMOR:	Padded, leather, or hide or any other nonmetallic armor; no shield
MAJOR SPHERES:	All, animal, charm, elemental (earth, water), healing, plant, sun, travelers, weather
MINOR SPHERES:	Combat, divination, necromantic
MAGICAL ITEMS:	As clerics
REQ. PROFS:	Spear, animal lore, set snares
BONUS PROFS:	Herbalism, survival (forest)

- Fastpaws must be gnomes. Most fastpaws are forest gnomes, but gnomes of every subrace except spriggans can be fastpaws.
- Fastpaws are not allowed to multiclass.
- Fastpaws may select nonweapon proficiencies from the rogue group without penalty.
- Fastpaws understand and use thieves' cant.
- Fastpaws have limited thieving skills as defined in the Limited Thieving Skills section of "Appendix 1: Demihuman Priests."
- Fastpaws cannot become *entangled*.
- Fastpaws can cast *find familiar* (as the 1st-level wizard spell) once per year. If the spellcasting is successful, the type of familiar acquired is always a raccoon (80%) or giant raccoon (20%), with all the attendant benefits and restrictions normally associated with the spell. Such creatures receive an extra +1 hp per Hit Die.
- Fastpaws can cast *locate animals or plants* or *pass without trace* (as the 1st-level priest spells) once per day. (Forest gnomes can *pass without trace* at will in woodland settings.)
- At 3rd level, fastpaws can cast *barkskin*, but with a –2 bonus to Armor Class and a +2 bonus to saving throws, or *warp wood* (as the 2nd-level priest spells) once per day.
- At 5th level, fastpaws can cast *messenger* (as the 2nd-level priest spell) or *tree* (as the 3rd-level priest spell) once per day.
- At 7th level, fastpaws can cast *call woodland beings* or *plant door* (as the 4th-level priest spells) once per day.
- At 10th level, fastpaws can cast *speak with plants* (as the 4th-level priest spell) once per day.
- At 10th level, fastpaws can cast *commune with nature* or *pass plant* (as the 5th-level priest spells) once per day.
- At 13th level, fastpaws can cast *animal summoning III* or *speak with monsters* (as the 6th-level priest spells) once per day.
- At 15th level, fastpaws can cast *changestaff* (as the 7th-level priest spell) or *transport via plants* (as the 6th-level priest spell) once per day.

Baervanian Spells

2nd Level

Arboreal Scamper (Pr 2; Alteration)

Sphere:	Plant
Range:	Touch
Components:	V, S, M
Duration:	1 hour/level
Casting Time:	5
Area of Effect:	Creature or creatures touched
Saving Throw:	None

An *arboreal scamper* spell enables the recipient to climb about or hang from trees as easily as a squirrel. The affected creature must be no larger than man-sized (7 feet tall) and have bare hands and feet in order to climb in this manner at MV 6 (3 if encumbered). While under the effects of this spell, the creature, barring outside interference, will not fall from a tree. *Arboreal scamper* does permit jumping up to 10 feet to a neighboring limb, although a successful Dexterity check is required to accomplish the feat. Even falling is not necessarily disastrous as the creature can easily grab any tree limb contacted.

The caster can divide the base duration between multiple creatures, to a minimum of one-half hour per creature. Thus a 3rd-level caster can confer this ability to two creatures for 1 ½ hours. The recipient can end the spell effect with a word.

Material components for this spell are the priest's holy symbol and an acorn purloined from a squirrel's secret stash.

Whisperleaf (Pr 2; Alteration)

Sphere:	Plant
Range:	Touch
Components:	V, S, M
Duration:	4 rounds+2 rounds/level
Casting Time:	5
Area of Effect:	1 oak branch
Saving Throw:	None

This spell transforms the still-living and still-attached branch of an oak tree into a stout magical wooden spear that the priest can easily remove from the tree and use in combat. A spear created by this spell gains a +1 bonus to attack and damage rolls. This bonus increases by +1 at 5th and again at 10th level, to a maximum of +3. The caster must wield the spear. When the spell terminates, the branch reverts to its original form, but it cannot be rejoined to the tree.

The material component of this spell is the priest's holy symbol.

4th Level

Tree Nap (Pr 4; Illusion/Phantasm, Necromancy)

Sphere:	Plant
Range:	0
Components:	V, M
Duration:	Special
Casting Time:	1 round
Area of Effect:	The caster
Saving Throw:	None

By means of this spell, the caster can draw on the healing power of a living tree while cloaked in an illusionary guise resembling part of the tree. This spell must be cast after the caster places himself in contact with the chosen tree in a position she or he can maintain for an extended period of time.

As long as the caster does not move (aside from small shifts in position) or break contact with the chosen tree, she or he is cloaked by a simple illusion resembling a natural part of the tree. For example, a priest who sits on the ground and leans against the base of the tree might appear to be an exposed root. However, any method that can discern illusions or reveal hidden creatures reveals the caster's position immediately, although that will not automatically end the spell effect.

A caster who gets a full night's sleep (8 hours) while the spell is in effect can tap into the life force of the tree. A night's sleep under the effect of *tree nap* is equal to complete bed rest and naturally heals 3 points of damage for the day. If the tree is an oak, the healing potential is doubled to 6 points. If the oak is the home of a dryad or hamadryad, the healing is doubled again to 12 points for a single night's sleep.

The material components are the caster's holy symbol and a drop of tree sap.

Baravar Cloakshadow

(The Sly One, Master of Illusion, Lord in Disguise,
Bane of Goblinkin)

Lesser Power of Bytopia, NG

PORTFOLIO:	Illusions, deceptions, traps, wardings
ALIASES:	None
DOMAIN NAME:	Dothion/the Golden Hills (the Hidden Knoll)
SUPERIOR:	Garl Glittergold
ALLIES:	Azuth, Brandobaris, Clangeddin Silverbeard, Erevan Ilesere, Leira (dead), Mystra, Sehanine Moonbow, Tymora, Vergadain, the gnome pantheon (except Urdlen)
FOES:	Abbathor, Cyric, Kuraulyek, Kurtulmak, Mask, Urdlen, the goblinkin pantheons
SYMBOL:	Cloak and dagger
WOR. ALIGN.:	LG, NG, CG, LN, N, CN

Baravar Cloakshadow (BARE-uh-vahr CLOKE-sha-doh) is a sly, sneaky protector of the Forgotten Folk. His defenses and protective strategies are rooted in deceit—illusions, traps, ambushes, and the like—and his jests and tricks may cause their victims some pain (emotional if not physical). In addition to teaching the arts of disguise, stealth, and spying to the gnomes, the Sly One creates traps and illusions of incredible depth and cunning, a skill he has passed on to gnomes throughout the Realms. As the patron of illusions, Baravar is the preeminent gnome god of magic. The Sly One oversees the magical arts of gnome magical craftsfolk as well. All those who survive by their wits venerate Baravar, particularly those who must often combat kobolds, goblins, and other humanoids. Most gnome wizards venerate the Sly One as well, though they do not necessarily participate in their god's ongoing war with the goblinkin powers.

Baravar is closely allied with the other gods of the gnome pantheon, and despite Baravar's somewhat mean-spirited nature, the Sly One follows Garl's lead in emphasizing trickery over strength. Baravar works closely with Segojan Earthcaller, as the Lord of the Burrow once included illusions in his portfolio, and Callarduran Smoothhands, for many deep gnomes are well versed in the art of magical deception. While the Baravar and Gaerdal Ironhand share similar concerns, Baravar's deceits do not sit well with the Shield of the Golden Hills and Gaerdal sometimes chooses to foil the Sly One's plans. Baravar has a genuine dislike for deities of many goblinkin races, particularly the powers of the goblin and kobold pantheons, and unlike the other gnome gods, he is none too restrained about expressing his view. Baravar and Leira were once closely allied, and the apparent death of the Leira at the hands of Cyric has earned him Baravar's eternal vengeance.

Baravar is a crafty, vengeful power who specializes in deceptions. He is unforgiving of any who threaten his charges, and he feels no compunctions about acting against those who have earned his enmity. Although he shares Garl's love of a good practical joke, Baravar's jests and tricks may cause no small discomfort to the victims. He is also a thief and enjoys using illusions to confuse creatures before robbing them. Baravar most often steals out of sheer boredom. The Sly One dispatches avatars to defend gnomes oppressed by humanoids; he often sends one to harass goblinkin from a distance even before they threaten gnomes: "Do unto them before they have a chance to do unto you" is a philosophy he often acts upon.

Baravar's Avatar (Illusionist 30, Thief 29, Cleric 18)

Baravar appears as a dark-haired, beady-eyed, very alert and vigilant young gnome. He is always dressed in dark clothes. He favors spells from the spheres of all, astral, charm, creation, divination, guardian, healing, protection, sun, thought, travelers, and wards and from the school of illusion/phantasm, although he can cast spells from any sphere and any school except necromancy, invocation/evocation, or abjuration.

AC –2 (–4 with *Shadowcloak*); MV 12; HP 145; THAC0 6; #AT 1
Dmg 1d4+5 (*dagger +4*, +1 STR)
MR 70%; SZ M (4 feet tall)
STR 17, DEX 21, CON 17, INT 23, WIS 18, CHA 16
Spells P: 10/10/9/9/6/4/2, W: 8/8/8/8/8/8/7/7*
Saves PPDM 4, RSW 1**, PP 5, BW 7, Sp 1**
    *Numbers assume one extra illusion/phantasm spell per spell level. **Includes gnome +4 CON save bonus to a minimum of 1.

Special Att/Def: Baravar wields *Nightmare*, a *dagger +4* that drips a paralyzing venom. Targets struck by this dagger must make a successful saving throw vs. paralyzation to avoid being immobilized, as by a *hold monster* spell, for 1d4 turns. While paralyzed, a victim suffers from the effects of a *nightmare* (the reverse of the 5th-level wizard spell *dream*) and the beneficial effects of the previous night's sleep are canceled. Any points of damage healed through resting from the previous night's sleep are lost in addition to the damage caused by the *nightmare*, and, upon emerging from the *nightmare*, the victim feels as if she or he had missed an entire night's sleep. Although memorized spells are not lost, replacement spells cannot be gained until the victim has a full night's sleep.

In addition to casting two spells a round if he makes no physical attacks, he has the ability to cast any illusion/phantasm spell. He can use this ability to continue to cast an illusion/phantasm spell once a round even after he runs of his normal number of spells (given above).

The Sly One wears the *Shadowcloak*, a unique magical item with all the benefits of a *cloak of displacement* and a *robe of blending*. He can become *invisible* or use *dimension door* or *rope trick* at will. He can also create at will 1d4+2 *mirror images* as shadowy duplicates within a 60-foot radius of his current position. He can be struck only by +1 or better magical weapons. He is immune to the effects of any illusion/phantasm spell that he does not wish to be affected by, including those created by deities of equal to or lesser power than himself.

Other Manifestations

Baravar commonly manifests through the form of widely varying illusions. Such manifestations often serve to hide a favored worshiper from enemies or mislead those who seek to do harm to a particular follower. Sometimes the Sly One communicates to his faithful via illusions, depicting scenes of what may come to pass or speaking through sounds that seem to emanate from stone statues, babbling creeks, giant boulders, or ancient trees.

Baravar is served by a variety of creatures, including blink dogs, brownies, change cats, dopplegangers, ethyks, faerie dragons, leprechauns, pixies, sprites, and thylacines. He demonstrates his favor through the discovery of aventurine, jade, scapras, star diopside, and zarbrina. The Sly One indicates his displeasure by causing illusions to flicker and fade, destroying their effectiveness.

The Church

CLERGY:	Clerics, specialty priests, illusionists
CLERGY'S ALIGN.:	NG, CG, N
TURN UNDEAD:	C: Yes, SP: No, Ill: No
CMND. UNDEAD:	C: No, SP: No, Ill: No

All clerics (including fighter/clerics, cleric/illusionists, and cleric/thieves) and specialty priests of Baravar receive religion (gnome) and reading/writing (Ruathlek) as bonus nonweapon proficiencies.

The church of Baravar is highly regarded for its efforts on behalf of the Forgotten Folk in the ongoing battles between goblins, kobolds, and gnomes over he same tunnels and caves, even if the more cultured gnomes find the priesthood's methods somewhat brutish. Baravar's faithful are deservedly admired for their skill in manipulating the Weave and crafting illusions of incredible realism. But their penchant for deception has earned them a measure of distrust among most gnomes, even those who seek to emulate the trickery of Garl Glittergold. Baravar's faithful maintain a low profile around humans and other demihuman races, and they are often viewed as little more than a priestly variant of the gnome illusionists. Dwarves in particular exhibit a degree of distaste for the priesthood of the Sly One, for Baravar's faithful embody nearly everything the Stout Folk dislike about gnomes.

Temples of Baravar always appear to be anything but a house of worship. Cloaked in the guise of another business, the Sly One's priests assemble in secret chapels behind hidden doors guarded by an elaborate array of tricks, traps, and illusions. The interiors of Baravar's churches are cloaked in a mosaic of shifting illusions and omnipresent shadows that befuddle and mislead intruders.

Novices of Baravar are known as the Cloaked. Full priests of the Sly One are known as the Illusory. Baravarian priests employ a wide variety of titles, seemingly changing them to suits their purposes in any given situation. It is not clear that any true hierarchy of titles actually exists. Specialty priests are known as hoodwinkers. The clergy of Baravar includes rock gnomes (60%), deep gnomes (30%), and forest gnomes (10%). Males comprise a slight majority of his priesthood (60%). Baravar's clergy includes specialty priests (40%), cleric/illusionists (30%), illusionists (12%), cleric/thieves (10%), fighter/clerics (5%), and clerics (3%).

Dogma: The world is a dangerous place, and the only sure defense is to cloak oneself in shadows under a web of deception. Strive to master the art of illusion and the game of deceit for therein lies security. Protect yourself and other gnomes. Do not completely trust anyone who has not proven himself or herself. Hope for the best, but prepare for the worst in life and in others' behavior. If folk do you or yours ill, do not fear showing them the error of their ways through making them the butts of a few pointed jokes. Desperate times call for desperate measures, and in time of battle or war, use the craft of illusion and camoflage to make sure that the right side wins—yours. Do not flout laws openly, but do what is best for those in your care whether or not that course of action is the one approved of by those in authority. Finally, devote yourself to your art and those you love with equal fervor, for one must have a reason to live beyond mere survival.

Day-to-Day Activities: Baravar's priesthood is deeply involved in refining the art of illusions. A sizable number of the clergy are adventurers, charged with finding new spells and magical items that allow the creation and control of effects from the school of illusion/phantasm. Other priests work as researchers, ever-refining their magical craft. Priests of Baravar are generally sneaky, smart gnomes, and they serve their communities as spies and investigative agents and by teaching skill such as disguise, camouflage, hiding, and the like.

Holy Days/Important Ceremonies: The clergy of Baravar venerates the Sly One in a monthly ritual known as the Cloaking. Although such rituals are always observed on the night of the new moon, the exact location and nature of the ceremony varies every time. The Cloaking is often held in public places, and it is considered a point of honor by the participants that such assemblies are never detected as such by outsiders. This practice has led to a common joke among the Forgotten Folk that any unexplained gathering of two or more gnomes must be "another meeting of the Illusory." Baravar's priests make offerings to their god by creating illusions of items they have seen or heard or otherwise sensed. The greater the realism of such deceptions, the more the god is pleased.

Major Centers of Worship: The Hill of Tombs, a prominent knoll at the southern extent of the Earthfast Mountains of western Impiltur, has long served as the burial ground of Impiltur's monarchs and war-captains. If the tales are to be believed, this is an ancient tradition begun by the long-lost realms that preceded the kingdom founded by Imphras I, War-Captain of Lyrabar. Unbeknownst to the human inhabitants of this young land, a secret temple of Baravar is located in the hill's heart. The Vault of Seven Mysteries houses a small community of priests and illusionists who gather beneath the tombs of the dead to develop their craft in utter secrecy. The only clue to their presence is the inordinate number of reported hauntings in the vicinity of the hill, coupled with a comparable lack of sightings of the undead. The folk of Impiltur ascribe the reports of numerous spirits guarding the Hill of Tombs to the dutiful service of pious lords whose souls linger after death to safeguard the populace of Impiltur in times of danger. In truth, the gravesite is overrun with gnome pranksters who nevertheless serve much the same function.

Myth Dyraalis, a mythal-cloaked town of elves and gnomes in the Forest of Mir, has served as a safe haven for the Fair Folk and Forgotten Folk who have dwelt therein since the settlement's inception in the Year of Clutching Dusk (−375 DR). The elven and gnome clergies of Sehanine Moonbow and Baravar claim that the two demihuman powers of illusion keep the "Phantom City of Drollus," as it is mistakenly called, a secret, locked away from the rest of the world. Many worshipers of the Moonlit Mystery and the Sly One may be found within the borders of Myth Dyraalis. They gather to worship both powers at the Twin Spires of Mystery, a temple jointly administered by the clergies of Baravar and Sehanine.

Affiliated Orders: The Knights of the Shadowy Cloak is a mysterious organization with cells in most gnome communities where Baravar is venerated. Members of this order include specialty priests, illusionists, cleric/illusionists, fighter/illusionists, and illusionist/thieves. The Knights work alone and in small groups. Their guiding principles hold that goblins, kobolds, and other humanoid races are an ever-present threat to the safety of the Forgotten Folk, and that, as a rule, members of these races cannot be redeemed. As such, the order is dedicated to driving away or exterminating humanoid tribes that might someday threaten neighboring communities of gnomes. Their methods are chosen not to draw attention or incite retaliatory attacks against those they are trying to defend. Many members of this order are members of multiracial bands of adventurers, for it is considered more effective to direct the militant talents of nongnomes against the enemies of the Forgotten Folk.

Priestly Vestments: The ceremonial garb of priests of Baravar consists of a hooded black cloak, a gray cloth mask, and an ornate silver dagger with a wavy blade. The holy symbol of the faith is a tarnished miniature of the silver dagger.

Adventuring Garb: Baravar's priests favor the garb of rogues, including leather armor, light weapons, and a concealing dark gray or black cloak.

Specialty Priests (Hoodwinkers)

REQUIREMENTS:	Dexterity 15, Intelligence 15, Wisdom 9
PRIME REQ.:	Dexterity, Wisdom
ALIGNMENT:	NG
WEAPONS:	Club, dagger, dart, hand crossbow, knife, lasso, short bow, short sword, sling, staff, staff-sling
ARMOR:	Leather armor, studded leather armor, or elven chain mail
MAJOR SPHERES:	All, chaos, charm, creation, guardian, healing, protection, thought, wards
MINOR SPHERES:	Combat, divination, sun, travelers
MAGICAL ITEMS:	As clerics or thieves
REQ. PROFS:	Dagger
BONUS PROFS:	Disguise, set snares

- Hoodwinkers must be gnomes. While most hoodwinkers are rock gnomes, gnomes of every subrace except spriggans are called to be specialty priests of Baravar's clergy.
- Hoodwinkers are not allowed to multiclass.
- Hoodwinkers may select nonweapon proficiencies from the rogue group without penalty.
- Hoodwinkers may cast wizard spells from the illusion/phantasm school as defined in the Limited Wizard Spellcasting section of "Appendix 1: Demihuman Priests."
- Hoodwinkers may hide in shadows as a ranger of the same level, with any appropriate racial, Dexterity, and armor modifiers and thieving skill modifiers.
- Hoodwinkers can cast *audible glamer* or *phantasmal force* (as the 1st-level wizard spells) once per day.
- At 3rd level, hoodwinkers can cast *mirror image* or *rope trick* (as the 2nd-level wizard spells) once per day.
- At 3rd level, hoodwinkers receive a +2 bonus to saving throws vs. illusion/phantasm spells.
- At 5th level, hoodwinkers can cast *improved phantasmal force* or *invisibility* (as the 2nd-level wizard spells) once per day.
- At 7th level, hoodwinkers can cast *dimension door* (as the 4th-level wizard spell) or *suggestion* (as the 3rd-level wizard spell) once per day.
- At 10th level, hoodwinkers can cast *phantasmal killer* (as the 4th-level wizard spell) or *spectral force* (as the 3rd-level wizard spell) once per day.
- At 13th level, hoodwinkers can cast *mislead* (as the 6th-level wizard spell) once per day.
- At 15th level, hoodwinkers can cast *prismatic spray* (as the 7th-level wizard spell) twice per tenday.

Baravarian Spells

1st Level

Mistake (Pr 1; Illusion/Phantasm)

Sphere:	Protection
Range:	0
Components:	V, S, M
Duration:	3 rounds+2 rounds/level
Casting Time:	4
Area of Effect:	The caster
Saving Throw:	Special

This spell creates a false impression in the minds of those interacting with the caster. When *mistake* is cast, the priest is not altered in any way, nor is she or he cloaked with any visible illusion. Instead, any sentient being that interacts with the subject must make a successful saving throw vs. spell in order to perceive the subject as she or he truly is. If the saving throw is failed, the creature encountering the caster mistakes him or her for someone else, the exact identity will be one that is least likely to provoke an encounter or cause difficulty for the caster. When viewed by multiple creatures simultaneously, the magic of this spell might create a different impression in each creature's mind or cause the subject of the spell to appear the same to the entire group, again depending on which is least likely to provoke an encounter. Viewers receive any magical defense adjustment modifier they are entitled to for high or low Wisdom scores. Creatures with an Intelligence of semi-intelligent or less (Int 4 or less) or supra-genius or better (Int 19 or more) or a Wisdom score of 18 or better are not affected by this spell. Creatures who rely primarily on scent to identify friend or foe are not fooled by this spell either.

This spell does not ensure the caster is not detected or detained, it simply enhances the probability that she or he is not. Viewers who plainly see the caster before or while she or he casts *mistake* are not fooled by the spell. This effect is not permanent, and if the attention of someone influenced by this spell is drawn back to the encounter after the spell expires, she or he will recognize that she or he has been duped, though his or her general Intelligence and Wisdom determines to what degree she or he is able to figure out what they really saw. Viewers with high Intelligence and Wisdom scores will remember more of the truth than those with lower scores; those with low scores (7 or less) may simply think that there was something odd.

For example: A priest casts this spell upon himself in order to rescue some prisoners. When she or he passes a bugbear guard, it might perceive the priest to be a goblin child who passes this post each day to get water from a nearby stream. If the priest continues past goblin warriors, they might perceive him or her as a subchief who does not like to be disturbed. When the priest reaches the prisoners, they would perceive him or her as a cloaked ally trying to free them while not raising an alarm.

Material components for this spell are the priest's holy symbol and a small piece of thin, translucent material.

2nd Level

Gull (Pr 2; Enchantment/Charm)

Sphere:	Charm
Range:	30 yards
Components:	V, M
Duration:	1 round+1 round/level
Casting Time:	5
Area of Effect:	One creature
Saving Throw:	Neg.

When this spell is cast, the priest's words become very persuasive to the target of this spell who becomes gullible if she or he fails a saving throw vs. spell. If the saving throw succeeds, this spell dissipates without effect. Targets apply their magical defense modifier (a function of their Wisdom score) to this saving throw. A target failing his or her saving throw is temporarily convinced of any one plausible excuse or fact that other information does not blatantly counter.

For example: If a priest attempts to *gull* a guard outside a private club, assuming that the priest is dressed appropriately, she or he might be able to convince the guard that she or he is a member of the club but has forgotten the password. However, the priest would have no luck convincing the guard that she or he is a particular member of the club if the guard has already seen that member enter just moments before, nor would the caster have any luck convincing the guard if only humans are permitted to join the club and the priest is obviously a gnome.

The material components are the priest's holy symbol and a pinch of sugar.

5th Level

Mantle of Baravar (Pr 5; Abjuration)

Sphere:	Charm
Range:	Touch
Components:	V, S, M
Duration:	1 hour/level
Casting Time:	8
Area of Effect:	One or more creatures
Saving Throw:	None

This spell confers a special magic resistance against illusion/phantasm spells. This magic resistance functions in a similar manner as standard magic resistance, but only against illusion/phantasm spells. Those protected receive 2% magic resistance per caster level, in addition to saving throws normally allowed. The priest can divide the duration evenly among several creatures, to a minimum duration of one-half hour each. Thus, a 10th-level priest can protect one creature for 10 hours, two creatures for 5 hours, three creatures for 3 hours and 20 minutes, and so on. A successful *dispel magic* spell ends the effect prematurely.

The material component for this spell is the caster's holy symbol.

Callarduran Smoothhands

(Deep Brother, Master of Stone, Lord of Deepearth, the Deep Gnome)

Intermediate Power of Bytopia, N

PORTFOLIO:	Stone, the deep underground, the Underdark, mining, the svirfneblin
ALIASES:	None
DOMAIN NAME:	Dothion/Deephome
SUPERIOR:	Garl Glittergold
ALLIES:	Clangeddin Silverbeard, Cyrrollalee, Dumathoin, Eilistraee, Grumbar, Psilofyr, Shevarash, Urogalan, Vergadain, the gnome pantheon (except Urdlen)
FOES:	Blibdoolpoolp, the Blood Queen, Deep Duerra, Diinkarazan, Diirinka, Great Mother, Gzemnid, Ilsensine, Ilxendren, Laogzed, Laduguer, Maanzecorian (dead), Urdlen, the drow pantheon (except Eilistraee)
SYMBOL:	Gold ring with star pattern
WOR. ALIGN.:	NG, N

Callarduran Smoothhands (KAAHL-ur-duhr-an SMOOTH-hands) is the gnome god of the earth's depths. He oversees the deepest mines and provides protection against the horrors of the Underdark. The Deep Brother is the patron deity of svirfneblin, also known as deep gnomes, who dwell in the lightless tunnels of Deepearth. Unlike the other demihuman powers whose worshipers reside largely in the Underdark, Callarduran is not an outcast; he voluntarily led the ancestors of the svirfneblin deep underground to encourage diversity among the Forgotten Folk. It was Callarduran who taught the deep gnomes how to summon and befriend earth elementals. A svirfneblin legend tells that his hands are worn smooth from his polishing of a massive *stone of controlling earth elementals* that he hides at the center of the world, granting deep gnomes their summoning abilities. Ignored by the other gnome subraces, the Deep Brother is venerated primarily by svirfneblin as their patron, with a strong emphasis on his protective aspect and his lordship of the all-encompassing earth and the treasures to be found within. Svirfneblin warriors and illusionists who defend and hide the deep gnomes from their numerous enemies form the core of the Deep Brother's faithful.

Callarduran is closely allied with the other gods of the gnome pantheon, with the exception of Urdlen, despite the geographic division that separates his worshipers from the rest of the gnome race. The Deep Brother encourages his followers to communicate with the other gnome races and faiths. In particular, Callarduran works closely with Segojan Earthcaller, the god of the earth, Flandal Steelskin, the god of mining, and Gaerdal Ironhand, the god of protection, all of whom have portfolios related to that of the Deep Brother but who are more involved with rock gnomes than deep gnomes. As a matter of practicality, Callarduran has forged alliances with other nonevil powers with interests in the Underdark, including Eilistraee, Psilofyr, Shevarash, and Urogalan. The Deep Brother despises drow, charging his people to drive away the Spider Queen's worshipers whenever possible. He is always battling Lolth, Ghaunadaur, and the other evil drow powers. Similarly, Callarduran opposes the gods of other evil creatures of the Underdark, including those powers venerated by aboleths, beholders, duergar, kuo-toa, illithids, ixzan, and troglodytes.

The Deep Brother is by nature solitary and thoughtful. He rarely consorts with others, even other gnome gods. He is a benign, but secretive deity, caring only for his own people and their defense. He frequently dispatches his avatars to defend his followers from dangers of the Underdark. The avatar's arrival is heralded by the sound of its humming, which can be heard through solid rock.

Callarduran's Avatar

(Earth Elementalist 33, Illusionist 33, Fighter 30, Cleric 23, Thief 20)

He appears as a handsome, brown-skinned svirfneblin wearing chain mail and a gold ring with a star pattern. He favors spells from the spheres of all, charm, combat, creation, elemental (earth), guardian, healing, protection, summoning, and wards and from the schools of abjuration, alteration, elemental (earth), and illusion/phantasm, though he can cast spells from any sphere or school.

AC –5; MV 12, Br 6; HP 209; THAC0 –9; #AT 5/2
Dmg 1d8+9 (*battle axe +3*, +4 Str, +2 spec. bonus in battle axe)
MR 70%; SZ M (4 1/2 feet tall)
Str 18/76, Dex 21, Con 19, Int 23, Wis 19, Cha 22
Spells P: 12/11/11/10/9/7/3, W:8/8/8/8/8/8/8/8/8*
Saves PPDM 2, RSW 1**, PP 4, BW 4, Sp 1**

*Numbers assume one extra elemental earth or illusion/phantasm spell per spell level. **Includes gnome +5 Con save bonus to a minimum of 1.

Special Att/Def: Callarduran wields *Spiderbane*, a *battle axe +3* that can slay drow and spiders outright (no saving throw allowed) on an attack roll of 17 or greater. Once per round, the Deep Brother can summon any creature from the Plane of Earth, typically a xorn with maximum hit points or a 24-HD earth elemental. Callarduran can determine the safety and composition of rock within 300 yards of his position at will. Once per round he can cast *animate rock*, *earthquake*, *meld into stone*, *move earth*, *passwall*, *spike stones*, *stone shape*, *stone tell*, *transmute rock to mud* (or its reverse), *wall of iron*, or *wall of stone* at will.

He wears a suit of *chain mail +3*. If he presses his ring against stone, he can form a star gem, a unique type of jewel worth at least 5,000 gp. He can be struck only by +2 or better magical weapons.

Other Manifestations

Callarduran can manifest as a deposit of smoothed stone or a stone-shaped ring, a subtle clue to guide poor svirfneblin to a cache of gems the god has hidden. He is served by dao, earth elementals, galeb duhr, khargra, mineral quasielementals, xorn, and

countless other creatures from the Elemental Plane of Earth and the Quasielemental Plane of Minerals. He demonstrates his favor through the discovery of rubies, or in truly rare circumstances, star rubies or star gems. The Deep Brother indicates his displeasure by causing the earth to tremble and shake as if a minor, localized earthquake.

The Church

CLERGY:	Clerics, specialty priests
CLERGY'S ALIGN.:	NG, N
TURN UNDEAD:	C: Yes, SP: Yes, at priest level –4
CMND. UNDEAD:	C: No, SP: No

All clerics (including fighter/clerics, cleric/illusionists, and cleric/thieves) and specialty priests of Callarduran receive religion (gnome) as a bonus nonweapon proficiency.

Callarduran's church is little known beyond the Underdark cities of the svirfneblin, even among the other gnome subraces. Among the deep gnomes, the Deep Brother's priests are highly regarded for their wise council and steadfast dedication to protecting their kin. The drow are well aware of this cult's zeal in hunting the minions of the Spider Queen, and they return the favor whenever possible. Other evil-aligned Underdark races mark this church as anathema to their people, an opinion that is a positive measure of the priesthood's effectiveness in safeguarding the communities and mines of the svirfneblin.

Temples of the Deep Brother are constructed in natural caverns worn smooth by a centuries-long process of Callarduran's priests rubbing the rough stone with their bare hands. At the center of such subterranean chapels is a stalagmite altar raised from the stone floor by *stone shape* spells and inlaid with hundreds of tiny rubies. Suggestive of the Deep Brother's giant *stone of controlling earth elementals*, such solitary menhirs are said to house a great deal of magical power derived from the Elemental Plane of Earth, including the ability to animate itself as a 24-HD earth elemental should the temple ever come under attack.

Novices of Callarduran are known as the Unworked. Full priests of the Deep Brother are known as the Smoothed. In ascending order of rank, the titles used by Callardurian priests are First Facet, Second Facet, Third Facet, Fourth Facet, Fifth Facet, Sixth Facet, Seventh Facet, Eighth facet, and Ruby. High-ranking priests have unique individual titles. Specialty priests are known as earthbloods. The clergy of Callarduran includes deep gnomes (97%), rock gnomes (2%), and forest gnomes (1%). Only males are permitted in the priesthood (100%). Callarduran's clergy includes cleric/illusionists (45%), specialty priests (40%), fighter/clerics (8%), clerics (5%), and cleric/thieves (2%).

Dogma: Callarduran led his chosen people into the deepest depths of the earth so that they might discover the joyous beauty of rubies and other gems. Beware the dangers of Deepearth, and guard against evil races who employ any means necessary to seize what is not rightfully theirs, such as the drow. Protect and serve the interests of your community. Preserve and nurture the depths that give you and your people life, cradling you in their dark safety. Celebrate the intricacies of minerals, especially gems, and their many forms, uses, and subtle variations—including their latent magical potentials.

Day-to-Day Activities: Callarduran's priesthood is ever vigilant against the very real threat of drow incursions into the territories of the deep gnomes. Many lead small war bands against the drow in the hopes of exterminating them before they inevitably turn against nearby svirfneblin enclaves. The Deep Brother's priests are teachers of magic, particularly that of the schools of elemental earth and illusion/phantasm, and work within their communities to spread such knowledge among all the deep gnomes.

Gnome Powers: Callarduran Smoothhands

Holy Days/Important Ceremonies: The followers of Callarduran assemble on Midsummer day and on Midwinter night to venerate the god in sister ceremonies known as the Festivals of the Ruby and the Star, respectively. The Festival of the Ruby marks Callarduran's hiding of rubies and other gems in the depths of the earth for the deep gnomes to find, a story symbolized in svirfneblin mythology by tales of the Great Red Ruby (the setting sun) sinking into the earth (dipping below the horizon). The Festival of the Star celebrates the continued protection the Deep Brother provides to the descendants of the svirfneblin who followed him into the Deepearth. The holy day is marked by deep gnomes who assemble on the shore of a subterranean lake or pool to observe an annual event when small patches of a specially bred species of phosphorescent fungi in the cavern roof light up like stars, creating an illusion of the night sky reflected in the waters below. For deep gnomes this event reaffirms their ancestral ties with the surface world and reassures them that they have not been abandoned in the hostile environment deep beneath the surface of the earth.

Major Centers of Worship: Of the score or more major cities of the deep gnomes, only three are reasonably well known to surface dwellers: Blingdenstone, an ancient city of svirfneblin astride the tunnel route from Menzoberranzan to Mithral Hall, Corundruby, in the depths of the Bloodstone Mines beneath the Galenas, and fallen Mycaern, deep beneath Caer Callidyrr in the Underdark of the Moonshaes. These cities have achieved some measure of renown of late in the Lands of Light as a result of their recent alliances with surface dwellers against the evil races of the Underdark. However, many far larger communities of deep gnomes are hidden in the deepest caverns of the Underdark, far beyond the knowledge of most surface dwellers.

The Vault of the Star Ruby is a great temple-city of Callarduran located at least three miles beneath the floor of the Sea of Fallen Stars, roughly beneath the Pirate Isles on the maps of surface dwellers. Legendary even among other deep gnome communities, this is said to have been among the first settlement of the gnomes who followed Callarduran into the depths of the Underdark. At the heart of the central cavern hovers a gigantic star ruby nearly 10 feet in diameter. Said to be the heart of the Deep Brother, the Star Ruby of Callarduran is the greatest relic of the faith and the source of incredible magical power. For centuries, Callarduran's followers have studied the great gem and hidden the secret of its location from other creatures. With the god's assistance, it is believed that the priests of the Vault have learned how to call forth a veritable army of earth elementals and how to awaken volcanoes anywhere in the world. Such power, if it fell into the wrong hands, would create a disaster of incredible proportions, and so, the svirfneblin have avoided calling on the gem's powers and thus calling attention to its existence.

Affiliated Orders: The Wardens of the Webspinners are a tightly knit order of warriors, warrior/priests, and priests with chapters in most cities of the Forgotten Folk that must regularly battle drow for control of territory. Members of this group are trained in battle tactics designed for use against the followers of the Spider Queen. Many members of this elite company are deep gnome burrow wardens (6th or greater level fighters), hence the name of the order.

Priestly Vestments: The ceremonial garb of Callarduran's priesthood includes simple, slate-gray robes adorned with tiny gems of varying hue (although red is favored). A silver or mithral circlet is worn on the brow and steel sandals on the feet. The holy symbol of the faith is a ruby, with the size of the gem identifying the relative importance of the priest in the church. The highest ranking priests of the faith use star rubies as their holy symbols.

Adventuring Garb: Priests of Callarduran favor leather jacks sewn with rings or scales of mithral over fine chain mail shirts, providing an effective Armor Class of 2. In addition to battle axes, they favor picks, daggers, *stun darts* as weapons, and crystal caltrops that release a powerful *sleep* gas when stepped on.

Specialty Priests (Earthbloods)

REQUIREMENTS:	Intelligence 12, Wisdom 12
PRIME REQ.:	Intelligence, Wisdom
ALIGNMENT:	NG, N
WEAPONS:	Any
ARMOR:	Leather, studded leather, or chain mail and shield
MAJOR SPHERES:	All, charm, combat, creation, elemental (earth), guardian, healing, protection, summoning, wards
MINOR SPHERES:	Divination, elemental (air, fire, water), necromantic, travelers
MAGICAL ITEMS:	As clerics
REQ. PROFS:	Battle axe, stonemasonry
BONUS PROFS:	Gem cutting, mining

- Earthbloods must be deep gnomes or rock gnomes.
- Earthbloods are not allowed to multiclass.
- Earthbloods receive a +2 bonus to all saving throws against spells cast by drow spellcasters.
- Earthbloods can cast *strength of stone* (as the 1st-level priest spell detailed in the Moradin entry in the "Dwarven Pantheon" chapter) once per day.
- At 3rd level, deep gnome earthbloods can summon an earth elemental (as the natural ability of deep gnomes) once per day with a 25% chance of success. This chance is only 5% for rock gnomes. The type of earth elemental is determined by the following table:

Die Roll	Elemental
1	24-Hit Dice earth elemental
2–6	16-Hit Dice earth elemental
7–10	12-Hit Dice earth elemental
11–15	8-Hit Dice earth elemental
16–18	Xorn
19–20	Summoning fails

At 6th level, this chance increases to 65% for deep gnomes and 15% for rock gnomes.
- At 5th level, earthbloods can cast *meld into stone* or *stone shape* (as the 3rd-level priest spells) once per day.
- At 5th level, earthbloods can subtract 5% per their level (to a maximum of 50%) from the magic resistance of drow that they cast spells against.
- At 7th level, earthbloods can cast *dig* or *stoneskin* (as the 4th-level wizard spells) once per day.
- At 10th level, earthbloods can cast *lower resistance* (as the 5th-level wizard spell) or *wall of stone* (as the 5th-level wizard spell) once per day.
- At 13th level, earthbloods can cast *move earth* (as the 6th-level wizard spell) or *stone tell* (as the 6th-level priest spell) once per day.
- At 15th level, earthbloods can cast *animate rock* or *earthquake* (as the 7th-level priest spells) once per day.

Callardurian Spells

In addition to the spells listed below, priests of the Deep Brother may cast the 1st-level priest spell *detect metals and minerals* detailed in *Powers & Pantheons* in the entry for Geb, the 1st-level priest spell *strength of stone* detailed in the entry for Moradin, and the 3rd-level priest spell *depress resistance* detailed in the entry for Shevarash.

1st Level

Animate Stalactite (Pr 1; Alteration)

Sphere:	Elemental Earth
Range:	Touch
Components:	V, S, M
Duration:	Special
Casting Time:	1 round
Area of Effect:	One stalactite
Saving Throw:	None

Animate stalactite temporarily awakens a stalactite to act like a piercer (see the MONSTROUS MANUAL tome). A stalactite animated by this spell remains active until it detects prey, at which point it reacts exactly as a living piercer. When it can attack, the animated stalactite drops from the ceiling and attempts to impale prey with its sharp tip. Whether or not the attack succeeds, the animation is dispelled and the stalactite shatters upon impact if it does not successfully pierce a creature.

The attack score of an *animated stalactite* depends on the size of the stalactite selected and the level of the priest. The size of the stalactite gives a base value of 1 Hit Die if Small-sized, 2 Hit Dice if Man-sized, and 3 Hit Dice if Large-sized or greater. An *animated stalactite* is treated as +1 Hit Die per every three levels of the priest (round down), to a maximum of +3 Hit Dice. A successful *dispel magic* deactivates the *animated stalactite*, returning it to its normal state. The priest can animate and control no more than one stalactite per experience level.

The material component is the priest's holy symbol.

Animated Stalactite: AC 3; MV 1; HD 1–6; THAC0 19 (1–2 HD); 17 (3–4 HD); 15 (5–6 HD); #AT 1; Dmg 1d6 per 2HD; SA surprise; SZ varies by selection of stalactite size; ML fearless (19–20); Int non (0); AL N.

3rd Level

Ruby Axe (Pr 3; Alteration)
Sphere:	Combat
Range:	Touch
Components:	V, S, M
Duration:	5 rounds+1 round/level
Casting Time:	5
Area of Effect:	One hand axe or battle axe
Saving Throw:	None

Ruby axe causes the caster's axe to glow with a faint red light along its cutting edge. The axe temporarily becomes magical (if it was not already) and gains a +1 bonus to attack and damage rolls. The attack and damage bonus increases by +1 at 8th level, and the damage bonus increases by another +1 at 12th level, to a maximum of +2 to attack rolls and +3 to damage rolls. These bonuses are cumulative with any magical bonuses the axe may already have. The caster must wield the axe; if it is given to another to wield, all bonuses the spell grants do not apply, though the spell does not end. When the spell duration expires, the axe reverts to its normal state.

The material component for this spell is the priest's holy symbol.

4th Level

Stone Form (Pr 4; Alteration)
Sphere:	Elemental Earth
Range:	Touch
Components:	V, S, M
Duration:	3 rounds+1 round/level
Casting Time:	7
Area of Effect:	One creature
Saving Throw:	None

By means of this spell, the recipient is transformed into living stone, not unlike a stone golem or stone guardian. This spell has no effect if cast upon an unwilling target. As a creature of magical stone, the subject receives an effective Armor Class of 5 or a +1 bonus to current Armor Class, whichever is greater, and immunity to nonmagical attacks (such as acid, normal fire, normal weapons, and so on). However, a being in *stone form* is affected by all spells that affect stone, including *stone shape*, *transmute rock to mud*, etc. Any spell effect or physical blow that transforms or shatters the *stone form* in any way immediately ends the spell effect and inflicts 4d6 points of damage.

The material components for this spell are the priest's holy symbol and a shard of rock from a once-animate stone (perhaps part of a destroyed stone golem or a rock previously subjected to an *animate rock* spell).

Flandal Steelskin

(Master of Metal, Lord of Smiths, the Armorer, the Weaponsmith, the Great Steelsmith, the Pyromancer)

Intermediate Power of Bytopia, NG

PORTFOLIO:	Mining, physical fitness, smithing, metalworking, weaponsmithing, armoring
ALIASES:	None
DOMAIN NAME:	Dothion/the Golden Hills (the Mithral Forge)
SUPERIOR:	Garl Glittergold
ALLIES:	Clangeddin Silverbeard, Cyrrollalee, Dumathoin, Geb, Grumbar, Kossuth, Moradin, Urogalan, Vergadain, the gnome pantheon (except Urdlen)
FOES:	Abbathor, Gaknulak, Kuraulyek, Kurtulmak, Urdlen, the goblinkin pantheons
SYMBOL:	Flaming hammer
WOR. ALIGN.:	LG, NG, CG, LN, N, CN

Flandal Steelskin (FLAN-dahl STEEL-skin) is a master of mining and one of the finest and strongest smiths in creation. The Forgotten Folk hold that he helped create the craft of metalworking along with several of the dwarven powers. In particular, Flandal devised an alloy first employed by gnomes known as telstang, and he was the first to discover the properties of arandur, a legendary metal once known only to the Forgotten Folk.

Flandal is physically the strongest of the gnome gods, and his prodigious nose gives him an uncanny ability to sniff out veins of metal that thread the earth. The Master of Metal is the patron of gnome miners, artisans, craftsmen, and all smiths—not just blacksmiths, but goldsmiths, silversmiths, and all other workers of metal. They venerate Flandal in the hope of gaining a fraction of his skill. A large number of gnome warriors venerate Flandal the Armorer as well, for his skills help ensure their continued survival.

Flandal has excellent relations with the other gnome powers, with the notable exception of Urdlen. It was Flandal who helped forge and enchant *Arumdina*, Garl Glittergold's battle axe, and the Master of Metal is a trusted advisor to the head of the gnome pantheon. Flandal is friendly toward Segojan Earthcaller, for both oversee the safety of gnome miners. Similarly, Flandal and Nebelun (Gond) share a strong bond as fellow craftsmen, though the Master of Metal despairs that the Meddler will ever get his projects to actually work. Flandal is also closely allied with many of the good-aligned deities of the dwarven pantheon, and he shares a particularly strong bond with Moradin the Soul Forger. Like all gnome powers, Flandal opposes the various humanoid powers, particularly the kobold pantheon. The role the Master of Metal takes in combating them is indirect, for his primary focus is to pass on secrets for forging armor and weapons to the Forgotten Folk, so that they may defend themselves.

Flandal is a true master craftsmen. He is ever-demanding of his own work and strives tirelessly to increase his skill. He is also a patient tutor; only lazy and indifferent craftsfolk draw his ire. The Master of Metal is often found traveling with one or two of the other gnome powers in search of new ores and veins of metal to use in his forges. When Flandal is not traveling, he can be found in his workshop, planning or making a new magical weapon. He is no stranger to battle, trusting in the creations of his forges to see him to victory. Although Flandal's war hammer *Rhondang* is capable of conversing with all fire-using creatures, its language proficiencies in no way means that Flandal is friendly toward those beings. Still, this god is prone to talk first in preference to combat. On rare occasions, Flandal dispatches an avatar to instruct gnomes in some very tricky smithing process or to guide them to hidden veins of ores. He may also send an avatar to deal with any disputes between gnomes and fire-dwelling creatures.

Flandal's Avatar

(Fighter 33, Cleric 33, Earth Elementalist 30, Fire Elementalist 30)

Flandal often appears as a balding, slightly aging, huge-nosed gnome with skin the color of blue mithral and eyes that appear as flaming coals. His hair and beard are brilliant blue-silver, and he wears a leather apron over (or in lieu of) beard are brilliant blue-silver, and he wears a leather apron over (or in lieu of) his other clothing. He favors spells from the spheres of all, combat, creation, divination, elemental (earth, fire), guardian, protection, sun, and time and from the schools of divination and elemental earth and fire, although he can cast spells from any sphere or school.

AC –6; MV 12; HP 223; THAC0 –10; #AT 5/2
Dmg 1d4+20 (*war hammer* +5, +12 STR, +2 spec. bonus in war hammer)
MR 70%; SZ M (4 feet tall)
STR 24, DEX 19, CON 21, INT 18, WIS 18, CHA 16
Spells P: 12/12/11/11/9/9/9, W: 9/9/9/9/9/9/9/8/8*
Saves PPDM 2, RSW 1**, PP 4, BW 4, Sp 1**
  *Numbers assume one extra elemental earth and elemental fire spell per spell level. **Includes gnome +6 CON save bonus to a minimum of 1.

Special Att/Def: Flandal wields *Rhondang*, a *war hammer* +5 of gold-plated mithral with an axe back. *Rhondang* inflicts double damage against cold-using and cold-dwelling creatures, can hurl a 6d6 *fireball* once per round in addition to its normal attacks, can flame like a *flame tongue* at will, and speaks the languages of all fire-using creatures (chimerae, fire elementals, red dragons, etc.).

Once per round, Flandal can cast *heat metal*, *ironguard*, or *pyrotechnics* at will. Once per day, Flandal can summon 2d4 16-HD fire elementals. These elementals are quite friendly to him and serve without question for up to 1 hour before returning to the Elemental Plane of Fire.

The Master of Metal wears an *apron of fire resistance* that reduces to half all damage suffered from heat and fire. He can be struck only by +2 or better magical weapons.

Other Manifestations

Flandal may manifest as flares of fire in a forge or hearth or jets of flame dancing about a bare floor or earth. Such flaming manifestations can erupt into a *fireball*, *flame strike*, or *pyrotechnics* effect or serve as a pyromantic scrying device.

Flandal is served by earth elementals, fire elementals, helmed horrors, iron golems, khargra, living steel, metal masters, mineral quasielementals, rust monsters, steel dragons, xavers, and xorns. He demonstrates his favor through the discovery of precious metals of any sort (particularly arandur and telstang), beljurils, fire agates, fire opals, flamedance, and mellochrysos. The Master of Metal indicates his displeasure by causing small tremors in the earth and by causing metals to crack or shatter as they cool or are struck by a hammer.

Gnome Powers: Flandal Steelskin

The Church

CLERGY:	Clerics, specialty priests
CLERGY'S ALIGN.:	LG, NG, CG
TURN UNDEAD:	C: Yes, SP: No
CMND. UNDEAD:	C: No, SP: No

All clerics (including fighter/clerics, cleric/illusionists, and cleric/thieves) and specialty priests of Flandal receive religion (gnome) as a bonus nonweapon proficiency.

The church of Flandal is highly regarded by most gnomes, for its priests are typically master smiths, a very respected occupation in the societies of the Forgotten Folk. They are known to share the secrets of their crafts with gnome artisans and craftsfolk without prejudice. The Stout Folk also hold the Master of Metal in high regard, and Flandal's followers are considered on the average to be the equal of dwarven smiths, a high compliment from the proud children of Moradin, and the followers of Flandal Steelskin are seen to embody nearly

everything dwarves like about the gnome character. Humans, elves, and half-elves respect the workmanship of the Forgotten Folk, but their work lacks the mystique that enfolds dwarven smithcraft, and as a result, Flandal's faith is less widely known than that of Moradin.

Temples of Flandal are typically subterranean forges that serve the faithful as both houses of worship and working smithies. Most temples are built atop the mines from which the ore for the priesthood's smithy is brought to be smelted.

Novices of Flandal are known as the Unworked. Full priests of the Master of Metal are known as the Tempered. In ascending order of rank, the titles used by Flandalian priests are Tinsmith, Bronzesmith, Brasssmith, Coppersmith, Silversmith, Electrumsmith, Goldsmith, Platinumsmith, and Steelsmith. High-ranking priests have unique individual titles. Specialty priests are known as pyrosmiths. The clergy of Flandal includes rock gnomes (65%), deep gnomes (25%), and forest gnomes (10%). Males make up the majority of his priesthood (88%). Flandal's clergy includes specialty priests (55%), fighter/clerics (35%), clerics (7%), cleric/illusionists (2%), and cleric/thieves (1%).

Dogma: The treasures of life were buried within the earth's embrace at Segojan's hand, and only hard labor, dedication, and great craftsmanship, as taught by the Master of Metal, can reveal their hidden beauties and wonders. Dig mines, extract ores, and forge suits of armor, weapons, and other items of metal. Strive to refine known techniques of metalworking, invent new processes for tempering and refining it, and discover new alloys and test their potentials. Finally, stay physically fit to enable you to pursue the rigors of the forge and mine with your whole heart.

Day-to-Day Activities: Members of Flandal's priesthood are inveterate miners and smiths. They continuously hone their skills in underground environments, seeking an intuitive understanding of the earth and stone. Many serve as teachers, instructing other gnomes in the art of detecting veins of ore, unsafe environments, and the presence of hostile creatures. Priests of the Master of Metal oversee the safety of gnome miners and inspect the output of gnome smithies. Nearly all members of the clergy are considered master smiths when working with one or more types of metal, and they produce fantastic weapons and suits of armor whose quality rivals that of priests of Moradin. Flandal's priests are expected to undergo regular strength and stamina training, a practice that keeps them physically fit for mining, smithing, or battle, as needed.

Holy Days/Important Ceremonies: Members of Flandal's priesthood assemble annually on Midsummer's Day in great moots to celebrate the holy day known as the High Forge. The faithful gather in the morning to make offerings of forged metal weapons to the god and offer praises to him through rhythmic, percussive hammer hymns culminating at midday with a brief period of utter silence. In the afternoon and evening, the participants exchange ideas and new techniques and exhibit the finest of their wares, and by evening the gathering is overwhelmed by merchants seeking to acquire new trade goods.

Major Centers of Worship: In the Cold Lands north of the Moonsea, a small mountain range runs east-west along the northern edge of the Border Forest, dividing the Tortured Land from the Ride. On the southern flanks of the White Peaks, as the snow-capped range is known locally, lies the small town of Whitehorn. Like Ilinvur to the south and west, Whitehorn is an outpost of Melvaunt and Thentia where the ore brought from nearby mines is crudely smelted before shipment to the cities to the south. Although individual gnome and dwarven miners are a regular, if infrequent, presence in Whitehorn, the humans who make up the majority of the town's population believe they are simply a handful of isolated miners who eke out a living by trading ore for food and equipment. Unbeknownst to the merchants of the Moonsea, the White Peaks are home to a large city of gnomes (as well as a few dwarves) named Forharn.

Forharn was founded over five centuries ago by an order of Flandalian priests after their leader, a gnome priest known only as the Arandhammer, discovered a massive vein of arandur in the heart of an ancient volcano. Begun as a temple-foundry consecrated to the Master of Metal, the Vitreous Forge has since grown into a city of over 10,000 gnomes and nearly 500 dwarves. Forharn is ruled by the Hammers of Flandal, a ruling council composed of senior miners, master smiths, and the Arandhammer (the seventh high priest of Flandal to hold that title). Arandur from the city's mines is smelted and forged into iron-plated trade bars and then sold to allied merchant concerns in Whitehorn by gnomes and dwarves pretending to be miners from isolated iron mines in the surrounding mountains. When Forharn's trade bars reach Melvaunt or Thentia, they are repurchased discreetly by traders in the employ of gnome-owned trading companies and shipped to communities of the Forgotten Folk throughout the southern Realms. By this means, the followers of Flandal are able to ship great quantities of this legendary metal across the Realms from mines right under the nose of the Zhentarim. When the occasional caravan carrying the trade bars of Forharn is lost, an elite company of gnome warriors and priests is dispatched to recover the lost trade bars before anyone discovers their arandur cores. A fact that would greatly alarm the human miners of Whitehorn, if they only knew, is the presence of a young red dragon and an adult blue dragon in the catacombs of Forharn. Raised from birth by the temple's clergy, both wyrms have reached a mutually beneficial agreement with the city's smiths in which they lend their breath weapons during the smelting of arandur in exchange for a significant tithe of the profits.

Affiliated Orders: The Fellowship of Steel is an order of fighters, clerics, fighter/clerics, and specialty priests that defend the mines of the Forgotten Folk. Members of this order serve their god by guarding miners and clearing regions of tunnels which gnomes are planning to mine of any dangerous creatures.

Priestly Vestments: The ceremonial garb of Flandal's priests is a steel helm and a suit of metal armor, typically chain mail or plate mail. Senior priests tint their metallic vestments the red-orange hue of the forge. The holy symbol of the faith is a miniature steel hammer engraved with a flame.

Adventuring Garb: Priests of Flandal favor the most durable metal armor available when adventuring, trusting their safety to the quality of workmanship and strength of materials. They only employ weapons made at least in part of metal, and solid metal weapons are always preferred.

Specialty Priests (Pyrosmiths)

REQUIREMENTS:	Strength 12, Constitution 12, Wisdom 9
PRIME REQ.:	Strength, Constitution, Wisdom
ALIGNMENT:	NG
WEAPONS:	Any metal-bladed or metal-headed weapon
ARMOR:	Any metal armor
MAJOR SPHERES:	All, combat, creation, divination, elemental (earth, fire), guardian, protection, sun, time
MINOR SPHERES:	Elemental (air, water), healing, war
MAGICAL ITEMS:	As clerics
REQ. PROFS:	War hammer; armorer or weaponsmithing
BONUS PROFS:	Blacksmithing, endurance, mining

- Pyrosmiths must be gnomes. Most pyrosmiths are rock gnomes, but gnomes of every subrace except spriggans can be pyrosmiths.
- Pyrosmiths are not allowed to multiclass.
- Pyrosmiths may select nonweapon proficiencies from the warrior group without penalty.
- Pyrosmiths receive Constitution hit point adjustments to their Hit Dice as if they were warriors.
- Pyrosmiths can cast wizard spells from the elemental school of fire as defined in the Limited Wizard Spellcasting section of "Appendix 1: Demihuman Priests."
- Pyrosmiths can cast *resist fire* (as the 2nd-level priest spell) twice per day.
- At 3rd level, pyrosmiths can cast *heat metal* (as the 2nd-level priest spell) once per day.
- At 5th level, pyrosmiths can cast *protection from fire* (as the 3rd-level priest spell) once per day.
- At 5th level, pyrosmiths gain a +1 bonus to their Strength or Constitution ability scores. They gain an additional +1 to either of these at 10th level and at 20th level. Neither score can exceed 25 in this way.
- At 7th level, pyrosmiths can cast *minor creation* (as the 4th-level wizard spell) or *shades of Rhondang* (as the 4th-level priest spell) once per day.
- At 10th level, pyrosmiths can cast *major creation* (as the 5th-level wizard spell) once per day.

- At 13th level, pyrosmiths can cast *fireball* (as the 3rd-level wizard spell) or *Malec-Keth's flame fist* (as the 7th-level wizard spell) once per day.

Flandalian Spells

In addition to the spells listed below, priests of the Master of Metal may cast the 1st-level priest spell *detect metals and minerals*, detailed in *Powers & Pantheons* in the entry for Geb. In addition, members of Flandal's clergy have developed fire-based variants of many clerical divination spells, a subspecialty of divination known as pyromancy. Typically, the medium of divination in such variants is replaced by fire. For example, the Flandalian variant of *magic font* involves a flickering flame, not a basin of holy water.

1st Level

Steelskin (Pr 1; Alteration)
Sphere:	Protection
Range:	Touch
Components:	V, S, M
Duration:	3 rounds+1 round/level
Casting Time:	4
Area of Effect:	One creature
Saving Throw:	None

By means of this spell, the caster transforms the hide of a creature into an alloy of flesh and steel. The added protection of the spell is sufficient to give a +1 bonus to Armor Class for every three levels of the priest (round up), to a maximum bonus of +5. However, the *steelskin* reduces the recipient's Dexterity to two thirds normal (rounded down) with a corresponding adjustment to Dexterity related abilities.

The material components for this spell are the priest's holy symbol and a forged steel rod.

3rd Level

Metal Shape (Pr 3; Alteration)
Sphere:	Elemental Earth
Range:	Touch
Components:	V, S, M
Duration:	Instantaneous
Casting Time:	1 round
Area of Effect:	9 cubic feet+1 cubic foot/level
Saving Throw:	None

By means of this spell, the caster forms an existing piece of nonmagical metal into any shape that suits his or her purposes. For example, she or he can make a metal weapon, a special trapdoor, or a crude idol. While metal coffers can be formed, metal doors made, and so forth, the fineness of detail is not great. If the shaping has moving parts, there is a 30% chance they do not work. If the shaping has a sharp edge, there is only a 30% chance it is sharp enough to cut. However, if this spell is employed on metal prior to it being worked by a smith, it reduces the time and expense to create the final product by 50% or more, as adjudicated by the DM.

The material component for this spell is lead that must be worked with a hammer into roughly the desired shape of the metal object.

4th Level

Shades of Rhondang (Pr 4; Evocation)
Sphere:	Elemental Fire
Range:	Touch
Components:	V, M
Duration:	1 round/level
Casting Time:	7
Area of Effect:	Caster's hammer
Saving Throw:	None

This spell gains its name by allowing the caster to temporarily duplicate certain powers of Flandal's magical hammer, *Rhondang*.

When the spell is cast, the caster's hammer bursts into flames, taking on the magical characteristics of a *flame tongue* sword. Thus, while the spell lasts, the hammer is regarded as a +1 weapon, +2 vs. regenerating creatures, +3 vs. cold-using, flammable, and avian creatures, and +4 vs. the undead. It produces light equal to a torch and can ignite flammable objects upon contact.

Shades of Rhondang functions only if used on a nonmagical hammer. If cast on a magical hammer or any other type of weapon, the spell automatically fails. Furthermore, the hammer to be affected must be owned and used by the caster and cannot be passed to another creature. Attempting to cast the spell on someone else's hammer or seeking to pass the hammer to another creature immediately negates the spell.

Shades of Rhondang ends if subjected to a successful *dispel magic* or similar effect, if the caster is slain, rendered unconscious, or releases his or her grip on the hammer's handle. Since the caster must retain a hold of the hammer to prevent the spell from ending, she or he cannot cast spells that require somatic components nor perform any actions that require the use of both hands.

The material components for this spell are the caster's holy symbol and the hammer to be affected, neither of which are consumed by the spell.

Gaerdal Ironhand
(The Stern, Shield of the Golden Hills)

Lesser Power of Bytopia, LG

Portfolio:	Vigilance, combat, martial defense
Aliases:	None
Domain Name:	Dothion/the Golden Hills (Stronghaven)
Superior:	Garl Glittergold
Allies:	Arvoreen, Clangeddin Silverbeard, Cyrrollalee, Gorm Gulthyn, Helm, Torm, the gnome pantheon (except Urdlen)
Foes:	Abbathor, Gaknulak, Kuraulyek, Kurtulmak, Urdlen, the goblinkin pantheons
Symbol:	Iron band
Wor. Align.:	LG, NG, CG, LN, N, CN

Gaerdal Ironhand (GAIR-dahl EYE-urn-hand) is the stalwart defender of the Forgotten Folk, the most martial deity of the gnome pantheon. His serious nature garners him sober respect, instead of the gentle affection that is lavished on the other deities. The Shield of the Golden Hills guards against threats from above and below and teaches gnomes to hold their own in combat with larger and more powerful creatures by using their size and natural abilities to their advantage. Gaerdal has a small but devout following among gnome warriors and those responsible for defending gnome communities against outside threats, and he has earned the respect of the Forgotten Folk in general.

Gaerdal has generally good relations with the rest of the gnome pantheon, with the notable exception of Urdlen, but his stern nature keeps him somewhat aloof from the mischievous antics of the other gods of the Forgotten Folk. In particular, the Shield of the Golden Hills is somewhat hostile toward Baravar, disliking deceitfulness, and to a lesser extent Baervan, disliking foolish pranks and other jests, and he may work to thwart their plans if he learns of them. In times of danger for the Forgotten Folk, however, Gaerdal cooperates with all the gnome gods, except the Crawler Below. Among other pantheons, Gaerdal is closest in temperament with the gods of the dwarven pantheon, particularly Gorm Gulthyn and Clangeddin Silverbeard. Gaerdal works well with Helm and Torm of the human Faerûnian pantheon. The Shield of the Golden Hills is ever vigilant in guarding against Urdlen's insidious attacks, and he battles the gods of the kobold and goblin pantheons regularly.

Gaerdal Ironhand is the most dwarflike deity of the gnome pantheon, rarely smiling, and he is the only gnome god who could be considered stern. Gaerdal takes his duties as the protector of gnome burrows very seriously, at the cost of sacrificing a playful spirit. The Shield of the Golden Hills has no use for tricks, jokes, or deceits, and he remains unsmiling at gnome tales and pranks (save those of Garl himself). The other gnome deities say he chuckles in private, but this is uncertain. Gaerdal often sends an avatar to assist gnomes preparing for battle.

Gaerdal's Avatar (Fighter 30, Cleric 27)

Gaerdal most frequently appears as a stern, strong gnome in the prime of life clad in chain mail. He has thick, sleek brown hair and brown eyes. He favors spells from the spheres of all, combat, guardian, law, protection, war, and wards, although he can cast spells from any sphere.

AC –4; MV 12; HP 204; THAC0 –9; #AT 5/2
Dmg 1d4+16 (*war hammer +4*, +9 Str, +2 spec. bonus in war hammer)
MR 55%; SZ M (4 feet tall)
Str 21, Dex 18, Con 21, Int 17, Wis 18, Cha 19
Spells P: 12/12/11/11/9/9/5
Saves PPDM 2, RSW 1*, PP 4, BW 4, Sp 1*
  * Includes gnome +5 Con save bonus to a minimum of 1.

Special Att/Def: Gaerdal wields *Hammersong*, a *war hammer +4* that, when it strikes a hard surface, utters a loud clanging sound equal in effect to a *deafening clang* (see "Gaerdalian Spells"). The Shield of the Golden Hills can create a *wall of iron* or *wall of stone* at will, once per round. Three times per day he can create a *wave of telekinesis* with a sweep of his hand.

He wears *chain mail +3* and carries a *shield +1*. He can be struck only by +1 or better magical weapons.

Other Manifestations

The Shield of the Golden Hills may manifest as an aura of shimmering silver and gold light that envelops a living creature and then withdraws into his or her body. The effects of Gaerdal's manifestation are three-fold: the recipient receives the benefits of *blessed watchfulness*, *iron vigil*, and *protection from evil* spells.

Gaerdal is served by earth and fire elementals, galeb duhr, guardian nagas, helmed horrors, incarnates of courage and faith, maruts, noctrals, per, sapphire dragons, silver dragons, and spectators. He demonstrates his favor through the discovery of alestones, alexandrites, amaratha (also known as shieldstone), carnelian, hypersthene, peridot, sapphires, star rose quartz, star sapphires, and topazes. The Shield of the Golden Hills indicates his displeasure through slightly exaggerated and rather bombastic omens: underground rumblings, a statuette cracking very loudly, rocks detonating, and the like.

The Church

Clergy:	Clerics, specialty priests
Clergy's Align.:	LG, NG, LN
Turn Undead:	C: Yes, SP: Yes, at priest level –2
Cmnd. Undead:	C: No, SP: No

All clerics (including fighter/clerics, cleric/illusionists, and cleric/thieves) and specialty priests of Gaerdal receive religion (gnome) as a bonus nonweapon proficiency.

Gaerdal's stern nature is faithfully matched by his priests, and as such, while his faith is well respected among the Forgotten Folk, it is not greatly loved. The faithful of the Shield of the Golden Hills have more in common with the Stout Folk than their own kin, and Gaerdal's church is well respected by those dwarves who venerate Gorm Gulthyn. Although the existence of this cult is not widely known among other races, it is well regarded by those halfling followers of Arvoreen and human followers of Torm and Helm who have learned of their gnome analogs.

Temples of Gaerdal are fortified subterranean strongholds formed from worked caves that serve as both houses of worship and defensive fortifications. Small statues of the god are erected at the center of such shrines, symbolizing Gaerdal's unflagging vigilance, but otherwise each temple is relatively austere, adorned only with the shields of the fallen.

Novices of Gaerdal are known as the Eyes of Shield. Full priests of the Shield of the Golden Hills are known as the Vigilant Host. In ascending order of rank, the titles used by Gaerdalian priests are Stern Watcher, Stern Observer, Stern Guard, Stern Sentinel, Stern Sentry, Stern Guardian, Stern Defender, and Stern Protector. High-ranking priests have unique individual titles. Specialty priests are known as sternshields. The clergy of Gaerdal includes rock gnomes (75%), forest gnomes (15%), and deep gnomes (10%). Males make up the majority of his priesthood (85%). Gaerdal's clergy includes specialty priests (60%), fighter/clerics (24%), clerics (13%), cleric/illusionists (2%), and cleric/thieves (1%).

Dogma: The best defense is unswerving vigilance. Gaerdal charges his followers to serve him with absolute dedication and devotion. Defend and protect communities of the Forgotten Folk against all invaders, both obvious and hidden. Never cease to hone the skills of battle and war, and use times of peace to pass such talents on to gnomes at large so that they can eventually preserve peace for all the Forgotten Folk forever by presenting a defense that none dare challenge. Be fair to those in your charge, and ask of them nothing that you would not do yourself—including laying down your life for your friends, relatives, and brothers and sisters of battle. Follow orders given you to preserve the efficient function of the chain of command, but do not be blind to the consequences of your actions or the implications of a command. You have a right to question once any order that seems to run counter to the common good or the ideals of our society, for in doing so you may unmask a spy, a traitor, or an invader cloaked by magic.

Day-to-Day Activities: Gaerdal's priests are as close to being a warrior caste as one could find among gnomes. Their numbers are fairly small. They are much less given to levity than most gnomes and may often be administrators, judges, and the like. Their role as protectors is of major importance to both their religious teachings and the safety of the communities where they dwell. Although temples of the Shield of the Golden Hills are rare, Gaerdal's priests usually erect small statues of Gaerdal at major entrances to gnome settlements to remind other gnomes of their daily duties. The closest most members of Gaerdal's clergy get to actively seeking enjoyment is their perennial and self-assumed task of making life difficult for the followers of Baravar, and to a lesser extent, Baervan and Garl.

Holy Days/Important Ceremonies: The followers of Gaerdal refer to tenday periods as Tenhammers, a name referring to the marking of the passage of each day by striking a great hammer against a metal shield, for such is the typical length of service for guard duty for members of this faith. The tenth day of every ten Tenhammers is a holy day of the faith, known to gnomes everywhere as the Great Clang and on such days the cult of Gaerdal assembles to pay homage to the god through battle hymns and rhythmic chants.

Major Centers of Worship: The Rathgaunt Hills, located due east of Lake Lhespen and the Shaar, midway between the cities of Shaarmid and Sebben, are a dangerous and unforgiving region for surface dwellers, for many predators who hunt on the plains of the Shaar and Eastern Shaar, including perytons, wyverns, and manticores, dwell amidst these rocky crags. A scattered community of rock gnomes, well skilled in the art of camouflage, dwell in shallow burrows throughout the range of hills working small, scattered veins of gold and silver.

The ever-present need to defend the burrows of the Forgotten Folk, coupled with the need for armed caravans to bring their wares to Shaarmid and the Great Rift for trade, has given unusual prominence to the cult of Gaerdal. At the heart of Sevenstones Hill, a prominent tor whose rounded peak overlooks the northern branch of the Traders' Way to the east, lies the Shield of the Rathgaunt Hills, a fortified abbey of 200 warriors and priests whose vigorous efforts keep the range relatively safe for its gnome inhabitants. The temple's high priest and de facto leader of the scattered gnome enclaves is Shield General Martak Ironwall. The most notable aspect of Martak's term as Shield General has been the amicable resolution of many long-standing points of friction between the Forgotten Folk of the Rathgaunt Hills and the Stout Folk of the Great Rift, a development that recently led to a treaty of mutual defense between the two races and regions.

Affiliated Orders: The Shields of the Golden Hills are a strictly organized militant order with semiautonomous chapters in most large gnome communities. Strictly divided into four individual branches according to skill, this group includes specialty priests, fighters, fighter/clerics, and clerics. The Shields are charged with defending the Forgotten Folk against attackers as well as serving as both the champions and officers of any larger force raised by the gnomes in time of need.

Priestly Vestments: The ceremonial vestments of Gaerdal's clergy include a suit of chain mail, an open-faced helm, and a shield emblazoned with the god's device. The faith's holy symbol is an iron or steel band worn on the right forearm.

Adventuring Garb: The strictly functional ceremonial garb of priests of Gaerdal serves them well in dangerous situations. Nevertheless, members of the clergy acquire the best armor that they can afford, and most senior priests commission a suit of gnome-sized plate mail at some point in their lives.

Specialty Priests (Sternshields)

REQUIREMENTS:	Strength 13, Wisdom 9
PRIME REQ.:	Strength, Wisdom
ALIGNMENT:	LG, LN
WEAPONS:	Any
ARMOR:	Any
MAJOR SPHERES:	All, combat, divination, guardian, healing, law, protection, summoning, war, wards
MINOR SPHERES:	Elemental (earth), necromantic
MAGICAL ITEMS:	As clerics
REQ. PROFS:	War hammer, blind-fighting
BONUS PROFS:	Alertness, endurance

- Sternshields must be gnomes. While most sternshields are rock gnomes, gnomes of every subrace except spriggans are called to be specialty priests of Gaerdal's clergy.
- Sternshields are not allowed to multiclass.
- Sternshields may select nonweapon proficiencies from the warrior group without penalty.
- Sternshields receive Constitution hit point adjustments to their Hit Dice as if they were warriors.
- Sternshields can cast *blessed watchfulness* (as the 1st-level priest spell detailed in the Gorm Gulthyn entry in the "Dwarven Pantheon" chapter) or *strength* (as the 2nd-level wizard spell) once per day.
- At 3rd level, sternshields can cast *iron vigil* (as the 2nd-level priest spell detailed in the Gorm Gulthyn entry in the "Dwarven Pantheon" chapter) or *spiritual hammer* (as the 2nd-level priest spell) once per day.
- At 5th level, sternshields can cast *glyph of warding* or *protection from evil, 10´ radius* (as the 3rd-level priest spells) once per day.
- At 7th level, sternshields can cast *abjure* (as the 4th-level priest spell) or *shout* (as the 4th-level wizard spell) once per day.
- At 7th level, sternshields can make three melee attacks every two rounds.
- At 10th level, sternshields can cast *cloak of bravery* (as the 4th-level priest spell) or *defensive harmony* (as the 4th-level priest spell) once per day.
- At 13th level, sternshields can cast *clairaudience* (as the 3rd-level wizard spell) or *minor globe of invulnerability* (as the 4th-level wizard spell) once per day.
- At 13th level, sternshields can make two melee atacks per round.
- At 15th level, sternshields can cast *blade barrier* (as the 6th-level priest spell) or *symbol* (as the 7th-level priest spell) once per day.

Gaerdalian Spells

In addition to the spells listed below, priests of the Shield of the Golden Hills may cast the 1st-level priest spell *blessed watchfulness* and the 2nd-level priest spells *alert allies* and *iron vigil* detailed in the entry for Gorm Gulthyn.

1st Level

Deafening Clang (Pr 1; Enchantment)

Sphere:	Combat
Range:	Touch
Components:	V, S, M
Duration:	Special
Casting Time:	4
Area of Effect:	One metal item
Saving Throw:	None

This spell is only effective when cast upon a metal item. Once cast, the object enchanted by this spell rings with a *deafening clang* if struck against a hard surface and a command word is spoken. The item can create no more than one such effect per round. The spell expires once three *deafening clangs* have been sounded or once 10 rounds have passed from the time of casting.

All creatures (except the wielder) within 10 feet of the point of contact when a *deafening clang* is sounded must make a successful saving throw vs. spell or be deafened for 2d4 rounds. An affected creature has a –1 penalty to its surprise rolls unless its other senses are unusually keen. Deafened spellcasters have a 20% chance to miscast any spell with a verbal component. The deafness fades in 2d4 rounds or can be cured magically (by *cure blindness or deafness*, for example).

The material components for this spell are the priest's holy symbol and a small round metal gong.

3rd Level

Nature's Eyes (Pr 3; Divination)

Sphere:	Animal, Divination
Range:	0
Components:	V, S, M
Duration:	1 hour+1 hour/3 levels
Casting Time:	1 round
Area of Effect:	30-foot radius/level
Saving Throw:	None

This spell attunes the priest to the natural world and links the caster, at will, to the senses of the creatures of animal intelligence or less in the area of effect. If there are too few living creatures in the area of effect (such as in true deserts, underground complexes, and areas haunted by the undead), then this spell confers no real benefit. If, however, the surrounding region teems with animal life, the caster is instantly aware of intruders in the area of effect and their approximate positions provided that living creatures can detect them. Although the priest cannot be surprised while employing *nature's eyes*, no information other than the approximate position of intruders can be determined by this spell. The spell lasts 1 hour, plus 1 hour per three levels of the caster (rounded down).

The material components for this spell are the priest's holy symbol and a pair of acorns held in the caster's fists.

4th Level

Wave of Telekinesis (Pr 4; Alteration)

Sphere:	Combat
Range:	0
Components:	V, S
Duration:	Instantaneous
Casting Time:	7
Area of Effect:	60¡ arc, 10 yards/level
Saving Throw:	Neg.

By means of this spell, the caster moves one or more objects within a 60° arc and within 10 yards per level with a single short, violent thrust in a generally uniform direction. Affected objects weighing 25 pounds per level or less are hurled directly away from the caster at high speed to a distance of up to 10 feet per caster level (175-pound or lighter objects are thrown to up to 70 feet for a 7th-level caster). Creatures within the weight capacity of the spell are hurled only if they fail a saving throw vs. spell. Damage caused to hurled creatures is decided by the DM but cannot exceed 1 point of damage per caster level. Those able to employ as simple a countermeasure as an *enlarge* spell, for example (making the body weight exceed the maximum spell limit), can easily thwart this spell. The various *Bigby's hand* spells also counter this spell.

Garl Glittergold

(The Joker, the Watchful Protector, the Priceless Gem, the Sparkling Wit)

Greater Power of Bytopia, LG

PORTFOLIO:	Protection, humor, trickery, gem cutting, finesmithing and lapidary, the gnome race
ALIASES:	None
DOMAIN NAME:	Dothion/the Golden Hills (Glitterhome)
SUPERIOR:	None
ALLIES:	Brandobaris, Clangeddin Silverbeard, Corellon Larethian, Cyrrollalee, Dumathoin, Erevan Ilesere, Gorm Gulthyn, Grumbar, Moradin, Tymora, Vergadain, Yondalla, the gnome pantheon (except Urdlen)
FOES:	Abbathor, Gaknulak, Kuraulyek, Kurtulmak, Urdlen, the goblinkin pantheons
SYMBOL:	Gold nugget
WOR. ALIGN.:	LG, NG, CG, LN, N, CN

Garl Glittergold (GARL GLIHT-ter-gold) is the Watchful Protector of the Forgotten Folk and the leader of the gnome pantheon. He is said to have discovered the first gnomes while exploring a new cavern and then told them a joke before leading them into the world. All gnomes who embrace the communal life of the Forgotten Folk venerate the Joker, even if they also worship another deity. His name is invoked by gnomes involved in smithcraft (particularly those who work with gold) and gem cutting. Gnomes who wish to play a prank or tell a joke invoke his name, as do those who seek to protect and strengthen gnome communities.

Garl is on excellent terms with the rest of the gnome pantheon, with the notable exception of Urdlen. He insists they cooperate in all endeavors, and he shares with them his responsibilities and concerns, thus mining and smithing are also overseen by Flandal Steelskin, illusion is also the province of Baravar Cloakshadow, protection and combat are responsibilities shared with Gaerdal Ironhand, and so on. Garl's boon companion is *Arumdina the Justifier,* a great intelligent two-headed battle axe, commonly referred to as female, who serves him as both weapon and friend. The sight of the gleaming weapon that cleaves through stone as easily as through air and slices through metal armor as if it did not exist has probably encouraged more than one victim of one of Garl's jokes to laugh it off with good humor rather than get too mad. The Joker is often found in the company of other powers of other pantheons of similar perspective, including Brandobaris, Erevan Ilesere, Tymora, and Vergadain. The various powers worshiped by humanoids and creatures of the Underdark are often the target of Garl's jests, and he usually leaves them helpless and humbled, a victim of self-inflicted folly. As a result, despite his ever-optimistic hope that they might learn a lesson about overweening pride and pomposity, the Joker has garnered many enemies from among their ranks, particularly among the kobold pantheon. Notable among the Joker's exploits are the story of how he pretended to be caught by Kurtulmak before escaping as he collapsed the kobold god's cavern on top of Kurtulmak, and the story of how Garl dressed up as a deer to lure Grankhul, the bugbear hunter god, out into the open before trapping him with an illusion and leaving him trussed up like a turkey.

Garl is a gentle and approachable power, one who values quick thinking and a clear head more than almost anything. He rarely stays in one location for very long. Though physical prowess and spiritual might are important, nothing is more crucial than keeping it all in perspective. Garl watches over cooperation among gnomes at all times; he may send omens, even an avatar, to resolve strife and serious disputes. Garl prefers trickery, illusion, and wiles to direct physical confrontation, although if forced to fight he is hardly weak. The leader of the gnome pantheon often steals evil weapons and magic intended for malefic ends from their owners and then disposes of them. The Joker is also a mischievous trickster, said to have the largest collection of jokes in the multiverse, and he has always got one appropriate to the situation. The Joker usually carries plenty of props for his illusions and practical jokes as he never knows when they might come in handy. There is another side to Garl than that of the witty adventurer who collapsed the kobold god's cavern. The Watchful Protector is ever alert to threats to the Forgotten Folk and watches directly over their affairs. If such threats cannot be forestalled, Garl will defend his people as needed and appropriate. Although his military prowess is almost always used defensively, when Garl's people are physically threatened, the god is a grim and determined war leader who out-thinks as well as out-fights his opponents.

Garl's Avatar (Thief 37, Illusionist 34, Cleric 32, Fighter 30)

Garl often appears as a handsome golden-skinned gnome with gemstones of ever-changing hue for eyes. He is well dressed, usually with a flowing cloak of silk, and always with a significant quantity of gold about his person. He favors spells from the spheres of all, animal, charm, combat, creation, divination, elemental (earth), guardian, healing, law, necromantic, plant, protection, sun, travelers, and wards and from the school of illusion/phantasm, although he can cast spells from any sphere or any school except the wizard schools of necromancy or invocation/evocation.

AC −5; MV 15; HP 220; THAC0 −9; #AT 5/2
Dmg 1d8+15 (*vorpal battle axe +5*, +8 Str, +2 spec. bonus in battle axe)
MR 80%; SZ M (4 feet tall)
Str 20, Dex 24, Con 19, Int 25, Wis 20, Cha 23
Spells P: 13/13/12/10/9/9/8, W: 9/9/9/9/9/8/8/8/8*
Saves PPDM 2, RSW 1**, PP 4, BW 4, Sp 1**

*Numbers assume one extra illusion/phantasm spell per spell level. **Includes gnome +5 Con save bonus to a minimum of 1.

Special Att/Def: Garl wields *Arumdina* (or rather an avatar of his companion weapon), an intelligent mithral *battle axe +5* that cuts earth, stone, and metal as easily as it does enemies, either passing through them as if they were air or cleaving them in twain. Once per day, *Arumdina* can *heal* Garl's avatar completely. Garl always carries a pouch with 3d4 applications of *dust of illusion* and a *bag of beans*. Within a *portable hole*, Garl carries many props for his practical joking and trickery, including several *wands of wonder*. In his *portable hole*, he also carries a variety of gems of all types, shapes and values (a seemingly endless supply.)

Garl is immune to all illusion/phantasm spells. He can cast *mirror image*, *glitterdust*, *gembomb* (see below), *improved invisibility*, *taunt*, and *Tasha's uncontrollable hideous laughter* once per round at will. Targets roll saving throws against *Tasha's uncontrollable hideous laughter* with a −4 penalty. He can be struck only by +3 or better magical weapons.

Other Manifestations

Garl commonly manifests as an enchanted mouth similar a *magic mouth* spell. Such manifestations may speak, cast spells (even those that would normally require somatic or material components), or most frequently, tell a joke or a tale. The Joker sometimes manifests as a cloud of glittering, golden particles. Such manifestations may hover in place, equal to a *glitterdust* spell, or coalesce on a bladed weapon, equal to an *edge of Arumdina* spell. Either effect lasts 7 rounds.

Garl is served by aurumvorae, badgers, chipmunks, golden hamsters, moles, raccoons, shrews, ground squirrels, weasels, and a handful of sentient magical weapons. He demonstrates his favor through the discovery of exquisitely carved gemstones of all sorts or by a ghostly chuckle in response to some particularly humorous jest. Omens take the form of gentle proddings through trickery, mischievously telekinetically moved objects bobbing about, or some illusion that makes a gnome appear momentarily foolish. The Joker indicates his displeasure by spoiling some achievement, causing some prized object to break, shattering a gemstone, etc.

The Church

Clergy:	Clerics, specialty priests
Clergy's Align.:	LG, NG
Turn Undead:	C: Yes, SP: Yes, at priest level −2
Cmnd. Undead:	C: No, SP: No

All clerics (including fighter/clerics, cleric/illusionists, and cleric/thieves) and specialty priests of Garl receive religion (gnome) as a bonus nonweapon proficiency.

The church of Garl is highly regarded throughout gnome society for its role in bringing the community together, and the Joker's priests often serve as both the spiritual and temporal leaders of their communities. In the conscious emulation of the overlapping interests of the god and the other members of the pantheon, the church of Garl works closely with most other gnome churches, engendering a great deal of good will. A significant minority of the church clergy seeks to emulate the adventures of Garl, and it is this subgroup that is primarily visible to members of other races. As such, the other human and demihuman races commonly regard the Joker's faithful as a loosely organized, ebullient, and friendly bunch, forever getting involved in shenanigans of one sort or the other and inveterate practical jokers. The mischievous exploits of both god and clergy are told and retold around the hearths of gnomes throughout the Realms.

Temples of the Joker are typically located in worked caves just below the surface at the heart of gnome communities. The central sanctuary is usually circular with a domed ceiling divided into four quadrants by great soaring arches. Each arch is carved with depictions of gnomes from all walks of life engaged in all of life's activities, a recurring theme in the church of Garl suggesting the contribution of each individual member of the community to the collective prosperity. The walls and ceilings of such temples are typically plated with gold leaf or studded with brightly polished gold nuggets that gleam in the light of flickering torches. Concentric circles of stone pews, split into four quadrants by narrow aisles that run beneath the arches, face inward to the central, slightly raised dais. The church of Garl encourages the use of the Joker's temples for more than just worship services, for this advances the interests of the god. Entertainers of all types, particularly joke tellers and illusionists, hold many concerts and shows in the round that are open to all members of the community.

Novices of Garl are known as the Uncut. Full priests of the Joker are known as Jewels. In ascending order of rank, the titles used by Garlian priests are Amethyst, Topaz, Opal, Jacinth, Diamond, Emerald, Ruby, and Sapphire. High-ranking priests have unique individual titles, but high female priests are known collectively as Star Rubies whereas high male priests are known as Star Sapphires, although neither gender-based group is considered senior to the other. Specialty priests are known as glitterbrights. The clergy of Garl includes rock gnomes (73%), forest gnomes (25%), and deep gnomes (2%). His priesthood is split roughly even between female and male gnomes (48%/52%, respectively). Garl's clergy includes specialty priests (40%), cleric/illusionists (19%), cleric/thieves (17%), fighter/clerics (15%), and clerics (9%).

Dogma: While life may sometimes be hard, it is important to keep a sense of humor and always welcome opportunities for laughter and delight. Communities are forged through the cooperation and communal spirit of a group of individuals who work and play together. The strength of a community is the cooperation that binds individuals into more than the sum of their contributions. A great prank can help to lighten hard times and make good ones shine. Those who are in authority should never take themselves too seriously, or they lose touch with those they direct and care for. Teach and preserve the tales and traditions of the Forgotten Folk, so that they are never forgotten among their own kind. Do not fear change or the unorthodox, for therein lies the future. Finally, in all things, do what works.

Day-to-Day Activities: Garl's priests serve their communities as craftsmen, educators, entertainers, mediators, and protectors. Even those who wander in search of adventure serve this function, for their exploits are incorporated into the oral tradition of the Forgotten Folk and related for generations thereafter. In their teaching of the young, members of the Joker's clergy combine a very earthy practicality with a streak of humor that keeps their young charges entertained and their interest and subsequent learning heightened. Many also work as smiths (particularly goldsmiths), miners, and gem cutters, and they are expected to contribute to the best of their ability, regardless of their seniority. The priesthood maintains a careful vigilance to protect against hostile races, especially kobolds, and watches over the welfare of the Forgotten Folk. The priesthood must maintain a good archive of jokes, jests, and tales, and priests are expected to be able raconteurs capable of enthralling an audience through a combination of all three.

Holy Days/Important Ceremonies: The church of Garl holds monthly worship services on the 13th day of each month—an auspicious day in gnome folklore. Known as the Communion of Laughter, the Forgotten Folk venerate the head of the gnome pantheon through a variety of activities that last the entire day. Although the order varies from temple to temple, the Joker's rituals include a period of prayer and quiet contemplation, dancing atop the central dais, the sharing of communal meals, storytelling to the accompaniment of visual displays of magic, and joke telling contests that last late into the night. Individuals are expected to offer a bit of gold (or other precious metals, if gold is not available) to the god, even if it is just a handful of gold dust. The moneys so collected are used by the temple for the collective benefit of the community.

Major Centers of Worship: At the headwaters of the northwesternmost tributary of the River Murghol, on the eastern slopes of the Sunrise Mountains, midway between the Lake of Mists and the ruins of Delhumide, lies the Hidden Kingdom of Songfarla. Although it is commonly known throughout the region that a few isolated communities of rock gnomes survive in the shadow of Thay, learning of the existence of an entire kingdom of the Forgotten Folk so close to the borders of the land of the Red Wizards would shock even the Zulkir of Divination. The Hidden Kingdom is largely self-sufficient, although it does trade with its neighbors in ways designed to continue its anonymity and preserve its sanctity and security. The inhabitants of Song-farla have a few representatives in the city of Almorel who trade the Hidden Kingdom's wares with traders traversing the Golden Way, in the city of Murghyr who trade with merchants on the River Rauthenflow, and in the city of Duirtanal who trade with merchants embarking on the Silk Road. Gnome goods are brought into all three cities in small quantities in the wagons of gnome merchants pretending to be itinerant peddlers and are then sold by a handful of gnome merchant families who have dwelt in each city for centuries. The secret of Songfarla's existence has thus been kept secret, even from the fanciful tavern-tales of bards that inspire adventurers.

At the heart of Songfarla is the Gilded Nugget, so named for the giant chunk of gilded granite or iron pyrite (tales vary) with which the lands of the Hidden Kingdom were purchased centuries ago. This vast cavern at the heart of a great vein of gold studded with gems (an unexplained natural phenomenon) and a web of innumerable illusion-cloaked passages connecting the burrows of the Hidden Kingdom, this great amphitheater serves as a center of worship, government, commerce, and the arts for the entire community. Under the able leadership of an aged rock gnome known only as the Laughing Mime, the clergy of the Joker knit this disparate kingdom together in common purpose and harmony.

Although it is hardly the preeminent temple of the leader of the gnome pantheon, the Temple of Wisdom, called the Shrine of the Short by some humans, is one of the few gnome temples that regularly admits human supplicants, having even won a few converts among them, and it is thus the most widely known temple of Garl outside the insular communities of the Forgotten Folk. The Temple of Wisdom, run by the quiet, observant Gellana Mirrorshade, is located in the Friendly Arm, a waystop for caravans passing along the Coast Way between Beregost and Baldur's Gate. Gellana and her husband, Bentley Mirrorshade, run an inn also called the Friendly Arm as a safe, secure place for travelers. Located within the secure walls of the holdfast, the Temple of Wisdom is a low building whose interior walls are studded with gems and gold nuggets and which is guarded by many illusions.

Affiliated Orders: The Companions of Arumdina are a military order of Garlian fighters, clerics, fighter/clerics, and specialty priests with strong links to the church of Gaerdal Ironhand. Dedicated to the defense of gnome communities across the face of Faerûn, members of this order are unusually stern by the standards of the church. Justifiers, as members of this order are sometimes known (not to be confused with the ranger kit of the same name), are skilled in defensive military tactics, particularly in the rolling hills and deep forests where most gnome communities may be found. Individual members often double as marshals, although their duties in this regard are usually light given the general law-abiding character of gnome society. Members of this order are commonly called in to combat ankhegs, bulettes, and other burrowing monsters that pose a threat to gnome settlements and they specialize in tactics to combat such beasts.

The Glittering Jesters are a loosely affiliated band of individuals who seek to relate and/or imitate their god's most outrageous exploits. Many travel from community to community, acting as performers and pranksters to the delight of common folk at the expense of the pretentious and highbrow. An elite minority of Jesters become adventurers in the hopes that their exploits will make their way into the oral tradition of the Forgotten Folk, to be told and retold for generations thereafter. Participation in events worthy of relating as a tale is considered to be an offering to the god. In the gnome oral tradition, the better the tale, the more likely it is to be attributed to a great, legendary hero of the gnomes or even to one of the gnome gods themselves. To the members of this group there can be no greater measure of their deeds than to have a tale relating their actions eventually attributed to Garl himself. It is the quality of the tale a deed inspires, not the accuracy of the tale or even the deed itself, by which their offerings are judged.

Priestly Vestments: The ceremonial garb of Garl's priests includes a gold-plated war helm, a golden belt, and if possible, a suit of gold-plated chain mail or plate mail. The holy symbol of the faith is a brightly colored gold nugget worth at least 10 gp.

Adventuring Garb: Garl's clergy employ a wide variety of weapons, including battle axes, crossbows, darts, flails, hand axes, maces, short bows, short swords, slings, spears, picks, and war hammers. Although those who wish to exercise their rogue or illusionist skills often prefer lighter armor or none whatsoever, most priests of the Joker favor the heaviest defensive mail available.

Specialty Priests (Glitterbrights)

REQUIREMENTS:	Dexterity 11, Intelligence 11, Wisdom 9
PRIME REQ.:	Dexterity, Intelligence, Wisdom
ALIGNMENT:	LG, NG
WEAPONS:	Any
ARMOR:	Any
MAJOR SPHERES:	All, astral, animal, charm, combat, creation, elemental (earth), guardian, healing, necromantic, protection, wards
MINOR SPHERES:	Divination, sun, travelers
MAGICAL ITEMS:	As clerics
REQ. PROFS:	Battle axe, gem cutting
BONUS PROFS:	Appraising, blacksmithing

- Glitterbrights must be gnomes. While most glitterbrights are rock gnomes or forest gnomes, gnomes of every subrace except spriggans can be glitterbrights.
- Glitterbrights are not allowed to multiclass.
- Glitterbrights have limited thieving skills as defined in the Limited Thieving Skills section of "Appendix 1: Demihuman Priests."
- Glitterbrights may cast wizard spells from the illusion/phantasm school as defined in the Limited Wizard Spellcasting section of "Appendix 1: Demihuman Priests."
- Glitterbrights can cast *taunt* (as the 1st-level wizard spell) or *messenger* (as the 2nd-level priest spell) or *ventriloquism* (as the 1st-level wizard spell) once per day.
- At 3rd level, glitterbrights can cast *fool's gold* or *glitterdust* (as the 2nd-level priest spell) once per day.
- At 5th level, glitterbrights can cast *phantasmal force* (as the 1st-level wizard spell) or *Tasha's uncontrollable hideous laughter* (as the 2nd-level wizard spell) once per day.
- At 7th level, glitterbrights can cast *improved invisibility* (as the 4th-level wizard spell) or *mirror image* (as the 2nd-level wizard spell) once per day.
- At 7th level, glitterbrights gain a +2 bonus to all saving throws vs. illusion/phantasm spells.
- At 10th level, glitterbrights can cast *animal summoning I* (as the 4th-level priest spell) or *mirror image* (as the 2nd-level wizard spell) once per day.
- At 13th level, glitterbrights gain the ability to function in all ways as if they were wearing a *cloak of displacement*.
- At 15th level, glitterbrights can cast *gate* (as the 7th-level priest spell) once per tenday.

Garlian Spells

3rd Level

Gembomb (Pr 3; Enchantment/Charm)

Sphere:	Combat
Range:	Touch
Components:	V, S, M
Duration:	1 turn
Casting Time:	6
Area of Effect:	1 gem/5 levels
Saving Throw:	½

This spell converts up to 1 gem per five levels into a grenade-like missile that can be lobbed by the caster only at an enemy target. The casting priest must hold the gems in his or her hand when the spell is cast. Gems enchanted by *gembomb* can only be thrown by hand (Ranges: 10/20/30). If the attack fails to hit, consult the Scatter Diagram for Grenade-like Missiles in the "Missile Weapons in Combat" section of the "Combat" chapter of the DUNGEON MASTER's *Guide* for where the gem lands.

A *gembomb* explodes in a rainbow-colored shower of magical energy when it is thrown to impact any hard surface. It will not explode if dropped or held temporarily in a pouch. On a direct hit, a *gembomb* inflicts 1d6 points of damage per 50-gp value of the gem, to a maximum of 3d6 points of damage. *Gembombs* have a 10-foot-diameter area of effect and inflict incidental damage of 1d3 points of damage per 50-gp value of the gem to a maximum of 3d3 points of damage to all creatures within the area of the explosion who are not struck by the bomb. Those who suffer damage from a *gembomb* and succeed with a saving throw vs. spell suffer only half damage.

One gem can be thrown per round. A caster cannot have more than one *gembomb* spell active at one time. Gems that have not been thrown when the spell expires disappear; all gems that explode are destroyed.

The material component is one or more gems worth at least 50 gp.

5th Level

Conjure Aurumvorax (Pr 5; Conjuration/Summoning)

Sphere:	Animal, Summoning
Range:	30 yards
Components:	V, S, M
Duration:	2 rounds/level
Casting Time:	8
Area of Effect:	Special
Saving Throw:	None

The *conjure aurumvorax* spell enables the priest to magically create an aurumvorax to attack his or her opponents. The conjured creature remains for 2 rounds for each level of the conjuring priest, or until slain. It understands and obeys the caster's verbal commands. A conjured golden gorger will unfailingly attack the priest's opponents, but it will resist being used for any purpose other than combat and consuming gold. If a conjured aurumvorax is directed to act otherwise, it becomes difficult to control and may refuse any action or attack the caster, depending on the situation. A conjured aurumvorax disappears when slain or when the spell expires.

The material components for this spell are the priest's holy symbol and a solid gold figurine of an aurumvorax worth at least 100 gp. The latter is consumed in the casting.

> **Aurumvorax:** AC 0; MV 9, Br 3; HD 12; THAC0 9; #AT 1; Dmg 2d4 (bite); SA jaw lock and rake; SD half damage from blunt weapons, immune to normal fire, half damage from magical fire, immune to poison and gasses; SZ S (3′ long); ML fearless (19–20); Int animal (1); AL N; XP 9,000.
>
> *Jaw Lock and Rake:* When an auromvorax successfully bites, it locks its jaws and hangs on, inflicting an addition 8 points of damage per round until either it or its enemy is dead. Only death causes it to let go. While hanging on with its jaws, it automatically rakes its victim with 2d4 paws each round after the first; each paw that hits inflicts 2d4 points of additional damage.

Edge of Arumdina (Pr 5; Enchantment)

Sphere:	Combat
Range:	Touch
Components:	V, S
Duration:	1 round/2 levels (round down)
Casting Time:	8
Area of Effect:	One axe, dagger, knife, or sword
Saving Throw:	Neg.

This spell enchants an axe, dagger, knife, or sword with the magical sharpness of Garl's boon companion, *Arumdina*. Any weapon enchanted by means of this spell can pass through earth, stone, or metal as though it did not exist. This is not to say the effects of this spell enable a weapon to cleave earth, stone, or metal. Rather, such materials are simply treated as air as far as the enchanted weapon—in its entirety, not just the edge—is concerned. While this enchantment confers no additional damage bonus to targets struck by such an enchanted weapon, metal armor of any sort, stone walls, and such provide no protection against a weapon enchanted with the *edge of Arumdina*, although magical item bonuses, if any, are unaffected. The Armor Class of all opponents clad in such armor or behind cover is adjusted accordingly. This spell does not give this enchanted weapon the ability to harm creatures that can only be wounded by magical weapons if the weapon does not already possess a magical bonus equal to the creature's special defense. For example, creatures only hit by +1 or better magical weapons could not be struck by a weapon enchanted with *edge of Arumdina* unless they were +1 or better magical weapons.

Nebelun

Nebelun (NEHB-eh-luhn) the Meddler is the name by which the Forgotten Folk of the Realms refer to Gond the Wonderbringer, although a new, small but emerging cult believes that Nebelun and Gond are separate gods. See the entry for Gond in the "Faerûnian Pantheon" chapter in *Faiths & Avatars*. In truth, Gond is a distinct entity unrelated to the lesser god Nebelun venerated by gnomes of other worlds, but that gnome power is not active in the Realms. Gond has assumed his aspect within the crystal sphere of Realmspace.

Perhaps Nebelun's most famous devotee is the former hermit Nadul Da-Roni who lives in the wilds outside of High Horn. This peculiar gnome has, over the past decade, become quite famous through the marketing of his mechanical contraptions and inventions in *Aurora's Whole Realms Catalong*. As a result, he unwittingly developed a small following that became a community of gnome inventors, all dedicated to Nebelun.

Nebelunan Spells

3rd Level

Analyze Contraption (Pr 3; Divination)

Sphere:	Divination
Range:	Touch
Components:	V, S, M
Duration:	Instantaneous
Casting Time:	6
Area of Effect:	One contraption
Saving Throw:	None

This spell enables the caster to determine the intended purpose of unfamiliar mechanical devices. The priest touches the object in question and receives a mental picture depicting what the object is supposed to do. Note that what a contraption is supposed to do is not necessarily the same as what the contraption will do; contraptions are notorious for reacting in unexpected ways. Note also that while this spell tells the caster how a device works, it does not tell the caster how to operate the device.

In addition to the complex devices sometimes associated with gnomes, this spell can also be used to analyze contraptions like mechanical traps and locks, and clockwork monsters and devices like the *apparatus of Kwalish* (both magical and not), and even unique artifacts.

The material component for this spell is the caster's holy symbol.

Segojan Earthcaller

(Earthfriend, the Rock Gnome, Lord of the Burrow,
Digger of Dens, the Badger, the Wolverine)

Intermediate Power of Bytopia, NG

PORTFOLIO:	Earth, nature, the dead, rock gnomes
ALIASES:	None
DOMAIN NAME:	Dothion/the Golden Hills (the Gemstone Burrow)
SUPERIOR:	Garl Glittergold
ALLIES:	Clangeddin Silverbeard, Cyrrollalee, Dumathoin, Geb, Grumbar, Kelemvor, Psilofyr, Sehanine Moonbow, Sheela Peryroyl, Urogalan, various Animal Lords, the gnome pantheon (except Urdlen)
FOES:	Abbathor, Cyric, Gaknulak, Kuraulyek, Kurtulmak, Laogzed, Myrkul (dead), Urdlen, Zuggtmoy
SYMBOL:	Glowing gemstone
WOR. ALIGN.:	LG, NG, CG, LN, N, CN

Segojan Earthcaller (SEH-goe-jann URTH-cahl-ur) is the gnome god of earth and nature whose primary concern is creatures who dwell within the ground and burrow through the earth. He is a friend to all living animals that move above and below the earth and one who speaks to the very rock itself. Segojan gifted rock gnomes with the ability to communicate with burrowing animals and taught them how to befriend moles, badgers, and other subterranean creatures. Much like Urogalan of the halfling pantheon, the Lord of the Burrow has assumed oversight of funerary rituals and the dead, for the Forgotten Folk inter their fallen kinfolk in his domain. Segojan was one of the first gods to be worshiped by the gnomes of the Realms, second only to Garl Glittergold. Some scholars of other races have postulated that the Lord of the Burrow has declined in influence and power over the centuries. In truth the emergence of other powers—Baervan Wildwanderer, Baravar Cloakshadow, Callarduran Smoothhands, and Flandal Steelskin—who took over responsibility for aspects of gnome life that Segojan once oversaw is more an indicator of the maturation of gnome religious beliefs than a suggestion of weakness on the part of the Lord of the Burrow. Segojan is widely worshiped by those who dwell within the earth, particularly rock gnomes, and to a lesser extent, deep gnomes. The Lord of the Burrow is revered by gnome miners, jewelers, illusionists, and artificers, but most members of these professions venerate Flandal Steelskin, Garl Glittergold, or Baravar Cloakshadow, respectively.

With the notable exception of Urdlen, Segojan is closely allied with the rest of the gnome pantheon, for his areas of control overlap the portfolios of the other gnome powers. Segojan works closely with Baervan Wildwanderer, the gnome god of forests, travel, and nature, and their shared oversight of the natural world is divided between burrowing animals of the deep earth for Segojan and forest animals and plants for Baervan. Similarly, the Lord of the Burrow is closely allied with Callarduran Smoothhands, and their shared oversight of those who dwell within the earth is divided between creatures of the shallow earth for Segojan and creatures of the deep earth on the Deep Brother's part. To a lesser extent, the portfolios of Segojan and Flandal Steelskin overlap as well, for the Master of Metal governs mining by the Forgotten Folk, a particular type of burrowing. Both powers work closely together to ensure the safety of gnomes engaged in extensive tunneling beneath the earth. In addition to his oversight of earth and nature, Segojan was once venerated as a gnome god of magic as well. The growth of Baravar Cloakshadow's cult in the Realms and the predominance of specialists in the school of illusion/phantasm among gnome spellcasters—gnome artificers being a rare exception—has led to the Sly One being revered as the sole gnome god of magic by the Forgotten Folk. Segojan is no longer seen as having influence in this aspect of gnome life. Nevertheless, Segojan and Baravar work closely together overseeing the development of gnome wizardry.

Outside the ranks of the gnome pantheon, Segojan is most closely allied with other gods of nature and the earth, and to a lesser extent, death. He has a particularly close relationship with many of the Animal Lords of the Beastlands. He is an ardent foe of the kobold gods and often battles the various humanoid powers. The ancient enmity between Urdlen and the gnome pantheon unfolds in large part in endless battles between Segojan and the Crawler Below, for of all the gnome gods, Segojan's area of concern is most directly threatened by Urdlen's campaign of bloody terror and destruction. Much more than the other members of the gnome pantheon, Segojan and Urdlen are engaged in an ongoing and brutal war of attrition.

Segojan is an earthy and pragmatic deity who always communicates in a direct and straightforward fashion. Although he attempts to defuse and avoid conflicts if possible, he is a fierce opponent if he or his followers are attacked, particularly when he or his followers are threatened in their homes. The Lord of the Burrow is only likely to dispatch an avatar when gnomes who dwell within the earth are threatened, usually in situations when interactions between rock gnomes, deep gnomes, and other races who inhabit the Underdark conflict.

Segojan's Avatar

(Earth Elementalist 34, Druid 34, Illusionist 24, Bard 20, Fighter 18)

Segojan often appears as a gray-skinned gnome who wears armor made of grass and roots. He favors spells from the spheres of all, animal, elemental (earth), and plant and from the schools of alteration, elemental (earth), and illusion/phantasm, although he can cast spells from any sphere or school.

AC –3; MV 12, Br 12; HP 230; THAC0 –2; #AT 5/2
Dmg 1d8+15 (rod of smiting +3, +7 Str, +2 spec. bonus in rod)
MR 70%; SZ M (4 ½ feet tall)
Str 19, Dex 15, Con 20, Int 22, Wis 22, Cha 16
Spells P: 14/14/13/13/11/9/9, W: 9/9/9/9/9/8/8/8/8*
Saves PPDM 2, RSW 1**, PP 4, BW 4, Sp 1**

*Numbers assume one extra earth elemental or illusion/phantasm spell per spell level. **Includes gnome +5 Con save bonus to a minimum of 1.

Special Att/Def: Segojan wields *Earthcaller*, a crystalline quartz *rod of smiting* with two unique powers, each usable once per day. When pressed against a mass of rock of sufficient size (at least 3,000 pounds) *Earthcaller* can call forth a stone golem of average intelligence from the stone. The golem serves the god for an entire day. When struck sharply against a floor, wall, or ceiling, *Earthcaller* can generate the effects of an *earthquake* spell if Segojan so desires. It has an apparently limitless supply of charges when wielded by him.

Segojan burrows easily through earth, clay, and even stone. Once per day he can summon 2d4 16-HD earth elementals who serve him without question for up to one hour before returning to the Elemental Plane of Earth. The Lord of the Burrow is immune to acid, petrification attacks, and all spells from the school of illusion/phantasm. He can be struck only by +2 or better magical weapons.

Other Manifestations

In keeping with his penchant for plain-speaking, Segojan rarely sends omens to members of his clergy, preferring to either dispatch an avatar or manifest in the form of a *magic mouth* spell that speaks directly to one or more of his followers.

Gnome Powers: Urdlen and Segojan Earthcaller

When discretion is required, the Lord of Burrows dispatches a small burrowing animal to communicate in a fashion similar to that of a *messenger* spell.

Sometimes Segojan manifests as a newly constructed tunnel. In most cases, such tunnels move with the intended traveler, collapsing behind him and opening before him as he moves through the earth. In other cases such tunnels are permanent and can be traversed in either direction as desired. In rare situations, when a follower is besieged by a potentially deadly opponent, the Lord of Burrows has been known to manifest as an earthen pit that suddenly appears directly beneath the opponent, enabling the gnome to flee.

Segojan is served by aurumvorae, badgers, earth elementals, galeb duhr, groundhogs, moles, raccoons, shrews, stone golems, stone guardians, weasels, wolverines, and voles. He demonstrates his favor through the discovery of small tunnels dug by burrowing animals, the discovery of gems of any sort (but diamonds are especially favored) in the soft earth or other types of ground where they do not occur naturally, and by gentle zephyrs that blow through tunnels opened by gnomes bringing fresh air and the god's good will. The Lord of Burrows indicates his displeasure by causing tremors in the earth that lead to localized cave-ins and by causing gems to change to water and soak into the earth.

The Church

CLERGY:	Clerics, specialty priests
CLERGY'S ALIGN.:	LG, NG, CG
TURN UNDEAD:	C: Yes, SP: Yes, at priest level –4
CMND. UNDEAD:	C: No, SP: No

All clerics (including fighter/clerics, cleric/illusionists, and cleric/thieves) and specialty priests of Segojan receive religion (gnome) as a bonus nonweapon proficiency.

The church of Segojan holds a prominent position in most rock gnome communities for the god is the patron of this subrace and his priests are involved in nearly every important aspect of gnome society. Although the clergy of Callarduran Smoothhands and Baervan Wildwanderer occupy more prominent positions in deep gnome and forest gnome communities, respectively, Segojan's church serves an important secondary function and works closely with the other clergies. In particular, forest gnome priests of Segojan emphasize their god's oversight of the natural world, while deep gnome priests of the Lord of Burrows emphasize their god's interest in the earth.

Segojan's temples are always constructed underground in a series of linked caverns connected by twisting passages. Such houses of worship share the traits of both a museum and a zoo. The creations of generations of gnome artisans adorn nearly every surface and include metal sculptures, sparkling jewels, elaborate illusions and others. Running wild amidst the displays of gnome craftsmanship are hundreds of small animals, ranging in size from tiny shrews to giant badgers.

Novices of Segojan are known as the Unearthed. Full priests of the Lord of Burrows are known as Earthcallers. In ascending order of rank, the titles used by Segojian priests are Shrew, Mole, Vole, Ermine, Groundhog, Wolverine, Badger, and Aurumvorax. High-ranking priests have unique individual titles. Specialty priests are known as earthfriends. The clergy of Segojan includes rock gnomes (80%), deep gnomes (18%), and forest gnomes (2%). Females make up the majority of his priesthood (70%). Segojan's clergy includes specialty priests (50%), clerics (30%), fighter/clerics (10%), cleric/illusionists (9%), and clerics/thieves (1%).

Dogma: The earth is the heart and soul of the Forgotten Folk. From its nurturing embrace spring forth the children of Garl; on its surface and amidst its tunnels and caves they dwell in life, and beneath its silent shroud they rest in death. Many are the treasures, both living and mineral, that Segojan has hidden beneath the earth's surface; preserve and protect the natural world that lies beneath the roots of those who dwell on the surface. Dig burrows, tunnel, and explore, for Segojan welcomes all gnomes into his domain. Beware the evil that ensnares those blinded by avarice and the destructive impulses from the Crawler Below. The Lord of Burrows shall protect those who dwell in his demesne and live in harmony with his teachings.

Day-to-Day Activities: Members of Segojan's clergy work closely with the priesthoods of other gnome gods. In conjunction with the clergy of Baervan Wildwanderer, they work to preserve and protect the natural world, particularly the diverse ecology found beneath the surface. In conjunction with the clergy of Flandal Steelskin, Segojan's faithful supervise mining operations and oversee the safety and protection of gnome miners. In conjunction with the followers of Callarduran Smoothhands, they work to forge ties between gnomes who dwell on or directly beneath the surface and the deep gnomes of the Underdark. Segojan's priests go further than others in actively seeking to protect boundaries between the various races of the Underdark whose tunnels and cavern homes lie deeper underground than gnomes usually explore. Rock gnome priests, who form the core of Segojan's clergy, often serve as emissaries to deep kinfolk on behalf of surface communities of gnomes, and many seek to establish and maintain trading between the two subraces. In accordance with their god's supervision of the dead, the priests of the Lord of Burrows preside over most funerary rituals for the Forgotten Folk, interring the mortal forms of gnomes in his domain.

Holy Days/Important Ceremonies: Segojan is venerated at quarterly holy days that mark the first day of each new season. His faithful gather in plainly adorned earthen dens and offer up gemstones, both worked and unworked, in honor of the treasures of the earth that the Lord of Burrows provides. Such treasures are then placed in small holes dug by badgers before covering them with dirt. Segojan is said to command small burrowing animals to move the jewels elsewhere for gnomes to discover anew. Those corrupted by the taint of Urdlen have occasionally returned to the burrows where Segojan is worshiped in hopes of stealing the offerings. Despite timely excavation, none of the buried offerings have been found where they were buried.

The Earthen Embrace is a relatively widespread funerary ritual observed in most gnome communities, particularly among rock gnomes. Gnome customs regarding the interment of the dead are believed to date back to the enslavement of the Forgotten Folk by the Netherese before their emancipation in the latter half of Netheril's Silver Age in 1472 NY. In gnome communities, the bodies of the fallen are rarely placed in any form of coffin or sarcophagus (except for some communities of forest gnomes who employ wood coffins). Instead gnome corpses are slathered with a thick coating of specially prepared mud by priests of Segojan. This coating dries and hardens over a period of three days until it achieves the consistency and strength of stone. During the three days it takes to prepare an earthen mummy, gnome illusionists work small magics into the hardening earthen shell to replicate the image of the deceased as she or he appeared in life. After preparation, an earthen mummy is adorned with lifelike illusions and then carried on a carpet of furs of small burrowing animals to the central gathering spot of the community, or in larger settlements to the temple with which the deceased was most closely associated. Friends and relatives, a group that often encompasses the entire community, then gather around the body to recount favored stories of the deceased and to tell tales of his or her life. Finally, the body is blessed by the assembled clergy and borne off by the priests of Segojan to its final resting place in an earthen burial niche.

Burial practices vary slightly from community to community, but generally changes to the basic ritual are performed only for gnomes who have received some measure of renown and thus entered into the rich oral tradition of gnome folklore. A fairly common practice in such cases is the placement of small gemstones and other treasures in the coating of mud before it hardens. This practice has resulted in grave robbers (including avaricious followers of Urdlen) plundering gnome burial sites in search of hidden treasures and the desecration and destruction of mummies thus unearthed. As a result, gnome burial sites are unmarked so as not to betray their location to nongnomes. They are often located deep beneath the surface at the end of narrow winding tunnels that are then completely collapsed. Other prominent gnomes are recognized by permanent illusions that persist long beyond the three-day mourning period that may actually move about as the gnome did in life. In the rarest of ceremonies, gnomes of great renown are honored by wrapping their earthen shell in the hide of an aurumvorax.

Major Centers of Worship: The fortified village of Hardbuckler sits astride the Dusk Road, midway between the cities of Hill's Edge and Triel. Inhabited largely by gnomes, the village sits at the heart of an incipient realm of the Forgotten Folk whose small communities may be found in the neighboring Trielta Hills, Northdark Wood, and Reaching Woods. Hardbuckler's major industry is the provision of secure storage facilities, and innumerable caverns have been tunneled beneath the village's streets to house the valuables of several score merchants and adventuring bands. Deep below the storage caverns lies a hidden temple of Segojan called the Den of the Great Badger. It is said to have been the site of a great struggle during the Time of Troubles between the avatars of the Lord of Burrows and the Crawler Below. The temple stood inviolate thanks to the heroic defense mounted by its resident priests and warriors from the surrounding region in the face of the disorganized assault mounted by the ragtag army of followers of Urdlen. Nicknamed the Impregnable Den ever since, Segojan's preeminent house of worship has been greatly expanded in the decade since it was nearly overrun. Seven primary hollows (caverns hewn from the surrounding earth) are linked to each other and the storage caverns above by a labyrinth of tunnels, most of which are barely wide enough for an unarmored gnome to pass with difficulty. Countless burrowing animals make their way through the gnome-carved tunnels as well as their own smaller passageways. Illusions and simple traps are everywhere, placed to hinder invaders but not those who dwell in the Segojan's warm embrace. In addition to the temple's resident priesthood, a large community of gnome scholars, sorcerers, and artisans, as well as their extended families, dwell amidst Segojan's hallowed halls. They seek to preserve the cultural heritage of the Forgotten Folk and to develop new modes of cultural expression. A group of tinkerers continues to experiment with the rich trove of Netherese artifacts stored within the temple, a legacy of their emancipated ancestors who took their fair share of magical trinkets in payment for generations of labor without recompense. This bustling hive is presided over by Heart of the Wolverine, Finn Hollowward, whose regal demeanor and extensive contacts among the gnome communities above has led to legends of a gnome king among visitors to Hardbuckler.

Affiliated Orders: The Watchers Below are a loosely structured order of gnome fighters, fighter/clerics, clerics, and specialty priests found in most rock gnome communities, as well as among the svirfneblin. The members form semiautonomous chapters that are affiliated with one or more gnome communities. These groups govern themselves with fairly flat hierarchies. The primary aim of the Watchers Below is to guard gnome homelands against the ever-present threat of Urdlen and depraved Forgotten Folk who follow the Crawler Below. In addition, members of this fellowship defend the subterranean borders of gnome communities against the numerous evil races of the Underdark who seek to extend their reach into gnome-held territories through conquest and raids.

Priestly Vestments: The ceremonial vestments of Segojan's priesthood include a fur cap and a suit of leather armor of gray or dark brown hue. The Lord of Burrows insists that no part of any animal that must be hunted for sustenance go to waste, and the use of animal furs and skins in the vestments of the church is a way of abiding by this teaching. The holy symbol of the faith is a large and skillfully cut gem into which a *light* or *continual light* spell has been cast. The power of the god changes this incantation causing the jewel to glow from within for as long as it serves as a holy symbol of one of Segojan's priests.

Adventuring Garb: In times of potential danger, priests of Segojan are permitted to use any armor or weapon that is a product of the earth. As this command is interpreted by the church to include any item made of wood, metal, or stone, priests of Segojan are essentially unlimited in their choice of armor and weapons (although clerics must still abide by the restriction to use only blunt, bludgeoning weapons). At other times, members of the clergy favor leather armor and usually carry a stone or metal rod as a weapon (treat as a club that inflicts 1d6+1 points of damage), even within the sanctity of their own burrow.

Specialty Priests (Earthfriends)

REQUIREMENTS:	Constitution 12, Wisdom 9
PRIME REQ.:	Constitution, Wisdom
ALIGNMENT:	LG, NG
WEAPONS:	Any
ARMOR:	Any
MAJOR SPHERES:	All, animal, creation, elemental (earth), guardian, healing, plant, protection, summoning
MINOR SPHERES:	Divination, elemental (air, water), sun, travelers, wards
MAGICAL ITEMS:	As clerics
REQ. PROFS:	Blind-fighting
BONUS PROFS:	Animal lore, mining, stonemasonry

- Earthfriends must be gnomes. While most earthfriends are rock gnomes or deep gnomes, gnomes of every subrace except spriggans can be earthfriends.
- Earthfriends are not allowed to multiclass.
- Earthfriends can cast *animal friendship* (as the 1st-level priest spell) or *meld into stone* (as the 3rd-level priest spell) once per day.

- At 3rd level, earthfriends can cast *Maximilian's earthen grasp* (as the 2nd-level wizard spell) or *messenger* (as the 2nd-level priest spell) once per day.
- At 5th level, earthfriends can cast *animal summoning I* (as the 4th-level priest spell) or *stone shape* (as the 3rd-level priest spell) once per day.
- At 7th level, earthfriends can cast *animal summoning II* (as the 5th-level priest spell) or *conjure earth elemental* (as the 7th-level priest spell, but an 8-HD earth elemental is conjured) once per day.
- At 7th level, earthfriends can shapechange into the form of any burrowing animal (normal or giant-sized) in a fashion similar to that of a druid with the abilities and restrictions thereof.
- At 10th level, earthfriends can cast *animal summoning III* or *stone tell* (as the 6th-level priest spells) once per day.
- At 13th level, earthfriends can summon an 8-HD earth elemental to do their bidding for up to 1 hour three times per tenday. The elemental never turns on its summoner.
- At 15th level, earthfriends can cast *sink* (as the 8th-level wizard spell) once per tenday.

Segojan Spells

1st Level

Segojan's Armor (Pr 1; Abjuration, Enchantment/Charm)

Sphere:	Plant
Range:	Touch
Components:	V, S, M
Duration:	1 day
Casting Time:	1 round
Area of Effect:	Creates one suit of armor
Saving Throw:	None

Prior to casting this spell, the priest gathers an armload of grass and roots and places the material in a pile. Next, an ounce of powdered iron is sprinkled over the collected foliage, and the spell is cast. As the incantation is uttered, the roots and grass weave themselves into a suit of armor tailored specifically to fit a specific individual of man-size or smaller. Others cannot wear it.

Once donned, *Segojan's armor* provides protection equal to scale mail (AC 6). Although it does not possess any magical plusses (+1, etc.), it does radiate magic. Because of its composition, it is nearly weightless and has an encumbrance value equal to normal clothing. It completely negates *magic missile* and similar spells, preventing them from damaging the wearer. *Segojan's armor* is regarded as actual armor, so magical items like *bracers of defense* and spells like *armor* cannot be used with it.

When the spell expires, the armor immediately unravels into its component parts. A successful *dispel magic* or similar effect can end the spell immediately.

The material components are the caster's holy symbol and an ounce of iron powder.

2nd Level

Burrow (Pr 2; Alteration)

Sphere:	Elemental Earth
Range:	0
Components:	V, S, M
Duration:	1 turn +1 round/level
Casting Time:	5
Area of Effect:	Special
Saving Throw:	None

When this spell is cast, the priest's fingernails lengthen and become as hard as stone. For the duration of the spell, the caster can use these claws to burrow through earth, sand, clay, and gravel (but not solid rock), excavating with enough speed to provide MV Br 3, much like a badger or other burrowing mammal.

In addition, the caster can use the claws as weapons. The priest can attack with both claws, each successful attack inflicting 1d4+1 points of damage, plus any Strength damage adjustment.

The spell ends early if subjected to a successful *dispel magic*, if the caster dies, or by the caster's silent command.

The material components for this spell include the caster's holy symbol, a tuft of fur from a burrowing mammal, and a tiny replica of a shovel.

7th Level

Call Stone Guardian (Pr 7; Conjuration)

Sphere:	Elemental Earth
Range:	Touch
Components:	V, S, M
Duration:	1 turn/level
Casting Time:	1 round
Area of Effect:	3,000 lbs. of stone
Saving Throw:	None

This powerful spell enables a priest to temporarily form a stone guardian from a solid block of stone of sufficient volume (3,000 lbs. minimum) with all the abilities and restrictions of a creature of this type. The guardian called forth is nonintelligent and can only follow simple commands issued by the priest involving direct actions with simple conditional modifiers.

The material components for this spell are the priest's holy symbol and a specially crafted rod of pure quartz that requires at least 10 days to shape at the cost of at least 1,000 gp. The priest must hold the rod to control the stone guardian and its premature shattering ends the spell. At the conclusion of the spell, the rod shatters into worthless shards.

Stone Guardian: AC 2; MV 9; HD 4+4; THAC0 15; #AT 2; Dmg 1d8+1 (punch)/1d8+1 (punch); SD one-quarter damage from edged weapons; one-half damage from all cold, fire, or electrical attacks; immune to normal missiles; SW can be instantly destroyed by *stone to flesh*, *trasmute rock to mud*, *stone shape*, or *dig*; SZ M to L (6´–8´ tall); ML fearless (20); Int non (0); AL N; XP 420.

Urdlen

(The Crawler Below, the Evil One)

Intermediate Power of the Abyss, CE

PORTFOLIO:	Greed, bloodlust, blood, evil, hatred, uncontrolled impulse, spriggans
ALIASES:	None
DOMAIN NAME:	399th level of the Abyss/the Worm Realm
SUPERIOR:	None
ALLIES:	Zuggtmoy
FOES:	Gaknulak, Grumbar, Kuraulyek, Kurtulmak, the dwarven pantheon, the gnome pantheon, the halfling pantheon, Psilofyr
SYMBOL:	White mole
WOR. ALIGN.:	LE, NE, CE

Urdlen (URD-len), a neuter and sexless being, is the epitome of the evil impulse that rules some gnomes and is feared by the rest. A mindless force of malicious evil and destruction, Urdlen serves as a warning for every gnome to beware the taint of greed that lies within the gnomish delight in gems and jewelry. It is telling that gnomes have no myths of how this evil arose, but that they simply fear Urdlen's vicious, life-hating evil and bloodlust. Just as the Crawler Below can burrow into the earth of the Abyss, so it hopes evil will burrow into the hearts and souls of gnomes everywhere. Urdlen thrives on trickery that harms the innocent and the good. It is commonly venerated by evil thieves and fighters, although gnomes from all walks of life have succumbed to its evil taint. Spriggans are said to be the twisted offspring of gnomes who succumbed to Urdlen's taint early in the history of the Forgotten Folk, and they honor their god and patron by perpetuating its reign of terror.

Urdlen's place in the gnome pantheon is oddly unquestioned, though the god is greatly feared and secretly reviled by nearly all the Forgotten Folk. Urdlen hates all the other gods of the gnomes with a passion, and they in turn war against it. Further, the Crawler Below has garnered the enmity of dwarven and halfling powers as well. Urdlen contests with Flandal Steelskin, Garl Glittergold, Segojan Earthcaller, Callarduran Smoothhands, and Urogalan, for those gnomes and halflings under their protection are most often the target of Urdlen's attacks. Although it may be more of a

rivalry, the Crawler Below and Zuggtmoy, the Demoness Lady of Fungi, are supposed to have an understanding of some sorts, an alliance that allows isolated followers of the Crawler Below to eke out a living on the wild fungi and lichens of the Underdark.

The Crawler Below crushes all life without regard. It wants to spoil or destroy everything. Urdlen is a half-mad, blindly destructive impulse; the blindness of its chosen avatar form is very tellingly symbolic. No one can predict where it will strike or what its plans are to further the cause of evil among the Forgotten Folk. The nature of its plans to bring evil into the hearts of gnomes is not understood even by the other gnome deities. It is said that Urdlen lusts for precious metals, jewels, and the blood of any human, humanoid, or demihuman.

Urdlen's Avatar (Fighter 33, Thief 30, Illusionist 28, Mage 28, Cleric 18)

Urdlen most often appears as a huge, dead-white furless mole with claws of steel. It favors destructive and damaging spells from any sphere or school.

AC –4; MV 12, Br 12; HP 235; THAC0 –10; #AT 2
Dmg 4d6 ×2 (claw)
MR 70%; SZ L (8 ½ feet long)
STR 23, DEX 19, CON 24, INT 18, WIS 15, CHA 1
Spells P: 10/9/8/8/6/4/2, W: 7/7/7/7/7/7/7/7/7*
Saves PPDM 2, RSW 1**, PP 4, BW 4, Sp 1**
 *Numbers assume one extra illusion/phantasm spell per spell level. **Includes gnome +6 CON save bonus to a minimum of 1.

Special Att/Def: Urdlen can attack twice per round. If both of its claws strike the same target in a single round, the effect is similar to that of a *sword of wounding*: These wounds cannot be healed by *regeneration* or any magic short of a *wish*, and each strike bleeds for an additional 1 point of damage per round for the next 10 rounds or until bandaged. The scent of blood—which is always spilled when an opponent is *wounded*—drives Urdlen into a frenzy, during which time it always attacks a bleeding target and gains a +2 attack and damage bonus and a –2 penalty to its Armor Class. Urdlen can infect gnomes with the weremole (see below) form of lycanthropy at will, but it does not seem to do so with any rhyme or reason; there is a 15% random chance any gnome struck by his avatar is infected.

The Crawler Below is immune to acid and paralyzation attacks. Although it is totally blind, its other senses can detect the presence of any living or undead creature within 300 yards. It can breathe a *stinking cloud* centered around its head with a 60-foot radius three times per day, and it is protected by a permanent *blur* spell. Also, it can be struck only by +2 or better magical weapons.

Other Manifestations

Urdlen almost never uses manifestations, preferring to ignore its followers and appear in avatar form. On occasion the Crawler Below has manifested in a worshiper as the effects of a *blur* spell. However, if the worshiper is slain anyway, Urdlen dines on the gnome's soul in the Abyss. Even more rarely, it is sometimes known to manifest as an *earthquake* spell, and tremors in the earth are commonly attributed by the Forgotten Folk to Urdlen's destructive impulse.

Urdlen is served by ankhegs, brain moles, bulettes, crysmals, dao, earth elementals, earth elemental vermin (crawlers), earth grues (chaggrins), earth mephits, earth weirds, garmorm, giant white moles, gnome vampires, imps, incarnates of covetousness, envy, gluttony, lust, and sloth, khargra, larvae, metal masters, white moles, nightshades, osquips, purple worms, spriggans, thoqqua, tieflings, vargouilles, werebadgers, weremoles, will o' deeps, and yeth hounds. The Crawler Below largely ignores its followers, but it occasionally gives cryptic omens in the form of blood bubbling from the earth, claw marks in rock, foul odors of blood or sulfur, and sudden severe nosebleeds (inflicting 1d2 points of damage) suffered by its faithful worshipers.

Lycanthrope, Weremole: AC 3; MV 6, Br 3; HD 4; THAC0 17; #AT 3 or 1; Dmg 1d3 (claw)/1d3 (claw)/1d6 (bite) or by weapon; SA command burrowing creatures, summon a host of burrowing creatures; SD hit only by silver or +1 or better magical weapon, standard gnome racial abilities; SW effective blindness vs. flying opponents; SZ S (3´ long); ML very steady (13–14); Int very (11–12); AL CE; XP 650.

Notes: Only gnomes are believed to be susceptible to this form of lycanthropy. Weremoles can assume their original form or the form of a large, blind, furless, dead-white mole with massive claws. Although blind in giant mole form, while underground weremoles can sense any creature within 90 feet as effectively as a gnome can see in full daylight. While on the surface weremoles can sense any creature touching the ground within 50 feet. Weremoles first appeared during the Time of Troubles in rural gnome communities that were attacked by the avatar of Urdlen.

SA—Weremoles can speak with any burrowing animal up to the size of an osquip and once per day can command them via a natural ability akin to *suggestion*. Once per day, a weremole can raise a host of burrowing creatures through a power similar to the 2nd-level wizard spell *summon swarm*.

SD—Weremoles have all of the standard gnome detection abilities, resistance to magic, and combat bonuses vs. humanoids and giants.

SW—In giant mole form, weremoles are effectively blind to airborne opponents, suffering the standard –4 attack penalty for blindness.

The Church

CLERGY:	Clerics, specialty priests
CLERGY'S ALIGN.:	LE, NE, CE
TURN UNDEAD:	C: No, SP: No
CMND. UNDEAD:	C: Yes, SP: Yes, at priest level –2

All clerics (including fighter/clerics, cleric/illusionists, and cleric/thieves) and specialty priests of Urdlen receive religion (gnome) as a bonus nonweapon proficiency. Clerics of Urdlen are allowed to use and become proficient in claws of Urdlen (see below), a type of slashing weapon.

Those who follow Urdlen are despised and feared by the Forgotten Folk. Its cult is a particular threat to rock gnomes and deep gnomes, but even forest gnomes suffer from its followers' depredations. Spriggans both venerate and fear the Crawler Below, and most are members of its cult. Urdlen's cult is opposed by good-aligned dwarves, gnomes, and halflings, and tales of the god's hunger for blood and destruction are a growing part of the mythology of the Small Folk. Other surface races have little knowledge of this obscure cult, typically merging tales of the god's rampages into stories of a wide range of horrors from below. Subterranean races are more likely to have been assaulted by Urdlen's avatar or that of its followers, and as such, its cult is a more credible threat.

Temples of the Crawler Below are few and far between, for rarely do its followers set aside their proclivities for destruction long enough to build a house of worship. Those few temples that do exist are typically little more than blood-spattered shrines, always located underground in lightless natural caverns dominated by a crude stone altar stained with the lifeblood of countless sacrifices.

Novices of Urdlen are known as the Unblooded. Full priests of the Crawler Below are known as Deep Crawlers. Individual priests have their own unique titles. Specialty priests are known as bloodstalkers. The clergy of Urdlen includes rock gnomes (60%), deep gnomes (18%), forest gnomes (12%), and spriggans (10%). Males make up the majority of its priesthood (70%). Urdlen's clergy includes specialty priests (60%), cleric/thieves (15%), clerics (12%), fighter/clerics (10%), and cleric/illusionists (3%).

Dogma: Succumb to bloodlust. Seize power—directly. Hate, covet, crush, despoil, and kill. Revel and exult in orgies of death and destruction. That which is living or created by life must be murdered or destroyed because that is the ultimate end of all and to deny it is to deny the truth of all existence. The strong survive and the weak are their cattle. Do what Urdlen wants first; second, do whatever you want. Give in to every evil impulse, for what use is there in covering over the truth of your nature? Propitiate the Crawler Below with sacrifice so that it does not come for you. Existence is a cosmic joke before death, the truth behind it all, comes at Urdlen's claws. Sharing the cruel ironies and harsh humor of existence with others is only kind, for it helps to toughen them for what is coming in the end.

Day-to-Day Activities: From their subterranean warrens, Urdlen's priests wage an unending war on communities of the Forgotten Folk, particularly the clergies of the other gnome gods. When not hunting other creatures, members of the priesthood work to steal, deface, or destroy objects of value, particularly gems and works of art. They share their lord's love for evil and deadly pranks directed against all creatures, including gnomes.

Holy Days/Important Ceremonies: In a regular ritual known as the Feeding, Urdlen's priests appease their god by spilling the blood of their prey on the ground and burying it. Jewels and valuable metal goods are also sacrificed to him by ruining, breaking, tarnishing, or melting them and then burying them. On Midwinter night, followers of the Crawler Below gather in subterranean caverns to offer blood sacrifices to the god to appease its wrath. If Urdlen is displeased by the volume of blood or the value of the despoiled goods offered on the Night of Blood, it may appear and slay all the assembled worshipers in an orgy of unbridled destruction.

Major Centers of Worship: All manner of beasts wander the Bandit Wastes north of Halruaa, including a pack of blood-crazed gnome weremoles with priest abilities led by a gnome vampire priest known only as the Blood-Curdling Scream. The Blood Screamers, as the greatly feared band is known, hunt all manner of living creatures from the Shaar to the Nathaghal, as the mountain range that forms the North Wall of Halruaa is known. The band is a recurring foe of Forgotten Folk who dwell in the mountain valley of northeastern Halruaa known as the Nath, as well as the well-entrenched communities of gnomes in the Rathgaunt Hills, located due east of Lake Lhespen on the road between Shaarmid and Sebben. If the Blood Screamers have constructed a temple to their god or even a warren in which to retreat, its existence has survived undetected for decades, despite the efforts of brave gnome adventurers seeking to end the reign of terror.

Affiliated Orders: Aside from small family groups of spriggans, Urdlen's followers are too chaotic and consumed with bloodlust to organize into long-lasting bands, let alone militant orders. At most they gather together in small groups to maximize their opportunity for destruction, but such bands rarely stay together for more than a few raids.

Priestly Vestments: During depraved ceremonies, priests of the Crawler Below wear blood-stained white cloaks made from the pelts of animals such as polar bears, winter wolves, and the like. The holy symbol of the faith is a blood-soaked skull, although most of Urdlen's priests keep a blood-fed white mole as both a pet and a symbol of their god.

Adventuring Garb: Members of Urdlen's clergy employ the best armor and weapons available. Specialty priests of Urdlen prefer edged weapons to maximize the amount of blood shed, and all priests favor weapons that inflict a great deal of pain on their victims. Some members of the priesthood employ magical steel claws similar to that employed by the cult of the Beastlord (see *Faiths & Avatars*). *Claws of Urdlen* are metal gauntlets with a row of large, curved knives affixed atop the knuckles. A priest must allocate a weapon proficiency to use them. A priest trained in their use can strike once per round with each hand without disadvantage. *Claws of Urdlen* weigh 4 pounds total (2 pounds each), have a speed factor of 6, are size S, and inflict 1d6+2 points of piercing and slashing (Type P/S) damage to size S or M targets or 1d6 points of damage to size L or larger targets. In addition, due to their enchantment, it is possible to burrow through soft earth once a day with a Movement Rate of 1 for as many rounds as the priest has points of Strength or Constitution (pick the minimum) using the *claws of Urdlen* as crude tools.

Specialty Priests (Bloodstalkers)

REQUIREMENTS:	Strength 11, Wisdom 9
PRIME REQ.:	Strength, Wisdom
ALIGNMENT:	CE
WEAPONS:	Any slashing and piercing (Type S and/or Type P) weapons
ARMOR:	Any
MAJOR SPHERES:	All, animal, chaos, combat, elemental (earth), healing, protection, sun (reversed only), war
MINOR SPHERES:	Divination, elemental (fire), necromantic, summoning
MAGICAL ITEMS:	As clerics
REQ. PROFS:	None
BONUS PROFS:	Blind-fighting

- Bloodstalkers must be gnomes. While most bloodstalkers are rock gnomes, gnomes of every subrace including spriggans can be bloodstalkers.
- Bloodstalkers are not allowed to multiclass.

- When casting a reversed form of a healing sphere spell that causes damage in hit points, bloodstalkers gain a bonus to the damage they inflict. This is equal to +1 point per point of their Wisdom ability score equal to or above a Wisdom of 14 (Wisdom score of 15 give a +2 bonus, etc.). If they cast a reversed form of healing spell that does not inflict damage in points, the saving throw of their target, if the spell has one, is made at a −2 penalty.
- Bloodstalkers can cast *cause light wounds* (as the reverse of the 1st-level priest spell *cure light wounds*) or *stinking cloud* (as the 2nd-level wizard spell) once per day.
- At 3rd level, bloodstalkers can cast *blindness* or *blur* (as the 2nd-level wizard spells) once per day.
- At 5th level, bloodstalkers can cast *cloak of fear* (as the reverse of the 4th-level priest spell *cloak of bravery*) or *soften earth and stone* (as the 2nd-level priest spell) once per day.
- At 7th level, bloodstalkers can cast *confusion* or *dig* (as the 4th-level wizard spells) or *passwall* (as the 5th-level wizard spell) once per day.
- At 10th level, bloodstalkers can cast *conjure earth elemental* or *creeping doom* (as the 7th-level priest spells) once per tenday.
- At 13th level, bloodstalkers can cast *slay living* (as reverse of the the 5th-level priest spell *raise dead*) once per day.
- At 13th level, bloodstalkers can cast *wither* or *destruction* (as the 7th-level priest spells) three times per tenday.

Urdlenian Spells

In addition to the spells listed below, priests of the Crawler Below may cast the 2nd-level priest spell *burrow* detailed in the entry for Segojan Earthcaller.

2nd Level

Soften Earth and Stone (Pr 2; Alteration)

Sphere:	Elemental Earth
Range:	10 yards/level
Components:	V, S, M
Duration:	Permanent
Casting Time:	5
Area of Effect:	10-foot square/level
Saving Throw:	None

When this spell is cast, all natural, undressed earth or stone in the area of effect is softened. Wet earth becomes thick mud; dry earth becomes loose sand or dirt; and stone becomes soft clay, easily molded or chopped. The caster affects a 10-foot square area per caster level to a depth of 1 to 4 feet, depending on the toughness or resilience of the ground at that spot (DM option). Magical or enchanted stone cannot be affected by this spell.

Creatures attempting to move through an area softened into mud are reduced to a move of 10 feet per round. Any creatures caught within the mud when the spell takes effect must make a saving throw vs. paralyzation or lose the ability to move, attack, or cast spells for 1d2 rounds as they flounder about in the muck. Loose dirt is not as troublesome as mud, and creatures are only reduced to half their normal movement rates, with no chance of being incapacitated for a round or two. However, it is impossible to run, sprint, or charge over either surface.

Stone softened into clay does not hinder movement, but it does allow characters to cut, shape, or excavate areas they may not have been able to affect.

Natural vertical surfaces such as cliff faces or cavern ceilings can be affected by *soften earth and stone*. Usually, this causes a moderate collapse or landslide as the loosened material peels away from the face or roof and falls. A moderate amount of structural damage can be inflicted to man-made structures by softening the ground beneath a wall or tower, causing it to settle. However, most well-built structures are only damaged by this spell, not destroyed.

The material component is a bit of slip (wet clay) from the wheel of a master potter.

4th Level

Summon Earth Grue (Pr 4; Conjuration/Summoning)

Sphere:	Elemental Earth, Summoning
Range:	10 yards
Components:	V, S
Duration:	3 rounds/level
Casting Time:	1 round
Area of Effect:	Special
Saving Throw:	None

The spell opens a *gate* to the Elemental Plane of Earth, summoning an earth grue, also known as a chaggrin or soil beast, to the spellcaster. The caster need not fear that the summoned grue will turn on him or her. Neither concentration on the activities of the grue nor protection from it is necessary. The summoned grue helps the caster in whatever manner possible: attacking the caster's foes, tunneling in the general direction desired, and so on. It remains for a maximum of 3 rounds per level of the caster or until it is slain or sent back by a *dispel magic* spell or similar magic.

The material components for this spell are the priest's holy symbol and unworked raw metals worth at least 50 gp. The latter is offered as a bribe to the creature during the casting and is handed over to the creature before it will enter the Prime Material Plane.

Grue, Earth: AC 4; MV 12, Br 3; HD 5+5; THAC0 15; #AT 2; Dmg 1d4+2 (claw)/1d4+2 (claw); SA quills, clinging claws, hide in stone; SD hit only by +1 or better weapon, spell immunity; SZ M (3´ long); ML average (8–10); Int average (8–10); AL NE; XP 1,400.

Notes: Earth grues summoned by this spell to the Prime Material Plane can assume the shape of a large mole, a yellowish hedgehog with a skull-like head, or a humanoid of lumpy, wet clay with an asymmetrical, vicious face and small, feral eyes. Although only 3 feet long, earth grues weigh 140–200 lbs.

SA—In any form, after a successful hit, an earth grue can dig its razor-sharp foreclaws into its victims and inflict 1d4+2 points of damage, and in subsequent rounds it inflicts 1d6+6 points of damage per round. (The victim must succeed at a Strength check to dislodge an earth grue.) In hedgehog form, unprotected flesh in contact with an earth grue's quills suffers 1d4 points of damage per round. Earth grues in humanoid form can merge with natural soil or a stone surface and be only faintly perceptible to careful observation as a damp, dark outline. They can then emerge suddenly to surprise opponents (−5 penalty to surprise rolls).

SD—Earth grues are immune to earth-based and earth-affecting spells such as *earthquake*, *passwall*, *transmute rock to mud*, *stone to flesh*, and the like. Their mere presence dispels such magic within a 40-foot radius even if it had been permanent. Magical items are not affected.

6th Level

Curse of the Everbleeding Wounds (Pr 6; Necromancy)

Sphere:	Necromantic
Range:	Touch
Components:	V, S, M
Duration:	1 turn
Casting Time:	9
Area of Effect:	Creature touched
Saving Throw:	Neg.

This spell inflicts a curse upon a victim similar to the effects of a *sword of wounding*. If the touched creature fails a saving throw vs. spell, all wounds suffered during the next full turn cannot be regenerated or cured by any sort of potion, spell or other magic short of *remove curse*, *limited wish*, or *wish*. They must heal naturally. The target suffers 1 point of damage each round after a wound is inflicted until the wound is bandaged or the spell expires. Multiple wounds are cumulative. A *periapt of wound closure* may provide complete immunity to the spell, as may other spells or items that prevent ongoing bleeding.

A round of tending to a particular wound with no other actions taken or enemy interference is sufficient to bandage an everbleeding wound and halt ongoing damage from that wound. Those with the healing nonweapon proficiency who succeed at a proficiency check can bandage a second wound in the same round.

The spell requires the priest's holy symbol and a small knife or sharp-edged item that is used to nick the creature for 1 point of damage as the priest's hand comes into physical contact with the creature.

HALFLING PANTHEON

The Small Folk of the Realms worship a pantheon of deities known collectively as Yondalla's Children. This group includes Yondalla herself, according to the tangled reasoning of halfling theologians, and the term is sometimes used to apply collectively to all halflings. The names by which the gods and goddesses of the halfling pantheon are known vary widely from community to community and have little correlation with subrace distinctions. The myths associated with the various halfling powers are often intermingled with tales of local halfling heroes and heroines of earlier generations who embodied the teachings and approach to life of one or more powers. For example, halfling villages scarcely two dozen miles apart might each have a different name for Yondalla. The citizens of each community might believe the Protector and Provider is a local deity concerned far more with their village than with the race of halflings as a whole. Finally, the name Yondalla is known by and the tales associated with her would most likely be derived independently from two widely respected halfling matriarchs, each of whom was a leader of her respective village early in its history. (To suggest the countless local names associated with each halfling power, each of the deity entries that follow have the notation "none widespread" in their list of aliases.) The names of the halfling powers of the Realms listed hereafter—Arvoreen, Brandobaris, Cyrrollalee, Sheela Peryroyl, Tymora, Urogalan, and Yondalla—are simply the names by which the individual halfling powers are most commonly known across the planes and the names by which religious scholars of other races refer to them.

Yondalla is the universally acknowledged leader of the halfling pantheon and the other powers defer to her authority without dissension, but in practice the entire pantheon works together in a collective fashion for the good of the whole race, even dispatching avatars to work together as needed. The closest the Small Folk have to an evil power among the gods that they acknowledge is the gnome god Urdlen, the Crawler Below, who is held in a few tales to tunnel up into halfling burrows as well as gnome dens. While the primary deities of the halflings are female and the male gods are seen as presiding over somewhat peripheral (if necessary) aspects of life, all are equally respected. The roles of the various halfling gods are closely related and sometimes overlap, at least from a mortal perspective. As a result, in some communities two or three powers—usually Yondalla, Cyrrollalee, and/or Sheela Peryroyl—are viewed as aspects of a single power. Divine coordination of portfolios is tightest among Yondalla, Arvoreen, Cyrrollalee, Sheela Peryroyl, and Urogalan, with Brandobaris and Tymora cooperating for the most part with each other.

Tymora is fully detailed in *Faiths & Avatars* and not in this volume because she is most commonly worshiped by humans, not halflings. Although Lady Luck is in some sense an interloper goddess in the halfling pantheon, the fragmented mythology of the Small Folk has allowed Tymora to be included as a local goddess under a wide variety of guises in halfling communities across Faerûn. Tales of adventurous, lucky, tricky halfling damsels have long been part of halfling folklore, and Tymora is commonly seen by the Small Folk as a long-standing local halfling deity who has simply conned the Big Folk into worshiping her as well.

As suggested by the conflicting representations of the halfling gods in various communities across Faerûn, the mentality of a typical halfling holds that the only really important things are those that happen close to home. The Small Folk are far more interested in worshiping an immediate and beneficent deity—one whose responsibilities are to *them*, and no one else—rather than an abstract power who is presumed to oversee the entire race. The remoteness of most human deities, for example, bewilders many halflings, as does the deference human worshipers show to their deities. Halflings are not irreligious; while they treat Yondalla and her brood with respect, they are far less in awe of their pantheon than is the norm between deity and follower for other races. As halflings see it, they have a simple bargain with their gods. In return for their veneration by the Small Folk, the powers promise to take care of all halflings. Halfling priests exist to see that both sides of the bargain are kept—to remind halflings to give the powers their due and to remind the halfling powers that they are responsible for the safety and comfort of their loyal followers. Many stories from halfling folklore remind the Small Folk that before they began to worship Yondalla and her Children, halflings were a shy and fugitive people who lived as hunter-gatherers on the edges of civilization and who hid in isolated burrows from the humanoids and monsters that preyed upon them. As a result, most halflings feel both gratitude for the gifts of Yondalla's Children and affection toward their deities.

The Small Folk are inclined to see evidence of small local deities—the Small Gods or the Thousand Home Gods of halfling folklore—in many aspects of their surroundings and daily lives. Each house commonly has a protector of its own hearth, often inspired by some matriarch or patriarch in the clan's history. The homesteader who starts a small community might well be accorded a similar status in later years—that is, his or her spirit might be invoked on matters relating to the health and prosperity of the village. Local myths may name a goddess of breadmaking and credit her if a particularly good batch of bread comes out or celebrate a local god of winemaking and demand a toast to him after the first drink of any exquisite vintage. If game is plentiful, the power of the neighboring woods, often pictured as a hare or a fox, is thanked and token morsels of food are left to him or her as offerings. Halflings who fish commonly revere venerable river denizens, such as an ancient or battle-scarred trout, and fisherfolk always throw back the river deity if she or he allows himself or herself to be caught. Some theologians of other races speculate that the Thousand Home Gods of the Small Folk are simply aspects of the established halfling powers, while others say that at most they are nature spirits. Halflings see little need to differentiate between Yondalla's Children and the Small Gods and rarely bother to do so.

In a variety of mythic forms, Yondalla is seen as the mother or adopted mother of the halfling people. In one tradition, sometimes Yondalla gives birth to the halfling race, sometimes she creates them from disparate elements of nature, and sometimes (rarely) she transforms some saddened solitary sylvan creature (usually a brownie) into a halfling, making the race her creation alone. Other more common mythic traditions hold that Yondalla adopted the halflings after finding one of them hiding in a thicket, walking along a riverbank, or tricking one of the Big Folk into doing something foolish to the advantage of the Small Folk. Whatever myth is told, halflings have a deep identification with Yondalla at a physically rooted level. In many versions of their founding myths, Yondalla uses her powers of persuasion with the powers of the other human and demihuman races to gain the fertile fields and meadows of the lands usually settled by halflings.

Halfling history is maintained by an oral tradition, and thus the origins of the Small Folk have long been lost to time. While most halflings today claim that Luiren is their ancestral homeland, there is little in that southern nation's archeological record or in the history of other lands with sizable halfling populations to suggest more than 12 centuries of residence by the Small Folk south of the Toadsquat Mountains. Dwarven and elven records suggest that the genies who founded the Calim Empires brought with them both human and halfling slaves approximately 7,800 years before the Standing Stone rose in Cormanthor. While many of the descendants of those early halflings still live (and are still enslaved) in Calimshan today, fragmentary historical records from the countless realms that have risen and fallen along the Sword Coast since the arrival of the Djen chart the steady northward migration of Small Folk since their arrival in the lands of what is now Calimshan. Today, sizable halfling population clusters are found in the Purple Hills of Tethyr, amidst the ruins of long-fallen Meiritin in eastern Amn, in the Sunset Vale west of Darkhold, and along the lower reaches of the River Delimbiyr. However, even the great Calishite diaspora cannot account for the widespread distribution of halflings throughout Faerûn, leaving the ancient history of the Small Folk to the realm of legend and myth.

All native Faerûnian halflings are divided into three distinct subraces: hairfeet, stouts, and tallfellows. There is some circumstantial evidence that hairfeet comprise the original racial stock of the Small Folk, but halflings generally find scholarly questions on such matters ridiculous as they themselves pay little attention to the differences between the halfling subraces. Sages of other races who have studied the Calishite halfling diaspora have suggested that stouts have a trace of dwarven ancestry and that tallfellows have a trace of elven ancestry, accounting for their distinctive appearances and close relations with the Stout Folk and Fair Folk, respectively. As evidence in support of their theories, scholars cite dwarven and elven records of Shanatar and Wealdath which indicate that escaped halfling slaves took refuge beneath the peaks of the Marching Mountains and the boughs of the Darthiir Wood, joining the dwarven and elven societies found therein for several generations before moving on to found their own communities. Complicating matters is the fact that halfling natives of Luiren have pointed ears, unlike their kin elsewhere in the Realms; however, they too are divided into the same three subraces. The decidedly recessive pointed-ear trait vanishes permanently in the first generation of descendants of any Luiren halfling who takes a mate from the ranks of the halflings of the rest of the Realms.

Finally, it should be noted that Anadian halflings, residents of the polar regions of Anadia, an inner planet of the Realmspace system, are almost unknown in Faerûn (and are not discussed in the deity descriptions that follow). According to Elminster, the total population of Anadian halflings resident in the Realms is countable on a single halfling's fingers and toes.

Despite the divisions in the halfling race across Faerûn, halflings of all subraces continue to venerate the same core pantheon, albeit under a variety of names. While some halfling powers draw a greater fraction of one subrace or another to their faith than the overall population balance found in the Realms (55% hairfoot, 30% stout, 15% tallfellow), such variances are slight. The only real difference in the way the various subraces worship the halfling pantheon is that hairfeet tend to adopt the occasional human power (such as Tymora), whereas stouts sometimes give homage to individual members of the Morndinsamman (the dwarven pantheon) and tallfellows sometimes give homage to individual members of the Seldarine (the elven pantheon).

General Halfling Priest Abilities: The general abilities and restrictions of halfling priests, aside from the specific changes noted later in this section for each halfling faith, are summarized in the discussion of halfling priests in "Appendix 1: Demihuman Priests."

Arvoreen
(The Defender, the Vigilant Guardian, the Wary Sword)

Intermediate Power of Mount Celestia, LG

PORTFOLIO:	Martial defense, war, vigilance, halfling warriors, duty
ALIASES:	None widespread
DOMAIN NAME:	Venya/Green Fields
SUPERIOR:	Yondalla
ALLIES:	Clangeddin Silverbeard, Haela Brightaxe, Helm, Gaerdal Ironhand, Gorm Gulthyn, Gwaeron Windstrom, the halfling pantheon, the Red Knight, Torm, Tyr
FOES:	Bane (dead), Bhaal (dead), Cyric, Iyachtu Xvim, Talona, Talos and the gods of fury (Auril, Umberlee, and Malar), Moander (dead), the goblinkin pantheons (orc, goblin, hobgoblin, bugbear, kobold, and urd deities, among others), Urdlen
SYMBOL:	Two short swords
WOR. ALIGN.:	LG, NG, CG, LN, N, CN

Arvoreen (ARE-voh-reen) the Defender, fiery guardian of the home, is the nearest thing to a halfling war god. He is a god of stern defense and aggressive watchfulness, who is always preparing for incursions into halfling lands and making ready to repulse hostile creatures at the first sign of trouble. Arvoreen is venerated primarily by halfling fighters, but also by fighter/thieves who prefer the former set of skills over the latter.

Arvoreen has cultivated good relations with most of the good and neutral deities, particularly of the dwarven, elven, gnome, and human pantheons. Of the halfling gods, Arvoreen is most closely aligned with Yondalla, Cyrrollalee, and Urogalan, although he has strong ties with the entire halfling pantheon. The Defender has little patience or understanding of the principles or priorities of unreliable rogues such as Brandobaris and Tymora, but he does value their contributions in defending his charges from external threats. As a large fraction of halflings live in and among human communities, Arvoreen finds that most of the divine threats to his charges are a result of the plots of the evil deities of the halflings' human neighbors.

Arvoreen is anxiously protective of the halfling race, and he is always alert to impending dangers. The Defender, although quite powerful, is not a particularly aggressive deity. He only engages in combat if he is attacked, though he does seek out his enemies and actively confront them to get them to desist from their evil practices. He does not go very far out of his way to avoid combat if it occurs, however, and fights to the finish. Although he stops short of advocating war, Arvoreen is not shy about pointing out folks who are acting suspiciously—after all, they just might be evil in disguise. He is more serious and less carefree and joyful than the typical halfling (or halfling deity) and serves as a reminder that the safety they currently enjoy was hard won and can be easily lost.

Arvoreen sends avatars to defend and patrol halfling communities very readily. Arvoreen may reward warriors who have defended halfling communities with a minor magical item, even if of another race.

Arvoreen's Avatar (Ranger 35, Cleric 29, Paladin 20)

Arvoreen appears as a handsome young halfling warrior, muscular of build and generally dressed in unencumbering and lightweight clothes and fine chain mail. He commonly carries twin short swords or, more rarely, a short sword and gleaming shield. He favors spells from the spheres of all, combat, guardian, healing, law, protection, sun, war, and wards, although he can cast spells from any sphere.

AC −4; MV 12; HP 222; THAC0 −10; #AT 7/2
Dmg 1d6+16 (*short sword +4*, +10 Str, +2 spec. bonus in short sword) and 1d6+16 (*short sword of dancing +4*, +10 Str, +2 spec. bonus in short sword)
MR 65%; SZ M (4 ½ feet tall)
Str 22, Dex 19, Con 21, Int 18, Wis 18, Cha 19
Spells P: 12/11/11/10/9/9/7
Saves* PPDM 1, RSW 1**, PP 2, BW 2, Sp 4
 *Includes +2 bonus to saving throws to a minimum of 1. **Includes halfling +6 Con save bonus to a minimum of 1. The Con save bonus also applies to saves vs. poison to a minimum of 1.

Special Att/Def: Arvoreen is specialized in the use of short swords and is considered proficient in the use of all weapons. He wields *Aegisheart*, a *short sword +4, defender*, and *Hornet*, a *short sword of dancing +4*. Even when dancing, the latter weapon gains his Strength bonus to damage. The Defender can employ *weapon shift* on either weapon at will (ignoring the usual prohibition on using this spell on magical weapons). He wears *chain mail +3* that can cast *heal* three times per day.

Arvoreen never attacks an opponent first, but the first attack upon him (if it hits) does only half damage, regardless of its power. The first magical attack upon him is automatically reflected back upon the caster; thereafter, spells are cast upon him normally. The Defender is only hit by +2 or better magical weapons, and he suffers only half damage from weapons of +2 or lesser enchantment. Arvoreen can become *invisible* at will and can *blink* and *dimension door* three times per day each.

Arvoreen is always accompanied by one of the Keepers (see below), with maximum hit points, and can summon 10d4 others once per day. (Additional Keepers arrive within 1d4 rounds and remain for the duration of the combat.)

Other Manifestations

Arvoreen manifests as a nimbus of silver fire that envelops a being, weapon, or object. This radiance typically gives any or all of the following aids to affected beings, for 1 turn: *haste* (without the aging effect), *ironguard* (as the 5th-level wizard spell detailed in *Pages from the Mages*), or *enlarge* (as the 1st-level wizard spell, tripling the affected being's normal size). It typically gives an affected weapon the attack and damages bonuses and the special abilities of a *sword +4, defender* for 1 turn.

If the object enveloped is a pool of water, Arvoreen manifests as a *magic mirror* effect (as the 4th-level wizard spell). Any devout worshiper who stares into the pool can scry the most pressing threat to the local halfling community. Otherwise, Arvoreen manifests as a *glyph of warding* or a *symbol of hopelessness* placed upon an item or portal to be warded.

Arvoreen is served by Keepers, elite halfling warriors (fighters of 6th–9th level) who died in battle and now defend and patrol the halfling burrows of Green Fields in the Outer Planes. In some situations, the Defender dispatches a small group of Keepers to the Realms to protect an embattled halfling community. Arvoreen is also served by aasimon; archons; bloodhounds; brownies; dobies; einheriar; guardian nagas; hybsils; incarnates of courage, faith, and justice; lammasu; maruts; noctrals; owls; pers; silver dragons; silver falcons; sunflies; and war dogs. He demonstrates his favor through the discovery of amaratha, rustine, trios of stones suitable to be used as sling bullets, figurines depicting halfling warriors formed from dlarun, and crossed sticks (which are seen as representing his symbol). The Defender indicates his displeasure through thunderclaps suggestive of two shields smashing together. His omens to his priests are usually direct warnings of impending danger and the need for battle readiness.

The Church

CLERGY:	Clerics, specialty priests
CLERGY'S ALIGN.:	LG, NG, LN
TURN UNDEAD:	C: Yes, SP: Yes, at priest level −2
CMND. UNDEAD:	C: No, SP: No

All clerics (including fighter/clerics, a multiclassed combination allowed to halfling priests of Arvoreen) and specialty priests (including fighter/specialty priests) of Arvoreen receive religion (halfling) as a bonus nonweapon proficiency. If the DM allows kits from *Demihumans of the Realms* and/or the *Complete Book of Gnomes and Halflings*, clerics (and fighter/clerics) may take either the sheriff or marshal kits.

Arvoreen is not exactly a popular power among most halflings and his priests are often perceived as overly serious and "grumpy as dwarves" by the Small Folk. However, the Defender and his clergy are respected and revered for their teachings and their role in protecting the halfling way of life.

Temples of Arvoreen are usually small fortified redoubts built partially above and partially below ground in strategic locations in regions inhabited by large numbers of halflings. The Defender's houses of worship serve their communities as armories, training grounds for the local militia, and as sanctuaries of last resort if the region they guard is ever overrun. Although the defensive fortifications of such temples vary widely so as to best suit their location, most are characterized by a maze of narrow, low hallways large enough only for a halfling or gnome to fight comfortably, cellars filled with weapons, supplies, and other stores, and large numbers of subterranean tunnels exiting far from the central structure through which halfling guerrilla fighters can launch lightning raids behind the lines of any besieger.

Novices of Arvoreen are known as Shieldbearers. Full priests of the Defender are known as Arvoreen's Marshals. In ascending order of rank, the titles used by Arvoreenan priests are Warder, Guardian, Defender, Protector, Magistrate, Sheriff, Marshal, and High Marshal. High-ranking priests have unique individual titles. Specialty priests are known as trueswords. The clergy of Arvoreen includes hairfeet (55%), stouts (30%), and tallfellows (15%). Males (54%) slightly outnumber females (46%). Arvoreen's clergy includes specialty priests (34%), clerics (26%), fighter/specialty priests (22%), and fighter/clerics (18%).

Dogma: Keep the community's burrows secure, and always be prepared for threats and attacks. Prepare an active defense, drill continuously, and leave nothing to chance. Put down danger before it even rears its head. Seek out allies, no matter how unorthodox. Those who give aid against a mutual foe are friends to be rewarded and trusted. Stealing from other halflings and allies is never acceptable, but thieving is not necessarily dishonorable, as long as it is employed against enemies to better the odds in combat later.

Day-to-Day Activities: Arvoreen's priests are the protectors and defenders of halfling communities. They spend their days constructing defensive barriers, signaling systems, beacons, and traps, and reviewing defenses already in place. Priests of the Defender regularly patrol their communities, always investigating the slightest hint of a threat. Many priests organize the local militia, procure weapons for volunteers, and train every able-bodied halfling in the use of weapons and other defense strategies or at least in how to best seek safety. Many of Arvoreen's Marshals regularly adventure to gain magical weapons and defensive items of all kinds.

Holy Days/Important Ceremonies: If time permits, Arvoreen's priests and lay followers come together prior to every battle (either in a temple or at a makeshift altar in the field) to ask for the blessings of the Defender. After a brief, inspirational sermon and a period of private prayer, the *Battle Hymn of the Keepers* is sung in unison and silvered weapons—at most one per worshiper—are sacrificed to the god by placing them on the altar. If Arvoreen is pleased with the diligence of his followers' preparations, the Defender receives the silver plating from the sacrificed arms, leaving behind the actual weapons. For the next 24 hours, all such once-silvered weapons are enchanted to strike at a +1 bonus on attack and damage rolls.

The Ceremony of Remembrance is celebrated annually on the Feast of the Moon. During this holy day, Arvoreen's followers gather in his temples and on battlefields where their comrades have fallen to remember the names of those who gave their lives in defense of the community. Close friends and relatives often report a brief, wordless encounter with the spirit of a fallen loved one during Ceremonies of Remembrance, but no evidence of such, aside from the statements of individuals who report such spiritual visitations, has ever been found.

Major Centers of Worship: The halfling realm of Meiritin was established north of the Tejarn Hills along the eastern shore the great lake in the Year of the Raised Banner (227 DR) by Small Folk who had been forcibly removed from their vineyard homes in the Purple Hills of Tethyr. The halflings of Meiritin were remarkably resilient in the face of several tyrants who threatened their realm. Notable among the threats they faced were the conquering of the Meiritin's largest settlement by Ilhundyl the Mad Mage in the Year of the Mist Dragon (231 DR), border skirmishes with the forces of Lord Ashar Tornamn of Valashar beginning in the Year of Blessed Sleep (321 DR), the loss of much the realm's territory to the Duchy of Cortryn in the Year of Faltering Fires (491 DR), and Meiritin's eventual collapse in the Years of Trials Arcane (523 DR) due to abuses and enslavement at the hands of the Duke of Cortryn.

Many halflings still dwell in eastern Amn, east of Lake Esmel, in the lands of fallen Meiritin, and not a few dream of the day when halflings in the Lands of Intrigue can once again call a realm their own. Chief among them is High Marshal of the Banner Raised Anew Brenth Stoutshield, once an officer of Arvoreen's Marchers (see below) who resigned his position in the Year of the Shield (1367 DR) after his secret dream of founding a halfling realm in the Purple Marches crumbled with the restoration of Tethyr's monarchy. After discovering a trove of gems during a foray into the ruins of Lost Xandar, Brenth began rebuilding his dream in southern Amn in the hinterlands of fallen Meiritin. He established the Citadel of the Banner Raised Anew across the river Hyrzashyr from the fishing village of Zinner atop ruins sacred to Arvoreen dating back to the establishment of Meiritin. Beginning with a small core of young priests and devoted worshipers, the High Marshal of the Banner Raised Anew attracted halfling parishioners from the surrounding farms of the region by supplementing the Amnian patrols from the Hillforts and by culling the monster populations in the western Tejarn Hills. With the increased tithes, the High Marshal could afford to grow the citadel into a large—by halfling standards—temple and to increase the size of the temple militia and the number of patrols it could mount.

As part of his efforts to integrate the newly founded temple in power structures of the region, Brenth forged a close relationship with Major Olehm of Hillfort Torbold. This close bond between halfling and human was first tested in the Year of the Tankard (1370 DR) as the Sythillisians began to carve out their empire in southwestern Amn. As the troops of Sythillis rampaged through the region, the Citadel of the Banner Raised Anew found itself on the front lines of the war. The High Marshal quickly pledged himself and a large fraction of his troops to Major Olehm's command, leaving only a small reserve to continue patrolling the farmlands surrounding Zinner. If the commander of Hillfort Torbold emerges as major player in post-war Amn (assuming the Sythillisians are eventually defeated), Brenth may very well find himself in a position to see at least part of his dream of refounding Meiritin come to fruition.

Affiliated Orders: During the chaos of Tethyr's Interregnum, a group of halflings and few gnomes active in the Purple Hills under the leadership of Estemal Talltankard were largely responsible for keeping the anarchy consuming the rest of the country at bay. Estemal's band, known as Arvoreen's Marchers, are now recognized by the crown of Tethyr as a knightly order and are responsible for patrolling the Purple Marches, particularly County Vintor. Members of the March include warriors, priests of Arvoreen, and rogues (the latter operating as spies and couriers). Their chapter house, Keeperstone, is located a mile or two north of the halfling community of Barrowsmorn in a forsaken manor destroyed during the Ten Black Days and later rebuilt by halflings and gnomes under Estemal.

Priestly Vestments: The clerical raiment of Arvoreen's Marshals includes silvered helms and suits of chain mail, dark blue tabards with the god's symbol displayed prominently in silver, and twin short swords. The holy symbol of the faith is a miniature silver buckler that is typically worn on a medallion hung around the neck.

Adventuring Garb: Priests of Arvoreen wear the most appropriate armor available, whether it be leather or studded leather in situations requiring stealth or chain mail or plate armor when straight melee combat is

expected. In times of peace when simply patrolling, the most common armor worn by members of Arvoreen's clergy is chain mail. Although they are trained in the use of a wide variety of weapons appropriate for their diminutive statures, most priests of Arvoreen prefer short swords, short bows, and slings.

Specialty Priests (Trueswords)

REQUIREMENTS:	Strength 12 or Constitution 12, Wisdom 9
PRIME REQ.:	Strength or Constitution, Wisdom
ALIGNMENT:	LG, NG, LN
WEAPONS:	Any
ARMOR:	Any
MAJOR SPHERES:	All, combat, divination, guardian, healing, law, protection, sun, war, wards
MINOR SPHERES:	Necromantic, summoning, travelers
MAGICAL ITEMS:	As clerics and fighters
REQ. PROFS:	Short sword, engineering, reading/writing (common)
BONUS PROFS:	Alertness, blindfighting, set snares

- Trueswords must be halflings, but they can be of any halfling subrace.
- Trueswords are allowed to multiclass as fighter/trueswords.
- If the DM allows kits from *Demihumans of the Realms* and/or the *Complete Book of Gnomes and Halflings*, trueswords and fighter/trueswords may take either the sheriff or marshal kits.
- Trueswords may select nonweapon proficiencies from the warrior group without penalty.
- Trueswords may hide in shadows and move silently as a ranger of the same level, modified by the truesword's race, Dexterity, and armor type.
- Trueswords can cast *blessed watchfulness* (as the 1st-level priest spell detailed in the Gorm Gulthyn entry in the "Gnome Pantheon" chapter) or *detect evil* (as the 1st-level priest spell) once per day.
- At 3rd level, trueswords can cast *strength* (as the 2nd-level wizard spell) or *weapon shift* (as the 2nd-level priest spell) once per day.
- At 5th level, trueswords can lay on hands (like the paladin ability), restoring 1 hit point per level once per day.
- At 5th level, trueswords can invoke courage in themselves and up to six others within a 60-foot radius with a word, granting those affected immunity to fear and a +1 bonus to attack rolls and saving throws. They can use this ability up to once a day per level. It lasts 1 turn.
- At 7th level, trueswords can make three melee attacks every two rounds.
- At 7th level, trueswords can cast *glyph of warding* (as the 3rd-level priest spell) or *strength of one* (as the 3rd-level priest spell) once per day.
- At 10th level, trueswords can cast *easy march* or *unceasing vigilance of the holy sentinel* (as the 5th-level priest spells) once per day.
- At 13th level, trueswords can cast *champion's strength* (as the 5th-level priest spell) or *haste* (as the 3rd-level wizard spell, on themselves only, with no penalty for aging) once per day.
- At 13th level, trueswords can make two melee atacks per round.

Arvoreenan Spells

In addition to the spells listed below, priests of Arvoreen can cast the 1st-level priest spell *blessed watchfulness* detailed in the entry for Gorm Gulthyn.

1st Level
Warning Shout (Pr 1; Alteration)

Sphere:	Protection
Range:	0
Components:	V, S
Duration:	Instantaneous
Casting Time:	1
Area of Effect:	One-half-mile radius
Saving Throw:	None

The priest who casts a warning shout can project a single word loud enough to be heard outdoors approximately one-half mile away. The sound is magically amplified so that it is the same volume close to the spellcaster as it is at the edge of the spell's radius. Only one word may be projected using this spell (such as "Intruders!" or "Help!"). As a side effect of the noise, this spell automatically awakens sleeping creatures within the area of effect who can be naturally awakened by noise who are not extremely deep sleepers. They do not necessarily know what awakened them when they wake up, however.

2nd Level

Weapon Shift (Pr 2; Alteration)
Sphere:	Combat
Range:	Touch
Components:	V, S, M
Duration:	2 rounds+1 round/level
Casting Time:	5
Area of Effect:	One weapon
Saving Throw:	None

This spell enables the caster to transform a particular weapon (that perhaps the caster cannot use) into an entirely different weapon (that the caster can use). However, the spell has several important limitations, as follows:

First, the final product must be a weapon that the caster can use without penalty, with regard to both class restrictions and proficiency status.

Second, the weapon to be changed must be of similar size and composed of the same material as the weapon it will become. For example, a wooden club cannot be turned into a steel short sword, though a steel short sword could be transformed into a steel club. Likewise a quarterstaff could be transformed into a short bow, as they are of a similar size.

Third, weapons that carry a magical dweomer, even if it is only temporary (for example, *Nystul's magic aura*, *light*, etc.) cannot be influenced by this spell. Casting it on a magical weapon simply wastes the spell.

Fourth, the transformed weapon receives no bonuses to attack or damage rolls, nor is it able to strike creatures that can only be hit by magical weapons. The altered weapon radiates magic if detected, however.

Finally, the caster must keep the weapon in hand for the duration of the spell or else it immediately reverts to its true form. Thus, the caster cannot pass the weapon to another being, nor can she or he cast spells that require somatic components or perform actions that require two hands.

Weapon shift can be negated if subjected to a successful *dispel magic* or more powerful effect.

The material component for this spell is the priest's holy symbol.

3rd Level

Humansize (Pr 3; Alteration)
Sphere:	Combat
Range:	Touch
Components:	V, S
Duration:	6 rounds+1 round/level above 5th
Casting Time:	6
Area of Effect:	One halfling
Saving Throw:	None

This spell makes a halfling grow to the size of a human and appear exactly human in all ways. Everything the halfling is wearing and carrying also grows proportionately. A short sword, for example, grows to the size of a long sword. The spell does not cause the halfling to be disoriented or clumsy; the recipient is adjusted to and in control of the larger body as if it were normal-sized. The larger halfling also gains two additional points of Strength. If the halfling's Strength goes above 18, it goes to the first percentile rank on Table 1: Strength in the *Player's Handbook*, becoming effectively 18/01. The true race of *humansized* halflings cannot be discovered except through the use of *true seeing*. If the casting priest cast the spell on himself or herself, she or he can return to normal at will. If the spell is cast on another, that halfling remains *humansized* until the spell expires.

Sparkling Sword (Pr 3; Evocation)
Sphere:	Combat
Range:	0
Components:	V, S, M
Duration:	1 round or 5 rounds+1 round/level above 5th
Casting Time:	6
Area of Effect:	The caster's melee weapon
Saving Throw:	None

When this spell is cast on the priest's melee weapon (usually a sword in the case of specialty priests of Arvoreen), it takes on a bright, sparkling silver glow. There are two applications for the spell, and only one can be used for a particular casting:

(1) The round following the spell's casting for 1 round and one attack, the caster gains a +2 bonus to attack rolls and a +3 bonus to damage rolls with the weapon on which *sparkling sword* has been cast. The spell allows the caster to strike creatures hit only by +2 or better magical weapons. If the attack misses, the spell is wasted.

(2) The caster gains a +1 bonus to attack rolls and a +1 bonus to damage rolls with the weapon on which *sparkling sword* has been cast. This effect lasts for 5 rounds plus 1 round for each experience level above 6th the caster has. The spell allows the caster to strike creatures hit only by +1 or better magical weapons.

When either version of the spell expires, the weapon on which it is cast must succeed at an item saving throw vs. crushing blow or be ruined. If there is 10 gp or more worth of silver in the weapon or its hilt or decorations, the weapon receives a +2 bonus on the saving throw.

The material component is a pinch of sulfur, which is tossed upon the weapon.

4th Level

Blazing Sword (Pr 4; Evocation)
Sphere:	Combat
Range:	0
Components:	V, S, M
Duration:	1 round or 4 rounds+1 round/level above 7th
Casting Time:	7
Area of Effect:	The caster's melee weapon
Saving Throw:	None

When this spell is cast on the priest's melee weapon (usually a sword in the case of specialty priests of Arvoreen), it takes on a bright, sparkling silver glow. There are two applications for the spell, and only one can be used for a particular casting:

(1) The round following the spell's casting for 1 round and one attack, the caster gains a +3 bonus to attack rolls and a +5 bonus to damage rolls with the weapon on which *blazing sword* has been cast. The spell allows the caster to strike creatures hit only by +3 or better magical weapons. If the attack misses, the spell is wasted.

(2) The caster gains a +1 bonus to attack rolls and a +2 bonus to damage rolls with the weapon on which *blazing sword* has been cast. This effect lasts for 4 rounds plus 1 round for each experience level above 7th the caster has. The spell allows the caster to strike creatures hit only by +1 or better magical weapons.

When either version of the spell expires, the weapon on which it is cast must succeed at an item saving throw vs. crushing blow or be ruined. If there is 10 gp or more worth of silver in the weapon or its hilt or decorations, the weapon receives a +2 bonus on the saving throw.

The material component is a pinch of sulfur, which is tossed upon the weapon.

5th Level

Giantsize (Pr 5; Alteration)

Sphere:	Combat
Range:	Touch
Components:	V, S
Duration:	9 rounds+1 round/level above 9th
Casting Time:	8
Area of Effect:	One halfling
Saving Throw:	None

This spell makes a halfling grow to the size of a hill giant and appear exactly like a hill giant; however, the halfling's Armor Class does not change, as the halfling lacks a real hill giant's tough hide. Everything the halfling is wearing and carrying also grows proportionately. A short sword, for example, grows to the size of a bastard sword (which a giant could wield for full effect with one hand). The spell does not cause the halfling to be disoriented or clumsy; the recipient is adjusted to and in control of the larger body as if it were normal-sized. The halfling's Strength become 19 for the duration of the spell. The true race of *giantsized* halflings cannot be discovered except through the use of *true seeing*. If the casting priest cast the spell on himself or herself, she or he can return to normal at will. If the spell is cast on another, that halfling remains *giantsized* until the spell expires.

Brandobaris

(Master of Stealth, Misadventure, the Trickster, the Irrepressible Scamp, the Friendly Rapscallion)

Lesser Power of the Planes, N

PORTFOLIO:	Stealth, thievery, adventuring, halfling rogues
ALIASES:	Kaldair Swiftfoot, otherwise none widespread
DOMAIN NAME:	Wanders
SUPERIOR:	Yondalla
ALLIES:	Baervan Wildwanderer, Baravar Cloakshadow, Dugmaren Brightmantle, Erevan Ilesere, Garl Glittergold, Haela Brightaxe, Mask, Quorlinn, Vergadain, the halfling pantheon
FOES:	Abbathor, Beshaba, Urdlen, Vaprak
SYMBOL:	Halfling's footprint
WOR. ALIGN.:	Any

Brandobaris (BRAN-doe-BARE-iss) is the master of adventure and misadventure, a favorite of halfling adventurers. Tales of the Trickster's wild exploits are almost beyond counting. The followers of Brandobaris, as might be expected, are mostly thieves and fighter/thieves. The more ardent followers are usually also the ones to take the greatest risks on adventures, and the Master of Stealth views them almost as favored apprentices.

Brandobaris is the errant rogue of the halfling pantheon, regarded with exasperated tolerance by his fellows. Only Tymora regularly accompanies the Trickster on his jaunts, and Lady Luck and the Master of Stealth are said (by halflings) to be romantically linked. Conversely, Brandobaris is routinely cursed by Beshaba, but, for the Trickster at least, Tymora's favor always seems to prevail over the Maid of Misfortune in the end. Brandobaris is an irrepressible scamp who gets along well with most powers who can let themselves smile at his antics. Helm and Torm are notable exceptions, and even Arvoreen finds his patience tried at times by the Trickster. Brandobaris is a good friend of Baervan Wildwanderer, Erevan Ilesere, Garl Glittergold, and Vergadain, and all have accompanied him at one time or another on some of his many misadventures. Brandobaris and Mask have a healthy rivalry, although the halfling god of thieves dislikes the Shadowlord's penchant for cruelty. The Master of Stealth will have nothing to do with Abbathor, as the Great Master of Greed is literally in the game only for the gold.

Brandobaris is always ready with a joke or a jug, yet he is such an agreeable, friendly rapscallion that he rarely makes an enemy. He's always well dressed and ready with a smart reply to any attempt at conversation. He has a bawdy sense of humor and little sense of propriety. Brandobaris often goes on adventures to find some item he believes will make life more comfortable for him, though this does not always prove to work out as he had planned. The moral lesson of many of his journeys and scrapes is that it is better not to dash off unprepared into danger, let alone on foolish dares. Nonetheless, Brandobaris does come across as an appealing sort of scamp. He has much of the trickster in him; he is primarily a clever thief who fools his opponents into thinking him harmless, then steals them blind and escapes their wrath. No matter how awful a situation in which he finds himself (and he's found some pretty awful ones), Brandobaris manages to find his way out again—and make a profit from the episode as well.

The mischievous Master of Stealth is always on the lookout for a worthy risk and challenge to face, and he may even seek out a highly skilled halfling thief or two to join him in some caper as he wanders the Prime. Other thieves may come along on such jaunts, but if they do not worship Brandobaris they might find some of their valuables missing when the adventure is over. Brandobaris reveals his identity only after the adventure is over, and only to his followers. Brandobaris's adventures can be exceptionally challenging and dangerous, but hold the promise of great reward for the fast, the clever, and the quiet!

Brandobaris's Avatar (Thief 30, Ranger 24, Mage 18, Druid 18)

Brandobaris appears as a plump, jolly, cheeky-faced young halfling dressed in smart leather jerkin, silk blouse, and cotton pants. He favors spells from the spheres of all, charm, creation, numbers, protection, sun, and travelers and from the schools of alteration, enchantment/charm, and illusion/phantasm, although he can cast spells from any sphere or school.

AC −2; MV 12; HP 190; THAC0 −3; #AT 2 (or 3/1)
Dmg 1d4+10 (*dagger +3*, +7 STR) or 1d4+11 (*sling of seeking +4* and stone bullet, +7 STR)
MR 60% (see below); SZ S (4 feet tall)
STR 19, DEX 23, CON 18, INT 20, WIS 18, CHA 22
Spells P: 10/10/9/9/6/4/2, W: 5/5/5/5/3/3/2/1
Saves PPDM 2, RSW 1*, PP 4, BW 4, Sp 5
*Includes halfling +5 CON save bonus to a minimum of 1. The CON save bonus also applies to saves vs. poison to a minimum of 1.

Special Att/Def: Brandobaris wields *Vamoose*, a *dagger +3* that magically points out the fastest and safest direction of escape from any maze or trap (making Brandobaris immune to *maze* spells when holding it). It can also transform into *sling of seeking +4* that hurls a sling bullet or a ball of dust whenever it is used. The dust ball has a maximum range of 100 yards (25 yards short range, 50 yards medium range) and does not harm the victim it strikes. The victim feels nothing but must succeed at a saving throw vs. spell at a −6 penalty or fall deeply asleep for 6d6 turns. Sometimes he uses *Vamoose* and another *dagger +3* with no other known special abilities. When doing so, his number of attacks per round is 3/1 rather than 2.

Brandobaris is so skilled at moving silently that he cannot be heard by any mortal being or god, should he desire to conceal his movements. He can also hide so well as to be completely invisible (detectable only with a *true seeing* spell or some magical item of similar power). The Master of Stealth has permanent powers of *feather fall*, *free action*, and *spider climbing*, and he has 90% magic resistance against all detection spells from the school or sphere of divination. He can be struck only by +1 or better magical weapons.

Other Manifestations

Brandobaris rarely manifests, preferring to interact directly with his worshipers in avatar form. When the Master of Stealth does manifest, it is usually subtly and the recipient of his beneficence is rarely even aware of the divine sponsorship of his good fortune. For example, a halfling thief who blows the use of a thieving skill (such as Climb Walls or Remove Traps) or an ability check (such as a Dexterity check) in a potentially fatal situation might find a small protuberance on which he can stop his fall, grab a trip wire before it can fully trigger, or recover his balance before tumbling off a narrow ledge. In such situations, Brandobaris's manifestation permits a second chance at the thieving skill or ability check.

An especially daring risk (one that places the halfling in considerable jeopardy) that pays off is looked upon favorably by Brandobaris. He might reward the perpetrator of such a daring act—though he does so only once in that halfling's lifetime, so as not to encourage the mortal to be *too* fool-hardy. Such rewards commonly take the form of a manifestation, and the recipient of such might gain the ability to employ *feather fall*, *free action*, *spider climb*, or a similar spell-like effect in some future situation.

Brandobaris is served by azmyths, blue jays, boggles, brownies, campestris, copper dragons, crows, crystal dragons, dobies, ethyks, faerie dragons, firefriends, firestars, fremlins, kenku, leprechauns, luck cats, mercury dragons, mice, monkey spiders, pixies, pseudodragons, raccoons, ravens, snyads, sunflies, and the occasional tiefling. He demonstrates his favor in the form of footprint marks leading toward a clue, key, treasure, or the like and by causing objects to appear in a pocket. The Master of Stealth indicates his displeasure in the form of footprint marks leading the tracker astray and by causing objects to disappear from a pocket.

The Church

CLERGY:	Clerics, specialty priests, thieves
CLERGY'S ALIGN.:	NG, CG, N, CN
TURN UNDEAD:	C: Yes, SP: No, T: No
CMND. UNDEAD:	C: No, SP: No, T: No

All clerics (including cleric/thieves, a multiclassed option available to halfling priests of Brandobaris) and specialty priests (including specialty priest/thieves) of Brandobaris receive religion (halfling) as a bonus nonweapon proficiency.

Like Brandobaris himself, the church of misadventure is filled with appealing scamps who regularly find themselves embroiled in trouble, but who usually emerge better off than not. Tales of the exploits of Brandobaris's followers are told and retold in most halfling cultures. However, despite their fondness for such tales, most halflings would prefer that the church of Brandobaris keep far away from their own lives and are personally unwilling to get involved in the misadventurous capers of the Trickster's entourage.

While most halfling gods are worshiped predominantly in small shrines within the home or local community and true temples are rare, Brandobaris is unique in that his church has no actual temples or permanent shrines at all. The Master of Stealth is honored instead through adventurous activity and by relating tales of his exploits and those of his followers. In a sense, a shrine of Brandobaris is temporarily created whenever a story involving the Trickster is told or whenever an item commemorating one of his misadventures is brought out and remembered.

Novices of Brandobaris are known as Wayward Rascals. Full priests of the Master of Stealth are known as the Hands of Misadventure. In ascending order of rank, the titles used by Brandobarian priests are Scamp, Rascal, Swindler, Blackguard, Trickster, Rapscallion, Knave, and Master Rogue. High-ranking priests have unique individual titles. Specialty priests are known as misadventurers. The clergy of Brandobaris includes hairfeet (60%), stouts (30%), and tallfellows (10%). Brandobaris's clergy includes specialty priests (30%), thieves (25%), specialty priest/thieves (22%), fighter/thieves (18%), and clerics (5%). Males (65%) outnumber females (35%).

Halfling Powers: Brandobaris and Tymora

Dogma: Adventure and risk are the spice of life, and stealth and subtlety are the tools of the trade. Seek excitement and danger wherever your feet take you, for risk-taking leads to life's greatest rewards. Lust for the thrill, not for the treasure, for greed obscures the true prize of the experience. At the end of the day, the wildest tale is the greatest reward. Learn to tell a good yarn, and sometimes your tongue will get you out of trouble.

Day-to-Day Activities: Members of Brandobaris's clergy are active adventurers who seek lives of excitement and danger by taking active risks and by employing the skills taught to them by the Master of Stealth and his most accomplished apprentices. Most Hands of Misadventure are stricken with wanderlust, seeking to see as much of the world as they can. While Brandobaris's priests are often involved in daring thefts, smooth cons, and other larcenous behavior, they are thrill-seekers, not bandits. They are driven by the acquisition of treasure, not the holding of it, and many benefit their communities by lavish spending of newly acquired wealth at halfling-owned establishments. Those who cannot adventure, whether due to age or infirmity, serve the faith by running safehouses and by spreading glorious tales among the sedentary majority of the halfling populace.

Holy Days/Important Ceremonies: As one might expect, followers of Brandobaris have little in the way of formal ceremony when they venerate the Master of Stealth. On nights of the new moon, no matter where they are, followers of Brandobaris are expected to hide one or more stolen items from the previous month's take in the best hiding place they can find as part of a ritual known as the Trickster's Tithe. If Brandobaris is pleased with the offering (which has less to do with the value of the offering than it does with the amount of risk required to acquire it), it vanishes from its cache by morning, and the worshiper is blessed with the Trickster's favor for the following month. (In game terms, this translates into a +1 bonus on a single saving throw that must be used within the next month at the character's discretion.)

Major Centers of Worship: As noted above, Brandobaris has no true temples. Instead, the Master of Stealth is worshiped through daring deeds and wild tales of his exploits. In some sense, cities and kingdoms where many of Brandobaris's followers practice their craft—such as Athkatla, Baldur's Gate, Berdusk, Calimport, Everlund, Iriaebor, Silverymoon, Riatavin, Waterdeep, and Zazesspur as well as Amn, Calimshan, Cormyr, Damara, Deepingdale, Luiren, Ravens Bluff, Tethyr, Turmish, and the Vast—are the Trickster's major centers of worship.

Legendary sites of Brandobaris's greatest adventures can also be considered major centers of worship, for many of his followers visit the settings of the Trickster's tales in simple homage to his daring and skill and to tell the tales of the Trickster's exploits. One such tale involves the founding of Luiren, legendary land of the halflings, centuries ago on the shores of Luirenstrand (also known as Hambone Bay), long before the fall of Myth Drannor. The founding myths of Luiren claim that the Lluirwood (now split into the Long Forest, the Granuin Forest (also known as the southern Lluirwood), and the Gundar Forest) at that time stretched from the foothills of the Toadsquat Mountains to the shore of the Great Sea and from the eastern bank of the River Ammath to the western bank of the River Gundar, incorporating all the territory that now composes Luiren and Estagund. At that time, the Lluirwood was inhabited by ogres, whose descendants still populate the Toadsquat Mountains, and the first Small Folk to settle along the shores of the Luirenstrand were hard-pressed to defend their homesteads from the relentless raids of the beast-men. At that time, a young halfling by the name of Kaldair Swiftfoot—now believed to have been an avatar of Brandobaris—encountered an avatar of the rapacious and violent ogre god, Vaprak the Destroyer. For 10 days and nights, Kaldair toyed with the Destroyer, leading him on a merry chase through a trap-filled tract of woodlands, but the ogre god could not kill or capture the elusive halfling rogue nor could Kaldair permanently thwart Vaprak's murderous designs on the halflings of the region. Finally Vaprak collapsed of exhaustion, while Kaldair danced about him and taunted the ogre god for his weakness. In his rage, the Destroyer hurled trees ripped from the ground at the elusive halfling, but to no avail. Kaldair then proposed a feat of strength—uprooting a tree without breaking the roots—with the loser withdrawing to the mountains and the victor claiming the forest, and Vaprak readily agreed. The Destroyer went first, ripping the great hardwoods from the forest floor, but he failed to remove a single tree without tearing apart its root structure. Kaldair, on the other hand, succeeded on his first attempt after carefully dislodging a tiny sapling with a single taproot. Vaprak roared in fury at the trick, but the ogre god had no choice but to concede defeat and adhere to the terms of the contest, for to do otherwise would simply add to his humiliation. The ogres then withdrew to the mountains and the halflings settled the forest glades. To this day, when a great tree falls to the ground outside the town of Beluir, a region known as Vaprak's Glade, a follower of Brandobaris sits on the trunk and relates the tale of Luiren's founding to the next generation of Small Folk, seeking to inspire them to pursue a life of adventure.

Affiliated Orders: The Midknights of Misadventure are an informal fellowship composed primarily of halfling clerics and fighter/thieves. While hardly a formal military order, small bands of Midknights perform jailbreaks and other rescue operations in situations where an imprisoned follower of Brandobaris faces death or torture and escaping without assistance is very unlikely. The composition and membership of a particular band varies widely, but half a dozen or so Midknights of widely varying skills and abilities are typically available at any given time in cities or regions with sizable halfling populations.

Priestly Vestments: Given the informal nature of the church of Brandobaris, regular adventuring gear serves as the ceremonial garb of priests of the Master of Stealth. For most priests, this includes leather armor, a cloak in a subdued hue, and when feeling particularly jaunty, a feathered cap of some sort. The holy symbol of the faith is a small purloined object of great value that the priest has personally *blessed*, typically a gold or platinum coin or jewel of some sort.

Adventuring Garb: Brandobaris's priests favor leather armor, or, in very rare cases when they can acquire it, silenced elven chain mail. They employ the weapons and tools of the trade, favoring clubs, daggers, knives, slings, and short swords for situations where combat cannot be avoided.

Specialty Priests (Misadventurers)

REQUIREMENTS:	Dexterity 13, Wisdom 9
PRIME REQ.:	Dexterity, Wisdom
ALIGNMENT:	NG, N, CN
WEAPONS:	Club, dagger, dart, hand crossbow, knife, lasso, sap, short sword, sling, staff
ARMOR:	Leather, padded leather, studded leather, or elven chain mail; no shield
MAJOR SPHERES:	All, charm, chaos, creation, divination, healing, protection, sun, travelers
MINOR SPHERES:	Animal, combat, guardian, time
MAGICAL ITEMS:	As clerics and thieves
REQ. PROFS:	Tumbling, ventriloquism
BONUS PROFS:	Disguise, gaming

- Misadventurers must be halflings. Most misadventurers are hairfeet, but they can be of any halfling subrace.
- Misadventurers are allowed to multiclass as misadventurer/thieves.
- Misadventurers may select nonweapon proficiencies from the rogue group without penalty.
- Misadventurers understand and use thieves' cant.

- Single-class misadventurers have limited thieving skills as defined in the Limited Thieving Skills section of "Appendix 1: Demihuman Priests." Multiclassed misadventurer/thieves receive no extra thieving skill points or bonuses for their misadventurer class; their thieving skills are based solely off their thief class.
- Misadventurers can cast *feather fall* or *spider climb* (as the 1st-level wizard spells) once per day.
- At 3rd level, misadventurers can cast *find traps* or *silence, 15´ radius* (as the 2nd-level priest spells) once per day.
- At 3rd level, misadventurers can create an illusionary *calling card* once a day. This calling card is the illusion of a simple item, whether it be a white glove, silk scarf, or rose. Upon its creation, the item must be immediately placed in a fixed location or it fades away into nothingness. Once placed, the illusionary item does not move or disappear until touched by a sentient being (animal intelligence or greater) other than the caster. Once touched, a *calling card* instantly melts away into nothingness.

  Much like a wizard's sigil, the *calling card* of a priest of Brandobaris is unique to that individual within the faith. Each acolyte of the Master of Stealth must choose an illusionary item to be created by this spell the first time *calling card* is cast. Once chosen, the type of object created can never be changed. *Calling cards* are typically left behind at the scene of the crime to take oblique credit for the theft.

  For every three levels above 3rd, a misadventurer can create an additional *calling card* per day.
- At 5th level, misadventurers can cast *invisibility* or *knock* (as the 2nd-level wizard spells) once per day. They gain the potential to do this once more per day at 15th level.
- At 7th level, misadventurers can cast *deeppockets* (as the 2nd-level wizard spell) once per day.
- At 10th level, misadventurers can cast *fumble* (as the 4th-level wizard spell) or *undetectable lie* (as the reverse of the 4th-level priest spell *detect lie*) once per day.
- At 13th level, misadventurers can cast *legend lore* (as the 6th-level wizard spell) once per tenday.

Brandobarian Spells

1st Level

Daydream (Pr 1; Phantasm)
Sphere:	Creation
Range:	20 yards+10 yards/level
Components:	S, M
Duration:	1 round/level
Casting Time:	4
Area of Effect:	One creature
Saving Throw:	Neg.

This spell causes the target's thoughts to drift away from the task at hand, diminishing his or her chance of noticing anything unusual. For the duration of the *daydream* effect, small clues or discrepancies are blithely ignored, and only obvious events are noted, as adjudicated by the DM. A successful saving throw vs. spell negates the *daydream*. If the casting of the *daydream* was done discreetly, regardless of whether the saving throw was made or not, the target does not even realize that a spell was cast.

While under the effects of a *daydream*, the target is penalized by 10% on any checks related to perception or observation. Thus checks for surprise are made with a –1 penalty, thief skill checks to move silently and hide in shadows are made with a +10% with respect to the subject of the *daydream*, Intelligence checks to notice or observe anything unusual are made with a –2 penalty, etc. If and when the target does notice anything unusual, the *daydream* effect comes to an immediate end.

The material components are the priest's holy symbol and a pinch of fine sand.

2nd Level

Charm of Brandobaris (Pr 2; Alteration)

Sphere:	Travelers
Range:	0
Components:	V
Duration:	1 day/level
Casting Time:	1
Area of Effect:	1d4 beings in a 30-foot radius
Saving Throw:	Neg.

This spell is useful when the caster has been captured. The spell convinces one to four target creatures that the caster is too valuable a prize to execute (or eat) out of hand. It creates lingering doubts in the targets' minds that make them think that the caster is worth ransoming, that higher authorities should be consulted, or in the case of evil beings, that it might be more fun to forcibly interrogate the caster later. In any case, the net effect is that the caster is not immediately killed, thus allowing for a possible escape. Even creatures of animal intelligence or less are more easily distracted from the caster—for example, other creatures available for consumption will be eaten first.

Charm of Brandobaris does not affect the caster's ability to communicate with his or her captors, nor does it otherwise alter their behavior: It does not, for example, make guards less watchful than usual.

The effect is centered on the caster, and it affects beings selected by the caster within the area of effect. If the spell is cast at three or four beings, each gets a normal saving throw vs. spell. If only two beings are to be affected, each has a saving throw penalty of –1. If the spell is cast at one being, the saving throw has a –2 penalty. Saving throws are adjusted for Wisdom.

The verbal component of this spell varies according to the situation, but typically *charm of Brandobaris* is invoked with an apropos comment along the lines of: "This isn't exactly what it looks like . . ." or "Let me explain . . . ."

3rd Level

Stealth of Brandobaris (Pr 3; Alteration)

Sphere:	Guardian
Range:	0
Components:	S, M
Duration:	1 turn+1 round/level
Casting Time:	6
Area of Effect:	The caster
Saving Throw:	None

When this spell is cast, the priest temporarily gains the ability to move silently and hide in shadows as a thief of his or her level as found on Table 19: Thief Average Ability Table in the DUNGEON MASTER *Guide* (or Table 18: Ranger Abilities in the *Player's Handbook*). Dexterity and racial adjustments apply, as do armor penalties. If the caster is a multiclassed priest/thief or a specialty priest of Brandobaris, his or her chance of success when using either skill is instead increased by 20%. *Stealth of Brandobaris* is canceled if exposed to a successful *dispel magic* or similar power.

The material component is the priest's holy symbol.

Cyrrollalee
(The Hand of Fellowship, the Faithful, the Hearthkeeper)

Intermediate Power of Mount Celestia, LG

PORTFOLIO:	Friendship, trust, the home, the hearth, honesty, hospitality, crafts (especially weaving and needlework)
ALIASES:	None widespread
DOMAIN NAME:	Venya/Green Fields
SUPERIOR:	Yondalla
ALLIES:	Azuth, Chauntea, Deneir, Eldath, Gond, Hathor, Helm, Ilmater, Kelemvor, Lathander, Lliira, Mielikki, Milil, Mystra, Nephthys, Oghma, Selûne, Shaundakul, Silvanus, Sune, Torm, Tyr, Waukeen, the Morndinsamman (except Abbathor, Deep Duerra, Laduguer, and Vergadain), the elf pantheon (except Erevan Ilesere, Fenmarel Mestarine, and Shevarash), the gnome pantheon (except Baravar Cloakshadow and Urdlen), the halfling pantheon
FOES:	Abbathor, Cyric, Leira (dead), Mask, Talona, Talos and the gods of fury (Auril, Malar, and Umberlee), Urdlen, Vhaeraun
SYMBOL:	Open door
WOR. ALIGN.:	LG, NG, CG, LN

Cyrrollalee (SEER-oh-LAH-lee) is the halfling power of friendship and trust. She is also a protective deity, like Yondalla, but whereas the concern of the Protector and Provider lies with the overall race, Cyrrollalee cares more for the sanctity of the home itself. The Hearthkeeper is specifically a goddess who protects the hearth and home while keeping the inhabitants from being too defensive and closed in. She oversees many of the mundane and day-to-day aspects of halfling home life. Her real interest is in the hospitality, generosity, and kindness halflings can show to others, and she is most displeased with those who fail to display proper hospitality and good fellowship. Her worst enemies are those who betray the trust of a host or who break into homes (of halflings) to steal. She is also the enemy of oath-breakers. Cyrrollalee's followers are largely regular halflings as well as a few warriors.

As a power of trust who embodies the spirit of good fellowship and friendship, Cyrrollalee is the halfling deity who has the largest number of good relations with deities of other races. Some believe her to be an aspect of Yondalla rather than a separate entity, but in truth, the two are closely allied but distinct goddesses. The Hand of Fellowship is allied with the rest of the halfling pantheon as well, particularly Arvoreen and Sheela Peryroyl, but she is ever wary of the antics of Brandobaris and Tymora. Although Cyrrollalee is by nature very forgiving and friendly, the Hand of Fellowship has despaired of certain powers ever changing their ways. She regularly opposes the machinations of those powers that inflict destruction upon the home—such as Talona, the Gods of Fury, and Urdlen, those powers who habitually lie or deceive—such as Cyric, Leira, and Mask, and those gods who steal from the home—such as Abbathor, Mask, and Vhaeraun.

As a rule, Cyrrollalee is warm, friendly, and welcoming, and even nondivine beings feel comfortable in her presence. Her words and her touch are always gentle, and she never raises her voice in anger. Cyrrollalee does not get too involved in the day-to-day lives of her followers except on a small level, watching over everyday events of the home. Naturally, she hates liars, swindlers, and (especially) thieves who would break into a person's home. If roused, she can be a most fearsome foe indeed; any halfling whose burrow has been violated knows the feeling of Cyrrollalee's fury swelling within him. Cyrrollalee does not often send her avatars to the Prime; this is usually only done in response to major oath-breaking, to punish the offender. When she does visit the Prime, Cyrrollalee sometimes takes the form of a stooped halfling of indeterminate years, worn by poverty and work into a frail shell. In this guise, she often visits halfling burrows to see if the inhabitants are truly hospitable; woe to the family that turns her away!

Cyrollalee's Avatar (Cleric 32, Paladin 25, Wizard 28)

Cyrollalee appears as a humble female halfling of homely appearance, the brown of her peasant's clothing matching that of her hair. She favors spells from the spheres of all, animal, charm, creation, guardian, healing, law, protection, summoning, and wards and from the schools of abjuration, alteration, and enchantment/charm, although she can cast spells from any sphere or school.

AC –3; MV 12; HP 203; THAC0 –4; #AT 2/1
Dmg 1d6+1 (quarterstaff +1, +1 Str)
MR 75%; SZ S (4 feet tall)
Str 16, Dex 19, Con 19, Int 20, Wis 24, Cha 21
Spells P: 14/13/13/12/12/11/8, W: 6/6/6/6/6/6/6/6/6
Saves* PPDM 1, RSW 1**, PP 2, BW 2, Sp 2
  *Includes +2 bonus to saving throws to a minimum of 1. **Includes halfling +5 Con save bonus to a minimum of 1. The Con save bonus also applies to saves vs. poison to a minimum of 1.

Special Att/Def: Cyrollalee wields *Camaradestave*, a *quarterstaff +1* that charms, as the 4th-level wizard spell *charm monster*, any creature it strikes who fails a saving throw vs. spell. She carries two pairs of *iron bands of Bilarro* that possess half the usual escape probability.

Cyrollalee is affected only by weapons of +2 or better enchantment. She is cloaked in a permanent mantle equivalent to *Serten's spell immunity*. She *detects lies* automatically, and she can manifest a 30-foot radius mantle with the effects of a *zone of truth* (as the 2nd-level priest spell) that moves with her, at will. Three times per day, Cyrollalee can *animate* any or all objects within a 60-foot radius at will for as long as she wishes, as the 6th-level priest spell *animate object*, and any such *animated* object remains animated and continues to serve her will even if she leaves the area.

Other Manifestations

Cyrollalee manifests in many ways, both large and small, to aid or gently instruct her followers. When a follower is about to be burgled or cheated, she often manifests as a chill sense of foreboding and an intuition that something is wrong within the home. If offended by the dishonesty of someone speaking with one of her priests, the Hearthkeeper may manifest as a *zone of truth* in which no saving throw is allowed to avoid its effects. When the life of a defenseless worshiper is threatened by someone who has entered his or her home, Cyrollalee often manifests by *animating*, as the 6th-level priest spell *animate object*, one or more objects to drive off the home invader.

Cyrollalee is served by aasimon, archons, asuras, baku, bronze dragons, brown cats, brown dogs, brownies, bumblebees, campestris, cave crickets, dobies, einheriar, formians, friendly fungi, giant sundews, guardian nagas, hollyphants, house hunters, incarnates of charity, faith, and justice, killmoulis, ki-rin, lammasu, maruts, noctrals, oathbinder genies, pers, porcupines, skunks, sprites, squirrels, sunflies, tressym, t'uen-rin, and woodchucks. She demonstrates her favor through the discovery of small household chores completed by unknown hands, with warm breezes in winter and cool breezes in summer, with baking aromas that waft through a room, with small fires that appear in the hearth for a few moments without consuming any visible fuel, and with doors that swing open untouched. The Hand of Fellowship indicates her displeasure by the sound of clanging pots, the sudden slamming of a door, or a sudden chill felt by a worshiper when he or she shakes the hand of a liar, cheat, or thief.

The Church

CLERGY:	Clerics, mystics, specialty priests
CLERGY'S ALIGN.:	LG, NG, CG, LN
TURN UNDEAD:	C: Yes, Mys: No, SP: Yes, see specialty priest description
CMND. UNDEAD:	C: No, Mys: No, SP: No

All clerics, mystics, and specialty priests of Cyrollalee receive religion (halfling) as a bonus nonweapon proficiency.

Cyrollalee's faith is little known outside of halfling communities, but the fruits of her teachings and the efforts of her priesthood are in large part responsible for the halfling way of life that is so admired by other races.

Among halflings, Cyrollalee is quietly appreciated by all and quietly venerated by those who build homes and families. Many invocations to her are day-to-day minor oaths and fussing by busy halflings, but underlying such daily minutia is a solid core of faithful veneration. While halfling adventurers, particularly those drawn to the errant ways of Brandobaris and Tymora, may tease devout followers of the Hearthkeeper for their sedentary habits and quiet lives, in most cases such wayfarers were raised in homes whose inhabitants performed monthly oblations and, in truth, they too continue to give quiet thanks to the Hand of Fellowship on the first day of every month.

Typically the manse of the local priest of Cyrollalee serves the surrounding halfling community as both a temple and as a home away from home. As such, there is little to differentiate such structures or burrows from those that surround a Cyrollaleen house of worship. One distinguishing feature of any temple dedicated to the Hearthkeeper is that the entrance door is always open whenever at least one priest is in residence. Halflings unable to return to their own beds for the night are always welcome to stay for a night at such temple-homes, and Cyrollaleen churches along major trade routes serve as de facto halfling hostels.

Novices of Cyrollalee are known as the Befriended. Full priests of the Hand of Fellowship are known as Homefellows. In ascending order of rank, the titles used by Cyrollaleen priests are Cheery Homemaker, Hearth Warden, Hand of Friendship, Hale Host (or Hostess), Homespun Companion, Neighborly Householder, Open Door, and Burrow Patriarch (or Matriarch). High-ranking priests have unique individual titles. Specialty priests are known as homesteaders. The clergy of Cyrollalee includes hairfeet (65%), stouts (25%), and tallfellows (10%). Cyrollalee's clergy is nearly evenly divided between specialty priests (35%), mystics (34%), and clerics (31%). Females (85%) far outnumber males (15%)

Dogma: Be generous in friendship, and welcome all friends into your home. Earn the trust of your neighbors and repay them with kindness. Guard fiercely the burrows in which you and your friends dwell, and keep a benignly watchful eye on the home of your neighbor. Never betray the trust of your host, break an oath, or violate the sanctity of another's home. Busy hands make a happy home, and things crafted with love will serve you and others well.

Day-to-Day Activities: Whereas Yondalla's priests are often the visible leadership of a small halfling community, Cyrollalee's priesthood are the quiet caretakers and nurturers of halfling society, serving their charges with generous hearts and graceful friendship. As such, their role is often overlooked, but their absence is sorely noted. Cyrollalee's priests are specifically defenders of the home, and they view their role as both protecting the home from outside threats and cultivating the familial bonds of those who dwell within. In addition, Homefellows oversee the drawing up of contracts and agreements of all kinds, and they also look after and educate young halflings. The priesthood is quite a homely and prosaic one, not an adventuring priesthood.

Holy Days/Important Ceremonies: Worship services for Cyrollalee are held on the first day of each month, known in halfling communities as Hearthday. Devout halflings gather in the home of one of their fellow parishioners, rotating to a different dwelling in the local community each month. The Hand of Fellowship asks for nothing in the way of propitiation aside from simple prayers requesting her blessing. Friendship among her worshipers is considered the highest praise one can raise to her name.

Major Centers of Worship: The Grapevine's Root, located in the Purple Hills of Tethyr on a low, wide knoll overlooking the town of Vineshade, is a sprawling cloistral villa built in the heart of a great vineyard. Cyrollalee's rustic temple consists of half a dozen open courtyards surrounded by covered walks with open colonnades overgrown with grapevines and wisteria on either side. At the intersections of the orthogonal cloisters are small circular chapels with domed roofs. Within each quadrangular acre, Cyrollaleen priests and their families dwell amidst the grapevines in small, homey burrows forming small neighborhoods within the greater temple community. Administering the clergy of the Grapevine's Root like an extended, multigenerational family is Enduring Vintage Glissando Homebody. Glissando has lived amidst the Purple Hills for over three centuries already, and this venerable halfling matriarch with the tightly wrapped silver bun has never lost her sweet smile or generous heart despite presiding over half a dozen generations of joy and sorrow, glad tidings and tragedy. The temple is justly famous for its homegrown vintage, Cyrojubilee, but the role its priests play in nurturing halfling home life in the hamlets scattered throughout the region is arguably the priesthood's more important role. Cyrrollaleen acolytes based in the Grapevine's Root visit parishioners the length and breadth of Tethyr's County Vintor, and their efforts are largely responsible for the close knit, familial feel of the local culture.

Affiliated Orders: The Cyrrollaleen church currently has no affiliated knightly orders, choosing to rely on militant priests and warriors affiliated with the faiths of Yondalla and Arvoreen. According to the church's oldest archives, previous halfling diasporas that led to the settlement of new lands by the Small Folk were preceded by small bands of scouts sent by the elders of the Hearthkeeper's faith to seek out likely regions for colonization. Tales of their exploits have faded into legend, however, as it has been many centuries since the last hordelike wave—as opposed to the creeping expansion that is now the norm—of halfling settlement.

Priestly Vestments: The ceremonial garb of Cyrrollalee's priesthood is the rustic clothing of halfling peasants, devoid of ostentatious display. Typically Homefellows wear simple brown habits bound with a deep golden or muted green girdle, and keep their heads and feet bare. The holy symbol of the faith is a carved wooden acorn, often hung on a leather cord around the neck.

Adventuring Garb: Members of Cyrrollalee's clergy adventure only in extremis, preferring to stay close at home if at all possible and within the bounds of civilization at all costs. When expecting their homes to be attacked or if travel through a region of some danger is required, Homefellows garb themselves in the best armor available, usually leather or padded armor. As no particular weapon is associated with Cyrrollalee, her followers tend to select one of the handful of weapons commonly associated with halfling village militias. Clubs, staves, slings, and staff-slings are common.

Specialty Priests (Homesteaders)

REQUIREMENTS:	Charisma 9, Wisdom 9
PRIME REQ.:	Charisma, Wisdom
ALIGNMENT:	LG
WEAPONS:	All bludgeoning (wholly Type B) weapons
ARMOR:	Any
MAJOR SPHERES:	All, animal, charm, creation, divination, guardian, healing, law, protection, wards
MINOR SPHERES:	Combat, necromantic, plant, sun, travelers
MAGICAL ITEMS:	As clerics
REQ. PROFS:	Cooking, weaving
BONUS PROFS:	Etiquette, fire-building, local history, seamstress/tailor

- Homesteaders must be halflings, but they can be of any halfling subrace.
- Homesteaders are not allowed to multiclass.
- Homesteaders turn undead at two levels lower than their actual level when outside a home, at their their level when inside a home, and at two levels higher than their level when inside a halfling home. For these purposes, a home is a dwelling in which beings of at least low intelligence live, though they may not be currently on the premises. A home implies at least a semipermanent status. An adventurer's campsite would not count as a home, but a tent in the camp of a nomad clan would.
- Homesteaders can cast *detect evil* and *protection from evil* (as the 1st-level priest spells) once per day each.
- At 3rd level, homesteaders can cast *friends* and *mending* (as the 1st-level wizard spells) and *sanctuary* (as the 1st-level priest spell) once per day each.
- At 5th level, homesteaders can cast *detect lie* (as the 4th-level priest spell), *zone of truth* (as the 2nd-level priest spell), or *knock* (as the 2nd-level wizard spell) once per day.
- At 7th level, homesteaders can cast *emotion* (*friendship* or *hope*) (as the 4th-level wizard spell) or *wall of force* (as the 5th-level wizard spell) once per day.
- At 10th level, homesteaders receive a +3 bonus to saving throws vs. nonmagical or magical *fear*.
- At 10th level, homesteaders can cast *word of recall* (as the 6th-level priest spell) twice per tenday.
- At 13th level, homesteaders can cast *succor* (as the 7th-level priest spell) twice per tenday.
- At 13th level, homesteaders can cast *symbol* (of *persuasion*) (as the 7th-level priest spell) twice per tenday.

Cyrrollaleen Spells

1st Level

Comforts of Home (Pr 1; Phantasm)

Sphere:	Travelers
Range:	Touch
Components:	V, S, M
Duration:	8 hours
Casting Time:	1 round
Area of Effect:	Creature touched
Saving Throw:	None

This simple spell allows a willing recipient to pamper himself or herself with all the *comforts of home*. For the duration of the spell, even the most meager trail rations warm the belly like a favorite home-cooked meal, the hard-packed ground feels like a soft, warm bed, upon awakening the recipient feels like she or he has bathed and changed into a fresh, clean set of clothes, etc. While this spell does not alter the reality of the recipient's current environment, it does alter his or her perception of that environment, mitigating the psychological rigors of travel.

This spell does provide two tangible benefits: Any night's sleep had while under the effects of this spell is equivalent to complete bed rest, allowing the recipient of the *comforts of home* to heal 3 points of damage for the day and be fully rested for the purpose of praying for spells.

The material component is the priest's holy symbol.

2nd Level

Seal of Cyrrollalee (Pr 2; Alteration)

Sphere:	Law
Range:	Touch
Components:	V, S, M
Duration:	Special
Casting Time:	Special
Area of Effect:	Two or more creatures
Saving Throw:	None

This spell can only be cast on two or more willing creatures who wish to make a pledge or contract with each other overseen by Cyrrollalee. A *seal of Cyrrollalee* ceremony requires each participant to swear an oath governing his or her future behavior or deeds (thus the variable casting time), and if the oaths so sworn are acceptable to all participating parties during the casting of the spell, requires each participant to uphold his or her oath or face very severe consequences. This spell fails if any party is not a willing participant, is under the effects of a *charm* spell (or similar effect or ability), or is not in his or her right mind, as adjudicated by the DM.

If any party should fail to meet the terms of the successfully cast *seal of Cyrrollalee* due to factors beyond his or her control and despite his or her best efforts, the participant who broke his or her oath suffers from the effects of a *curse* spell (as the reverse of the 1st-level priest spell *bless*) until such time as she or he receives an *atonement* cast by a priest of Cyrrollalee.

If any party should *deliberately* fail to meet the terms of the successfully cast *seal of Cyrrollalee*, Cyrrollalee's wrath afflicts the oathbreaker by reducing one ability of the victim to 3 (the DM randomly determines which ability), as one of several possible effects of *bestow curse* (the reverse of the 3rd-level priest spell *remove curse*). Cyrrollalee's wrath persists until such time as the oath breaker makes amends for his or her broken pledge and receives an *atonement* cast by a priest of Cyrrollalee.

The material component is the priest's holy symbol.

4th Level

Improved Sanctuary (Pr 4; Alteration)

Sphere:	Protection
Range:	0
Components:	V, S, M
Duration:	2 rounds+1 round/level
Casting Time:	7
Area of Effect:	Friendly creatures in a 30-foot radius
Saving Throw:	None

When the priest casts an *improved sanctuary* spell, those friendly creatures in the area of effect the instant the spell is completed receive the effect of the 1st-level priest spell *sanctuary*. Any opponent attempting to strike or otherwise directly attack a protected creature must roll a saving throw vs. spell at a −1 penalty. (This penalty increases by −1 per every four levels the caster is above 7th to a maximum of 3: −2 at 11th, −3 at 14, etc.) If the saving throw is successful, the opponent can attack normally and is unaffected by that casting of the spell. If the saving throw fails, the opponent loses track of and totally ignores the warded creatures for the duration of the spell. Those not attempting to attack the subject remain unaffected. Note that this spell does not prevent the operation of area attacks (*fireball*, *ice storm*, and so on). While protected by this spell, subjects cannot take direct offensive action without breaking the spell, but they may use nonattack spells or otherwise act in any way that does not violate the prohibition against offensive action. This allows a warded priest to heal wounds, for example, or to *bless*, perform an *augury*, *chant*, cast a *light* in the area (not upon an opponent!), and so on.

The material components are the priest's holy symbol and a small silver mirror.

Sheela Peryroyl

(Green Sister, the Wise, the Watchful Mother)

Intermediate Power of the Outlands, N

PORTFOLIO:	Nature, agriculture, weather, song, dance, beauty, romantic love
ALIASES:	None widespread
DOMAIN NAME:	Outlands/Flowering Hill
SUPERIOR:	Yondalla
ALLIES:	Aerdrie Faenya, Angharradh, Baervan Wildwanderer, Chauntea, Hanali Celanil, Isis, Mielikki, Rillifane Rallathil, Segojan Earthcaller, Sharindlar, Shiallia, Silvanus, various Animal Lords, the halfling pantheon
FOES:	Talos and the gods of fury (Auril, Umberlee, and Malar), Talona, Moander (dead), Urdlen
SYMBOL:	Daisy
WOR. ALIGN.:	LG, NG, CG, LN, N, CN

Sheela Peryroyl (SHEE-lah PAIR-ree-roil) is the halfling goddess of agriculture, nature, and weather. She balances the concern for wild untamed lands and habitats with strong roles as a goddess of cultivation, seasons, and especially harvests. She is also concerned with the pleasures of life—feasts, revelry, romance, and the general desire to live with passion. Her followers often wear a small flower in her honor and strive to work in harmony with nature and the earth.

The image of Sheela is often mixed, almost interchangeably, with Yondalla herself. Some hold that Sheela and Yondalla are different aspects of the same goddess, but in truth, they are simply closely allied. Sheela is on good terms with the rest of the halfling pantheon, particularly Urogalan in his aspect as Lord in the Earth, as well as other nonhalfling powers concerned with nature, agriculture, weather, and the balance between them. Sheela's concern with finding a middle ground between civilization and pristine nature sometimes results in her being called on to mediate between other powers such as Silvanus and Waukeen or even the Oak Father and Chauntea. Sheela strongly opposes those powers she sees as corruptive distortions of the natural way, such as the Gods of Fury and Moander.

Sheela is generally quiet, although she's rarely seen without a smile on her face and a dance in her eyes. At other times, Sheela is laughing and just generally delighted by life. Though she appears naive, even simple, she can wield great powers of nature magic. Sheela is sometimes credited with creating many species of flowers and has a strong aesthetic sense. When she sings she causes flowers to bloom, trees to bud, and seeds to sprout, and living plants to grow and flower in her wake as she walks along the earth. Sheela brings good weather to her favored worshipers but can easily send drought or floods to those who worship her poorly. Sheela dispatches an avatar to counter any main threat to halfling land (not just halfling people or homes). She is greatly angered by wanton despoiling of nature, and her avatar pursues offenders in order to punish them.

Sheela's Avatar (Druid 30, Mystic 25, Mage 21, Ranger 18)

Sheela appears as a pretty young halfling maiden dressed in garlands of wildflowers with brilliant flowers in her hair. She favors spells from the spheres of all, animal, divination, elemental, healing, plant, sun, travelers, and weather and from the schools of elemental air, earth, and water, although she can cast spells from any sphere or school.

AC −3; MV 12; HP 192; THAC0 2; #AT 2/1 (or 3/1)
Dmg 1d6+5 (*quarterstaff +4*, +1 STR)
MR 75%; SZ S (4 feet tall)
STR 16, DEX 19, CON 20, INT 19, WIS 23, CHA 24
Spells P: 13/12/12/12/11/10/8, W: 5/5/5/5/5/4/4/2
Saves PPDM 2, RSW 1*, PP 4, BW 4, Sp 4
　　*Includes halfling +5 CON save bonus to a minimum of 1. The CON save bonus also applies to saves vs. poison to a minimum of 1.

Special Att/Def: Should she need to, Sheela can create a powerful *quarterstaff +4* with all of the powers of a *staff of the woodlands* from a single blade of grass in an instant. Sheela can cast *changestaff* on one such staff once per day and then create another one to use for her personal defense. Sheela does not usually fight with two weapons, but if she should decide to, she is considered proficient in all weapons, and her melee attacks per round would increase to 3/1.

Sheela can cast *entangle* or *Sheela's entangle* once per round at will. The use of *entangle* and *Sheela's entangle* spells is her favored method of attack and defense. She can also cast *call lightning*, *call woodland beings*, *control weather*, *creeping doom*, *hallucinatory forest*, *hold plant*, *liveoak*, *plant door*, *plant growth*, *rainbow*, *snare*, *speak with animals*, *speak with plants*, *spike growth*, *sticks to snakes*, *transport via plants*, *trip*, *wall of thorns*, and *warp wood* three times per day each.

Sheela travels freely on all terrains (for example, *pass without trace*, *free action*, *water walk*, etc.). She cannot be *entangled*, *held*, or paralyzed. She regenerates 3 points of damage per round if her feet are on bare earth. Sheela is immune to all weapons with wood in them and can only be affected by +2 or better magical weapons. She is also immune to electrical attacks of any kind, including lightning.

Other Manifestations

Sheela's typical manifestation is that of a shimmering green, blue, or amber radiance that envelops a living thing, whether it be a person, animal, or plant, or wooden weapon. This manifestation typically gives affected beings the ability to cast, as a 12th-level priest, one or all of the following spells within the next turn: *call woodland beings*, *commune with nature*, *entangle*, *Sheela's entangle*, *locate animals or plants*, *speak with animals*, *speak with plants*, *tree*, or *weather summoning*.

Any animal enveloped by Sheela's manifestation becomes instantly calm and at peace (or if actively hostile, neutral and disinterested), and if Sheela desires, is affected as if by an *animal growth* spell. For the duration of the manifestation, the Intelligence of any creature of animal (1) Intelligence is raised to low (1d3+4) Intelligence.

Any plant or group of plants enveloped by Sheela's manifestation is affected as if by *entangle* or *improved entangle*. Any berry or fruit bathed in Sheela's radiance confers the benefits of a *goodberry* or *royalberry* spell on any creature eating it. Sheela manifests in trees in a fashion similar to that of a *liveoak* spell.

Sheela is served by amber dragons, badgers, bees, brownies, butterflies, dobies, dryads, earth elementals, firefriends, firestars, grigs, hamadryads, hybsils, kilmoulis, korreds, leprechauns, mice, moles, moon dogs, nature elementals, needlemen, nixies, nymphs, pixies, porcupines, pseudodragons, raccoons, satyrs, singing trees, snapper-saws, sprites, squirrels, sunflies, thornslingers, treants, twilight blooms, umplebys, unicorns, water nagas, wild cats, and wolverines. She demonstrates her favor through the discovery of daisies, plant fossils encased in amber, seeds that sprout instantly when placed in the ground and other sudden plant flowerings, flowers of any species that bloom at the wrong time of year, playful behavior by small woodland animals, and benign weather changes (sunbeams through clouds, very localized dewfall, etc.). Green Sister indicates her displeasure by dispatching a swarm of grasshoppers, locusts, or velvet ants.

The Church

CLERGY:	Clerics, specialty priests, druids, mystics,
CLERGY'S ALIGN.:	LG, NG, CG, N, CN
TURN UNDEAD:	C: Yes, SP: Yes, at priest level –2, D: No, Mys: No
CMND. UNDEAD:	C: No, SP: No, D: No, Mys: No

All clerics, specialty priests, druids, and mystics of Sheela receive religion (halfling) as a bonus nonweapon proficiency.

The church of Sheela is widely revered among halflings, nearly as much as that of Yondalla herself. While not all halflings are farmers, most share the Green Sister's reverence for growing things and appreciate the balance she works to maintain between untamed and settled lands. Dwarves, gold elves, moon elves, and gnomes generally work well with the church of the Green Sister, while many wild elves feel that Sheela's priests care more about new farms than preserving those wild spaces that remain. Humans tend to view the church of Sheela as a mix between that of Chauntea and Silvanus.

Temples of Sheela are typically woven into the surrounding landscape. Constructed of earth, stone, and plants, such houses of worship seem to be a part of the land itself. The Green Sister's temples contain both well-tended gardens and untamed thickets, and they are usually found in the heart of agricultural valleys surrounded by wilderness. Interior rooms are overflowing with life, both animal and plant, and most are constructed so that streams meander through the central courtyards and so that summer breezes and sunlight bathe every chamber.

Novices of the Green Sister are known as Seedlings. Full priests of Sheela are known as Green Daughters and Green Sons and are collectively known as Green Children. In ascending order of rank, the titles used by Sheelite priests are Daisy Maid (or Lad), Seed Sower, Nature Nurturer, Plant Grower, Crop Harvester, Seed Pollinator, Sun Shower, and Watchful Sister (or Brother). High-ranking priests have unique individual titles. Specialty priests are druids and greenfosters. Greenfosters concentrate on operating in and around halfling villages and farms, while druids go wherever they are needed. The clergy of Sheela includes hairfeet (65%), stouts (10%), and tallfellows (25%). Females (78%) greatly outnumber males (22%). Sheela's clergy includes druids (51%), mystics (23%), specialty priests (21%), and clerics (5%).

Dogma: Living in harmony with nature requires a careful balance between the wild and the tame, the feral and the tended. The need to preserve wild growth is just as important as the need to till the fields and provide ready food. Seek to understand the natural processes that envelop and work within them. While nature can be adapted, it should be evolved, never forced; work within the framework of what already exists. Celebrating life requires one to live with passion and romance. Revel, feast, and thrive—this is the zest of life.

Day-to-Day Activities: Sheela's priests are concerned with nature and agriculture, and they work closely with halfling farmers and settlers to preserve the balance between cultivation of fertile lands and the need to leave some areas wild and in a pristine state. Many Green Children tend gardens of their own, seeking to develop new strains of crops and flowers. Others protect wilderness regions from careless exploitation of their resources. Members of Sheela's clergy oversee the integrity of halfling lands, leading their inhabitants through the annual calendar of seed-sowing and harvest festivals. They also try to keep the wild creatures from running rampant through settled halfling areas by guiding them to travel, live, or grow around the communities, not in or through them.

Holy Days/Important Ceremonies: Sheela is venerated at twilight under the full moon in monthly celebrations known as Gatherings. Halflings from the surrounding community gather to celebrate the bounteous produce of the earth, whether it be brought from the fields directly or brought from root cellars dug within the earth. Gatherings are as much community-wide feasts as religious ceremonies, and all are expected to contribute, even if it be only a stone for the soup. (Halflings have a tale similar to that of most human cultures in which a wayfarer comes to a town suffering after a terrible harvest. After learning there is nothing to eat, the hungry stranger begins to cook stone soup. As the visitor boils his water containing naught but a rock under the watchful eyes of the incredulous villagers, he comments how much better it would be if he only had a carrot. After one villager reluctantly offers up a hoarded carrot, the stranger muses how much better it would be with some cabbage and a single head is found

as well. The tale continues until every family in the entire village has contributed something to the soup, at which point the stranger pronounces it done and shares it with all the contributors.)

The major festivals of the church of Sheela are usually celebrated around Greengrass and Higharvestide, although the starting date varies from year to year. The first festival—called the Seeding, New Spring, and other titles, depending on the region—comes at the traditional time of planting the first crops of the year. At dawn, Sheelite priests dispense seeds from the temple stores while giving homage to the goddess, and the entire community aids in the sowing of the fields. The second festival—called High Harvest, the Reaping, and other titles, depending on the region—comes at harvest time. At this time, offerings of seeds are made to the temple to be stored for the coming year, as are the fruits of the season's labors. Community-wide revelry is common at these celebrations starting in the evening when the work has been finished and continuing late into the night. The length of these festivals varies from area to area, averaging about 10 days.

Major Centers of Worship: Sunset Vale encompasses the verdant, prosperous farmland between the arcing arms of the River Reaching and the upper Chionthar River and the natural wall formed by the Sunset Mountains and the Far Hills. The Dusk Road runs through the heart of the Vale, east of the Reaching Woods, carrying the traffic of this vital region back and forth. Many halflings dwell in the Vale, particularly in the vicinity of Corm Orp, despite the loom shadow and ever-present threat of Zhentarim-occupied Darkhold. The handful of buildings that make up the small road-hamlet seem unremarkable, but under the hills east of Corm Orp are hundreds of halfling burrows and their number grows by leaps and bounds every year. In fact, Corm Orp is the fastest-growing halfling community north of the land of Luiren. Every Shieldmeet, more halflings gather in Corm Orp to do business with their fellows, trade native goods, and exchange tales, doubling or trebling the already sizable nonhuman population. Liking what they see, many decide to move there. The halflings of Corm Orp are rightfully proud of the food they produce, especially their mushrooms and free-range hogs. Another product of pride is mass-produced red clay pottery—simple, sturdy items widely used throughout Faerûn.

The agricultural, spiritual, and social heart of the Corm Orp region is the Ladyhouse, a deceptively large temple of Sheela the Watchful Mother nestled in a hollow among the green, pig-roamed hills east of the village and emblazoned with the symbol of the daisy. The Ladyhouse is filled with flowers and climbing vines inside and surrounded by gardens outside, including wild gardens that are preserved plots of tangled weeds, shrubs, and scrub trees. The gardens, as well as the roadside wood lot in Corm Orp, are sacred to the goddess and are not to be despoiled. Halfling worshipers bring their best flowers and plants to the temple for use in breeding and in rituals, and the clergy spend their days working with the halfling farmers, keeping watch over the hills for Zhentarim raids, thieves, wolves, and other wandering beasts who might harm the crops or pig herds, and chanting the praises of the Green Sister.

The clergy are led by the widely respected matriarch Honored Mother Alliya Macanester, the Old Lady of Corm Orp. Revered by halflings, she knows the local weather and way of nature better than almost any other living thing and can tell exactly where, when, and how to plant or nurture for best results. Her touch is said to give life to withered plants, and she is rumored to be able to tell by looking at it if a seed will germinate. Her wisdom and foresight have prevented weather spoiling the crops on two important occasions: the Great Frost early in the Year of the Bloodbird (1346 DR) and the drought of the Year of Lurking Death (1322 DR), which brought down desperate attacks on Corm Orp, as on so many other places on Faerûn, from starving monsters. Alliya is a wise, diligent leader of the farmers of Corm Orp as well as the local halflings and her temple. The Honored Mother is the true ruler of Corm Orp, and the village's human lord, Dundast Hultel, obeys her in all things. Alliya is a fierce foe of the Zhentarim and even deals with poisons, adventurers, and other violent things not in keeping with nature in order to eradicate the threat from Darkhold, which she calls the Devouring Shadow.

Of late, many of the younger halflings of the Sunset Vale have begun to speak of founding a halfling realm, Sheeland, with the Honored Mother as its first queen. To date, Alliya has always responded to such ideas with a chuckle and an observation about the fate of the succession of petty rulers and robber barons who sought to rule the region in the past, but, as Darkhold's shadow looms ever-farther over the Vale, events may necessitate such a measure.

Affiliated Orders: The church of Sheela does not have any affiliated knightly orders. It has firm connections to several orders of halfling warriors who serve Arvoreen by defending the fields and silos from those who would despoil or loot the fruits of halfling labors. Likewise, Sheela's church works closely with individual rangers, many of whom venerate Mielikki and whether they be human, half-elven, or elven, to preserve the wilderness as well.

Priestly Vestments: Sheelite priests favor simple green robes festooned with garlands of vibrant hue and embroidered with flowers. In their hair they wear only flowers, and their feet are left bare so as to feel the earth from which Sheela's bounty flows. The holy symbol of the faith is mistletoe or a sprig of holly with berries in a pinch.

Adventuring Garb: Members of Sheela's clergy avoid situations requiring combat, if possible. Few carry more than a blade of grass, trusting the favor of the goddess to allow them to create a *reed staff* and enhance it with a *shillelagh* spell. When conflict is inevitable, Sheelite priests favor armor made from natural components—leather armor and wooden shields—and weapons associated with nature or the harvest—clubs, quarterstaves, sickles, and slings.

Specialty Priests (Druids)

REQUIREMENTS:	Wisdom 12, Charisma 15
PRIME REQ.:	Wisdom, Charisma
ALIGNMENT:	N
WEAPONS:	Club, sickle, dart, spear, dagger, scimitar, sling, staff
ARMOR:	Padded, leather, or hide and wooden, bone, shell or other nonmetallic shield
MAJOR SPHERES:	All, animal, elemental, healing, plant, sun, weather
MINOR SPHERES:	Divination, travelers
MAGICAL ITEMS:	As druid
REQ. PROFS:	Herbalism
BONUS PROFS:	Agriculture, modern languages (pick two from: brownie, centaur, dryad, elvish, gnome, korred, nixie, pixie, satyr, sprite, treant, unicorn)

Most of the specialty priests of Sheela Peryroyl are druids. Their abilities and restrictions, aside from the changes noted above and later in this section, are summarized in the discussion of halfling priests in "Appendix 1: Demihuman Priests" and detailed in full in the *Player's Handbook*.

- Druids of Sheela must be halflings. While most halfling druids are hairfeet or tallfellows, halflings of every subrace are called to be specialty priests of Sheela's clergy.
- Druids of Sheela are not allowed to multiclass.

Specialty Priests (Greenfosters)

REQUIREMENTS:	Constitution 12, Wisdom 13
PRIME REQ.:	Constitution, Wisdom
ALIGNMENT:	CG, NG, N, CN
WEAPONS:	Bow, club, crossbow, dagger, dart, flail, knife, net, staff, sickle, sling, staff-sling, whip
ARMOR:	Padded, leather, hide, or studded leather; no shield
MAJOR SPHERES:	All, animal, creation, elemental (air, earth, water), healing, plant, sun, travelers, weather
MINOR SPHERES:	Charm, divination, guardian, necromantic, protection
MAGICAL ITEMS:	Same as clerics and druids
REQ. PROFS:	Herbalism, weather sense
BONUS PROFS:	Agriculture, animal handling, local history

- Greenfosters must be halflings. Most greenfosters are hairfeet or tallfellows, but they can be of any halfling subrace.
- Greenfosters are not allowed to multiclass.
- Greenfosters can analyze and identify domestic grains and garden plants native to Faerûn. They can look at a field and tell what is growing, how far along it is in the harvest year, what the state of the crop is (healthy, diseased, drought problems, etc.), and even what species planted and is tending it.

- Greenfosters cast all plant sphere spells as if they had an additional two levels of experience.
- Greenfosters can cast *speak with domestic animals* (as the 2nd-level priest spell *speak with animals*, but greenfosters can only speak with domesticated animals) or *speak with plants* (4th-level priest spell) three times per day.
- At 3rd level, greenfosters can cast *entangle* or *reed staff* (as the 1st-level priest spells) once per day.
- At 5th level, greenfosters can cast *Sheela's entangle* or *plant growth* (as the 2nd- and 3rd-level priest spells) once per day.
- At 7th level, greenfosters can cast *hold plant* or *plant door* (as the 4th-level priest spells) once per day.
- At 10th level, greenfosters can cast *speak with domestic animals* and *speak with plants* at will.
- At 10th level, greenfosters can cast *anti-plant shell* as the 5th-level wizard spell) or *anti-animal shell* (as the 6th-level priest spell) three times per tenday.
- At 13th level, greenfosters can cast *charm plant* as the 7th-level wizard spell) or *sunray* (as the 7th-level priest spell) once per tenday.

Sheelite Spells

1st Level

Reed Staff (Pr 1; Alteration)

Sphere:	Plant
Range:	Touch
Components:	V, M
Duration:	3 rounds+1 round/level
Casting Time:	4
Area of Effect:	One blade of grass
Saving Throw:	None

This spell transforms a normal blade of field grass into a quarterstaff that can then be used as a weapon. Although the quarterstaff possesses no bonuses to attack or damage rolls, it is considered a magical weapon for determining what creatures it can successfully strike.

Only the caster may use the *reed staff*; if another creature attempts to use it, the spell is negated. The caster need not remain in contact with the *reed staff*, however. The priest is free to set down the weapon in order to perform other actions, including fighting with another weapon, casting a spell, and so forth. The spell can be ended prematurely if it is exposed to a successful *dispel magic* or brought into contact with an *anti-magic shell* or similar effect.

The material components are the caster's holy symbol, a splinter of wood, and the blade of grass to be affected.

2nd Level

Sheela's Entangle (Pr 2; Alteration)

Sphere:	Plant
Range:	80 yards
Components:	V, S, M
Duration:	1 turn
Casting Time:	5
Area of Effect:	40-foot cube
Saving Throw:	Special

Like the 1st-level spell *entangle*, this spell enables the caster to cause plants in the area of effect to entangle creatures within the area of effect. The grasses, weeds, bushes, and even trees, wrap, twist, and entwine about the creatures, holding them fast for the duration of the spell. Any creature entering the area is subject to this effect. A creature that succeeds at a saving throw vs. spell can escape the area, moving at only 10 feet per round until out of the area. Exceptionally large (gargantuan) or strong creatures may suffer little or no distress from this spell, at the DM's option, based on the strength of the entangling plants. *Sheela's entangle* inflicts 1d4 points of damage per round on all creatures trapped therein from constriction and abrasion if so commanded by the caster. (There is no saving throw for this, and it makes no difference if the victims are able to move or not.)

Unlike the weaker version of this spell, however, the effects of *Sheela's entangle* are cumulative (although not with *entangle*) if cast several times over the same area. For each additional casting, creatures entering the area of effect suffer an additional penalty of −2 to their saving throw. Only one saving throw is still required, however. Likewise the escape movement rate is reduced by 2 feet per round until out, to a minimum of 2 feet per round.

The material components of this spell are the caster's holy symbol and a small piece of vine.

5th Level

Royalberry (Pr 5; Alteration, Evocation)

Sphere:	Plant
Range:	Touch
Components:	V, S, M
Duration:	1 day+1 day/level
Casting Time:	1 round
Area of Effect:	2d4 fresh berries
Saving Throw:	None

When cast upon a handful of freshly picked berries, this spell makes 2d4 of them magical. The caster (as well as any other caster of the same faith and 9th or higher level) can immediately discern which berries are affected. A *detect magic* discovers this also.

Royalberries (the enspelled berries) enable a hungry creature of approximately man size to eat one and be as well nourished as if a full normal meal were eaten. They also cure 2 points of physical damage from wounds or other similar causes, subject to a maximum of 16 points of such curing in any 24-hour period. Finally, if any poison exists in the consumer when a royalberry is consumed, it is slowed (as the 2nd-level priest spell *slow poison*). If three or more berries are eaten, such a poison is neutralized (as the 3rd-level priest spell *neutralize poison*). Consuming six royalberries (total) at a time additionally acts as a *cure disease* spell.

Unlike the more commonly known *goodberry* spell, there is no reverse of this spell.

The material component of this spell is the caster's holy symbol passed over the freshly picked, edible berries to be enspelled.

Tymora

See the entry for Tymora in the "Faerûnian Pantheon" chapter in *Faiths & Avatars*.

Urogalan

(He Who Must Be, the Black Hound, Lord in the Earth, the Protector, the Shaper)

Demipower of Elysium, LN

PORTFOLIO:	Earth, death, protection of the dead
ALIASES:	None widespread
DOMAIN NAME:	Eronia/Soulearth
SUPERIOR:	Yondalla
ALLIES:	Callarduran Smoothhands, Dumathoin, Flandal Steelskin, Geb, Grumbar, Jergal, Kelemvor, Segojan Earthcaller, Sehanine Moonbow, the halfling pantheon, Osiris
FOES:	Abbathor, Cyric, Myrkul (dead), Urdlen, Velsharoon
SYMBOL:	Black dog's head silhouette
WOR. ALIGN.:	Any

Urogalan (URR-roh-GAH-lan) is the protector of the dead and god of the underground. His deathly aspect is as a protector of the souls of the dead and as an adviser-judge with Yondalla. His earthy aspect is one of reverence for the very earth itself and protection from threats beneath the surface, rather than concern with natural growth. Few halflings worship him, but he is respected and revered by most as a protector. Although the Small Folk generally do not fear death, most halflings shiver at the sight of the Black Hound's symbol.

Urogalan is on good terms with the rest of the halfling pantheon, particularly Yondalla, Arvoreen, and Sheela, but he holds himself somewhat removed from their joyous embrace of life. The Black Hound is closely allied with those powers of human and demihuman pantheons concerned with earth, death, and the protection of the dead, but he abhors those whose portfolios include necromancy and the undead.

Urogalan rarely speaks or displays much emotion, and when he does, the Black Hound's quiet-spoken voice is tinged with loss. The Lord in the Earth prefers observation to intervention and has the disconcerting habit of appearing in the shadows and simply watching and waiting until he is noticed. Urogalan dispatches his avatar to gather in the souls of great, wise, or exceptional halflings, and he may also dispatch his avatar underground to watch over perils that may come from within it.

Urogalan's Avatar (Cleric 24, Wizard 23, Fighter 13)

Urogalan appears as a slim, dusky-skinned halfling, dressed in a pure white robe (death aspect) or brown robe (earth aspect). He favors spells from the spheres of all, elemental (earth), guardian, necromantic, protection, and wards and from the schools of abjuration, conjuration/summoning, elemental earth, and necromancy, although he can cast spells from any sphere or school.

AC −2; MV 12; HP 176; THAC0 6; #AT 5/2
Dmg 2d4+6 (*double-headed flail +3*, +1 STR, +2 spec. bonus in flails)
MR 70%; SZ S (4 feet tall)
STR 17, DEX 19, CON 19, INT 18, WIS 22, CHA 16
Spells P: 12/12/12/12/11/8/3, W: 5/5/5/5/5/5/5/3
Saves PPDM 2, RSW 1*, PP 5, BW 5, Sp 4
*Includes halfling +5 CON save bonus to a minimum of 1. The CON save bonus also applies to saves vs. poison to a minimum of 1.

Special Att/Def: Urogalan wields *Doomthresher*, a *double-headed flail +3* whose touch inflicts *flesh to stone* on any living creature that fails its saving throw vs. spell and acts as a *mace of disruption* against the undead, and wears a *ring of protection +3*.

The Lord in the Earth can see in magical *darkness* of any sort. He cannot be blinded or deafened, nor can he be dislodged from the earth unless he so chooses. He can move through earth or stone at will. When he wishes, Urogalan radiates a *cloak of fear*. He can generate an *earthquake* up to three times a day simply by stamping his foot on the ground. He can be struck only by +1 or better magical weapons.

Urogalan can command any nonevil creature from the Elemental Plane of Earth within 100 yards. Urogalan is always accompanied by a completely silent black hound that can follow the Lord in the Earth through earth or stone if the god wishes.

Halfling Powers: Urogalan

Black Hound: AC 2; MV 24; HD 12; hp 96; THAC0 9; #AT 1; Dmg 2d8; SA radiates *fear* 5´ radius, double damage on a natural 20 attack roll; SD immune to fear; MR 15%; SZ M (4´ high); ML fearless (20); Int high (14); AL LN; XP 7,000.

Other Manifestations

Urogalan manifests by causing the earth to move or transform as he wishes. Such manifestations typically duplicate the effect of one of the following spells: *animate rock, earthquake, Maximilian's earthen grasp, Maximilian's stony grasp, meld into stone, move earth, sink, soften earth and stone, spike stones, stone shape, transmute rock to mud* (or the reverse), or *wall of stone*. The Lord in the Earth communicates with his priests through an effect similar to that of *stone tell*.

Urogalan is served by baku, blink dogs, brownies, earth elementals, earth elemental vermin (crawlers), einheriar, galeb duhr, hollyphants, hound archons, lupinals, maruts, mist wolves, moon dogs, oreads, pech, pers, sapphire dragons, stone wolves, war dogs (typically black hounds), and weredogs. He demonstrates his favor through the discovery of chalcedony, chrysoberyl, epidote, ivory, jade, meerschaum, samarskite, silkstone, tiger eye agate, tomb jade, white lilies, and deposits of dlarun. He Who Must Be indicates his displeasure by creating tremors in the earth or, when gravely displeased, by dispatching a hound of ill omen. He sends omens and manifestations of black hounds, including their baying, as premonitions of death and to garner souls.

The Church

CLERGY:	Clerics, specialty priests
CLERGY'S ALIGN.:	LG, NG, LN, N
TURN UNDEAD:	C: Yes, SP: Yes
CMND. UNDEAD:	C: No, SP: No

All clerics and specialty priests of Urogalan receive religion (halfling) as a bonus nonweapon proficiency.

Urogalan is propitiated by many halflings, but his priesthood is very small. While his followers are respected for their services and rituals and while death is not generally feared by halflings, few of the Small Folk want to associate with symbols of the Black Hound, as they are generally considered unlucky. Other races, even humans among whom halflings often dwell, are generally unaware of Urogalan's faith, its reverence for the earth, or the god's role as protector of the dead, for halflings rarely discuss their beliefs regarding death. Dwarven priests of Dumathoin note a great deal of similarity between the practices of the two faiths, and they are likely to welcome a male member of Urogalan's clergy as one of their own.

Temples of Urogalan are typically located in shallow basins open to the sky, natural caves, and halfling-dug catacombs. Nearly any site that naturally emphasizes the surrounding geography is acceptable. The floor is always covered in at least six inches of soft dirt, and the central altar is usually a large limestone rock with a shallow depression, etched by rain or a small stream, at the center of the flat-topped surface. Only rarely do Urogalan's priests dwell within the temples of the Lord in the Earth. More often a temple of Urogalan is little more than a shrine, tended by a single priest who resides in a nearby community of the Small Folk.

Novices of Urogalan are known as Earthlings. Full priests of He Who Must Be are known as Vassals of the Black Hound. In ascending order of rank, the titles used by Urogalanan priests are Earth Embracer, Soil Digger, Clay Potter, Dlarun Smith, Grave Guardian, Crypt Sentinel, Vault Marshal, Barrow Warden, and Black Hound. High-ranking priests have unique individual titles. Specialty priests are known as grimwardens. The clergy of Urogalan includes hairfeet (25%), stouts (65%), and tallfellows (10%). Urogalan's clergy is nearly evenly divided between specialty priests (54%) and clerics (46%) and between men (55%) and women (45%).

Dogma: Earth is the giver and the receiver of life, providing shelter, food, and wealth to those whose toes embrace it. The sacred soil is to be revered as the mantle of Those Who Have Been and the shelter of Those Who Will Be. The thanatopsis of He Who Must Be reveals that death is to be embraced as the natural end of life and in doing so gives honor to life.

Day-to-Day Activities: Urogalan's priests are responsible for presiding over the internment of the dead and for the caretaking of graves. They administer last rites, preside over burial rituals, and memorialize the fallen. They maintain much of the history of the Small Folk, keeping records of genealogies and deeds of those who have "gone to the fields of green." In halfling cultures where ancestor worship is practiced, the Black Hound's priesthood safeguards the sacred tokens of the deceased used in rituals to contact them. Urogalan's priests also have a role in consecrating the foundations or first diggings of buildings and new burrow complexes.

Holy Days/Important Ceremonies: Nights of the full moon are considered holy days by the Urogalanan priesthood and are collectively known as Earthrisings. Halfling theology holds that the full moon is a manifestation of Urogalan, symbolizing both the ascendance of earth and the inevitable coming of death after life. Priests and followers of Urogalan, as well as halflings whose loved ones have passed away within the past month, gather in natural earthen basins at night to propitiate He Who Must Be. Offerings to the Lord in the Earth at such ceremonies are made on a large, low, flat rock placed at the center of the bowl and typically include precious gifts of the earth such as uncut gems, dlarun, and clay statuettes depicting the god. During such rituals, participants sing soft dirges and chant elegies to the percussive pounding of bare feet while making slow rotations around the central stone.

Among the various burial practices used by priests of Urogalan, there are only three set precepts that must be met. The body must be encased in earth or stone—either a wooden casket that will quickly rot away or a stone sarcophagus—and a stone tablet engraved with the name of the deceased. Urogalan's symbol must be placed upon the corpse's chest. The priest presiding over a burial must carve from stone or shape from clay twin figurines depicting a pair of black hounds, *bless* them, and place them on the palms of the deceased. Finally, members of the community who were friends of the departed soul must come forth and return a gift the deceased gave to them. Such gifts are typically tales of the generosity, kindness, cleverness, wit, or escapades of the deceased and are sometimes accompanied by a small token of remembrance suggestive of the tale. Typical tokens include a clay pipe, an apple, a jug of wine, or a simple woodcarving.

As an example of a fairly wide-spread burial practice, halfling gravestones often include clay statuettes of Urogalan placed in a small niche at the base of the grave marker. Regional practices exist as well. Many halflings of the Sword Coast are descended from emigrants from what is now the Calim Desert who fled enslavement at the hands of the genies and the human rulers who followed them. The early hin—an archaic name for halflings derived from Alzhedo—often lacked the simple pleasures and quiet security halflings treasure, and it was feared that a life lived in tragedy would leave the deceased unprepared for the afterlife in the Green Fields of Mount Celestia. Thus began the practice, which continues until this day among the halflings of the Purple Hills, eastern Amn, Sunset Vale, and the lower Delimbiyr river valley, of covering the face of the deceased with a terra cotta mask depicting the face of the deceased with contented expression. Such burial masks were believed to aid the spirit in its initial adjustment to the afterlife and to symbolize the true peace escaped slaves found only in death. Of course, the reasoning behind this practice has been forgotten by most of its practitioners, and if pressed by nonhalflings questioning the custom, most halflings explain it away with the quizzical rejoinder, "Undead don't smile!"

Although burial practices vary somewhat from community to community, few changes occur upon the passing of a halfling deserving of special status, for the Small Folk feel ostentatious tombs for particularly individuals are inappropriate in their relatively egalitarian society. Acceptable enhancements to the common burial practice include interring favorite possessions along with the deceased, chiseling elaborate carvings representing the life and deeds of the deceased on the exterior of a sarcophagus, and employing rare stone, gems, and metals in the construction of the sarcophagus and gifts interred within. As a matter of necessity, elaborate safeguards to deter tomb robbers must sometimes be included as well. For example, the last Margrave of Meiritin, Samovar Amethystall, who died in battle with the armies of the Duchy of Cortryn in the Year of the Phoenix (519 DR), was entombed in a small vault in the western Tejarn Hills of what is now southern Amn. The halfling prince was interred in a red marble sarcophagus elaborately sculpted with friezes depicting his heroics as well as his beneficence. Engraved in the lid of the stone coffin was a stylized map of the lands he ruled, before the rise of Cortryn, with important sites marked. Within the marble casket, along with the margrave's body, was placed a terra cotta mask with bronze filigree and green eyes of carved tomb jade, a pair of *onyx dogs* (*figurines of wondrous power*), an ornate silver snuffbox, a dlarun weed-pipe, and the *Crystal Crown of Ilhundyl*. The location and current state of the tomb are unknown, although the margrave's distant descendant, Count Krimmon Amethystall of Tethyr, has discreetly funded several expeditions to find it.

Major Centers of Worship: Since the fall of Athalantar, the Realm of the Stag, a thousand years or so ago, halflings have lived along the banks of the River Delimbiyr near its confluence with the Unicorn Run and the Hark River (also known as the Hawk River or Highmoorflow). While the flood plains north of the River Shining, as the River Delimbiyr is also known, are rich farmland, the southern shore of the river, south of the confluence with the Hark River, is demarcated by the steep (80-foot high) limestone and pink granite Red Cliffs. To ensure the continued sanctity of the honored dead, both from the orc hordes that periodically sweep down Delimbiyr Vale and from enterprising farmers seeking to expand their acreage, the earliest Small Folk resident in the region dug shallow burial niches in which to inter their kin in the escarpment midway between the two forks. The lack of funerary riches accompanying halfling burial rituals at the time minimized the risk of later plundering by tomb robbers, and careful attention to the placement of graves lessened the possibility of erosion washing away the bodies of those interred within the cliff face.

The founding of Phalorm, Realm of Three Crowns, at the Council of Axe and Arrow at the Laughing Hollow led to the formal establishment of a halfling nobility in the Lower Delimbiyr Vale and slowly changed the character of the burial niches dug in the High Moor escarpment. The first (and only) halfling duke of Imristar, Corcytar Huntinghorn, survived the collapse of the Realm of Three Crowns, known thereafter as the Fallen Kingdom, and led his people in battle for many years thereafter. After his death at the grand old age of 197, Duke Corcytar was interred, along with his armor and weapons, in Urogalan's Bluff with great honor and ceremony in a pink granite casket inlaid with jade carvings placed within a true tomb. This began a practice of carving formal tombs in the Red Cliffs and including rich grave goods along with the body of the deceased among the halfling noble and mercantile elite of the region. When the duke's second wife passed away three decades later, however, his former subjects were horrified to discover, upon reopening Huntinghorn's tomb, that all of the precious grave goods within had been plundered by tomb robbers, as had several other nearby vaults. This unsettling discovery led to the founding of the Cliffbarrow Cloister of Imristar, an Urogalanan abbey carved into the Red Cliffs whose resident cadre of priests tended the burial niches and tombs Urogalan's Bluff.

Although the other races of the region mistakenly assume Urogalan's Bluff is simply the site of an unusual halfling hamlet, the priests of Cliffbarrows, as the cloister is now commonly known among Secomberite halflings, continue in their role as caretakers and protectors of the cliffside burial ground. The abbey has been slowly expanded in the centuries since its founding and its limestone and granite halls now extend deep beneath the High Moor. The Cenotaph of Corcytar serves as the Urogalanan altar and the surrounding Vault of the Fallen Hin as the abbey's chapel. Other chambers within the maze of tunnels serve as crypts, cubiculums, mortuaries, and living quarters for Urogalan's priests. The high priest of Cliffbarrows is High Moor Hound Cornelius Monadnock, a stout halfling hailing from the Llorkh region originally. During his adventuring days, the Moor Hound, as Monadnock was then known, recovered the long-lost *Imrisword* and *Coronet of the Shining Hart* of the halfling duke of Phalorm in the deepest reaches of the Dungeon of the Hark (known as the Dungeon of the Hawk in earlier times), and those funerary relics are now stored within the temple vaults. The *Solium of Huntinghorn*, however, has yet to be found despite Monadnock's chartering of several adventuring bands to recover it.

Affiliated Orders: Urogalan's priesthood is segregated into two religious orders with overlapping responsibilities and memberships. (In small communities with but a single Urogalanan priest, the resident Vas-

sal of the Black Hound serves both roles.) The Wardens of the Dead are primarily responsible for the protection of halfling gravesites and ensuring the peaceful transition of halfling spirits to the afterlife. The role of the Children of the Earth is to honor the ground from which halflings extract their livelihood and to defend against dangers from below that might emerge in the midst of halfling communities on the surface.

Priestly Vestments: Urogalan's priests wear simple, ankle-length robes of tied with a belt of rope. Depending on whether they are performing rituals in honor of death or earth, their robes are white or brown, respectively. They are always barefooted and, if at all possible, keep two feet firmly planted on the ground at all times. Priests typically shave their pates, while priestesses bind their hair in twin braids hanging down their backs. The holy symbol of the faith is a small (2 inches high) statuette of a hound carved from dlarun, meerschaum, or tomb jade.

Adventuring Garb: Although they can wear any type of armor, members of Urogalan's clergy strongly prefer suits of mail and shields forged from the bounty of the earth (in other words, made of metal). Likewise, they favor stone and metal weapons such as flails, slings, daggers, and short swords.

Specialty Priests (Grimwardens)

REQUIREMENTS:	Wisdom 13
PRIME REQ.:	Wisdom
ALIGNMENT:	LG, NG, LN, N
WEAPONS:	Any
ARMOR:	Any
MAJOR SPHERES:	All, combat, divination, elemental (earth), guardian, healing, necromantic, protection, summoning, wards
MINOR SPHERES:	Creation, law, sun, time
MAGICAL ITEMS:	As clerics
REQ. PROFS:	Flail (horseman's or footman's), ancient history, stonemasonry
BONUS PROFS:	Gem cutting, necrology, netherworld knowledge, pottery

- Grimwardens must be halflings. Most grimwardens are stouts, but they can be of any halfling subrace.
- Grimwardens are not allowed to multiclass.
- Grimwardens can affect triple the number of zombies and skeletons when destroying undead.
- Grimwardens gain a saving throw vs. petrification against any form of energy-draining attack that could drain them of experience levels or hit points.
- Grimwardens can cast *Maximilian's earthen grasp* (as the 2nd-level priest spell) or *protection from evil* (as the 1st-level priest spell) once per day.
- At 3rd level, grimwardens can cast *invisibility to undead* (as the 1st-level priest spell) or *soften earth and stone* (as the 2nd-level priest spell detailed in the Urdlen entry in the "Gnome Pantheon" chapter) once per day.
- At 5th level, grimwardens can cast *meld into stone* (as the 3rd-level priest spell) or *protection from evil, 10´ radius,* (as the 4th-level priest spell) once per day.
- At 5th level, grimwardens can cast *negative plane protection* (as the 3rd-level priest spell) once per day.
- At 7th level, grimwardens can cast *call hounds* (as the 4th-level priest spell) or *dig* (as the 4th-level wizard spell) once per day.
- At 7th level, grimwardens gain immunity to all petrification attacks.
- At 10th level, grimwardens can cast *stone shape* (as the 3rd-level priest spell) or *transmute rock to mud* or its reverse (as the 5th-level priest spell) once per day.
- At 13th level, grimwardens can cast *stone to flesh* or its reverse (as the 6th-level wizard spell) twice per tenday.

Halfling Powers: Cyrrollalee, Yondalla, Arvoreen, Sheela Peryroyl (foreground)

Urogalanan Spells

In addition to the spells listed below, priests of Urogalan can cast the 2nd-level priest spell *soften earth and stone* detailed in the entry for Urdlen.

2nd Level

Earth Anchor (Pr 2; Alteration)

Sphere:	Elemental Earth
Range:	10 yards
Components:	V, S, M
Duration:	3 rounds+1 round/level
Casting Time:	5
Area of Effect:	30-foot radius
Saving Throw:	Neg.

This spell causes creatures within the area of effect who are in contact with the ground to be magically bonded to the earth or stone on which they stand. Thereafter, while it is possible to slide forward or backward at one-third normal movement, it is impossible to lift any body part in contact with the ground away from the earth to which it is anchored. Any being exiting the spell's area of effect is no longer bound by the effects of the *earth anchor*. Beings entering or reentering the area of effect after the casting of the spell are affected, however. Likewise, any being within the area of effect who brings other parts of its body into contact with the ground finds those parts similarly anchored as well. Only living, corporeal creatures in physical contact with the ground are affected by this spell. Boots, clothing, armor, and the like do not count as a gap between an individual and the ground.

Any creature within the area of effect when the spell is cast or any creature that enters (or reenters, even if it has already succeeded at a saving throw vs. spell) must succeed at a saving throw vs. spell to avoid the effects of the *earth anchor*. Targets of this spell can willingly forgo their saving throw vs. spell if desired.

The material components of this spell are the priest's holy symbol and a small amount of mud.

3rd Level

Doomhound (Pr 3; Phantasm, Necromancy)

Sphere:	Necromantic
Range:	10 yards
Components:	V, S, M
Duration:	Special
Casting Time:	6
Area of Effect:	One creature
Saving Throw:	Special

This spell creates a shadowy mastiff visible only to the caster and the intended target of the spell. Once created, a *doomhound* inexorably stalks its target, never approaching closer than 10 feet or falling more than 100 yards behind, creating a unshakable premonition of death.

The initial appearance of a *doomhound* causes fear in the target creature, as the reverse of the 1st-level priest spell *remove fear*. A successful saving throw vs. spell obviates the *fear* effect, but it does not dispel the *doomhound*. Regardless of whether or not the target of this spell attempts to flee the *doomhound* when it first appears, for as long as the *doomhound* stalks the target, the victim rolls all subsequent saving throws with a –2 penalty and fails all morale checks or saving throws vs. magical or nonmagical fear unless a 20 is rolled.

Creatures immune to magical fear are unaffected by this spell. Only one *doomhound* can stalk at target at any time. The effects of this spell can be ended at any time by a *remove curse*, *limited wish*, or *wish* or by the death of the target, but physical or magical attacks are otherwise ineffective against a *doomhound*.

The material component of this spell is the priest's holy symbol.

4th Level

Call Hounds (Pr 4; Conjuration/Summoning)

Sphere:	Animal, Summoning
Range:	10-foot radius
Components:	V, S, M
Duration:	1 turn/level
Casting Time:	1 round
Area of Effect:	Special
Saving Throw:	None

When cast, a pair of jet-black hounds appear anywhere within the spell's range, as desired by the caster. The hounds are completely loyal to the caster and attempt to carry out the caster's every command so long as such actions do not contradict the tenets of Urogalan's faith. If ordered to undertake a task contrary to the tenets of Urogalan, the hounds simply vanish, ending the spell. The caster's control over the hounds is nearly absolute; only a full *wish* or divine intervention is sufficient to subvert the hounds' loyalty to the caster.

The hounds are the equal of war dogs, as described in the MONSTROUS MANUAL tome, with maximum hit points (18 hp) and lawful neutral alignment. They are more intelligent than normal war dogs (low intelligence) and can understand complex instructions.

Call hounds ends if the hounds are slain or subject to a *banishment* spell, if the caster is slain or rendered unconscious, or if the caster wills the spell to cease. *Dispel magic* has no effect on the hounds. *Protection from good, protection from evil*, and similar powers can keep the hounds at bay, however.

The material components for this spell are the caster's holy symbol and a silver dog whistle (worth at least 50 gp) that the caster sounds during casting. Neither are consumed in the casting.

Yondalla

(The Protector and Provider, the Nurturing Matriarch, the Blessed One)

Greater Power of Mount Celestia, LG

PORTFOLIO:	Protection, fertility, the halfling race, children, security, leadership, diplomacy, wisdom, the cycle of life, creation, family and familial love, tradition, community, harmony, prosperity
ALIASES:	Dallillia (Sword Coast south of Waterdeep), Perissa (Moonshaes), otherwise none widespread
DOMAIN NAME:	Venya/Green Fields
SUPERIOR:	None
ALLIES:	Angharradh, Berronar Truesilver, Chauntea, Corellon Larethian, Garl Glittergold, Hathor, Helm, Moradin, Nephthys, Sharindlar, Shiallia, Torm, Tyr, the halfling pantheon
FOES:	Bane (dead), Bhaal (dead), Cyric, Iyachtu Xvim, Talona, Talos and the gods of fury (Auril, Umberlee, Malar), the goblinkin pantheons, Urdlen
SYMBOL:	Shield with cornucopia
WOR. ALIGN.:	LG, NG, CG, LN, N, CN

Yondalla (Yon-DAH-lah) is the Protector and Provider of halflings and the chief matriarch of the halfling pantheon. She is responsible for the race's creation and for blessing them with peace, comfort, and plenty. As the goddess of protection, Yondalla fends off evil influences and intrusions into the homes and lives of halflings. Yondalla gives her people the strength of character and the determination to defend themselves. Her protection is part of the very souls of her creations, for of all the demihuman races, the halflings have most rarely succumbed to evil. As a provider, Yondalla is a goddess of fertility and growing things, of birth and youth, of nature and plants. She can make barren places and creatures fertile and increase the growing rate of plants and animals, almost as she chooses, although she uses such powers sparingly and almost never confers such benefits on other demihumans or humans for fear of giving offense to their deities.

Yondalla's portfolio can be interpreted to somewhat overlap those of Sheela Peryroyl, Cyrrollalee, Arvoreen, and Urogalan, but in truth this is mainly as she is their leader and both directs their efforts and works with them in harmony to provide for both the good of the divine and the mortal halfling communities. Only Brandobaris and Tymora walk their own paths, but even they work closely with the Nurturing Matriarch in ensuring the peace and security of halflings throughout the Realms. The Protector and Provider has forged strong alliances with the patriarchs and matriarchs of the other demihuman races to ensure the mutual survival of their charges, and she is closely allied with agricultural and guardian deities of all the goodly races.

Yondalla is a kind and merciful goddess to her people. Although she brooks no evil, she despises no part of her creation, and always seeks to guide halflings who have lost their way in the world, physically or spiritually, back to their homes and friends. Although Yondalla is tolerant of thieves among her people, she does not approve of them and tries to have her priests guide such errant folk to use their skills more usefully. However, appropriating an extra share for oneself from the big folk is no great sin if no real harm or damage is done. Yondalla has given plenty of gifts to her worshipers, not the least of which is her temperament. From her, the halflings have learned to stand up for themselves, to defend their homes and families, and to seek peaceable solutions—or else turn their foes against each other and slip away unnoticed. Yondalla is a charming and persuasive power of peace, and though she can take life and health as easily as she gives it, she never seeks out opportunities to harm those who do not richly deserve it. When she is aroused to ire, however, Yondalla is a truly fearsome goddess, for all her apparent gentility and diminutive stature. Although not a power of war, Yondalla is a skilled warrior that other powers do not readily seek to challenge. If a community of halflings is faced with extermination, Yondalla acts first through her priests and with manifestations and then by having Arvoreen dispatch his avatar. If all else fails, Yondalla is very likely to send an avatar herself to defend her charges. If she does this, she fights within the area of the halfling communities and homes rather than venture attacks outside of that area.

Yondalla's Avatar (Cleric 37, Paladin 30, Wizard 29)

Yondalla appears as a strong, proud, vibrantly attractive female halfling, determined of bearing, with long golden hair, a skirt of forest green, a corn yellow and earth brown tunic, and a stout wooden shield. She favors spells from the spheres of all, animal, combat, creation, divination, elemental (air, earth, water), guardian, healing, law, necromantic, plant, protection, sun, and wards and from the schools of abjuration, illusion/phantasm, and elemental air, earth, and water, although she can cast spells from any sphere or school.

AC –5; MV 12; HP 218; THAC0 –10; #AT 5/2
Dmg 1d6+14 (vorpal short sword +4, +8 STR, +2 spec. bonus in short sword)
MR 75%; SZ M (4 1/2 feet tall)
STR 20, DEX 18, CON 20, INT 24, WIS 24, CHA 25
Spells P: 16/15/14/14/13/12/10, W: 7/7/7/7/7/6/6/6/6
Saves* PPDM 1, RSW 1**, PP 2, BW 2, Sp 2
    *Includes +2 bonus to saving throws to a minimum of 1. **Includes halfling +5 CON save bonus to a minimum of 1. The CON save bonus also applies to saves vs. poison to a minimum of 1.

Special Att/Def: Yondalla wields *Hornblade*, a *vorpal short sword +4* that glows silver when it strikes, and she is specialized in short sword. She is proficient in all other weapons. Her *shield +3* reflects all bolt spells back at their caster.

The Protector and Provider is immune to magically caused wounds (the reversed forms of many healing spells), energy drains, paralyzation, gaseous attacks, blinding, deafness, disease, and spells from the illusion/phantasm or enchantment/charm schools that she does not want to affect her. Yondalla can only be struck by +3 or better magical weapons, and she radiates a permanent full-strength *protection from evil, 20´ radius*. Once per round by a wave of her hand, she can cast *curse of Yondalla* on any creature within 30 yards. Yondalla can cast *plant growth* and *animal growth* at will, and, if among a community of halflings, she can cast each of the *Bigby's hand* spells once per day.

Other Manifestations

Yondalla commonly manifests as a warm, golden radiance that envelops a creature, item, or region. If Yondalla's radiance envelops a halfling, her power cloaks them in the power of an *armor* spell, *cures* 1d8 points of damage, and grants them *invisibility* and/or *free action*. A hollowed-out horn or other container enveloped in Yondalla's aura spills forth great quantities of food and or drink, like the effects of a *horn of plenty* spell, in sufficient volume to feed every worshiper or ally present. A weapon bathed the goddess's manifestation is wrapped in a nimbus of soft light and attacks with a +3 attack and damage bonus for the next turn. If Yondalla manifests in a region of open space, any halfling touching her manifestation passes through or into an extradimensional space or tunnel such as that created by spell such as *rope trick*, *dimension door*, or *gateway*.

Yondalla is served by aasimon, archons, asuras, baku, bariaurs, black bears, brown bears, brownies, dobies, einheriar, gold dragons, guardian nagas, hollyphants, hybsils, incarnates of charity, faith, and justice, lammasu, maruts, nature elementals, noctrals, pers, sheep (normal and giant), silver dragons, sunflies, and t'uen-rin. She demonstrates her favor through welcome but sudden changes in the weather or natural surroundings. Conversely, the Protector and Provider indicates her displeasure through unwelcome, but sudden, changes in the weather or natural surroundings. Her favor is also demonstrated through the discovery of amber pellets, daffodils, dlarun, malacons, meerschaum, peridots, pipestone, serpentine, silverbark trees, star rose quartz, and telstang.

The Church

CLERGY:	Clerics, mystics, specialty priests
CLERGY'S ALIGN.:	LG, NG, CG, LN
TURN UNDEAD:	C: Yes, Mys: No, SP: Yes
CMND. UNDEAD:	C: No, Mys: No, SP: No

All clerics, mystics, and specialty priests of Yondalla receive religion (halfling) and reading/writing (common) as bonus nonweapon proficiencies.

The church of the Protector and Provider, under all the guises by which she is known, plays a central role in halfling society. Throughout the Realms, communities of the Small Folk are led by members of Yondalla's clergy, and they are widely credited for their efforts in ensuring the safety and prosperity of halflings across Faerûn. Among the other human and demihuman races, Yondalla's priests are respected for their determined defense of halfling communities and their defensive skill, belying their diminutive natures.

Temples of Yondalla are remarkably rare, despite the goddess's widespread veneration by halflings. The Provider and Protector is most commonly worshiped in small shrines and in the home, and her formal houses of worship are usually little more than the home of the local priest or priestess. In those few halfling communities where churches of Yondalla do exist, they are usually carved into an earthen hillside, resembling a halfling burrow more than anything else. Although smoothly blended with the surrounding environment, such temples serve as fortified redoubts, well stocked with arms and food to allow the halflings of the community to hold out indefinitely against invaders. Gardens, armories, cisterns, and granaries are nestled among chapels, residential quarters for the resident priests, and bubbling springs.

Novices of Yondalla are known as the Blessed Children. Full priests of the Protector and Provider are known as Revered Councilors. In ascending order of rank, the titles used by Yondallan priests are Blessed Sister/Brother, Sacred Guardian, Revered Nurturer, Blessed Mother/Father, Eminent Prodigal, August Warden, Hallowed Provider, and Exalted Protector. High-ranking priests have unique individual titles. Specialty priests are known as horn guards. The clergy of Yondalla includes hairfeet (55%), stouts (30%), and tallfellows (15%). Yondalla's clergy is nearly evenly divided between specialty priests (37%), mystics (33%), and clerics (30%). Women (60%) slightly outnumber men (40%) among the clergy.

Dogma: Those who seek to live in accordance with the way of the Provider will be blessed with a cornucopia of riches. Seek peace and comfort, for a life lived with both is true wealth. Although violence should never be welcomed, the Protector's aegis will extend to those willing to fiercely defend their home and community. Lead through example, and know the activities of those you lead so that you can help shoulder their burdens when need be. Treasure your family, for your parents gave you life and your children are your future. Care for the aged and the weak, for you never know when you may be one of the strong laid low.

Day-to-Day Activities: Priests of Yondalla are concerned with all spheres of halfling life, save thievery. They protect halfling communities from outside threats. They serve as ever-vigilant sentinels overseeing fields and burrows. Many double as secular leaders of their communities as well as religious authorities. Yondalla's priests officiate at weddings and funerals, the latter in conjunction with members of Urogalan's clergy.

The primary mission of the priesthood of the Provider and the Protector is to pass Yondalla's teachings on to the community at large and to knit such communities tightly together. Areas of instruction include collective and self-defense, concealment, agriculture, brewing, wine-making, gardening, and cooking. Spells granted by the goddess are used to demonstrate or enhance such activities. Communities are brought together through regular feasts, revels, and celebrations with few spiritual overtones other than a celebration of the collective purpose of the community.

Holy Days/Important Ceremonies: Halflings set aside one day per Realms week—the fifth day of each tenday—for worship of Yondalla. Safeday, as it is known, is a day that is mostly spent in rest and play. In the morning, families gather together in the home, collectively offer up the fruits of the goddess's bounty in homage to the Provider, and then spend several hours preparing a tenday's feast from those offerings. During these activities, local members of the clergy of Yondalla go from house to house to lead each family in brief devotions, offer the goddess's blessings, and share any concerns a family may have. When the tenday's feast is prepared, each family, sometimes joined by a local priest, joins together in eating, laughing, and the telling of tales. In the late afternoon, the Small Folk emerge from their homes and assemble in the central square. The highest-ranking priest of Yondalla (or in the absence of a priest, a pious lay representative) then leads the assembled Small Folk on a walk around the central community, symbolically joining Yondalla in her defense of the settlement. Such tours are hardly armed patrols; they usually involve contests to see who can pick the most perfect apple or the like and other gentle reminders of how bountiful are the goddess's gifts. When the promenade returns to the central square, the community-wide dinner feast begins. Extra food prepared during the morning hours is heated and served, while the community elders relate traditional tales of halfling folklore. Such festivities can last far into the night as the community reforges their communal bonds. Unlike the religious ceremonies of other races and powers, allies and even strangers are often invited to contribute and partake in the feasting and merriment, although those unknown to the community are discretely observed just in case.

Major Centers of Worship: As noted above, large temples of the Nurturing Matriarch are few and far between, for most halflings worship in the home, and most communities are served by at most a handful of priests who tend the local shrine, if any exists outside of individual homes. Nevertheless, Yondalla's priesthood has found it expedient to found the sprawling Abbey of the Bountiful Horn in the town of Ammathluir on the western border of Luiren. The abbey and the town of Ammathluir are led by the aging matriarch, Cornucopia of Blessings Sara Fallowguard and her lifelong mate, High Marshal Bernarth Hornguard (a fighter/specialty priest of Arvoreen). Under their combined stewardship, both town and temple have bloomed with gardens and other signs of the goddess's bounty, masking the extensive defensive fortifications that have been erected in every home and burrow and along every path and stream. Like the town itself, the temple is far larger and more extensive than it initially appears. The abbey is dug into the side of a large hill on the western edge of the town, and its earthen tunnels honeycomb the heart of the hill and connect with most of the burrow-homes of Ammathluir. This deception enables Yondalla's numerous resident priests to blend in among the surrounding community, dwelling in individual burrows with their families, but in times of war to assemble in the abbey's heart into small guerrilla bands and then emerge from countless holes to defend the town from attack.

The Bountiful Horn has also guarded Luiren's western forest since the halfling nation threw off the yoke of the Arkaiun invaders in the Sixth Century DR. The encircling Toadsquat Mountains and Lluirwood have long stymied would-be invaders, restricting access to Luiren to the sea and a single east-west route through the forest connecting Ammathluir and the Trader's Way. It is along this route that the great war chief of the Arkaiuns, Reinhar, and the people of the wind, as the original humans of Dambrath were known, invaded the halfling realm in the Year of the Pernicon (545 DR), and it is along this route that any future invasion, such as a horde of the Shebali warriors led by the Crintri of Dambrath, would likely come. To guard against any such invasion, the abbey's priests have created an exten-sive array of fortifications, traps, and ambush points along the length of the Ammathvale road as it passes through the forest, and any army passing through would be severely weakened, if not routed, by the combined assaults that can be unleashed by a handful of defenders as they fall back along the length of the gauntlet.

Affiliated Orders: The Wayward Wardens are a loosely organized fellowship of Yondallan priests stricken with wanderlust who wish to see the world. Estranged by choice from forming a long-term relationship a single community, Wayward Wardens serve the Provider and Protector by coming to the defense of besieged or threatened halfling communities in need of additional protectors. For example, during the Tethyrian Interregnum, many Wayward Wardens lived for a time among the halflings of the Purple Hills. The addition of two score elite defenders to the halfling communities of the region did much to keep the chaos of interregnum at bay.

Priestly Vestments: Members of Yondalla's clergy dress in loose-fitting green and brown robes and a saffron overcloak, keeping their heads bare. Priests typically wear their hair long, dying it golden blonde if it is not naturally that color. Yondallan priests always carry a shield, usually wooded, emblazoned with the cornucopia symbol of the goddess. The holy symbol of the faith is an animal horn of any type, except in Luiren where it is a wheat stalk crossing a silver tree, representing the meadows and the forests.

Adventuring Garb: When expecting combat, Yondallan priests wear the best armor available and always carry a shield, again usually emblazoned with Yondalla's cornucopia. They favor short swords, hand axes, slings, short bows, spears, small lances, hammers, and morningstars.

Specialty Priests (Horn Guards)

REQUIREMENTS:	Wisdom 13
PRIME REQ.:	Wisdom
ALIGNMENT:	LG
WEAPONS:	Any
ARMOR:	Any, but must always carry a shield
MAJOR SPHERES:	All, animal, astral, combat, creation, divination, elemental (air, earth, water), guardian, healing, law, necromantic, plant, protection, summoning, sun, wards
MINOR SPHERES:	Weather
MAGICAL ITEMS:	As clerics
REQ. PROFS:	Short sword, agriculture, local history
BONUS PROFS:	Ancient history, cooking

- Horn guards must be halflings, but they can be of any halfling subrace.
- Horn guards are not allowed to multiclass.
- Horn guards receive a +2 attack bonus, in addition to the normal halfling thrown-weapon bonus, when using rocks they have selected. Thrown rocks do 1d4 points of damage, and horn guards can hurl three rocks per round.
- Horn guards can cast *protection from evil* (as the 1st-level priest spell) or *shield* (as the 1st-level wizard spell) or *magical stone* (as the 1st-level priest spell) once per day. Note that the *shield* ability horn guards use has no problem working in conjunction with nonmetallic armor, but it cannot work in conjunction with any metal armor save elven chain mail.
- At 3rd level, horn guards can cast *bless* (as the 1st-level priest spell, but with twice the normal duration) or *wyvern watch* (as the 2nd-level priest spell) once per day.
- At 5th level, horn guards can cast *create food and water* (as the 3rd-level priest spell) or *efficacious monster ward* (as the 3rd-level priest spell) once per day.
- At 7th level, horn guards can cast *animal growth* (as the 5th-level priest spell) or *plant growth* (as the 3rd-level priest spell) once per day.
- At 7th level, horn guards gain immunity to paralyzation and to fear effects of any kind.
- At 10th level, horn guards can cast *heroes' feast* (as the 6th-level priest spell) or *restoration* (as the 7th-level priest spell) once per month.
- At 13th level, horn guards can shapechange (similar to the druid ability) into a mammalian form. They are restricted to assuming the form of burrowing mammals, mammals that live above the ground but not in trees, and mammals that live in water. Horn guards are not allowed to become reptiles or avians, nor do they heal damage when shapechanging.

Yondallan Spells

In addition to the spells listed below and those spells common to all halfling priests, Yondalla's clergy can also cast the 1st-level priest spell *reed staff* detailed in the entry for Sheela Peryroyl.

4th Level

Badger Form (Pr 4; Alteration)

Sphere: Animal
Range: 0
Components: V, S, M
Duration: 2 turns/level
Casting Time: 1 round
Area of Effect: The caster
Saving Throw: None

This spell transforms the priest into the form of a giant badger, with all the abilities and attacks thereof as detailed in Monstrous Compendium® Annual, *Volume Two*. No system shock roll is required.

> **Giant Badger:** AC 4; MV 6, Br 3; HD 3; hp as caster; THAC0 17; #AT 3; Dmg 1d3 (claw)/1d3 (claw)/1d6 (bite); SA saves as caster; SZ M (4´ long); ML as caster; Int as caster; AL as caster; XP as caster.

When the change in form occurs, the priest's equipment, if any, melds into the new form. (In particularly challenging campaigns, the DM may allow protective devices, such as a *ring of protection*, to continue operating effectively.) The priest retains all mental abilities and granted powers but cannot cast spells. Hit points and saving throws remain the same as well. The priest can return to its normal form at any time, ending the spell prematurely. When the *badger form* ends, whether due to the spell expiring or the priest willing it to do so, the priest returns to his or her own form and heals 1d12 points of damage. The priest also returns to his or her own form when slain or when the effect is dispelled, but no damage is healed in these cases. A system shock check is not required to transform back to the caster's normal form, whether voluntarily or involuntarily.

This spell is commonly employed to assist in the digging of halfling burrows and to defend them against attackers.

The material components of this spell are the priest's holy symbol and a claw, tooth, or tuft of hair from a badger (normal or giant sized).

Horn of Plenty (Pr 4; Conjuration)

Sphere: Creation
Range: Touch
Components: V, S, M
Duration: 1 turn
Casting Time: 2 rounds
Area of Effect: The hollowed out horn of a ram or giant ram
Saving Throw: None

This spell temporarily transforms a hollowed out horn into a magical cornucopia. In the first 5 rounds after the spell is cast, fresh vegetables, fruits, and grains tumble forth from the *horn of plenty*, in quantities sufficient to feed up to six human-sized creatures or two horse-sized creatures for one day. In the second 5 rounds, wine, water, or ale gushes forth from the *horn of plenty* sufficient to quench the thirsts of up to six human-sized creatures or two horse-sized creatures per level of the caster for one day. During the casting, the caster must specify the type or types of fruits, vegetables, and grains and the type of liquid to be dispensed. It is up to the caster to determine how, if at all, the food or beverage is to be contained so that it does not spill all over the ground; caster's often arrange to have containers placed on the ground to catch the bounty. The enchantment of the *horn of plenty* fades once the spell expires, but any food or drink created by means of this spell is permanent and nonmagical in nature and spoils and decays normally.

The material component of this spell is the priest's holy symbol.

5th level

A Day in the Life (Pr 5; Alteration, Abjuration)

Sphere: Law, Combat
Range: Touch
Components: V, S, M
Duration: One day
Casting Time: 8
Area of Effect: Creature touched
Saving Throw: Neg.

This spell transforms a living, sentient, intelligent creature touched by the caster (successful attack roll required) into a normal halfling with no character class abilities (see the Monstrous Manual tome) provided the creature fails a saving throw vs. spell. The creature transformed retains its alignment, its memory and mental capacity, its normal saving throws, and its hit points. It does not gain any bonuses that halflings normally possess; the spell gives halfling form and THAC0. Items carried or worn are not changed with the spell's target, who may now be awash in ill-fitting armor or holding a weapon too big to wield effectively. Magical items usable only by character classes other than fighters no longer function for the target. A creature transformed by *a day in the life* cannot cast spells, although these are not forgotten and can be cast when the creature once again assumes its normal form; similarly, the use of psionic abilities granted by the psionicist class is not possible. The spell does not require a system shock roll for the target creature when it is transformed or when it assumes its normal form at the spell's expiration.

The material components are the priest's holy symbol and a hair from a halfling's foot.

7th Level

Curse of Yondalla (Pr 7; Alteration, Abjuration)

Sphere: Time
Range: 20 yards
Components: V, S, M
Duration: Special
Casting Time: 1 round
Area of Effect: One creature
Saving Throw: Neg.

The curse of Yondalla is reserved for creatures who have greatly offended Yondalla—for example by completely destroying a halfling community or killing innocent and defenseless halflings, such as the aged or very young. A creature afflicted by curse of Yondalla is stunned and unable to act offensively if it fails a saving throw vs. spell. It then returns to infancy over the period of a turn, growing younger slowly at first and then rapidly, until it is once again an infant specimen of its species. No system shock survival roll is required. The infant has no memory of its previous life. Commonly, a halfling community or the priest then raises the infant to respect halflings and the ways of Yondalla. An infant of a species inherently unsafe for such folk to raise (say, a troll or a dragon), it is placed with a foster parent of a species able to properly raise it in a positive moral and ethical fashion.

An undead creature of less than divine status that fails its saving throw is destroyed by this spell, but a creature of extraplanar origin that fails its saving throw is merely cast back to its home plane and unable to return to the Prime Material Plane for 10d10 years. A creature with magic resistance has it reduced by a −25% penalty against the effects of a curse of Yondalla. A creature that successfully saves still suffers 3d8+3 points of damage or half its remaining hit points in damage, whichever is less.

The bestowed curse of Yondalla cannot be dispelled. It can be countered by a remove curse from the same priest of Yondalla who cast it or by any good priest whose level exceeds the original caster's level; it can also be negated by a full wish. When the curse if removed, the creature returns to its normal age over the course of 1 turn (requiring no system shock survival roll), but it remembers any events that took place during its second youth in addition to those of its previous older life. Destroyed undead creatures can be restored or extraplanar creatures allowed to return before the end of the allotted time only by a full wish or divine intervention.

Priests of Yondalla do not cast this spell lightly. Yondalla's divine servitors or Yondalla herself are said to watch over its use and will prevent it from being successfully cast if they feel its is being misused.

The material component of this spell is the priest's holy symbol.

APPENDIX 1: DEMIHUMAN PRIESTS

The basic classes of the priest group in use in the FORGOTTEN REALMS campaign setting, aside from the specifically defined specialty priests detailed in the entries for each deity discussed in the bulk of this book, are detailed in *Faiths & Avatars*. (Most of these classes are also discussed in the *Player's Handbook* and/or PLAYER's OPTION: *Spells & Magic*.) Note that the crusader class referenced in this work is not the crusader class described in *Warriors and Priests of the Realms*. The crusader class found in *Warriors and Priests of the Realms* has been renamed the holy crusader to differentiate it from this class.

Nonhuman Shamans: In the Realms the demihuman civilizations (even that of the jungle dwarves) have matured past the point that their religions use shamans; their faiths are much too civilized and traditionbound. This is not to say that only humans in the Realms are shamans, but the other races who have shamans tend to be humanoids with less sophisticated cultures, such as the kobolds, goblins, trolls, etc.

Racial Level Limitations and Slow Advancement: In general, the FORGOTTEN REALMS setting allows a few more races to belong to certain classes than the core rules for the AD&D® game would permit. It also is strongly suggested that DMs pursue the optional Slow Advancement rule in the Racial Level Restrictions section of "Chapter 2: Player Character Races" in the DUNGEON MASTER Guide to allow demihumans unlimited level advancement in the FORGOTTEN REALMS campaign setting. Specifically, it is recommended that demihumans be allowed to rise normally to their racial maximum level and then be required to earn triple normal experience points to advance beyond that point. It is not recommended that the optional Exceeding Level Limits rule for extremely high ability scores be used.

Specialty priests of any race in the Realms are technically unlimited in the maximum level they may obtain. If they are not human, however, they are *always* required to earn triple normal experience points to advance beyond the listed level limits.

Racial Class and Level Limits

	Human	Drow	Dwarf	Elf	Gnome	Half-elf	Halfling
Cleric	U	12	10	12	9	14	8
Crusader	U	12	13	12	—	12†	—
Druid	U	12†	—	12†	—	9	—
Monk	U	—	—	—	—	—	—
Mystic	U	12	—	12	—	14	13
Shaman	U	—	—	—	—	—	—
Specialty Priest	U	16	14	16	13	18	12

†Character race and class combinations normally not allowed in the AD&D game rules. These changes are recommended specifically for the FORGOTTEN REALMS campaign setting; however, Dungeon Masters are free to exclude these races from the given classes.

Multiclassed Characters in the Realms: How multiclassed characters function has been subject to considerable debate. These rules explain exactly how to assign hit points, proficiencies, class abilities, and armor to multiclassed characters in the Realms:

- For hit points, roll all the character's Hit Dice, adjust each die for Constitution, and note the total somewhere. A character's hit point rating is the average of all the dice (the total divided by the character's number of classes). Drop all fractions, but do not discard the total; it will be used to help determine the character's hit points as she or he gains levels. Each time the character gains a level, roll the appropriate hit die, adjust for Constitution, and add it to the recorded total. Recalculate the character's hit points by dividing the new total by the character's number of classes, again dropping any fractions.
- Multiclassed characters get all the abilities from their classes (except armor and weapon use, see below). A character can use only one ability at a time, however, and cannot combine abilities as part of a single action. A fighter/mage, for example cannot make a melee attack while casting a spell, though she or he could use his or her fighter THAC0 when targeting spells that require attack rolls. A thief making a backstab attack must use his or her thief THAC0 to get his or her attack and damage bonuses (selecting the right spot to hit puts a crimp on her overall fighting ability).
- Except as noted above, a multiclassed character uses the best THAC0 from his or her classes.
- A multiclassed character always uses the best available saving throw from all his or her classes.

- To assign proficiencies to a multiclassed character, choose the highest number of initial proficiencies from among all the character's classes. Thereafter assign a new proficiency whenever the character would normally earn them for each class.
- Multiclassed characters generally must abide by the worst armor restrictions among their classes. Multiclassed elf and half-elf mages can wear elven chain mail if one of their other classes is normally allowed to use chain mail. Multiclassed thieves suffer penalties to their abilities if they wear armor better that leather. Elven chain mail, padded armor, and leather armor impose the penalties noted on Table 29: Thieving Skill Armor Adjustments in the *Player's Handbook*. Other types of armor negate all thief abilities except open locks and detect noise. (These abilities still suffer the penalties from the "Padded or Studded Leather" column on Table 29.) Note that *The Complete Thief's Handbook* extends Table 29 to cover most types of armor.
- Multiclassed characters generally enjoy the best weapon selection from among all their classes, except for priests, who remain bound by their priest class's weapon restrictions. The sole exception to this exception is priests who multiclass with the ranger class, as in the ranger/cleric combination. These priests are allowed to use the ranger's weapon selection to supplement their allowed weapon selection.

Demihuman Racial Spell-like Abilities: Unless otherwise noted, racial spell-like abilities function at a casting level equal to their user's level or Hit Dice.

Optional Experience Point Progression Table: The specialty priest column of the Expanded Priest Experience Levels table in "Appendix 1: Priest Classes" in *Faiths & Avatars* exhibits most of the characteristics of the druid experience point table. Specialty priests using this table experience relatively rapid advancement at low to mid-range levels and relatively slow advancement at high levels when compared to clerics and other classes. The following optional table follows the pattern of the cleric experience point table, but with a higher base value. If the DM so desires, nondruid specialty priests may use it in lieu of the table given in *Faiths & Avatars*. Note that if the DM decides to use the optional table given here, the mystic class should not use it, but should use either the specialty priest column of the Expanded Priest Experience Levels in *Faiths & Avatars* (preferred) or the cleric experience point progression table.

Optional Specialty Priest Experience Levels

Level	Specialty Priest Experience Points	Hit Dice (d8)
1	0	1
2	2,000	2
3	4,000	3
4	8,000	4
5	17,000	5
6	35,500	6
7	71,000	7
8	142,000	8
9	289,000	9
10	578,000	9+2
11	867,000	9+4
12	1,156,000	9+6
13	1,445,000	9+8
14	1,734,000	9+10
15	2,023,000	9+12
16	2,312,000	9+14
17	2,601,000	9+16
18	2,890,000	9+18
19	3,179,000	9+20
20	3,468,000	9+22

Specialty Priests: Specialty priests gain an additional level for every 289,000 experience points above 3,468,000. They gain an additional 2 hit points for every level after 20. They gain additional spells as shown on the Extended Priest Progression Table in the "Pantheons of the Realms" chapter of this work.

Drow Priests

Drow priests may be clerics, crusaders, druids, mystics, and specialty priests, although no member of the drow pantheon accepts druids openly into his or her service. Rumors hold that perhaps a smattering of gray druids who formerly served Ibrandul may be unknowingly serving Lolth, but in general the only drow druids would be neutral drow who have renounced the life below and have joined some of the Faerûnian human faiths under special circumstances.

Drow cannot be shamans. Drow priests may not normally multiclass, although Ghaunadaur, Lolth, and Selvetarm permit fighter/clerics, and Vhaeraun permits cleric/thieves. Drow clerics, crusaders, druids, and mystics are limited in level to 12th level. Specialty priests are limited to 16th level before they must earn triple normal experience to advance in level, and most drow deities have not allowed their specialty priests to exceed 22nd level in any case.

All drow receive the modern languages (low drow) nonweapon proficiency, which is essentially the same as the modern languages (Undercommon) nonweapon proficiency, and the modern languages (drow silent speech) nonweapon proficiency.

Nonplayer Characters: As discussed in *Drow of the Underdark* and the MONSTROUS MANUAL tome, all drow have innate base powers usable once per day that fade with time on the surface world, including the ability to evoke *dancing lights*, *faerie fire*, and *darkness*. Drow of 4th level or greater gain mature powers also usable once per day, including *levitate*, *know alignment*, and *detect magic*. These powers also fade with time on the surface world.

All drow priests and priests receive additional spell-like powers through divine favor, in addition to their spells, that do not fade with time on the surface world, including *clairvoyance*, *detect lie*, *suggestion*, and *dispel magic*. At the DM's option, these can be extended to such abilities as *detect undead*, *ESP* (other drow only, 20-foot maximum range), and *invisibility to undead*. It is suggested that drow priests and priests have a 20% chance of improving an existing power and a 10% chance of gaining a new power for each new level attained; augment these chances to simulate deities rewarding truly exceptional service.

Drow of noble blood or name typically gain the ability to use all of their base, mature, and priestly powers more than once a day. An additional daily use is gained at the end of each decade of life. All drow with Intelligence scores of 16 or higher and of 6th or greater level can wield a natural spell-like power and a spell simultaneously (for example, casting a spell while levitating) or employ a maximum of two natural spell-like powers simultaneously (for example, levitating while launching *darkness* to enshroud the head of an opponent).

The presence of strong light hampers drow concentration. All drow priests are considered to have received at least some training for such occurrences. Noble drow and drow priests must succeed at a saving throw vs. spell to launch any spell or spell-like power (already active ones are automatically retained), and all drow are reduced to the use of one spell or spell-like power at a time; no combinations are possible.

All adult drow, including drow priests, have a base magic resistance of 50% that increases by 2% for every level of advancement above 1st. (Multiclassed drow gain this bonus from the class in which they have the highest level, not from both or all three classes.) All drow receive a +2 bonus to all magical attack saving throws—that is, both against spells that overcome their natural resistance, and against the effects of magical items wielded against them. Both magic resistance and the saving throw bonus fade with time on the surface world.

Player Characters: According to the 2nd edition AD&D game rules, player character drow (dark elves) receive exactly the same racial abilities as elves. (See the Elves section in "Chapter 2: Races" in the *Player's Handbook*.) The FORGOTTEN REALMS campaign setting follows this rule. Optionally, the DM may allow player character drow to retain some drow abilities and penalties. The player and the DM must then carefully track the loss of those powers when the PC is out of the Underdark (and their gradual reappearance when reentering the Underdark) and consistently apply the drow light sensitivity penalties. In no case is it recommended that player character drow have magic resistance. If the DM really wants to allow a player character to have racial magic resistance, then a stiff experience point penalty of at least doubling the amount of experience required to gain each level would be a first recommended step toward balancing this huge benefit.

Dwarven Priests

Dwarven priests are individuals who feel a special affinity for a particular deity, usually from birth. They must want to further the aims of the deity and feel a love and kinship for the god, and they often hear the god speak, feel the deity's emotions, or (by vision) see the god act in their minds. There is a particular look about the eyes and face of a dwarven priest that is readily discernible (in good light and within 20 feet) to another dwarf of the same race, but never to strangers or nondwarves. This is a subtle look of devotion, not a flashing sign that proclaims a priest's level and deity.

Dwarven priests try to hide their class from nondwarves. When they must cast spells, they try to do so from hiding or from a distance. They have generally succeeded in keeping the understanding of their spells or even recognition of their existence secret from most nondwarves in Faerûn. This is particularly true in the North, where dwarves walk more softly and more often live among nondwarves. Dwarven priests may dress and act as nonclerical dwarves do and often try to keep worship and rituals hidden from nondwarven eyes.

Dwarven priests may be clerics, crusaders, fighter/clerics, and specialty priests. Normally the only multiclass combination permitted to dwarven priests is that of fighter/cleric, although Abbathor and Vergadain permit cleric/thieves, Clangeddin Silverbeard and Haela Brightaxe permit fighter/specialty priests, and not all powers permit fighter/clerics or even crusaders. Dwarven clerics are limited in level to 10th, dwarven crusaders are limited in level to 13th, and dwarven specialty priests are technically unlimited in the maximum level they may obtain, but only a handful have ever risen above 14th level. Due to long-standing tradition, dwarven priests of most dwarven deities before the Time of Troubles had to be of the same gender as their deity. Since the Time of Troubles, this stricture is not longer the absolute that is was, and all dwarven faiths now accept priests of either gender—reluctantly. Priests of the gender opposite their deity are likely to be treated gingerly or with slight resentment by their same-gender fellows and to be called upon to prove their commitment to their vocation often. Dwarven culture is very slow to adopt new customs.

Half-dwarves are treated as dwarves of the appropriate subrace. There are no sundered dwarves or deep dwarves (both of which appear in *The Complete Book of Dwarves*) in the Realms.

Dwarven priests cast spells as priests of other races do, with one important difference: spell energies are always channeled through a stone or metal holy symbol worn next to the skin or grasped by the priest. Without this stabilizing focus, dwarven priest spells are 40% likely to go wild when cast. (The only exception to this rule are the priests of Thard Harr; the Disentangler's priests must be in physical contact with the earth or a plant firmly rooted in the earth to avoid any chance of their spells going wild.) This instability is also the reason most dwarven priest spells involve material components, fragments of the Prime not subject to any innate magical resistance. Note that spell-like granted powers never go wild. All dwarven priests are allowed to use all magical items not specifically denied to priests, but the usual chances for malfunctions, as described in the *Player's Handbook*, apply.

To determine the effect of wild spell energies, the DM should consult the *wand of wonder* effects, using the table of suggested results given in the DUNGEON MASTER *Guide* and devising new ones. It is not unheard-of for a wild spell to duplicate the effects of *chain lightning, reverse gravity, Mordenkainen's disjunction*, and *dancing lights* all at once. They have also been known to cause other upheavals of nature that are just as dramatic and deadly. Wild spells may be even more deadly attacks than the standard spells they started out as. They are not deliberately caused by priests more often simply because they can be as deadly to friend as to foe, having unpredictable side-effects. Moreover, most dwarven deities think such behavior reckless and disrespectful of their grace (in granting the spells in the first place) and of the safety of the dwarven people. A dwarven priest casts spells without a stone or metal holy symbol only unwittingly or when desperate. An attack that damages or removes a holy symbol during casting does not ruin the spellcasting but always causes the spell to go wild. Most dwarven priests carry spare holy symbols with them at all times to prevent their magic becoming ungovernable due to loss or theft of a holy symbol.

Dwarven clerics (as well as multiclassed clerics) differ somewhat from clerics of other races. They cannot turn undead before 7th level, but they always strike at +2 on all attack and damage rolls against undead creatures.

At 7th level and above, dwarven clerics can turn undead as other clerics do, but as a cleric of four levels less than their current level. These modifications apply only to the cleric class and not to crusaders or specialty priests, unless specifically noted. Dwarven clerics of Abbathor, Clangeddin, Gorm, Haela, and Thard are allowed the use of any type of weapon.

Dwarven priests of 7th level or greater are collectively known as High Old Ones, although each individual faith has its own title for members of this elite group. The High Old Ones are the most respected elders of the Stout Folk, especially in the North, where clan power and the pride and prosperity of young dwarves is weakest, and they often function as direct servants and speakers of their deities. Dwarves of all races and faiths (including gray dwarves, wild dwarves, and those who follow evil powers such as Abbathor, Laduguer, and Deep Duerra) respect High Old Ones. Unless mentally controlled or unable to identify such a dwarf, they never willingly attack a High Old One, whatever the situation. High Old Ones are also the only dwarven priests capable of employing dwarven rune magic.

Gray Dwarves (Duergar)

Gray dwarven priests are considered to be dwarven priests, with all of the abilities and limitations thereof, as described above. In addition, duergar priests have the abilities and weaknesses common to their race including *enlargement, invisibility*, surprise bonuses, susceptibility to bright light, and immunities to poison, paralysis, and illusion/phantasm spells, as detailed in the MONSTROUS MANUAL tome. The *enlargement* racial ability of duergar is used at a level equal to their hit point total, to a maximum of 10th level.

If the Invisible Art (psionics) is permitted in the campaign, many duergar have psionic abilities as well. While most gray dwarven priests can be considered multiclassed priest/psionicists, at the very least they are all wild talents, as discussed in the *Complete Psionics Handbook* and PLAYER'S OPTION: *Skills & Powers* supplement. If the DM desires to use psionics in his or her campaign, the use of the PLAYER'S OPTION: *Skills & Powers* system is recommended over the somewhat dated version found in the *Complete Psionics Handbook*.

Elven Priests

Elven priests may be clerics, crusaders, druids, mystics, and specialty priests. Normally no multiclass combinations are permitted to elven priests, although Corellon Larethian permits fighter/clerics, Erevan Ilesere permits cleric/thieves, fighter/cleric/thieves, and specialty priest/thieves, Solonor Thelandira permits cleric/rangers, and not all powers permit clerics, crusaders, druids, and/or mystics. Elven clerics are limited in level to 12th, elven crusaders are limited in level to 12th, elven druids are limited in level to 12th, and elven mystics are limited in level to 12th. Elven specialty priests are limited to 16th level before they must earn triple normal experience to advance in level, and only a handful have ever risen above 16th level.

Gnome Priests

Gnome priests may be clerics and specialty priests. Although gnome specialty priests can never multiclass, all gnome powers allow gnome fighter/clerics, cleric/illusionists, and cleric/thieves as members of their clergies. Gnome clerics are limited in level to 9th. Gnome specialty priests are limited to 13th level before they must earn triple normal experience to advance in level, and only a handful have ever risen above 13th level.

Deep Gnomes (Svirfneblin)

Deep gnome priests are considered to be gnome priests, with all of the abilities and limitations thereof, as described above. In addition, svirfneblin priests have the abilities and weaknesses common to their race including casting *blindness, blur*, and *change self* once per day each; radiating *nondetection;* surprise bonuses; immunities to illusions, phantasms, and hallucinations; base magic resistance of 20% plus 5% per level above 3rd; saving throw bonuses; and if they are at least 6th level and are not illusionists or cleric/illusionists, the ability to summon an earth elemental once per day as detailed in the MONSTROUS MANUAL tome.

Forest Gnomes

Forest gnome priests are considered to be gnome priests, with all of the abilities and limitations thereof, as described above. Forest gnomes have the potential to know the languages of treants, elves, and the simple common speech of forest animals (rather than burrowing mammals) rather than the common rock gnome tongues listed in the Player's Handbook und the description of the gnome race. Forest gnome priests have the abilities and weaknesses common to their race, including the innate ability to *pass without trace* and to hide in the woodlands (90% chance of being undetected); an Armor Class bonus when they are fighting larger opponents; an attack bonus against orcs, lizard men, troglodytes, and any creature they have directly observed damaging woodlands; and normal gnome saving throw bonuses based on their Constitutions, as detailed in the MONSTROUS MANUAL tome and *The Complete Book of Gnomes & Halflings*.

Spriggans

Spriggan priests are considered to be gnome priests, with all of the abilities and limitations thereof, as described above. In addition, spriggan priests have the abilities and weaknesses common to their race including casting *affect normal fires*, *shatter*, and an enhanced variant of *scare* at will when small, and changing to giant or normal size at will, as detailed in the MONSTROUS MANUAL tome. Most spriggan priests can be considered multiclassed priest/thieves.

Half-elven Priests

Half-elven priests may be clerics, crusaders, druids, mystics, and specialty priests. Generally the only multiclass combinations permitted to half-elven priests are fighter/cleric, fighter/druid, cleric/ranger, cleric/mage, druid/mage, fighter/mage/cleric, and fighter/mage/druid, although not every power allows every multiclass combination. Half-elven druid/rangers are only found in the clergy of the human deity Mielikki, detailed in *Faiths & Avatars*. Half-elven clerics are limited to 14th level, half-elven crusaders are limited to 12th level, half-elven druids are limited to 9th level, and half-elven mystics are limited to 14th level. Half-elven specialty priests are limited to 18th level before they must earn triple normal experience to advance in level, and only a handful have ever risen above 18th level. Half-elves are welcome in the faiths of most of the elven deities if they have been raised in elven society; if raised in human society, they feel more of an affinity for the human powers. Most human powers detailed in *Faiths & Avatars* and *Powers & Pantheons* accept half-elves into their clergy unless their descriptions seem to explicitly or implicitly state otherwise, so long as the half-elf was raised in human society.

Halfling Priests

Halfling priests may be clerics, mystics, and specialty priests, and Sheela Peryroyl allows druids as one of her two types of specialty priests. Normally no multiclass combinations are permitted to halfling priests, although Arvoreen permits fighter/clerics and fighter/specialty priests and Brandobaris permits cleric/thieves and specialty priest/thieves. Not all halfling powers permit mystics, though many do. Halfling clerics are limited in level to 8th, and halfling mystics are limited in level to 13th. Halfling specialty priests (including Sheela's druids) are limited to 12th level before they must earn triple normal experience to advance in level, and only a handful have ever risen above 12th level.

Nonweapon Proficiencies

A number of the specialty priest classes make use of some special nonweapon proficiencies. The alertness proficiency originally appeared in *The Complete Ranger's Handbook*. The necrology and netherworld knowledge proficiencies originally appeared in *The Complete Book of Necromancers*. The sea lore nonweapon proficiency originally appeared in *Night of the Shark*.

Alertness: A character with this proficiency is exceptionally attuned to his or her surroundings and is able to detect disturbances and notice discrepancies. A successful proficiency check reduces his or her chance of being surprised by 1. (This replaces the description of this proficiency in *The Complete Thief's Handbook*.)

Proficiency	Group	No. of Slots Required	Relevant Ability	Check Modifier
Alertness	General	1	Wisdom	+1
Necrology	Priest, Wizard	1	Wisdom	0
Netherworld knowledge	Priest, Wizard	1	Wisdom	–3
Sea lore	General	1	Intelligence	–1

Necrology: A character with this skill is well versed in necrology, the lore of undead creatures. This proficiency may be used to help determine the probable lairs, dining habits, and history of such creatures (no ability check needed). Whenever a character with this skill confronts an undead creature, she or he may be able to specifically identify the creature (discerning between a ghast and a common ghoul, for instance) with a successful ability check. In addition, provided the character makes another successful ability check, she or he recalls the creature's specific weaknesses and natural defenses or immunities. At the DM's discretion a failed ability check (in either of these cases) reveals misleading or even completely erroneous information that may actually strengthen or otherwise benefit the undead creature.

Netherworld Knowledge: With this proficiency, a character learns about the cosmology and organization of the AD&D game multiverse, focusing primarily on the ultimate destination of spirits after death: the Outer Planes. In addition, the character learns about the behavior of the dangerous creatures that inhabit the nether regions, including such fiends as tanar'ri and baatezu. As with necrology (which applies exclusively to undead creatures), netherworld knowledge can reveal the specific weaknesses and natural immunities of beings from the Outer Planes. Netherworld knowledge can also be used to classify the exact type of extraplanar creature encountered. Both of these abilities require a successful ability check, however.

Sea Lore: This skill gives a basic understanding of the sea and its denizens; someone with sea lore can identify various species of fish and plant life, as well as predict tides, currents, and even storms. When making a sea lore proficiency check, a character normally rolls an ability check against his or her Intelligence score with a –1 penalty (–6 when attempting to predict storms).

Limited Thieving Skills

A number of specialty priest classes have some thieving skills. Specialty priests defined in *Demihuman Deities* who have limited thieving skills noted in their bullet point list of special abilities have the thieving skill base scores as set out in the *Player's Handbook* (including Dexterity, race, and armor adjustments) but gain *no* initial discretionary points. Each time a such a specialty priest gains a level, 20 points may be applied to thieving skills. No more than 15 points may be assigned to a single skill. Such specialty priests cannot backstab as thieves, nor do they ever gain the ability to use magical scrolls that a thief does.

Limited Wizard Spellcasting

A number of specialty priest classes defined in *Demihuman Deities* are allowed to cast some wizard spells. In addition to priest spells, such specialty priests can cast wizard spells from the wizard school or school that is indicated in their bullet point list of special abilities. These spells are cast as if the specialty priest were a mage of the same level. For example, a 3rd-level specialty priest casts wizard spells as a 3rd-level mage. Specialty priests with this special ability pray for their wizard spells instead of studying to memorize them, and chosen wizard spells replace priest spells potentially available for use that day. (In other words, the wizard spell occupies a priest spell slot.) These specialty priests gain access to 8th-level wizard spells at 16th level and 9th-level wizard spells at 18th level. A specialty priest with this special ability must have a Wisdom of 18 or higher and an Intelligence of 16 to gain access to the 8th-level spells, and a Wisdom of 18 or higher and an Intelligence of 18 to gain access to the 9th-level spells. If a specialty priest with this special ability is able to gain high-level wizard spells, every 8th-level spell prayed for occupies a 6th-level priest spell slot and every 9th-level spell prayed for occupies a 7th-level priest spell slot. Such specialty priests are always able to read spells of the school designated in their special ability on scrolls or in wizard spellbooks as if they knew *read magic*, but studying spells from a spellbook is useless to them. No more than three-quarters of the total number of spells available (round down) to a specialty priest with this special ability can be taken as wizard spells.

APPENDIX 2: SPELL INDEX

T he following abbreviations are used here: "Pr"=priest spell; "Wiz"=wizard spell; "DD"—found in *Demihuman Deities*; "F&A"—found in *Faiths & Avatars*; "FD&D"—found in *For Duty & Deity*; "HHK"—found in *Halls of the High King*; "P&P"—found in *Powers & Pantheons*; "PFTF"—found in *Prayers From the Faithful*; "PFTM"—found in *Pages From the Mages*; "VGtATM"—found in *Volo's Guide to All Things Magical*. A deity's name in the spell name indicates the religion a spell is associated with; most of these are religion-specific spells, with the exception of *starharp*, which is also available to Harpers, and certain wizard spells originally derived from *Pages From the Mages*. Spells with no deity name (or group of deities, in the case of the Emerald Enclave spells) listed with them are broadly available if prayed for or otherwise acquired. Duplicate source codes indicate the spell is found in two sources; with such spells, *Faiths & Avatars* and *Powers & Pantheons* take precedence over earlier sources. Italicized spells are reversible. The reverse name follows the slash. An asterisk (*) indicates a cooperative magic spell.

A

A day in the life (Yondalla; Pr 5, Law, Combat).................*DD* 182
Abbathor's greed (Abbathor; Pr 3, Divination) ....*DD* 46
Abeyance (any; Pr 5, All) ....*VGtATM* 27
Acorn barrage (Rillifane Rallathil; Pr 2, Combat, Plant)..........*DD* 124
Advanced sunshine (Amaunator; Pr 4, Sun).....................*F&A* 29
Akadi's vortex (Akadi; Pr 7, Elemental Air) ....*F&A* 26
Alert allies (Gorm Gulthyn, Gaerdal Ironhand; Pr 2, Thought) ......*DD* 67
Alert vigil (Torm; Pr 1, Charm, Necromantic) ....*PFTF* 107
Alicorn lance (Lurue; Pr 3, Animal)...........................*P&P* 40
All-seeing crystal ball (Savras; Pr 6, Divination) ....*P&P* 51
Amanuensis (Deneir; Pr 3, Creation)..........................*F&A* 56
Amaunator's uncertainty (Amaunator; Pr 2, Law)................*F&A* 29
Amber prison (Rillifane Rallathil; Pr 4, Plant)..................*DD* 124
Amorphous form (Ghaunadaur; Pr 5, Animal)...................*DD* 22
Analyze contraption (Nebelun/Gond; Pr 3, Divination) ....*DD* 154
Analyze opponent (Red Knight; Pr 1, Divination)................*P&P* 46
Animal sight (Malar; Pr 4, Animal)..........................*F&A* 107
Animal transfer (Malar; Pr 6, Animal)........................*F&A* 108
Animal vision (Osiris; Pr 4, Animal) ....*P&P* 124
Animate stalactite
    (Callarduran Smoothhands; Pr 1, Elemental Earth)............*DD* 145
Anyspell (Mystra; Pr 4, Charm, Creation).....................*F&A* 130
Arboreal scamper (Baervan Wildwanderer; Pr 2, Plant) ....*DD* 140
Archer's redoubt (Solonor Thelandira; Pr 3, Protection)...........*DD* 135
Arm hammers (Geb; Pr 2, Combat) ....*P&P* 101
Armor of darkness (Shar; Pr 3, Protection, Sun) ....*F&A* 142
Assess value (Nephthys; Pr 1, Divination) ....*P&P* 119
Assume undead form (Velsharoon; Pr 4, Necromantic) ....*P&P* 78
Astaroth's augmentation (Pr 3, All) ....*P&P* 25
Attraction/disdain (Bhaal; Pr 2, Charm).......................*F&A* 47
Augment artistry (Corellon Larethian; Pr 1, Creation) ....*DD* 103
Augment psionics (Deep Duerra; Pr 2, Thought).................*DD* 56
Awaken magical item (any; Pr 7, All, Creation)..............*VGtATM* 30
Awakening; renamed "Awaken magical item"
    (any; Pr 7, All, Creation)...........................*VGtATM* 30
Awakening (Lathander; Pr 4, Protection).....................*PFTF* 99
Axe storm of Clangeddin
    (Clangeddin Silverbeard; Pr 4, Combat)....................*DD* 53
Azuth's alteration mantle (Azuth; Pr 6, Protection)............*PFTF* 112
Azuth's exalted triad (Azuth; Pr 5, Thought; Wiz 5, Alteration) ....*F&A* 36
Azuth's fedensor (Azuth; Pr 4, Thought; Wiz 4, Alteration)........*F&A* 36
Azuth's firing frenzy (Azuth; Pr 6, Combat) ....*PFTF* 112
Azuth's immobility (Azuth; Pr 5, Charm)....................*PFTF* 111
Azuth's spell shield
    (Azuth; Pr 7, Protection; Wiz 7, Abjuration).................*F&A* 36

Detect spirits (Sehanine Moonbow; Pr 3, Divination) . . . . *DD* 129
Detect weapons (Haela Brightaxe; Pr 1, Divination) . . . . *DD* 70
Determine final rest (Jergal; Pr 3, Divination) . . . . *P&P* 34
Disentangle (Thard Harr; Pr 2, Protection) . . . . *DD* 88
Dispel silence (Finder Wyvernspur & Milil; Pr 3, Combat;
   Wiz 3, Abjuration, Alteration) . . . . *F&A* 118, *P&P* 17, *PFTM* 24
Dispel ward (Set; Pr 2, Wards) . . . . *P&P* 129
Divine bloodline (Siamorphe; Pr 1, Divination) . . . . *P&P* 61
Divine investiture (Siamorphe; Pr 5, Law, Time) . . . . *P&P* 61
Divine purpose (Gond; Pr 3, Divination) . . . . *PFTF* 7
Divine romantic interest (Hanali Celanil; Pr 1, Divination) . . . . . *DD* 116
Dolorous decay (Myrkul; Pr 6, Combat, Necromantic) . . . . *F&A* 128
Doom of Bane, The (Bane; Pr 4, Necromantic) . . . . *F&A* 40
Doomhound (Urogalan; Pr 3, Divination) . . . . *DD* 179
Doomtide (Beshaba; Pr 4, Combat, Guardian) . . . . *PFTF* 13
Doublecoin (Waukeen; Pr 4, Creation) . . . . *F&A* 180
Dragon scales (Tiamat; Pr 4, Protection) . . . . *P&P* 137
Dumathoin's rest (Dumathoin; Pr 2, Necromantic, Wards) . . . . . . *DD* 63
Duplicate (Oghma; Pr 4, Creation) . . . . *F&A* 134
Dust shield (Geb; Pr 3, Elemental Earth) . . . . *P&P* 101
Dweomer divination (any; Pr 7, Divination) . . . . *VGtATM* 30
Dweomerflow (any; Pr 4, All) . . . . *VGtATM* 27
Dying curse (Horus-Re; Pr 6, Protection) . . . . *P&P* 114

E

Earth anchor (Urogalan; Pr 2, Elemental Earth) . . . . *DD* 179
Earth walk (Dumathoin; Pr 6, Elemental Earth) . . . . *DD* 64
Earthenair (Grumbar; Pr 3, Elemental Earth) . . . . *F&A* 68
Earthenport (Grumbar; Pr 5, Elemental Earth) . . . . *F&A* 68
Earthshake* (Geb; Pr 5, Elemental Earth) . . . . *P&P* 102
Ease labor/inflict labor (Shiallia; Pr 3, Healing) . . . . *P&P* 57
Edge of Arumdina (Garl Glittergold; Pr 5, Combat) . . . . *DD* 154
Eilistraee's moonfire (Eilistraee; Pr 2, Sun) . . . . *DD* 17
Elder eye (Ghaunadaur; Pr 5, Necromantic) . . . . *DD* 22
Elsewhere chant (Milil; Pr 7, Summoning) . . . . *PFTF* 116
Embattlement (Ilmater; Pr 3, Protection) . . . . *PFTF* 104
Enchant phylactery (Mystra; Pr 5, Guardian, Protection) . . . . . . *PFTF* 81
Enchanted hammer (Laduguer; Pr 3, Creation) . . . . *DD* 74
Endless dance (Shiallia; Pr 6, Charm) . . . . *P&P* 58
Endurance of Ilmater (Ilmater; Pr 4, Necromantic, Protection) . . *F&A* 77
Enduring ward (Nephthys; Pr 6, Wards) . . . . *PFTF* 120
Eternal flame (any; Pr 5, All, Elemental Fire, Necromantic) . *VGtATM* 28
Everchanging self (Mask; Pr 6, Chaos, Protection) . . . . *PFTF* 57
Everfull quiver (Solonor Thelandira; Pr 3, Combat) . . . . *DD* 135
Exaltation (Helm; Pr 3, Combat, Healing) . . . . *F&A* 70
Excessive indulgence (Sharess; Pr 1, Charm) . . . . *P&P* 54
Eye of fire (Horus-Re; Pr 3, Combat, Sun) . . . . *P&P* 113

F

Faerie form (Erevan Ilesere; Pr 7, Animal) . . . . *DD* 111
Faith armor (Helm; Pr 5, Protection) . . . . *PFTF* 39
Faith magic zone (Emerald Enclave; Pr 4, Protection, Wards) . . *PFTF* 127
Faithful mount (Malar; Pr 7, Animal, Charm) . . . . *F&A* 108
Falling wall (Silvanus; Pr 6, Elemental Earth, Weather) . . . . *PFTF* 53
False dawn (Lathander; Pr 6, Sun) . . . . *F&A* 93
Fangs of retribution (Ilmater; Pr 2, Combat) . . . . *PFTF* 104
Fantastic machine (Gond; Pr 6, Creation) . . . . *F&A* 65
Favor of Ilmater (Ilmater; Pr 3, Necromantic, Protection) . . . . . *F&A* 77
Favor of Shaundakul (Shaundakul; Pr 2, Travelers) . . . . *F&A* 144
Favor of the goddess (Chauntea; Pr 2, Plant) . . . . *F&A* 50
Favor of Tymora (Tymora; Pr 2, Protection) . . . . *F&A* 168
Favor of Valkur (Valkur; Pr 5, Charm, Elemental Water) . . . . . . *P&P* 75
Favor of Yathaghera (Lurue; Pr 3, Animal) . . . . *P&P* 40
Feat (Tymora; Pr 4, All) . . . . *F&A* 168
Feline form (Nobanion; Pr 7, Combat) . . . . *P&P* 44
Fertility (Shiallia; Pr 4, Creation) . . . . *P&P* 58
Find companion (Malar; Pr 4, Animal) . . . . *F&A* 108
Find drinkable water (Mielikki; Pr 1, Divination) . . . . *PFTF* 119
Find sustenance (Fenmarel Mestarine; Pr 3, Divination) . . . . *DD* 113
Fire eyes of Gorm (Gorm Gulthyn; Pr 4, Combat) . . . . *DD* 67
Fire of justice (Tyr; Pr 5, Combat) . . . . *PFTF* 11

Fireward (Silvanus; Pr 5, Elemental Fire) . . . . *F&A* 148
Fist of faith (Helm; Pr 2, Combat) . . . . *PFTF* 39
Fist of Gond (Gond; Pr 6, Combat) . . . . *PFTF* 8
Flame shield (Eldath; Pr 3, Elemental Fire) . . . . *F&A* 60
Flight of Remnis (Aerdrie Faenya; Pr 4, Animal, Summoning) . . . . *DD* 97
Float (Pr 5, Creation) . . . . *PFTF* 124
Flock of birds (Thoth; Pr 4, Animal, Summoning) . . . . *P&P* 132
Flowstone (Sharindlar; Pr 5, Elemental Earth) . . . . *DD* 85
Focal stone (any; Pr 5, All, Elemental Earth) . . . . *VGtATM* 28
Foesight (Any; Pr 4, Divination) . . . . *FD&D* 16
Forceward (Helm; Pr 3, Wards) . . . . *F&A* 70
Foresight (Savras; Pr 1, Combat, Divination) . . . . *P&P* 51
Forgotten melody (Milil; Pr 5, Charm, Combat) . . . . *F&A* 119
Fortitude (Selvetarm; Pr 2, Necromantic) . . . . *DD* 36
Fortitude of Uthgar (Uthgar; Pr 1, Charm) . . . . *P&P* 71
Fortunate fate (Tymora; Pr 7, Healing, Protection) . . . . *PFTF* 28
Free will (Ubtao; Pr 2, Charm) . . . . *P&P* 93
Frost breath (Auril; Pr 2, Combat, Elemental Water) . . . . *PFTF* 87
Frost fingers (Auril; Pr 1, Combat, Weather) . . . . *F&A* 33
Frost whip (Auril; Pr 2, Combat, Weather) . . . . *F&A* 33

G

Gaseous form (Velsharoon; Pr 5, Necromantic, Elemental Air) . . . *P&P* 79
Gate of doom (Jergal; Pr 7, Summoning) . . . . *P&P* 35
Gauntlet of winds (Shaundakul; Pr 4, Elemental Air, Weather) . *F&A* 145
Gembomb (Garl Glittergold; Pr 3, Combat) . . . . *DD* 153
Ghost knight (Kelemvor; Pr 4, Summoning) . . . . *PFTF* 90
Ghost pipes (Finder Wyvernspur; Pr 3, Charm;
   Wiz 3, Alteration, Illusion/Phantasm) . . . . *P&P* 17, *PFTM* 73
Giantsize (Arvoreen; Pr 5, Combat) . . . . *DD* 166
Glowglory (Marthammor Duin; Pr 3, Combat, Creation) . . . . *DD* 77
Glyph of revealing (Deneir; Pr 2, Divination) . . . . *F&A* 56
Glyph of warding: Telatha (Pr 3, Guardian) . . . . *PFTF* 122
Goad of misfortune (Beshaba; Pr 6, Combat) . . . . *PFTF* 14
Greater creature of darkness (Shar; Pr 6, Sun) . . . . *PFTF* 36
Greater mantle of Mystra (Mystra; Pr 6, Protection) . . . . *PFTF* 83
Greater shield of Lathander (Lathander; Pr 7, Guardian) . . . . *F&A* 93
Greater touchsickle (Eldath; Pr 5, Combat, Plant) . . . . *F&A* 60
Greenwood (Eldath; Pr 3, Plant) . . . . *F&A* 60
Ground trace (Mielikki; Pr 4, Divination) . . . . *PFTF* 120
Guardian hammer (Berronar Truesilver; Pr 4, Guardian) . . . . *DD* 49
Guardian mantle (Dugmaren Brightmantle; Pr 7, Protection) . . . . *DD* 60
Gull (Baravar Cloakshadow; Pr 2, Charm) . . . . *DD* 143

H

Haela's battle blessing (Haela Brightaxe; Pr 2, Combat) . . . . *DD* 70
Hamatree (Hanali Celanil; Pr 5, Plant) . . . . *DD* 116
Hammer of justice (Tyr; Pr 5, Divination) . . . . *F&A* 171
Hand of Hoar (Hoar; Pr4, Law) . . . . *P&P* 31
Hand of Torm (Torm; Pr 4, Guardian) . . . . *F&A* 165
Handcandle (Oghma; Pr 3, Elemental Fire) . . . . *PFTF* 43
Handfang (Moander; Pr 2, Combat, Necromantic) . . . . *F&A* 122
Handfire (Sune; Pr 1, Combat) . . . . *PFTF* 75
Hard water (Pr 5, Elemental Water) . . . . *PFTF* 125
Harp of war (Milil; Pr 7, Combat) . . . . *F&A* 119
Haunted reverie (Kiaransalee; Pr 5, Necromantic) . . . . *DD* 25
Haunted visions (Savras; Pr 3, Divination) . . . . *P&P* 51
Healing hand (Ilmater; Pr 4, Healing) . . . . *PFTF* 105
Heart of ice (Auril; Pr 7, Combat, Necromantic) . . . . *F&A* 33
Higher consecration (any; Pr 6, All) . . . . *VGtATM* 29
Histachii brew (Sseth; Pr 4, Animal, Creation) . . . . *P&P* 87
Hold metal (Pr 4, Charm) . . . . *PFTF* 123
Hoar's revenance (Hoar; Pr 6, Necromantic) . . . . *P&P* 31
Holy flail (Tempus; Pr 3, Combat, Creation) . . . . *F&A* 160
Holy might (any; Pr 6, All, Creation) . . . . *VGtATM* 29
Holy star (Mystra; Pr 6, Combat, Protection) . . . . *PFTF* 83
Holy vesting (any; Pr 6, All, Creation) . . . . *VGtATM* 29
Home port (Valkur; Pr 3, All) . . . . *P&P* 75
Horn of plenty (Yondalla; Pr 4, Creation) . . . . *DD* 182
Horns of Hathor (Hathor, Pr 2, Combat, Animal) . . . . *P&P* 108
Humansize (Arvoreen; Pr 3, Combat) . . . . *DD* 165

Resplendence of renewed youth (Tyr;
Pr 7, Necromantic, Healing)........................F&A 171
Restore rune (Deneir; Pr 6, Divination, Guardian)...........PFTF 62
Retarget (Emerald Enclave; Pr 5, Combat, Protection) ....PFTF 127
Reveal/conceal (Tempus; Pr 4, Divination) ....F&A 160
Revenance; "renamed "Hoar's revenance"
(Hoar; Pr 6, Necromantic)..............................P&P 31
Right of might (Gilgeam; Pr 5, Charm, Combat)...............P&P 106
Ripen plant (Chauntea; Pr 2, Plant).........................PFTF 30
Rising rot (Moander; Pr 5, Combat, Necromantic)............F&A 122
Rites of Istishia (Istishia; Pr 3, Elemental Water)............F&A 81
Ritual of transference* (any; Pr 7, All Creation) ....VGtATM 31
Roar of the king (Nobanion; Pr 4, Combat)...................P&P 43
Rockburst (Clangeddin Silverbeard; Pr 2, Combat).............DD 53
Roots of the assassin (Moander; Pr 6, Summoning, Plant) .....F&A 123
Rosemantle (Lathander; Pr 1, Protection) ....F&A 92
Rosetouch (Lathander; Pr 2, Protection) ....F&A 92
Rosewater (Lathander; Pr 2, Healing) ....PFTF 98
Royalberry (Sheela Peryroyl; Pr 5, Plant) ....DD 175
Ruby axe (Callarduran Smoothhands; Pr 3, Combat) ....DD 146

S
Sacred link (Tempus; Pr 7, Creation) ....F&A 162
Sacred strike (Loviatar; Pr 4, Combat, Necromantic)..........PFTF 47
Sacrosanct (any; Pr 7, Guardian)...........................VGtATM 78
Sanctified marker (Deneir; Pr 4, Creation) ....PFTF 60
Sanctify crypt (Nephthys; Pr 7, Wards)......................P&P 120
Sanctify sacred site (Chauntea; Pr 7, All, Sun, Plant)..........F&A 51
Sanctify spirit host (Osiris; Pr 6, Necromantic)..............P&P 124
Sap (Rillifane Rallathil; Pr 1, Plant) ....DD 124
Sarcophagus of death (Set; Pr 4, Necromantic)...............P&P 129
Scent of vengeance (Hoar, Pr 2, Animal).....................P&P 31
Scouring wind (Talos; Pr 5, Elemental Air)...................PFTF 21
Sea legs/land legs (Valkur; Pr 1, Healing) ....P&P 74
Seal of Cyrrollalee (Cyrrollalee; Pr 2, Law) ....DD 171
Searing song (Milil; Pr 4, Combat) ....PFTF 115
Seed of Moander (Moander; Pr 5, Plant) ....F&A 123
Seedstorm (Isis; Pr 5, Plant Combat) ....P&P 117
Seek eternal rest (Jergal; Pr 4, Necromantic, Time) ....P&P 34
Seeking mote (Chauntea; Pr 1, Sun)..........................PFTF 30
Seeking sword (Helm; Pr 4, Combat)..........................F&A 71
Segojan's armor (Segojan Earthcaller; Pr 1, Plant) ....DD 157
Sentry of Helm/Gorm
(Helm, Gorm Gulthyn; Pr 1, Guardian, Travelers) ....F&A 70
Shades of Rhondang (Flandal Steelskin; Pr 4, Elemental Fire) ...DD 148
Shadow sword (Shaundakul; Pr 3, Combat, Sun) ....F&A 145
Shadowcloak (Mask; Pr 3, Sun, Protection)...................F&A 111
Shark charm (Deep Sashelas; Pr 2, Animal, Charm) ....DD 107
Shatter circle (Thoth; Pr 5, Protection) ....P&P 132
Sheela's entangle (Sheela Peryroyl; Pr 2, Plant) ....DD 174
Shevarash's infravision (Shevarash; Pr 3, Sun)................DD 132
Shield of Lathander (Lathander; Pr 5, Guardian) ....F&A 93
Shield of the god (Helm; Pr 5, Protection) ....PFTF 40
Shift glyph (Deneir; Pr 3, Creation, Divination) ....F&A 56
Ship shield (Valkur; Pr 5, Elemental Air) ....P&P 76
Silver tongue and starry eyes (Lurue; Pr 6, Animal) ....P&P 40
Silverbeard (Clangeddin Silverbeard; Pr 1, Combat) ....DD 53
Singing stone (Milil; Pr 4, Divination, Elemental Earth) ......F&A 118
Sixth sense (Corellon Larethian; Pr 1, Protection) ....DD 103
Skulk (Ibrandul; Pr 4, Protection) ....F&A 74
Skull of secrets (Cyric; Pr 4, Guardian) ....F&A 53
Sleep of dragons (Tiamat; Pr 6, Charm) ....P&P 137
Slicing shadow (Mask; Pr 5, Combat) ....PFTF 56
Slow boon (Ilmater; Pr 3, Healing) ....PFTF 104
Smoke ghost (Silvanus; Pr 4, Elemental Fire).......F&A 148, PFTM 61
Snake charm (Sseth; Pr 1, Charm) ....P&P 87
Snake skin (Sseth; Pr 4, Animal) ....P&P 88
Snow boots (Auril; Pr 1, Elemental Water)....................PFTF 87
Snow snake (Auril; Pr 5, Combat, Elemental Water)...........PFTF 88
Soften earth and stone (Urdlen; Pr 2, Elemental Earth) ....DD 160
Solitude (Fenmarel Mestarine; Pr 4, Wards)...................DD 113

Song of compulsion (Milil; Pr 3, Charm, Law) ....F&A 118
Song of healing (Milil; Pr 5, Healing) ....PFTF 116
Soul forge (Moradin; Pr 5, Creation, Law) ....DD 82
Soultheft (Vhaeraun; Pr 7, Necromantic).....................DD 40
Sparkling sword (Arvoreen; Pr 3, Combat)....................DD 165
Spawn of Tiamat (Tiamat; Pr 6, Combat).....................P&P 137
Speak with ancient dead (Labelas Enoreth; Pr 5, Divination) ...DD 120
Speak with avians (Aerdrie Faenya; Pr 1, Animal, Divination)....DD 96
Speak with birds (Thoth; Pr 1, Animal Divination)............P&P 132
Speak with drowned dead (Umberlee;
Pr 3, Elemental Water, Divination) ....F&A 174
Spectral manticore (Malar; Pr 4, Summoning) ....PFTF 17
Spectral stag (Malar; Pr 4, Summoning) ....PFTF 17
Speed rot (Moander; Pr 3, Plant) ....F&A 122
Speeding trident (Umberlee; Pr 2, Combat) ....PFTF 70
Spell shield (Mystra; Pr 3, Protection)........................PFTF 81
Spell ward (Mystra; Pr 7, Protection) ....F&A 131
Spellbind (Oghma; Pr 7, Necromantic, Protection) ....F&A 134
Spellsong (Eilistraee; Pr 6, Creation) ....DD 18
Spider bite (Lolth; Pr 6, Combat) ....DD 33
Spider summoning (Lolth; Pr 5, Animal) ....DD 32
Spiderform (Lolth; Pr 5, Animal, Necromantic) ....DD 32
Spirit annihilation (Bane; Pr 6, Necromantic)..................F&A 40
Spirit mask (Ubtao; Pr 1, Divination) ....P&P 93
Spirit quest (Uthgar; Pr 6, Divination) ....P&P 72
Spirit trap of the Darkbringer (Moander;
Pr 5, Plant, Necromantic) ....F&A 123
Spiritual corruption (Gargauth; Pr 6, Charm) ....P&P 26
Spring mastery (Eldath; Pr 6, Creation, Elemental Water) ......F&A 61
Sprite venom (Erevan Ilesere; Pr 3, Combat) ....DD 110
Stalk (Eilistraee, Mielikki; Pr 2, Animal).....................F&A 115
Starflight* (Mystra; Pr 3, Elemental Air, Travelers)............F&A 130
Starharp (Finder Wyvernspur; Pr 6, Healing, Protection;
Wiz 6, Alteration, Necromancy) ....P&P 17, HHK 51
Steal psionic strength (Deep Duerra; Pr 1, Thought)............DD 56
Stealth of Brandobaris (Brandobaris; Pr 3, Guardian) ....DD 169
Steelskin (Flandal Steelskin; Pr 1, Protection)................DD 148
Still waves (Valkur; Pr 4, Elemental Water) ....P&P 75
Stone form (Callarduran Smoothhands; Pr 4, Elemental Earth) ...DD 146
Stone seeing (Dumathoin; Pr 5, Divination, Elemental Earth) ....DD 64
Stone storm/stone quench (Moradin; Pr 7, Elemental Earth) .....DD 82
Stone trap (Vergadain; Pr 4, Guardian) ....DD 91
Stone walk (Bane; Pr 7, Elemental Earth) ....F&A 42
Stoneblend (Laduguer; Pr 1, Elemental Earth) ....DD 74
Stonefall (Dumathoin; Pr 4, Elemental Earth) ....DD 63
Stonefire (Moradin; Pr 4, Elemental Earth, Elemental Fire) ......DD 81
Storm cone (Talos; Pr 5, Elemental Air, Weather) ....F&A 158
Storm shield (Talos; Pr 3, Protection, Weather) ....F&A 158
Stormcloak (Umberlee; Pr 4, Elemental Water, Protection) .....F&A 175
Stormrage (Talos; Pr 6, Combat) ....PFTF 21
Stormvoice (Horus-Re; Pr 2, Weather)........................P&P 113
Strength of stone
(Moradin, Callarduran Smoothhands; Pr 1, Elemental Earth) ..DD 81
Striking shadows (Mask; Pr 6, Guardian) ....F&A 112
Striking wave (Umberlee; Pr 4, Elemental Water)..............F&A 175
Stumble (Anhur; Pr 1, Combat) ....P&P 99
Succor of Berronar (Berronar Truesilver; Pr 5, Healing).........DD 49
Summon ancestor (Uthgar; Pr 3, Necromantic)................P&P 71
Summon cetacean
(Deep Sashelas; Pr 3, Elemental Water, Summoning) ....DD 108
Summon divine minion (Mulhorandi pantheon;
Pr 7, Summoning, All)...................................P&P 96
Summon earth grue
(Urdlen; Pr 4, Elemental Earth, Summoning)...............DD 160
Summon lock lurker (Waukeen; Pr 3, Summoning, Animal) ...F&A 180
Summon shadow spirit (Eshowdow; Pr 4, Summoning) ....P&P 83
Summon spectator (Helm; Pr 5, Summoning, Protection) ......F&A 71
Sun scepter (Amaunator; Pr 6, Sun, Law) ....F&A 29
Sunrise (Lathander; Pr 3, Sun) ....F&A 92
Sunstroke (Horus-Re; Pr 3, Elemental Fire, Sun) ....P&P 113
Surface sojourn (Deep Sashelas; Pr 1, Elemental Water) ....DD 107